SW

David Epps

Writers Guild of America, East - Reg. No. 125279-00

ISBN: 1-58898-819-8

This book is dedicated to

Marine Second Lieutenant Carl Jason Fisher
(1958-1981)

1980 Junior Sword Drill

"We die proud!"

ACKNOWLEDGMENTS

In 1981, only one year after the graduation ceremonies for the Class of 1980, I received a phone call that would start the journey towards writing *Sword Drill*. A senior cadet at The Citadel called my home to tell me that my friend, classmate, and former roommate had been killed in an auto accident. At that very moment I knew that his story had to be told. The loss was significant, and it was clear that the world had been robbed of a favorite son whose passion for life defined how we all should live. Carl Fisher was a true Citadel man, and in his pursuit to become a member of the 1980 Junior Sword Drill he found both himself and a gift that the Military College of South Carolina has bestowed on men from countless generations.

In 1983 I made my first attempt at putting his story into words on paper. The effort was to be a true and accurate account of Carl's pursuit of Sword Drill. As his roommate, I observed some of what he went through, yet because I lacked many facts about his life prior to entering The Citadel, and what actually occurred to the 1980 aspirants inside McAlister Field House, that effort soon failed. Though his story remained a goal, it wasn't until 1989 that I made a second attempt by trying to write a purely fictional story about the Sword Drill journey that would indirectly tell of Carl's dream. But that too was a stymied effort as I was soon frustrated with not having enough facts about what really happened because of the long standing secrecy of the organization. I thought about making everything up, but feared violating the true spirit of Sword Drill by merely guessing.

In 1991, I took a chance that the Commander of the 1992 Junior Sword Drill would talk openly with me about the secret life of the organization, and Cadet First Sergeant Dan Mackie became my first source of vital information to do this book. With countless hours of interviews with him, I had enough inside information to make my story one of fiction based on fact. Riding on my successful interview with Mr. Mackie, I decided to probe further. I approached other Sword Drill members from years as early as the 1950's up through the early 1990's, concentrating heavily on the years surrounding Carl's journey through the process. Some would talk to me, while others flatly refused. Yet, as the successful interviews began to mount, so did the recurring facts that defined the core activities and essence of the Junior Sword Drill.

A full time job, outside interests, and family matters made the reality of writing a book extremely difficult, if not sometimes impossible. However, long nights and full weekends of writing finally yielded the story I wanted to tell.

Sword Drill is based on the actual events and facts surrounding the 1980 Sword Drill. It describes one young man's dream in a way that reveals the passion, spirit, and sacrifice that comes with the aspiration. Over its 60-year history, some Drills were not as harsh, while others were far more brutal. I believe that this book fairly represents the typical Sword Drill experience during the late 1970's and early 1980's.

This effort could not have been possible had it not been for the cooperation and understanding of many Citadel graduates. Their willingness to speak to me honestly was based on a consensus that this was indeed a story that needed to be told. I respect those who refused to talk to me, but I feel that it is important that the world know the true depth of the Sword Drill experience. Though I fully expect that many will not understand or even approve of what took place over the decades with the Junior Sword Drill, I am extremely proud of what these men stood for and accomplished.

The one aspect relative to the history of the Junior Sword Drill that I find truly sad is that the organization no longer exists on The Citadel campus. As society changed, so did its tolerance for hazing, personal servitude, and male-only organizations. Each year it seemed that another unfortunate mishap occurred, and despite intense intervention and supervision by the faculty, they just could not stop the annual misfortunes that plagued the Junior Sword Drill. In 1993, an aspirant was hospitalized after being beaten over 100 times with a sword in the confines of a Drill member's room. The offending senior was expelled, and the Junior Sword Drill was deemed out of control, and disbanded forever.

I would like to thank those who so kindly contributed. They are:

COL Floyd W. Brown Jr. - Class of 1955
COL Walter B. Clark, USA,(Ret.) — Class of 1951
Lt. Col. Harvey M. Dick, USA, (Ret.) – Class of 1953
CDR Gary G. Durante, USN - Class of 1980
Billy Gordon - Class of 1993
MAJ James Scott Green - Class of 1980
Rev. William W. Hendry II - Class of 1973
2LT Daniel Patrick Mackie, USA - Class of 1992
CAPT Ronald Keith Miller, USAF - Class of 1982
CAPT William M. Moser, USMC - Class of 1978
Danny Quirk, Jr. - Class of 1980
Robert James Richter - Class of 1992
Edward Raymond Moore III - Class of 1993
James A. Rembert - Class of 1961
Wallace I. West - Class of 1970
Michael S. White - Class of 1978
Lt Col Fredrick J. Whittle, USMC, (Ret.) – Class of 1980

The real members of the 1980 Junior Sword Drill are:

Charles Manzione - Commander
Charles Lee - Voice
Gary Durante
John Ference
Frank Figueroa
Carl Fisher

James Green
James Hall
James Koppenhaver
Daniel Quirk
Daniel Renaldi
Paul Rogers
Charles Stewart
Frederick Whittle

A book like this cannot go without the mention of those who either directly or indirectly made a contribution to this effort that made it a reality. I give special thanks to the following:

Sam and Taylor Epps, my son and daughter, who are the definition of love in my life; Leroy S. Epps, Jr., my deceased father, who also loved to tell a good story; Betty Lou Graves Epps, my deceased mother, who created within me a love for art and music; my sister Debbie Epps Ipock, who has been a standard of class that every man and women should hope to achieve, and will forever be the subject of my deepest admiration; my brother Roy Epps who has always inspired and protected me (and isn't Charles IV); Tripp Player, my forever friend who taught me that life is for living, and the hell with everything else; Jay Etheridge, Class of 1981, Junior Sword Drill, for the full arc, which meant something then, and still means something now; Mary Ham, my high school English teacher, who used Keats' "Ode to a Grecian Urn" to break through a closed, stubborn mind, and taught me the beauty of written words; Q. Curtis Lee, my high school principal, for believing in me when everyone else had given up; Ken Palka, Citadel Class of 1964, for being such an excellent friend and mentor, and for opening so many doors; Don Couch, Class of 52, whom I share as a father with my classmate Tim Couch; Craig Ellis and Carter Hayes, for their generous help and friendship when things got tough; Steve James, for being the best lawyer around, as well as a good friend; Leigh Murray, actress/producer/manager, for being an outstanding professional, and helping me get my act together; the taxpayers of South Carolina, and the alumni, faculty, and staff of The Citadel, for a precious gift that I shall forever cherish.

There are so many more I should mention and I sincerely apologize to those whom I have left out.

And finally, please, give generously to:

The Citadel Foundation
The Citadel
171 Moultrie Street
Charleston, South Carolina 29409-6230

CHAPTER 1

I have always had the motivation. I could walk through hell and back to obtain my heart's true desire. Still, I couldn't help but feel anxious. Hell was where I was headed, and the front gates of The Citadel would be my entry into that abyss. It was my decision to accept such a challenge, assuming that my deep southern pride would always get me through tough times no matter how bad they got. Yet, I knew my life was about to drastically change, and that the greatest challenge I would ever know would soon be upon me.

As we drove down Highway 52 towards Charleston, it was deathly quiet in our car as I was nervous and my parents' minds were somewhere adrift. They were probably lost in thoughts, considering the impending fate of their second born. The tough reputation of The Citadel was indeed renowned, and they were concerned about the struggle I had chosen to face. But they knew my past had not been an easy one, and that at age eighteen I was as hardened as any other taking the same route.

Like my ancestors before me, I was driven to accept and meet challenges head-on. It had become an inbred family trait resulting from centuries of struggle that began many years prior to the birth of the nation. As a part of the King of England's plan to settle South Carolina in the mid 1700's, the O'Bryan family arrived at a location on the northern banks of the Black River, distinguished only by a marked white pine called the "King's tree." They were among the original Scotch-Irish settlers of Williamsburg County who found little relief from the hardships they had left in the Counties of Down and Antrim in Ireland. Industrious and thrifty, they transformed with sweat the swamp lands and sandy pine barrens into fields that would first yield corn to make bread, then later indigo that would make money. They hunted whitetail deer and wild turkey until their cows and hogs had multiplied to a stable resource. The wool from sheep and cotton from the ground provided the raw materials to make their clothes. They learned to survive in a world that presented new struggles each day.

They were a God-fearing people who were intimate with hardship. Only half of their children would live to see adulthood and experience the opportunity to own and work a piece of land. Generations lived and died on our land as the nation gained its independence, only to later divide itself. My family lost loved ones in both struggles, and we have always carried with us the pride that we have both worked and fought for the right to call a part of this earth our own.

Even in my earliest days of growing up on our farm near the town of Kingstree, I was told of the ties I had to the land. It was a celebrated honor that ran deep in my family. I actually thought we were royalty, and that our two thousand acres was a kingdom.. I thought of my father and grandfather as great monarchs who ruled over some boundless domain. It was rural South Carolina, decorated with tobacco barns and cotton pickers and optimistic dreams of a good crop.

My father made his living growing corn, cotton, soybeans, and tobacco. He had no desire at all to raise livestock, considering their time consuming needs and the hassles of dealing with diseases. His focus was putting seeds in the ground and selling what eventually came from them.

I was introduced to farm work in my early years, quickly learning what it meant to get up with the sun and stare at the passing rows of crops all day from atop a tractor. Our busiest time was always summer, and the combined heat from the sun and machinery was usually enough to bake a boy to well done. When a combine or picker broke, we would cook a perlow right in the field as we worked into the night to fix it. We lived the work, and the life I knew on the farm might have been harder to accept had I known any different. But I never once questioned it.

My dad was both a good businessman and a respected member of the community. Yet, much of his respect was given to him at birth by the mere fact that he was the son of Charles O'Bryan, Jr., who was already revered as a successful farmer. From birth, my Dad was weaned on the intricacies of farming with the understanding that one day he would eventually assume full responsibility. It was a family tradition as natural as the passing seasons. My father's mission in life was to maintain and hopefully improve on the assets of his father, and then pass everything on to the next generation for their use and continued contribution.

In my early years, I heard many a conversation that hailed our family's history, and my elders accentuated with passion the wealth and pride that the line of Charles O'Bryan's had brought to the family throughout the years. Yet those conversations were for the benefit and edification of my older brother of two years, Charles IV. Even at an early age, it was clearly evident that Charles held a special place with our father and grandfather based on the constant attention and praise they bestowed on him. I too was loved, yet shadowed by the blatant partiality shown towards Charles. I would eventually come to realize the significance of a name, and how an eldest son tradition would shape my destiny.

But this seemingly dark cloud did have a silver lining. The environment would equip me with a strong sense of independence as it became obvious that the farm was not the key to my future. By design, that was my brother Charles' destiny. I was but a second thumb in that sacred grand design.

Yet, my knowledge and acceptance of my standing would not be enough to shield me from its consequences. From day one, Charles resented my presence, and he could never dismiss me as a threat to his sovereignty. I was a possible caveat to his birthright, so he made it his mission to keep a cap on my advancement and success. His world was one that demanded a total domination of attention and praise. He could never allow any thoughts to develop that I too might be deserving or even capable of sharing in the future of the farm. He schemed to place disaster around each corner I turned. He painted me as worthless and incompetent, and under the pretense of trying to make me tough, he beat me on a regular basis in an attempt to fix the problem. The taste of blood soon defined for me the term brotherly love. I became tough all right, but at the price of living through a battered childhood.

CHAPTER 2

I will have to give my brother Charles most of the credit for my choice of attending The Citadel. Though he and I never discussed colleges or anything that might improve my status, he remains the single greatest influence in my approach to the future. Many have questioned why any guy would voluntarily sign up for the kind of misery dished-out at The Citadel. Thanks to Charles, I had my reasons. My burning ambition was created by a need to escape to a world where I would no longer be ranked as a second-class citizen. I had no desire to remain where I wasn't wanted, and had already suffered enough because of my brother's fear that I might just decide to stay. So I searched for my identity in life in a new place; I wanted to be anything other than a farm hand in the sticks of Carolina.

Like so many gullible young boys before me, I imagined football as my vehicle to an exodus and a prosperous future. But even my youthful ignorance was not enough to disguise that this was for me an ambitious concept. I was far too lean and scrawny to be much of a threat to anyone. But with blinding determination obscuring my drawbacks, I became hell bent on converting myself into something other than an untouchable in the O'Bryan family caste system.

The lack of meat on my bones put me in the defensive backfield early on, where I learned well the positions of cornerback and safety. I was at least blessed with above average speed, and was as much of a threat as the bigger guys. I was a fine example of the junkyard dog theory, in that if you kick a mutt enough, sooner or later he will become ornery and start biting back.

During my first year of eligibility to move up to the varsity, I became a recognized favorite player of the coaches. It was a real story to have a sophomore winning a starting position over the older juniors and seniors on the squad. But not all were so impressed. Those beaten out, along with my brother who was a senior on the team, were not at all pleased with my early rise. Bitterness ran high among those who had paid their dues by riding the bench through their sophomore and junior years only to have some sophomore punk strip them of their earned time in the limelight. Furthermore, the attention and prestige I had received as an above average player was gut wrenching to my brother who himself was just mediocre as a defensive end. There was little doubt that I had enemies, and I made it a point to keep my guard up at all times.

But the consequences relative to my resented rise to fame quickly came to a head. During a practice scrimmage, the defensive line consistently failed to execute as the offense ran plays. Time after time, the ends got burnt as the quarterback alternated between short passes and runs. There was an obvious weak spot, and he was happy to take full advantage of it to show his stuff. The patience of the defensive coordinator was fading, as Charles and the other guys playing on the line appeared to be either overwhelmed or unmotivated. Each time they would miss the play, the defensive backfield would be forced to make a score saving tackle.

The defensive coordinator finally reached his wit's end, and called for an immediate motivational session, yelling out, "You guys want to screw up? We'll screw up with some 'bull in the ring.'"

Those words sent a shock wave of distress to my brain. As a meager sized player, I had barely survived "bull in the ring" in earlier practices, and now it was even more risky. I was on the field with a group of players who had an ax to grind.

"Bull in the ring" was a hard lesson in pain. The bull was a man in the middle of a circle of players, and it was his job to escape wherever he could. That meant a balls-to-the-wall run through whoever was in the way of getting out. With the bull possessing a full head of steam and the need to penetrate, this meant some poor guy was going to get hit hard.

The circle was formed, and Charles, because his side was constantly messing up, was nominated by the coach as first to be the bull. As he started running in place, his infuriation seemed to seethe through the openings in his helmet. He had performed so badly, yet it was surely the scolding in front of the team that made his blood boil. And even with the comprehension of his nonperformance, his hateful, twisted mind somehow equated the problem's source with my presence.

With all of the energy Charles could muster, he ran straight towards me on his first try to exit the ring. He hit me hard with a full head of steam. I was sure it was the hardest hit Charles had ever delivered to anyone. I was a bit dazed by the tremendous impact, but managed to slowly get back up and resume my place in the ring.

Since Charles had made it out of the ring, another player was brought forth as the bull. Unfortunately, it was Terry Elliott, who was one of the team's starting linebackers and nothing less than a Mack truck. I had not previously participated in the "bull in the ring" drill with the linebackers and the linemen since most of the time we were separated into groups sensibly based on players of common height and weight . But this was a punishment situation, and the defensive coordinator's mind was more focused on payback than safety.

With my slow recovery, it was easy to recognize the path of least resistance. I had also been deemed a deserving target, thanks to my brother's mouth. So naturally Terry clobbered me again, but this time, with the significant addition of size and speed. He dispensed upon me the worst hit I had ever experienced, and I felt like a homerun baseball coming off a bat. The bone jarring strike knocked me into oblivion. I instantly had a concussion, and was totally out of it. In an effort to truly help, my teammates assisted me in standing back up. But this only set me up for the *coup de gras*. The coach was so busy preaching that he hadn't noticed that I was hurt and helplessly out of my senses. The next "bull" was Alvin Bunch, a defensive tackle, and a monster of pure meat and bone. As Alvin began chopping up, Charles could only smile at the sight of me stunned and unprotected.

"What are we doing?" I mumbled to a player standing beside me.

"This ought to be good," said Charles to a teammate who then

7

realized my state of vulnerability.

A few of the more sensible players could see that I was in trouble, but the defensive coordinator blew his whistle before anyone could react, and Alvin took off for the preferred weak point. He ran his two hundred and twenty-pound body straight into me as if I were a burlap sack filled with cotton. With me in another world, I took the hit standing straight up without the slightest preparation. There was a popping crack as I was knocked through the air for several feet. Alvin's helmet hit me square in the chest, which not only knocked the wind out of me, but shattered several ribs. The coach watched as the event unfolded, then raced over in a horrified panic, convinced I was dead after such a massive unguarded blow.

I was admitted to the Williamsburg County Hospital, and three hours after arriving the amnesia started to pass such that I finally began to come out of my fog and recall the story of what had happened. Though my broken ribs were painful, my main concern was finding out just how debilitating my injuries would be. My father, Charles, and the doctor were in the room as the volley of questions rolled out with the restoration of my memory.

"How's it look, Doctor Morgan?" I asked with fear.

"How many times we gotta tell ya, ya loon!" replied Charles with a laugh.

"He's starting to remember things now, Charles," replied Doctor Morgan. "Be patient. Now John, you have serious fractures in three of your ribs. Those that aren't broken are badly bruised. You must have taken a real shot out there on the field."

"I don't remember. I have no idea what happened."

Charles looked at me and said with an insinuating tone, "It was bull –in –the ring. You weren't paying attention and got nailed."

I shook my head not remembering a thing, then looked up at the doctor and asked, "Am I still going to be able to play?"

"You'll recover from this with time, but you can forget about any more football this year."

I was immediately devastated by the words that seemed to ring in my head. Even with a concussion and pain, I was shattered by the revelation. I had worked so hard to win my starting position and now, for some reason that I did not fully understand, it was being taken away.

I stewed for hours in my confusion as the cobwebs faded and I finally gained the ability to reason. I couldn't imagine what circumstances had landed me in the hospital. Then later that evening, it all started to become clear when I was visited by two of my friends who were also football players.

"The last time we saw you," said one of the boys, "you were somewhere out there in la la land."

"I'm just beginning to get my stories straight, but still have a lot of questions about what went wrong."

"There's no question about what happened, man," said one of my friends. "They tried to take you out."

"What do you mean? And who are 'they'?" I asked.

"The goons just ganged up on you. It all started with your brother. He really tried to clean your clock."

"Damn! I somehow knew Charles had a part in all of this."

"He started it, Elliott creamed you, and then Bunch finished you off."

The pain in my ribs was soon overshadowed by the knowledge that my own brother had done me in. Abuse from Charles wasn't anything new; it was that it had now reached a new level of potency. It was clear that I had a serious enemy who would exercise every opportunity to make my life miserable. Worse was that I lived with that adversary, and there was little I could do to get away.

But I was most devastated over being put out of action. I had come so far in developing myself as a player, and before I could even get into my first varsity game, all was stolen in a mean and vicious way. I was robbed, violated, and I just couldn't accept it without a fight. I argued unsuccessfully with Dr. Morgan and my mother, trying hard to convince them that the injuries would heal in a few weeks.

They could see the tears welling up in my eyes, and they struggled to understand how, after such an injury, I could be so stubborn over the obvious. What they couldn't see was the depth of my anger over my sense of defilement. Charles had taken what was most important to me, just because he felt threatened that I was somehow invading his precious world at the top. This was something I had earned, and not something he had inherited.

Doctor Morgan could see that no further conversation was needed. He asked Mom to step outside so they could talk, and they left me unaccompanied in the room. As tears streamed down my face, sundry emotions gathered, and a burning hate ignited deep within me. A serious message had been sent to Mr. John O'Bryan, that I was going to have to fight to get anywhere in life, and to escape the unjust clutches of my twisted brother's birthright. Sitting there in that hospital bed, bathed in both the physical and mental pains of having been wretchedly violated, I swore to myself that I would never again play the role of victim, and would fight back at every challenge sent my way. I would break free and flee from the shadow of the O'Bryan legacy, and intensify my efforts to the point of obsession to make it, and make it big, on my own. That would be my vindication towards this rotten world. Charles could take the farm and shove it up his ass. My direction would be something, anything other than a life in Kingstree. Even if I had to become the biggest son-of-a-bitch in Williamsburg County, I would take no more crap from Charles or anyone else. I wiped the tears from my eyes, and swore it would be the last time I would ever cry again about anything, and I fucking meant it.

CHAPTER 3

It seems that the harsh realities of life are too often the primary influence in the shaping of a young man. My heart soon grew cold and hard, and I entered my late teens carrying a chip on my shoulder, vowing never to take a back seat to anyone, and to always stand my ground. This attitude brought me an occasional brush with trouble, and often times, real grief to my parents.

My worst boondoggle was during my most celebrated summer while in high school, just prior to my senior year. I enjoyed those warm nights immensely, but not without adversity. I was bodybuilding for the approaching football season, and beer provided lots of calories to help keep the weight on as I worked out like a mad man and busted ass daily on the farm. I spent many an evening in the joints, both good and bad ones, and I turned into a pretty rough character for seventeen. I not only had the age and privileges to basically do what I wanted, but had also grown into a force to be reckoned with. I had developed the strength of body so as to not to have to take any crap from anyone while out in the crowds. No longer the ninety-pound weakling, I was up to most anyone's challenge. I had adopted some of my brother's coldhearted meanness, and made it a mission to educate others that John O'Bryan was not the person to seek out if fucking with someone was the objective. I wasn't out working Charles' family superiority gig, it was just that I had taken too much abuse from others over the years, and now that I had the ability to do something about it, it was time to adjust a few attitudes. I wanted to make it clear to everyone once and for all that if you wanted trouble with me, it would cost something to play. I never started any shit, yet I wouldn't hesitate to bust someone's ass if they asked for it.

Word soon got out that I was now fighting back, and some of my long time adversaries saw a need to confirm their place of superiority in the local pecking order. What they found was more than they bargained for. But after about the fourth or fifth fist fight during the summer, that shit soon got old. I started to grow weary of the busted knuckles and constant battles every time I went out.

One Saturday night, I went to this redneck dive down on Lake Marion, and enjoyed the company of trashy friends and lots of ice-cold beer. As the late hours arrived, and the more civilized members of the crowd departed, the more rowdy troublemakers started to take over. You could easily sense that unrest was on the rise; right up until a group of low rent smart-asses consummated the spirit of things by trying their best to start something. The mistake made was when an asshole named Arnold Finch decided he would slap my buddy Gary Hinson around just because he was too wasted to defend himself. So I stepped in and nicely asked the oaf to stop, which seemed to be just what the crowd was waiting for. Then Arnold let his mouth overload his ass, saying he had always known I was a pussy. My friends stepped in to put a halt to it becoming four against one, then it became just him and me. Alcohol made him brave but slow, and I punched quick, clean, and hard as he missed every throw. Unfortunately for Arnold, he had caught me at a time when I was plain sick and tired of people not knowing that things were now different, and that I was no longer everyone's punching bag. He was the poor soul with a big enough mouth to nominate himself as someone to make an example of. I beat him like a drum. I then decided to use his face as a message board to the rest of the world, so I also kicked his teeth in after he went down. At the time, it seemed like the right thing to do.

Little did I know the trouble I would find from that evening's events. Arnold's clan threatened to prosecute, but the family attorney worked wonders to convince them that there were people lined up to say he had started it. Word passed through the area like wildfire that I was in trouble, and I even got a visit from the sheriff. It was a big mess all right, but I got out of it after Dad pulled some strings. He wasn't happy about the incident, but for me, it was the last time anyone ever played me for a chump. My reputation went to the bad, but at the time, I kind of liked it that way.

***

My decision to go to The Citadel was one that sort of grew on me over time after experiencing several instances of being "encouraged" to attend. One noteworthy bit of coaxing occurred during my high school senior year and actually came from a man I considered more adversary than advisor.

As I sat in the clerical area of the Kingstree High School office, I ignored the stream of warm blood that ran down from my nose and dripped to stain my favorite Lynyrd Skynyrd T-shirt. The secretaries fought back their temptation to look at me, knowing well my partiality towards confrontation, and my total lack of respect for authority. I was at odds with all of the disciplinary ideals they held so high, which was in essence the only thing that protected them from guys like me. Their power was only as strong as their intimidation; except I wasn't convinced they were strong enough to even play the game.

"My office Mr. O'Bryan!" said Mr. Coswell as he walked by as if in a hurry.

I gradually rose without a hint of haste, my body language indicating what a pain in the ass this all was to me. I entered the principal's chambers as if climbing into a boxing ring, and there were no exchanges of smiles or impromptu pleasantries as I plopped myself down in the hot seat. I knew the procedure well.

"Another fight John? How many does this make?"

I said nothing, just tried to burn holes through Mr. Coswell's head with my best Charles Manson stare. I already knew he despised my appearance with my sandy blond hair down past my shoulders and my scraggily youthful beard, but with my piercing eyes I sent him a clear message that I wasn't in the mood for any of his shit.

"Who started it?" continued Mr. Coswell.

I said nothing, and continued just to stare.

13

"You want three days' suspension?"

"He did."

"Over what?"

"His brain skipped time…I don't know. You ask him?"

"He said you started it."

"Then he's a liar."

"He said you threw the first punch."

"I threw the last one, when I laid his ass out. He started it when he sucker punched me. What did your snitches tell you?"

"That you could have walked away from this."

"I don't start trouble, but I don't walk away from it either."

"What's with you John? So full of hate, so hell bent on making your own rules. Your teachers can't do anything with you. What is it that goes through that troubled, deviant head of yours?"

I silently turned to look out the window, knowing the sort of insubordination it would represent.

"Am I wasting your time here?" reacted Mr. Coswell.

"Let's just get on with it," I said. "I don't need another lecture."

This started to push Mr. Coswell over the edge.

"Is it because you think you're God's gift to football or is it because you're just a no-good, cocky little shit who should be in a jail and not in a classroom?" The fact that Mr. Coswell stooped to foul language actually got my attention. "You should be ashamed, coming from the family you do."

"They might enjoy parading around town on a high horse, but I've decided to skip that show."

"Your brother never gave us this kind of trouble."

"My brother's an asshole."

"Watch your language young man. Despite your attitude, we've tried to work with you here. Your faculty advisor has taken a great interest in your future, and you act like you haven't heard a word she's said."

"What does some prissy woman know about me? Who does she think she is, telling me what I should do with my life?"

14

"She cares about you!"

"She doesn't know a thing about me."

"And you do?"

"I know you folks are wasting your time trying to twist my mind. The teachers in this school are all wimps. They haven't a clue what it means to survive out there."

"They're not the pushovers you profess."

"You know, I just need to haul off and slap the fire out of one 'em, just kick 'em right square in their butt, then they'll understand what the world is like for me."

"It's talk like that that'll get you arrested, son."

"You arrogant people think you have all the answers."

"We know what it takes for you to be a contributing part of society."

"Speech number 962: just act civilized so we can hold hands and sing Kum-ba-ya."

"Nothing wrong with having peace in this world."

"You know what's wrong with you hippies from the 60's? You live in a flower child dream world. You think that everything is just peachy keen. Well, sometimes you have to fight to get away from those who try to make your life miserable."

"I just don't get it. You come from a successful family. You could have a football scholarship to any school in this state. What do you have to fight for?"

"Respect…and the right to be left alone."

Mr. Coswell shook his head, and then walked over to look out the window.

"Didn't The Citadel offer you a full ride?"

"So? What if they did?"

Mr. Coswell snapped around, growing tired of my disrespect. "Because you need to seriously consider accepting it. You've got an attitude that stinks, and no one around here can seem to deal with it. What you need is a rude awakening, and a swift kick in your backside. They won't stand for your ill disposition down there. You may think you're bad, but you'd meet your match down in Charleston."

"Why would I go to a prison when I can go to a party school... with women?"

"Because you need it. You think football is the answer, don't you? Let me tell you something young man, football won't always be there. One day you're gonna find you've got to make a living, and that piece of pigskin will be the last thing to do it for you. You'd better wise up. You'd better realize what's really important."

"Can I go now?"

With a sigh, Mr. Coswell could see he was getting nowhere. "Get the hell out of my office. I can't give you but five days' detention for this, but next time you'll be suspended! Understand?"

I walked out of the office without answering.

CHAPTER 4

Being the hoodlum I was, I probably would have never been accepted to The Citadel had it not been for the Vietnam War. In 1976, a post war anti-military attitude made admissions to military schools drop like a rock. That was to my benefit. With my average grades and above average wild life, I was not what one would consider as a hot recruit for such a reputable school. Luckily, the institution was also state-supported, and the fact that I was a South Carolinian gave me an added edge over those from out of state who had better credentials. In different times, I would have likely not been accepted.

When we entered Charleston on arrival day I felt an admiration for the port city's history and beauty. But as my parent's car passed through The Citadel's main gates I soon felt a sense of departure from the safety of a more civilized world. We arrived in front of Stevens Barracks, more commonly referred to as 4th Battalion. Mom and Dad walked in with me to report to R Company, and we all quickly picked up on the domineering, no bullshit atmosphere found inside. We were told what to do by the upperclassmen who were all dressed in perfectly shined shoes, brass, and fresh pressed uniforms. They were helpful, but didn't mince words or ever smile. They were pure business, and in an authoritative voice stated what they wanted us to do. My parents soon started to worry about me, and actually felt as threatened as I did. I had prepared myself both mentally and physically for what was about to happen, but I couldn't help but find my host's welcome unnerving.

My parents and I followed the upperclassmen's directions and took my things up to what they called third division. After climbing two flights of spiral stairs we found a screen door that had two yellow cards in permanent holders, one having my name on it. Inside was an amazingly simple room, with furniture that was green and metal. My roommate and I each had a chair, desk, chest of drawers called a half press, and a freestanding closet called a full press. There was a set of stacked bunk beds with plastic mattresses on each. A medicine cabinet/mirror was mounted above an old sink that had separate spigots for hot and cold water. There was a transom window above the wooden door at one end, and a large window with bars on it at the other. The floors were stained hardwood and the walls and ceilings were a rough texture plaster painted a light green. The room had obviously seen many years of occupancy, and there was no question that this was an old structure. My mother noted the absence of air conditioning, and my father swore that the prisoners at the Central Correctional Institution in Columbia had better accommodations. It was definitely nothing fancy.

I could see other incoming freshmen milling about outside the room on the quarry-tiled walkway called "the gallery." As I made trips to the car to move my things, I gave a faint hello to my classmates-to-be, and could tell that they too were nervous as they returned my greetings.

With my things all in the room, I knew it was time to cut the umbilical cord with my parents. We were all edgy and nervous, and I saw no need to sit around and beat our fears to death.

"Do you have everything?" asked Mom. "Is there something else we need to do?"

"Pray for me," I said without humor.

The three of us walked out onto the gallery, down the spiraling steps, and across the red and white checkerboard quadrangle to the outside. We struggled with conversation, as there was so little to say over the mounting concern. The closer we got to the car, the more my mother seemed to be getting upset and she soon began to cry.

"Come on, Mom, why are you crying?"

"I'm just worried about you. This place looks so rough, and although I know you're strong willed and all, I just hate to see you subjected to what this place is known to dish out."

"Come on, Frances. John will be all right. He's as tough as nails. Anyone who could play football the way he did can certainly take whatever these guys have to dish out."

My dad put his hands on my shoulders and said, "We're proud of you son. You're going to do just fine here. If things get too tough, you know how to get in touch."

"We'll write to you often," said Mom, reaching up and hugging me, "We love you. Just try to take care of yourself."

"I will, Mom," I said as I hugged her back tightly. And in a display of affection not normally found between my father and I, I hugged him too.

As they got into the car, I could see Mom struggling to hold back the tears. Even Dad, as strong-willed as he was, seemed a bit concerned.

I stood on the sidewalk and watched as they drove down the avenue towards the main gate. As I walked back towards the battalion, I acknowledged that I had reached a major threshold in my life. I was now on my own. I accepted it, and actually looked forward to the challenge that lay before me. I was confident that no matter what happened, I was going to get through this like I had gotten through so many of the other tight spots in my life. But no matter what kind of hell they dished out, I felt I could take it.

***

The next morning I arrived on the quadrangle where a bunch of cadets were milling around, so I just strolled up to one and asked if he could tell me where to check in.

"Get in this line over here smack!"

I moved into the line but was concerned that I came down empty handed. I flagged down a cadet to let him know.

"Excuse me. But I didn't bring any of my…"

"Shut up. From this point forward, I never want to hear any statements from you other than your three answers. 'Sir, yes, Sir. Sir, no, Sir. Sir, no excuse, Sir.' Say them."

I stood silent for a second, basically stunned.

"Say them," the upperclassman yelled.

"Sir, yes, Sir. Sir, no, Sir. Sir, no excuse, Sir."

"Fine, let me hear nothing else out of your mouth, understand?"

"Sir, yes, Sir."

"Good! Now, eyes straight ahead. Don't look around, don't move around, stand at attention. We'll be with you in a moment."

What a reception. It seemed that all the upperclassmen were pissed off at the incoming freshmen, not only those standing in the line, but all over the quadrangle. There was a table set up in every corner of the battalion that represented each company's area. There was N, O, R, and T Companies, with each having a huge six-foot letter painted on the side of their respective stairwells.

As freshmen checked in, they were taken over to the side and immediately given marching lessons in small groups. I was looking at a group move away when a cadet came up to address me.

"Didn't we tell you not to look around!"

"Sir, yes, Sir," I said answering his question.

"What's your name, boy?" asked the upperclassman.

"John O'Bryan," I answered.

"No, no, no!" said the cranky upperclassman.

"That's not the way you answer. What are your three answers?"

"Sir, yes, Sir. Sir, no, Sir. Sir, no excuse, Sir."

"I see that you've at least got that down. When someone asks your name, scumbag, nobody wants to know what your mamma calls you. You just give me your last name and your first two initials. You're what's known as a Cadet Recruit, better known as knob. When someone asks your name, the answer is, 'Sir, my name is Cadet Recruit last name, two initials' and then Sir. So, let's try it again. What's your name knob?"

"Sir, my name is Cadet Recruit O'Bryan, J. S., Sir."

"Good! Don't forget it."

I was soon next up at the receiving table. The Cadet sitting behind it didn't even look up and asked, "Name?" I looked down at him and answered, "Sir, my name is Cadet Recruit O'Bryan, J. S., Sir."

Seemingly having eyes on the top of his head, the upperclassman quickly looked up and said, "What are you looking at O'Bryan? Didn't they tell you to look straight ahead at all times?"

I quickly looked back up and began staring across the quadrangle. "Ok, O'Bryan. You're checked in. Your ID number is 244076." The upperclassman put several items into a plastic sleeve that had a chain connected to it that he called an "idiot bag," then hung it around my neck. "Get in line over there knob."

I quickly ran over and got in line with the three other freshmen.

Once there were eight of us, another upperclassman then began to speak saying, "Knobs, when I give you the command of right face, I want you to turn ninety degrees and face me. Ready? Right face!"

In the most uncoordinated fashion, we all turned towards the upperclassman. He then looked at the ground and shook his head.

"I can tell right now this is going to be a long day. Good morning knobs. My name is Cadet Sergeant Pewter. You, by either misfortune or fate of God, have become members of my squad. I am a member of the training cadre that will indoctrinate you into the corps, and it is my job today to get you into uniforms, teach you how to march, and introduce you to your new life here at my Citadel. I'll first try to teach you morons how to march so we don't bump into each other throughout the day. Then we'll be on our way."

Cadet Sergeant Pewter began whipping us into shape by teaching us the essentials of marching. We then proceeded outside of the barracks and marched across the Parade Ground, which was a big open field that served as the center of campus. We moved through the dew-covered grass towards Mark Clark Hall, which was a point of high activity. Groups of freshmen with hair were standing in lines outside, with other groups coming out with freshly shaved heads. For some reason, they all looked really stupid.

It wasn't long before my squad was inside the barbershop. There were five chairs with barbers transforming long heads of hair into nice shiny bald ones. I instantly understood where the name knob came from since heads became doorknob look-alikes after such a buzz job. Once in a chair myself, I felt a bit violated as the shearing razor brought a new coolness to the top of my head. I felt my long hair falling on my shoulders, and could see the new me in the mirror across the room. Once out of the chair I rubbed the fine bristles left as I moved back into line, and knew there was no turning back at that point.

After each victim suffered his moment of humiliation, we marched over to a huge warehouse, where countless yelling upperclassmen issued uniforms and other items that would become a part of us for the next four years. With each item added in my laundry bag, a check mark was placed on an inventory card found in my idiot bag.

After receiving uniforms, we went back to the barracks, where we immediately put them on. Every step of the way we were being hollered at and pushed to the limit. It seemed everything we were told to do, we were given only half the time needed. As if that wasn't bad enough, there was always some upperclassman in my face, throwing me off as he yelled constantly. I was trying frantically to get things done, but these guys didn't let up for one second. I was sweating like hell, and frustrated beyond belief.

I soon found myself back over in Mark Clark Hall, finally sitting down, and obviously there to hear someone important speak. The auditorium was filled with my freshman class, all with shaved heads. The smell of sweat rose from over 700 steaming bodies, and I couldn't recall air-conditioning that had ever felt so good. We all sat silently, absorbing the coolness of the building, marveling at the tranquility of no one yelling.

The moment soon came to an abrupt end when an upperclassman walked in and demanded that we all rise. Four men came marching in through the center, one wearing a high-ranking uniform that was genuine Army. I assumed him to be a General. The party made its way up to the front and up onto the stage. After a few brief introductions, I saw for the first time the President of The Citadel, Lieutenant General George M. Seignious, II.

General Seignious opened his speech with a few welcoming remarks, then got down to business. Though he spoke with authority, he seemed to address us with a certain passion, as if he understood everything we were going through. He made no secret that we faced a tremendous trial over the coming nine months, but encouraged us to give it our best, and live up to the challenge. He said we were to be admired for having accepted the unique test of The Citadel. He promised that if we had the stamina, courage, and commitment necessary to make it through such a demanding curriculum, the rewards would be immeasurable.

I appreciated what the General was saying. He seemed intimate with my very reasons for being there, as if he knew the commitment I had made in that hospital room years earlier. Although my head was shaved and I was in a sweat soaked uniform, I actually felt fortunate to be there.

At lunch that first day, my frustration seemed to peak. The upperclassmen were all over us to set the table up in exactly the fashion they desired. We were told that the purpose of our presence was not to eat, but to serve. Only when the mess was properly set up, and the upperclassmen were well attended to would we be allowed to eat. Try to eat that is. Food had to be offered when their serving was finished, and glasses, under no circumstances, were ever to become empty. It wasn't beyond these guys to throw a glass if we weren't fast enough, and the yelling just never seemed to cease. They continuously queried us on what they called "mess facts," which were mostly questions right out of the freshman's information book called *The Guidon*. They were irate to find we didn't already know it backwards and forwards, and swore we would pay dearly if we didn't quickly become experts in Citadel trivia.

That afternoon we were issued rifles over at Jenkins Hall where they told us that we would rather jump off the Cooper River Bridge than to have something happen to it. Once back in our rooms, they showed us where and how to store it, and later in the days to come, how to take it apart and clean it.

What became a real pain in the ass was that every time we came back in the battalion, we had to duck into this small service elevator room to get what they called a "shirt tuck." I mean these guys were fanatical about that crap. They taught us that we were incapable of giving ourselves an acceptable one, and showed us a better two-man method. We would loosen our pants and a classmate would tuck in the tails of our shirts so that they were skin tight, then we would attempt to buckle everything back while keeping it that way. The real test was to then "pop off" to the upperclassmen who would be standing on the stairs, waiting like vultures.

"Sir, Mr. Pewter, Sir. Cadet Recruit O'Bryan, J.S., request permission to drive up your stairs, Sir."

The first challenge was getting the upperclassman's name right while also addressing the ranking cadet on the stairs. Then, you go up the stairs and the jerks inspect your shirt tuck. If not absolutely perfect, they would grab the back of your shirt, pull it up, and send you back down to try again, thus starting the process all over again. Man did this get on my nerves. It could take fifteen minutes just to get up the stairs, when time was already critical and your ears were ringing from the constant yelling.

Later I saw one guy finally break down and cry when he was ganged up on by three upperclassmen that chewed him out for all he was worth. I also heard that one of my classmates had already decided to quit. It was easy to see why.

When late afternoon arrived, the upperclassmen made us line up on the first floor gallery to get ready for Evening Formation. They explained that there would be at least three formations a day, one before every meal. At any formation, no matter what the occasion, we were expected to be immaculate in appearance, or else suffer the consequences. The cadre would yell at us constantly until it was time to leave the battalion.

At evening mess the upperclassmen were again relentless. They said we had been trained at lunch, and we should now know how to do everything. But the mess hall was like a mad house.

You couldn't hear a word above all the yelling, much less maintain your concentration. There were threats by the truckload, and promises that after Wednesday, we would start to pay dearly for our mistakes. I couldn't imagine how this could get any worse.

After mess we spent the evening in our rooms learning how to put away all of our new things. Everything had its place, and had to be folded or hung just so. We learned to make our beds using hospital corners such that the spread could bounce a quarter off the middle. We learned to shine brass and shoes, and how to prepare our uniforms to meet the strict standards of the upperclassmen. We worked right up until 2300 when they blew taps, and we turned our lights off and got into our racks.

I lay there in the dark and ran my hand over my tennis ball-like hair and wondered how my girlfriend Donna would react to it. I also realized the absence of yelling, and my first real opportunity to truly relax since I exited the rack that morning. I felt the sticky remnants of an entire day's worth of sweat as my body clung to my new sheets. It was still hot, but I knew I would be asleep within minutes. The fan in the window gave only minor relief, but the hum it made wasn't quite enough to cover the sounds of my roommate softly crying in the bunk below. It had been true agony, but at least day one was finally over.

CHAPTER 5

I soon found life as a knob every bit as bad as I heard it would be. Actually, it was worse. Although I had tried to prepare both mentally and physically for the experience, it was still very hard to make it through the exhausting demands and mental anguish. I didn't stand out as a screw up among my classmates within R Company, yet I also hadn't done that great either. It seemed as if the system was designed such that you were doomed to make mistakes. It seemed every upperclassman's mission was to make your life miserable. They were masters at finding fault with us.

At the end of our third day, the cadre turned up the heat on us in our life of torment. We had been taught everything about being a squared away knob, and a lack of conformance could no longer be the result of a lack of knowledge. That meant violations represented a lack of motivation, and failure to comply. Incentives were now deemed necessary to inspire us. That Wednesday night was what would become known as "Hell Night," and with it, the Fourth Class System would shift into high gear.

That memorable evening started with us being told to remove our belts, nametags, and any insignia from our uniforms for safety reasons. We were lined up on the quadrangle with all lights in the battalion off, and then we were left alone in the silent darkness. Taps were played in an expiring way, and then someone closed the huge squeaking gates and locked them. An announcement came across the loudspeaker saying, "Gentlemen, the Fourth Class System is now in effect!" and the doors of every first floor room flew open and an explosion of upperclassmen poured out. They started yelling and screaming at us as if in a panic, then told us to get into push-up position and start pumping them out. The inner walls of the dark battalion echoed their endless yelling of commands and ridicule, and the noise served to support the chaos of us all coming under attack. The members of the cadre chewed us out for ever existing as they moved us through push-ups, sit-ups, running in place, and then back down to push-ups again. In that one spot I did endless physical drills, all while being hollered at for being unmotivated and too slow. Each knob seemed to be doing something different, yet we were all in constant motion. It would be our first time being "racked," which was the signature activity of the Fourth Class System. It was a physical penalty in support of discipline that we would all come to know well and hate.

The cadre racked us for the longest time until we were all soaked with sweat and exhausted, and my arms and legs felt as if made of lead. They then screamed for us to move up the company stairs to fourth division, where they packed us into the showers with the faucets all running full blast on hot. The steam was so thick you couldn't see your hand in front of your face, and the heat made our already scorching bodies seem on fire. They pushed us all up against the wall until we were packed in like sardines, then made us start running in place, each kicking and stepping on the other with every stride. I was tired, hot, thirsty, out of breath, and could hardly find air. I thought I was going to die.

The yelling and pushing started again, and through the blindness of the steam we were herded out onto the gallery and down into the large corner room called an alcove. The windows were all closed, and it felt like an oven inside. They packed us into a corner, and then pushed on the front few to get rid of any possible free space between us. The upperclassmen had burning cigars and only heat and smoke was found in the air as we gasped to breathe. It was so hot I thought I was in the top of a heated tobacco barn, and I was so thirsty my mouth cracked with the movement of my tongue. The upperclassmen yelled at us constantly, and quiet came only after the Company Commander, Mr. Beach, stood in a chair to address us. He greeted us with threats, and assured us that our lives were going to take a turn for the worse. He welcomed us to the only true hell on earth.

One by one, each of the major ranking cadets within the company stood on the chair to tell us of our mistake of thinking we could make it in their school. With the unbearable heat and our battered bodies packed so tightly, it took great effort to make our chests and lungs expand enough so as to breathe. A few of my classmates were spared having to hear the words of intimidation as they passed out. I couldn't believe the malice, and I then realized just how serious this game had gotten.

The final words of peril were spoken, and we were told to get out and go back to our rooms. We left carrying those who couldn't walk. Through the evening's process, some had not made it, and they took a ride on a stretcher in the meat wagon to the infirmary. We survivors found the safety of our rooms, but the cadre were once again screaming at us to get out of our sweat soaked uniforms and to hit the showers. We were paraded naked through streams of water like members of the Holocaust, given only seconds each under the flow. The night ended with the mandatory lights out only minutes after returning to our rooms. Lying in my rack, I was drained beyond belief, and I caught myself occasionally moaning from the soreness until I was finally lost in sleep.

The next day, just like on Tuesday and Wednesday mornings, we were all up again at 0530 for our daily death run. I had somehow thought that after killing us the night before they would have cut us some slack. The joke was on me. They ran us just as hard and threatened those having trouble keeping up. All of the same headaches with shirt-tucks, driving up the stairs, inspections at formations, and doing the impossible at mess were in full strength, except this time we got racked every time we screwed up. They had a rule that no freshman could do more than 15 push-ups or 15 minutes in one rack session. But there was no limit on the number of sessions per day, and those bastards could make you die in that quarter of an hour. They were masters of physical torture, and they measured the effectiveness of their work by the size of the sweat puddle you left on the gallery.

We quickly became experts in the mannerisms of the Fourth

Class System. We learned to brace, which was an exaggerated position of attention accomplished by locking up your whole body by pulling your chin in such that it nearly touches your throat and holding your shoulders back and your arms locked to your sides.

The cadre would often pull and jerk on our arms when least expected just to see if we were really bracing. When inside the battalion, a freshman had to brace at all times, except when in his room. The room was safe except when an upperclassman entered, and then we had to "pop to" until he left.

We also got into the "freshman trot," which was a braced shuffle-run used to move about while on the galleries. Our arms had to be at ninety-degree angles with our forearms parallel to the deck. We had to "square" our corners as we maneuvered around obstacles like trashcans, or just changed directions. We had to ask for an upperclassman's permission to pass if he was in the way, similar to the routine used on the stairs. We had a side assigned to us that we had to use on both the stairs and the gallery, and it just happened to also be the side where all of the obstacles were.

We also had to brace in the mess hall, and could sit only on the front three inches of our chair. Meals quickly grew nasty as they placed more requirements and pressure on us. We stayed in trouble, either for failing to perform, being slow, or not knowing one of our thousands of mess facts. We were told to "drive by" an upperclassman's room for a rack session when we didn't meet their impossible standards. We were lucky if we ever got to eat at all.

I just couldn't believe the amount of emphasis that the cadre placed on shining shoes, brass, and keeping up with one's personal appearance as we were racked constantly for not getting it right. Every minute detail was checked at every formation. The standards were extremely high, and there was never an exception. I made every effort to keep my appearance in top form, but no matter how hard I tried, either my shoe shine was dull, my brass was tarnished, my cover had lint on it, or I just didn't shave well enough that morning. If I did manage to get by on my personal appearance, then the upperclassmen would just find some bit of freshman trivia that I didn't know to nail me on. There was no way to win. We did push-ups all day, and every time I came into contact with an upperclassman it was always an unpleasant experience. To remain unseen and unheard was the best way to go about getting through the day. But even that was a challenge. A freshman's room was the only oasis of peace while in the barracks; that is unless an upperclassman decided to come for a visit. During that first week, they were a constant interruption.

As each day passed I found myself perfecting my cadet skills. I also learned to better organize my time. We were constantly reminded that cadet life would only get harder once academics were added to the system. I just couldn't believe it could possibly get any worse. I felt like they were already pushing us beyond our limits, and once classes started, they would surely have to back off so we could study.

On Sunday we went to church at the Summerall Chapel, and I stood in awe at the beauty of the building. I could not ever remember being in a grander sanctuary, and I thought the Chaplain was one of the best I had ever heard, and by far the funniest. Chaplain James was a perfect choice to preach to the Corps, and his great first impression would be a lasting one with me.

On Monday the place was overrun with the return of the upperclassmen that were not on cadre. They weren't supposed to mess with us, but were still an added nuisance since we did have to pop off to them on the stairs. That meant another hundred or so jerks to give us hell for not knowing their names.

The next day was tough as everybody rushed around to get registered for classes and buy books. It was especially hard for freshmen because we weren't allowed to walk anywhere on campus accept in the gutter and behind the buildings. While in the barracks, if we had anything in our hands, like books, and were dropped to get racked, we gained an additional twist to the burden as we had to place our hats and anything we carried on our backs while in the le an and rest.

When classes began on Tuesday, my assumption that the upperclassmen would have to back off at least some was partially correct. It wasn't because they curtailed their assaults out of kindness; it was just that certain time periods were set aside for classes and to study. They too were in class most of the day, and actually didn't have the time to fool around with us either, that is unless we had really stepped on our meat.

But for me the real eye-opener was getting into my initial classes in Electrical Engineering. It was one hell of a challenge. I counted twenty-three students there that first morning, ready to start into the undisputed hardest major on campus.

The head of the department had the first crack at us. He began his speech in a cold-hearted fashion saying, "Gentlemen, I want you to note the individual sitting to your immediate right, and then to your left. Out of the three of you, only one will finish this college with a degree in Electrical Engineering."

That fact certainly got my attention. It was a sobering statistic. It was easy to question why so many would choose such a difficult course when statistics showed they would not likely make it through.

"This course is not for everyone. Many of you may be here now because you do not fully realize the commitment. We cut no breaks here. The grades you make are the grades you receive. We pass no one unless they pass themselves."

These were stern words of warning, and it was hard to accept such an attitude that seemed opposed to encouraging individuals to pursue the curriculum. The department head seemed to be persuading us to leave and go to other disciplines of study.

But I would soon find that this was indeed an appropriate introduction. When asked by the cadre as to what my major was, I received consistent reactions to my answer. They all knew by reputation that both the Civil and Electrical Engineering disciplines at The Citadel were considered nightmares. They called both courses "pre-Business" based on the historic dropout rate. I prayed I would have the brainpower to back up my choice of a major.

As I got into my studies, I quickly found myself loaded down with an abundance of homework in subjects that were extremely complex as compared to those in high school. Everything required so much more concentration in class, and the time needed to do the homework was more than I had available. I was thankful that I had already learned to better organize my time. If I had not done so, there would have been no way to keep up with both academics and my military responsibilities.

As if all the pressure wasn't enough, there were other problems. Sleeping in the barracks was tough as I tried to get used to the sweltering nights with no air conditioning, sweating in bed as I lay there waiting for sleep. I often found myself perspiring just trying to do homework, merely sitting at my desk, leaving sweat stains on the papers I was writing. It seemed I was in the worst of circumstances, yet was expected to perform at my peak. The mental and physical challenges seemed more than anyone could ever fulfill, and I couldn't imagine that this was how I would spend each day over the next four years.

***

After two weeks of being locked in, I relished the thought of getting off campus and hitting the town. It would be an opportunity to once again taste a beer. Though fully cognizant of my academic workload, I knew I needed and deserved a break. The upperclassmen had actually stressed that there was a time and place for everything. The Citadel wanted to create an individual who was well rounded, and no one had to tell me that all work and no play made John a dull boy.

The weekend would bring with it our first Saturday Morning Inspection. An SMI was a formal and quite thorough inspection of a cadet and his room, and it represented a lot of hard work for even the upperclassmen. This was to be a practice run for the 4th Class, giving us a chance to screw up before being put through the real thing with the rest of the Corps. But to the cadre, and to us, it was serious enough. Our rooms and uniforms were expected to be blitzed down and perfect.

I spent Friday night polishing brass and cleaning my room until the wee hours of the morning. With looming threats, it was understood that failure would yield unmerciful penalties, including restriction from going on leave, which would indeed be severe.

The next morning after mess I carefully dressed into the uniform and brass I had so meticulously prepared the night before. When the bugle blew, I went down to formation scared out of my wits with the prospect of making a mistake with my rifle manual, or forgetting one of the thousand minute details to be covered.

But it had been useless to worry. I survived personal inspection without a single negative comment. When the inspection team made it into our room, I was surprised to find that with an intense search they could only come up with a little dust from inside the light cover, which yielded only a minor verbal scolding. I had expected much worse. It seemed like a gift based on what could have gone wrong.

After the inspection concluded, all of the freshmen were assembled and the cadre had a talk with us. This was to be the first indication that they actually cared about us other than just having someone to rack. In almost a big brother way they emphasized that we needed to be careful outside the gates since potential trouble lurked in large quantities, and to avoid it at all costs. They also indicated what kind of conduct was expected when out on the town and when we later returned to the barracks. It was all right to go drinking and to have a good time, but it was unacceptable to get into trouble or cause any dishonor to the school. That meant no fights, no getting arrested, no lewd conduct. We were expected to conduct ourselves as gentlemen. They especially made it clear we were to be back no later than midnight.

Although we had all lived and struggled closely together for two weeks, we really didn't know each other all that well, except for those who were roommates or who had found small opportunities to have short visits with each other. Those vague connections served to form us into large groups as we made plans to hit the joints. I felt like I ended up in a pretty good group of fellows, though at that point, no one really knew who was a stud and who was a dork. It was amazing what The Citadel had done to completely break each of us down so that we all had blundered many times.

As we struck out for frolic on the town, we first found ourselves at Dino's. The bar was about three blocks from campus and was an easy walk. It seemed that every freshman at The Citadel had been told about the place and I found myself sitting at a big round table where ten of us had bought five pitchers as a starter. I couldn't believe the pleasure that first taste of beer brought.

We went from bar to bar, sharing taxi rides, buses, and walking as much as we could. It was great to be out, even though we felt like we were walking around naked based on the stares. It seemed to me that Charlestonians would not have been so astonished at seeing knobs. The city had certainly hosted its share over the previous century and a half. Maybe they gawked because they knew what kind of crap we were going through.

It didn't take long before we were all intoxicated. I had hoped to pace myself for a long afternoon and evening out on the town, away from the hellhole I had been confined to for the previous twelve days. I guess the incredible taste of those initial beers and the mere freedom just to be able to drink was more than we could stand.

We constantly watched the time, counting the precious hours until that dreaded moment arrived when we had to return. We all felt a nervous, sinking sensation as we stood at the main gate, depressed in knowing the freedoms enjoyed that day were behind us, and that we once again faced our regimented life. In small groups of two and three we finally began our journey towards the battalion, with most walking peculiarly, some even stumbling at times. I wasn't crawling drunk, just far from sober, and was more concerned about some of my classmates than I was for myself. There was no way they would make it up three flights of stairs without a problem. I would do what I could to get them to their rooms. I knew they would do the same for me.

When we got to the first set of stairs it didn't take long to discover that the vultures were waiting. Lingering at the top were two juniors who were obviously expecting us. "Sir, Mr. Toucan, Sir. Cadet Recruit Moore, D. N., requests permission to drive up your stairs, Sir."

"Moore, you smack, have you been out drinking?"

"Sir, no excuse, Sir!" said Moore slightly laughing.

"Moore, are you crazy, laughing at the bottom of my stairs?"

"Sir, no, Sir!"

"Get the hell up here."

I was petrified. I knew that Moore was drunk and headed for trouble. I was next up to the steps.

"Sir, Mr. Toucan, Sir. Cadet Recruit O'Bryan, J. S., requests permission to drive up your stairs, Sir!"

Just as the words came out of my mouth, Moore tripped, yet got up quickly and started moving the rest of the way up the stairs.

"Moore you stupid shit. What's the matter with you? I didn't tell you to lie down on my stairs. Get the hell up here!"

The two juniors at the top of the stairs were so pre-occupied with what was going on with Moore that they never bothered to answer my request. As I looked up, I noticed Assistant First Sergeant Schmidt standing with Squad Sergeant Toucan.

"Are you drunk Moore?" yelled Schmidt.

"Sir, no excuse, Sir."

"Then let me rephrase the question. Have you been drinking?"

"Sir, yes, Sir."

"You must be drunk. You look like shit!" said Schmidt, who then turned his attention towards me. "Who's down at the bottom of the stairs?"

"Sir, my name is Cadet Recruit O'Bryan, J. S., Sir."

"You just gonna stand there?" said Toucan.

"Sir, no, Sir. Sir, Mr. Toucan, Sir, Cadet Recruit O'Bryan, J. S., requests permission to drive up your stairs, Sir."

"O'Bryan, you waste bag!" yelled Schmidt. "Who outranks who? A Squad Sergeant or an Assistant First Sergeant?"

"Sir, Mr. Schmidt, Sir, Cadet Recruit O'Bryan, J. S., requests permission to drive up your stairs, Sir?"

"O'Bryan," said Schmidt calmly, "You're such a dumb shit. Neither one of us is standing on the stairs."

I started up the stairs, but just as I did, Toucan stepped over to them, so I immediately stopped and popped off again.

"Sir, Mr. Toucan, Sir, Cadet Recruit O'Bryan, J. S. requests permission to drive up your stairs, Sir."

"Get the fuck on up here O'Bryan!" said Toucan.

When I reached the top I had two upperclassmen's faces poking right in mine, sniffing around. "Are you drunk too?" asked Toucan.

"Sir, no excuse, Sir," I answered.

"Where have you knobs been?" asked Schmidt.

"Sir, no excuse, Sir," I said.

"Go ahead knob and speak. Tell me where you've been tonight."

"Sir, we went to Dino's, The Ark, Clay's Lounge, Gene's Haufbrau, and Big John's, Sir."

"What?" yelled Schmidt. "No wonder you're so wasted."

"Who the hell's down there at the bottom of the stairs, now?" barked Toucan.

"Sir, Mr. Schmidt, Sir, Cadet Recruit Connors, C. J., requests permission to drive up your stairs, Sir."

"Drive, Connors!" answered Schmidt.

Connors came up to the top of the stairs. "Get up here beside your two classmates, hurry up," said Toucan.

The two upperclassmen moved to the other side of the gallery and began to look at the three of us as we braced our asses off. Don Moore, however, had an ever so slight shit-eating grin on his face that quickly perturbed Schmidt.

"Moore, I know you're not smiling. My eyes must be deceiving me that you're standing on my gallery, inside my barracks, with a smile on your friggin' face. Hit it asshole!"

Don immediately went down into the lean and rest.

"You hit it too, Connors," said Toucan, and Connors also fell into the push-up position, which left only me standing.

Schmidt walked up and got right up in my face. "Well, O'Bryan, looks like it's just you and me. What happened to you guys tonight?"

"Sir, no excuse, Sir."

"That's right. There is no excuse. You went out drinking and got drunk. Pretty irresponsible on your part I'd say."

I just stood there silent.

"So where are you from O'Bryan, with such a shitty Southern accent?"

"Sir, I'm from Kingstree, South Carolina, Sir."

"Just what we need. Another local grit!"

I could tell immediately that I was in trouble since Schmidt's accent made it clear he was from up north. To my relief, he turned his attention back towards Don.

"Where are you from, Moore?"

"Sir, I'm from Greenwood, South Carolina, Sir."

"Oh, another Carolina boy. How 'bout you, Connors. Pop off!"

"Sir, I'm from Greenville, South Carolina, Sir."

"O-o-o-h, isn't that just sweet? All of you South Carolina boys stuck together tonight. Didn't even bother to take your out-of-state classmates out and show them around.

This wasn't even close to the truth. Most of the R Company knobs had been together all day as we made it through the town. Only by chance did we come back together.

"Boy, you southern folks sure like to talk about how friendly and accommodating you are. But look at this! You just leave your classmates stranded to fend for themselves. Tell you what, O'Bryan, I'm tired of looking at your face. Hit it!"

I also went down into the lean and rest.

Toucan turned to Schmidt and said, "I can't believe this class of freshmen. They only think about themselves, and never help out their classmates. They're just a bunch of little snobs."

"Especially these from the South," said Schmidt. "Get up!"

We all three stood up and Schmidt began to really jump on us. "You knobs need to know one thing. I hate southerners. I can't stand the way you talk, the way you walk, the way you dress, and the way you waltz around with this facade of being so nice when in reality you just want to screw people. This college may be in the South, but you're on my campus now, and you'd better quit thinking about yourselves and start including your classmates. Hit it."

We all fell back down into the lean and rest.

Toucan, in turn, then said, "Get up!" and we stood up.

The cycling up and down became constant. Each time we got up out of the push-up position, seconds later we were right back down again. This was always the initial way to wear out a freshman before really getting down to some heavy-duty push-ups.

This racket went on for a good while, with the three of us constantly getting up and down, stopping every so often to do a push-up. It was still hot and the sweat started to pour, and before long our backs began to bow as fatigue set in. The fact that we had been drinking made things even worse. We all began to feel it, especially Don, who was by far the drunkest. With all the up and down movement, he also started feeling a bit queasy.

"Sir, Mr. Schmidt, Sir, Cadet Recruit Moore, D. N., requests permission to ask a question, Sir."

"What the fuck do you want now, Moore? Can't you see I'm in the middle of racking you?'"

"Sir, Cadet Recruit Moore, D. N. is sick, Sir, and is about to throw up, Sir."

"What?" said Toucan with a smile.

Both Schmidt and Toucan became very excited, and turned their full and enthusiastic attention towards Moore.

"What are you saying, Moore?" asked Schmidt.

"Sir, I'm nauseated, Sir, and I feel like I'm going to throw up,

Sir."

"I can't believe this," said Schmidt, "I'm in the middle of racking you, and you decide you're going to get sick? Don't do it Moore. I'll let you go, but after I'm finished racking you."

Toucan began to chime in, "Moore, if you throw up, you're gonna lick it up. You understand? Hit it, every one of you!

Toucan had an expression of pure pleasure as he squatted beside Don. "Moore, you don't expect Mr. Schmidt and I to change our schedules just because you and your stupid knob buddies decided to go drink a bunch of beer and eat a bunch of greasy food do you?"

That was all it took. With one massive gush, Don blew his whole stomach out onto the gallery. By pure accident, the surge went all over one of Toucan's shoes, as he was standing too close.

Toucan sprang up and started jumping and shaking his foot as if it were on fire. "Oh shit!" he screamed, "He puked on my shoe!"

Toucan was leaping about and slinging the hash like substance everywhere. Schmidt backed up, and Chuck and I crab-walked away to keep from getting it all over us as it gushed out across the gallery. Don could do nothing but go to his knees and continue to puke his guts out.

Schmidt backed up with a sick smile on his face, and I wasn't sure if it was because he had accomplished his mission or if he was just entertained with Toucan's dance exhibition. He wanted to laugh out loud, but struggled to keep a semi-serious attitude in front of us freshmen. However, he soon became concerned since it was not legal to physically abuse a freshman, or ignore the fact that one is sick.

"Get up you knobs," said Schmidt, still fighting the urge to laugh. "Moore, get to your room right now. O'Bryan, you and Connors get a mop and bucket and clean up this mess you've made."

Chuck and I got up and started running to where the mops and buckets were stored, knowing damn well we weren't responsible. But like all other injustices within the 4th Class System, we again found ourselves screwed. We could only take pleasure in knowing that

Toucan had a shoe full of puke.

Though cleaning up the gross mess was a pain, we laughed about the incident for a long time. I saw myself coming through the event unscathed, not realizing what it would mean for me down the road. Schmidt had revealed his deep dislike for southerners that night, and I would later find that to indeed be true. I was from the Deep South all right, and our introduction that evening left an impression of me on Schmidt's Yankee mind.

CHAPTER 6

The next morning I found myself in relatively good shape considering the amount of beer I had consumed the day before. We were glad to have the day to recover, but we soon learned that Sundays were a free day for freshmen only in theory. On those afternoons we were expected to paint company banners made from sheets to show support for the football team in the game the following weekend. This was like the ultimate test. We were given the freedom to leave campus, but we dared not since we were under the constant scrutiny of the cadre. As Schmidt had mentioned the night before, we had to be willing to support our classmates in every endeavor. Although the privilege was given, we knew better than to dare use it.

At formation that evening it was announced that all freshmen were to report to Mr. Beech's room immediately following ESP. Beech was R Company Commander, and I knew that whatever the subject, it had to be important being held in the head honcho's room.

All freshmen showed up after Evening Study Period at the exact prescribed moment of 2230. When we entered the room we were surprised to be told by Mr. Beech to let our chins out and to stand at ease. He spoke in a calm voice as he sat up on his bed, talking to us as if he were our big brother.

"OK, knobs, I've called you in here to explain another part of your life as a Citadel freshman. It's time to assign each of you to your seniors. Your first and foremost responsibility is to perform whatever reasonable tasks your senior asks of you. That may include things like emptying his trash, sending out his laundry, making up his bed, sweeping his floor, or any type of service or menial task that a senior should not have to deal with. Fellows, this is a tradition. You may not understand how this could be fair, yet if you'll notice, as freshmen you have few rights or privileges. But as you work hard and move up in the system, you acquire more freedoms and benefits. When you become a senior, you'll have the world by the balls. In other words, a freshman ain't shit, and seniors are gods. Does everyone understand that?"

The whole crowd replied, "Sir, yes, Sir."

"Good. Now that we've gotten the negative out of the way, let's discuss the positive side of this relationship. Your senior is there for you to talk to. He is someone at the top of the totem pole. If you treat him right, he'll treat you right. But let me warn you. Don't think that every time you get into trouble, that you can run to your senior and he's going to get you out of it. If I find any of you manipulating the system, I'm gonna do something about it. Do you all understand that?"

We all once again responded, "Sir, yes, Sir".

"OK, let me read off the list just who your seniors are."

There was quite a moment of anticipation in the room. Most of us had heard this was coming, and some had even been "interviewed" for the position. There were rumors of how some seniors treated their freshmen well, and some not so well. Some provided a positive influence, while others were nothing but trouble. It was said that those who ended up with a really good senior found themselves taking off in a positive direction for the rest of their cadet life, while those with bad seniors became products of poor advice or misguided directives. This was indeed a matter of serious concern for us all.

Each freshman's name was read off the list, followed by the name of the senior he was assigned to. I hoped that I would be lucky enough to get an officer, but when Beech got down to my name, the name of Arthur Benson was read off after mine. I had never heard of him. This immediately told me that Benson had to be a senior private since I was required to know every officer within the chain of command.

This was immediately disappointing to me. I already knew what it meant to have rank within the Corps of Cadets, with the privileges it brought and the many doors it opened. But I had no choice in the matter. I had to make the best of what I had been given.

As we exited Beech's room, we found most of the seniors

standing outside the door waiting for us to come out. They grabbed us and led us away to their rooms. Mr. Benson was also standing there and I found myself following him up to 4th division. I entered his room only to see another freshman already there. It was James Nixon who I had barely gotten to know since we arrived, and he was the knob of Benson's roommate, Craig Lever, who was the Academic Officer for R Company. This was somewhat comforting in that I may not have gotten an officer as my senior, but I did pick up one within the same room. I had met Mr. Lever once before when he called all of the company freshmen together to tell us that we needed to study hard and take our grades seriously. He had seemed like a decent guy, even if he was one of "them."

Mr. Benson and Mr. Lever made James and I continue to brace as they initially talked to us, acting as if they were going to be tough. "OK, you knobs," said Lever, "I hope you guys are ready to do some cleaning and take care of our shit! You are to make our beds and sweep the floor each morning, then make sure our laundry goes out and gets picked up when it comes back in. Understood?"

"Yes, Sir," we answered.

"OK, then. We'll try to make it worth your while, but don't piss us off by doing something stupid like not sending out our laundry or getting us burned during morning inspection. Y'all head on back to your rooms and we'll see you in the morning."

"Yeah, and be on time," said Benson with an obvious effort to sound tough.

That evening I thought about who I had gotten as a senior. I actually perceived Benson as being somewhat of a "give a shit" type since his personal appearance was very much borderline. My perception was partially based on the stereotype that went with most senior privates. But, he was my senior, and there was nothing I could do but make the best of it.

The next morning after mess, I went by and did all the chores Benson and Lever had spelled out before rushing back to clean up my own room. I was really pushed to get everything done, and with an eight o'clock class on the other side of the campus, there wasn't much time to tarry.

That evening after formation and mess, I made my way back to my room and jumped right into my books. I studied with the anticipation of driving by Benson's room again since he had mentioned to do so that morning. He insisted that I arrive promptly at 2230 since a knob was not allowed in his senior's room during ESP. This was a sacred study time to insure that the military did not interfere with academics, and even a freshman's senior couldn't interfere during Evening Study Period.

Around ten o'clock I was still sitting at my desk trying diligently to make some headway with some of the difficult subjects I had to conquer. My roommate, Jim Schafer, was also studying hard. Even though he wasn't an engineering major, he too had a lot of homework in his business subjects, and we were both buried deep in concentration. The window was open in an attempt to sample the coolness of the evening, and above the noise of the fan, off in the distance, I could hear a faint chant by a group of cadets.. It sounded somewhat like the cadence we used during our early morning runs during our first week. But it was ESP, and I knew better than think that someone would be out running in formation at this time of night. ESP was an untouchable study time that I thought was sacred. I tried to forget what I heard, but as I tried to concentrate the sound got louder. Turning off the fan I could partially make out what they were saying. It sounded something like "We love Cord Hill," which certainly made no sense to me. The chant got louder and louder, and before long, I realized that they were saying, "We love Sword Drill."

I immediately got excited. Was this the activity that my classmates and I were so sternly warned against observing? I stopped working and turned around to look at Jim who had also paused. I could see the wonder on his face as he too listened.

"Is that them?" I asked.

"Yeah, I think so."

All of a sudden we heard shouting out on the galleries, "Get in your rooms, knobs! And close the doors!"

We had been forewarned earlier by the upperclassmen that if at any time we found that the Sword Drill was going to come near us, we were to immediately seek a building or room to enter so as to insure that we would not observe their activities. This only made me all the more curious. I had no idea what the group was about, other than what was written in *The Guidon*, which described the Junior Sword Drill as a precision drill unit made up of the top NCO's from the junior class. I also knew that both First Sergeant Anderson and Assistant First Sergeant Schmidt were both trying out to make it, but that was it.

Both Jim and I started looking out of our window to see if we could see anything, even though we were strictly told not to.

"You think we should be doing this?" asked Jim.

"Why not? No one's gonna see us peering out the window."

"You know much about the Sword Drill?"

"I don't," I said. "A couple of guys in class said upperclassmen really don't like for freshmen to see what was going on because the aspirants had to brace and even got racked like knobs! You know, the assholes that normally rack freshmen getting racked themselves."

"I guess I can understand that," said Jim. "But what are they trying to accomplish?"

"According to *The Guidon*, they just do one performance on Parents Day."

"Seems like a lot of bullshit to go through just for that."

"I'd still like to see them getting their asses busted!"

The two of us laughed, knowing how pleasurable it would be to see Anderson and Schmidt having to take what they had been dishing out to us for the last two weeks. Nothing like having the barrel of the abuse gun turned back on them.

The sound of the Drill soon grew to a tremendous volume. Although we couldn't see anything outside of our window, we knew they were close to the battalion. It wasn't long before the chant developed an echo as they apparently entered through the sally port and moved onto the quadrangle, and the battalion soon came alive with clapping and cheering.

"I think they're inside the battalion now," said Jim. "Let's take a look out the transom."

"Not on your life. You want to get us killed."

Just as I finished speaking an upperclassman walked right by our room shouting out, "Close your doors, knobs. I better not see any of you looking out!"

We looked at each other to silently confirm our relief for having made the right decision. To be caught would surely mean many long hard rack sessions.

Based on the increasing noise there seemed to be more and more upperclassmen onlookers who were cheering. After what sounded like a couple of circles run around the quadrangle, the voices soon came to what sounded like a stationary position, and then their chanting ended. The applause died down to silence, and I wondered what the hell was happening. After a few moments, the crowd resumed their cheering, and in the R Company area, it appeared that two chanting voices started making their way up the stairs. It had to be Anderson and Schmidt making their way back up to their rooms, but their voices seemed strained and winded as they shouted "We love, Sword Drill!"

I checked my watch and found that there were only ten minutes left in ESP. Soon I was to report to my senior's room. Though it was servitude, I somewhat liked the opportunity. It was nice to be able to get to know an upperclassman whose number one agenda wasn't to rack you.

At exactly ten-thirty I knocked on the door of Benson's room. When I entered I found him watching television and Lever working at his desk.

"Hey, it's Knob O'Bryan," said Benson. "Come on in."

I walked in, and Nixon soon knocked and entered behind me.

"Have a seat on the bed," said Benson.

Both Nixon and I sat down on what appeared to be Benson's bed, which was unstacked out of the usual bunk bed arrangement. It was a senior privilege to arrange your room the way you wanted, including taking the beds apart.

"Ok, let's find out a little more about you guys," said Benson, more talkative than ever. Lever was sitting at his desk working on something quite seriously, leaving Benson with the lead on this exchange. "Tell me something O'Bryan, what bars have you been to here in Charleston?"

"Sir, I've been to probably a half dozen or so downtown, but my favorite so far is Big John's."

"Big John's!" Benson livened up a bit. "That's one of my favorites, but not many knobs go to Big John's, except the brave ones," chuckled Benson.

"I did notice that there were mostly upperclassmen in there, but I still think it's a neat place."

"So what do you guys think about this military life so far? Do you guys want to grow up to be officers like Mr. Lever here?"

I could see that Lever was listening and lightly snickered.

"Sir, no excuse, Sir," I answered hoping the subject would go away.

"What?" replied Lever. "You guys don't want to wear a set of shoulder boards? You don't want to be a Senior Private like old Benson here?"

"Shut the fuck up," said Benson. "Listen. Being a Senior Private is the life. You don't have any responsibility, and you get all the privileges. Lever here has to do inspections, check haircuts, burn people..."

"That's not true," said Lever. "I'm the Academic Officer. I just skate on by. I leave all the burning up to the Platoon Leaders, the CO, and XO."

"Yeah, yeah," said Benson. "I know you get a really hard dick when you see that kind of stuff going on." Benson turns his attention back to us. "I'm telling ya, after they put that piece of sheepskin in your hand, nobody looks back to see who had rank and who didn't.

Now, if you want to go around pissing off all your friends by burning people, maybe rank is for you. Me, I don't want any part of it. I've got too many important things to do like drinking beer, chasing women, and occasionally sitting down to study so I can graduate. O'Bryan, didn't you say you were a double E major?"

"Sir, yes, Sir."

"My god. There should be no question what you should do. You're barely going to have time to study as it is without wasting it on this military crap. You need to spend time on books, beer, and babes, and less time polishing those damn shoes and brass."

Lever looked up, starting to feel too distracted by all the talk, and said, "Hey, it was good for you guys to come by tonight, but I've got something I've got to finish here. Are you through with them yet Arthur?"

"Yep. I think I've got these boys on the right track."

I went back to my room and thought about what Benson had said. It did make some sense. What was the reason for trying to get rank? It didn't provide that many additional privileges. It was a big ego boost that took up valuable time when there were so many other important things to do. Benson had a point.

As the days passed I continued to go to Benson's room to both work and visit, and over time heard lots of his opinions towards the military and the burdens of having rank. I could never figure out if his attitude was based on analysis or just sour grapes. Whatever his reasons, Benson made a real effort to influence me to not pursue the military aspects of school and to concentrate on the fun life. I felt I already had the right perspective on grades, having decided that I would do the minimum just to pass. I saw no reason to kill myself for A's when catching hell as a knob. Though EE was a bear, I felt that to study most of every ESP was a reasonable enough effort, one that would yield at least C's. I could live with that.

So almost as a routine, I would study each evening until I heard the "We love, Sword Drill" chant heading towards the battalion. It became the symbol that marked the end of ESP. I'd quit the books and relax until time to go to our senior's room. For a while, that study plan seemed in perspective, yet, in actuality I was steadily falling behind. Unfortunately, I didn't see this as a strong reason to change. I was convinced ESP was sacrifice enough in that I often struggled just to concentrate for over three straight hours. My mind would just drift to other things, like my girlfriend Donna, and what she was possibly doing. I often wondered how she would react to my new lifestyle, with my nearly bald head and wearing uniforms all the time. Would she see me as a handsome soldier, or just think I was some sort of clown? Before I left she talked of how proud she was of me for pursuing such an ambitious direction for my life. But I often worried about not ever getting to see her. More than anything, I just missed her, and the footloose wild life of my past.

CHAPTER 7

I soon realized just what I had committed to with Electrical Engineering. Unfortunately, this conclusion was reached as a result of seeing test grades coming back that were far less than acceptable. I was soon behind to the point of feeling overwhelmed. It wasn't as if studies were all I had to deal with either. Intramurals, company drill, shining shoes and brass, and keeping my room in perfect order also demanded their share of attention. Between the books and the Fourth Class System, my weeks were high stress chains of endless tasks. On the weekends, when finally free to escape, I flew like a jailbird. It was a necessity to help me keep my sanity.

One evening on my regular visit to Benson's room I found him excited about the coming weekend and the first Senior Party of the year. He told me these were really big blowouts that were sponsored by the senior class. The events were an infamous tradition at The Citadel for years where cadets consumed large amounts of alcohol and got wild and crazy.

"Got a hot date for the party?" asked Benson. "You are going, aren't you?"

"I guess I am, but I haven't made any plans yet."

"You'd better get hoppin'. You can start by buying yourself a ticket and calling up some women cause it's gonna be one of the better parties we'll have this year."

"Will there be a band at this thing?"

"A band? You kidding? They're gonna have "The Tams." You'd better jump on the horn right now and call your best girl, and if she can't go, then get your worst one, cause you'll need to take a date. With "The Tams," everybody's gonna want to dance. Think you can scrounge up a woman?"

"I'm not really sure, Sir. My girlfriend goes to Clemson, and I doubt if she'll come down just for a party."

"That's too bad," said Benson. "But you should get yourself a date anyway. Your girl will understand. Ya know, you don't have to screw every girl you go out with. Just consider this as one of those times where you really do take a girl out just to have a good time."

"My girlfriend would probably understand. But with the way I look, I doubt if I could even get a date."

"Sure you can. Girls over at the College of Charleston would give their right tit to get a date to a Senior Party. All it takes is enough balls to give one a call. Whatever it takes man! Don't ass around! Somebody will show you some mercy."

It would indeed be an act of mercy for someone to go out with me. They'd find out quick that I didn't have a car, hair, or freedom.

"Tell you what, O'Bryan. You come up with a date, and I'll even give you a ride to the party."

"Thanks, Mr. Benson. I'll do what I can to get one, but I know it's gonna be hard."

"Don't take that kind of attitude. I'll let you off early tonight. You head on down to the phone room and see if you can call up some chick. I know you can think of one. When you get all that straight, come and see me with some ticket money."

Like most of the other freshmen, I was without a date and had no idea how I could get one. But luck did come my way. I talked with my classmate Don Moore about my dilemma, and not only did he have a date for himself, but was looking for someone willing to date her friend. I had learned during my high school dating experiences that the "friend of a friend" scenario was usually a bad deal, yet under the circumstances, I was in no position to be picky. I was determined to go to the party with a dance partner, so I graciously accepted the offer and thanked my friend for looking out for me.

I later told Benson the good news and he seemed surprised. Though he had encouraged me, I really don't think he ever really expected me to come up with someone to go with.

That Saturday I got into my leave uniform and grabbed my laundry bag that held my civilian clothes. I followed Mr. Benson out to the senior parking lot. Once outside the gate we stopped by a favorite spot of Benson's to stock up for a party. They had beer, ice, and some really inexpensive styrofoam coolers. Benson advised me to go as cheap as I could, explaining that my use of the cooler would likely be just once and that I would have to consume all the beer I bought. I sure as hell couldn't bring the extras back to my room.

Once stocked, we took off towards the Medical University's women's dorms, and not long after going in, Benson walked out with his girlfriend. She had a pretty good figure, but I couldn't consider her anything more than just cute. Benson wasn't a terribly handsome guy either, and they seemed like a pretty good match. She did have a bubbly personality, and that made it easier for me to relax.

But as we drove towards the C of C I got nervous again. I had no idea what this girl was going to look like, nor if she would even be nice. Whoever she was, I swore I would have a good time one way or another.

We pulled up to Craig Dormitory and I hopped out. Inside I could see other cadets already waiting for their dates. I called her from the lobby to say I was there, and couldn't believe how nice she sounded. I hoped it was a good sign. I watched as each girl entered the lounge area, anticipating who might be the one. I then saw a girl walk in who had a nice smile. She asked, "Are you John?"

"That's me," I answered.

"Great. I'm Julie, nice to meet you."

I was both pleased and relieved. She seemed nice right off the bat. She wasn't a model, but she was far from ugly.

Twenty-five minutes later we pulled into the beachside parking lot of the Folly Beach Pier that already held hundreds of cars. The long structure stretched out into the ocean waves to a large weathered wood building that stood high above the water on pilings. Swarms of people were making their way towards the blaring music coming from within, and I suddenly got a feeling it was going to be a good night, and I hoped that Julie was ready to party.

The four of us moved through the pier entrance, then made our way down the long wooden walkway. Inside was a huge room with a large dance floor and stage at one end. The place was old, and had obviously seen its share of parties. I remembered back in my very early youth, in the late fifties and early sixties, when beachfront dance piers were the rage of the Carolinas.

It was an excellent spot to have a Senior Party. Rowdy cadets couldn't hurt the joint even if they tried. It was built from thick timbers, with open wood rafters in the ceiling and tongue-in-groove boards as walls. It was built to take it.

Three bands were scheduled for that evening, two of which would play beach music. The music of The Drifters was blasting away on the speakers as cadets and their dates slugged down beers in an attempt to get into the mood for what was predicted to be a big blow out. Julie and I parted from Kathy and Benson and wandered around looking for my classmates from R. I finally spotted four R Company knobs at a table tucked over on the side, and we made our way towards them. They were the earliest to arrive, but only because they had no dates. I introduced Julie to each of them and observed their unspoken curiosity as to how I ended up with a date.

As the building began to fill, Don Moore and his date soon arrived, and the two girls were glad to be hooked up. Surrounded by a group of drooling, skin headed sperm banks, I think Julie was a lot more comfortable having her friend there.

A member of the senior class introduced the first band and things heated up fast. It was a good rock and roll band and I felt a big rush when their initial song reached my ears. I had already killed one beer, and I couldn't tell if it was the alcohol, music, or freedom that was the most exhilarating. Being out of the hellhole again intensified even the slightest pleasure. I asked Julie if she was ready to dance and she said she was. Other couples moved out with us, and I couldn't recall a party where so many piled out to shake a leg on the very first song. Everyone was ready to get down, and my unleashed spirit fit right in.

The energy of the party steadily built on itself and Julie and I maintained a heavy pace in consuming the beer. We were both getting a buzz and it was comforting to know that I didn't have to drive us home. I felt at ease to just cut loose, and indebted to both Benson and Moore for setting me up with such a great evening.

Julie and I weren't the only two at the party who were consuming alcohol like crazy. The whole building seemed full of drunks who were dying of thirst. It was clearly the biggest and wildest party I had ever attended. The band was really kicking in and the cadets were going crazy. The upperclassmen seemed as happy to be out as the freshmen.

The building was soon packed with cadets dancing on the floor, standing on top of the tables and chairs, and sitting in the windows that were open to the ocean. They were even up in the wooden rafters climbing over the crowd. Everyone was going crazy. For a highly disciplined college, restraint seemed far away.

After the first two bands finished playing, there was a brief moment for the roadies to clear off the stage and set up for "The Tams" performance. It was a good time to go catch a breath of fresh air before the main event started.

The building had a walkway completely surrounding it, and Julie and I moved out on it with others who shared the same idea. We leaned by the rail, looking out towards the open sea. The night was warm and beautiful, and the freshness of the ocean breeze blew across our faces as the waves crashed against the pilings below us. It was a romantic setting like I had rarely seen before.

With my knob looks I was short on confidence, especially with a date I had only met a few hours earlier. But with the alcohol, and Julie's easy-going style, I actually felt comfortable.

"Are you surviving amongst the cadets tonight?"

"I sure am. I appreciate you asking me."

"Have you ever been to a Senior Party before?"

"This is my first. But it's everything I heard about and more. There are a lot of wild people here."

I smiled and said, "I hope you're not too offended."

"Not one bit! I've just never seen so many people in one room going so strong."

"We freshmen really needed it. It's been tough so far."

"You poor guys. I know you have it rough, but from what I hear, it's gonna be worthwhile in the long run."

I could hear "The Tams" being introduced on stage, and Julie's big smile indicated she was ready for the next round.

Moving in we noticed everyone heading towards the dance floor and to the edge of the stage. With a loud "Ladies and gentlemen, The Tams" introduction, we rushed out just as the band jumped into a popular song. Julie and I started to dance with the rest of the building's occupants, and the enthusiasm for the moment was unreal. There were people shaking on the floor, the tables, the edge of the stage, and even up in the rafters. Cadets from every class were exercising a well-deserved great time.

I had a blast dancing my butt off, and I hated to think about such an incredible evening coming to an end, but there was soon a final song and the band paraded off the stage. It was clear that everyone had a ball, but was tuckered out from dancing hard and guzzling down the spirits.

Julie and I weaved our way back to the table and then looked around for my cooler. We soon concluded it was a part of the pile of styrofoam, ice, bottles, and cans that were scattered across the table and muddy floor. Benson's advice and foresight had been right on the money. I was surprised anything had survived.

On our way out we got a kick out of watching those leaving who looked like victims of a fight. Some had crud all over their clothes and looked totally wiped out. There were lots of crazies heading towards the door, yelling, making a spectacle of themselves, having obviously exceeded their sanity limit for booze.

Walking down the long pier towards the parking lot I held Julie's hand. Even after the wild night, I started to get a little tense as the situation felt a little complicated. I still had Donna to think about, and I was also self-conscious about my appearance. I had no measure of the impact that my shaved head had on women. I at least knew it killed the confidence I once had.

I didn't want to over-complicate things in my mind, yet I felt like I needed to decide what was the right and proper thing to do. Once in the car, we all talked about the party as we drove down the boulevard that leads out of Folly Beach. But things began to quiet down on the dark open road that led back to Charleston. Benson and Kathy were pretty much whipped, and she soon put her head on his shoulder to catch a catnap as we drove home.

Following Kathy's lead, I slid myself closer to Julie and put my arm around her. She responded by snuggling up and putting her head on my shoulder. Without being too obvious, I let out a small sigh of relief. The modest victory was enough to confirm I had done the right thing by not polishing the doorknob.

Julie stayed cuddled close as we drove the distance down Folly Road. When we reached Charleston, and were only five minutes away from Julie's dorm, I felt compelled to do something more.

"I really had a good time tonight," I said to break the ice.

Julie responded in a meek, low voice, "I did too, John."

I leaned down and began kissing her. She showed no resistance, and I was again relieved. We kissed as Benson drove through downtown. I enjoyed the small sampling of intimacy, and was instantly encouraged that there was indeed hope for a social life during the next four years.

It wasn't until Benson stopped at Julie's dorm that I ended the kiss. As I looked up, I could see Kathy's head lift from Benson's shoulder and say, "It was so nice meeting you Julie."

"You too, Kathy. And it was nice meeting you also Arthur...I mean, Mr. Benson," said Julie laughing.

"Sure thing, Miss Julie," said a smiling Benson.

We got out of the car and walked into the dorm's lobby. Julie turned to me with a sincere smile and said, "I really had a good time. Got a little drunk, but I enjoyed every minute of it."

"Thanks for going with me." I rubbed my hand across the top of my hair bristles. "I don't know whether it was a sympathy date or not, but I really appreciate it."

Julie responded laughing by saying, "That makes no difference. I understand what you guys are going through."

She kissed me nicely, and then turned to move up the stairs. As I walked away, I felt a rush of confidence. The night couldn't have gone any better, and it was a hell of a break from the hell back at school. Though Donna still held the number one place in my heart, it was comforting to know I now had someone local if I ever needed a date. I just had to be careful not to jeopardize what I had waiting for me at Clemson.

As I crawled into the back seat of Benson's car, he said, "You did real good tonight, Kiddo. She's a nice girl. Cute too. Saw you in the rear view mirror giving her the lip lock."

"Oh, shut up, Arthur," said Kathy, slapping Benson's shoulder.

"You don't understand. I know what the boy's been going through. He's been without any for a long time!"

Kathy just shook her head.

"I'll set a course for home," said Benson. "I've got an overnight pass tonight John, so I'll just swing back by the school and drop you off."

"Thanks! I really appreciate the ride, Sir."

"Don't thank me now," said Benson, "There's laundry that needs folding back at the room!"

I laughed as Kathy looked at Benson and said, "Asshole!"

CHAPTER 8

That evening was one of my all time best dates, and I looked forward to the next Senior Party that would take place Parents Day Weekend. I had a grand time with Julie, but was dying to see Donna again, and my hope was that somehow she could come down from Clemson for that weekend. Parents Day was considered the biggest event of the year for cadets. For the 4th Class, it was the first big happening where parents are encouraged to come to the school and get a first-hand look at how their sons were doing. For the seniors, it was their big moment to receive their coveted Citadel rings. There would be the formal Ring Hop and the Junior Sword Drill performance on Friday evening, then a Senior Party following the football game on Saturday. It would be an action packed weekend, and a great time for a girlfriend to see a freshman cadet in his new life.

Although Parents Day was more than a month away, I wanted to plan ahead and make arrangements so that everything would be perfect. I had been writing to Donna regularly, and she had written me back once. Her letter indicated that it was a big change for her to go to Clemson, getting lost in a student body so big. She described it as exciting and fun, and that she had made a lot of new friends. She also said she kept busy to pass the time while away from me.

I felt a little uneasy as Donna mentioned the many parties and the fraternity rushes. I knew those gatherings were filled with opportunities for her to meet other guys, and like me, would almost have to date in order to attend without feeling awkward. It was this sort of understanding that justified in my mind getting a date for the Senior Party. But I just had this feeling that the combination of distance, loneliness, and opportunity was going to make our relationship a challenge.

Sunday evening following the Senior Party, I spent ESP writing a letter to Donna, telling her more about my challenges and how I was missing her. I also told her about going to the party and having a wonderful time, yet didn't include any details about having a date. Although I would understand if she did the same thing, I certainly didn't want to encourage it. I only brought it up to build some excitement about Senior Parties so she would want to come. I invited her for the entire weekend and indicated how much I sincerely wanted to be with her.

As I further pondered over Donna and our situation, my thoughts were again interrupted by the now familiar sound off in the distance of "We love Sword Drill."

"My God," I said to Jim, "not them again. How often do these guys go out? We just came off of a big weekend where everyone got wasted, and these guys are already back playing soldier again."

I just couldn't fathom the sort of dedication to military life these Sword Drill guys possessed. Benson said they were a bunch of whackos, but there was something very strange about the mystery surrounding the whole deal. I had to admit I was a little curious about it. Based on the stories, these guys were going through some ridiculously sick and painful stuff just to put on a single show Parents Day weekend. To me, the weekend meant all kinds of things, including seeing Donna again. I could care less about Sword Drill.

But ignore them I could not. Every evening, I would again hear the upperclassmen, moving down the galleries, hollering for freshmen to get inside their rooms. I wasn't sure what these guys were so secretive about, but I longed to somehow relay to the upperclassmen that I couldn't give a shit about their almighty Sword Drill secrets. I just wished they would quit disturbing my ESP's with that stupid chant. I sure didn't like the assholes who were trying out for it. It was loaded with the biggest pricks in the Corps, and if this was their clientele, then I surely wanted nothing to do with it. I had enjoyed the Senior Party, and being out with Benson, and I now had a real appreciation for his give-a-shit attitude concerning military life. He was right! Instead of wasting time playing army one would be better off concentrating on more rewarding things. Free time should be dedicated towards chasing leg and slamming' down cold beers.

Although the highly disciplined and structured life of The Citadel was one of the things that had attracted me to the school, I was not about to devote a tremendous amount of time or effort to the pomp and circumstance of the military. I was not at The Citadel to set the world on fire militarily or academically. It was fine with me just to make my way through as a private with average grades. I just wanted to do the minimum to pass and then have some time to get out on the town. No one could tell me I wasn't already sacrificing enough.

And for the first couple of weeks after that first Senior Party, I felt really comfortable with what I was doing. It seemed that there was less pressure on me by taking on a more laid-back attitude. However, I was in a system that was designed and refined over the years to push an individual to his limits. Though my outlook might have seemed justified, it was in reality as dangerous and faulty to a freshman cadet as any. In order just to survive as a freshman at The Citadel, one must give a hundred percent at all times. The system was conceived with high standards as its basis, and the only way to meet them was by doing one's best and then some.

On a Thursday evening, I went to see my good buddy Don Moore. He not only liked to have a good time, but also seemed to have the sort of attitude that I now had adopted. Since he was nice enough to set me up with a date, I felt indebted to him. I felt that I should extend some sort of invitation to him.

Under the guise of going to ask an academic question, I ventured over to Don's room during ESP. "Why don't you let me take you out and buy you a beer for setting me up?" "Sounds good, but why don't you just come with us tomorrow

night. We're really gonna go do something fun."

"What's that?"

"There's a drive-in theater up on Rivers Avenue called The Port that shows nothing but X-rated porno flicks. I haven't told you this yet, but I now have a car parked outside the gate."

"You have a what?"

"No shit. My brother brought it down and dropped it off for me this last weekend. It's a real heap, but it's transportation."

"Man, that's great."

"We want to christen the car right. So what I'm gonna do is get a bunch of guys together and do something crazy. Man, we're gonna set the standard for R Company knobs."

After we finalized our plans, I went back to my room where I tried to get back to studying, but my mind kept drifting to the weekend's plans. Even the pleasurable memories of what happened at the previous senior party kept coming to mind, and I could hardly study. I concluded I just needed to get out on the town again to release the frustrations that clouded my concentration.

As if I wasn't already having a hard enough time studying, I could once again hear that now aggravating chant. "How much longer is this gonna last?"

Jim lifted his head from his studies and turned towards me saying, "Not much longer I hear. The guys that have survived Drill to this point will soon be going through the final tests. I heard the juniors at my mess talking about it. I think they will have something like a marathon night where they compete in these endurance tests. Then they have something called 'cuts' where they all get graded to see who is the best. Only the top 14 will make it."

"I sure will be glad when they finish," I said. "I won't be happy to see Schmidt and Anderson back with more time to harass us, but damn, right now they always seem so tired and in a shitty mood, giving everybody a hard time. I don't know what the hell it is they're doing to those guys, but they're looking kinda rough, and it's sure making them mean. Actually, I hope the two assholes get fucked in the deal."

"Really! You talk about a couple of pricks. I hope they don't get squat out of this thing."

Jim and I tried to get back to studying, but our concentration just wasn't there. We just sat back and listened to the same old routine of the upperclassmen running through the galleries, yelling their heads off.

When taps played I hit the rack. My Friday class schedule included three in the morning and one in the afternoon and I had a test scheduled for my eleven o'clock Chemistry. I had tried to study for it during ESP, but between making plans with Don and Sword Drill coming in, I really didn't feel adequately prepared. I guess I could have stayed up late to study, but felt that would be counter-productive. Actually, I just didn't want to be tired the next day since I had plans to go out with Don and the guys and being worn down would certainly take the edge off the fun.

The next day I entered the classroom and the test was passed out. I took a quick scan over the questions and found that I was indeed in trouble. By the time the bell sounded, I not only failed to answer many of the questions, but the ones I had answered were neither precise nor complete. I worked right up until the last minute, but it was probably of little consequence since I was mainly guessing.

I felt really bad about the work I had done, yet it was too late to do anything about it. I needed to get back to the barracks as quickly as I could since noon was always prime time to get inspected. I would really have to bust ass because my brass and shoes had recently been neglected.

By the time I got up to my room and managed to put just a bit of a shine on my shoes it was too late for me to even look at my brass, so I slapped my best belt on and got down to formation. When I arrived I found that I was the last one in my squad to get there. Waiting for me was Mr. Mauldin, who was the sophomore Corporal in my squad.

"Where the hell have you been O'Bryan?" yelled Mauldin.

"Sir, no excuse, Sir.

Already mad, Mauldin checked my appearance. Looking down he could see that my shoes were polished, but borderline at best. He let them slide, but when he looked at my brass, all hell broke loose. In my rush to get down to formation, I had smudged the front, and there was already tarnish on the back of it.

"O'Bryan, you're just really stepping all over your meat today," shouted Mauldin. "First, you get down here late, and now your brass looks like shit. Hit it smack!"

And that was it. Mauldin racked the piss out of me from that moment until it was time to roll out. It was noon, and it was hot, and it didn't take long for him to thoroughly kick my butt. He didn't have the full fifteen minutes, but he used what time he had to its fullest potential.

Marching over to lunch, I just tried to put both the test and Mauldin out of my mind. After the platoon was dismissed, I moved on into the mess hall for what I hoped would be a non-eventful meal. Once inside I made my way on over to my mess to start setting up the table, but to my surprise, I found different guys at the table. Then it hit me. Today was the first day of new mess changes. I was supposed to look at the company bulletin board before noon formation to see where my new mess assignment was. Running late, I never had the chance.

"What the hell are you doing here O'Bryan?" said Mr. Horton, the Company XO. "You're not on my mess!"

I could only answer, "Sir, no excuse, Sir," since I really didn't know. Suddenly, the fear of being in real trouble overtook me."

You dumb ass," said Horton, "Don't tell me you didn't look at..."

Someone walking up to the mess table interrupted Horton yelling, "O'Bryan, what are you doing over here douche bag?" It was Mr. Wells, a Squad Sergeant.

"Sir, no excuse, Sir," I answered.

Both Horton and Wells then dove on my case with a royal ass chewing so intense that I was unable to really comprehend what they were saying, that is until Mr. Wells ordered me to follow him. I hurried over to my correct table with half the mess hall watching me. When I arrived I found my classmate Keith Wright already working to set up the glasses and the other mess items.

"OK smack," yelled Wells, "Now that you've shit all over your classmate, you think you might want to lend a hand in getting this table set up."

I was really flustered. It seemed that I had died and gone to knob hell in a matter of minutes, and my only relief was to work as quickly as possible to make up for the lost time. I grabbed Mr. Wells' glass and immediately put ice in it. Keith was right there with the pitcher of tea and poured the glass full. As I was putting Wells' glass back in place I was looking to see what others had not been prepared, and by not paying close attention I put the glass down on the side of his plate which caused it to spill. The shit I was in just got deeper.

It took a while for Wells to stopped yelling such that the rest of the mess hall could turn their attention away from me to eat. Wells of course wanted to know if I had a one o'clock. Hardly able to speak, I indicated to him that I did. But he was also available at two, so I knew where I was going to be then.

After mess I made my way back to the barracks, got my books, then quickly headed on out to my one o'clock class. I sat down in the classroom and felt momentarily relieved that I was no longer under fire. But when class was over, I rushed back to my room to put my books up, then without delay went up to fourth division to Wells' room where I suspected I was already in a whole lot of extra trouble for being late. I sprinted down the gallery and knocked on his door saying, "Sir, Mr. Wells, Sir, Cadet Recruit O'Bryan, J. S., reporting as ordered, Sir."

I then backed up over to my side of the gallery and could see Wells through the screen door sitting at his desk. He stood, walked slowly towards the screen door, opened it, and then lazily walked over to within inches of my face saying, "O'Bryan, what time is it?"

"Sir, no excuse, Sir," I answered.

"I'm not sure what your watch says, but according to mine, you're almost five minutes late. Hit it dip-shit!"

I fell into the lean and rest and could tell by Wells' tone that he was still upset about the incident at mess, and that the rack session was going to be a mean one. He began with a long series of cherry picking exercises, where I was forced to squat and put my hands above my head, and bounce as if I were picking cherries out of a tree. This was murder on the legs, and quite uncomfortable. I was actually in pretty decent shape from a month of rackings, but my thigh muscles really began to hurt. Wells was one of the most effective and thorough rackers on cadre, and I knew I was in for a tough stretch.

After the cherry picking, Wells returned me to the push-up position, and then had me right back up again. He then kept me moving up and down in a constant cycle as another ploy to generate a lot of intense physical activity. The only thing the fifteen push-ups or fifteen-minute rule did was to prevent a rack session from running on forever. The limits were a blessing, but with other innovative exercises available, they had more than enough time and ways to break a freshman's endurance.

Wells pushed me as hard and fast as he could, moving me from one position to another, with me constantly giving it my all. I quickly grew tired and felt myself sweating and breathing really heavily, yet the session seemed to go on forever.

Finally I approached my fifteenth push-up. Although I had no way of knowing how much time had elapsed, I suspected it was the full fifteen minutes. The aggregate of all of the exercises had me feeling that I had neither the strength nor the willpower to do the last one. But with every ounce of strength and strain I had left, I managed to execute a quasi form of a wobbling push-up. At its completion I was told to stand back up and brace. I was soaked, the gallery held a puddle of sweat, and I was exhausted. It was the worst 15 minutes of physical agony I had ever been through, and I knew it was hard payment for spilling a glass of tea.

"Ok, knob," said Wells, "I hope you learned your lesson. Any freshman on my mess has got to perform at peak, with no excuses whatsoever. I'll be watching you smack. Now get the hell out of here."

I returned to my room and plopped myself down in my desk

chair. The sweat was still pouring, as the September heat showed no sympathy for my plight. My legs felt like rubber, and my back muscles were in knots. But the relief from sitting down was shattered by thoughts of the approaching formation for parade. I wanted to have my brass and shoes shined up exceptionally well so that I wouldn't make matters any worse with Mauldin. By showing up with everything blitzed, it might help me gain at least some compassion for having messed up earlier.

I worked on my brass and shoes right up until it was time to go down for parade. When I arrived early, I found Mauldin wasn't even in sight. But after five minutes of steady arrivals by others, I heard footsteps coming up behind me. Mauldin then walked in front of me and said, "Well, O'Bryan, I see you've made it down to formation on time, this time."

He looked closely at my appearance and after a glance said "My, my! Check out those shoes and brass. You must really want to make up for earlier. The effort is appreciated, but hit it anyway!"

I immediately dropped into the lean and rest. But this time, instead of my flat and stable cunt cap, I had my oval shaped Garrison hat and rifle to deal with. The hat as usual was to go on my back, which was hard to keep balanced unless I remained perfectly still. The rifle had to be placed between the back of my legs such that the barrel was resting on my butt and the stock was cradled in the valley created by my two legs being held together. This was hard to pull off.

I remained in push-up position as Mauldin looked over the other freshmen in the squad, and very quickly I began to feel the strain coming over my body. It wasn't long before I was fighting hard just to keep my back straight enough to keep my hat from sliding off.

After several minutes my back began to sway badly, and the more I fought to keep it straight, the more my hat fell off my back. Each time it did I would have to reach back, pick it up off the gallery, and return it to my back while remaining in push-up position. Mauldin began to see that I was having a hard time, yet provided neither sympathy nor relief for what I was going through.

Mauldin finally decided to show me some attention and turned towards me saying, "OK, O'Bryan, down."

As soon as I went down, the pain and fatigue became dominant, and there wasn't enough strength left in my arms to do the move gracefully. And soon as I bottomed out I could hear my blitzed brass hit the gallery and scrape. I knew from the sound of the metal hitting concrete that it would be gouged such that the entire piece would probably have to be trashed. With all the work it took to get it right in the first place, I hated to think of starting all over again. I began to wonder when this nightmare would end.

Mauldin finally said "up," and I came back up straining to say "Sir, one, Sir."

I could not believe how acutely my arms, back, and shoulders were sending me painful messages that they had had enough. The sensation was only broken by Mauldin's voice again saying "down," and I again heard my brass hit the gallery.

"O'Bryan, is that your brass on the gallery?"

In a very strained voice I replied, "Sir, yes, Sir."

"Get up maggot!"

Mauldin immediately positioned himself in front of me, looked down at my brass, and then shook his head saying, "You dumb shit, you've ruined this piece of brass. Why are you such a wuss? If you hadn't been wimping out you'd have never ruined this breastplate. O'Bryan, I'm gonna cut you a break here. I'm not even gonna rack you until after parade. As soon as we get back to the battalion, I want you to drive by my room and we'll take care of this matter once and for all."

What a major bummer. I still had to go through another rack session after parade? This was unreal. How much longer would this ordeal last?

Though physically exhausted, I tried as hard as I could not to screw up during Parade, knowing that this running tragedy had to end. Even if my body was killing me, I was going to do everything necessary to keep from advancing my plight. But even that commitment was tested while out on the Parade Ground as sand gnats began biting me on my neck, despite the fact I had worn bug spray. For an upperclassman to see me move or scratch would be my end. The normal punishment for moving was ten confinements, so that would at least be the starting point for a knob.

When parade concluded, we were marched back to the battalion and dismissed. I quickly got up to my room, changed back into my gray nasties, and then took off towards Mauldin's room.

"Sir, Mr. Mauldin, Sir, Cadet Recruit O'Bryan, J. S., reporting as ordered, Sir."

I could see both Mauldin and his roommate inside, still getting undressed from parade, readying for their weekend since General Leave was in effect. For a moment, he seemed a bit surprised I was there, possibly forgetting that he had told me to come by.

"O'Bryan, you tool, it's time for the weekend you idiot. Now you're cutting into my plans. Hit it!"

I quickly went down into the lean and rest just as I had done so many times during the day. I knew that I was in for a really kick ass rack session. There was nothing to provide interruptions. But Mauldin turned and went back into his room and began to change his clothes. I could hear him talking to his roommate, going on about plans for the weekend. I could hear him yell out, "down!" and I immediately reacted. I could hear him talking away and in between words I heard, "up!" I responded with, "Sir, one, Sir."

This went on, as Mauldin seemed too busy to deal with me. The rack session was apparently a low priority for him, and I was thankful. I pumped out push-ups as he slackly called the cadence. After what seemed like only a few minutes, I completed my fifteenth push-up, and then remained in the lean and rest as I heard Mauldin and his roommate continue to talk. He soon came out of his room wearing his robe, heading towards the showers. As he moved down the gallery walking away from me, he suddenly stopped and turned back as if he had forgotten that I was there and said, "Stand up,

O'Bryan."

I stood up.

"O'Bryan, you're lucky I don't have time to fuck with you today, cause you deserve to have the living shit racked out of you. But being the nice guy I am, I'm gonna let you off since it's Friday.

Now, get the hell out of here scum bag, and come Monday, I expect that you'll be back in tip-top shape! Understand me knob?" Sir, yes, Sir," I answered with approving enthusiasm. "Get the hell out of here!" I couldn't believe my good fortune. I finally reached the end of the problems that had started so many hours earlier. I was free, with only the weekend ahead of me.

CHAPTER 9

The neighborhood just outside The Citadel's main gate was old, yet well maintained. Still, one had to question the sanity of leaving a car parked and unattended for weeks at a time. I doubted the judgment of taking such a chance, not knowing if it would get stripped, stolen, or even towed. But when our group arrived at the car, we quickly understood how Don could live with such a risk. It was a working automobile all right, but one that few would waste time stealing. It was an old four door 1966 Chevrolet Impala, with a few spots on it where the white paint had peeled off. It had obviously had some rough years.

"My god," said Rosellini, "look at this piece of shit."

"You don't have to ride in it you know," reacted Moore.

"Shut the fuck up, Hank," said Palmer, "You got any wheels better than this?"

"At home!" replied Hank, "But since I don't have it here, I'd better not say this is a genuine turd."

"I have no complaints, as long as it'll get us there and back alive!" interjected Bullard.

Ten minutes later we arrived at the Piggly Wiggly where we all piled out and bought a six-pack each, three bags of ice, and a big, cheep styrofoam cooler. Once we had the collection assembled in the truck, we climbed back in amidst fighting over who would sit where.

"You guys can figure this out on the way to the theater," yelled Don. "It's a triple feature. Maybe you guys can rotate from time to time. One guy takes a turn in the middle, the next guy takes a turn by the door."

"Yeah," said Bullard, "everybody needs to have their turn in the middle."

Through careful negotiations we worked it out. Each person would sit in a given seat for half of a feature, then we would move clockwise. It was settled.

We soon pulled in at the theater marquee with its big triple X's and started down the long avenue that took us behind a shopping center. We could see the large billboard-like screen and the rows of speaker posts, and at the ticket booth we traded bills back and forth until we had a full kitty to get in. Moore didn't seem to want a debate over where we were going to park and just drove towards the middle to seek the best possible viewing position.

"Hey, dumb ass," yelled Bullard, "don't get too close to that bunch of cars. We gotta keep going back and forth to the trunk gettin' beer."

"You think anybody really gives a shit whether we're drinking beer at the porno flicks?" asked Palmer.

Don finally pulled into a choice parking space and positioned the car sort of catawampus on a grass ridge where the speaker posts were positioned. Though still daylight and no movie was yet on the screen, Don grabbed a speaker and pulled it in.

"Hey, I think it's about time for a round," demanded Bullard, "How 'bout it Conners? Your ass is first to fetch."

Conners jumped out of the car and headed back to the trunk. He quickly opened up the lid, grabbed six beers, then jumped back in with them under one arm and a handful of ice in the other, which he immediately threw at Palmer.

"You faggot," yelled Palmer, "you must want your ass cut!"

"Where's your fuckin' army?" laughed Conners.

"Hey! Don't be messin' up the ride!" yelled Moore. "It may be old, but I don't need you to fuck it up any worse."

"Y'all shut your whinny mouths," said Rosellini, "the movie is starting."

We quickly quieted down and looked up at the screen only to see some really outdated and wacky looking advertisements for the concession stand.

"OK, dip shits, the screen says we need refreshments," said Bullard, "Hand out those beers, Palmer."

In no time there were six stunned guys sitting in that old beat up car, watching the close up shots of these two so-called actors going through the motions of their art.

"Man…that guy's gonna drill that hose bag to death," said Bullard.

"Nothing but amateurs…" replied Connors coolly. "If you guys were to ever see a pro like me in action on a Saturday night, you'd jump off the Cooper River Bridge."

We all recognized the statement as just another innovative attempt by good ol' Chucky boy to again remind us that he was God's gift to women. His arrogance was entertaining, but his cockiness also made him a good target.

"Hey, Connors," said Palmer, "if I could buy you for what you're worth, and sell you for what you thought you were worth, I'd be a millionaire."

"You know Connors," chimed Rosellini, "I don't know how you can just sit here and watch your mother do those kinds of things up on the screen and not be embarrassed."

"You know, I saw your sister doing squat thrusts on a fire hydrant out in front of third battalion the other day," said Connors barking back.

That started it. The bell had rung and we all went slashing at it back and forth. The beer and the flicks just seemed to set the stage for it. Most of these guys were pretty sharp, and there always seemed to be a bit of competition between us all, especially with Rosellini, Palmer, and Connors, who each possessed massive cocky attitudes. It was hilarious to watch and listen to their battle of wits as they jousted with words.

"Would you guys shut the fuck up," I said. "I'm trying to hear what's happening on the screen. I don't need to hear your jaws flapping."

"Hey, you shut the fuck up," said Rosellini. "All they ever do is moan and groan and play that cheap, silly ass music."

We all soon found the bottom of our beer cans, and based on our best guess it was about halfway through the first feature. Along with a refill, it was about time for a change in seating. We did our clockwise rotation with two people having to get out of the car. All in all, it was a pretty good plan. It even had the efficiency of timing, with the shotgun rider able to perform his duty as he inherited the beer seat.

That old car quickly became an interestingly tough place. We were primed, ready to kick ass, and having a magnificent time. We were on a freedom high, with booze and quick wit to enhance the effect. We were entertained and amazed as roosters and whores grinded away on the screen. In our cockiness, some would try to convince the others that he had experienced similar encounters prior to knob-hood. It was one big bullshit game, but we loved every minute of it. Connors had always portrayed himself as a ladies man, and Rosellini, who possessed the deadliest tongue among us, also tried to sell himself as the dominant buck. Palmer, the right hand of the devil, just loved to egg them both on, while the rest of us just sat back and called bullshit as they all boasted away.

We killed off our first three beers of the evening in no time. I knew everyone's tolerance for alcohol was different, but working on our fourth, I could see the effects kicking in.

The party went on until we found ourselves in the final feature film. Compared to the first two flicks, it was easily the best of the three. It even had a recognizable plot and was of recent vintage. Its improvement, however, did nothing to curb our now extreme level of rowdiness.

At that point in the rotation, I was in the middle of the front seat with Rosellini and Connors, with Palmer, Bullard, and Moore in the back seat. All of a sudden the entire car filled up with the most awful stench, and it quickly became obvious that someone in the car had passed gas. Palmer quickly placed its intensity at a nuclear grade, and even with the windows rolled down, it was devastating. We maneuvered for fresh air, tying frantically to open the door to both escape the fumes as well as to release them. Half of us were laughing as we tried to get our heads outside the window. I had to climb over

Rosellini just to get my head out of the stench and into the fresh air.

"Get the fuck off of me, O'Bryan," yelled Rosellini.

"You get the hell out the way asshole," I screamed. "Open that door! It smells like shit in here."

I was hacking and coughing as Rosellini finally managed to open the door. I was trying so hard to get air that I actually fell over Rosellini and out the door onto the ground. We were all scrambling wildly, laughing at the blast. I was in the dirt with my white pants on, knowing they would have a horrible stain on them, yet, was laughing my head off.

After we recovered by getting enough air to function again, an effort was initiated to seek out the culprit. It was definitely a silent but deadly violation, which by all established rules of the common man was a severe offense, especially if the infraction occurred in the confined quarters of a car holding six guys. Based on his lack of effort to get fresh air, it was obvious that the guilty party was Bullard who was sitting in the middle of the back seat. Palmer, Rosellini, and Connors immediately lit into him, threatening to kill him for doing such a nasty thing. Palmer was especially upset since he was sitting right beside Bullard and had received a maximum strength dose of the violation.

Palmer dove back inside the back seat and grabbed Bullard by the neck and began choking him and yelling, "You son-of-a-bitch, I'll murder you if you do that again. You almost peeled the skin inside my nostrils. My fucking eyes are watering. What the hell did you eat?"

Moore, who occupied the other seat beside Bullard quickly acknowledged his deep lack of appreciation for the foul stench. "Damn, Bullard, what the hell crawled up your ass and died?"

Although we weren't parked directly beside anyone else, we were still noticed as we all bailed out of the car gasping for air. It had to be apparent to the other cars that we were suffering from the remnants of an unannounced fart. Although totally offended, we began to somewhat settle down and get back in. We were all laughing, but seriously threatened Bullard with a violent death if he were to try something like that again.

"Hey guys, don't blame it on me," laughed Bullard. "It's that mess hall food! Blame them and that sloppy shit we had to eat tonight. The beer just activated what was already in there. You know what they say, there's more room outside than there is in."

"But we're gonna turn you inside out if you try that again," returned Connors. "You'd better get outside the fucking door if you've gotta fart. Either that or you need to go to the rest room and take a big dump!"

We tried to settled back down and resume our gawking and drinking. But in the process of getting out the car so quickly, Rosellini and I spilled most of our beers. He was upset at me for scrambling so hard and causing the loss, but I easily placed the blame on Bullard, which everyone readily accepted.

Into the last half of the final feature, Rosellini was next scheduled for the beer hot seat. The last round was coming up, and he and I were already ahead of the others since most of our beer had spilled in the scuffle. So Rosellini got out and opened the trunk lid and grabbed the entire styrofoam cooler and brought it forward. He opened the back door and put it right into Bullard's lap saying, "OK, mother-fucker, I'm not getting out twice because of your screw up. You hold the cooler until the others are ready. Maybe if I put this son-of-a-bitch in your lap it will help hold the stench in."

"You gotta be fucking crazy," said Bullard. "You don't think I'm gonna hold this cooler for the rest of the movie."

"Damn right you are," said Rosellini. "I'm not getting in and out all night because of you."

"Well suppose I gotta fart again," laughed Bullard, "one of you guys is gotta let me out."

"That's what you think," replied Palmer. "You'd better hold that son-of-a-bitch in unless you have your last will prepared."

"Don't you dare let another one go," said Moore.

"Well, you guys better let me out now if you don't want to get blasted again," said Bullard.

"Listen asshole," snapped Palmer, "it's your turn to sit in the fucking middle. That doesn't mean that we sitting on the ends have got to make some special exception for you. You just hold it in until the damn movie's over."

"I don't know how I can," replied Bullard.

"You just fucking better," demanded Connors. "We'll bust your smelly ass if you do that again."

The guys made every possible threat in order to prevent Bullard from violating us again. Yet, they all knew that it would be tough for him to hold it for the rest of the movie. Palmer or Moore would have to let him out if the pressure elevated.

Rosellini and I were the first to pop new beers. What was salvaged from our last ones had lost their appeal after being shaken and spilled. We began nursing our fresh ones while the other guys finished drinking theirs and then asked Bullard to open up the cooler and hand them another.

It wasn't long before the third feature neared its halfway point, and needless to say we were getting pretty looped from the beer. For cadets, who drank so rarely, half a dozen beers can do you in. For Bullard, the effects were not only inebriation, but also bloating. The carbonation continued to work its mischief in his gut, and pretty soon he was again in need of relief. But his natural tendency to purge was overridden by the fear of his fellow passengers. He was convinced it was best to cooperate.

"It's that time again fellows," said Bullard.

"One of you assholes let him out before he burns a hole in the car seat," said Connors.

"Palmer, Moore, get your fucking asses out of the way," yelled Rosellini, "We don't want him to blow up again."

"You guys shut the fuck up," said Palmer. "Nobody's asking you to be disturbed. Anyway, you're the one's that made him hold the cooler. The movie's about over anyway. He can last 'til then."

"Bull shit!" interjected Bullard. "You guys need to let me out or suffer the consequences."

"Suffer, my ass," said Palmer. "You'd better not rip one. Let him out Moore."

"You must be fucked up," replied Moore. "You let him out!"

"I can't wait much longer," said Bullard.

"You fart and your ass is history," said Palmer.

"Let him out you stupid dickweeds," I yelled.

"Here, hold this," said Bullard as he passed the cooler over to Moore and put it in his lap. "Let me out Palmer, I can't fucking wait any longer."

"Damn, I'm really getting shit on here," protested Palmer.

Palmer reached down to grab the door handle , but just as he did, the fat lady sang. Bullard just couldn't hold it any longer, and he let it rip with a long and loud one.

Moore quickly shoved the cooler back over towards Bullard as he again started his scrabble to get out of the car. At the same time, Palmer lunged to grab Bullard by the neck. Bullard was shoved from one side while a heavy, fragile cooler was being thrust from the other. The result was the styrofoam container broken into a million pieces, with water, ice, and beer flying throughout the car and all over its occupants. The interior exploded with chaos as our bodies reacted to the icy water, and the four doors flew open and we all bailed out screaming and yelling.

It had to be an unbelievable sight to the surrounding cars. Who were these guys? Wasn't it possible to go someplace hush-hush like an X-rated movie and find some peace and quiet?

I again found myself on the ground in what was now mud. But this time, I was not alone as Rosellini was right beside me. I could see that three others had also managed to bail out. Palmer looked to be the worst casualty as he was soaked from head to toe, sitting up in the mud with the whiteness of his once clean pants gone. Arms spread and sitting statuesque in the car, Bullard was both soaked and stunned.

As if five guys bailing out of the car was not enough of a

spectacle, we were all yelling, cussing, and screaming at Bullard. Not only had he caused the turmoil, but got the car and us soaked in the process, and broke our brand new six-dollar cooler.

"You stupid fucking idiot," yelled Connors. "Look what you did to the cooler."

"Look what he's done to my beautiful car," hollered Moore.

"That car was a piece of shit to start off with," said Rosellini.

"But its a wet piece of shit now," I said.

"Shit that we've got to ride back in," said Moore.

Filthy and wet, Palmer was beyond speech as he sat dumbfounded. He could only turn to face Bullard who was still sitting in the back seat of the car, soaked to the bone and shivering in a state of shock. Everyone was ranting and raving outside the car, but before Bullard could even react, Palmer jumped back inside and again grabbed him by the neck and started choking him and hitting him in his stomach. The struggling two rolled out the open door on the other end onto the soggy ground.

We quickly ran around to the other side hoping to save Bullard from the now crazed Palmer. When we got to them, we found Palmer on top of Bullard still choking him. We grabbed Palmer and pulled him off and held him down until he calmed down.

"Shit Palmer, leave Bullard alone," I yelled, "You're gonna kill him."

"I vote that we let him kill him," said Connors.

"Ah, shut the fuck up," said Bullard sitting up in the mud. "It ain't nothing but a damn fart that you pussies can't handle."

"Pussies?" yelled Connors. "You shit in your pants and call us pussies for not putting up with it? I tell you what... I think you need to have your ass wiped. Palmer, grab his other leg."

Connors grabbed Bullard by his leg, and he immediately started kicking. Rosellini jumped on top of Bullard and held him such that Palmer was able to grab the other one even though Bullard was thrashing wildly in the mud. Just as Palmer got a grip, Connors took off running. They pulled Bullard along through the dew slick grass as he fought unsuccessfully to get loose. He was grabbing at their hands to remove them from his legs, which left him sitting up as they pulled. He was sliding around on his butt through the grass and mud in his once white pants.

"There," grunted Connors as he pulled. "We'll wipe your tail clean for you."

"It's the proper procedure after a shit like that," grunted Palmer as he pulled.

Bullard was screaming madly, "Let go of me you assholes."

There had to be many at that drive-in theater that were suspecting that six fools had somehow escaped from the asylum with a car and a cooler of beer. Patrons locked their doors as they watched in shock as the two guys dragged Bullard around, screaming as he skimmed across the grass on his rear. Some even cranked their cars to leave. Rosellini, Moore, and I just struggled to stay on our feet as our sides ached from laughing so hard.

It was fortunate that Bullard had such a good sense of humor. I think I would have had to kill those guys had they done the same to me. But fortunately, no real harm was done, except for our clothes and Moore's car.

We finally calmed down, and began the damage assessment as the last few minutes of the movie were being shown. We bailed out what remaining ice and water we could, but the efforts seemed futile. The car was both wet and muddy, and there was a terrible stench coming from the old fabric on the seats, as the moisture seemed to unlock years of odors stored in them.

We finally got ourselves in at least enough order to leave. Moore was back in the driver's seat and we were still raising hell as we made our way out to the main road. Although we all were wasted and rowdy, Palmer seemed the most untamed. The beer was like fuel that kicked his ruffian mind into overdrive.

Don drove through North Charleston to I-26 that would take us back to school. The car's crummy radio was tuned to a local rock station and was blaring out a good Molly Hatchet song that only fired us up even more. All the windows were rolled down and the night air was whipping through to somewhat help dry us out as we screamed down the road. The noise was deafening as our mouths tried to compete with the radio. It was a mad house on wheels.

Suddenly, I noticed that the interior light was on. That idiot Palmer had opened the back door, and as we moved at over 60 miles an hour, he stuck his foot out on the interstate pavement as it was whipping by. Because he had taps on his heels, sparks flew like fireflies. It scared the life out of us, and we couldn't fathom what the hell Palmer was doing. He was screaming with an ear piercing howl as he continued to wear his heal down on the pavement. Bullard, sitting beside him, grabbed Palmer by the arm and pulled him back in.

"Are you fuckin' nuts?" yelled an irritated Bullard.

Bullard was now all over Palmer, choking him and screaming, "You crazy bastard! Suppose a cop was behind us, or a pothole knocked your fuckin' foot off!"

Connors, Rosellini, and I were laughing hysterically. Everyone had already suspected that Palmer was nuts, but this was a proving point. Drunk or not, the guy was crazy.

We made it down the road hoping there wouldn't be another crisis before we got in, then parked the car back on the side street where we had found it.

"This has been quite a night for the old bomb," said Moore as he turned off the motor.

"We gave the bitch a workout, didn't we?" said Connors.

"I don't know," I said. "I'm drunker than shit!"

"You fuckin' wus!" said Bullard. "I was just getting started."

"Speaking of getting started," said Rosellini, "we'd better get our asses started. We don't have but five more minutes 'til all-in."

"Oh, shit!" said Connors.

We hadn't realized we were cutting it so close. It would take a fast walk or even run to get back in time. With Rosellini leading the way, we all took off towards the main gate. Once inside, we were again under the stringent rules of the 4th Class System. But at that time of night, usually no one except the Main Gate guard was in the area. We were able to walk swiftly, and as we moved along at a quick pace, we stayed close behind one another as if we were drafting in a stock car race. Every now and then, one of us would pass the other as if making a final slingshot move for the finish line. For extra effect, some made car noises as they moved into high gear. It was obvious we were a band of drunks.

When we reached the corner near 4th Battalion, we speed walked down the final short stretch of sidewalk before making the final turn into the sally port. As we went by the guard at the gate, he knew that we were cutting it close and said, "You guys had better hurry up or you'll be late for all-in."

The six of us moved briskly, and when we got to the R Company stairs, we made it up the first flight without a hitch. We turned onto the 2nd division gallery, but when Rosellini stopped to look up the second flight, he noticed that standing at the top was a sophomore corporal, Mr. Braddock. Braddock was on cadre, and was considered by every freshman to be the biggest prick in the sophomore class. Of all times, we now had to run into him drunk, with our clothes in terrible shape.

Rosellini immediately popped off with a slur, "Sir, Mr. Braddock, Sir. Cadet Recruit Rosellini, H.C., request permission to drive up your stairs, Sir."

"Drive Rosellini!" replied Braddock.

Next was Bullard. "Sir, Mr. Braddock, Sir. Cadet Recruit Bullard, M.D., request permission to drive up your stairs, Sir."

"Drive Bullard!" he answered. He then looked back down the stairs and yelled, "All you knobs, drive! You're supposed to have already been here for all-in."

I started coming up the stairs, and behind me followed Connors, Palmer, and then Moore.

"You idiots line up against the rail here. What's the idea of coming in at the last minute...and shit, look at you! You're a fuckin' mess! What the hell happened?"

"Sir, no excuse, Sir," answered Bullard and Moore with the rest of us not saying anything.

"Son-of-a-bitch, I can't believe this. You knobs follow me."

Braddock turned and started walking up the stairs towards third division, and as he walked he yelled, "Leon!"

A response came back, "What!"

"Come here a second. I've got a bunch of drunk knobs down here! They're probably the ones you're looking for."

Soon, someone came down from the 4th division stairs. It was Mr. Runey, who was the Guidon Corporal and highest-ranking sophomore in R.

"Get a load of this crew," said Braddock. "Not only are they drunker than shit, but look at their pants."

Runey walked down the line with a look of amazement.

"Did you knobs get into a fight or something?" asked Runey.

No one said a word.

"Well, pop off," yelled Braddock, "What about it Bullard?"

"Sir, no excuse, Sir!"

"You bunch of dip-shits," yelled Runey. "You barely made it in. You had one minute left before you were all AWOL."

Runey slowly walked down the line and checked each of our names off, then said, "OK, that's everybody. I've got to get the all-in sheet over to the guard room, so I'll leave you knobs to straighten this matter out with Mr. Braddock."

Runey walked away and I immediately began to worry. Braddock was not about to let the situation pass as his expression quickly copped an appearance of control.

Braddock was one who had obtained rank for reasons obviously other than his leadership abilities. He was a knob's nightmare in that he showed little integrity in the way he used his authority that came with being a Corporal. He looked for faults in freshmen just so he could rack them, and they were always harsh sessions, even for the slightest problem. Braddock seemed to rack knobs just to get his rocks off.

Unfortunately, Braddock now had a multitude of reasons to kill us. I could see the twisted pleasure in his eyes as he now had a crew of troublemakers needing his intense corrective actions.

"You stupid, fucking knobs! You've been out on the town looking like this! Your pants are a mess. Your blouses aren't in bad shape, so obviously you were also out of uniform. Where were you knobs?"

"Sir, no excuse, Sir!" answered a couple of the guys.

"Well, I'm not going to have any freshmen from my company walking around like this. Hit it!"

Considering the late hour, I actually looked at the whole situation as a foul on Braddock's part. He tried to get into a rack session as if it were daytime. For about five minutes, he tried to push us hard with push-ups, running in place, and giving us a hard time verbally. But I soon noticed a door had opened and a junior walking out of the room. He just stood there staring with disgust. He obviously had been sleeping and felt that Braddock's actions were uncalled for at such a late hour. I could see that Braddock quickly got the message, and immediately finished up the rack session, then sent us to our rooms with threats of taking care of us later.

We all made our way up to Connors' fourth division alcove, and as the six of us filed in the comments began to fly.

"How about that fuckbag Braddock!" said Connors.

"He's the biggest asshole I've ever seen," said Rosellini. "He had no right to rack us this late at night. The stupid ass probably got himself in trouble for making so much noise while everyone else is in the rack!"

"We need to get that son-of-a-bitch!" said Palmer.

"You gonna go down to his room and kick his ass?" I said.

"Hell no. I've got a better idea. Isn't Rosier's room right over Braddock's?" said Palmer with a scheming look.

"Yeah, it's the room directly over his," Rosellini answered.

"Let's all go there right now. I've got an idea," said Palmer.

"What the fuck you guy's gonna do?" yelled Connors.

But before Palmer answered, he was heading out the door. We couldn't do anything but react by following. When we got to Rosier's room, we found it dark and unoccupied. Rosier had a good senior who had a television, and he and his roommate were probably there watching the late show, and the fact that they were gone fit right into Palmer's plan.

"OK guys, what we need to do is stand up on the top bunk and jump off to the floor, all at the same time. We'll give Braddock a hellacious boom below."

"Are you crazy?" yelled a shocked Rosellini, "That'll probably knock the whole damn ceiling out."

"All the better," said Palmer.

"You guys are fuckin' crazy," said Bullard. "That son-of-a-bitch'll kill us. We'll be walkin' tours for ever."

"Bullshit. Now you guys wait here. I'll go down and make sure Braddock's in."

Palmer again headed out the door before anyone could say a word. As soon as he left, we looked at each other and started to debate the sanity of his crazy idea. We were drunk all right, but not totally immune from recognizing the risk.

Just as we concluded this was idiotic at best, the door flew open and in ran an excited Palmer. "Alright, I can hear him and his roommate in there talking. There's not a soul out on the gallery either."

"Listen Palmer you psycho, I'm telling you, we're looking at an ass load of trouble here," interjected Rosellini.

"Shut the hell up you wus," replied Palmer. "If we do this thing right, we'll have it made. Now, we can't all fit up there on the bed, so two of you get on a desk. I'll look outside the door and make sure the coast is clear. When I say go, then you guys jump, but you've got to be synchronized and hit the floor at the same time to get the maximum effect."

"Man, we're getting ready to fuck-up here," said Moore.

"No we're not," insisted Palmer, "Just listen to me and don't screw up. As soon as you hit the floor I'll have the lights out and the door open. Just get back to your rooms fast."

"What about us?" said Bullard, "we live on third division. How are we going to make it down there."

"Just dive into one of our other classmate's rooms and act like you're in there visiting. They'll never catch us. They'll come up here and find Rosier's room empty. They'll think some upperclassman did it. Now go ahead! You guys get up on the bed and I'll cut out the lights."

We reluctantly started to climb up on the bed and desks with Moore complaining, "Man, we're in for a world of shit."

"Shhh...keep quiet!" said Palmer.

Even though he was standing on top of a desk, Moore was still whispering that we were surely going to get caught. But Palmer was pushing us so hard and fast that there was really no way to get out of it. We were already in position.

"Ok, looks good," said Palmer. "On three!"

Don started protesting faster and louder, but Palmer just started counting louder. "One, two, three!"

On three, the five of us launched ourselves, and with great timing, we all hit the floor at the same time with a tremendously loud boom. Before the echo of the sound had ceased, we were all six busting out the door and tearing down the gallery. Under the circumstances, one would think that we would have just run haphazardly, but being drunk and so fully conditioned to the 4th Class System, second nature had us sprinting down our side of the gallery. We were in a single file line running full speed towards the corner of 4th division where the alcove was.

Normally we would have also had to square our path around the trashcan located about halfway down the gallery. That thing was always a pain in the ass as it presented itself as a constant obstacle. The first person in line was Palmer, with Rosellini, Connors, and then the rest of us following. Palmer darted out and around the trashcan and then back to his side of the gallery with Rosellini just able to react to what Palmer was doing. But Connors was unfortunately running too close to Rosellini to respond and made a direct hit on the metal container in a full-fledged run. He fell in an awesome wipeout while the can made an alarming amount of racket as it rolled down the gallery in its dented form. Right behind him was Bullard whose momentum took him right into the calamity, causing him to trip on Connors as he rolled down the gallery. Moore and I looked like hurdlers as we jumped over the bodies and never broke stride.

The noise was alarming, and at the same time that Connors was trying to get himself up he was cussing profusely. Moore and I rounded the corner and Palmer and Rosellini darted into the alcove. I could hardly run since I was laughing so hard, but quickly darted into my room just as doors began to open. Both Connors and Bullard got themselves up quickly and also tried to sprint towards the safety of a room. But it was too late for them. By a matter of seconds they missed getting inside without first being seen by Arnold Beech, R Company's Commander, who stepped out on the gallery just as they opened the screen door to Connors' room. Before they could sit down, Beech walked in and immediately began to question them. He had heard the enormous boom, and apparently so did everyone else within the company. The intensity of the effect was a bit more than we had expected. The addition of the trashcan had made it a noise orgy.

At the same time that Beech began to question Connors and Bullard, there rose quite a stir outside on the gallery. Obviously the combination of the boom and the tumbling trashcan had awakened the world. But before the two freshmen could come up with any real answers, an angry Sid Horton entered the room. He had obviously been roused and was demanding blood. "What the hell are you knobs doing this late at night."

"I'm trying to get to the bottom of this now," said Beech. "OK knobs, I want some answers. What happened?"

"Sir, no excuse, Sir," said Connors.

"Not this time assholes. What the hell was all that racket? I heard a boom and then all of a sudden you guys are falling all over my gallery with a trashcan. I want to know what you were doing, and who was with you. Start talkin' Bullard."

"Sir, no excuse, Sir," answered Bullard.

"Enough of that shit!" screamed the short-tempered Sid Horton. "You mother fuckers woke me up, so you'd better stop playing games with the three fucking answers. Now what the hell were you doing?"

"Sir, we were just running some shit, Sir," replied Bullard.

"Running shit on who?" asked Beech.

"Sir, no excuse, Sir," answered Bullard.

"Enough of that horse shit we told you," yelled a now pissed Beech. "I want to know who you were running shit on and the names of the others involved. We'll start with you Connors. Who were you running shit on? I want a name."

The two guys could see that both Beech and Horton were mad as hell and getting intensively worse. Connors hesitated and then spoke, "Sir, Mr. Braddock, Sir."

"Braddock? The sophomore?" asked Beech.

"Sir, yes, Sir," answered Connors.

"OK, Bullard! I want another name. Who was involved with you?"

"Sir, Cadet Recruit Palmer, Sir."

"Palmer!" said a discerning Beech, "I should have known that radical was involved. Who else? Connors, give me a name."

Conners and Bullard were forced to name us all, but there was more noise and yelling out on the gallery, which grabbed the attention of Beech and Horton. Awakened sleepers were obviously mad and demanding answers.

One by one, Beech and Horton rounded up the guilty. As they moved from room to room searching, an irate Braddock showed up, pissed off and yelling profusely, "Look what some asshole did!"

Braddock was covered with plaster dust, and was as upset as he was mad, "My fuckin' ceiling fell in and beaned me and my roommate. Some son-of-a-bitch is gonna die for this."

Although concerned, Horton began to laugh, but quickly held back, knowing that his position as XO did not allow displays of amusement at such a belligerent act. "Just calm down man. We've got the situation under control. We know who did it, and we're rounding them up now."

"Who's the asshole? Who's the son-of-a-bitch that did this shit?" yelled Braddock with a cry.

"Knobs," said Beech.

"Knobs!" screamed Braddock in disbelief.

Beech and Horton proceeded with their search for the damned. I was feeling lucky that I was at least in my own room, and that Jim was asleep in his bed. But I knew by the noise that things had gone to hell. Drunk, I felt a need just to hide. I quickly turned out the lights and crawled up under the bed. If someone were looking for me, they would look in the room, see the lights off, Jim asleep in the rack, and assume that I wasn't there.

I laid there for about a minute, listening to the noise outside, then began to think about how lame it was for a grown man to be hiding up under a bed like some three year old. I immediately realized that if I were to get caught doing this that it would surely make things worse.

But just as those thoughts ran through my head, I could hear the screen door screeching, and the big wooden door come flying open. The lights went on, and without a word I felt someone grab my ankles and pull me out from underneath the bed. When I looked up, I saw in terror both Arnold Beech and Sid Horton with killer looks on their faces.

"Taking a fucking nap there O'Bryan?" asked Beech.

I knew I looked really stupid laying on my back on the floor in a full brace. I answered, "Sir, no, Sir."

Beech reached down and grabbed me by the shirt saying, "Get your ass up. We know you're involved with this shit."

It wasn't long before I was heading down the gallery and could see the other guys also being ushered into Beech and Horton's alcove room. When I got inside, I looked around and noticed that all six of us were present. There were also about a dozen upperclassmen gathered, all of whom were trying hard to cover their smiles with official looks of concern, all except for Braddock, who wasn't faking it. He was definitely pissed.

From that point on, there were a lot of questions and ass chewings. Everyone but Braddock calmed down, and there was almost a carnival-like atmosphere as those in charge tried to discover the details of the daring escapade.

As bad as things seemed, there were a few positive points on our side. We had bonded together to pull off something considered to be ballsy. It was impressive that we had the guts to try it, and we were at least smart enough to pick on a sophomore who was often considered by the upper two classes as a pain in the ass.

But the bad points far exceeded the good. We were freshmen, and had displayed not only a complete non-compliance towards the 4th Class System, but had demonstrated disrespect towards an upperclassman. It was also a late hour, and our folly had awakened many. I guess it was our belligerence that really set the upperclassmen's minds rolling.

The seniors in the room seemed most prone to see the humor in what we had done. No one wanted a bunch of goody-two-shoe knobs. They could tell we were sauced, and that under more sober circumstances, we probably wouldn't have tried such a stunt. But in the swashbuckling spirit of cadet life, we took a chance, but got caught.

"You shit heads are gonna pay for waking me up!" said Horton. "Not only are you gonna get racked for the rest of your miserable freshmen lives, but we're gonna set your asses on fire with tours. You'll be walkin' until you're seniors!"

As Horton was talking, Beech reached under the sink and grabbed two shoeshine boxes that were used to store the polish, Brasso, and rags needed to shine shoes and brass. He also grabbed a trashcan, turned it upside down, and put it beside the two wooden boxes. We were all bracing our butts off, yet I could tell these guys had something in mind for us.

"Rosellini, O'Bryan, Moore!" yelled Beech. "Get your asses up on top of those shoe shine boxes and grab that pipe hanging from the ceiling."

Still bracing, we all looked up and saw a pipe close to the ceiling, so we quickly stood up on the small boxes and trashcan as Bullard, Connors, and Palmer were instructed to give us each a boost so that we could grab the pipe. I could immediately feel the worn out muscles in my arms stretch as the helping hands left me. My day filled with rack sessions had left a painful signature.

Beech walked over and grabbed two brooms and a transom stick. "You other assholes, hold these above your heads, and squat on top of those boxes up under your classmates."

The others one by one squatted in a balance on top of the shoe shine boxes under us. I was hanging with Bullard directly under me. Rosellini had Connors under him, and Moore was over Palmer, who was squatting on the trashcan.

By this time the other upperclassmen had pulled up chairs to get comfortable. Someone turned the radio on and Beech lit a cigar. We had obviously opened the door up for some exotic punishment we had never experienced before. We had heard all kinds of stories about "the Old Corps" which had a harsh reputation for doing things like making freshmen hang from pipes and beating them with swords, but we had always heard this might come around recognition time.

Though I knew we were about to experience a kick ass racking, in an odd way, it made me feel better about the future consequences of our little escapade. As I hung there I could still see that Braddock and his roommate were still ticked, yet the other upperclassmen were enjoying the opportunity to have some real fun with a band of smart-ass freshmen that were in no position to do anything about it.

So there we hung. One, two, three, four minutes. As we got close to five, I started reaching the point where I could hardly hold on anymore. Beech, Horton, and the other upperclassmen were laughing and betting on who was going to be the first to fall, and whether the freshman underneath would get his neck broken or not. Even Braddock was beginning to loosen up a bit as the humor of the moment gained the upper hand, as I'm sure we looked ridiculous with our legs dangling in the faces of those under us. Although those below did not have to hang, it had to be a challenge to stay balanced in a squat on their pedestal while both holding a broom up and having someone threatening from above. But it soon became obvious that the end was near as we groaned and struggled to maintain our grip. I didn't want to be the first to drop, but I was at a disadvantage having been racked several times during the day.

The guys below were now openly talking, urging us to literally hang in there as best we could, but we couldn't hang on all night, and for me, the time had arrived where I could hold no more. I finally fell and landed on top of Bullard, which caused him to fall with me. This somehow started a domino effect, which knocked Palmer and Connors off balance, finishing off what little grip Rosellini and Moore had left. With one huge fall we all came down into a pile. The already over stressed shoe shine boxes exploded into pieces, and the bent trash can shot noisily across the floor. The laughing and cheering upperclassmen stood and scrambled out of the way as the sea of knobs blew out across the floor.

Beech started yelling over the laughter, then grabbed us up, opened the door, then threw us out on the gallery. "Get your asses out of here and get back to your rooms!"

All of the upperclassmen present then started yelling, and we scrambled to get on our feet and catch our hats as they too flew out the door. Apparently no one was hurt, and even a few of us were laughing as we started running down the gallery trying to get our hats on.

I somehow knew the event was a gift from the punishment gods.

The stupid fun the upperclassmen assholes had with us would surely relieve some of the serious trouble we were in. It seemed somewhat fitting anyway; smart-ass punishment for a smart-ass violation.

We all made a beeline for our rooms without any further activity or discussion. The day had been long, and there was little left in me for further adventure. I was beat. I had no agenda other than to hit the sack and rest my battered body. I was wasted from the beer and worn out from an overwhelming day of racking. The spinning bed was my only obstacle, but that effect soon faded as sleep found me. It was a long, hard day that needed to end.

CHAPTER 10

The next day, we all woke up suffering from our sins of drinking. I had a good time all right, but picked up lots of trouble and a whopping hangover as a result. I began to wish I hadn't done some of the things I had the night before as I remembered why I was so painfully sore. The rackings, the drive-in dirt, and the pipes were enough to pulverize anyone. The alcohol hadn't helped either.

I continued to feel rough throughout the day. I could not remember a hangover that hurt so much. We freshmen had a lot to do that day with the painting in the company area and our football banner of the week. As I worked I longed for the banner to get finished so I could get back into my rack and hopefully sleep away my clouded, aching head.

When the banner was nearly completed, I decided I would leave the guys with it and head back to my room. I had worked most of the afternoon and no one could deny I had done more than my fair share of the work. Besides, Sunday afternoon would bring another chance to contribute, and I was sure that I would feel much better then. I had just enough time to catch a couple of hours sleep before evening mess at 1800. Once I was in the rack, it took only a few minutes find sleep.

The privilege of rest, however, was going to cost me dearly. Shortly after I left my classmates, R Company's Assistant First Sergeant Kevin Schmidt decided to visit the knobs. His main purpose was to chastise the infamous six who had gotten in trouble the night before. Finding me not there, Schmidt was infuriated. No one bothered to explain that I had more hours in than most since I had worked hard earlier. But I couldn't blame my classmates, since opportunities for explanations were a rarity for a freshman.. Schmidt told my classmates that he would take care of me later.

Schmidt's main purpose in visiting the guilty was to relate the news that we were only going to receive demerits for our mischief the night before, and that we were lucky that it wasn't left up to him, since he would have "packed it up our ass."

My cohorts were happy and relieved with the punishment handed down. Getting racked along with a few demerits wasn't bad at all considering the violation, especially when we clearly deserved confinements or even tours. I would forever believe that this was more than just an act of charity by the upperclassmen. The hanging from the pipes escapade was strictly against the rules. I was certain that came to mind when the "official" punishment was being considered. They probably thought it best to go light on us since if the penalty did involve something heavy, and the TAC Officer wanted details, it may just mean trouble for them too. We could even turn them in for hazing, but none of us was that stupid, or that much of a wimp.

When a freshman at The Citadel turned in an upperclassmen for such a violation, there was always a clear signal that went with it. Everyone would assume that the freshman was a whiner or a crybaby, even when rules had not been followed. The 4th Class System was a bad deal for any freshman, and there was an endless arsenal of perfectly legal ways to make his life miserable without having to break the rules. No matter how much you hated the upperclassmen, to start taking them to the mat on technicalities was stupid and self-defeating. There were a lot of guys who just didn't belong at the school, sissy boys sent by their parents to get toughened up. Some could take the daily abuse better than others, while some couldn't take it at all. No doubt the curriculum was extremely hard, and any way you looked at it, we were all catching a whole lot of hell. Life as a knob sucked big time. But that was the challenge. Most of us were learning to deal with it, and that was how we would grow. But some wanted special treatment by trying to modify the 4th Class System into something that best fit their own set priorities and standards. To cry hazing was a way for them to justify their own shortcomings, and have an excuse as to why they just couldn't hack it. We saw it all the time.

In most cases, when freshmen were hazed such as we were, there was seldom a stink about it. It actually made a good impression with the upperclassmen, and in a weird way, brought us closer to them. The fact that it was unfair really had very little to do with it. Life, especially in the military, is never fair, and neither was any part of a freshman's existence at The Citadel. My worst moments as a freshman were all results of things that were done by the book. Granted, on rare occasions, some guys took unofficial things too far, and needed to be hung out to dry, but most things that were considered as hazing, were in actuality a joke. It was a technical dime for wimps to use to call their mamas.

Schmidt never broke a Blue Book rule his entire cadet life, yet he was the meanest upperclassman I would come to know. After his discussion with the others working on the banner, he made his way up to my room, where he opened the door and found me asleep in the rack. But he said nothing. It was General Leave, and I had every right to be there. He couldn't touch me, at least not then. He went by the rules, but he also never forgot.

The next day, I felt much better. I worked hard most of the day hanging the banner and painting in the company area. Over the two days, I had done a lot of work, and was even a bit perturbed at those who hadn't carried their share of the load. I never saw Schmidt until Sunday evening formation. He walked up to me while I stood with the rest of my squad on the gallery. General Leave was over. He could do what he wanted.

"Hit it O'Bryan!" yelled Schmidt loudly as he approached.

I went down into the lean and rest. I felt bad since I had reported to formation with everything blitzed, and had passed Mauldin's detailed inspection with flying colors. Now I was going down anyway.

"O'Bryan! What the hell were you doing in the rack yesterday afternoon?" yelled Schmidt as he squatted down beside me.

"Sir, no excuse, Sir!"

"In the rack while the rest of your classmates were working on the football banner!" he yelled.

"Sir, no excuse, Sir."

"You're damned right there's no excuse. Man, you're just shittin' all over your classmates. I can't believe it. You go out Friday night, get all drunked up, come back to the barracks looking like a total dirtball, then run shit on an upperclassman. If that wasn't bad enough, you're in the rack sleeping while the rest of your classmates are out working. Tell you what son, you and I are going to be seeing a lot of each other from now on. But for now, down!"

And that started it. Schmidt racked the living hell out of me until the bugle blew for us to roll out into formation. I just couldn't believe my bad luck. I had carried more than my share of the load, but now I found myself in trouble with the meanest bastard in R Company.

Kevin Schmidt was a leader in his class. As an English major, he wore Gold Stars, which meant he had a 3.7 or higher GPR. He had a full Navy scholarship, and was going out for the prestigious Junior Sword Drill. He was capable and effective in almost everything he did, including racking knobs. But he was from the North, and had a most unusual and deep dislike for anyone from the South. We could never figured out why, but every opportunity he had to pick on someone from Dixie, he would, especially those who were from the Charleston vicinity. Maybe he had a hard time when he was a freshman, so far away from his home in New York. He probably saw that those who lived close had an opportunity to go home at any given moment. Maybe this was his idea of how to balance out the advantage guys from South Carolina had.

As the next few weeks passed, I found myself at the mercy of Schmidt every time I turned around. I rarely got racked or even inspected by my squad sergeant since Schmidt came over at every formation. I found his attitude towards me troubling, because I knew he hated me, and there was no way to redeem myself.

I didn't think he could make matters any worse for me, but he did. As Assistant First Sergeant, he was in charge of assigning cadets to tables. Without explanation, I found myself transferred over to his mess, and soon learned it was the worst thing that could have happened to me. Schmidt could care less whether I ate or not. He pushed me to set up the table and cater to the upperclassmen and constantly interrogated me on impossible mess facts. After only a few days, I found myself constantly hungry. This was really bad since I soon lacked the energy necessary to get through my days filled with his rack sessions. I also found it hard to concentrate over the hunger while in class or trying to study in the evening.

I soon accepted the fact that Schmidt really had it out for me in a serious way. He was a pure asshole, and seemed out to punish me over a matter of regional hatred. Maybe he suspected that my Great-Great Grandfather had blown away one of his relatives during the big war, or maybe his quest for the mysterious Junior Sword Drill just made him mean and nasty. He always looked rougher than any freshman, and his hair was shorter than mine as part of being an aspirant. He always looked over-stressed and ragged. Whatever they were doing to him was showing both physically and mentally.

As the days went by during what was called the 14 Nights, I could see Schmidt progressively looking worse as his physical condition began to deteriorate. Each day only seemed to make him meaner, causing him to lash out and crack down on me even further. I had heard that the Nights were almost over, and I was more than ready to have this escalation in viciousness come to an end. Maybe then he would leave me alone.

But during the day after the eleventh night, I found out that Schmidt was no longer in the running for Sword Drill. Something bad had happened. Somehow he injured his leg. I wasn't sure how, but he was limping badly, and it was enough to disqualify him from continuing. I was curious to know the details, since it could effect my situation with him, but it was hard to get any information, especially anything that had to do with Sword Drill. All I could see was that his leg was wrapped up in an ace bandage and he had to walk with a cane. His physical pain from the injury seemed to be overshadowed only by the letdown of being out of the running. He seemed crushed by that fact alone. I figured he must have put a whole lot of effort into it by the physical deterioration that had taken place, and his great disappointment at not succeeding.

That day at lunch, for the very first time, Schmidt barely said two words to me. He just sat there and ate. It was as if someone had died. Even the other upperclassmen at the table failed in having much conversation with him. Whatever had taken place, neither Schmidt nor the other upperclassmen wanted to talk about it.

After a couple of days, Schmidt started to gain some of his physical strength back, and slowly recovered from the mental burden of the disappointment. He soon resumed his attack on me with his endless yelling and harassment. The only disappointment I ever saw out of him was when they announced over the mess hall speaker that several roaches had accomplished certain feats of strength and stamina. Loud cheering arose from the company areas of the successful Roaches. There was no cheering in R Company.

I knew that both Schmidt and First Sergeant Anderson had gone out for Drill, and as far as I knew, Anderson was still in the running. Even though his name was not called out over the loudspeaker for accomplishing one of the great feats, he was still hanging in there for the final cuts. Even with all the hoopla, the whole ordeal was unimportant to me. The Junior Sword Drill was nothing more than a mess fact and a disturbance to my ESP. I couldn't understand the reason for all the mystery and secrecy. I only knew I hated it because Schmidt wanted to be in it.

Days later, the final cuts night took place. During that ESP, there wasn't the normal loud entry into the barracks by the Roaches. There was, however, a great deal of commotion over in the other companies with the upperclassmen yelling for knobs to get their transom sticks and brooms and come down to the quad. It seemed that the entire battalion, with the exception of R Company, was going berserk. There was great celebration for a long time, and I could just guess that roaches from N, O, and T must have made the Drill, and Anderson had not.

Benson later told me that First Sergeant Anderson had indeed not made the cut. It wasn't because he was injured like Schmidt, but he had not performed well enough to make the team. I felt bad for R Company in that no one had made it, but felt no loss for Anderson, and especially for Schmidt. As far as I was concerned, the assholes got what they deserved.

As the days passed, I couldn't tell if Schmidt was over the ordeal or not. I had no way of telling other than observing his attitude at mess, which was usually so violent towards me that every other issue seemed overshadowed. I was just glad that the whole Sword Drill bit was over. I strongly suspected that it had fueled the frustrations that caused Schmidt to declare war on my life. My hope was that he would soon start to ease up a bit.

But in the coming weeks I found Schmidt's attitude would not change. He didn't seem to be as worn out, but he continued to carry a chip on his shoulder, one that seemed to have my name on it. Over the weeks that I sat on his mess, he made a point to keep me so busy that there was never time to eat. I could see my clothes getting looser day by day and my face becoming thinner. I stepped on a scale in the Athletic Department and to my horror found that I had lost thirty pounds. I could only think back to the endless days and nights during high school of working out with weights and eating like a madman just so I could bulk up. Although I was no longer playing football, I certainly wanted to maintain the physique I had worked so hard to obtain. This was a case of deliberate starvation that was ridiculous and uncalled for. I could take all that The Citadel had to dish out, because I could see a purpose behind most of the games. But Schmidt's starvation scheme lacked any purpose or value at all. Even worse was that it was directed only towards me. My classmates were catching hell at mess too, but I knew of no other who was completely denied the opportunity to eat. This guy, in a large-scale deviation from the normal freshmen curriculum, was singling me out.

I knew that the only option I had was to go to someone and

complain. But after some thought, this turned out to be no option whatsoever. If I were to do so I would simply bring upon myself a reputation of being a cry baby, and would surely lay the ground work for a very miserable finish to my freshman year. Somehow, I had to get more food, even if I ate in the canteen between classes, or hid a stash of supplies in my room.

Most of all, I hated that I was looking so rough. I had developed dark circles around my eyes from a lack of nutrition and sleep. I was behind in most subjects, and almost to a point of desperation in a few. I started staying up late trying to get caught up, but that only made me weaker and less attentive in class. I felt regret that I had been so careless with my study time in the previous weeks, and now I was in deep trouble because of it. I was playing catch-up while under the added stress of hunger, weakness, and the constant rackings from Schmidt. I had no choice but to keep trying, but it seemed so difficult without the strength.

Each day seemed to bring a new twist in the wrath of my abuser. He made federal prison seem like a nice place to escape to. I waited for something to happen, anything that would release me from the grips of Schmidt's vengeful mind. I would take relief any way I could get it.

A week away from Parents Day weekend I began to worry about how I would appear to my parents, and to Donna if she came down as I hoped. I thought of her possible reaction every time I looked in a mirror and saw what was anything but an attractive guy that a girl of her beauty would be proud to be with. I had nothing more than bristles for hair and eyes that seemed to sink into my skinny face. The uniforms that fit so well on my first day now flapped loosely on my thinned out body. My only hope was to somehow get away from Schmidt so I could eat better and recover at least some before I saw those who would notice.

I decided to call Donna Sunday night before the big weekend after struggling to study through the evening. Since we had no phones in our rooms, I had to go to the battalion telephone room where phones were lined up on the walls for cadets to stand and make calls. I hated the set-up, especially since it was used by both freshmen and upperclassmen. It was hard to carry on an intimate conversation with an upperclassman standing right beside you who was equally unhappy about the lack of privacy.

I dialed Donna's number at Clemson, then stood there shaking as it rang, hardly able to control myself when she answered.

"It's so nice to hear your voice again," said Donna. "It's been a long time you know."

"Yes, a long time for a lot of things."

"I've missed those things too."

"I hope you got my letter, and that we can do something about this problem," I said.

"Yes, I do want to come, that is if you still want me to."

"Are you kidding? I can't wait to see you."

"I've been so worried about you. Tell me, are they still trying to starve you to death?"

I wished that I could laugh and portray the situation as not serious, but I could find no humor. I knew that I was being taken advantage of by Schmidt, but I wasn't keen on letting Donna know that someone was pushing me around. I still had my pride. I had only made her aware of not getting enough food so as to lighten the blow of seeing me.

"I'm gettin' by," I said.

"That's good. I'm really looking forward to going out to one of those great restaurants in Charleston."

"I've got an excellent one picked out for you."

"I can't wait. Are your parents also coming down for the weekend? You did say it was Parents Day."

"I've written to my mother to set aside the weekend."

"Great! I'll be anxious to see them again," she said.

"When do you think you will get here?"

"I know in your letter you had indicated there would be a dance and the sword thing on Friday, and really, I do want to come for it, but I can't. As I told you in my last letter, I'm rushing a sorority here, and Friday night we're having a party. I'd miss it if I could, but it happens to be the most important evening for those who are rushing because we're responsible for setting everything up. It's sort of a test to see who is willing to sacrifice for the sorority. It would make a bad impression if I weren't there. I'm sure you understand."

"Oh, yeah," I said very disappointed, "We too have to do things for the company, and if you don't carry your weight, they act as if you're stabbing knives in your classmates. Well, when can you make it?"

"I'll be sure to leave school first thing the next morning. It's a five hour drive down to Charleston, so I can probably make it there by eleven if I leave at six."

"I really hate for you to have to get up so early," I said.

"It's no problem. I just hate that I can't come for Friday night. I hope that you're not disappointed."

"I'm disappointed only because I won't be able to see you until the next day."

"That's so sweet John. I'll at least get to see you some on Sunday too."

"Good. I wasn't sure how that was going to work out."

"My parents are a little concerned about me being on the road by myself at night, so I'll need to leave shortly after lunch on Sunday. That should give us at least some time together."

"Yeah, I guess so," I said with more disappointment. "What seems like it's supposed to be a weekend only turns out to be partial days. But I understand the circumstances."

"We'll just have to make the best of the time we have together. Where will I be staying?"

"I have a classmate whose girlfriend is also coming for the weekend. You'll share a room with her."

"Won't you be staying with me?"

My frustration peaked with Donna's question. I knew without a doubt that I wanted to, but I thought I had explained to her that freshmen were not allowed any type of overnight or weekend pass until we were into our second semester.

"Gosh, Donna, it doesn't look like I'll be able to stay out all night."

"Oh, John, I don't know if I'll be able to stand it. I really wanted so much to be with you...and I mean...really be with you."

"I know," I said with disappointment, "It seems like going to this school requires a sacrifice that never seems to end."

"Yes, I'm beginning to see that."

The next day I called my parents to coordinate the weekend with them. I was pleased to hear they had already made plans after receiving my letter, though I was immediately disappointed to hear that they too would not be able to make it Friday night. It was harvesting season, and Dad was still trying to pick cotton and cut corn. The early fall rains had delayed getting into the fields, and he was now desperately trying to get the crops in while the ground was firm enough to hold up the machinery. He was, however, able to leave the operation on Saturday to visit that morning and go to the football game. Though they wanted to stay longer, they would have to leave that evening after dinner.

I was discouraged that I would spend Friday evening alone only to then have to share Saturday with both my parents and Donna. It didn't seem fair to have to jam everyone in on Saturday with Friday and Sunday afternoons left open.

CHAPTER 11

The Friday afternoon of Parents Day Weekend finally arrived, and following my last afternoon class, I could see the excitement building on campus. By the time we marched out for parade, the place was packed. Family members and girlfriends always seemed to make a real point to be there for Parents Day, yet other cadets were obviously more fortunate than I in getting them to the school early. Though excited about the weekend, I was also saddened to know that everyone else would be taking advantage of the first day's events while I was going to be alone. What was really ironic was that I was actually closer to home than most other freshmen.

After parade I went back to my room and stripped off my sweaty clothes. I sat in my underwear feeling the late afternoon breeze as it came in through the window, bringing slow relief to my hot body and feet. My thoughts centered on the fact that I had no idea what I was going to do that evening, certainly not wanting to sit alone in my room all night. It was a really awkward feeling.

I just sat in my chair thinking as Jim rushed around to get changed to meet his folks. With my limited options I decided to catch mess on campus, then possibly watch the Sword Drill performance. Although I was curious about it, I still had a bad taste in my mouth about the group since in my mind it still so much represented Schmidt. But I couldn't help having an interest after the months of secrecy, and possibly by going to the performance, I thought I might then understand. Besides, I had nothing better to do.

After mess I returned to a battalion that was almost empty. As I entered my room and flipped on the light, a weird feeling came over me, one that signified that for the first time in months, I was inside the barracks without something I had to do or someplace I had to be. Even during ESP, I at least always had the philosophical requirement to be studying, even if only for appearance's sake.

As I sat at my desk, my books were in sight as I wondered how to fill the time until the 8:00 p.m. performance. I smiled, knowing I wasn't about to study, having just come out of a full week of it. I just wasn't programmed to do school work during the weekend, even with the knowledge that I was in real trouble with my grades. I did nothing but sit and think of how lonely and uneventful the evening would be, and just how much I looked forward to seeing Donna the next day. I thought of the relationship I had with her only months earlier, and how close we had gotten after my many years of knowing her at a distance.

***

Donna Brown and I became a couple almost a year earlier to the day. She was a cheerleader, and I was a football player for the Kingstree Bowl Weevils. Our team was facing our sixth game of the season, which was Homecoming. Due to unfortunate circumstances, we were playing Manning, one of the toughest teams in the area. It was hard to understand how my senior Homecoming game could have been scheduled with the number one ranked team in the division. We were good, but reality warned of a real possibility to lose. Losing Homecoming my senior year was unthinkable, but Manning was undefeated and so were we. They had beaten some very good teams by sizable margins, and were number one for genuine reasons. To win, we would have to be extraordinary.

I was on the defense as a free safety, and our commitment that night was evident as there was no score in the first half by either team. Everyone was frustrated with the offense, especially since they run only a few plays and would quickly leave us with a critical need to hold Manning. But we knew what our job was, no matter what the offense did. We had to shut down every play, one at a time.

During half-time, the coaches never even addressed the defense. It was as if we didn't exist. There was no need. The defensive coach stood alone, silent, and just stared at the wall as the offense scrambled for answers. We saw it as respectful homage. There was no need to fix something that wasn't broken.

The start of the third quarter revealed a renewal of the defense's rock solid commitment. The game remained scoreless as each team's offense was continually shut down. As the third quarter was coming to an end, it appeared a score by either team was not going to happen.

My coach had always tried to make us thinking players. Any opportunity to read the plays and establish patterns was encouraged. But we were cautioned about using this approach, having gotten burned a few times in the past. I saw a pattern in a dead giveaway play where every time the opposing offensive team lined up in stacked side formation, there would be a short pass in that direction. I saw it as a perfect opportunity to break up a play. But I also understood the consequences of risk taking, and was cautious.

When Manning lined up in that pattern, it was just a split second decision by me. I knew what was about to happen without a whole lot of analysis. As if not in control of myself, I moved out of position and started stepping forward, shifting towards the left side of the field. I was sneaking as the quarterback began calling signals, watching his eyes closely to see if he noticed me. Surely if I got caught, he would go to an option and burn me for sure.

On the sideline the defensive coach started moving and saying, "What in the hell is he doing?" He could see that I was moving quickly out of position. At the instant the ball was snapped, I was in a full run towards that side, still honed in on the actions of the quarterback who had dropped back for a pass, looking left. When he released the ball, I jumped and soared in front of the end and actually caught the ball. I was as surprised as anyone. I landed on my feet with somewhat of a stumble, yet managed to keep running. There was nothing anyone could do. I blistered the sixty-yard run and entered the end zone all alone.

The entire stadium was in an uproar. I had scored the first touchdown of my life in organized sports. I was clobbered by my teammates as they mobbed me with their approval. They were going crazy. I was stunned. It all felt like a dream. I was so disoriented that I had to look at the scoreboard to confirm that it was indeed six to nothing. I got off the field as the extra point team came on. The crowd was still cheering madly, and I didn't know what to say or do. The players swarmed me again on the sideline, and it was hard to absorb the significance of the moment.

When the game ended, the final score was seven to nothing in the Homecoming game of my senior year, and I was an instant household name. I could barely make it to the dressing room because of all the people congratulating me. It was a moment I had dreamed of. All the weight lifting, running, and working hard had finally paid off. I always knew there was a reason for it all. The team had won, and I had the greatest moment of my life.

The celebration went on as I showered up and changed into my nicest clothes. Immediately following the game was the traditional Homecoming dance. I was tired and sore, but still felt like a million bucks. I tried to control my emotions, and promised myself not to get cocky and blow a good thing. But I knew that I was going to own the dance that night.

Arriving at the gymnasium, I saw many an eye turn as I walked into the huge decorated and dimly lit auditorium. Although not used to such attention, I savored the extraordinary feeling of the moment. Before I could find my friends among the crowd, they found me, greeting me at the door. I was showered with congratulations as we discussed the details of the game and how great it felt to make the interception. It was a splendid time to be John O'Bryan. I had never had so much positive attention in my life and was enjoying every minute of it. I was surprised when Becky Lawrence, who was one of the girls I dated from time to time, walked over and grabbed me by the hand, and without a word pulled me out onto the dance floor. It was a perfect gesture. Things were so good for me that I just started laughing as I danced. Becky understood and threw her hands up with a yell. She knew this was going to be a splendid party night for everyone.

I seemed to be dancing every dance, and when I wasn't, folks were carrying on about the game. I was having a big time talking, dancing, and listening to the band. But I also developed a second agenda. I had serious hopes to end up with a choice girl for some later activities following the dance. That would cap my dream night off in a really nice way. I didn't want to let the precious opportunity go to waste.

There were many girls within the school I had always wanted to go out with. But based on my new found popularity, I felt like it was possible to have the favor of almost any available girl I wanted, including those considered the most desirable. But I realized I had one particular girl in mind.

Donna Brown was also a senior. She was a tall, black haired beauty that I had known since the first grade. I had always liked her, and thought of her as the prettiest girl in school, but for some reason, had never dated her. She was always going steady, whether it was with someone from Kingstree High or from another school. Boys simply flocked to her. Her piercing magnificence took control of a young male's heart with authority, and she was so pretty that she could make you nervous just being in her presence. She was a varsity cheerleader, and I saw her often since they usually practiced the same time as the football team. For one of the first times in my memory, she was not dating anyone. That is, no one steady. I was thrilled to see she was at the dance. When she wasn't dancing, I could see her from a distance as she stood with a small group over to the side of the gymnasium.

The attention made it difficult to time things correctly so as to break away and ask her for a dance. Under normal circumstances, I wouldn't have been so shy about approaching a girl. But this was Donna Brown, and her popularity made me nervous. But this was my night, and I was feeling cocky. It was time for me to execute my second great play of the evening, but like the interception, it wouldn't be easy.

For the first part of the night, I often found myself on the opposite side of the large room from Donna and her group of friends as everyone constantly moved around in the crowd. But then I noticed that Donna and her clique had joined mine as I was on the dance floor. When the song ended, I told my dance partner that I was ready to take a break and we moved back over towards the crowd. As I walked into the group, I watched Donna to see if she noticed me. She smiled, and I smiled back. I quickly became chillingly nervous as neither of us looked away. It was exactly what I had wanted, but I couldn't believe it was happening. There was a confirmation in our smiles. Already astonished by the event, I was shocked to see her start walking towards me. She came right up to me with her unwavering confidence and began to speak as my heart raced.

"So, you're the hero tonight."

"Everybody gets lucky!" I said with a newfound coolness.

"Am I gonna get lucky and work in a dance tonight?"

I reached down and grabbed her hand and began backing out on to the dance floor. I was surprising myself with my smoothness as I held her hand and pulled her through the crowd. We went out on the floor and danced to the fast song already playing. I could not remember ever dancing with her through the years that I had so distantly known her. I marveled at the sight of such a beauty on display for me to behold, and I could see in her eyes a look interest I had never seen before. At that moment, I loved where I was, and who I was. I felt myself hitting the pinnacle of my life.

When the song came to an end, the band said a few words and went into a really nice slow song. Without a word Donna drew close and wrapped her arms around me and we began dancing again. She felt wonderful in my arms, and her fragrance ignited my senses as I held her close. I started thinking that this must be a reward from God for all of the sacrifices for good I had done in my life. Not only had I gotten all the glory for making such a great play, but also now I was holding the girl of my dreams. I didn't know where this dance was going to take me, or how this night would end, but I felt magnificent.

We held each other with conviction as we moved to the music.

Donna lifted her head as if to say something, then surprised me as she slipped her hand around my neck, and pulled me into a long and lasting kiss. Although consumed with astonishment, I reacted coolly and just danced on, pulling her closer, kissing her in front of the whole school. Our lasting kiss ended with Donna putting her head on my shoulder, pulling me even closer to her.

I was extremely happy. What a monumental day I was having. Not only had I proven myself a true champion on the football field, but I had also won over the most beautiful girl in the school. I had scored big with my peers, and the fact that the ever-popular Donna Brown and I were now a couple was enough to seal my place in the local social order. It took no time at all for the entire gymnasium to realize what had happened. With so many eyes on us while on the dance floor, there was no way to keep what was happening between us a private matter. It brought answers to a dream, and it seemed quite possible that evening would be the best of my life.

***

I loved what that Homecoming night did for me, and as I sat alone in the quiet of my room, I wondered if I would ever experience such a thrill again. My life at The Citadel seemed so hard and negative, I was sure I had indeed seen my peak in life.

I sat back and savored the year old memories that seemed like an eternity ago, then got up and walked over to the mirror to stare at a totally different person than the guy I used to be, the one that owned Kingstree High on Homecoming night. "Now look at me," I said to myself. I was an inmate in a glorified prison, only two months into a four-year sentence. I looked like hell, and my once annihilated hair had grown out just enough to look completely awkward and unmanageable. I had dark circles around my eyes from the constant racking, lack of sleep, and deficiency of diet thanks to the personal attention from Schmidt. I could see myself begin to frown, and a look of hate came over my face as I thought of how unfair it was that he had singled me out. But I knew that I would never complain. I was not going to let Schmidt get to me, even though it was clear I was suffering badly. He might physically hurt me, but never would I let him break me. No Yankee asshole would ever get the best of me.

Staring into the mirror filled with my reflection of hate, I closed my eyes, tried to clear the image from my mind. I wanted pleasant thoughts instead, so I returned to my chair, and tried to resume my visions of being with Donna. But my daydreams were now contaminated, and I couldn't forget where I was, and what I had become. I prayed that Donna would understand through my letters what was going on, and that if she did have a reaction, it would be one of sympathy, seeing through the negative changes, realizing the good that would come from me going to The Citadel. In less than a year I would become an upperclassman and move out of the harsh conditions I was currently under. If she could just wait, things would surely get better.

I looked up at the clock and noticed that I had spent a lot of time daydreaming and thinking about the past that now occupied such a cherished place in my mind. I had about fifteen minutes to get to McAlister Field House and find a seat for the performance..

The Ring Ceremony was viewed as a big deal. Each senior, one by one, would walk through a huge replica of a Citadel ring accompanied by his girlfriend or mother. While in the center, they would then have their picture taken, and after stepping through, the Sword Drill would arch their swords in salute to that senior. A formal dance known as the Ring Hop took place next door in Deas Hall during the many hours it took for the hundreds of seniors to pass through. It was definitely a ceremonious occasion.

I made a start towards the event, and in my freshman trot, I ran through the battalion, and when I got to the sally port, I found a small crowd of civilians waiting for other cadets. There was the pleasant sight of girls dressed in formal evening gowns. Their beauty seemed so profound, and their drifting fragrance took my breath away. I felt so distant, so far severed from their normality.

Intimidated, I just walked on by as if they didn't exist.

At McAlister Field House, I was shocked to find myself in an unbelievably huge crowd trying get into the arena. I began to think I had made a big mistake in waiting so long to come. Ten minutes before the performance would start, there were people in large groups still piling in. I was also surprised to see the number of non-senior cadets there, not realizing there was such interest within the Corps for the annual event. It was apparently worth seeing.

As I stood in line and made my way in, I was surprised to see just how large the facility was and how many people it could seat. It appeared to be a miniature coliseum, with large bleacher stands surrounding the floor and huge balconies of seats going high up to the ceiling. To my astonishment, I could see as I looked around that there were very few seats left, and hundreds still looking for one. There were some folks who had already resigned themselves to the fact that they would be standing to watch the performance. I saw a single seat that was apparently open and I was happy to hear a confirmation that it was available.

There was a tremendous air of excitement in the McAlister, and the noise level was high as people talked, laughed, and moved through the sea of humans. There were a lot of smiling conversations, with cadets' having their first real talks with girlfriends and families in some time. I could hear joyous reunions all around me, with people rambling on about events from home and cadets explaining details of Citadel life. I was actually quite jealous.

Finally, the lights began to dim, and the noise slowly subsided. The event's facilitators apparently left the last glimmer of light for those final stragglers to make their way to sit down, that is, if someone still had a seat for them.

The lights continued to dim until there were none in the Field House. It was an eerie feeling to be inside such a large, dark building filled with people. As soon as there was complete silence, a small light came on down on the floor. It was a reading light at a podium, and standing at it was a Cadet Sergeant. He began to read, and his subject was the history of the Junior Sword Drill. He described how it was put together, but provided little detail over and above what I already knew. He emphasized that it was extremely important that there be no noise made during the performance. He then said something about a silent count, which seemed such a paradox that I didn't understand. His words ended, he turned the podium light off, and then moved away into the dark silence. One could hear a pin drop.

All of a sudden a set of bagpipes began to play. It was both surprising and ghostly, yet, absolutely beautiful. I had often heard the bagpipes being played at parade by the cadets in Band Company, but the instrument was still quite foreign to me. It sounded so hypnotic and mysterious.

The piper played, and it soon sounded as if he were actually walking away, moving down some corridor leading out of the building. As I strained to hear the fading music, the silence once again took over as the last notes escaped my ears. Sitting in the darkness amidst the enormous crowd, I waited for something to happen.

Like a bolt of lightening cracking on a peaceful day, there came a strange sound through the air of the Field House that appeared to be a cross between a siren and a high-pitched scream. As it sounded out through the darkness, I could not figure out through my shock the source of the noise. It was obviously human, and it held some resemblance to a command. Whatever it was, it was the most unusual voice I had ever heard. I then detected footsteps of a group marching down on the floor, and a spotlight suddenly snapped on, and was pointed at 14 perfectly uniformed cadets, lined up in a platoon formation made up of pairs. It was impressive and beautiful as the spotlights reflected off of the numerous pieces of shined brass. I was awestruck.

There were no further commands given as the squad went through a series of parade rest and dress-right-dress motions, all in complete silence. They started moving again, this time using an odd

113

stepping motion. It was the wildest way of marching I had ever seen. The cadets would lift a foot, bringing it up beside their other leg, balancing and almost stepping backwards. They then brought that foot back and onto the floor, and then slid it forward in a step. The thrilling thing was that they all did this in perfect unison. Everything was obviously shined to perfection, and even the brass that was on their shakos twinkled as if they had tiny stars resting on their golden edges. The aureate stripes that clad their upper arms showed that each was a high-ranking sergeant of some kind. They wore feather plumes in their shakos and a long burgundy sash. Their shoes gave off brilliance, slightly covered by their pressed white pants. Together they marched through the spotlights, creating a haunting beauty, wearing the uniform that had caused me so much heartache since entering The Citadel. But I immediately understood the obsession with perfectly shinned brass and shoes, and having a perfect personal appearance. This was a complete definition of why these things were legitimately important. I could not believe how impressive they looked out on the floor as they marched and performed moves that looked both difficult and majestic. These were all very special moves and marching patterns that had apparently been created by the Sword Drills over the years. They were challenging both in balance and in concentration, and the difficulty was obvious. I caught a few little mistakes here and there, and actually saw one doozy, but considering the complexity, it seemed impossible to do it all perfect. We were witnessing an attempt at the insurmountable.

I looked around and noticed that everyone was mesmerized. It was a widespread amazement that something could be so unique, so impressive. It was so much more than I had imagined. There had been so little information about the Drill to go by, and the upperclassmen certainly laid the groundwork to make it seem mysterious. That enigma was obvious even in the performance, which had a ghostly awe about it with the obscure lights and eerie silence. The beauty of the uniforms complimented the high degree of skill obviously earned through many hours of practice needed to pull off the amazingly coordinated moves.

I watched in astonishment, as the pace of the Drill seemed to change from a slow, unusual step to a very quick tempo that sent the cadets in many different directions across the floor. They would time and again do awesome ripple moments with their swords, and it was hard to consider that these 14 guys could know exactly when they were supposed to make their moves, turns, stops, and starts, all in silence. There was no visible means of passing a signal, and many times the cadets were turned away from each other such that they couldn't even see what the other was doing.

The performance went on for a duration that had to be physically demanding on the performers. With one impressive move right after the other, all 14 guys ended up in two long lines with half on one side and half on the other. They all turned inward to face each other, then arced their swords up into the air as their final move.

At that point the entire McAlister Field House erupted into an standing ovation with the most enthusiastic cheering that I had ever witnessed. It was the type of sincere appreciation that came from the heart, something far greater than that found at sporting events or even concerts. People were really moved. The Junior Sword Drill had given a performance that was above and beyond anything anyone would ever expect to see from a bunch of cadets. It was obvious that there had to be extreme circumstances that would lead a group of individuals to come together and work so hard on something. Everyone at the performance could see that, and they acknowledged their discovery with vivacious applause.

I too couldn't help but clap and cheer with them, forgetting that I was showing appreciation for probably the meanest upperclassmen in the Second Class. I hated many of the juniors that were in the Corps of Cadets, especially the ones like Schmidt, who had high rank and constantly used it to make my life miserable. But I just couldn't help but admire what the members of the Drill had just done. It actually made me feel a lot of pride and enthusiasm for the school, even more so than when I saw the Citadel football team make a great play or win a game. This was different, something very different. This was a unique demonstration to the public that went straight to the heart as to exactly what The Citadel stood for.

After only a few months in the school, most of which had been pure hell, I really couldn't say that I could predict just what the Citadel experience would ultimately mean to me. But out on the floor that night, there was a clear definition of what excellence and dedication was all about. It was built into every step of the Sword Drill's performance. It was enough to make any cadet proud of The Citadel's high standards. I felt so enthused about the performance that I actually felt good about my decision to attend the school. For at least that brief moment, I forgot about all of Schmidt's abuses and the many hard rack sessions from the other upperclassmen.

It wasn't long until I saw the seniors with their escorts lining up behind the big ring. The Regimental Commander was the first to walk through with his date, where the Drill members then raised their swords in a full-arced position. A picture was then made of the couple inside the ring, then after a kiss, they walked down between the two rows of arced swords.

I sat there and watched as the other seniors went through the motions. One by one, each walked into the ring with his best girl, had a picture taken, then walked down through the middle of the arced swords.

But the crowd soon started to disperse, some leaving the building, while others lined up to go through the ring. There were others such as I, still sitting in the seats, just watching and savoring the performance they had just witnessed. I wanted to absorb what had taken place. I was that impressed. I was instantly fascinated with the Drill. It excited me more than anything else since entering the school. I started thinking about how Schmidt was so disappointed when he was forced out due to his injury, and it was easy to see why he was so crushed. For someone to be selected to participate in something as prestigious, as glorious as the Junior Sword Drill, they would probably go to any extent to gain such an honor. Rumor had it that this was the second year in a row that no one from R had made it. Maybe there was something wrong with us. Maybe there was a jinx, or some sort of conspiracy by the other companies to purposely prevent R's cadets from making it. For whatever reason, the prestige of the Drill was not in my company.

As I sat there thinking, I watched as the Drill arced swords over and over again as the line of seniors progressed through the ring. It was hard to imagine that these 14 guys still faced many hours of standing at attention, punishing what already had to be tired arms. Even standing in one place for so long would be murder. Maybe that was why they trained so hard. Maybe that's why the seniors chose the best the 2nd Class had to do the job.

Although still impressed, I had seen enough of the arching. I stood up in the once crowded balcony and made my way down the stairs to the floor. I observed the sweat soaked faces of the Drill as I walked towards the door, and noted how serious their expressions remained. These guys were focused on their jobs, all right.

As I walked along in the darkness behind the dimly lit battalions, my imagination seemed to really take off. I laughed at myself wondering if I could ever make it as a member of the 1980 Junior Sword Drill. It was an absurd thought, but one that I soon started to take seriously. I knew there was some sort of minimum rank requirement, of having to be a high ranking sergeant in order to even consider going out for the Drill, which on a company level, left only a few juniors even able to qualify. I knew that there were many things that qualified an individual to get rank as an upperclassman, since the cadre had already bombarded us with the fact that a cadet's grades were the most critical factor. I immediately swallowed a huge dose of doubt knowing that my grades sucked. In my cadet life to date, I had considered rank as unimportant and a waste of time. This was at least the attitude Benson had tried to lead me to adopt. But now I was puzzled. I somehow had the feeling that possibly Benson may have given me some bad advice. It seemed as if many of the privileges that were to be had within the upper classes were given to those with rank. Those without it certainly suffered from among other things, a lack of power. The most apparent so-called benefit was the ability to rack knobs, but to a large extent, even that really couldn't be considered as some tremendous benefit. Racking knobs might provide a sensation of power for those who felt like they needed to prove something, but for the most part, the privilege wasn't substantial. As I saw it, the most important aspect of having rank was the ability to exist in a position of accomplishment, and to show that you are a leader among your peers.

I knew that in addition to grades that leadership ability was also considered in the rank selection process. Many privates would say that rank was often chalked up to one's ability to "brown nose," or as Cadets would say, "sucking nuts." I knew this wasn't necessarily true, and that there was sometimes a cloud of resentment present. But no matter how others felt, I knew that consciously shunning rank was contrary to the commitment I made many years back, when I swore that I would try to excel in everything I did. I wanted to prove myself based on my own performance, and not on my last name. In high school, football seemed to be the route that would have allowed me to achieve that goal, but football was now gone forever.

At that point, the Junior Sword Drill was the most impressive thing I had seen on campus. Even over the influences of Benson, the 1980 Junior Sword Drill was something that I wanted to be a part of. Even though it seemed an unrealistic thought, it was a true desire in its purest form. I smiled as I considered my former opinions of Sword Drill, but as I walked down that dark sidewalk, I knew without a doubt what I wanted to do.

But my smile faded as the truth of the present day brought me back to reality. I was really in deep trouble with my grades, and based on my most recent escapades, I was also in trouble with many of the cadre, including the ultimate pain with Schmidt. I had made a bad start indeed.

Arriving at my room, I again sat in my desk chair where I had earlier reminisced about my glory days in Kingstree, missing being on top of the world and having the admiration and respect of so many. Now I seemed to have Sword Drill in my sights, and new questions came to mind as to how I would approach the rest of my cadet life.

Even through high school, I always wanted to prove that I was no backwoods dummy who lacked both the motivation and intelligence to accomplish worthwhile goals. It was a combination of being perceived as a "farm boy" and constantly living under the Charles O'Bryan dynasty that formed that desire. I wanted to break out of the world of traditional family hierarchy that had established who I was based on birth order. No matter what anyone said, I would never except that I was only worthy of second place.

At 2300 I climbed into my rack to get an early start on a good night's rest. As I lay in my bed, I felt a longing come over me in anticipation of the next day's festivities. Desire consumed me just thinking about Donna in my arms, and I hated that she had not been there that evening for me to hold, and to also experience the Sword Drill performance. She would have loved it, and it may have shown her a purpose for the sacrifices of being a cadet.

I could have savored my thoughts and ambitions for hours, but I knew that I had to put everything out of my mind for the night and get some sleep. I thought about my understanding of God, and of life, and felt that if I were willing to make the effort, and provide the dedication, He would grant me the ability to rise above the obstacles that seemed to be shackling my life. I somehow knew this freedom could be won if I proved myself worthy. I felt an uncanny peace in that thought, and soon, with that accord, I found sleep. The seed that would change my life had been planted.

CHAPTER 12

The next day, I was up with my roommate's early alarm clock. The room was in good shape, but there were several last minute things that we freshman had to do before the parents and other civilians entered the barracks. I tried to hold back my excitement, but found it hard. I was finally going to see Donna and my parents after such a long and trying time. But the safety from the upperclassmen was not yet in hand, and they were raising hell, instructing us to finish sweeping and blitzing the company area to make the right impression.

We got the last few chores done with only minutes left to get back to our rooms and change into the proper uniforms for the open barracks. When the front gates opened, the civilians started pouring in, and we were allowed, better yet told, to be "at ease". It was standard policy that at no time was a freshman to brace when the public was around. It was not only a negative image for the parents and guests, but simply bad taste. It was a rare time for us just to tool around on the gallery without bracing. But my classmates and I felt awkward as we leaned over the gallery rail under the pretense of being relaxed. It was actually an uncomfortable feeling. During the preceding months, it was the most vulnerable place for a freshman to be, and it was hard to dismiss the threat. We were safe to relax, but knew that to do something really stupid, we would surely pay dearly later.

We all continued to stare across the quadrangle to the front sally port, each of us hoping that our loved ones would be next to come through the gate. I watched as classmates spotted familiar faces until I too noticed my parents walking across the quad. They were looking towards the R Company area, and like my brazen classmates, I too yelled and waved until their eyes matched mine. I could see that they were happy to see me, and I scrambled down the stairs and met them with a big hug for my mother and a strong handshake for my dad.

"John!" said Mom who had a lot of concern in her eyes, "What in the world has happened to you?"

"What do you mean, Mom?" I said still trying to smile.

"Just look at you!" she said with no change in her concerned expression. "Are they not giving you anything to eat? And look at your eyes! What's going on here?"

I could see that my mother was genuinely upset and concerned. I was so excited about seeing them that I had forgotten about my appearance and how my mother might react.

"We've had a lot of physical activity, Mom," I said trying to take control before she caused a scene.

"But you've been involved with physical activity all your life, and you always seemed to get bigger then. You look terrible!"

I could see that mom was so concerned that tears were starting to build up in her eyes. She was truly shocked at how thin I was.

I put my arm around her and said, "Come on, Mom. Don't worry about it. It's a tough system, but there are lots of guys who have lost weight around here. Heck, there's one guy who's gone from being a lardo down to a lean, mean, fighting machine."

"I don't care," she said, "I know the son that I raised, and I can tell that something is not right here. They're obviously not giving you enough to eat."

Dad drew near to us and said, "Now, Frances, you and I both know that this is a tough school, and we expected John would have a challenge here. Let's just leave it up to him. He knows what he's doing, and is tough enough to handle it."

I looked at Dad as he spoke and could see that there was also concern in his eyes for my well-being. I knew that he was merely handling the situation to reduce the concerns of my mother. It was his way of quickly weighing out the reality that if I needed their help I would have asked for it. But I could see in his stare that he too was troubled with my condition.

I knew I looked bad, but I had two months to grow into it. I didn't like my appearance, but I never thought that it would be such an enormous shock for my parents.

Mom pulled herself together, finally realizing that her tears would only embarrass me and actually do nothing to help my situation. I was sure she felt like going to someone on the faculty and giving them a piece of her mind for ever letting this happen to her son. But she knew it would tag me to have someone from the outside mettle in what was my dilemma. For decades, this place had dispensed its unique brand of challenges and heartache, and that I deserved the chance to get through this on my own.

My mom finally forced herself to put on a happy face, and I led her and Dad up to my room. We sat and talked about what was happening at school, and though I didn't want to, I felt it necessary to bring up the problems I was having with my grades. My parents understood, with my mother even questioning how I was surviving at all under the circumstances. They both wanted me to do well, but had been expecting the worst during the first semester, knowing my pursuit of an engineering degree was indeed very ambitious. I was failing two of my subjects, chemistry and calculus, and was doing poorly in the others. But my parents felt confident that I would pull it all up once I got through the initial stages of cadet life. I was surprised at their faith. Most others would be quick to say that electrical engineering was far beyond the intellectual reach of John O'Bryan.

My parents caught me up on the news from home, with how the farm was doing. But when the conversation began to center around Charles, concern entered Dad's voice and expression. Apparently Dad and Charles had been having a few debates over making some changes on the farm. Like any ambitious, yet naive young person, Charles thought he had a better way of doing things than his predecessors. He had attended several seminars that presented new ideas and methods of farming, and was obviously sold on several propositions that would add a touch of innovation to the O'Bryan family farming process. His favorite was a new aquatic farming scheme. I wasn't familiar enough with it to pass judgment, but Dad was clear that he was no fan of the idea. Mom, always concerned with fairness, thought that Dad should at least be open to Charles' suggestions, and that he may be acting a little too hard towards him. But I could see that Dad was in no hurry to change anything. It wasn't worth the risk to put family land on the line for some supposedly big money venture. In his opinion, it's too easy to lose what was built up over generations by taking unnecessary chances.

I could see this was not Dad's favorite subject, and he wanted to get back to what was going on with me. It was a lot more pleasant and interesting to discuss my life at The Citadel than the work and worries back in Kingstree. Although there had been years of favoritism shown toward Charles, I really think Dad was genuinely proud of me for selecting The Citadel on my own. He knew well that it was the most respected school in the state, and that any father would be proud to say that his son was a cadet. He wanted to hear the details, so I told him about the insanity of the 4th Class System. Funny, he seemed to somehow envy the challenge.

Our conversation consumed us until the announcement came over the loudspeaker indicating that it was time for the barracks to close to the public due to the upcoming parade. It was such precious time spent with my parents, but I took comfort in knowing the weekend was far from over.

I walked with my parents down to the quad, then said goodbye until after the parade. We planned to meet again at the front gate as soon as I was free, and I asked them to keep an eye out for Donna who would probably arrive just as parade would be ending.

I headed back up to my room to put on my parade uniform, making sure my brass and shoes were shined so as not to invite trouble. Under normal circumstances, knobs would start getting racked at the very onset of formation, but on this particular day, any problems would be taken care of later since civilians were peering in through the sally port gates. Racking knobs in front of their parents was not a good idea, even if it was no secret that it was a regular part of a freshman's life.

123

The parade that morning was symbolic in several ways. It was the first time we freshmen would march in the event with the upperclassmen. It also meant that I would no longer be referred to as Cadet Recruit O'Bryan, but Cadet O'Bryan. Parents Day was considered the culmination in a freshman's introduction to Citadel life. For two months we were under the coaching eyes of the cadre as we learned the ropes, but now we were expected to know everything about conducting ourselves as cadets. We would be absorbed into the Corps, along with the cadre members who had trained and nurtured us through those first difficult months. We were told that things would only get harder, and that after the weekend, any ranked upperclassmen could rack us. I knew some were just chomping at the bit, and it was clear that the liabilities of integrating into the Corps would far exceed any privileges. From that day forward, we would no longer be under what was loosely termed as "the protection of the cadre". It would now be open season on our asses.

Following parade, everyone raced to get into approved uniforms for leave. I moved frantically, anticipating that Donna had arrived and was hopefully hooked up with my parents. I felt a lot of anxiety as to whether she had made it, and felt compelled to expect the worst. But as I exited the sally port, I saw Donna and my parents standing in the crowd. She looked beautiful. I walked towards her and watched as she struggled to recognize me. When she did, she threw her arms around me and we hugged tightly for the longest time. The familiarity of her perfume made me lightheaded, and I felt a moment of ecstasy as I savored the sensation of holding her body close to mine. It seemed like an eternity since I had experienced such a feeling. Donna seemed as happy to see me as I was her, and she gave me a sweet kiss, then stood back to get a better look. I felt a rush of fear, and then watched as her jubilant smile weakened, and a look of concern entered her face.

"My God, John," she said, struggling to remain positive.

"Oh, no! Not you too," I laughed. "Come on you guys, cut me a break. It's all part of being at The Citadel."

Donna forced a smile as she searched for words coated with reserve, but I could see that she was both shocked and concerned.

"Wow, John, I can't believe it," she said lightening up, "and look at your hair."

Donna began to smile again and laughed as she reached up and took the hat off of my head, then ran her hand across the top. She giggled a bit at the bristly stubs that were the remnants of what used to be the long hair she once ran her fingers through.

"Come on. Don't take my hat off," I said laughing while putting it back on.

Donna quickly said with a smile, "Oh, it's cute! I like your hair, that is...what's left of it," then turned and laughed with my parents.

"Hey, let's get out of this crowd," said Dad.

"We'd better get going," I agreed. "I don't have a whole lot of time."

My parents, Donna, and I started moving through the crowd as best we could. I grabbed Donna's hand and gave her a smile, and she looked back with a sexy grin. She seemed thrilled to see me again, and I hoped her shock was fleeting, yet I knew it would take some time for her to get used to my new appearance. I was glad I had given her some warning before coming, using my letters to prepare her for the bombshell. She walked very close as we moved towards the car, and held my hand with a warm conviction.

We had just enough time to catch lunch at a restaurant and talk without having to choke our food down. But right after our meal I had to get back to campus to make formation and march over to the stadium. Donna and my parents would have to get to the game on their own, but I had purchased three football tickets during the week so that my parents and Donna could sit together. Unfortunately, I couldn't take a date to the game, since that was a privilege reserved for juniors and seniors. Although Donna and I had dated for nearly a year before we both departed for college, we had never spent much time with either her parents or mine. I knew they would get along, but I also realized that it would be awkward for them to sit through an entire football game together.. At least it was better than her having to sit by herself.

The opposing team for the Parents Day game was the Furman Paladins. Unfortunately, they were ranked quite high in the Southern Conference and this was to be a real challenge of a game for The Citadel. The first quarter was an even match-up with no score, but the second brought scores by both teams, with Furman leading at the half 14 to 7. It was unfortunate we were behind since by tradition cadets weren't allowed to take off their hats unless we were ahead. With the afternoon heat, we had a personal stake in the matter.

Even with the negatives, half time was still a treat. The Summerall Guards were to perform, and as soon as the field was clear, they marched on and started into their exhibition filled with difficult and impressive moves. Their style was more of a traditional form of marching than that of the Sword Drill, and they used rifles with fixed bayonets instead of swords. The Guards performed many times in various outdoor locations throughout the country versus the Drill's single performance in the dark silence of McAlister Field House. They both used a silent count, and had similar rippling techniques. Sitting up in the stands of the football stadium it was thrilling to watch the 51 cadets accomplish such difficult moves without someone messing up.

Though they had similarities, the Junior Sword Drill seemed so very different than the Guards. There seemed to be this cloud of mystery associated with the Drill. I was yet to witness any of the non-performance activities of the Guards other than seeing several of the seniors going to practice. In the spring they would have their tryouts and the aspirants would be known as Bond Volunteers, or BV's. There were a whole lot of jokes made with claims that the Guards were the varsity squad on campus and that the Drill was merely the JV. But there was something different about the Junior Sword Drill all right, and that cloud of mystery was a real source of curiosity for me, especially since I now harbored such a strong fantasy to be a part of the Drill.

But I had to laugh at myself as I thought about another dream I once had and lost. It was hard for me to attend The Citadel's games and not think about how much I once loved football. I had such grand hopes of one day being a dominant force on the gridiron, but that dream was dead, lost in an instant. After a year, it still hurt to think of the tragedy.

***

After making my grand Homecoming interception, my senior year of football was one for the books. I played well during every remaining game, and became known in Williamsburg County as the star of a winning team. Donna was thrilled with her popular boyfriend, alright, and in the back seat of my car her ability to say "no" weakened with each kick off until it perished in the twilight following our last regular season game.

Our conference held only two post-season games to determine the State Champion. The first for us was for the Lower State title, with the winner playing the Upper State for the number one slot.

That lower state championship game was tough and hard hitting with a lot of scoring by each team. It was during a long sweeping play where the opposition's quarterback and fullback took off around the right side that my tendency for extra effort would yield tragedy, and my dream season luck would finally run out. As the other team ran around the end it seemed as if most of the left side of their offensive line had pulled and was coming around to help block. I could see a lot of movement, and counted on most of the defensive line to stop the play and make the tackle. But I kept running to the right side of the field in case they missed the tackle. I soon could see the line all over the running back, and so I began to slow down. Just as I watched the runner go down, covered with Kingstree jerseys, I came to a stop with my attention locked on the play. I never saw the opposing player coming. I only heard the whistle blow, and then the snapping sound of my leg as he hit it. The sound was like a tree limb breaking, and I was immediately overwhelmed with extreme pain as I fell to the ground and screamed out in agony. I could hear more whistles blowing as I rolled in misery, and actually saw penalty flags flying in the air from the referees. But it made no difference; I knew I was hurt, and hurt badly. I never even saw who hit me, and was in such pain that I didn't even care. In seconds my teammates were huddled around me asking if I was all right. I was in so much pain that I could barely speak. Through my torment I could only say, "My knee! My knee!"

I was taken to the side, where the team doctor gave it a look. I knew Dr. Morgan well, since he treated me during my concussion and broken ribs two years earlier. He was the finest doctor the town of Kingstree ever had, and I trusted his opinion. He examined my leg and his worst fear came true when he realized that my pain was not in the bone but directly in the joint. I had a critical injury, and his look alone said it was very serious.

I couldn't believe what had happened. I was blind sided by some idiot who was too dumb to hear that the whistle had blown. Although flags were thrown, and the team gained a fifteen-yard penalty, it cost me my leg in the form of a serious injury. Worst of all, my days of playing football were over.

Although not wanting to accept it, the glory and prestige that I had gained from football was now to be a distant memory, and something I would never again experience. With the careless disregard for a whistle and the rules of game, my life was changed forever. All by a guy I never met. I wondered if he knew the dream he had ended with his stupidity.

***

The Corps and The Citadel cheerleaders came to a loud roar in preparation for the second half kick off, but the third quarter was not a good one for us. The Citadel was behind 21 to 10 when it ended, and my hopes to win on the big weekend began to fade.

The Corps really wanted to see this game won and the stubborn crowd came to its feet when the fourth quarter started. Cadets were relentless with their cheering. It appeared that the team was reacting to what we were doing, and with some ambitious passing, and hard runs, The Dogs steadily made their way down the field to score a touchdown to make the difference 21 to 17. Then with three minutes left in the game, both the fans and the team got serious, and with the miracle of determination, The Citadel scored another seven points with a remarkable and aggressive drive with only a minute left on the clock. The Paladins failed to get the ball inside the goal before time ran out, and The Citadel ended up winning 24-21 over Furman. It was a magnificent win over a tough team in an important game, and the close score and gallant effort made the victory even sweeter.

I was pleased with the triumph, and knew that it would charge up the Senior Party that evening, and my desire to get the night rolling was teeming. But the best news was yet to come over the stadium PA. "From the President of Citadel -- All cadets not currently on punishment orders are hereby granted an overnight!"

The Corps erupted into shouts and screams of pleasure. It was rumored that the President was prone to do such a thing on occasions, and to have it happen on such a weekend was a dream come true. With parents and girlfriends in town, it was a generous and timely gesture. The time for celebration was upon us!

CHAPTER 13

I found Donna and my parents waiting for me in front of the stadium, and as I walked towards them I could see that they were still excited over the game. I told them I was pleased with the win, but that I was ecstatic about the overnight. Everyone was in an excellent mood, and for me, it was a great moment to be a Cadet.

The four of us started heading back towards the Citadel campus while basking in the victory, and Dad took the lead on putting together a plan for the evening.

"Didn't you say in your letter that you had a party to go to tonight?" asked my Dad.

"Yes Sir. It's a Senior Party out at the Folly Beach Pier."

"Your Mom and I are heading back home this evening, but would you and Donna care to join us for dinner before we go?"

"That would be great, Dad," I answered.

"I've heard so much about Charleston's fine restaurants," said Donna.

"Then I'll treat the crowd to the best in town." said Dad. "Carolina's is our favorite, and I know you'll love it. Why don't we split up, get our cars, then we'll meet you at the restaurant."

I took Donna's hand and we moved through the heavy crowd back towards campus. With her vague description I determined she was parked at Washington Light Infantry Field, which was on the edge of the Ashley River. 4th Battalion was on the way and so I stopped in and grabbed my civilian clothes for the party.

The sun was just starting to go below the horizon when we reached Donna's car, and once in, we fell into a lip-lock of passion, ignoring others getting into cars around us. Even though it was dusk, others could still observe us. We kissed frantically, and I wasted no time in slipping my hand under her blouse.

"A little fast, aren't we?" said Donna with a non-resisting smile.

"You just don't know! I've thought about you constantly."

"I've missed our little rendezvous myself," she said looking out the window.

"I know. Damn! There's always too many friggin' people around this place!"

"Hold on tiger. Good things come to those who wait."

"I've been waiting for months!"

I regretfully curtailed my attack as I could hear the voices of those moving near cars parked beside us. Donna coolly adjusted her bra to better seat its contents, and then started the car. I thought I was going to die.

The view of the Ashley River made matters worse as the amber glow of the sun gave signature to the passing day. It would have been so nice just to sit and enjoy the scene, and address the burning desires that made me feel so desperately aroused. If not for the intrusion of the people walking around the car, my wanton urges would not have been ignored.

We exited the campus through the Summerall Gate and drove downtown, then learned my first lesson in the pains of trying to park there. It seemed that every spot was taken, with every nook and cranny occupied with a car crammed in it. We finally pulled into a dark vacant lot of a bank, but before Donna could get the key out of the ignition, my second attack was underway.

Donna laughed as I kissed her, and my hands again took off running. "No excuses now!" I said through connected lips. It was just dark enough such that we were barely safe from an observant glance catching us in the act. Donna took pleasure in removing my dress blouse, claiming it was the longest zipper she had ever had the pleasure of opening. Though I wanted to tear them off, I maintained enough control to remove a sufficient amount of her clothes before resorting to ripping them at the seams. I nearly fainted when our bodies merged, and she laid back on the front seat, laughing at me as I gasped in the consuming pleasure. It was probably the worst sexual performance of my life, but one that released months of lustful frustration. Not even concerned, Donna just giggled and kissed me, and enjoyed my rush of the moment.

"Now what stud?" she asked. "Guess I can just go home now."

"I'll cut your tires!"

"You mean there's more where that came from?"

"You'll get yours later!"

"Promises. Promises," she said with a smile and a kiss.

We looked none the worst from our little wrestling match as we innocently walked into the restaurant and were seated by the maitre d' at my parents' table. They were on their second drink, and I could see that they weren't concerned with our little delay in arriving.

Though not accustomed to drinking in front of my parents, I accepted my Dad's invitation to order something to wet the whistle before dinner. Donna had a glass of white wine, and I had my usual Miller Lite. The conversation was the most liberal I had ever had with my parents, and somehow, between the drinks and the dialogue, I felt I was no longer a kid in their eyes. They spoke to me as if I had been furloughed from their laws of conduct, and that the responsibility for my actions had now fully passed to me, and to The Citadel. I loved being treated like an adult, but felt a sense of losing something that was always there to turn to.

The food was extraordinary, though I placed the magnitude of the appreciation on the mess hall's menu and the starvation practices of Mr. Schmidt. Donna was in heaven as both the taste and elegance of the dinner touched her affection for the finer life. I was indebted to Dad for helping me make her visit a good one.

But the time passed quickly, and Dad and Mom had a long drive back to Kingstree, and we needed to get to the Senior Party. With sincere thanks and good-byes, we left my parents and drove towards the Holiday Inn Riverview that was just across the Ashley. Danny Burn and I had reserved a room for our dates to share, but I now suspected that the overnight would have the four of us in there together for the night. I wasn't sure how the girls would feel about it, but to me, I knew what I was going to do. I felt like the luckiest guy in the world.

When we entered the room we could see that Danny's girlfriend Linda had already come and gone, and from the looks of her things being unpacked, they were probably already at the Senior Party. My watch indicated it was just getting underway, and that Donna and I really needed to get going. Donna insisted on taking a shower after a long day and our impromptu encounter. I wanted her to hurry, but blew it when I joined her, then migrated to the bed for round two. It was a much more satisfying experience for the both of us versus the front seat of her car, but we still made it quick as we had to get out to Folly before we missed the entire party. I hated to push her since it had been long and frantic day for her, having gotten up so early to drive in from Clemson, and then bouncing from place to place on a killer schedule. I was in my civilian clothes in a flash, and I waited as she went through her make-up routine. After she finally got into a pair of jeans and an Izod shirt, I dragged her as fast as I could to the car and we raced towards the beach, stopping only to buy another cheap cooler and some beer.

When we entered the huge wooden structure of the Folly Beach Pier, the party was already in full swing. Everyone there had at least half a six-pack start on us, and after the meal and shower, we were stone cold sober. The second of the three bands was already playing, and it was tough to carry the cooler through the rocking crowd and find the table where my classmates were already set up. I could see that Donna was bewildered with the lunatic crowd, and I knew I needed to get her drunk as soon as I could. Sober is not the way one should approach a sloppy, wild ass Senior Party.

I found many of my classmates already three sheets in the wind when I located the group, and I had to squeeze my cooler onto a table that was already overloaded. I popped two beers and slugged away in an effort to catch up. Donna, however, seemed just too tired to attempt a quick drunk, and just slowly sipped on hers. My classmates stared at her striking good looks, and I hoped that she would take it for the compliment it was. Some of the more plastered guys though were talking a lot of bullshit, and I could tell she wasn't in the mood to hear it from a bunch of sloppy drunk skinheads. When I finished my beer, I took her by the hand and led her out onto the dance floor, hoping that would wake her up and get her going.

We had arrived in time to catch the final three hours of the party. I drank like a fish in an effort to catch up with my peers, but could see that Donna was not interested in much more than drinking a few to be sociable. I was a bit worried about how she just wasn't in the spirit of things, and just after midnight, she started to complain that she was just too tired to really get into a party mood. She said she had worked hard to help set up her sorority party on Friday afternoon, then had to stay late to help clean up at the end. She got maybe four hours sleep the night before, and it was taking a toll. I wished there was something I could do to get her fired up, but I knew she had bent over backwards just to be there and just wasn't in the mood to party. I was disappointed, but knew there would be other Senior Parties. I needed to get her to bed, but this time so she could sleep.

When the final band was in the prime of its set, Donna had gone as long as she could. I explained to Danny that we were leaving early, and he agreed we would indeed stay in the room with the girls. I walked out carrying a nearly full cooler of beer, and a girlfriend hanging on my shoulder who was dead on her feet. I drove us back to the Holiday Inn as Donna laid her head on my lap, and I had to wake her from a deep sleep when it was time to go in. She took off her shoes and pants and was out as soon as she was under the covers. My day had not been a short one either, and I went to sleep quickly. Neither Donna nor I heard a sound when Danny and Linda came in later and got themselves into bed. I guess we were that tired.

I wasn't sure if it was the lights coming on, or our intruder's big mouths that broke through my sleeping senses. It certainly wasn't the knocking. All hell broke loose, and I was completely confused and dazed as I sat up and saw Rosellini, Connors, and Palmer at the end of my bed, saying something about partying. A quick look around the room confirmed that I was still in the Holiday Inn, but I had no idea what these guys were doing there. Donna then awoke startled just as I wondered if they had come in with Danny and Linda. But seeing Danny in his skivvies, and Linda propping up in their bed, soon canceled that notion.

Fighting through sleep and confusion, I asked, "What are you guys doing here?"

"We're here to party man!" said Rosellini. "What are you wuss bags doing in the rack? We've got an overnight!"

"Have you lost your fucking minds?" I protested. "What made you think you could come here?"

"How'd we know you guys were gonna be asleep?" said Palmer. "Danny told us you were staying here."

"I didn't tell you to come here though asshole!" replied Danny.

"Hey, Man," said Rosellini as he jumped into my bed, "What about all for one, and one for all, and that sort of shit."

Donna screamed, dazed and not sure at all what was going on.

"Get the hell out of this bed you asshole," I yelled.

"No you get out," replied Palmer as he grabbed my leg, and tried pulling me out of the bed.

I kicked my feet a few times and halted that idea, but then that drunken assed Rosellini grabbed me and acted like he was going to kiss me saying, "Oh, darling can I be next!" I started to struggle with Rosellini who thought all of this was really cute. Donna was terrified and beyond speech over what was going on. She grabbed desperately for the sheets to try to cover herself, but it was difficult with Rosellini wallowing in the bed and me grabbing at him and trying to pull him out. Connors and Palmer were laughing hysterically, but I was furious, having reached my fill of their crap. I grabbed Rosellini by the back of his shirt and snatched him out of the bed. He landed on the floor with his shirt ripping in my hands as he hit. I started yelling at him, asking him who the hell he thought he was, and felt a real urge to start knocking his teeth out.

"You idiots!" I roared. "Get your asses out of here before I throw you out?"

Now I had Rosellini's attention, and with his nice shirt having been torn, I could see that he was pissed.

"Hey you asshole, you tore my fuckin' shirt!" he yelled.

"I'm fixin' to tear up your ass!" I answered firmly. "Just what the hell are you morons still doing here?"

Before Rosellini could answer, I could hear that Burn and Palmer were now getting into it.

"We just thought we would pay you a visit and party some, but it sounds to me like you guys just want to be a bunch of assholes."

"Assholes?" I replied, "My girlfriend and I are both tired as hell. You saw that we left the party early so that we could come back and get some sleep. Anyway, what the hell made you think you could just barge in here and violate our privacy like this."

"Screw you," said Rosellini, "If you guys want to be a bunch of pricks then we'll just leave."

"Don't let the door kick you in the ass on your way out," I answered.

I looked back at Donna who appeared to be in shock, and could see tears in her eyes. Palmer and Burn were just breaking up their part of the argument as Palmer probably realized that he had clearly made a poor choice in barging in. But Rosellini, who had quite a temper, was still raising hell as he left. He turned back towards me and yelled, "You're a shithead for tearing my damned shirt!" and then turned in rage and walked out the door with Danny slamming it just as Palmer stepped out.

I could not believe what had happened. I tried to console Donna, while hoping no one in the rooms near us had called the front desk and complained about the noise. All of the yelling and screaming and the door slam must have awakened someone. Before I could say a word, I noticed Donna really crying. Not only because she had been scared by the surprise, but also because of the close brush with violence between Rosellini and me. She had never seen anything like it before, and it really frightened her.

I tried my best to assure her that the jerks were gone and that they would not be coming back. Although Linda was not quite as upset as Donna, she was furious.

As I stood there, I realized I was in nothing but my underwear, but was too mad to feel any embarrassment in front of Linda. I just wanted an end to the bad situation and get Donna calmed down.

"Let's get back to sleep!" I said. "We'll deal with those jerks later."

"God, I can't believe their stupidity," said Danny.

Danny flipped the lights out and crawled back into bed where he and Linda continued to talk about how asinine the whole situation was. I tried my best to calm Donna, but she was just too upset to lie back down at the moment. I put my arms around her and found that she was shaking. She was both irritated and exhausted.

"I'm sorry Donna," I whispered to her in the dark.

"Its not your fault John. I guess I blame your situation. The Citadel just puts up so many overwhelming obstacles to us being together. It's beyond reason to have to put up with all of this."

It was easy for me to see her point. It had been a long and difficult day, and a whole lot of trouble just to see each other and find only brief moments of privacy. And now, in our exhaustion, we were under even further strains due to the arrogance and stupidity of my classmates.

Donna finally lay back down, and I put my arms around her, knowing she was upset with my situation. All I could do was comfort her as best I could with affection and caring. She hugged me tightly, and then quietly began to weep. I wasn't sure just what she was feeling, but I knew her frustration was at a peak. We just lay there holding each other until we both again drifted off into sleep, which had to be around 4:00 a.m.

The next morning, we all awoke with an obvious lack of rest. Through sluggish efforts we got up and struggled to get out of the room to meet the check-out time. Donna and I then drove back towards downtown to a very nice hotel called the Mills House. It was a long established, top quality hotel and restaurant that provided one of the most elegant and well-catered brunches in Charleston. I had planned what should have been a fitting culmination to a romantic evening, but instead it was more like treatment for a night of turmoil.

The Mills House was still a nice touch with its wonderful food and atmosphere to start us back on the road to recovery. But the rough night continued to take its toll on our romantic inclinations. The lack of sleep had us both worn out and not feeling well.. Our conversation required effort, and centered on chitchat subjects of friends, family, and activities in school. Donna talked a bit about her sorority, and about all of the festivities that centered on the Clemson football season that remained. She expressed how unfortunate it was that I couldn't even consider coming up to visit her for the exciting events that were coming up. It just didn't seem fair, and it was hard for Donna to see the justification. The first real opportunity to see her again would be Thanksgiving, which was over a month and a half away. She wasn't happy to hear about another long period of being apart, but accepted it. I was touched by the fact that she wanted to spend time with me as much as she did, but I also worried that the strain would surely affect our relationship.

I thought back to the way Donna was in high school, where she constantly had a boyfriend, and participated in every social event that took place. The sorority at Clemson had obviously provided a lot of activities to take the place of the many interests she had during high school, but I just knew that not having her boyfriend there for social functions had to be making it hard on her.

Although I was thrilled to spend time with Donna, I had a gut feeling that the weekend did nothing to help our relationship that was already strained from being apart. As I looked across the table at her, I gave her a smile every now and then, but saw that the returned look seemed more like an acknowledgment than an expression of love. It was far different from what I saw at Carolina's the evening before.

We finished our meal, and I could see that Donna appreciated that I had taken her to such a nice place. As we left I felt a need to spend more time with her, but knew there was no suitable place for us to go that would provide the kind of privacy we needed. I felt empty, almost sick as we drove towards school, like I had lost a chance to live out a dream I had relished for months. As Donna pulled up in front of the battalion, I knew that our short visit was about to end. We sat there in her car and tried to carry on further conversations, but we had a lot of time to talk through things at brunch, and what we really needed was quality time alone. But that would require rest, and privacy, and more than just a few minutes. I knew it was best that I get out of her car so that she could get started on her long drive back to Clemson. With her visit so short, I had imagined us spending every second together. But at that point, it seemed a lost cause.

I thanked Donna for her efforts to be there for my big weekend, and apologized for things being so hectic and laced with turmoil. She said she understood, and claimed that she enjoyed the weekend anyway. I gave her a long parting kiss, then got out of her car. I stood and watched as she drove away and disappeared through the main gate, then immediately felt a deep sense of sadness overtake me.

CHAPTER 14

Six o'clock would provide an official end to Parents Day Weekend. It had been a big recess from the harsh life of being a cadet, especially for us freshmen. Visits from loved ones, strolling around on the gallery with our chin out, and the overnight were all freedoms that gave a dangerous taste of relief that had the potential to distort just who we were and the strict standards that went with it. At evening formation, the upperclassmen went to great lengths to insure us that the party was over. There would be no further curtailment of grief.

On Monday I went to my classes, and felt the weight of their burden cut deep into my spirit. I was failing miserably, and it hurt to know I couldn't rally myself to do something about it. I wanted to pay attention and buckle down, but it was just so hard to do. I wanted to think about Donna, and what could be done to get our relationship back on track while being harnessed by the restraints of being a knob. Our short, chaotic weekend did more to elevate my need to see her than it did to relieve it.

I also thought a lot about Sword Drill. As much as I realized I was too far removed from the performance level in grades and military to even consider it, I just couldn't squelch my new desire. I felt a hunger deep within to become what they were. It was a burning paradox that caused my mind to debate my current choices. Was there honor and accomplishment in rebelling, copping an image and attitude of a give-a-shit party animal? Was having rank and prestige just a way to stroke one's ego at the price of manipulating others? How did one define one's own character? Was it already defined for us? Though not compelled to do anything different, I somehow felt I was at a crossroad.

After my first full morning of classes, I put on my best brass and shoes before going down to formation in anticipation of a kick ass noon inspection. But there was none. Instead, we were formed up in front of the company letter.

Our C.O., Mr. Beach, walked in front of us and commanded our attention. He said that during the Parents Day we became full-fledged members of the company, and that there would now have to be new squad and platoon assignments to disburse us among the ranking upperclassmen. He also announced that there were new mess assignments.

It was rumored that the change would make life just as difficult as it was at the beginning of school. All sophomore corporals, junior sergeants, and senior officers who had gone for months without being able to touch us could now make up for lost time. It was just what we didn't need, another flock of flaming assholes to make our lives even more miserable.

Beech left no doubt that change was in the air as he said we would also change roommates. He said as knobs we had no say so in whom we shared our living space with, and that by the time we became sophomores, we would have earned the right to choose for ourselves. He said that we would have several different roommates before the year was over, and then gave some bullshit explanation about us getting to know all of our classmates.

Beech told us that three lists would be posted on the company bulletin board that would indicate our new squad, mess, and room assignment. He said room changes would take place that afternoon immediately following class, and that we were to report to our new squads and mess at evening formation.

When I returned from noon mess, I stopped by the bulletin board to see how I had faired. My new Squad Sergeant was Mr. Toucan, whom I knew well from cadre. My Squad Corporal, however, was someone I didn't know. His name was Porter. I had heard his name a few times around the company, and thought I had popped off to him once on the stairs.

To my absolute delight, I was no longer on Schmidt's mess. I was now with a senior, Mr. Ramsey, who was R Company's Athletic Officer. I had no idea what he was like, but was thrilled knowing I would no longer be dealing with that sadist Schmidt. He had already done more than enough damage to last the rest of knob year.

Finally, I found that I was now to room with Larry Segars. I was pleased since I had come to know him as an easygoing, middle of the road type. He was a Business major and seemed to do well as a cadet. He was no military dick, but he wasn't a screw-up either. I felt I had gotten good news across the board.

That afternoon I said goodbye to my first room and roommate. In one massive move involving all the freshmen, half of us had to switch drawers and carry our things to a new room. It was fast and efficient as my favorite asshole Schmidt orchestrated the relocations.

At evening formation I joined my new squad where both Toucan and Porter were standing. Without a word Mr. Porter started to inspect us. Toucan, with his accent, started talking, explaining that he and Porter expected only the best out of the squad, and would only rack us when necessary. But he was quick to assert that any violations of poor personal appearance or misconduct would be dealt with appropriately. Toucan, having said his piece, then walked off to shoot the breeze with some of his buddies. He seemed more than willing to leave the rest to Porter.

Porter seemed to be a mild mannered individual, yet, was apparently sharp in many aspects. He inspected each of us with great detail, not racking anyone for violations, yet pointing out every little flaw he found.

After he finished with the fourth and final freshman, he stood back to speak. "I want you knobs to understand something right from the onset. Today, in this very first formation, I'm going to cut you a break. I told each of you the things that I think you have fallen short on, and I expect them to be corrected by tomorrow. I want us to start out on a good foot, and I will assume that you now understand the level of performance that is expected at every formation. Are there any questions?"

The four of us answered with a resounding "Sir, no, Sir!"

We marched over to the mess hall, and when my platoon was

dismissed, I rushed over to where Mr. Ramsey was standing and quickly moved to the open knob position on the mess table. I noticed that my freshman partner on this mess was Ken Wilson, who so far, had not demonstrated much to anyone since he had arrived as a freshman. He was slow natured and not very motivated. I knew immediately that it was going to be up to me to set the pace. The only other ranked cadet on the mess was Mr. Henderson, who was a corporal. Henderson had also not participated on cadre, so this would be my introduction to him. The other cadets on the mess included one Senior Private, one Junior Private, and a Sophomore Private.

"OK knobs," said Ramsey, "I'm here to eat. You're here to eat. I will only ask you one mess fact per day. Mr. Henderson here will be in charge of asking you all of the other crap that comes with being a knob. But I'm sure at this point, you already have that stuff perfected and understood. The mess fact that I will require, will determine whether you get dessert or not. You bring a sports question that must relate to football, basketball, or baseball. If I, or any member of my distinguished sports panel here cannot produce a correct answer, then you win the dessert. However, if one of us is able to answer your question, then you forfeit your dessert to this panel."

This was not too bad. Things were going to be a bit more fun than the simple down and dirty quizzing that the cadre put us through. Besides, I was sick of the detailed questions that pertained to the blow-by-blow history of the school.

"I do, however, want you to understand that I expect you to perform well your responsibilities of setting up this mess. I don't want to have to yell at you, nor does Mr. Henderson. You knobs can eat as much as you want, and I encourage you to do so. The price is that I want no screw-ups. Are there any questions?"

"Sir, no, Sir!" answered both Wilson and I.

We had been working to set the mess up as Mr. Ramsey was talking. I felt that I was leading the way on everything, from getting the upperclassmen's glasses fixed to getting the food served. I was clearly going to be the performer on that mess.

My week following Parents Day brought many changes, and some surprising news. Homecoming, another big Citadel weekend with an important football game and another Senior Party was less than a month away. Benson said it would be the most closely spaced parties of the year, and that the timetable was based solely on the home football schedule. To me it seemed like good news since I saw it as another chance to get Donna back into town. I felt I needed a reprieve from the Parents Day disaster and was unwilling to wait until Thanksgiving to see her. Maybe on that weekend she wouldn't have a sorority commitment to mess things up. I could make arrangements to get a motel room just for her so we could be alone. She could get all of the rest she needed, and be tucked away from any of my smart-ass classmates out to try something stupid again. Though I wouldn't be able to spend the night with her, we would have plenty of time to be alone together.

I wrote to her to find out if she could pull off the second visit, but as the days clicked off and I checked my mailbox, I received no reply from her. We had no set schedule to write to each other, but I was a bit concerned that I had not heard from her since our disastrous weekend. I soon felt it necessary to call.

At 2230 I went to the telephone room where I made the long distance call to Clemson. Donna's roommate answered the phone, and I asked if Donna was in. Her voice hesitated a second, then she said, "It sounds like this is long distance. Is this John?"

"Yes," I answered, proud to be recognized. "How did you know?"

"I can tell by the echo that you're calling from out-of-town."

Donna's roommate sounded distracted as she spoke, her mouth seemingly moving away from the receiver as she talked. She then said, "I'm sorry, but Donna's not here right now. I think she went down to the library to check out a book... or something. Can I leave a message for her?"

"Yeah...well...I guess so," I replied. "Would you just ask her if she would consider coming to Charleston, not this coming weekend, but the next? It's our Homecoming, and we're going to have another

Senior Party and football game. I was really hoping she could come since we had such a rough time at the last one."

"Yeah," laughed Donna's roommate, "She told me what a wild time y'all had."

"Maybe a bit too wild. But if you'd ask her to drop me a quick letter as soon as she can, I'd appreciate it."

"OK, I'll sure tell her."

I hoped that Donna would not delay in writing since Homecoming was fast approaching. I needed time to get all of the plans made, especially in reserving the motel room.

Over the next few days I failed to stay focused on my class lectures as my mind continued to drift. I was so worried about not hearing from Donna, and the pain of not knowing what was going on tore at me in a bad way. I stopped twice a day to check my mail, nearly convinced it was becoming a waste of time. But then one morning, during a quick glance through the scratchy glass of the box, I caught a glimpse of an envelope. I opened the door and held a letter from Donna in my hand. But time was running out to get to class, and I was forced to delay reading it until I got there.

My heart rate was high from my brisk walk to beat the bell and avoid demerits for being late. The math professor jumped right into his lecture on rational functions and derivatives, and I waited a few minutes for him to get lost in a problem before I cautiously removed the letter from my book and quietly opened it using a pencil. I placed the stationary between the pages of my textbook, and as best as I could started to read.

Dear John,

I was so sorry I was not in my room when you called. My roommate Jane gave me your message that you wanted me to once again come down for another game and Senior Party. She said this was to celebrate your Homecoming. I had already received your letter indicating how well things were going for you now that they have changed you to another table. Knowing you are doing better makes what I have to say a whole lot easier.

I was so happy to see you after being separated for so long. But what should have been a joyous reunion was ruined by the unreasonable restrictions The Citadel places on you. Being alone with you should not have been too much to ask. I have spent most of my time over the last few months trying to stay busy with the sorority and other activities to try to fill the void of you not being here. I have spent countless nights alone in the dormitory studying and watching TV., refusing to accept invitations to go out. John, you know that I have cared for you for a long time now, but it's clear that carrying on a relationship with so much distance between us makes it really hard. But add to this the restrictions of your school, and anyone can see it is just impossible.

I have thought about this very hard John, and that is why it has taken me so long to write you back. I am sorry if this may have delayed you in getting another date for your big weekend, but letting go is so hard to do. It's not that I don't care for you anymore, it's just that I can't carry on a relationship with someone I can't see.

I'm really sorry that circumstances have led us to this. I hope that you can see the situation the same way I do. I'm sure that there are many pretty girls in Charleston who would just love to go out with a handsome cadet like you, just as there are guys here who have continued to ask me out. I have so many times turned them down, but I just can't sit in my room forever. I know that this is what's best for the both of us, and it's my hope that you will agree. You know that we can always be friends no matter what, and I will always cherish the good times we had together.

Take care of yourself, and I wish you the very best in your pursuits at The Citadel.

Sincerely,

Donna

I couldn't believe what I read. I looked up to see if the professor had noticed me reading the letter and could see he was still lost in his equations. I knew I had a look of shock on my face as my heart raced and I felt myself starting to sweat. There was an enormous pain in my gut and my emotions began to run wild. I felt sick, nearly nauseated. Had Donna forgotten how much we cared for each other, or just how badly I needed her now. I was in the most grueling and challenging place of my life, a time when I needed support the most. Now, like every other part of my old life, she too was gone.

I had no idea how I was going to deal with this, especially while sitting in the middle of class. The only thing I could do was fight to maintain my composure, although I felt nearly consumed with hurt and anger. Surrounded by other cadets, I suddenly felt so alone, so betrayed. I had always known in the back of my mind that my relationship with Donna would be hard to maintain under such constraints. I had realized this even before entering the school, but now that the division was actually taking place, it was much harder to deal with than I had imagined. I guess I didn't know just how bad things would get for me, or just how much of a sacrifice this Citadel decision would be. I needed Donna to provide the assurance I required while trying to cope with all of the madness. I understood all of her reasons, and knew that it was a lot to ask of her to sit in her dorm waiting on someone who had no chance of getting there.

But understanding was of no consequence. It still hurt. I loved many things about Donna Brown. She was pretty, and popular with everyone who met her. I could remember how much I wanted to go out with her all during high school, and how fortunate I was to have finally caught her eye. But the flame that made me bright to her was now burned out. She just didn't want me anymore.

I sat through my class, ignoring the professor's lecture, thinking only of my situation and trying to accept what had happened. I searched for answers, and even looked for someone to blame. I condemned myself for ever wanting to go to The Citadel. I blamed

147

Donna for not trying harder to understand the situation. I even blamed Rosellini and his cronies for breaking into the motel room, creating a nasty situation that contributed to Donna's dislike for Citadel life.

But towards the end of the class, after thinking it through many times, there was nothing left to do but accept the situation. It wasn't the first time I'd been rejected, and probably wouldn't be the last. I had always known that in order to achieve, one must be ready to suffer a certain amount of failure. But this was one failure that came at a really rotten time. My plate was already filled with enough problems.

My day was marked with depression. My enthusiasm to meet the demands of being a student and a knob was all but gone. I felt no desire to give attention to that which I felt had ruined my life. I was lucky. I made it through formation, mess, and class without making matters worst, even though my unseen attitude was one of indifference.

In the late afternoon I found myself sitting at my desk, having finished class with two hours free until evening formation at 1800. But my mind was filled with a hazy gloom, and the pain in my heart was so very real. I had many negative feelings at that moment, and felt a need to somehow get away. I decided to deal with it by going for a run.

Physical activity wasn't a burning desire, but I just couldn't sit there any longer and wallow in the pain. The end of the day brought with it coolness in the air as the fall weather was now finally arriving. I knew I would feel better just getting out, even if I had to just walk. The walls of my room were closing in on me as my sorrow looked for a course to follow. I put on my winter PT's, then fled the confines of the battalion with no destination in mind.

It was weird to find myself out running by choice. Physical activity was not something I had lacked since entering school back in the summer. Between the PT runs, getting racked, and intramurals, I had never had a desire to run, lift weights, or do any physical exertion other than that already required.

The first mile or so felt pretty good, but I soon started getting winded, and had to apply effort to keep going. My motivation was probably at an all time low, and instead of keeping a nice quick pace, I fell off to a slow jog, and then down to nothing more than a running walk. I hadn't made it two miles when I decided to stop running altogether and just walk. I went to Washington Light Infantry Field, to the top of the hill there which provided a beautiful view of the marsh grass that ran out to the Ashley River. It seemed like a good place to sit and find a trace of peace in the middle of a campus filled with turmoil. I was tired, and had no desire to push any further than my new found oasis.

As I plopped down on the grass in a leisurely manner, I felt a sense of violation as I became so informal while still on campus. But athletics provided a few immunities for freshmen, and being in PT's, it was acceptable to sit and rest after the riggers of a physical workout.

It felt good to stop. The combination of the warm sun and cool breeze coming across the marsh was soothing. It relaxed the body and mind, although mental tranquility at that point seemed inconceivable. It took little time for me to start thinking about Donna, even though I knew it was best not to. I knew just why she dumped me, yet that helped little to dismiss the hurt. I thought of how pretty she was, and how I once held her exposed body to mine, and how I would never experience that sort of ecstasy with her again. I supposed there was some wild remote chance that we could one day get back together, but certainly not while I was at The Citadel. There was no denying the price I was paying to be a cadet.

I felt the hurt run deep, and it was laced with a hate for what I had done to myself. Before I allowed my emotions to take me, I vaulted up from the hill and took off running with a vengeance, hoping to generate enough bodily pain to take the edge off of my anguish, which was much harder to handle than any physical suffering I could muster.

I filled my short afternoon with attempts to tame my emotions and keep myself from thinking of Donna. I returned to the barracks in time to catch a shower and change into a fresh uniform before evening formation. The situation lurked like a predator in the back of my mind, as I just couldn't shake the emptiness and loss deep inside of me. The physical activity had done some good as it helped divert my musing, and I always heard that with time, even the worst of things would eventually pass. If I could keep my thoughts off of my misfortune, surely within a few days the whole thing would mean nothing.

Though feeling a bit better, my return to the barracks after mess brought a conservative decision to use caution and change my routine. I'd normally gather up my books and strike out towards the library or one of the academic buildings to study, but on this evening, I knew that going off into some secluded place would not be wise. I didn't need to be alone.

After we both got back to the room, Larry and I took a couple of minutes to tidy up the place. We soon settled down at our desks, and I worked on math problems for an hour, and with effort, kept my concentration and mind off of Donna.

As I moved into my second hour in the books, my mind started to drift more aggressively, and I knew I needed to take a break before my brain seized more detrimental thoughts of Donna. I quickly tried to change the atmosphere, so I asked Larry if he minded if I turned on my radio to hear a bit of music. He didn't, so I reached up and flipped the power on where it was already tuned to my favorite station. The music was just the right kind of distraction I needed, and I felt like I was back in high school, where I found it easy to listen to tunes while working math problems. The math was much more difficult now, but the background music was not enough to prevent me from concentrating on what I was doing.

For a while, the change was a positive one. I lost myself in the numbers and soothing sounds. But as I entered into the final stretch of ESP, I grew weary of concentrating and once again began to drift.

I really didn't want to think about Donna anymore, but my supply of discipline had been taxed, and I just couldn't keep her out of my mind. I could picture her lying close to me, looking at me with her beautiful dark eyes. I remembered our most romantic and memorable moments, when I held her close, and we made love. I still cared for her, even though I knew that memories were all I would ever have of her again.

I was getting knots in my stomach, and knew I had to stop thinking about her. But I couldn't. I felt a need to ache, and feel sorry for having lost my most prized link with the life I had left behind. I felt a sickness creeping in, and at the worst possible moment, the right wrong song was introduced on my radio. Chicago's "If You Leave Me Now" flowed from the speaker, and worked as a dagger to an already struggling heart. The song was beautiful with its horns sounding in the beginning, then drifting into the sad and slow vocals of a heart wrenching song. I lifted my head up from my work, then again drifted through my past with Donna. The song seized me with its lyrics, and hurled me into an emotional vacuum that quickly became more than I could endure. I turned my head away, as if it would provide relief from the song, but I only felt the chilling fall breeze on my face as it blew in through the open window. The words were too strong, too relevant. I tried to fight my grief, but I could feel my eyes starting to fill with tears. I quickly turned my head back from the window, not wanting Larry to by chance see my face or eyes and realize that I was losing it.

I had to hold back the pain. I closed my eyes and thought, "What have I done to my life? What have I gotten myself into?"

The ache was terrible, and I strained with all my effort to suppress it. I quickly rose from my desk and walked towards the sink with my back turned to Larry. I turned on the faucet, and then splashed water into my face and eyes.

"What's the matter man, falling asleep?" asked Larry with a slight laugh.

I buried my head in a towel that was hanging on the back of the door, and was grateful that Larry provided me with an excuse.

"Yeah...yeah, I guess the reading was getting to me. I was about to doze off there," I answered.

I knew that by rubbing my face in the towel I could cover up for the way my eyes might look, but Larry never lifted his head as I moved back to my desk and sat down.

I had always thought of myself as having the mental strength and personality to handle anything thrown at me, but this time, I had reached what seemed to be the lowest point in my life. I lost the only girl I had ever truly cared for, only because I voluntarily signed up to go through this shit hole of a college. I hated myself for trying to be so damned responsible, thinking I was going to do something good and different with my life.

I sat there, despising what I had done. I hated The Citadel, and the motherfuckers like Schmidt who made my life the miserable mess it was. I thought of what I could do to solve my problems. I even considered the consequences of just quitting. But I soon realized that the damage was done, and there was nothing more that could be taken from me. My appearance, my body, my freedom, and now my girlfriend had all been robbed. There was nothing I could do about it other than accept that I had royally screwed up my life, and that I was stuck with the results of doing so. But I would never, under any circumstances, give Schmidt or anyone else the satisfaction of knowing I couldn't hack it, especially after what they put me through. Quitting wouldn't bring anything back anyway. The only thing left to do was to suck it up and take my problems and shove them up everybody else's ass. I had made more than my share of the sacrifices. I now needed to reap some of the benefits of doing so. The Junior Sword Drill came to mind, and I thought of the desire it created the night I saw the performance. They were a picture of pure excellence. I knew without question I wanted it, but feared I could never muster the commitment necessary to change my ways. But at that very moment, I vowed to provide whatever effort and dedication it would take.

The aspiration was now more than just a good idea; it was a necessity. Everything I once had going for me was gone. For whatever reason, I had been torn down and given a clean slate. If I wanted to be a loser, the opportunity was there. But if I wanted to find a place among the best, I would have to devote every bit of effort I could muster to pull myself out of this mess. I would have to fight every step of the way to get myself back up, but nothing was going to stand in my way. The hell with Donna Brown! No bitch was ever going to burn me again.

I trembled with anger as my mind burned, fueled by hate and pain over the events leading up to the present. I put my head in my hands, and I found nothing as I tried to grab my hair to pull. I then felt the breeze from the window make an attempt to cool the burning thoughts in my head.

I sat back and looked up towards the God that seemed determined to make my life a hard one. I silently made a vow to Him that I would not falter again from that point forward, no matter how hard it got, or what price I had to pay. I had nothing left to lose.

With my convictions, I suddenly felt the strangest feeling of my life. It seemed that it was all somehow meant to be. My angry heart melted as the tension in my body began to ease. I felt a sense of peace enter my mind. Somehow the hurt and pain was overtaken with a new feeling of purpose. I would not grieve over Donna again. My emotions had to be channeled in a more beneficial direction. Desire would no longer be wasted on the unimportant. I now knew what it meant to be cold-hearted.

I sat out the remainder of ESP in silence, staring at my desk as though working; recovering from the emotional roller coaster ride I had taken in the previous 12 hours. I felt drained, and decided to skip Benson's room for that evening. I crawled into my rack, and lay there in silence as Larry continued to study. I eventually heard taps play as an encore to one hell of a day, and I soon drifted away into a world of silence and peace.

CHAPTER 15

I slept well having somehow cleared my mind of its obsessions. At times during the day I would momentarily flash back to Donna, but would quickly force myself to think of something else. There were many important things I had to do. Wasting time on that dead issue was not one of them.

It was very clear that the greatest challenge I faced was improving my grades. They were killing me. I was failing two subjects, and the others were sucking wind. My very hesitance to even consider Sword Drill was strictly based on my present state of scholastic non-performance. If there was a common trait among those who held high-ranking sergeant positions, it was having high GPR's. Being sharp and shined up was all very nice, but without the grades, dreams of numerous stripes were a waste of time. And there I was…failing…with an ambition of making Sword Drill.

It was so hard to even imagine a viable approach to tackling such an impossible feat. The reality of what it would take just to even pass was enough to shut down even my most motivated desires to straighten out the mess. Yet, it was my realistic understanding of the monumental task I faced to recover that provided the proper mindset to formulate the right solution. I would have to study every available minute just to pass. Period. The 21 credit hours of highly technical courses moved at a blistering pace, and I learned through my failures that it took one's undivided attention in class and a massive dose of outside study just to keep up. Add to it making up for months of sloughing off, and the sobering reality of the required effort became very clear. I would be in the books every waking hour.

I got really serious about ESP's. They became sacred. I went to empty academic buildings to find a distraction free environment so I could use every second to concentrate and work. During the day, I utilized any and all opportunities, including the few open classes in my schedule and the afternoons when I didn't have drill or mandatory intramurals. I had no time for messing around. When the weekend arrived, I made numerous gut wrenching decisions not to go out, providing endless excuses to my friends when they invited me to go drink beer. I claimed every reason possible just so I could lock myself in a room and do homework.

My alibis worked well enough such that the guys started to curtail their invitations. I hated to commit social suicide, but I had no choice. It was hard to be so responsible, and I sometimes had to struggle through a less than enthusiastic attitude towards my mountainous backlog.

It was hard to forsake the call of the wild over the entire weekend, but I fought back temptation with the reality that I had to stay focused. Each Monday I was glad that leave was no longer a choice, and I could center my concentration on giving maximum performance at all times without the regret.

Though I had made a rock solid commitment to change my ways, I was not going to be left alone to provide all the motivation. The day after midterm grades were published, a noon formation was taken over by Mr. Lever. As Benson's roommate, he had never really given me any flack other than some kidding around while I was up in their room. But as the Company Academic Officer, he looked rather stern as he read off a list of names of those who were directed to proceed to the "shirt tuck room." Over half of R Company's freshmen entered the confines of the space as the upperclassmen gathered to witness the show. I wasn't sure why, but since it was right after midterms, I had a good guess.

"Pack it in Knobs," yelled Lever.

We all pushed ourselves further back into the small space to the point of being stuffed in like sardines.

"I said to pack it in real tight you slack asses," howled Lever again.

I had never before witnessed Lever racking knobs, nor had I ever seen him even aggressive. What ever was happening, he certainly appeared to be pissed.

Being noon formation, I had on my best formation brass and

shoes, and in such tight quarters, it would be easy to get them both wiped out. I tried to maneuver a bit to avoid getting my shoes stepped on, but lost the notion as soon as Lever gave the command for us to start running in place.

It was the last thing I wanted to hear, but I had no choice but to remove my "cunt cap" from my head, hold it out as best I could with someone standing right in front of me, and then start running in place. It took only seconds before I was sure my shoes were totally wiped out as the other freshmen around me could not help but step on them, just as I stepped on theirs. Though an intense racking was still to come, destroying my very best shoes was already stiff punishment.

As if this was not already enough, Lever told us to hit it, which would seem impossible for such a large number of guys packed into a small place. But we had no choice, and we all went to push-up position, creating an intermingled sea of arms and legs. It was a terrible mess. I knew my brass was not going to escape damage, and I fought to keep it from totally being destroyed. But I could feel the weight of someone's chest draping across my knees, and I certainly couldn't consider it a foul since I too was over someone else.

"You smacks are probably wondering why I've invited you to join me for this little party," yelled Lever. "You're here because of shitty GPR's which you obviously decided to ignore."

I knew it. It was now time to pay the piper.

"You've done an outstanding job of proving that R Company freshmen are nothing but a bunch of stupid, dumb-ass fools. Look at this. It's almost your whole friggin' class in here. Hell, the GPR cut off point is super generous. Every one of you numb skulls had below a 2.0 at mid-term. Maybe it's my fault for thinking you idiots knew how to study and that you understood that R Company had a tradition of academic excellence. By the time I'm through racking you, you'll know all right! You'll think Deans List is too low. Get this straight. Small academic performance equates to big rack sessions. Do you knobs understand?"

As best we could in our push-up positions, we all responded with a "Sir, yes, Sir!"

"When you ladies get back from noon mess today, you will find a schedule posted up on the company bulletin board. This will indicate what time you are to report to my room for your first of many regular rack sessions. You can bring whatever excuses you want, but they won't matter one bit. The only thing I want to hear is how you're gonna straighten this shit out. Is that clear?"

"Sir, yes, Sir!" we replied.

"Fine, get up!"

All of us, as best we could, fumbled around and grabbed for our hats, then got back onto our feet, once again pushing ourselves back against the wall.

"Pack it in!" yelled Lever. "Push it in tight."

We all pushed in as best we could towards the closed door of the elevator, with the guys in the back getting the crap squeezed out of them.

"Listen you screw-ups, understand one thing before you leave out of here. You guys might not care about your grades, but I'll be damned if you're going to screw up this company's record. Not while I'm still Academic Officer. Now roll out!"

Lever stepped out off the way, and we poured out of the shirt-tuck room, yelling as we ran out onto the quad and lined up in formation where my academically proficient classmates were already waiting. I could feel the perspiration dripping down my face, and I knew my brass and my shoes were history. The hard life was once again going to take over.

For the hundredth time I cursed myself for not working harder on my grades, and I even started to question the sanity of choosing a major like double E. I was warned, but ignored the advice that it would be extremely difficult. Unfortunately, the 2.0 cut-off point applied no matter what major a knob had.

The situation sucked. Lever made it clear he was going to motivate us to improve by making life miserable for those not meeting the standard. My only condolence was that I was already working on a solution, and I was thankful that Sword Drill had already influenced me to get my act together. But in the mean time, I would still have to deal with Lever's motivational sessions to do better.

Lever racked the guilty on a regular basis, right in front of my senior's room that was supposed to be a safe haven for me. When I would come up to see Benson, I found Lever not as tolerant of me being there as he was. He took our grades very seriously, and at every given opportunity, he would ask why I wasn't spending the time studying instead of wasting it up in their room. Benson didn't appreciate at all what Lever was doing since he liked my visits and wanted their room to be a perk in exchange for my servitude. But deep inside, Benson also believed that I should have been concentrating more on grades than on anything else, especially the military.

Lever admitted that I was at a disadvantage being a double E major, but said that it was my decision to take on such an endeavor, and that I had to make the extra effort to make up the difference. He wanted everyone to contribute to the overall company GPR, not drag it down. I tried to assure him that I was working extra hard to correct the situation, but he acted as though he had heard the same story from the other knobs. "Results!" he said, were all that he was interested in.

***

Those first days and weeks of my new approach to school work were the greatest confrontations with temptation I had ever experienced. It was a sacrifice during the week, but staying in on the weekends was like torture. The Saturday night just one week prior to Homecoming was agony as I fought to stay true to a stubbornness not to give in. It was so hard to do that I couldn't help but wonder how many times I could endure such a test of will. Even further pains started when Larry and a few of my classmates returned from the bars, reeking of beer and tavern smoke. They were drunk, and I was sober, and they were in a real mood to give me a bunch of shit.

"Hey man, when are you going to decide that EE stuff is for eggheads and nerds!" said Joe Rosier who stumbled in with Larry.

"You engineering majors sit in here every afternoon and weekend doing these strange problems when you could be out drinking beer," yelled Larry.

"But when we graduate," I returned, "I'll be out sippin' the suds while you're out lookin' for a job!"

"That's a bunch of shit," said Rosier, "I've got a Navy contract! A job is waiting for me with my Uncle Sam."

"But not Mr. Segars here," I said. "He's majoring in business, and has no plans to play Army. If he's not careful, he's gonna end up driving a garbage truck."

"That's what you think asshole. I'll probably land a job as a stock broker, making probably double what you make, and triple more from my investments."

"Ripping off old ladies' pensions," I said with a cold twist.

"Fuck you, electron breath," said Rosier.

"Just get your stinking pickled asses out of here and go find some other drunks to harass. I'm ready to hit the hay."

"OK douche bag," said Larry, showing unusual aggression. "We'll go on up to my senior's room so we can let Cinderella here dream of his next satellite. Night, Night!"

"Fuck you," I said in a dragging, monotone voice as the crew exited laughing.

***

Homecoming was similar to Parents Day with the big crowds present on campus to watch the special events scheduled for the occasion. Instead of mostly parents and girlfriends, there were hoards of alumni and their families coming into the open barracks

159

and attending the football game. They lined the streets as we marched over to the stadium, and one could easily see they were reminiscing over days past when they were in our shoes.

Following the football game, I started walking back towards the battalion through the huge crowd milling around in the parking lot. As I weaved through the masses, I swore I heard my name being called. I turned to see an older couple calling and waving as they came my way. It was Mr. and Mrs. Johnson from Kingstree. I smiled at the familiar faces, and walked towards them, reaching out to shake Mr. Johnson's hand, then tipping my cap at Mrs. Johnson.

"Look at you!" said Mr. Johnson, "I never thought I'd actually see you wearing that uniform. This is great!"

"Thank you Sir. I appreciate all of the advice you gave me. I think, for the most part, it's turned out to be the right move for me, although freshman year's been no picnic."

The Johnson's smiled in an understanding way.

"I really don't know how you guys do it," said Mrs. Johnson.

"You have to remember dear, John was an excellent football player," said Mr. Johnson. "I'm sure he'll do just fine. Have you picked a major yet?"

"Yes Sir. I chose Electrical Engineering."

"I really had my fingers crossed that you would go the engineering route, and electrical is an excellent choice."

"I think so, but I've got my work cut out for me. By the way, how's Cindy doing?"

"She's doing just fine," said Mrs. Johnson. "You know she decided to go to Columbia College."

"I didn't know that," I replied.

"She decided to go to a smaller school, not wanting to get lost in some big university. She says she really likes it there."

"When you see her, tell her I said hello," I said sincerely.

"We will John," said Mr. Johnson as they began to walk off. "It was good to see you... and you take care of yourself... and don't let those upperclassmen get the best of you!"

"I won't," I said waving and laughing.

It was nice to see the Johnson's again. I hadn't laid eyes on either of them since high school. I wasn't sure Mr. Johnson had known what my final school decision was, but I would have been surprised if word of mouth had not gotten back to him. I was pleased to hear that their daughter Cindy was going to Columbia College, which was considered to be one of the finest all-girl schools in the state, and based on her academic abilities, it was a great choice for her.

***

Cindy Johnson was brilliant. She was valedictorian of our class, but achieved that position because of circumstances one would hate to be in. Though nice as the day is long, Cindy was nothing at all to look at. She wasn't ugly, just really fat. She was the brunt of every greasy joke told since we were in grade school, and the abuse dealt out through the cruelty of children can be as ruthless as an assassin's bullet. In elementary school, she was always plump, but through the years, her quandary with food seemed to grow, and by the time we reached high school, she was nothing less than obese. Coupled with the fact that she made little effort towards dressing herself up, she wasn't within anyone's criteria for a date. Though I once thought of her only as the best punch line in the county, I will forever owe her for saving my ass and allowing me to experience the greatest moment of my life.

It all started when I let my dreams of being a football star become obsessive to the point of self-destruction. I was totally committed to lifting weights and building a body that would make me a real threat. I had big dreams of playing college ball, and I knew my senior year had to be an outstanding one to attract the scouts. My obsession resulted in a 100% focus on bodybuilding and a 0% effort on grades. Mrs. Moore, my physics teacher, was more than pleased to see me devastated when she revealed I was failing and would not be playing football in the fall due to my own doing. One was disqualified from all extracurricular activities if academically deficient by flunking any course in the previous nine-week period, even if it was from the year before. She had my attention.

I thought hard about the girls in school that I had dated that may be willing and able to help out. Some were really bright, but none were in my physics class. The smartest person in the class was Cindy, and she was my best hope to pull me out of trouble. She understood the subject in detail, but the big question was would she help me?

I wasn't able to catch Cindy in the hall between classes, but I knew her routine having observed her mother always dropping her off at the front door in the mornings and then picking her up right after school. I figured that I could catch her as she was going out the door and talk to her then.

When the final bell rang that day, I headed straight for the door. Cindy was indeed there waiting for her mother. Although a little nervous about asking, I made a dash towards her.

"Cindy," I yelled.

Cindy noticed it was me, but hesitated thinking I wouldn't be calling her name.

"I've got a quick question for you."

"Sure, John, go ahead."

"I've gotten myself in a lot of trouble in physics, and I'm looking at making an F this grading period. You probably know I play on the football team, and they've got this crazy rule that if I fail a subject, I can't play. Do you understand how devastating this could be?"

"Yes," said Cindy.

I stood there, waiting for further response. But none came.

"I guess what I'm getting at is…well…do you think you may have some spare time to possibly help me study for the last test?"

"Sure. I'll help you," she said calmly.

I was shocked, but instantly grateful.

"Look Cindy, whenever it's convenient, I'll work around your schedule."

"My mom won't mind if I stay after school and help. You just tell me how much time and when you want to meet and we'll do it."

"I'd better be up front with you. I've got to make an A on this last test in order to pass."

"An A?" she said with concern.

I looked at her, thinking that she would surely back out now.

"This is going to take a lot of work. Do you think you can squeeze so much study time into your agenda?"

"I'll spend a thousand hours if necessary. I'm just concerned about your schedule."

"No problem. Would you like to start tomorrow?"

"Yes, that would be great! I'll stay after school and meet you here. I really appreciate this. Whether I pass or fail, I'm gonna owe you a real big one. I'll see you tomorrow. Thanks again."

She looked back as she was walking away, and in a very nice voice said, "You're welcome, John!"

The next day, I met her in the classroom. She was there waiting with some papers spread out on the desk. I walked over and sat down in the desk beside her saying, "Have you thought of how we're gonna pull this off?"

"Yes, I kinda know what we need to do. I think we may be able to do this if you're willing to work hard."

"I'm willing to give it my all, Cindy. It means everything."

"I'd hate to see you off the team too. I'll do whatever I can to help."

"Like I said before, I really appreciate this. I don't know how I'll ever pay you back, but one day I will, I promise."

"Don't worry about it! Let's just get started."

Cindy and I started into what seemed like a technical nightmare. Theorems, formulas, equations, factors. I was more than lost. I was confused and very worried. But Cindy knew her stuff, and took mercy on me by providing explanations I could understand. I was getting it, but we had to work hard right up until time to go.

"Gosh, I hate to stop," I said. "I feel like I'm really understanding this stuff."

"I know. It's too bad we have to quit. I did tell my mother what time to pick me up though, and she should be here in a few minutes. We'll pick up here tomorrow."

We made a great start, but I knew getting an A would be difficult. I knew I just couldn't leave anything to chance.

"Listen Cindy. I know I'm taking up a lot of your time, but if you want to I can give you a ride home after studying."

"If you don't mind, that would allow us some flexibility. My mother doesn't mind me staying longer if I have a way home."

"Just tell your mom I'll get you home tomorrow. Seems like we've got a lot left to do, and we'll never make it unless we increase our efforts."

The next day I showed up to meet Cindy at our regular time. With almost a sense of urgency, we got down to business. Cindy was well prepared to walk me through slowly, and she maintained her wonderful explanations as to what was going on with each of the problems. We wasted not a minute as we got focused on our goal, and worked diligently through that evening.

When we called it a night we walked to my Camaro, which was my pride and joy. With a top-notch stereo, it was not only fast, but also a pleasure to cruise in. Cindy was a little startled when I turned the key and the music came on. I had a really good tape in.

"Do you like the Doobie Brothers?" I asked.

"I really don't listen to that much music. But I think I've heard them on the radio."

"I really like 'em. They're one of my favorite bands, along with the Eagles and America."

"They sound great through your stereo."

I didn't know where Cindy lived, but she provided directions that started us on a course towards the west side of Kingstree. She directed me to a nice, well-established neighborhood. I wasn't sure what her parents did for a living, but I had always suspected that her mother was a nurse because she usually wore white. Judging from the neighborhood I suspected her dad probably had a decent job. Her house wasn't a mansion, but nice for Kingstree.

As Cindy got out and walked into her house, I considered how nice and helpful she had been. Always responsible, she had every reason not to want to help me after I had been so careless.

Instead, she was nothing less than supportive, and I was genuinely grateful.

On Fridays, everyone at school seemed more concerned about weekend plans than schoolwork, and it was normally a day when my attention was at its worst. But I knew there was no time to waste. I was a long way from getting the A I needed, so I again met Cindy that afternoon in the usual classroom.

"I hope this isn't ruining your weekend plans," I said.

"No. I really didn't have any," she answered nonchalantly.

I wasn't surprised. I suspected she didn't have much of a social life. In a way, I was pleased, because I knew I really needed her help. At the same time, I was a bit melancholy over her circumstance just knowing that someone so nice probably spent her weekends always sitting at home. I could easily tell that she was a genuinely nice person even though her appearance left much to be desired. It was a real shame, because underneath her weight problem, glasses, and her lack of attention to hair and make-up, I could see the features of a pretty girl. She had natural blond hair, but she did nothing with it. The most unstylish glasses covered her blue eyes, and she wore clothes that appeared loose and comfortable, but unflattering at best. She had large breasts that appeared to be nothing but extensions of her excess weight, and her clear complexion lacked the presentation found with even the slightest traces of make-up. She appeared to be a victim of her own self-neglect.

We worked through problems as I constantly checked the clock to track our progress. It soon appeared though that we were not going to get all that we needed done. As each problem was tackled, the next always seemed to be harder.

"It looks like our time is just about up, Cindy. I know we've got more to go, but I'm sure your parents are expecting you home for supper. I'll just have to go home and work through the rest as best I can."

"Nonsense, John. I've worked with you to this point. I'm not gonna give up now. Remember our goal is for you to get an A, and we're nowhere near that. We need to come up with another plan."

"What can we do?"

"Why don't we push on for a bit more. My parents are going out tonight, and they know I won't be home before they leave. Dinner's not a problem because my mom left a frozen pizza for me. I can fix it anytime I get home."

"I really do appreciate this, especially the extra effort."

"We've got a long way to go. It's too bad you have plans this weekend because we need to really work on this a lot more."

"Who said I had plans this weekend?"

"I just assumed you had a date or something."

"I've got a date alright...with these books."

"I was hoping you'd say that. We've made progress, but still have a lot to do. You'll have to know this stuff backwards and forwards to make an A. Let's meet again tomorrow evening, then finish up on Sunday afternoon."

"Suits me fine," I replied. "Are you sure this isn't going to put you out too much?"

"Don't worry about it. It's helping me to study too."

I knew that Cindy was just being nice. Based on the knowledge she had up to this point, she could blitz the test without ever cracking the book again.

"Listen, nobody likes to eat a frozen pizza. Why don't you at least let me buy you a real one after we're through here tonight?"

"That sounds great. "'m already getting a little hungry."

I smiled at Cindy, realizing that she was really pleased with my offer. I was sure her social life was probably slim to none.

When we finished it was already eight, and I too was hungry by then. We drove to the only pizza place in Kingstree, which on Friday nights was dominated by the high school crowd. Walking in I realized that many of my friends were there, and when we stepped through the door they all saw I was coming in with Cindy Johnson. I prayed that the stares and muted laughs were such that only I would see them. Most knew I was just getting help from her, and that we sure as hell wouldn't be out on a date. But because of the blatant scrutiny, I felt a bit embarrassed. They would surely give me a hard time about it later.

Although I knew the consequences of making such a drastic social mistake, I really didn't care. Cindy had gone out on a limb to help me not lose my dream. If my friends couldn't understand the situation, then they weren't my friends. I wasn't about to let the stares or unspoken comments bother me.

Cindy and I got a booth and ordered up a pizza and a pitcher of Pepsi. When it came we both tore into it. I was much more aggressive than Cindy, and I was surprised at how little she wanted. Maybe she was self-conscious, not wanting to do what everyone would expect.

While we ate we had a wonderful conversation. I was interested in finding out what her parents did for a living, and she said her mother was indeed a nurse who worked in a local doctor's office. She said her mom had gone to Columbia College, then later transferred to the Medical University of South Carolina to get her degree in Nursing. That was when she met Cindy's Dad, who was also in Charleston attending The Citadel. Cindy said he was currently employed as an engineer there in Kingstree.

Cindy asked questions about my family. Though we had known each other since kindergarten, she really lacked any sort of in-depth knowledge about me. I went into the details of my family's history and talked about what it was like to live and work on a farm.

We then turned the conversation towards our goals. Cindy was so definite on what she wanted to do. It was her desire to follow in the footsteps of her mother and become a nurse. I was astonished that at the end of our junior year she was already so sure as to what school she would go to and what her major would be. At that point in my life I had no idea what I would major in or where I would go. I told Cindy that my priorities were built on playing football at the most popular school that would take me, and that was it. My decision would be based on the athletic program and I could have cared less what was in store academically.

We continued to talk about our dreams and what lay ahead for us. In doing so, I couldn't help but feel that we were somehow becoming good friends. This was not something I had planned on, and it was actually something I had hoped to avoid. It was pretty clear that Cindy was developing a connection with me. I just hoped she was mature enough to recognize that this would never go any further than a study relationship. I didn't see it as any big deal, but was cautious about her not getting the wrong idea.

On the way home from our pizza there were times when small talk required some effort. For some reason, I felt awkward and she seemed the same. In an attempt to alter the somewhat uncomfortable atmosphere, I reached over and pushed in the cassette that hung half way out of the tape player. I knew it was my favorite tape, *The Eagles --Their Greatest Hits*, and hoped for a quick paced tune to liven things up. But this was a big mistake. There was already a strange ambiance about us already, but when the next song to play turned out to be "Best of My Love." I wanted to snatch the tape back out. It couldn't have come at a worse time. Here I was, trying to make sure that she didn't get the wrong impression about our relationship, and this song pops up to ruin the effort. It was more than enough to set the mood to romantic, and I knew the song's effect, having so often used it to create the right atmosphere while out on a date with a favorite girl.

Although Cindy wasn't saying anything, I had a feeling she was being taken in by the circumstances. The music, the warm spring evening, and the gentle air coming in through the open windows as we cruised were painfully seductive. I tried to convince myself she wouldn't notice, but my senses told me different.

When I got to her house I pulled up in the driveway in a cold sweat, and began to wonder what would happen next. I prayed she hadn't mistaken what had just happened, or wasn't thinking I was going to do something like walk her to the door and kiss her goodnight. When the car stopped, a few silent seconds went by that seemed like hours. She finally said, "Thanks for the pizza. It was a lot of fun and I enjoyed the company. I guess I'll see you tomorrow afternoon. What's it gonna be, about five-thirty or six?"

"Yes...Yes, that sounds about right. I'll see you then."

"Ok," she said, then got out of the car and walked on in. I took off without delay and started towards home.

On the way, my mind raced about what was happening. But nothing had happened. I felt both foolish about how vain I was for thinking that Cindy would mistake our situation. I started to examine my lack of humility in thinking that she would go that route. My mind had turned her simple friendship into something it wasn't. Surely she too only wanted to be just friends. I had let my lack of modesty and over-abundance of conceit overrule my own common sense.

When I arrived at Cindy's house the next day at 5:00 p.m., I found her waiting for me by opening the door after the first ring.

"Come on in, John, I've got the dining room set up for us."

"Hi, John, how are you doing?" said Cindy's mother.

It was the first time that I had ever talked to Mrs. Johnson. I had many times seen her from a distance when she picked up Cindy, but had never met her face to face. Though she was in her forties, I could see she was a very attractive, well-spoken lady.

"We're glad to have you over John," said Mrs. Johnson, "I know you've been studying hard, and I hope you'll do well on your test."

"Thanks. I'm sure grateful Cindy has been able to help me."

"I think she's enjoyed it. Maybe both of you will get an A. Sweetheart, why don't you let your father meet John?"

"OK. We'll just say hello," replied Cindy.

I followed Cindy into the den where her father was watching a baseball game on television, but when I walked in Mr. Johnson stood up to shake my hand.

"Hi, John, so nice to meet you. Hitting the books tonight, huh?"

"Yes, sir. This isn't something I usually do on a Saturday night, but I guess I'm kinda forced into it."

"That's alright. We're glad to have you over anyway."

Cindy motioned for me to follow her towards the dining room. Once in the room, she whispered, "I'm sorry! I didn't mean for you to have to go through that. You know how parents are."

"No problem. They seem like real nice folks."

"Thanks. You ready to get started? We need to jump on these problems so we can get an early start on our review."

We sat at the dining room table, and Cindy opened up the book to where we left off and we worked on problems until ten o'clock.

The next day in church, I said a special prayer that included two important things. First, I asked that Cindy be blessed for all of the efforts that she had put forth in trying to help me. I so hoped that she understood the situation that existed between us. She was too nice to hurt over something like this. Maybe God would see to it that nothing would be misconstrued. Maybe blessings of another kind would come to her. In God's hands, it would work out.

I also asked in the prayer that I be given the strength and the clear mind to be able to put to use what I had learned. I knew better than to ask God to just give me an A on the test, because I felt that I alone had created the situation, and that it was up to me to get myself out. I just asked for a fair opportunity to show what I knew based on the help provided by Cindy.

After lunch with my family, I left immediately for Cindy's. I actually arrived about fifteen minutes early and Cindy answered the door. When I entered I found Mr. and Mrs. Johnson still sitting at the dining room table finishing up their lunch. I was embarrassed at my interruption.

"Oh, I'm sorry. I didn't mean to disturb your meal."

"Don't worry about it, John, we were through. We were just

sitting here letting our food settle."

Cindy then said to me, "Have a seat in the den while we clean off the table. Five minutes and we'll get started."

I sat down in the den where the TV was already on a baseball game. I figured Mr. Johnson to be a baseball fanatic since both times over he was watching a game. He soon followed me in to chat while the women tended to the dishes.

"You like baseball, John?"

"I don't play on the school team, but I like pick up games."

"That's all I ever really did. I never got to play much organized ball. Cindy tells me you're some football player."

"I try hard."

"I look forward to coming out next year to watch you play. I don't come to every game, but do like to get out there every now and then. Now that I know somebody on the team, maybe I'll get there more often. I really like going to The Citadel football games more than anything else. I take Elizabeth and Cindy to every home game we can make."

"Cindy told me you graduated from The Citadel in engineering."

"Yeah, Civil Engineering."

"Isn't that like a military school or something, where you have to go into the service and all?"

"Well, yes and no. You have the option to go into the service if you want to, but it's not required. You do have to take ROTC each semester, and the day-to-day life there is something like the military."

"But why would someone want to go to a school like that if they aren't going into the service?"

"You have to understand something about The Citadel, John. It's a school that's built around a lot of tradition. The school has been there a long time. Matter of fact, it was a couple of smart behind cadets that made the first shot of the Civil War."

I was fascinated with that fact. "I didn't know that."

"Yep, it's true, and Citadel Cadets have been troublemakers ever since," said Mr. Johnson in a laughing voice. "I'm probably a bit on the biased side about this, but I believe from the bottom of my heart that The Citadel is the finest school in the world. It takes the full experience of going through it to truly understand why, and it's probably one of the most unpleasant experiences an individual can go through in trying to make it. But the school does offer a tremendous opportunity for a young man, sort of like you, to mature very quickly. It's a challenging situation that most guys can't even begin to try to put up with. By the way, have you decided where you're going?"

"No, Sir, I haven't. I'd love to play football for Clemson or Carolina."

"Don't forget to look into The Citadel. It's a fine school, and most guys never even consider it. Do me that favor and take a look at it before you make a final decision."

"I'll check it out. But I'll be honest, a lot of folks say you're crazy to go there, that it's a lot like a prison."

"There's a purpose for everything they do there, and I agree, it's definitely not for everyone. Most colleges try to educate you book-wise, and that's enough for some. The Citadel tries to prepare you for life, the good and the bad. Isn't that what a real education should be all about anyway? Some people are prepared to handle tough situations, and some are not. Wouldn't it be nice to have the best training possible and know that you can deal with just about anything?"

"That makes sense. By the way, are you getting a commission for drumming up new students?"

Mr. Johnson laughs and says, "No, I just want to see good people go to a good school, that's all."

"Ready John?" said Cindy poking her head in the room.

"Sure, be right there! You're the second person who has strongly suggested that school to me. I guess when I start really looking I'll take The Citadel into consideration. Thanks for the tip."

"Sure thing! And good luck on your test tomorrow."

I walked into the dining room where Cindy had everything cleared off the table and the books ready to go. We started working diligently, not taking any breaks, knowing that we needed to finish as soon as possible.

By six o'clock we had completed the review in detail.

"Think you're ready?" asked Cindy.

"I feel like I am. We've worked hard enough."

"It'll be worth it to see you get an A."

"I hope it turns out that way."

When I walked into the physics classroom the next day, I saw Cindy sitting there ready to go. I looked at her and we both smiled. She could see I was rested and ready to go.

"Let's get started class," said Mrs. Moore with a vengeance.

I dove in and worked steadily, only looking up once during the whole test just to glance over at Cindy. She looked so confident while working, as if not nervous one bit. I worked frantically, so worried I wouldn't finish.

When I completed all the questions, I had only a few minutes to check my work. At that point, few students had handed in their tests, yet it was nearly time for the bell. When I walked to the front and handed the folded paper to Mrs. Moore, she looked at me as if to say she knew this was just another F. But I smiled at her for the first time in our relationship, and that threw her off a bit. I strolled out the classroom and found Cindy there waiting.

"How about it?" she asked.

"If I don't make an A, it won't be my fault or yours. It's up to Mrs. Moore now."

The next day, at the beginning of physics class, I was almost at my wits end, just wanting to find out if my Senior year of football was over before it ever started. Mrs. Moore entered the classroom with the large bundle of test papers and her grade book. She looked around the room, her eyes scanning, and they finally stopped on me. I thought I would die. Good or bad, I had made some sort of impression.

Mrs. Moore stood in the front of the class and announced boldly, "Class, some of you didn't do so well on this test." My heart shot into my throat. "While others of you did excellent. It's so nice when I have a student make a perfect score."

Mrs. Moore walked over towards Cindy and handed her her paper.

"Cindy, you scored a perfect 100. Congratulations!"

Cindy smiled as she took the test paper from Mrs. Moore, but immediately looked over at me with concern.

Mrs. Moore continued, "And we have a second student that I will recognize, but I'm not sure what to think about this one. When a student goes from one extreme to another, I don't know whether to be happy because they've done well or mad because they've not used their potential all along. So, I'll let it balance out and simply hand John O'Bryan his perfect paper."

"Alright!" I yelled very loudly, hitting my desk.

"That's enough, John," said Mrs. Moore obviously understanding my enthusiasm, yet, never allowing her class to get out of hand. She handed me the test paper and shook her head negatively, then continued to hand out the others.

I was beside myself, and looked over at Cindy who was equally excited. We had done it. We had saved my football career and kept me from the humiliation of failing off of the team.

When I left the classroom, I found Cindy outside the door and I grabbed her with delight. My friends familiar with my plight patted me on the back as they walked past. We laughed and celebrated until we had to get to our next class. It was a great feeling.

On the last day of school we were all beaming knowing our senior year was in sight. I was especially happy to even be looking forward to the upcoming football season.

At the end of that final day I realized that I had not seen Cindy to say goodbye for the summer. Thinking she would probably be waiting for her mother, I rushed out to find her standing there. Her mother was right on time so I ran quickly to catch her before she left.

She turned and saw it was me and smiled in a trusting fashion, and we hugged like long lost friends.

"I probably won't see you again until next year," I said. "We'll be seniors then, and I'll be playing football thanks to you."

"It was you that did it, John. You're the one that studied."

"I wish it were that simple. You knew your stuff, and took the time to make me understand. I really owe you Cindy, and I don't know how I'll ever be able to pay you back, but I promise I will."

Cindy looked up at me as if to say something, but just stood silent. I could see tears beginning to swell up in her eyes. I found this uncomfortable based on where we were, yet I too felt a bit of sentiment having gone through such a heart filled predicament together. I think we also both knew the relationship we had developed was now over. For whatever reason, whether it was the break for summer or just the difference in our social groups, it was the end for Cindy Johnson and me.

Cindy looked warmly at me and said, "Goodbye, John, I guess I'll see you next year."

She then turned, overwhelmed by tears, and ran to her mom's car where she quickly got in.

I walked off confused about what had just happened. Yet, in truth, I felt I knew. I was sincere about wanting to do something to show my appreciation for her help, but the walls between us, constructed from social castings of high school kids, would in no way come down. I realized how unfair this situation was and knew that things unjust needed to be fought. But this was one war that I was not willing to enter. I was already battle weary from my own bout to gain acceptance. I would do anything to pay her back accept give up football or commit social suicide. I had managed to cover my night in the pizza parlor with her since everyone was aware of my plight with Mrs. Moore. But a real date was out of the question. Under no circumstances could I tolerate romantic activities with a fat girl, no matter how much she helped me. I would have to find some other way to pay Cindy Johnson back.

CHAPTER 16

After Homecoming weekend I had a two-week stretch until Thanksgiving furlough. It would be my first opportunity to go home, and I looked forward to the visit and the break from freshman life. It was nothing more than a long weekend, but to me it looked like a trip to heaven.

Like a sprint to the finish line, I worked hard through those two weeks, religiously holding on to my commitment of doing better. I had a few test scores come back with pretty decent grades and was pleased with how they helped pull my average up. But daily, I wanted to kick myself in the ass for creating such a deficit in the first place.

Just days before furlough I received a surprise visit from a senior who was a Cadet Lieutenant in Delta Company down in First Battalion. When he strolled into our room, he scared the life out of both Larry and me as we recognized that he was both a senior and an officer. We had no idea why he was there, but he calmly told us both to relax. He had seen my name on the freshman roster as a freshman cadet from Kingstree. He introduced himself as Lewis McKenzie from Kingstree. It was then that I recognized him.

Lewis seemed like a really nice guy, and although I had not known him well, I had seen him with much longer hair around Kingstree High when I was a freshman and he was a senior. He said he just wanted to offer me a ride home for furlough since he knew freshmen weren't allowed to have cars at school. It was really nice for him to offer since otherwise someone would have to drive to Charleston to pick me up.

We made arrangements for a place and time to meet, and I thanked him for the offer, and he just smiled and left as if it were no big deal. I felt almost confused, having an upperclassman treat me as if I were a human being and not the lowest form of life commonly referred to as a "knob."

On the last afternoon before the holiday, I watched as cadets left the barracks with bags in hand. For some it was a matter of driving a few minutes to get to their homes in Charleston, but for most, especially those from up north or from out west, there were planes, buses, and trains to catch. Most had grueling drives for hours to reach a distant hometown.

For Lewis and me, however, it was only a little over an hour's drive to get home. As soon as my last class was over, I made it back to the barracks, changed clothes, and with bag in hand walked down to 1st Battalion. Lewis was already sitting out front in his car as he said he would be.

Although Lewis had already been cool around me concerning the Fourth Class System, I was still a bit apprehensive as I climbed into his car. That all passed after a few minutes of riding as Lewis pointed out that he was in 1st Battalion and I was in 4th, and that there was no way we would ever meet on campus under circumstances that would matter. He told me to drop the yes sir/no sir bullshit, especially since we were out the gate and on our way home. I tried, but slipped often from habit.

We soon pulled onto the long driveway that led to the only home I had ever known. Returning from my first time being away from home for any real length, it seemed so weird as we drove down the lane.

I thanked Lewis for the ride, and confirmed the time that he would be back to pick me up on Sunday. When I walked into the house, my mother was there, ready to greet me with a big hug.

"Hmmm...I can see that you've put back on a few of those missing pounds," said Mom. "But you're still too skinny, and I've got some good food in store for you this weekend. Come sit down, and I'll fix you something."

I was surprised by Mom's enthusiasm to fatten me back up. The impact of seeing me at Parents Day must have been significant.

"Aren't you going to be fixing supper tonight?" I asked.

"Not really. Your father and Charles are down at the barn and they're cooking a hog for tomorrow's lunch. They're going to cook up a pot of perlow for supper tonight while they watch the coals. But you know those guys, they'll end up pullin' a cork and eatin' late. I think you may want a sandwich to hold you over."

I knew Mom was right. Dad, Charles, and the other men would be cooking the hog all night since the coals had to be maintained until morning. Barbecuing a hog was a southern art form requiring the proper amount of heat to slow cook the meat to perfection.

After the sandwich and conversation with my mother, I went up to my room, stopping at the door to look around at the space that was so much a part of my past, confirming that it was as I had left it. I decided to change into some real clothes, even though they felt strangely loose due to the weight loss.

I hurried out with a burning desire to fire up my car. It had only been driven a few times by Dad since I had left for school. Having had nightmares of Charles sneaking in a drive and rapping it around an oak tree, I was happy to find that it was in exactly the same shape I had left it in. Even my tape collection was still intact. I turned the 350 Chevrolet motor over, and closed my eyes in pleasure as I heard its eight cylinders sing their song through the headers and tailpipes. I slapped the Hurst shifter into reverse, then went to first and fishtailed wildly as I headed down the road. I savored the way it felt to be back in the driver's seat again with my favorite tunes blaring on my stereo and the freedom to go wherever I chose. I enjoyed the moment so much that instead of heading straight to the barn, I made a high speed swing through the back county roads. It was nice just to drive, and not have to worry about having to be somewhere.

I drove around for nearly an hour, and then made my way over to the barn. When I arrived, I found Dad, Charles, and several of the farm workers there, getting ready to kill the hog. I drove up just in time to allow the pig a brief stay of execution as everyone stopped to greet me for the first time in three months. I received an enthusiastic welcome home from everyone, especially from the farm hands who were surprised to see me with such short hair and a much skinnier frame.

Dad welcomed me home, and then Charles greeted me with a handshake saying, "Shit man! What got hold of you?"

"I guess a couple of assholes down there at school."

"You should have busted their ass back."

"It's not really that easy to do."

"Ida kicked their ass if they'da pulled any shit on me. But fuck it, we gotta get this hog dressed."

Standing near the hog was Henry, the unofficial foreman of the O'Bryan family farm. In his hand was an ax, and I knew exactly what was about to happen, having seen it many times before.

Charles turned back to me and said "Hey, how about a beer?"

"Sure, I guess I'll have one," I said.

Charles went walking off and talked loudly as he walked, "Don't tell me they don't allow y'all to take a drink down there?"

"We get one every now and then," I said.

I watched Henry reach down and step in front of the hog. He grabbed him right up under his jowls such that they were looking eyeball to eyeball. Henry smiled and said, "OK piggy, time to meet de Lord!"

With one hand gripping the pig, and the other holding the ax half way up the handle, Henry hit the pig right in the top of the head with the blunt end of the blade. Without so much as a flinch, the hog fell straight to the ground, dead as a doornail.

Charles came walking back with a beer for himself and one for me, and said as he popped open his beer, "You can see Henry still has the touch to put 'em down quick."

"Yeah, I see that, and that's a fine looking hog."

"Ought to be!" said Charles. "Lee was the one that growed it."

Lee was another of the workers who had lived on the farm for as long as I could remember. He, like some of the others, had little sideline ventures like growing hogs and truck crops to bring in some extra cash. Dad always bought hogs or cows from those who worked for him for more than a fair price. He was never interested himself in raising any livestock. He would simply patronize those who worked for him by letting them handle the pains. It seemed to be a pretty good deal for all concerned.

This was a big hog, and I could see that there was plenty of hardwood cut, and a pit already dug under the overhang that stood right in front of the entranceway to the old converted tobacco barn. We would soon start a big fire to begin the production of coals that would be needed to start the cooking, but in the mean time, we had to gut, scald, and shave the pig before we could throw him onto the wire over the pit. They already had all of the black and red pepper, salt, and vinegar lying out to season the meat as it cooked. Unlike most places, Williamsburg County barbecue was something unique. All the spices and flavoring were put on the meat while it was cooking, unlike where they just roasted the pork and later poured the sauce on after the meat had been stripped and shredded. Throughout the different areas of South Carolina, there seemed to be regional differences and arguments as to the proper way to barbecue a hog. For those who were from Williamsburg County, they had a perfected a way that could not be challenged. It was hot, but very good.

I jumped in and helped dress the hog. Once we got it cleaned and over the pit, I sat and talked with Dad as he prepared the perlow. Like barbecue, it too was a southern art form subject to preferences. However, perlow seemed to vary more between individuals in the area. I grew up in a part of the country where cooking was considered a risky activity, having witnessed many a heated discussion, and a couple of busted asses, over pork and greasy rice.

But to me, this was heaven. I was glad to be there. I was back home during what I always considered as my favorite time of year on the farm. The hot work of the summer and the frantic harvesting between rains was over. The tractors and pickers were silent. We were going to cook, eat, and maybe even do a little drinkin' and tell a few lies around the fire.

The group of men stayed together well into the late night. I told them some of what I had been through down in Charleston, but found it hard to explain the insanity to those so far removed from that sort of environment. Their lives had and would always revolve around the farm, and they seemed to take real pleasure in bringing me, now an interested outsider, back up to speed on the events of the previous months. It was an excellent evening. I was home, and around those I knew so very well. For a good while that night, I forgot about the misery I had left down in Charleston.

I didn't want to stay out too late since I knew Thanksgiving Day would be eventful. I said goodnight and got back in my car to enjoy the slow ride home, catching a few more tunes in the cool night air as I made my way in.

My room seemed huge compared to the small space I had occupied in the previous month. I got in my bed, and felt the fresh sheets, and comfortable mattress that I had slept on for years. The comfort of my bed, and the knowledge of being home, was enough to quickly send me off into the most peaceful sleep I had experienced in months.

The next morning brought with it the surprise that I had slept until eight o'clock. The farm was usually a busy place by this time in the morning, but Thanksgiving provided change to normal activities. Usually by seven o'clock there would be the sounds of tractors cranking and trucks running to and fro as most of the workers would be heading out towards the fields, and there would be banging on whatever broken down machinery or equipment needed attention. But this morning was quiet, except for the few sounds that I could hear coming from the kitchen. I got up and walked downstairs, embarrassed that I was the last to have gotten up, but nearly dizzy from the aroma of delicious food cooking.

"Good morning John," said Mom. "I thought you would want to sleep late, so I didn't disturb you."

"Where's Dad and Charles?"

"They've left already. They went back down to check on the pig. You want some breakfast?"

"That's alright. Everything's already been cleaned up."

"Oh no," replied Mom with a vengeance. "I can whip you up some eggs and ham from the smoke house. Have a seat."

"Yes mam!" I replied to the order.

I grabbed a cup of coffee, but decided that I would get dressed while Mom cooked. I wanted to get back down to the barn where I knew some sort of activity would be getting under way. I rushed to get my clothes on and shoveled breakfast down quickly.

"Now I know how you got so skinny. You don't even chew your food. Gracious me, don't be in such a hurry."

I finished off my breakfast and made my way back out to my car, where I again drove over to the barn. Once there, I found that the barbecue had already been taken off the fire, and that Dad and the others were already cutting it up. They had made hash out of the hog's head during the night, which was always delicious over rice. The gravy, made from the hog's drippings with lots of pepper and vinegar was also made. I was overwhelmed with the smell of the delicious, unmistakable fragrance of fresh, pit-cooked barbecue. Breakfast was now nullified, and I had an instantaneous appetite that I couldn't resist. I walked over and picked out a prime piece of loin meat and pulled it off. It melted in my mouth. It was incredible. Hot, spicy, and lean, with just enough vinegar. It was not the pork that the common people eat. It was marvelous. It was perfect. It would make your tongue slap your brains out. I knew then I could not wait until noon when we would finally sit down to our traditional Thanksgiving feast, with barbecue, ham, turkey, stuffing, sweet potato pie, macaroni pie, corn, butter beans, cranberry sauce, cornbread, biscuits, and iced tea. Dessert was an assortment of fresh baked cookies and cakes, and my favorite, peach cobbler with vanilla ice cream. But at the moment, that seemed too many hours away. It was an acceptable violation to participate in a premature pig pick.

"How'd you sleep last night John?" asked Dad who came walking up with Charles.

"He must have slept damn good," said Charles before I had an opportunity to answer. "Y'all always sleep late down at college?"

"Sure we do," I replied. "And the upperclassmen serve us breakfast in bed before they draw our baths."

I knew that it was time for Charles to start. The smart-ass comments and put-downs had somehow been dormant during the previous evening, but I knew that wouldn't last. Though I was prepared to provide comebacks, I didn't want to ruin my already too short vacation by getting into it with him. So as much as I could, I would just take his shit and do my best to keep my cool.

"By the way," I said to Dad, "what's on schedule for the rest of the day?"

"We thought we'd go put us on a little deer drive this afternoon. Then we'll just kind of open up the hunting to everybody the way they want to do it. If y'all want to go shoot some doves, or maybe even try your luck on the duck pond, it's up to you."

"That sounds great," I said. "Soon as lunch is over, we'll give 'em all a try!"

Dad laughed knowing I had always enjoyed hunting, and Thanksgiving was the premium time to take just about any kind of game. Dove season was open and according to Charles, they were pouring into the cut cornfield down at the old irrigation hole tract. Ducks were also in season, and I had some sure fire secret spots down in the swamp. The deer were still in the rut, and it was prime time to catch a granddaddy buck with his guard down as he chased the most recent doe in his harem to go into heat. It was a grand time to be in the woods.

I helped to finish up the work with the barbecue and transport it back to the house. The TV was already on as the parades were ending and the football games were just getting under way. Many of my relatives began to show up, and as I saw each one for the first time, they made a big deal over how I now looked, noting the positive change in hairstyle, and the negative loss of weight. The weight loss was understandably viewed as bad sign that they weren't feeding me well down there in Charleston, but most of them, being as old as they were, were thrilled to see my hair cut shorter. To them, the prevalent long hairstyles of the 70's were absurd, and it was nice to finally see a male my age with a proper haircut. They realized it lacked style, but it fully met their number one criteria. It was short.

As the afternoon progressed, I began to notice Charles getting irritated with the attention I was receiving. With every opportunity, he tried to change the subject from my experiences at The Citadel to something more local, like what was going on with the farm, and how hard he had been working to keep the season profitable. Everyone in the family was pleased with the way the farm had produced since it had indeed been a very good year. Charles took every opportunity to hint that the success was based on his extra efforts. Many of the family members wanted to provide him with encouragement, since they all wanted him to successfully carry on the proud tradition like those who came before him. They were willing to accept his cockiness as a trade off to possibly ensure that he would remain motivated. But as hard as Charles tried to keep the conversation centered on him, it would eventually drift back to what was going on with me down at The Citadel, and I could see that it didn't make him happy.

The meal was its usual masterpiece. Every member of the family ate to capacity, each retiring to the sitting rooms in order to relax and possibly catch a quick nap so as to recover from the fine work that Mom and the official hog cookers had accomplished.

After some rest, the male members of the O'Bryan family left with their shotguns and hounds to meet with other men from the area to start a good ol' fashion deer drive. Minutes after the pack was turned loose, they struck pay dirt, and the chase was like music as the barks and squeals echoed through the swamps and stands of timber. I wasn't lucky enough to get a shot, but the group did manage to bag a couple of nice bucks. Afterwards we gathered back at the skinning shed to butcher out the deer, and have a drink or two while arguing about whose dog jumped which buck. I enjoyed being with that group. It was quite a social event, one you would find on most holidays and Saturdays in the southeastern part of South Carolina. There was just something really right about being around so many people that I knew so well, who were sincerely happy to see me, even in my altered state.

I headed home after the crowd had dispersed and the long day had begun to wear on me. I wanted to get in bed since unlike my first morning home, I had plans to get up early and try to catch some ducks coming in when the sun rose.

When the alarm clock went off at five, I felt for a moment I was back at The Citadel. I sat up with my routine in mind, ready to prepare for formation. But I quickly snapped out of my disorientation with the pleasure of noticing that I was in my own bedroom at home. I crawled into my warm chamois and quickly made my way out into the pitch-black dark of the woods, to the small pothole duck ponds near the edge of Santee Swamp. I sat on a familiar log near the edge of the water, and watched the mist over the pond, breaking open to show the reflection of the stars that shined above. It was a peaceful moment, as the owls called through the mossy oaks, and unknown animals rustled through the leaves behind me. The cover of darkness slowly dissolved as the light of day approached. I could hear the distant call of Wood Ducks, and the whistling sound of their wings as they flew above me, searching for that perfect body of water that would yield their fill of submerged acorns. I could barely see the droves gliding by as they came in and landed on the water. When legal time to shoot arrived, I started folding them up with my Browning, and reached my limit in what seemed like only minutes. I then sat back on the log and relaxed as the remaining droves skimmed across and settled into the now quiet water. It had been an excellent hunt, and a great way to start the day.

I spent the rest of that Friday and all of the following Saturday hunting. I moved between dove shoots and deer drives that my family and neighbors were putting on. At a dove shoot on Saturday morning I ran into one of my old high school football cronies who was also a good friend of many years. We talked for a while after the hunt, catching up on what had happened in our lives since graduation. He revealed some welcome news of a party that was set for that evening. I had plans to go climb up in a tree and try to nail a buck in the late afternoon, but knew I would have plenty of time to make it over just as the party would be kicking in. I assured my friend I would be there.

The final few hours of my last full day of freedom were spent sitting up in a tree stand overlooking a cut cornfield. It was a peaceful setting, and the cool afternoon breeze brought with it the fragrance of cornhusks. It gave me an opportunity to think about many things, including what possibilities might come up at the party that night. I considered a mixture of scenarios, ranging from running into Donna, to possibly seeing other girls I had dated throughout high school. It would be an educational experience since I wasn't sure if everyone knew that Donna and I had broken up.

My concentration on the possibilities of the party was suddenly broken after spotting a nice eight-pointer walking down the edge of the cornfield. It was a long shot at over two hundred and fifty yards, but I knew I could take him with no problem. I waited until he stopped walking and was turned perfectly broadside as he checked out the field. With my .243 Winchester, I squeezed off a round, and dropped him in his tracks.

Until that point it had been an unproductive holiday for my deer hunting. I was thrilled to bag such a nice buck with this being my last chance to hunt during furlough. I had hunted all my life and had developed deadly skills in my 18 years. I normally took many a deer during each season, but based on my inability to leave school, my kills would be limited over the next few years. I had to make the best of the few chances I had.

I borrowed Dad's truck to haul the buck back to the barn. I quickly dressed it out, and nailed the horns up on the side of the barn right beside the other hundred or so that the O'Bryan men had accumulated over the years. I knew we had plenty at home, so I delivered the meat to several appreciative farm workers who normally expected it from me during the year.

I then hurried home so I could get changed and make it to the party. I rushed as I dressed, having used more time with the hunt than expected. I really wanted to see my old friends, some of whom I hadn't laid eyes on since we had all graduated back in May. My mother could see that I was in a hurry, but wouldn't allow me out of the house until I at least ate some of the leftovers from the wonderful supper I had missed because of the kill. I appreciated her enthusiasm for getting me back in shape, since it was also a high priority of mine.

I ate quickly as I couldn't help being excited about the possibility of seeing some of my friends, even though I was a bit apprehensive about seeing Donna, and what that situation might lead to. I tore out of the house, jumped into my car, and drove to the site of the party. It was a huge old house that was once the homestead of a local family from the area, but was now occupied by one of that family's latest members to move out on his own. He had a long way to go in making it livable, but it was perfect for a party. There was a huge tapped keg of beer in the back, with a second one sitting beside it in a washtub full of ice. Scattered throughout both the inside of the house and the yard were over a hundred people. I could hardly take five steps without someone stopping me with a handshake or a hug. Everyone was startled to see my hair so short and my body so thin. I probably spent my first hour there going from person to person, talking about the many changes I had gone through since August. Everyone seemed so interested in all that had taken place, and astonished that John O'Bryan, of all people, was so tolerant and passive towards what had been done to him. I could see touches of the same concern I saw in my mother's eyes when she first saw me during Parents Day. I began to get a strange, uncomfortable feeling about some of the reactions. Everyone was nice, and happy to see me, but I could see some at a distance staring at me. Some had frowns of concern, while others were pointing and laughing. I knew my appearance had changed, but I was still John O'Bryan, and certainly everyone should understand that. I thought that maybe I was just being paranoid, but I just couldn't help but feel that there was some sort of weird distance between myself and almost everyone else at the party. I felt so different, so out of place.

Though I kept an eye open for Donna, she never showed up. It was possible she hadn't heard about the event since it was only by chance that I had. There was also a strong chance that she may have wanted to avoid seeing me. But Donna had gone steady many times in her life, and breaking up with me would not be the first time she'd ever had to deal with the end of a relationship.

But I sure wasn't going to sweat it. I accepted the fact that our relationship was over, and as far as I was concerned, the best thing for me to do was to see how well I could do otherwise. But the party was not a dance, and making moves on girls was limited to how well a conversation would go. I moved through the crowd and talked with lots of females, but still seemed to sense a most uncanny standoffish response. I found that every girl I talked to was nice, but that was it. They showed no attraction. There was this common theme in their conversations as to how sorry they felt for me, and that they hoped The Citadel would be worth it in the long run. But I could detect a bit of cynicism as some measured the value of such a huge sacrifice, probably seeing it as extreme and fanatical.

I tried to shake it all off and not be so self-conscious, but by the end of the night was frustrated with what I perceived as a hint of alienation. My self-conscious mind began to even wonder if the break up with Donna was also in the thoughts of those who were at the party. Was that a part of their reaction towards me? Had Donna sold me out to others as having gone off the deep end?

I guess it really didn't matter anyway. My furlough was nearly over, and by the next evening I would be back in Charleston, bracing my ass off. Though I hated it, it seemed that my new life as a cadet was now all I had, and I was a visitor anywhere else, even at home.

The crowd at the party started to thin, and the fact that I had gotten there late made it a short evening for me. I walked towards my car alone, having not even come close to having an intimate conversation with a female, much less seducing one. As I drove home, even the music didn't seem to sound as good, and the seat beside me appeared to be more empty than usual. The void in my ego that was usually filled with close friendships and lovers seemed somehow very hollow. I felt separated from the rest of the world, except for the other 43 freshmen in R Company who were probably also finding that their lives had changed.

I woke up the next morning around 6:30. Even after a few days at home my body was still on Citadel time. I went downstairs and enjoyed coffee, my mother's wonderful Sunday breakfast, and a slow glance through the newspaper before I got myself ready for church. I had been enjoying my civilian clothes, but at my parent's request and insistence, I wore my uniform. My parents were very proud of what I now was, and they felt it only proper that I show up dressed accordingly. Attending the Kingstree Methodist Church in uniform would certainly be an event.

My parents and I drove the three miles to church and I found pleasant greetings as soon as I stepped out of the car. I was still a bit uneasy after my experience the previous night at the party, and I took time to try and notice how people reacted. All I could see was admiration and respect, and I began to think that maybe I had just been paranoid the night before.

After church, Mom capped off a weekend of bountiful food with another splendid meal. She had vowed on my arrival that she would replenish some of the weight that had been robbed from me, and I was happy to see that I had indeed put on about five pounds. Mom was also delighted to have accomplished part of her goal.

Shortly before Lewis was to arrive, I decided to take a walk in the nearly perfect November weather, just to enjoy my final moments of freedom, and look at the surroundings I had missed and often longed for. To my surprise, Dad joined me, and for the first time ever, he and I walked together down the long dirt road leading back through the farm. I felt a bit awkward, and could see the effort it took for Dad to speak. He and I were never prone to have father and son talks, but I think he felt a need, obviously having something on his mind.

I guess all he really wanted to say was how proud he was of me for having stuck through such adversity as a Citadel freshman. It was unusual for him to open up and reveal himself to be caring. I had always considered him to be an honest and decent man, but one who had never had much interest in my life. For what seemed like the first time, Dad appeared to be showing the kind of attention towards me that was once reserved only for Charles. It was a strange, yet wonderful moment.

I got almost a sick feeling as I climbed up the stairs to my room so as to put my uniform back on and prepare for the ride back to school. I knew I had a very challenging time ahead of me with final chapter tests and a week filled with exams. I packed my laundry bag, and before I knew it, Lewis was in the yard. I told my parents goodbye for three weeks, then rushed out the door. It had been four very short days.

CHAPTER 17

As we rode back towards Charleston, Lewis and I discussed our holiday activities, and how it sucked to be returning to the challenge of finishing out the semester with final exams. Although the distance was the same, the ride back to school seemed shorter than that going home. Getting closer to the asylum, it felt as if my body was slowly tying itself in a knot as it prepared for the shock of being tossed back into the 4th Class System. The site of the front gates gave notice that the party was over, and I became anxious when Lewis dropped me off in front of the battalion. I tucked my chin in, and entered through the front sally port, and felt I was being swallowed into the bowels of hell.

The moment we freshmen arrived on the first division gallery for muster formation the upperclassman yelled for us to stand in front of the company letter, a big blue R that was painted on the stairwell in the corner of the battalion. They explained to us that they wanted to hear some Christmas songs, sung with all the sincerity that we could gather. As I glanced across the quad to the other companies, I could see that they were apparently doing the same thing. I could sense another 4th class tradition being introduced, and they told us that we would sing at every evening formation until we left for Christmas furlough.

As silly as it seemed, we caught on quick, and started singing a very sick sounding version of "Jingle Bells." We sang terribly as we braced and tried to find harmony. The upperclassmen immediately commented on our lack of quality and enthusiasm and demanded improvement. It was actually very funny, but I knew better than to smile. Although entertaining for the upperclassmen, I actually found it humbling to have to brace and sing.

After muster formation I went up to Benson's room. Both he and Lever were in good moods, not because they were back, but because they were rejuvenated after getting away. Lever seemed much

191

calmer and open towards my presence, but still on his academic agenda.

"I hope you're ready to jump back into the books again, O'Bryan," said Lever.

"Yes, Sir. I made some progress on getting my grades up before I left for furlough, and I'm hoping to do well on my exams."

"Just do your damnedest to get those grades up above a 2.0, cause it'll make or break you on what kind of rank you might see next year."

"Rank next year?" I asked with concern, "Already? This is only the first semester, what about next semester?"

"I hate to tell ya this O'Bryan, but there's something called rank boards that take place long before your final grades come out for second semester. So the only thing the board will have to go on will be your academic performance this semester, with a bit of consideration put on your mid-term grades of second."

"Sir, I'm working as hard as I can to correct the problem."

"At least you're trying," said Lever. "Although I know you've got a difficult major, I've gotta stay on your ass. 2.0 is not really all that high. You've just got to study your ass off and get those grades up."

Furlough hadn't been exactly what I had hoped it would be, but I did feel somewhat revitalized from the break. I immediately set my mind to the purpose, and dove back into a policy of trying to utilize every free minute I had to play catch up. The days flew by and the blistering pace made the two weeks leading up to exams seem like one long sprint as I was consumed by the many final chapter tests in each subject. I managed to do well on them and entered into exams with a better than even chance of pulling off a passing grade in each of my subjects. It wouldn't be any outstanding GPR, but at least I would pass. My ambitious hope was to pull off the minimum 2.0, but in reality, that would take a miracle.

Exams are a pretty weird time around The Citadel in that the military aspects of cadet life are at their most relaxed point. Those last few tests play such an important role in the final grades that everyone understands it's not a good time to be overly concerned with the military. Unless some very unusual circumstances were to arise, there would be no racking, drills, parades, or anything to interfere with studying during that final week.

But just because the 4th Class System was relaxed, by no means was it over. To screw up at this point might not result in immediate reprisals, but the upperclassmen would not forget, and at the start of the next semester, they would quickly serve up justice for any past violations, with an intensity based on the knowledge that a knob took liberty with the generous privilege.

My exams brought the most serious dose of academics I had experienced in my life. In the previous month and a half, I had been studying as hard as I knew how, yet exams would be my most intense effort of the year. It was the deciding factor as to whether I would pass or fail my two most critical courses.

Each day while going to and from exams, I would check the classrooms to see if grades had been posted on tests already taken. With each posting, I was happy to find I had at least done as I had expected. It was bittersweet as I was relieved to pass, but knew it looked pretty grim getting an overall 2.0.

After my last afternoon exam, my brain was burnt as I dragged back to the battalion. I was relieved to have the burden behind me, but exhausted to a point of near illness. I had already called my parents and given them a time to pick me up since Lewis and I had different exam schedules and he had left the day before. As I walked across the campus and through the battalion, I noticed that I was one of the few cadets still there. Only engineering students remained, and it was clear that our courses were not only more difficult, but we took more credit hours. For the rest of my cadet career I could expect to be taking a minimum of 23 hours each semester, with two to five more courses and labs than most other cadets, all with a much higher degree of difficulty. It wasn't a pleasant thought.

When I got back to my room, I just sat there and absorbed the penalties I had endured because of my slackness and stupidity.

Wasting precious time and energies during the first part of the semester resulted in months of academic hell. I swore that the upcoming semester would not be the same story.

I changed into civilian clothes and then met my father at the front sally port. I was excited to see him again even if it had only been three weeks. I was ready to get the hell out of there.

Driving back to Kingstree, I found that I had few new stories to tell my father. My time at school had been consumed with nothing but studying since I had returned from Thanksgiving break. All of the exciting things had taken place earlier in the semester, so the ride home was filled with little conversation, which my brain actually welcomed. I was ready to do nothing but tune out and think only of how I was going to take it easy for a while.

By the time we arrived home it was already dark. Without surprise, Mom had supper waiting for us on the table. Charles was there with his feet kicked up, watching TV as Dad and I walked in.

"Hey, look at this, if it ain't the college boy home again."

"Yep," I said, "got another break."

"Damn, I sure wish I could take a break," said Charles. "I could use a little vacation myself. But you know us workin' people never seem to get to relax. Anyway...how ya doin'?"

I picked up on his deliberate shot, but let it go. I knew the outlook well. While we were supposedly off playing in college, hard working guys like Charles were home earning a living. I was supposed to feel guilty about that. I just chocked his attitude up to his ignorance. If he weren't so focused on his own little empire he could see the last four months of my life had not been a vacation. I wasn't surprised at Charles' sour attitude, just amazed at his quickness to show it.

It also didn't take long for my mother to address her concerns. "It doesn't seem that you've gotten much bigger since the last time I saw you."

"I haven't done a thing since I left except study."

"You've got a couple of weeks just to relax and eat right."

"OK Mom," I said with an appreciative, yet tired smile.

During my days home for Christmas break I managed to stay pretty busy. I helped with chores around the house and farm and also rushed out to do my part of the Christmas shopping. I took every opportunity I had to hunt and I found the companionship of the other hunters a welcomed interaction. I actually preferred the company of females, but felt lost trying to get reacquainted with the locals. Kingstree had no nightclubs or bars for the college crowd, and mostly the high school crowd frequented all of the so-called 'hangouts' in town. I just felt so detached and distant from others. Most people my age seemed hidden, and it was so rare to run into my old friends. When I did, they seemed willing to speak and ask how things were going, but few made any effort to involve me in social plans. I felt so out of place, so alien.

It was a disturbing conclusion to come to, but at least I was astute enough to realize that my life had changed, apparently in a way that was not popular with my old friends. This hurt more than I wanted to admit. Maybe because I knew there was no way to go back. I hated to think about the summer that would follow the upcoming semester. The break would be a welcome one, but I just hoped that it would not be as boring as my Christmas furlough.

When I reached the end of my furlough, Lewis McKenzie was again willing to provide me with a ride back to school. I told my parents that the next time I would see them would be during Spring break, which was a couple of months away. My parents expressed hopes that the coming semester would go smoother than the previous one. Mom had worked hard to feed me well, and I was sporting many more pounds than when I had arrived. She warned me that she didn't want to see her efforts eroded by some renegade upperclassman.

I left the house feeling the pride of my parents for what I was doing. With a handshake and a hug, I walked out the door feeling both pain and relief. Good or bad, the only real life I had now awaited me in Charleston.

Though it was sad that my vacation was at its end, I actually welcomed the fresh start on my grades. I was also leaving some less than pleasant things behind, like problems with Charles, and the boredom of a dead social life. The challenges of the 4th Class System were hard, but certainly not boring.

When Lewis and I drove through the front gates and up to Fourth Battalion, I could feel the familiar apprehension start to overtake me. The three weeks away from school was just enough to make me feel comfortable as a civilian again.

During that first week back, change was again in the air. I found myself on a new mess, this time with the company First Sergeant, Darryl Anderson, who as the carver, and Guidon Corporal Leon Rooney as the only ranking sophomore. Both of them were smart and well organized, and at first I actually felt my luck had taken another turn for the worse. But to my surprise, I found both Anderson and Rooney were calm at mess. They didn't look for trouble, just made it clear they would nail me hard if performance problems ever surfaced. They left me alone such that I was able to carry out my duties flawlessly.

Once, to my delight, Anderson started talking about Sword Drill after Rooney indicated a slight interest in possibly roaching. With his experience of making it through the 14 Nights, Anderson was both pleased and concerned with Rooney's interest. He warned Rooney that this was a commitment to be taken seriously, not only because of the time and effort required, but that it involved much more than meets the eye of an outsider. "Once the commitment is made," he said, "it's awfully hard to turn your back on it and quit." Rooney, as Guidon Corporal, would surely be considered for the kind of junior rank that would be high enough to qualify. However, I just didn't see any burning desire in him to do it.

Even more change came when we were told we were to again get new roommates. I reacted with both joy and concern when I found that mine would be Jay Palmer. I thought of the wild escapades with him when we all went out to the X-rated drive-in. He had pretty decent grades, but was definitely a wild man, constantly looking for someone to run shit on. It would be a real test to stay out of trouble while rooming with him, and I had a genuine fear of finding trouble in the form of guilt by association.

Shortly after classes resumed, so did our academic motivational sessions. During lunch formation I saw Mr. Lever calling out his list of names of those of us who were to proceed to the shirt tuck room for a conversation. Luckily there weren't quite as many in the shirt tuck room as before, meaning that a few had managed to pull their midterm grades up to a higher level. But unfortunately for most, including me with my 1.8, there was a failure to meet the magic cutoff point of 2.0 for the final semester GPR. The action soon started with Lever's famous "hit it" command. Packed like sardines, my shoes were once again wiped out and my brass was destroyed as it grinded against the concrete floor. But this time Lever did not stop with just a nasty speech. He began to rack us seriously. He poured it on until it was time to roll out to line up for formation. Although it was January, we exited the shirt tuck room in a cloud of steaming sweat.

For me the whole situation boiled down to simply having to pay the price for events that had taken place months earlier. I had several opportunities to discuss the situation with Lever when I was up in Benson's room visiting, but we both knew there was nothing that could be done. He emphasized to all of us that once mid-term grades came out, we would again have an opportunity to get off of his shit list. Until then, we just had to suck it up. There was no question in my mind that when midterms rolled around that I would not only meet, but also would far exceed a 2.0 GPR.

I found it easier to keep up with my studies since I had organized my time. Rooming with Palmer left little doubt that the barracks was no place to study during ESP. As soon as I returned from mess and took care of my sweep detail duties, I would grab my books and head towards an empty classroom or the library where I could find true peace and quiet. I tightened up my study schedule and got really serious about trying to do well on my tests. As the scores came back, I was pleased to find I was doing well with A's and B's and I looked forward to mid-term grades.

As the weeks flew by I continued to do well on my tests. I was comfortable with my GPR as it hovered around a 3.0, which I hoped to maintain in order to make the Dean's list. That would certainly help balance my awful first semester. I got used to spending a lot of my free time on the weekends trying to keep up with the massive work load, but I also knew I needed to get out sometime, and I tried to schedule conservative activities that would give me the break and still leave enough time to get the important things done.

It had been quite a few months since my buddies and I had made our memorable trip to the drive-in theater, and for quite some time Don Moore had been suggesting that we all do it again. For the longest time, I discouraged it since I wanted to use my weekends to really push for good mid-term grades. I kept putting Don and the other guys off, but promised that once midterms were posted that I would use that as a reason to go out and celebrate. They bought it as a reasonable approach and the future plans were made.

Finally, after two months of agonizing humiliation and rack sessions, midterms were posted in early March. Totaling up my GPR yielded a 3.2, and Lever was the first to praise me for making such tremendous improvement by nearly doubling my GPR from the previous semester. He even used me as an example when speaking to the other freshmen that had not been as successful in bringing their grades up. He packed all the regulars on his deficient list into the shirt tuck room, then told of the exceptional performances of a few freshmen that were no longer eligible to be on his academic shit list. This is when he told my classmates about my performance, and the vast improvement which no other cadet had shown. He emphasized that I had accomplished such a feat as an Electrical Engineering major, and this actually made things worse for my classmates with majors of much lesser difficulty. He ceremoniously dismissed all freshmen who were over the 2.0 level, then proceeded to rack the living hell out of those who remained. I felt really good as I ran over to my place in formation. I had worked my ass off not to be in that room. I felt the accomplishment, and I savored the positive recognition in front of my classmates.

It was a great feeling to be doing so well, for both the pride of achievement and for relief from the punishment. I swore right then not to rest on my victory and let up on my diligent pursuit. But I knew that I had promised the guys I would go out for a wild night after midterms, and I did have a good reason to celebrate. My pursuit would have to allow for at least one more wild night.

The following Saturday night, the original group of guys once again climbed into Don Moore's bomb for round two of the X-rated flicks. We set our sights on the Port Drive-in Theater with a prerequisite cooler full of beer in the trunk. But before leaving, I told Don up-front that I was going to limit my drinking to the legal limit and that I was going to drive home. It was my best underhanded excuse for maintaining a reasonable cap and still save face. Besides, I didn't want to get killed on the ride home either.

When we got to the theater, things got crazy fast. The guys were sucking down beers at a break neck pace, and I soon stood out as a conservative sore thumb. They could see I was not quite as loose as before, especially compared to that notorious first time out. To them, I was being a goody two shoes, and a far different person from the hell raiser they knew first semester. I hated the possible alienation this might create, but I knew I couldn't lose with my conviction to stay out of trouble. To cadets whose emphasis centered on the wild life, this was a bad sign.

We laughed and joked through the three films, and I watched as the others got really blitzed. The drunks were soon as entertaining as the flicks, and when the last credits started to roll, it was a timely end to their self-abuse. I took the wheel and started toward what I knew was just the beginning of part two of a wild night. We parked and hurried back to 4th Battalion, and as we ascended the stairs, I made an unannounced dash straight to Benson's room. I chose television instead of the trouble that the guys would surely be looking for, especially Palmer. During the ride home, he mentioned the need to maintain tradition, and to commemorate the mission run on Braddock, and that we just had to find someone else to run shit on. I easily chose not to go.

Indeed my decision to cut out was a good one, as on this night, Palmer would truly push the limits. Like me, Connors, Bullard, and Rosellini also wised up and opted to pass by calling it a night. Palmer and Moore were on their own, and there wasn't an ounce of sense between them as they swore to go for the gusto.

Palmer had Graham Copeland as his senior, who was R Company's Second Platoon Leader, who held the rank of First Lieutenant. Moore's senior was also a Platoon Leader, and since it was an open weekend, they were both away on overnights. Palmer and Moore each went to their senior's room and borrowed a field jacket and overseas cap, and once on, they were easily impersonating two senior officers. Their mission was to infiltrate the neighboring O Company, enter a freshman's room, and rack the hell out of him.

Although it was extremely uncommon for upperclassmen to rack freshmen from another company, any knob knows he has to follow the orders of a ranking upperclassman. Freshmen were so well trained not to question orders that they would surely not have the guts to put up resistance.

With their senior's jackets and cunt caps on, Palmer and Moore made their way to the first occupied freshman's room they came to in O Company. When they entered, they indeed found two freshmen inside. Terrified, the two popped to and started bracing their butts off, keeping their eyes locked straight ahead. Palmer immediately went into a long yelling speech explaining how he was sick and tired of the O Company freshmen not doing their part in keeping the common galleries clean. He and Moore yelled and verbally abused the two unsuspecting knobs to an extreme, and when they realized they had these guys completely fooled, they told them to hit it. From that point on, they racked them with the passion of a relentless First Sergeant. The two unsuspecting freshmen did pushups, ran in place, and picked cherries. It was all Palmer and Moore could do to keep from laughing as they observed the disbelief on their victim's faces.

When they walked out of the freshmen's room, they immediately noticed an O Company corporal standing right at the stairwell. They nervously started back down the dark gallery towards R. Glancing back, Palmer could see that the corporal had certainly noticed them, but banked on the fact that he would recognize them as officers.

The two quickly made it back to the Copeland's room. As he turned to go in, Palmer once again glanced back down the length of the gallery to see that the corporal was still standing there, staring as he and Moore opened the door and walked on in. Safely inside, he knew they had to remove their senior's uniforms and get out of there in case someone from O had questions about such an improper invasion.

Five minutes later Palmer and Moore were in the third division alcove laughing and bragging about their adventure. Even they could not believe what they had done. They had pulled off the mission of all missions. It was outrageous, and since there was no word of trouble, they were convinced they had gotten away with it.

But the sighting by the O Company corporal did not go unchecked. With accusations of fraternization, he later questioned the two freshmen on Sunday about their relationship with the officers from R. After hearing the knobs' bizarre explanation, the corporal found himself faced with questions as to why officers from another company were allowed to come over late at night and rack O Company freshmen. Word soon reached the O Company's CO who quickly became unnerved at the absence of common courtesy. On Sunday night he paid a visit to Romeo Company headquarters to have it out with Arnold Beach, and by Monday morning, the two Company Commanders had the corporal point out the room the two officers had entered. At noon formation the two CO's had a few questions for Graham Copeland. It was Copeland himself who first suspected the answer. He smiled at the thought, then reasoned that his knob, Palmer, wasn't that crazy. Or was he?

As he stood between the two confronting company CO's, he yelled "Palmer!"

At that point there was more yelling in R Company than could be found at a Wall Street selling frenzy. Palmer and Moore were taken into the shirt tuck room and upperclassmen from both companies tore into both of them with fury. Although the two Company Commanders managed to see a bit of humor in the situation, they knew that this was a problem that had to be dealt with seriously. Palmer and Moore were smart asses, and until the end of the freshman year, they would be the recipients of a lot of attention, going from one rack session to another. Unfortunately, these rack sessions would not be restricted to R Company. An agreement was reached that the O Company upperclassmen had R's full blessings to rack the pair, and since they had to run through O's area many times daily to get to R, they were often dropped and racked on site. There was also a special "get even" rack session scheduled for the two victims to try their hand at being upperclassmen. For Palmer and Moore, it was a problem that just wouldn't go away.

I was so pleased not to be involved. I once again reaped benefits from my new code of conduct as I otherwise would have been right with Palmer and Moore had I not changed my ways. It was in my blood to be wild. I was an extremist. I loved running shit on people as much as anyone, and deep down inside, I actually missed it. But I couldn't play the part of both a saint and a hellion. I had to choose one or the other: either Sword Drill or endless tours on the quad. But at that point, there was no question. I wanted Sword Drill like nothing else in my life.

For the rest of the semester I had to put up with listening to Palmer bitch about all of the punishment he was receiving for what seemed to him to be an innocent little prank. We all spent many a moment laughing at his bold, yet ever so stupid move. Having not forgotten getting racked constantly for my grades, this mess was best suited for him and Moore. I was out of trouble, and had no intentions of asking for it again.

CHAPTER 18

As second semester moved along, my responsibilities as a knob became almost second nature. I had learned and perfected all my duties and could deal with anything the upperclassmen threw at me. Other than a few freshman inconveniences, I had only my grades to worry about, and as the end of the semester neared, I encountered the most challenging parts of each of my courses. I was getting into the advanced theories that were an expansion of the earlier basics. I often struggled, but definitely kept my goal to finish the semester with at least a 3.0 GPR, and to end up on the Dean's List. But as I pushed myself through test after test, I found it harder to maintain the comfortable 3.2 I had at mid-term, and began to see its security start to dwindle. What I had accomplished during midterms was all well and good, but the only grades that really counted were the final ones, and as best I could, I worked hard to hold my position.

When we entered the final weeks I began to hear rumors about Rank Boards. Lever explained to me that it was a selection committee made up of ranking cadets and faculty. Their job was to look at the performance of the rising classes and determine who would receive what position for the upcoming year. There was no question that I wanted to be a Corporal sophomore year, but knew I only had a glimmer of hope. My bad academic performance from first semester was going to hurt me. Grades were everything when it came to assigning privileges.

When the Rank Board interview schedule was posted, I was extremely disappointed to find I wasn't even on the list. It was a very bad sign. There were fifteen freshmen being interviewed for the ten Corporal positions. I had no chance.

When Rank Boards for sophomores finally did arrive, I could see many of my friends getting haircuts and shining up in preparation to go before the panel. It only took one afternoon to do the interviews, and it wasn't long after that the results were published. Out of my group of six hell-raising friends, only one, Hank Rosellini, had become a corporal. It appeared that our group had conducted ourselves in a manner that was not conducive to showing responsibility. I immediately thought back to the things I should not have done, and the things that I wished that I could go back and correct. But it was water under the bridge at that point.

But I couldn't dwell on the situation. I had to prepare myself for the upcoming final exams. If I ever expected to get rank, I would really have to do well. I couldn't get discouraged. Rank was the first step to qualify for Sword Drill.

Regular classes soon ended, and the dreaded exam phase was once again upon me. Though I fought the good fight, my GPR had indeed fallen in the final weeks of classes. I went into exams just barely holding on to a 3.0. I braced myself for what was going to be an agonizing and grueling week of having two major finals each day. I at least had one advantage over my first semester in that I had studied hard over the entire period. It was now more a matter of re-memorizing formulas and getting a good night's sleep, but I often had to fight thinking about the rank situation. I couldn't let anything cloud my much needed mind.

As before, I got myself through the unpleasant task. Even though this set of exams was much nicer to me than my first time through, there was no question I was still worn out. My brain seemed to burn as I handed in that last test paper, but I knew I would not have to worry about academics again for months. I had only two days between my last exam and graduation, and then I would be free for the entire summer.

Before getting down to the final clean up of the barracks and graduation, there was one other major bit of business that had to be addressed. We freshmen had to be recognized as upperclassmen. This brought forth emotions and anticipation based on the endless rumors concerning what would take place. It was an end to our plight as freshmen, and the last opportunity the upperclassmen would have to rack us. The buzz was that they would leave us with a lasting impression and really kill us one last time. One of the more pleasing rumors though was that many a newly recognized freshman would beat the crap out of their most hated abuser. There were even tales of broken arms and separated shoulders during tremendous brawls between the classes.

But Benson told me that the killer rack session with unlimited push-ups, running, and other physical challenges had a real purpose. It was used more to wear the knobs out so much that they wouldn't have the energy or desire to fight. The hope was to see everyone shaking hands and ecstatic that it was all over. I wasn't so sure that would be the case.

Recognition activities started at 8:00 a.m. on the Thursday before Saturday's graduation. We were told to show up dressed only in our grey nasties and tennis shoes. We had to remove our belts, class and company insignia, and name tags before coming down. They again said it was for our protection.

After a speech or two from the juniors and seniors on how proud they were of us for making it, they proceeded with a hellacious rack session that tore into the best of us. They jumped into a series of endless push-ups, sit-ups, running in place, cherry picking, and any other drill to completely wear us down. It was nearly the same approach used during "Hell Night" only days after we had first arrived. I tried to preserve my strength as best I could, but I could see as I looked around that everyone was being taken beyond his limits. I could only think to myself that after this rack session and the handshakes, I would never again have to do this. But I also thought heavily about tracking down Schmidt to punch his lights out. The thought of getting even with that son-of-a-bitch was truly gratifying, and the anger caused by the thoughts of him helped me gain the motivation to get through the recognition process so I could kill him.

But there was no way to keep anything in reserve. The rack session went on until we were drained of all we had. Then just when we thought we could go no more, they announced that our last task was to pump out eighty push-ups for the Class of 1980. It was murder to get through them, and I don't even know how I did it. On the eightieth push-up we all collapsed on the quad in total fatigue. It took everything I had just to get back on my feet and line up so the upperclassmen could walk through and shake our hands and introduce themselves by their first names. Nearly dizzy with exhaustion, it was hard to believe that it was all finally over.

Each of the upperclassmen came by, one by one. As they did, I shook their hands in my exhaustion as I stood there panting for air. When Schmidt came by, I had nothing left in me to throw at him. I took the hand he offered and shook it. It was an insincere handshake with few words, and he was gone as fast as he walked up. But I just couldn't react. I was too tired. I was also too happy about finally getting through the 4th Class System. I just couldn't bring myself to spoil the moment I had worked so hard to see. Maybe there would be an opportunity later to get some revenge on the asshole, but for the moment, I would enjoy what my classmates and I would remember for the rest of our lives. We had survived the most difficult part of making it through The Citadel. We were no longer knobs. We were now upperclassmen.

***

No one from the Corps was allowed to leave to go home until graduation was over. Until then we were to use the free time to pack away all of our uniforms and other items into large boxes that would be stored in a warehouse until the following year. The barracks had to be emptied of all belongings since the rooms would be used over the summer for other purposes like summer school and sports camps.

With recognition behind us, we removed the 4's from our collars and replaced them with our new insignias. For some of my classmates that meant a set of Corporal wings. For me, it was a 3. It was good to be moving up, but it tore my heart out that I had not gotten rank after trying so hard. I was going to suffer much for my two months of carelessness. Powerless to do anything about it at that point, I accepted my 3 with a forced smile. As conciliation, the upperclassmen tried to give encouragement and reminded those of us not receiving rank about the customary second semester rank rotation. They presented it as a motivation for us to continue to improve our grades or discipline records.

But my contempt quickly turned to curiosity as I thought about my exam grades and the help they might bring to the situation. I really wanted to know how I would finish up with my GPR, and since I had free time before graduation, I started checking outside of the classrooms on a regular basis to find the posted slips that had ID numbers and final grades. I continued to check and collect my grades right up until the Friday afternoon before graduation. My final GPR ended up being a 2.94, less than one tenth of a point from crossing that 3.0 threshold. Although I was happy with the massive improvement, I was terribly disappointed not making the Dean's List. My name appearing on that published list would have brought the sort of attention that would make it much easier for me to pull out of my no-rank situation.

I found myself in a very unique position on the Friday evening before graduation. Along with the rest of the Corps, I was finished with classes and there was no more 4th Class System. If there was ever a time to go out and raise hell, it was then. I hooked up with my classmates as the masses headed out on the town. We all had much to celebrate. For some, it was the first chance to show off their new rank.

We had a large group of guys, and decided to make our way down to Big John's. It was an old bar, but very popular with the upperclassmen. When we got there, the place was already packed to the gills with cadets in a very good mood. School was almost out, and we were in an upperclassman hangout without fear. There was no longer such a thing as fraternization. Instead of avoiding the upper three classes, we were actually happy to see them. Although it was a bit awkward at first trying to chum around with the individuals who used to rack your brains out and verbally abuse you on sight, it was easier than I thought to put the past behind us knowing that we would never have to go through that again. We were now one of them.

That evening was also a night for good-byes. Most would not see each other during the summer, but as for the senior class, we would probably not see them again for years. Benson was there, and I helped him tie on a good drunk by buying him a pitcher of beer for being so nice to me over the last year. He thought it was great that I was a private, thinking he had trained me right to recognize that rank was of no value. I never told Benson about my dream of making Sword Drill, knowing it was just the sort of thing he disliked the most. I merely toasted his future, and he toasted mine. We were still the best of friends even though I secretly disagreed with all that he had stood for as a cadet.

The next day Benson and his classmates walked across the stage that had been erected just for the ceremony. There was a huge crowd of family members and girlfriends there to see loved ones go through the motions. The speeches were inspirational, but what I found to be the most impressive were the many cadets who had their fathers present them with their diplomas. Some of the dads were Citadel graduates themselves, and others were high-ranking NCO's and officers in various branches of the military. Through the pride displayed on their faces, it seemed to be a huge honor for both. It was also evident that the mothers were also just as proud of their sons for having put up with the unbelievable challenges that the school had thrown at them for four years. It was a wonderful moment for everyone, and with the final throw of hats into the air, the ceremony ended.

My dad picked me up in front of the barracks as the masses scrambled to leave, and on the way home my father and I talked constantly about all of the things that had happened since we had last seen each other. I was proud to tell him about the huge improvements in my grades over the previous semester, and he never expected in his wildest dreams that I would do as well as I did. He shook his head in disbelief, knowing the difficulties of my major, and admitted he had only hoped that I would be able to get C's. I had only one C, along with several B's and A's. He thought it to be so out of character for me, yet so outstanding. I could see he was really stunned by the news.

We then switched subjects to the farm, and Dad explained that things were normal but busy. Planting season was still going on with some of the crops, and with the current workload, my help would certainly be needed during the summer. But Dad encouraged me to take a break if I could, and use every free moment to take advantage of the vacation. He seemed to have a sense of what I had gone through, and considered it much more stressful than anything I had done in high school, where when summertime arrived, he fully expected me to work all the time.

Dad also mentioned that Charles was now getting more into the management oriented duties of the farm. He said it relieved him of some work, but left those things Charles used to attend to hanging, some of which were hard to find a replacement for. Some things were now starting to back up and I felt like Dad was hoping that I would help provide the relief needed in those areas. He seemed concerned about the unattended tasks, but I also got the impression that the decision process around the farm was turning into the "two women in the kitchen" predicament.

As I rode along and thought about our talk, I couldn't help but consider the 100+ degree tobacco fields, the sweltering barns, and the other harsh elements of summer farming I was heading towards. It was weird that I could envision it all as a cakewalk as compared to what I had just gone through at The Citadel. I truly believed that even hell had nothing on El Cid. I was without question ready and willing to get away from that place, even if it was only a change to hard labor.

From that point on, I found myself slowly establishing a summertime routine. During the week, I would work on the farm and then usually just hang around the house watching TV at night. Each weekend I hoped to hear of a party or some social event that would provide access to either old friends or at least a chance to make new ones. But those opportunities were scarce, and I felt too out of sync with others to create my own. Drugs and wild drunks were the sport of the day, and I looked more like a cop than I did a party animal. I felt a straight-laced stigma attached to my very appearance, and I could just sense the phobia others felt about me. I didn't know if it was a conscious decision by them or just a reaction, but it was clear that even out on summer furlough I was far from fitting the socially acceptable mold of a typical nineteen year old in 1977.

I found that things between Charles and I were the same as always, but I could detect that the full time workers on the farm were acquiring a growing concern as he took over more and more of the things that Dad had always handled. They knew Dad as a tough businessman, yet he was always concerned about those who worked for him. But for Charles, power and authority was all that mattered. He spared no one's feelings, and was bossy and rude when asking people to do things. Worse yet, he never seemed to care how his decisions affected the morale of the workers, and very rarely asked for or wanted to hear others' opinions. He had all the answers. For someone to even question his orders was nothing less than insubordination, and they were directed to just do as they were told and to leave the thinking to him. This brought nothing but a lot of aggravation for those who had been with the O'Bryan family for countless years.

With my mother's wonderful meals and the lack of pressure that I was normally used to while eating, I started to see some of the weight return that I had lost while on Schmidt's mess. I wanted to run and lift while putting the pounds back on, but found it hard to get motivated since the summer workdays were so long and the heat and physical exertion took most of the energy out of me. Sometimes on weekends, or on rainy days when the physical drain had not been so heavy, I would put on my running shoes and go for a two or three mile run or even hit my old weight bench and pump iron for an hour or two. I really missed the muscle tone I once had while playing football. Following the injury to my leg was when I first saw that excellent physique start to drift away. It was after getting on Schmidt's mess that I watched it completely disappear.

Though somewhat hidden, I started to see some of the real tension that existed between Dad and my brother. It seemed Charles had some pretty radical ideas for making changes. He wanted to modernize the equipment at a faster pace such that less labor would be needed, and he also had looked hard at a few new farming ventures. Worst of all, he wanted to borrow the money to pursue many of these endeavors. One of Charles' hottest ideas was picked up while attending a seminar on catfish farming. Apparently, he was convinced that there were mega-bucks to be made in constructing these huge ponds and fish tanks so as to raise thousands of catfish that would later be sold to fish markets and individuals, supposedly yielding outstanding profits. He saw it as a perfect opportunity, especially when compared to the temperamental nature of growing crops and dealing with the unpredictable elements.

I knew well that both my father and grandfather had traditionally shown no interest in going into any kind of livestock farming at all. Though it had potential, it presented too many problems that could affect one's ability for success. Charles knew that, but to him catfish farming seemed to be a huge opportunity.

As if he weren't irritating Dad enough already, I often heard Charles presenting the idea to him. Dad would constantly put Charles off and expressed mostly negative feelings about breaking out of the operation that had over the years provided a slow and steady buildup of the O'Bryan family assets. But more than anything, he didn't want to put anything on the line, especially when the risk meant possibly losing the farm because a mortgage couldn't be serviced.

I stayed clear of the mounting feud as I could see the pressure was rising between Dad and Charles. The wrong things were being said, and both sides had their minds made up. It appeared it was going to be a long and nasty battle.

As the weeks clipped along, I felt numb about the bland summer I was having. Soon though, the Fourth of July weekend arrived and I found myself invited to a big party down at a friend's lake house on Lake Marion. When I arrived I was pleasantly surprised by the number of people who were there. I was excited when I realized it was definitely going to be a blowout. There was a large spread of food and three full-sized kegs on ice.

My lagging summer spirits rose as I walked around and spotted many of my old friends from high school there. I knew this was going to be the highlight of my summer, that is, until I found that the crowd included Donna. First I spotted her from a distance, and then I felt an overpowering feeling of discomfort. I was able to stay lost in the crowd and clear of her through most of the afternoon, but eventually I found myself standing in a group where she and some guy walked up and joined us. There was immediately a bit of awkwardness, and I felt peculiar since this was the first time I had laid eyes on her since Parents Day Weekend. I could feel a strange alteration in the group's conversation, as most standing there knew that Donna and I had once dated seriously and that she had somehow caused the break-up by dumping me. If there was anyone in the group who was not tense it was Donna. To her, I was just another one of the many ex-boyfriends she had learned to deal with. Handling old flames was probably an art she had since mastered. She just walked over and greeted me with an ambush of enthusiasm and hugged me with a huge smile.

"Hey, John! How have you been?" she yelled, as I stood stiff with chagrin.

I certainly wasn't expecting such an enthusiastic greeting from her, especially from someone who had so coldly stabbed me in the back at the worst of times. But I knew there was no purpose in making a scene, especially under the circumstances.

I smiled back at her saying, "I'm doing fine. How are you?"

"Great," she replied with a gleaming smile. "John, I want you to meet Doug Thatcher. Doug, John's the one I told you about that goes to The Citadel."

I couldn't imagine what she had told Doug concerning school and me. Maybe it was that she had torn my heart out there.

"Hi, Doug!" I said with little conviction, "How're you doin'?" I reached out to shake Doug's hand.

Doug was tall, and a pretty good-looking guy. Donna had obviously found an excellent replacement. He reached his hand out to shake mine, but showed little enthusiasm while going through the motions.

"I'm fine," he replied.

Donna broke into the awkward moment by saying, "I'm glad to see that you've at least survived your freshman year, and gosh, look...even your hair has grown out some."

Donna reached up and lightly touched my hair. It was still short, but much longer than it was when I last saw her. I could see that Doug really did not appreciate her touching me. I guess he obviously didn't realize that I wasn't getting any thrill out of the big to-do reunion either.

"I survived. It was tough at times, but I made it."

"I'm so glad. I just wanted to check and make sure you had gotten through all right. We've all been concerned about you down there."

"Hey, I appreciate that," I said with no enthusiasm.

"Well, just wanted to pop over and say hello. We'll be seeing you around."

Donna grabbed Doug's hand and they walked away. An old friend of mine, Bill Morris, was standing in our group, and he just shook his head in a negative fashion as they left. I wondered if it was because Donna had dumped me or because her boyfriend Doug seemed like such a jerk.

When Bill's girlfriend noticed him shaking his head, she asked, "What's the matter with you?"

Bill answered in a low, quiet voice, "I know that guy. Everyone calls him Thatch. That guy's bad news."

214

"What do you mean?" prodded Bill's girlfriend.

"He's nothing but a jail sentence looking for a place to happen. He's the biggest coke dealer at Clemson."

"Does Donna know that?" asked the girl.

"She dates him, doesn't she?" replied Bill.

I found it a bit hard to swallow that Donna was now dating someone who was involved with dealing heavy drugs. What a change-up. The whole time we dated, Donna never used or had much tolerance for that crap, nor did either of us like to hang around anyone who did. This was a real change of pace for her, yet maybe it wasn't. Maybe ol' Thatch was making some real bucks off of what he was doing. The fact that he had looks to go with it probably made him attractive to Donna. She liked money and power and apparently didn't care how they were obtained. Although I still felt some hurt over what Donna had done to me, I hated to see that she had now chosen such a stupid path.

But there was nothing I could do about it. I just drew another beer from the keg and enjoyed the rest of the party feeling a bittersweet satisfaction that I had finally gotten that first meeting with Donna over with. I felt concern for her future, and a bit of pain for a love lost through rejection. Though hard to admit it, I felt a bit empty for the rest of the party.

The holiday weekend passed, and as July became August, I found myself in the final weeks of my furlough. My father again encouraged me to take some time off and try to do something entertaining and fun. I appreciated his offer, but also knew that my help was needed on the farm. I really had no burning desire to go anywhere, especially since I had no one to go with.

During the final week I did however decide to head back to Charleston a day or two early, since that was permissible by the school. Cadre had already started and the new freshman class had been there for almost a week. I could get an early start on getting my room set up and possibly take a day or so to knock around Charleston and go out with a few of my buddies who were already there. Rosellini and Burn were cadre corporals, and I knew that the three of us could probably go grab a beer.

But as my luck would have it, I was not able to leave before witnessing a pretty bad argument between Charles and my father. It seemed that Dad's continued refusal to yield an inch on the expansion ideas had finally caused Charles to hit his frustration limit over the matter. For some reason, Charles had it justified in his mind that he should be allowed to make at least one major decision concerning the family business. He was at the ripe age of twenty-one, and felt he deserved the opportunity to try the catfish venture. Dad had grown weary of Charles' refusal to accept "no" for an answer, and could see that he was hell-bent on pursuing the endeavor.

When the time finally arrived for me to head back to school, the conflict was still unresolved as Charles and my father remained at odds with each other. It was almost a relief to again head back to school since tensions were so high at home. I was also bored, and was now looking forward to pursuing the challenges of the upcoming sophomore year. I was more than ready to leave Kingstree and Williamsburg County.

As I prepared to go, it felt peculiar to be packing stuff into my Camaro. But now, as a sophomore, I had the privilege of having a car. I could even park it on campus, and could drive to and from school without having to rely on anyone else. No more buses, cabs, or hitching a ride. I already liked life as an upperclassman.

CHAPTER 19

Driving towards Charleston I was feeling a bit antsy as I looked into the rear view mirror to see what was now long hair as compared to Citadel standards. I knew that within 24 hours it would once again be short, and that the freedoms I had grown used to over the previous three months would disappear.

When I walked into 4th Battalion, I could hear the familiar yelling of upperclassmen at freshman, and wondered if it was one of my classmates. As I moved into the company area, the first person I saw was Rosellini. I laughed when I saw that it was indeed him who was tearing into a freshman. I had to stop and watch, knowing that this was the same hell-raising individual who used to bitch about upperclassmen who were such pricks and assholes for racking and yelling at us knobs. And now, here he was dishing it out like some hard ass.

I walked into Rosellini's sight, and when he saw me he stopped yelling and left the knob in the lean and rest to come over and shake my hand. He seemed genuinely happy to see me again and indicated that he looked forward to us going out and grabbing a beer later. I wanted to talk more about our summers, but then remembered that he was busy.

I left Rosellini with his duty and made my way on up the stairwell. I recalled that at this early stage, all of the knobs and the cadre were located on 3rd and 4th Divisions. I knew I needed to see Leon Rooney, who was now Assistant 1st Sergeant for Romeo Company. It was his job to make room assignments based on class standing, rank, and the desires for room choices that the seniors, then juniors, and then finally sophomores had made. Since the freshmen had to room on 3rd and 4th, that meant that by the time the top two classes had made their choices of a room, it left sophomores, especially the privates, with very little choice. During the final days of our freshman year, I had approached Larry Segars about again being my roommate. I was happy when he accepted, knowing he was the most compatible guy I had roomed with during freshman year. I also knew that we were both going to be privates. Rankless, there would be little pull between us to nail down a decent room.

On third division I found Rooney's room, but he wasn't there. Lonny Mauldin, however, who was now R Company's 1st Sergeant and Rooney's roommate, was in, and with a very strict and official mannerism, he instructed me that room assignments were posted on the Company bulletin board. Mauldin wasn't rude, yet acted as if he had little time to talk to me.

I left Mauldin's room and strolled down to the bulletin board where I indeed found floor plan drawings showing each of the division's rooms. With some degree of humiliation, I discerned that sophomore privates wouldn't even be given a choice among the leftovers. My degradation further heightened as I found that Larry and I had received one of the worst rooms in R Company. It was the 1st Division small alcove, which was not only the smallest room, but also it contained piping that was part of the fire sprinkler system. The large collection of painted iron pipes took up a significant part of the already scarce space and added the insult of an eyesore.

I felt put in my place. I had received my first hint that I was considered as nothing more than a freshman with his chin out. I hadn't even gotten my things into the barracks and I was already finding out that I had a room that was much worse than any I ever had as a freshman. I reminded myself that this was something I had expected, and confirmed that I would be relentless in my quest to obtain rank.

Shaking off the disappointment, I went out to my car and got the personal items I brought with me and began to haul them in. Once I had the car unloaded, I then made my way over to the warehouse and located my boxes of uniforms and other items I had stored for the summer. Too big to fit inside, I brought them back by placing them on the hood, then after lugging them to my room, I began to unpack and use the rest of the afternoon to get my things put away.

While working in my room, a few of my other cadre corporal buddies popped in to say hello and welcome me back. I appreciated them stopping by to speak, and respected their attitudes in handling their rank. But I knew that based on the personalities of some of my classmates, that it was just a matter of time before a certain few of them would be trying to pull rank for some ridiculous reason or another. From stories I heard from Benson, it was inevitable that such encounters would eventually happen.

During my freshman year I had both heard and observed upperclassmen in conflict with members of their own class because rank was used to carry out enforcement of rules that eventually led to discipline and sometimes even heavy punishment. When these actions were taken, especially against a classmate, it generally put everyone involved in a bad position. With my hopes of having rank one day, I didn't want to set a bad example by bucking authority or causing trouble for those who were in charge, especially when it might send perceived signals of sour grapes.

I finished the unpacking and found myself with a lot of extra time on my hands. I began to think that now was the time for my resolution to kick in. I sat at my desk for a moment and thought about the things that I wanted to accomplish during the coming semester, as well as for the rest of my cadet life. At the top of my list was my desire to make Sword Drill. I was haunted with the thoughts that to even qualify I was going to have to obtain a high sergeant's rank. To get it, I would need both outstanding grades and military performance. There was nothing at that moment I could do about grades since I had no books, but I certainly had everything available to work on my appearance.

I could hardly believe I was actually going to sit down, and without any pressure from anyone, jump right into those things that seemed so useless as a knob. Now, as a sophomore, with the freedom of being an upperclassman, and school not yet officially started, I was really going to take up my free time to shine brass and shoes. I smiled at the thought. But the commitment was there.

I could feel it calling. It was unquestionable and unwavering.

I worked hard on all my uniform items, bringing them to perfect shape, one after the other. While I was shining, I could hear formation going on outside as the knobs were getting racked and yelled at by what sounded like the entire cadre. I soon could hear them going through the motions of formation, and then march away to mess. I went back to work and was finishing up my last few items when Rosellini arrived from the mess hall.

"What the hell you doin' with all this shit out?" asked Rosellini, laughing as he talked. "Damn man, don't you even know how a private's supposed to act?"

"Hopefully, if I do some of this shit, I won't be a private for long."

"Oh yeah?" laughed Rosellini.

"You're damn right. It sure didn't take me long to find out what not having rank means. Look at this shit hole they put me in. What the hell am I supposed to do with all these pipes?"

"Don't sweat it. You'll get something when rank rotation comes around. Anyway, I don't think it's all that much better once you get these corporal wings on your collar. They keep all of us doing the shit work, and we get nothing for it."

"Oh yeah? You don't have a mouse hole for a room, do ya'?" I asked in contradiction.

"I guess not. But come on -- let's get the hell out of here. I want to drink some brews before I have to get back."

Hank and I headed out of my room and down the gallery. We still had to walk around and under the "O" Company stairwell on our way out. Unfortunately, it was a junior privilege to be able to walk across the quad. Although there was no freshman trot or bracing, we still had to take the same old route.

"We've got to swing by to pick up Burn," said Rosellini. "He's going with us."

"Oh yeah? How's he doin'?"

"Pretty good. He says being Guidon Corporal sucks since he has so much damn paperwork to keep up with, but he does get a couple of extra privileges."

"Good. Maybe he has a couple of extras to give me."

We got into my car and cut around to the mess hall entrance. Danny came running out of the doors as if he were running late and jumped into the back seat.

"Sorry I couldn't get away from mess earlier," said Danny.

"Yeah, right, you asshole," replied Hank. "If you'd just leave the friggin' knobs alone, you'd have your ass out here."

"Damn O'Bryan, when you gonna get a haircut? You look like a fuckin' freak!"

"I've made a decision, I'm gonna keep my hair long through this first semester."

"Schmidt will have your ass," said Burn. "He's already bent out of shape over us on cadre. Look how short mine is. He wants us to be knobs again."

"Schmidt?" I yelled with real anger. "I can't tell you how happy I'll be to see that jerk again."

"I thought you hated his guts," quizzed Rosellini.

"I just want to see him again so I can finally punch him in his smart ass mouth since I missed the opportunity when we got recognized."

"Ooooooo," rooted Burn, "I see you've come back as a badass."

"Bad enough to kick your Yankee ass," I replied.

"Damn," interjected Rosellini, "You must have been rackin' farm hands down there in Hooterville all summer."

Our cuts flew like sand gnats during parade. It was our way of welcoming each other back. To me, their slams were welcomed validation that two of my closest classmates had not copped an attitude. Burn was the highest-ranking sophomore in R Company, and Rosellini was obviously the biggest flame-on, yet they didn't show one ounce of snootiness towards me, their rankless friend. We had all been buddies during freshman year, and apparently we were still going to be, even with the changes.

The following day would mark the return of the remainder of the

221

Corps. When I was awakened in the early morning by the sound of the upperclassmen yelling at knobs during formation, I piled out of the rack with an agenda to get a jump on the process of transforming from quasi-civilian back to a squared away cadet. I knew the first day back would be hectic with long lines to get registered for classes and tackling the other countless time consuming tasks that would come with the start of a new cadet year.

The barbershop was open and there were already other cadets there who also must have anticipated problems with waiting until later. I jumped into the chair, and as I watched my hair falling to the floor, I felt a remnant of the same lump I had in my stomach when I got that first haircut as a freshman, even though this was not to be a complete skinning like before.

Back in my room, I pulled out my nasties and prepared a shirt by putting my nametag on my breast pocket and my R and 3 on my collars. I then put on my freshly shined brass belt and shoes, finishing off with my overseas cap. I then walked over to the mirror to see the image that had been absent for months. It was so wild to have seen myself all summer with longer hair and sometimes an unshaven face. I was now back in the groove as an upperclassman, but I still felt like a nobody.

I spent the rest of the day making rounds from room to room, hearing wild stories of events that had taken place during my classmates' summer. There was quite an assortment of tales. Some had good summer jobs. Some had excellent adventures. Some even got laid. Everyone seemed to have a story about good times away from prison. But as I talked to them, I began to see that for some strange reason, they were all happy in a way to be back. Somehow or another the school had changed them too, and in such a way as to make them understand that as long as they were cadets, the place where they were most wanted and were most comfortable was The Citadel. Love it or hate it, it was now our home.

When Larry finally showed up, he had left little time to get his act together. I helped him unload his stuff from the car of another cadet who he had caught a ride with and we lugged his possessions to our hole in the wall. I watched as Larry tore through the boxes to find his uniform and brass to wear to muster. He had just enough time to prepare, but had a long way to go to get his part of the room squared away. He would have a busy schedule the next day to get everything done.

As the muster formation bugle sounded, I could see that there were still a few guys missing. We all fell into our old positions from the previous year, which required a bit of memory, though those with rank hadn't seemed to forget. I was in First Platoon, Second Squad. Only after we had lined up did I recall that the Platoon Leader for Second was Darrell Wells, who had been promoted up from Squad Sergeant. The Platoon Sergeant was Don Henderson, who was once a corporal on one of my messes.

As soon as we were called to attention, the two of them started making their way through first squad, writing down the most outstanding deficiencies of the troops as they went along. Most everyone still needed haircuts, and uniforms and brass stood out as needing the most attention. As Wells made his way through the second squad, he seemed pleased to find a sophomore private like me looking so good for a muster formation. Henderson, who was right behind him making notes on his clip board, smiled at me and said in a fake Spanish accent "looking charp," then moved on to the next guy. Although it was subtle, I felt pleased to have already made a good impression, and was satisfied I was on my way to setting up the correct image.

The new chain of command within the company was very lenient towards the unruly for the time being, displaying an unusual understanding for those having difficulties getting back into the cadet mode of things. The inspection was performed to basically survey the company and make note of those things that were lacking. It was a low-pressure inspection with no demerits, and only gentle reminders that the time had arrived to get back on track. The fun was over. It was a new year.

With a quick short speech, our new Company Commander, Kevin Schmidt, welcomed us all back and confirmed officially that there would be a short lived toleration for those deficiencies noted that evening, and that he, as well as the other ranking members of the company, expected quick compliance to standards.

Once the company was dismissed, most everyone spent the rest of the evening unpacking boxes, visiting, and swapping war stories from the summer. Having unpacked already, I made my way around the company, shooting the shit with whomever I ran into. While walking down the gallery I passed by an individual who appeared to be George Porter, the Cadet Corporal that had worked so well with me immediately following Cadre. As we passed by each other, he spoke, but I had to do a double take since his head was now completely shaved. I had to stop for a moment and consider the fact that Porter was probably going out for the Junior Sword Drill. I felt a bit stupid that I had no idea who was aspiring for Drill out of R. I had seen Lonnie Mauldin the day before, and had not noticed that his head was shaved. Porter was Cadre First Platoon Sergeant, which left only Leon Rooney, the now company Assistant First Sergeant, as the only other individual within the company who was qualified. But I remembered seeing him at the muster, and recalled that his head wasn't even close to being shaved. It seemed that the only guy from the Company going out for Drill was George Porter.

I couldn't understand how anyone with qualifying rank would not go out for Sword Drill. To me, it seemed like the biggest honor on campus. Yet there were many things about Drill that I did not understand, and now that I was an upperclassman, I was going to use the opportunity to find out some real information that I was never privy to as a freshman.

The next day was eventful as the Corps rushed through annoying tasks such as registering for classes and buying books. It was a challenge to get everything done, and I laughed as I saw the long haircut line stretching all the way out of Mark Clark Hall, thinking how fortunate it was that I had not waited.

It really didn't take long for the Corps to get back into cadet life considering the sharp transition from freedom. The one day buffer before classes went like a flash, and on Tuesday, the real hammer came down. At noon formation, demerits were handed out for those who had not met the haircut standard or other personal appearance violations sighted during the Sunday night's muster.

For some, it was a bad way to start off the new year. For me, it was just another opportunity to shine. As I was inspected, both Wells and Henderson couldn't help but note the perfection of my brass and shoes. My Squad Corporal, Chris Davis, who had been a friend during freshman year, was also pleased. He handled his rank so well, and did his job without flaunting or abusing his corporal position. I began to wonder if the stories were true that there would be classmates who would be so mindless as to try to do stupid things with their rank.

As the days passed in that first week, I found my cadet life quickly getting back into a routine. I immediately started attacking my subjects, but this time with even more vengeance and enthusiasm than before. Dean's list had eluded me the previous semester by only a fraction of a point. That wasn't going to be the case again if I could help it. I now had too many reasons to do well.

One very exciting event that was supposed to happen that first week was the start of Sword Drill's 14 Nights. Finally, I would at least get to see first hand what was happening on the quad each night when the Drill returned. Though I tried to determine just which night they would begin, I felt a need to remain nonchalant in my inquiries, still not wanting to let the cat out of the bag about my secret dream. Being an upperclassman certainly didn't make one immune from catching a ration of crap for one's overly optimistic high hopes.

I also wanted to start training quite seriously. I already knew that Sword Drill activities were physically demanding. I was going to have to squeeze some weight lifting and running in whenever possible. I had become pretty efficient with my time, and rarely was there a moment wasted, but I also knew that my schedule would have to be even stricter if I wanted to accomplish all I wanted to do.

Friday came quickly as it had been a short, four-day week of classes. Saturday would bring our first SMI, which was scheduled to insure that cadets had returned uniforms and rooms to an acceptable standard. I saw this usually unpleasant event as another opportunity to hopefully score another positive impression. So after a good run immediately following parade, I headed back to my room and used the rest of the evening to make sure that my uniform and weapon were blitzed to perfection and ready to go for the inspection that next morning.

First, I cleaned my rifle with detail, and then worked on my brass and shoes until they were flawless. I carefully stored my rifle in the rack behind the door, put away my personal appearance items, and then proceeded to clean my room. Everything was still in pretty good order since I had just unpacked and put my possessions away. But the room was still dusty from the three months it sat empty during the summer. Dust was on top of the presses, desks, light fixtures, and especially on the tremendous piping conglomeration in the corner of the room. I spent almost an hour just trying to dust the place, finding it a challenge to finish since every time I would wipe something off, dust would fly and settle on the things I had already cleaned. It took awhile, but eventually I managed to blitz the whole place down.

The next morning following mess, I dressed with care and made my way out to line up for personal inspection. My shoes looked like black glass, and my brass like Christmas ornaments. As I stood in line in my squad waiting for the inspection, Chris Davis walked up to give me a friendly check over.

"Damn John," he yelled, "You trying to make me look bad?"

"No," I said smiling, appreciating the compliment.

"Are those patent leather shoes?" he protested. "You're not suppose to wear those down for SMI's."

"Wrong again, buddy," I said. "Those are leather."

Chris looked closely and could see that they were indeed leather.

"Hey, I'm the corporal!" he said, "I'm the one that's supposed to be setting the example."

"Better watch your ass then," I said with a smile.

The formation was soon called to order, and there was movement by the officers to indicate that the inspection process was about to begin. I hadn't asked or heard just who would be doing the inspecting that morning, thinking it didn't matter. But to my disappointment, I soon realized the SMI was going to be handled by none other than the new R Company Commander, Kevin Schmidt.

Though I wasn't happy about it, I knew how well prepared I was, and that this was probably my best opportunity to finally make a good impression on Schmidt. He had been a real pain in the ass all through freshman year, but since reporting back as a sophomore, I hadn't had contact with him other than just seeing him in passing on the gallery. As much as I disliked him, he unfortunately had the largest say in who held rank within the company. My hope was that freshman year was behind the both of us.

The SMI seemed to move along at a snail's pace, with each individual being inspected with a surprising amount of detail. Schmidt seemed to be checking everything on each cadet, and it took him almost ten minutes to make his way through the first squad of First Platoon. He was looking at every minute detail, even with the juniors and seniors, whether they held rank or not.

Finally, he made his way down through second squad until he made the left turn in front of me. As he did, I brought my rifle up to inspection arms position.

Kevin started looking me over with a fine tooth comb. When he looked down at my shoes, he looked back up at me and asked, "Are those leather?"

"Yes, they are," I answered.

Lonnie Mauldin, who was standing right beside Schmidt, also looked down closely at them, and after a few seconds said, "He's right. They're leather. Pretty good shoes!"

Schmidt showed no expression either way, and just as I looked over at Mauldin to give him a smile for saying such, Schmidt quickly came up with his hand and snatched the rifle from my grip. He caught me off guard, but I reacted by going to attention. I had obviously not failed on my brass, hair, uniform, or shoes, and I knew Schmidt could not view my appearance as anything but impressive. But as he looked over my rifle, then checked the bore, he turned to Mauldin and said "dirty rifle," then turned back and looked me in the eyes and said "You have dust in the bore. Make sure it's clean next time."

Schmidt then handed the rifle back to me where I then went to order arms as he turned to inspect the next cadet. After he moved down, Mauldin ended up in front of me, reluctantly writing down the dirty rifle charge with frustration on his face. It was obvious to anyone that my personal appearance was outstanding and that I had worked hard to look my best. My personal appearance was far above that which was expected out of any sophomore, much less a private.

As I stared forward, I was almost in shock. What was wrong with Schmidt? Had he not realized that knob year was over and that I was now an upperclassman? What was this guy's beef with me? I had always suspected as a freshman that I had been singled out by him for one reason or another, but I could never see any real reason why he could dislike me so much. But one thing was now obvious. Schmidt was not going to limit his antipathy for me to freshman year. He brought it with him to the new year, where I was hoping to get a fresh start.

I stood there in formation for almost another 30 minutes as Schmidt took his sweet time inspecting the rest of the company. When we were finally dismissed, I went back to my room and immediately kicked the door open, still furious at Schmidt for burning me.. More so, I was frustrated that I once again had some individual in my world always trying to make matters worse for me. I thought that when I left the farm and Charles that I had put an end to that sort of looming threat. But now, it was resurrected in the form of a Yankee asshole.

I tried to cool down while waiting for the room inspection to start, and looked around to make absolutely sure that nothing was out of order. But before putting up my rifle, I looked down into the bore to see if it had indeed been dirty. As I looked, I squinted hard to see that at the very bottom of the barrel there was indeed a tiny speck of dust. I was shocked. I thought I had cleaned it. As I stared across the room trying to think of what went wrong, the sight of the dustpan on the wall revealed the answer. Dust had probably gotten into the barrel as I was cleaning the room. It was flying everywhere. After putting my cleaned rifle back into rack with the open barrel pointed up, it was no wonder dust was able to get inside. Damn!

Wrapped in frustration, I put my rifle back in the rack just as I heard the inspection party making its way down the gallery to next door. Larry and I got into our positions, and when the group finally did enter, I could see Schmidt glance at me as he stepped in. He immediately begin going over the room, speaking as he looked.

"Well...Mr. O'Bryan and Mr. Seagers. Looks like you guys ended up with the pipe room, huh?"

"Yes, we did," responded Larry, without me saying a word.

I just stood there with a serious look on my face, not entertained at the moment with any small talk Schmidt might have to offer. He ran his hand over the sink, and the light fixture, both of which I had cleaned to perfection. Wearing a white glove, any speck of dirt or dust would be picked up instantly. But there was none. So Schmidt proceeded to walk through the entire room checking, not finding a thing out of place. Apparently desperate to nail us, he even went over to the pipes, which was well over and above what we should be held accountable to clean. Yet, I had given it my all, and knew there wasn't a nook or cranny in that room with dust or dirt in it.

First Sergeant Mauldin just stood with a puzzled look on his face, baffled by the intensity of Schmidt's inspection. But as Schmidt failed time and again to prove us guilty, Mauldin grew impatient, ready to move on to another room.

Schmidt finally conceded, but as he walked out, he couldn't resist one last attempt, and stopped suddenly to look at the bottom rack.

"Whose rack is this?" asked Schmidt.

Larry spoke up answering "mine."

Schmidt looked at Larry and said "tighten it up a little bit better next time."

"Okay," answered Larry.

Schmidt gave me a quick, cold glance, and then turned and walked out of the room. Mauldin looked at me too, but his face was full of frustration. He shook his head, and then followed Schmidt out the door. It was over.

"I thought you were crazy cleaning up so much," said Larry. "Boy was I wrong. I guess I owe you one."

"That son of a bitch. He's still after me!" I said with a very stern and serious look on my face.

"That's right! I had forgotten. He was the one that wouldn't let you eat during first semester."

"Yeah," I answered coldly.

"What is it with you two? What's got you's guys as enemies?"

"I think it's because I'm a Southerner, and he thinks that I have some sort of advantage. He's made it his business to even things up. All I really know is that he hates my guts."

"Sure looks that way."

I stayed pissed about the SMI for a while, but soon realized that there was nothing that could be done about it. I knew I would just have to stay out of Schmidt's way. He, more than anyone, possessed the ability to make or break me from ever becoming a corporal. It would have to be approved by him if it was to ever happen. My subconscious told me I'd probably never see rank as long as he was the CO.

CHAPTER 20

The following week brought many distractions. The first was the approaching weekend and the kickoff Senior Party of the year. It was to be a new experience for us all since the Folly Beach pier had burnt over the summer, and we would now have the infamous event at a huge, old facility located downtown called Charleston County Hall. Many things would be different, but as usual I was left with the problem of getting a date. But the first person that came to mind was Julie, and after giving her a call, she sounded pleased to hear from me again, and in her energetic voice agreed to go with me. I was proud to say I would pick her up in my car, and that I was now on the upperclassmen's curfew schedule.

The other diversion started that Monday evening when I heard at mess that the Junior Sword Drill had started into their 14 Nights. I was startled by the news since I hadn't heard a thing about it before that moment. It was as if it were done just to keep everyone in the dark. The activities of the Drill always seemed so far in the background, and being an upperclassman provided no more of an open door to their secret world.

When I got back to my room after mess, I ignored my normal routine of grabbing my books and heading out to some academic building to study. I was not going to leave the barracks that evening, even though I knew it would be towards the end of ESP when the Drill would return. I just didn't want to chance missing them, so I stayed at my desk studying, trying to concentrate while fighting the anticipation and curiosity about what was to happen. I wanted to finally see what took place as the Drill returned with their chant of "We love, Sword Drill." It was killing me to know what it was they did on the quad that required all knobs to be in their rooms with doors closed tight.

I struggled to concentrate on my work through most of ESP, and finally around 9:15, I could hear the faint chant off in the distance that brought back memories of the first time I ever heard it. It was such an eerie sound as the cadence echoed between the battalions, breaking through the night air and silence of The Citadel campus.

I wasted no time in getting up, and Larry asked, "Where are you going?"

"To see the Drill dummy," I answered. "Can't you hear them?"

Larry listened for a moment and then said, "Oh yeah, I can hear them. I guess we can finally see what those stupid asses are up to, huh?"

I was headed out the door, but stopped briefly to say defensively, "What makes you think they're stupid asses?" but didn't wait for an answer as I headed out the door. I then realized it was a foolish thing to say, and I was sure Larry would wonder if this was an sign that John O'Bryan, Mr. Sophomore Private, was dreaming of making Drill. But he exited the room and said nothing, and I felt I had gotten away with a major verbal blunder.

We were one of the first out, but I soon saw doors opening and upperclassmen coming out of their rooms shouting as they walked up and down the gallery, "Close your doors knobs! Get inside your rooms. Don't let me catch you looking out the transoms." Over the shouting, I heard the banging sounds of doors closing and the shuffling feet on the concrete of knobs as they rushed towards their rooms. All four companies came alive, and I could see an upperclassman on third division over in N chasing and yelling at a bracing knob as he sprinted in his freshman trot towards his room. I laughed at the sight, and enjoyed the explosion of sound that broke up the normal tranquility of ESP.

But the Junior Sword Drill was an obvious exception to the rule, and I could see that nearly all upperclassmen had come out, from first division all the way up to fourth. They were leaning up against the rails on the upper decks, and looking towards the front sally port as they waited to see the Drill make their way in. Within a matter of seconds I saw three running cadets enter the battalion wearing black shirts with what appeared to be the Junior Sword Drill name and emblem on the front. It was easy to see they were last year's Sword Drill, and following right behind them were six more cadets, all dressed in gray nasty pants, Citadel PT shirts, a sword and scabbard with breast plate webbing, a shako with a feather plume, and high top tennis shoes. It was an odd uniform with mixed items from a cadet's formal, daily, and PT uniforms.

As they thundered through the sally port, the old Drill ran in front, setting the pace as the aspirants followed. The group first ran a lap around the outer edges of the quad with the roaches still chanting words that bounced and echoed off the concrete encasement of the battalion walls. After the lap was completed, the old Drill dropped out and moved to the middle as the others continued to circle, staying in formation, and continually singing their song which fought to compete with the cheering and hell raising of those showing their appreciation.

As the guys passed by it was apparent that they looked pretty rough. They were drenched from head to toe in sweat, and though their faces were partially covered by the strap of their shakos, I could tell from their exhausted expressions that they obviously had caught hell during the evening.

The crowd continued to watch and cheer as the aspirants finished running laps and ended up in the middle of the quad. The old Drill put them in the lean and rest, where they soon began to pump out push-ups. They struggled to make their tired arms lift and lower their bodies, and I could feel their strain as they fought just to make fourteen. When they were completed, the old Drill leaned down and whispered something to them, and after a few seconds, they all stood and once again began chanting as they split apart and started towards their companies.

I could see George Porter heading our way, and it was plain that he had been through a very rough time. He ran by us, bellowing his chant, stopped to kiss the R painted on the stairwell, then headed up the stairway to the second deck, and then up to the third, where with the slamming of a door, I could hear his vocalization stop. Within seconds, all chants ceased. The sounds within the battalion were reduced to the talking of those who were out on the galleries to watch. The show was over and everyone headed back to their rooms.

I also went back to mine and sat down at my desk as if I were going to once again study, but instead spent the next few minutes talking with Larry about what we had seen. It was just enough to really whet my appetite to learn more about the Drill. Their return was an exciting event, and I was pleased to see the support received from all in the battalion.

But I couldn't help but think of how beat George looked. From my football days, I knew he was going to be a ball of pain and soreness in the morning, and would have a tough time in class and with his other duties on Cadre. He and the other aspirants would also have to keep their brass and other uniform items up to some super standard while under the scrutiny of the old Drill. I couldn't imagine how he would get it all done.

It was then that I realized an opportunity. I wanted to know more and get closer to this process. Maybe one way to do it would be to offer some assistance to George. It could be a way for me to get some real information on what was truly going on with the Drill. I had been unsuccessful finding someone who had any genuine knowledge about it. But if I were to help George out, he would probably talk about what was happening. If I were to somehow pull off getting the rank necessary to go out, and if George ended up making it, it would also serve as an opportunity to gain some points for the future.

My first concern for my sudden plan was the fact that I was still very much a Sophomore Private. George probably already had other ranking members of my class offering to help out. I didn't know of any, but through cadre some of my classmates who were dealing with him daily would surely have had the opportunity to offer help.

I also recognized that it was so easy at The Citadel to be accused of kissing ass. There were those just waiting to ridicule anyone over anything. I had a feeling I would catch hell from some of them, but since George was only a staff sergeant with little authority to affect rank selection, maybe it would be considered as merely assistance to a fellow upperclassman. Besides, my classmates on cadre were loaded down with handling the new knobs.

The next day at morning formation, I found it difficult to even see George. His responsibility as a Cadre Platoon Sergeant was to the knobs, and he was required to march over with them to the mess hall separate from the upperclassmen. I knew I would just have to be patient and catch him going to class.

I kept my eyeballs pealed for George through my morning classes, but didn't see him until we were at noon formation where he was completely surrounded by his classmates and a few seniors, all interested in hearing about what had taken place the evening before. From a distance he looked a bit weary, and was moving slowly as if he was indeed quite sore. I knew it was not a good time to approach him, and I chose to wait for a more appropriate setting.

By late afternoon it seemed I had missed every opportunity to get hooked up with George. I decided that my best approach would be just to head up to his room, knock on the door, and talk to him. That way I was assured to have the privacy to talk without unwelcome ears present.

I knew that George would probably be busy, so I tried to see him right after the company had completed afternoon drill. Once back in the battalion, I waited for things to settle down, then made my way up to George's room where I knocked and heard an immediate response of "What do you want?" in a raspy voice.

I was sure George was thinking I must be a knob reporting to his room, so I just walked on in instead of yelling through the door like some freshman. When I entered I could see that both George and his roommate, Bill Kay, were in the room. I had hoped for a private conversation, but I was there, and forced to speak when George turned and asked, "What can I do for you?"

"Hey, George," I said trying not to sound nervous, "How ya' doing Bill?"

Bill turned and looked and answered, "Fine...uhhh...O'Bryan," as his eyes found the nametag on my shirt.

"George, I saw you coming into the barracks last night and was impressed with you guys, except you really looked like you were pretty worn out."

"I'll say I was," replied George, "they're pretty rough on us out there, ya know."

"Sure looks that way. Well, I just thought I would come up and offer my help if you should ever need it. I know that you must have a lot to do, and I've got a little more time available than a lot of the other guys who are on Cadre, so if you need something, I'm more than happy to help, you know, like shining brass or shoes."

"I really appreciate that, uh, O'Bryan. I mean...well...I hate to ask this, but what is your first name? I've honestly forgotten it," said George, somewhat embarrassed.

"It's John," I said smiling.

"That's right. You know when we recognize you guys right there at the end of the year, we get about a forty man introduction with one first name after the next."

"No problem. I'm having the same trouble since all you guys used to have the same first name of 'Sir.'."

Porter and Kay barely laughed, not really impressed with my joke.

"Well it looks like you're busy with your brass. Is there anything that I can help you with?"

"I don't think so O'Bryan. I really prefer to do my own brass and uniform. That way if something goes wrong, I have no one to blame but myself. But, I'll sure keep you in mind if I do need something."

"Just let me know. And good luck tonight."

"You bet," said George.

I turned and walked out of the room, consumed with the feeling of just having made an ass of myself. They had to be wondering whom this sophomore private was, coming up to suck nuts by offering help. I shook my head, thinking how stupid I was. Surely these guys were going to put the word out as to what I had done, and I would be the laughing stock of the three upper classes.

I couldn't help but think that I had really screwed up. I realized that my comment to Larry the night before as I walked out to observe the Drill was enough to show more than just a passing interest. The two incidences, coupled with my high pursuit of personal appearance and academic performance, would now be more than enough to point out my true agenda.

That night at evening formation, I figured that word would have already spread through the company that I had approached George. But no one even mentioned it. I just concluded that there must not have been enough time for the rumor to get around. Obviously, after a day or so, I would be catching shit right and left.

But after mess, I knew I really needed to get back on schedule, so I walked over to the library and studied hard from seven until nine-thirty, returning early so as to not miss the Drill's arrival. Ten minutes after getting back, I heard the Drill's faint chant ringing through the evening air, and I moved out on the gallery to once again observe the show. The galleries again filled with cheering upperclassmen, and the evening almost seemed a carbon copy of the night before. But as the guys broke from the middle of the quad to head towards their respective companies and rooms, I couldn't believe the face of George as he passed by. He looked more than tired, and was moving much more sluggishly than he did the previous evening. It was probably the accumulative result of having been torn down two days in a row. It was common knowledge that these guys were going to endure one hell of a challenge, but seeing the actual results made one realize that this was indeed a no-kidder.

It was going to be a tough road for George to make it, but he had the pride of the company with him. I was concerned as a freshman when I learned that none of the R Company seniors wore the yellow Sword Drill patch on their field jackets, and then watched as both Anderson and Schmidt failed to make it. There were numerous suspicions that went with our company's two-year failure. No one was sure why, but we all hoped that George would put an end to the R Company losing streak.

The next day George's face appeared to be a lot more stressed-out and fatigued than it had been after the first night. It was evident that his body was now worn and battered. He had a hard time walking, as his muscles seemed tight and sore. His eyes appeared to be squinted and the color in his face pale. I had experienced all kinds of physical stress and workouts with football and rack sessions as a freshman, but these guys were being pushed well beyond even the most aggressive of limits. Seeing George so whipped, so soon, I could only speculate as to whether he was going to make it. There was a long way to go, and after only two nights, he already appeared to be in trouble.

My afternoon was pretty much open since there was no drill on Wednesdays. Around four o'clock I decided to go hit the weight room, and just as I was heading out the door, I could see George slowly hobbling towards me. He looked up, surprised to see me standing there in the doorway.

"Oh...there you are John. I had to ask where you lived."

I was just as surprised to see George.

"Come on in," I said.

George limped on into my room and looked around saying, "Hey, you got the pipe room!"

I laughed a bit and said, "All the privileges of being a sophomore private."

"I can see that," said George. "Listen, I want to take you up on your offer."

I could not believe it. He had something for me to do.

"Would you mind bringing me back some food from the mess hall?" he asked.

"I don't mind one bit. Is that all you need?"

"Yeah, that's all. It's just that my roommate...he really wants to help, but he's so damn slack about things. Just do me a favor. Try to wrap it up in something other than an old napkin. He brought me

238

back a piece of that mystery meat wrapped up in a couple of napkins, and by the time the gravy soaked through, I could hardly get the soggy paper off so that I could eat it. It's bad enough to eat cold meat like that, but damn, he could of at least made a sandwich. If you'd look out for me during the evenings and bring me back something, I'd really appreciate it."

"That's why I offered. I'll be more than happy to help."

"I do appreciate it. Let me get back up to my room. I've got some more brass and stuff to finish up before 1800."

"Okay," I said, "you hang in there!"

"I'm trying," said George as he painfully climbed the steps.

I could see George having to strain to lift his foot up as he climbed each step. He really must have been sore. As he ascended, I felt thrilled that he had asked for my assistance, and I lay to rest the anguish and doubts I had over my offer to him. There would probably still be some repercussions, but the potential damage somehow seemed more distant, having not been turned down cold.

Before going to the mess hall, I came up with an idea that would benefit both George and me. On my trip back to school, Mom had sent a batch of fresh baked Toll House cookies, which had quickly been devoured. But instead of sending them in a cake tin, she used a Tupperware container to keep them fresh longer. It was perfect for the task of saving a meal for someone.

At mess, I ate and waited for everyone else at my table to finish getting all that they wanted, and then filled the container with a meal as if George had come to the mess hall. I then carefully took it back to the battalion and left it on his desk, knowing it would be several hours before he would be back to eat it.

When the aspirants entered the battalion that evening, it was once again easy to see the intensity of the stress in their faces as they ended their third outing. The next night would be the last of that week, having a break on both Friday and Saturday. George would then get what appeared to be a critically needed rest.

The next afternoon, I headed up to George's room where I found him sitting at his desk, shining brass, already getting ready for the upcoming night.

"Hey George, how's it going?" I asked.

"Pretty rough John. Come on in," he answered. "Damn, I really appreciate you bringing the food back. I never expected to get it in a nice container like this, and it sure was better than what my slack assed roommate Bill was bringing back."

"I didn't mind at all. As a matter of a fact, I came back to get the container so I can do it again tonight."

"Great! But I hate to tell you this. I didn't have a chance to wash it out since last night. I just, well, didn't seem to...."

"Don't worry about it," I interrupted, "I told you I'd be glad to help out. Just eat the food and leave the container to me. I'll pop by the day after, rinse it out, and get it ready for the next night. Every time I see you, you're polishing brass. I can at least take care of this part."

"Thanks!" said George, who seemed to genuinely appreciate the help. He continued to work with a sense of urgency. "Tonight is the last night for this week, but I will need food again Sunday night," He said.

"Gotcha," I said, "Good luck tonight."

"I appreciate it, buddy."

On his last night out for the week I again watched as George and his classmates came in just as the clock approached the 10 o'clock hour. This time, he appeared to be in the worst shape yet. It had been hot that day. Extremely hot. As George ran up to his room shouting his chant, he seemed near collapse and gasping for air. I was really concerned for him, but knew that it was not my place to go up to his room at such a critical time. He had plenty of classmates to help him, and I would just have to hold my curiosity and trust that there were others more appropriately suited to help.

The next day, I worked through my classes and began thinking of the Senior Party that was to take place on the following evening. Although I had not been all that excited about it earlier, I was starting to appreciate that the weekend was near, and that I had earned the right to get out and cut loose. My last class that afternoon was at 1300, and following it I swung by George's room to pick up the container. When I got there, there was no one in the room, so I just walked in and found it sitting at the edge of his desk. But just as I turned onto the gallery after exiting through the screen door, I saw George creeping up the stairs, moving onto the gallery and heading towards his room.

"Boy, you look rough," I said.

"I feel rough. But at least I've got the weekend."

George walked up to me as best he could, and then stopped.

"I know you're looking forward to it. I guess you're gonna raise hell at the Senior Party after all you've been through."

"Senior Party?" laughed George. "Are you joking? Roaches don't go to Senior Parties."

"Why not?" I asked. "You got a lot of brass and stuff to shine? If you need my help so you can go..."

"No, you don't get it," interjected George. "Even if I had the strength, and had all my equipment in tip-top shape, I wouldn't dare let the old Drill catch me outside of these gates. When I'm not working on my sword manual or personal appearance, then I need to be resting. Anyone who's got the time or strength to be out partying while the Nights are going on is obviously not catching enough hell."

"I get your drift."

"That's Sword Drill. Many are called, but few are chosen."

I laughed with little enthusiasm.

"I've got to hit the rack," said George as he struggled to walk again. "I'm a hurtin' cowboy."

"Have a good weekend. I guess I'll see ya Sunday."

"Yeah, thanks again for the food. It's the only thing that's keeping me going."

As it got close to Senior Party time, it became clear just how much more convenient things were going to be as an upperclassman. I had a stock of civilian clothes in the truck of my car, along with a really nice cooler for my beer. I was Senior Party bound with no hassles and no hitching a ride. Life was good.

When we arrived, there seemed to be as much excitement in the air as Julie and I had discovered a year earlier when we attended our first party together. There were knobs already going crazy, and the upperclassmen seemed ready to kick off the pains of being back in school. For the first time, my classmates and I found ourselves at the same tables as the upper two classes. We were no longer considered social outcasts, and it felt good.

Julie and I danced, drank beer, and had a really good time as usual. I felt like it was a break well deserved since I had spent the previous evening and all that day studying. After so much work, the music seemed to sound that much better, and the beer seemed to be colder and more satisfying.

As I drove back towards campus at the end of the evening, I smiled as I thought about my relationship with Julie, and how uncomplicated it was. We seemed to get along so well together, not letting a lack of romance get in the way of our friendship. I was perfectly happy with that sort of arrangement, knowing well the extreme ups and downs of being in love. I didn't want any part of that mess again for a long time. Though nearly a year had passed since my breakup with Donna, I still had scars from the experience.

For the next two weeks, I set myself into a fine tuned routine of going to class, lifting or running in the latter part of the day, then studying like hell during the evening before watching the Drill return after their night of hell. There really wasn't a substantial reason for me to always be there, other than I just wanted to. Drill had become the greatest desire in my life, and any opportunity to witness even a small part of it seemed like a significant event. I guess I thought I might miss something if I weren't there.

During the third week of the Drill's activities I began to see George's condition steadily breaking down. After the many nights of stress and strain, the harsh reality of the struggle really showed in his face. He looked malnourished, like a prisoner subjected to constant torture. He reminded me so much of when I was on Schmidt's mess, not getting enough to eat, and looking like pure hell. His shaved head seemed to only increase the unattractiveness and exposed even more of the negative. The rackings as a knob seemed trivial when compared to the hours of torment that George and his classmates were obviously going through. This seemed much harsher in a major way, and in a far tougher league.

As the end of the Nights approached, I heard discussions about "Feats Night," where the roaches would try to accomplish feats of endurance that involved contests to see who could hold up a sword for a certain amount of time, do the most pushups, or run the fastest. At noon mess we heard the names of those who were the champions in the various events, and I wasn't surprised at all not to hear George mentioned. He said he was more concerned with surviving at that point than showing off.

Finally, the twelfth and final torture filled night arrived. The aspirants still had to go through Cuts, which consumed nights thirteen and fourteen. They would at least be as intense and nerve racking as the others, but not the usual physical torment in the heat. For George, that had become critical. He openly admitted that his body had reached a threshold in its ability to take the punishment, and I could tell he was thoroughly beaten down by both the physical and mental stress. When I talked to him in our brief moments when I was up getting the food container, I noted that his wit and sharpness had dwindled as his need to dig deep to get through yet another day had taken its toll.

George was always so exhausted and pressed for time that I found it hard to ever talk with him at length. The inside details that I had hoped to gain by helping him never seemed to surface. For some reason, George had very little to say about what went on after they left the battalion. I wondered if it was because of something to do with my relationship with him or if it was just a strict standard not to talk about Drill activities. Secrecy had always been the reputation of the Drill, and now it seemed to be true. I wanted to press George for more information, but also had the sense to know that it was a bad time to do it.

During the weekend before cuts, even I could feel the anxiety. That Monday and Tuesday would be the all-critical selection phase for the Drill, and I could only think of how worn George still looked, even with rest. This troubled me. Cuts were a huge undertaking, and I hoped that the condition of the other roaches was at least equal to that of George so that he would have an even chance going in.

On Monday afternoon I made my way up to George's room to get the food container, and when I entered, I found his brass, shoes, and uniform were laid out carefully on towels and the sheets of his bed. They had obviously been prepped to the max, and he had them protected and out of the way. George was really nervous. His adrenalin over cuts was flowing all right, and he seemed wired and on edge as he moved around the room.

That evening I made it through mess and ESP and came back to the barracks to catch George's return, not really knowing when he would come back or if there would be the normal show on the quad. The later it got with no disturbance, the more I began to think that the roaches would return without the pomp and circumstance.

Around 2230, my curiosity got the best of me as I felt I just had to know something, and decided to go up to George's room to at least ask what was going on. Surely George wouldn't mind.

When I knocked on the door, I heard the words "Come in," yelled out by George. When I walked in I found George was partially in his cuts uniform and in what appeared to be a close and tight conversation with three other juniors including his roommate, First Sergeant Lonnie Mauldin, and Assistant First Sergeant Leon Rooney. They were all there to obviously hear how cuts went, and instantly, I felt like an intruder.

"I'm sorry George, I didn't know you had others in here. I'll come back later."

"No! That's alright, John," he said. "Come on in a second."

Mauldin and Rooney did not seem to be shocked by my

appearance. They must have known that I had been assisting George.

"I was telling these guys how it went tonight," said George.

I walked in further and leaned up against the full press without saying a word.

"And to sum it up for you John, all I can say is that I did my best. I don't think I did too much worse than everybody else, but I certainly didn't set the world on fire either. I received my fair share of cuts, so it's really hard for me to say how I did."

"You have cuts again tomorrow night, right?" I asked.

I noticed that both Mauldin and Rooney were sitting there silent as I spoke, and I wondered if I was truly screwing up by butting in. But George answered me as if I were welcomed.

"Yeah, another night of cuts again tomorrow. I'd give you the Tupperware container back now, but I haven't even eaten yet."

I saw George's statement as the perfect opportunity for me to bow out gracefully. I didn't need a hint that they would be more comfortable talking among themselves.

"I was just curious. I'll just pick up the food container tomorrow," and I headed towards the door.

"Okay John," smiled George, "I appreciate the help."

I walked out the door, and with a sigh of relief headed back down to my room. Since I only stayed for a minute I was not overly concerned that I had busted into the meeting. I was at least happy to find out the night had not been disastrous for George. This meant with a good night on the following evening, he would more than likely make the Drill.

My afternoon the next day was busy with company drill and lifting weights. Just before evening formation I was headed towards the showers when I saw George as he was taking the last few steps across the quad to go out of the sally port. He was dressed in his cuts uniform and was carrying his shoes, probably not wanting them to get damaged while walking over. He had pieces of toilet paper wrapped around his shako and sword, probably guarding the brass so it wouldn't get tarnished or scratched on the way over.. It seemed extreme, but the whole Sword Drill process was already more than I ever imagined it would be.

I felt nervous for George, and hoped so much that he would make it. I had witnessed just how hard it was to make it through the Nights just to get the chance to go through cuts. He had a lot of dedication and hard work invested in the quest, and I just couldn't imagine someone doing so much just to come up short.

I went to mess, and for the last time filled the Tupperware container with a meal. I worried what was going on as each minute passed, and when it was time to go to the library I concluded it to be the wrong move. I wanted to be in the barracks in case final word came back, even though I knew it would probably be after ten before any news would surface. Cuts were rumored to be long and grueling with intense inspections of appearance, marching, and sword manual. It had to be hell on the nerves.

I tried to study, but found the waiting difficult. It was so out of character for a sophomore private with no obvious potential to qualify for Drill to be so emotionally evolved. Yet out of everyone in R Company, I felt like I was the most concerned for George's outcome. It was nerve racking, and I found that I had very little done by the time nine o'clock had rolled around.

While I sat there struggling, my ears suddenly caught a faint sound of interest on the gallery as I thought I heard an individual running up the stairs with a scabbard and sword rattling at his side. I wasn't sure who it was, but immediately popped up out of my chair and darted out the door. But by the time I made to the gallery, there was no one in sight. I stood there thinking that my ears must have deceived me, but then I noticed several guys running into the barracks, obviously very excited. One of them ran towards the O Company stairwell and began climbing at two step intervals yelling, "Knobs! Get your brooms and transom sticks and get out here now."

I thought back to freshman year and remembered my classmates in other companies having to arch transom sticks and brooms for those who had made the Drill, having never experienced it myself due to the R Company jinx. I could easily see that the commotion was beginning to intensify, and that cadets in O Company were pouring out of their rooms.

The same noise started taking place over in T company, and I started to get worried. To my disbelief, I heard nothing happening in R Company. Everything was quiet. There was no commotion. I hoped that it was simply a matter of word having not gotten back to the battalion yet that George had made it.

But then I saw Leon Rooney coming through the sally port, walking slowly across the quad heading back towards R. He walked and looked up at the commotion going on both in O and T, then looked down at the quad as he made it to the edge of the gallery. He noticed me standing there, and stopped, giving me a serious stare. I felt privileged by his recognition of my involvement, but agonized over what I feared he was about to reveal to me. Without saying a word, he just shook his head in a negative fashion, then turned and walked on up the stairs.

My heart sank. This was tragic. I couldn't imagine it had happened again. George had not made it. For the third year in a row, R Company would not have a Junior Sword Drill representative. And the work...all that George had put into it. The sacrifice, the dedication, the endurance, the devotion: it was all for nothing but a heart wrenching letdown.

As I watched the knobs in O and T line up in two rows in front of their company letters, I remembered the sound that I had heard while sitting at my desk that had brought me out on the gallery in the first place. It now made sense and had meaning. It was George apparently coming back, trying to get up to his room before the celebrations started.

The whole battalion went into complete turmoil, especially over in Oscar and Tango. November and Romeo were dead. Out of the five roaches from 4th Battalion, two were from O and one each from N, R and T. It was obvious that the guys from N and R had not produced. T's man must have made it, and at least one from O.

247

As the turmoil started to climax with all of the O and T freshmen lined up on the quad with the upperclassmen around them, I could see three guys running in through the sally port. The cheering erupted to a massive volume as one roach peeled away towards T while the other two ran towards O, each finding freshman with their brooms and transom sticks at full arch to run under. Each gave a final kiss to their company letter before the crowds swallowed them up, mobbing them with shared joy, then picking them up and carrying them around in a real celebration. The noise was unbelievable as the cheering was loud and sincere. This was obviously a wonderful night for the three who had made it. A dream come true. It was a beautiful end to a story that they had lived through for a long time, with many sacrifices along the way.

But I felt empty. There were guys devastated. There was the roach from N and George. I knew that no matter how hard they tried, there was no way they could drown out the cheering and celebration. At that point, I was sure it was the last thing they wanted to hear.

I felt sick, and really had no desire to stand there and watch the other companies celebrate. As I walked back to my room, I felt a real sense of loss. I had wished so hard for George to make it. I felt bad for our company, the junior class, and most of all, for George. I couldn't imagine his pain and disappointment.

Larry walked back in saying, "Shit, I guess he didn't make it."

"I think you're right."

"I know you're probably disappointed after helping him so much. I didn't lift a finger for him, and I know I am."

"I feel horrible. All the work on his equipment…the physical sacrifices…all for nothing!"

I knew it would be insane for me to go up to George's room, although I was curious to find out just what had gone wrong. But he would surely be consumed with distress, and he had the best thing in the world for that. His classmates. This was a burden better left to them.

CHAPTER 21

The next day I never even saw George during the morning hours. He never made it to breakfast formation, as I'm sure he had no desire to come out. It was not until everyone was gathering for noon formation that I finally saw him for the first time. It wasn't a good time to talk with him since his classmates and a few of the ranking seniors again surrounded him. Even from a distance I could see his disappointment as he tried to cover it up with an occasional smile while getting handshakes and endless condolences.

As formation drew closer, and I could see that everyone was starting to line up, I walked over to my place in the squad and waited for the next bugle to blow. But before the formation was called to order, I felt a tap on my shoulder, and was surprised to find George standing there with his hand extended.

"I guess you heard, huh?" he said.

"Yeah, I did. I would have said something but..."

"Don't worry about it. I just wanted to say that even though I didn't make it, I appreciated all your help."

I reached out and shook George's hand and he gave me a quick smile, then pulled away having to get out to his cadre platoon. As I turned around, I felt a lot of satisfaction knowing that I made what was an awfully hard journey for him just a little easier.

Cadet life seemed to quickly get back to normal for everyone. George didn't mention Sword Drill again for a long time, and hardly anyone wanted to bring it up. There was no word on what happened during cuts, and significant information on any Drill matter remained virtually nonexistent. Sword Drill had always been a mystery, and I still didn't know much other than just a few surface details. The big secret still loomed. What went on inside McAlister?

As the days passed, I often saw the two guys from O and the one from T heading out of the battalion with their swords and practice uniforms on. I also saw them in the afternoons, then again during the evening as they obviously had several practices a day. I once made it down to morning formation quite early and found them returning from a pre-dawn practice. It was apparent that once you made the Drill, there was still a long way to go before the performance would be perfected. They would apparently invest many hours before Parents Day, which was only a month away.

I continued studying, lifting and running hard, knowing that Parents Day Weekend would bring with it a need for a lot of free time. Although I had no big expectations of a hometown sweetheart coming as I had during my freshman year, I was at least going to play host to my parents. There would also be the Junior Sword Drill performance that Friday evening, and the big Senior Party on Saturday after the football game.

One week before Parents Day, an SMI was scheduled for the purpose of insuring that cadets and their rooms were squared away before the hoards of visitors arrived. I focused on the upcoming inspection like I never had before, working hard on my personal appearance and the room to make sure everything was just right. Larry still didn't think that so much effort was required, yet understood clearly that I was now bucking for rank, and that I also had a score to settle from the previous SMI.

That Saturday morning, Larry and I looked each other over in almost a microscopic way to ensure that every detail was covered. Every part of my uniform looked great, but my shoes were again absolutely amazing. There was not a place on them that didn't look like black glass. When the formation bugle was blown, I felt almost like George Porter going to cuts as I headed out to the quadrangle, being extra careful not to damage anything before the inspection.

When the SMI started, I was pleased to see that Schmidt would only be assisting, and that the actual inspector would be the company TAC officer, Army Captain Michael Donnel. Each company had assigned to it a liaison from Jenkins Hall who was actually a commissioned officer from one of the four branches of the armed forces. Captain Donnel had been with the company since the beginning of the semester, and it was his job to provide guidance and advice when it came to the company's administrative matters.

As Captain Donnel moved through the formation, he kept a pace that was much quicker than that which Schmidt took during the first SMI. He looked at each cadet accurately, but with speed, stopping only to take a rifle every now and then, showing little emotion.

The group eventually made it through first squad and then through second down to me. As the Captain turned in front of me I brought my rifle up to inspection arms with precision. Captain Donnel looked at my hair and shako, moving quickly down to my breastplate and webbing, then my shoes. It was there his eyes stopped and locked, with me knowing he was pondering the now all too familiar question.

"Are those patent leather?"

"No sir," I answered.

Schmidt disgustingly commented for his own sake, "His shoes always look like that."

Donnel stared towards my feet, obviously thinking hoax. He then looked back up and quickly slapped my rifle as he snatched it from my hands and looked it over quickly, even checking down the barrel for dust. He handed the rifle back to me where I immediately took it with authority and went to order arms with him watching my every move.

Captain Donnel simply said "Outstanding Personal Appearance," turned, and moved on down.

Outstanding Personal Appearance was something rarely handed out during an SMI, especially to a sophomore, or better yet, a sophomore private. Schmidt was then standing right in front of me and he quickly turned to Mauldin and echoed what Captain Donnel had said. But Mauldin was already writing with a kind of a smirk on his face. Schmidt simply showed no emotion and only glanced for half a second at my eyes as he turned to watch and observe the Captain.

I could hardly stand it. I was about to explode. I had done well, not only getting merits, but also I was face to face with Schmidt, loving the fact that he had to stand there and take it.

After personal inspection I headed back to my room, where the inspecting party soon arrived. Captain Donnel walked in and to my disappointment, inspected very little as he just strolled through the room and noticed that it was immaculate. I was hoping that he would challenge me on the room, knowing that I had spent many hours making sure that every square inch was perfect. Donnel stopped only as he was getting ready to head out of the door. He turned around as if it were a second thought and asked, "Your name is O'Bryan?"

"Yes Sir," I answered.

"What's your major?"

"Electrical Engineering, Sir."

"Tough major," he returned as he walked on out of the room.

I was still a bit disappointed that he had not checked more in the room, anxious to prove the work I had done. Yet, since he obviously found nothing out of order, I had indeed accomplished my goal. The icing was that someone in charge now knew my name. I finally had been noticed.

I really felt great, but could only think about what had gotten me to that point. It was the dedication and sacrifice. It was the foresight to get ahead when time was available. All I wanted now was to take the ball and run even further with it.

I utilized the entire weekend to get further ahead. But on Sunday night, I made my usual trip to the phone room in order to call Julie for our Senior Party date. There was a new twist to my invitation in that I not only asked her to go to the party, but also to the Sword Drill performance and Ring Hop. Julie was thrilled with the invitation, and delighted at the notion of dressing up and going to the formal dance.

I really looked forward to the Drill's performance, longing to again see the detailed marching and the flawless execution of sword manual. I wanted to absorb all of the details that my memory had lost of that first performance. I wanted to dream it was me who was down on that floor.

When I arrived to pick up Julie Friday night, I was impressed by how lovely she looked, having only seen her in blue jeans and sweat shirt for the senior parties. We didn't linger since I knew Julie's walking speed in her long dress and heels would make us slow. I also remembered well that during the first performance the place had filled up quickly, and I wanted a good seat this time.

I thought it took frustratingly long to get back on the campus with traffic jams at the gates as people arrived for the performance. When we finally entered the Field House, we wasted no time grabbing the best available seats we could. We were indeed early, which left us time just to sit, talk, and watch as the auditorium slowly filled to capacity.

The building was soon packed, and not long after the lights were dimmed the opening comments were made. I had learned that the individual at the dimly lit podium was a member of the "Sword Drill Platoon," that is, a roach who made it through the 14 Nights, but not cuts. I had also discovered that Platoon members would also be involved in the next year's selection process by participating in the 14 Nights. But, I knew it must have been very hard for him, having to introduce the dream performance he had failed to be a part of.

After the introduction, blackness filled the Field House when the podium light was secured, and the eerie music of the bagpipes began to play. Julie took my hand and gripped it firmly, not because she was scared, but the mystery and anticipation was enough to make her anxious. I couldn't help but smile, sensing her wonder as she peered into the darkness and listened to the music as it faded away. She was not prepared for the siren voice that cut through the darkness, ringing out the first commands as the Drill readied to start. She jumped as the sound hit her ears, and her nerves only settled slightly when the spotlights hit the Drill down on the floor.

They began their performance by making their way out to the middle of the floor. I didn't want to miss a single detail of what was happening, but couldn't help but glance back periodically to see the expressions of total amazement on Julie's face.

The performance started well for the Drill. I could only see just an ever so slight timing miss every now and then, of a foot not hitting the floor at the same time as a partner's, or a turn being a tenth of a second off from the rest of the squad. It was turning out to be a pretty darn good presentation.

Fortunately, the performance continued with only a few mishaps, and only one major mistake. All of the ripples, slow march, fast march, pin wheel, and other moves were pulled off precisely and elegantly, and as the Drill turned and made their final arch of swords indicating the end of their performance, there once again came the unbelievable roar and applause that indicated a grateful and impressed crowd. While clapping, I turned to see that Julie was cheering and clapping enthusiastically. Even with a few small errors, she apparently loved it.

After watching the Drill arch swords for some of the seniors, Julie and I then left McAlister Field House and went across the street to Deas Hall where the Ring Hop was already underway. As we walked, Julie grabbed my arm and pulled me close to indicate that the performance had been a wonderful experience for her. I had earlier made an assumption that the dance would likely be the highlight of her evening, but she questioned how I was ever going to top the Drill performance. I was surprised at how genuinely impressed she was.

Entering Deas Hall, we found ourselves in a receiving line. There were special guests, dignitaries, and faculty members from the school doing the greeting, including the school's President and Commandant of Cadets. I actually grew a bit nervous as we made our way from person to person, but I could see that Julie was eating it up. I think she was a zealot for formality, and to her, our evening was a visit with the pleasures of refinement. For me, I barely managed to make it through the President without passing out from anxiety.

Breathing again, we moved into the room with the huge dance

floor, live band, and refreshments. The place was filled with cadets in uniform, and pretty females in long evening gowns. I thought of "Gone with the Wind," and felt as if in a time warp going back to the formal celebrations of the Old South.

Julie and I moved onto the dance floor, where for the next hour we enjoyed dancing. There was an occasional fast song, but it was mostly slow waltzing music, which was certainly a far cry from that of a senior party. It was actually a pleasingly sophisticated and impressive way to spend a Friday night with a date.

It seemed Julie's only desire was to dance the night away. I could see she was having a wonderful time, but it was getting late, and I knew that we were going to have a late evening the following night at the Senior Party. As we left, I could see that she was a bit sentimental. It hadn't been in my plans to overly impress her, but I could see that the evening had really meant something.

As we drove back to the College of Charleston, she talked continually about how wonderful The Citadel was and how it seemed to bring back the lost days of romance and chivalry, something she dreamed of but thought was gone forever. But in Charleston, there was still a place to go that was right out of a storybook. I think she felt it a real honor to have been invited.

The following day brought an early start, and as soon as the front gates were opened and the visitors moved in, I could see that my parents were some of the first to come inside. I walked out to greet them, and escorted them back to my room.

Once they entered, Dad was quite entertained by the collection of pipes that occupied our living space.

"Damn son," he laughed, "they put you in charge of the sprinkler system?"

"This is what you get when you're a sophomore."

"You had a better room when you were a freshman!"

"I often believe the knobs sometimes have it better than we do," I said smiling.

My parents laughed, remembering just how bad freshman year

was for me, and that my current lack of privileges wasn't even close, even with the crappy room.

"How're things back at the farm?" I asked very light heartily.

"Not so good," said Dad in a serious voice.

"Oh, don't start," said Mom chastising Dad, then turning to me to provide the positive spin on what was happening. "Your father and Charles seem to have worked out some of their differences, dear."

"Right!" returned Dad. "In other words, I've given in to Charles to let him try his crazy catfish farming venture, even though I know it's a stupid move to allow it."

"You're acting like it's doomed without ever giving him an opportunity to try it," replied Mom. "Now we all weighed out the risks and agreed to let him borrow enough money to give it a go."

"Borrow the money?" I said quickly. "How much money?"

"Fifty thousand dollars!" said Dad firmly.

"Are we here to bring up sore subjects or enjoy the day?" asked Mom, clearly not pleased with where this was going. "Tell me dear, how are your grades so far this semester?"

"Great. I think I'm gonna be way above the Dean's List requirement for mid-terms."

"I can't tell you how proud we are of you John," said Mom.

"Dean's List?" said Dad shaking his head. "Never thought I'd see the day."

It was great to see my parents again, and my day with them was filled with one event after the other that made for a quick paced visit. As if a tradition, I met them again downtown at Carolina's for another elegant and superb meal, which was quite a contrasting prelude to the wild and crazy Senior Party Julie and I would attend to finish off the evening.

All in all, it was a splendid weekend, far better than my freshman year Parents Day calamity. In a way, the weekend seemed like some mid-point. I was one year into my dream of making the 1980 Junior Sword Drill, and one year away from the performance that they would give. But as a private, it was scary to think of just how far away I was from ranking in the top ten percent of my class, a prerequisite for those who wanted to go out for Drill. Time was quickly running out.

CHAPTER 22

Parents Day brought with it the end of Cadre, and the knobs were merged in with the rest of the company. It was an interesting week as many of my non-cadre classmates who were corporals got their first crack at supervising and racking knobs. It seemed like a free-for-all and an all out war on the freshmen as they lived under the gun all that following week.

That next weekend was relatively quiet as I chose to stay in the entire time to study and work out. It was pretty dull until evening formation on Sunday, when I noticed a crowd of my classmates standing huddled together talking. The conversation seemed volatile, so I decided to walk over and check it out.

Burn, Rosellini, and several other guys were giving one of our classmates, Rob Cornelius, a hard time. Cornelius was a non-cadre Corporal, so I figured he must have screwed up in handling his new squad of knobs. Not to my surprise, Rosellini was leading the charge giving him hell.

"I just don't understand it, man!" said Rosellini, "Why didn't you just get up and come on in."

"I'm telling you," answered Rob with some discontent, "I just thought it was too late. I knew that the gates were closed and that I was in trouble anyway. I guess I just didn't think."

"Didn't think is right!" said Danny Burn, "I'm not sure what you'll get out of this, but it won't be good."

"What happened?" I asked.

"This dumb shit went AWOL last night," said Rosellini.

"What?" I said with shock.

"Yeah, over a piece of ass," said Burn.

"Damn Rob, didn't you get enough last weekend?" I asked.

"Obviously not!" laughed Rob, "Shit! It was just a mistake. My girlfriend and I went to a big outdoor party thing this weekend and we drank beer all day long."

"Then what?" asked Chris Davis.

"We went back to her dorm and decided to take a quick nap."

"Was that the only reason you got in bed?" chuckled Keith Wright.

"Of course not," said Rob laughingly, "Getting in that bed got me two things…laid and in trouble."

"I still don't understand," I said with frustration. "What the hell happened?"

"He over slept," yelled Rosellini with conviction. "The dumb shit stayed there all night instead of getting up and coming back in."

"Holy shit, I said, "AWOL?"

"Yes, AWOL!" answered Rob shaking his head.

"Why didn't you just get up and come back in?" I asked. "You would have just been written up for being late!"

"I'm telling you assholes! I just didn't think. You know how it is when you wake up after drinking. I looked at my watch, saw it was 3 a.m., and knew the gates were all locked."

"Maybe they'll cut you some slack," said Keith Wright.

"Hell, you've got a perfect discipline record up to this point," I said. "And don't you still have an overnight left?"

"Yeah, I do," answered Rob. "That's the craziness part of it all. I would have signed up for one had I known."

"They'll probably give you a few confinements and charge you with an overnight," I said. "It shouldn't be that big of a deal."

It was pretty stupid for Rob to get himself into such a mess. We all hoped that he'd just get a slap on the wrist and that would be the end of it, but AWOL was often viewed as a semi-serious offense, even with the circumstances.

When I arrived for noon formation the next day, I could see Captain Donnel standing out on the quad, speaking with Kevin Schmidt, Lonnie Mauldin, and Leon Rooney. There was quite a serious conversation going on with a look on Kevin Schmidt's face that did not indicate approval of what Captain Donnel was saying. But it was no concern of mine so I turned my attention back to the entertainment of watching the knobs get racked as my classmates inspected them. It brought back lots of memories to watch them catch hell right up until time to roll out.

As I made my way out to my place in the platoon, I noticed that Captain Donnel, Schmidt, Mauldin and Rooney were now coming to some kind of an agreement. Captain Donnel started heading out the front sally port, and Mauldin and Rooney walked away leaving Schmidt standing at the front of the company where he normally stood. But as I watched Mauldin and Rooney walking away, I noticed that they were walking directly towards me, and as soon as they stopped, George Porter, who was now in the same platoon that I was in, also walked over and joined them. Mauldin began to speak as I wondered what in the world I had done.

"Listen O'Bryan," said Mauldin, "as soon as your last class is over with today, I want you to grab your blouses and immediately take them over to the tailor shop and get some stripes sewn on, and go by the cadet store and get some Corporal wings. Cornelius has been busted and you're now a Corporal. Got that?"

I didn't know what to say, and just stood there speechless.

"I said, you got that?" said the now smiling Lonnie Mauldin.

"Uh, yeah," I said, "but..."

"Okay, get it done as soon as you can," said Mauldin, and he and Rooney walked off smiling, knowing that they had caught me completely off guard. George just stood there also smiling.

"Hey man, it's too bad about your classmate. Seems like his loss is your gain. But don't worry about it, that kind of stuff just happens. Tell you what, swing by my room right after mess, and I'll let you have my old corporal wings. They're already blitzed down, and I'd be proud if you wore 'em."

I still didn't know what to say. This had not been in my plan at all. I never imagined that someone would get busted and that I would end up with rank that way.

As I marched along, Hector Reddick, my current Squad Corporal, patted me on the back saying "Hey, good job dude. You got yourself a set of wings now."

I wanted to feel good about the promotion, but was very concerned about Rob who was obviously going to be hurt by this. As soon as our platoon made it over to the mess hall and was dismissed, I just waited for Rob who was in the platoon behind me. Once they were dismissed, I walked up to Rob who was laughing and talking with another Corporal, James Nixon.

"Rob," I said, "wait a second."

"John boy," he answered. "What's happening?"

"They just told me I was gonna be a corporal at your expense," I said nervously and with a bit of shame.

"Hey, so you're the guy that's gonna get it. Man that's great. I couldn't be replaced by a more deserving guy. Shit with your grades in double E and you sucking nuts the way you do with that personal appearance of yours, you should have got it for Cadre."

"Damn man," I said, "you've got to really believe that I didn't want it this way."

"Ah shut the hell up, John," he answered smiling, "You had nothing to do with this, I mean the part about me getting busted. That's all my fault. I sincerely mean that. Anyway rank's been a pain in the ass, and I'm looking forward to a little bit of the 'private life.' So don't worry about it."

I couldn't believe the way Rob was taking this. He had always been a hell raiser, and usually placed a lot of priority on going out and having a good time, and to a certain degree, never was all that much into the military. But he did have really good grades, which was probably the main reason he had obtained rank in the first place. But for some people who go to The Citadel, rank just doesn't hold that much importance, and in this particular case, it appeared Rob wasn't all that concerned about the loss.

When mess was over, I went back to the barracks, but knew my one o'clock class left me little time to fool around. But I did want to go by George Porter's room since he had so generously offered me his old corporal wings.

When I got to his room, I could see that he already had them out.

He was sitting there rubbing them on a towel.

"Give me your cap," he said as I walked in.

George took the first emblem and put it on my cunt cap, and then reaching up without saying a word, he grabbed my collar and removed my three to replace it.

"I, George Porter, head honcho here at The Citadel, home of many flame-ons, do here by dub thee Corporal John. May you rack a hundred knobs till they drop, bleed, and die."

I couldn't help but laugh. This was all too much. At noon I was a sophomore private, and not an hour later, I had corporal wings on. It all happened too fast. It was like a dream.

"Listen John. I want to tell you something important," said George who all of a sudden got very serious. "I talked with Mauldin and Rooney at mess, and this was largely done by their influence and Captain Donnel's strong recommendation. First of all, Schmidt didn't want to see Cornelius busted, which is admirable on his part. But more important, you weren't really his first choice as Cornelius' replacement, so keep your eyeballs peeled."

I didn't find the news a surprise, and had even wondered during mess how the whole thing had come about with Schmidt's strong influence over who holds rank.

"I could have guessed that," I said calmly.

George seemed puzzled and asked "What is it between you two? I remember during rank boards last year when Schmidt was so down on you even being considered for corporal."

"So it was him," I said, now beginning to get angry.

"Listen," said George, "I shouldn't even be telling you this stuff. Just take my advice…if there's a problem between you and Schmidt, you need to get it solved. I think I know the direction you're wanting to head in, and if my guess is right, the last thing you need is some powerful guy like Schmidt gunning for you."

"I know," I answered, "but I'm not exactly sure what his beef is with me. If I did, I'd try to do something about it."

"Just do your job, watch your back, and try to keep your nose clean. I'd hate for that guy to find some way to take this from you just as fast as you got it."

"Don't worry," I said as I was heading out the door for class, "I won't mess up. And thanks for the wings. I couldn't be carrying on for a better guy!"

Just as I got down the gallery, George popped his head out the door and said, "By the way, don't try to impress too many people too quick by being a flame-on!" and then laughed after saying so.

"Who me?" I said looking back with a devilish look in my eyes.

I slapped my cap on my head, somehow feeling the difference that the insignificant weight of the corporal wings made. I had to really rush to make it to my class in time, and as I finally sat down in my chair huffing and puffing from having rushed so hard to make it, the guy sitting beside me said, "Running late, huh O'Bryan?"

"Yeah," I answered, "I had a busy lunch."

The guy looked over at me, did a double take, and looked even closer. "Hey, I thought you were a private."

Still panting heavily from having rushed so hard I simply answered, "Like I said, I had a busy lunch."

I immediately took over the squad that Cornelius had. My Squad Sergeant was Ralph Leupold, who left it to me to insure the freshmen were supervised and made to perform to the highest standard. After nine months of being a knob, it wasn't like someone had to explain what I was supposed to do to make that happen.

My first formation with them was that evening, only six hours after being promoted. I had three knobs to deal with, and it was obviously an awkward situation for them to switch again after only spending a week with Rob. I had no idea what he had set up, so there was nothing I could do but take charge and explain how I expected things to be done.

"Now listen here you three," I said in a normal tone of voice, "this first inspection is going to be a freebie, but your only freebie. I want your shoes shined so that I can see two fingers reflecting off the front of them from belt-buckle height. I want all the pits out of the front of your brass with the back also blitzed down so that there are no visible letters, and absolutely positively, no tarnish or green grunge anywhere on it. I want your nametags, Company letter, and 4's all blitzed. And finally, I want no lint on your hat or on any other part of your uniform. Got that?"

"Sir, yes Sir," they answered.

"I want no hair touching the ears, a fresh uniform every day at evening formation, a fresh shave in the morning, and finally, most important of all, improvement on GPR's. Even though I'm sure the Academic Officer has spoken to you guys about this, your GPR will set the stage for the rest of your cadet career. So, if you don't want to get the shit racked out of you, then I would suggest getting your grades up."

"Sir, yes Sir," they all answered.

"Good, have your shit together when I see you first thing tomorrow morning."

I was sure the knobs had already heard about the personal appearance stuff, but I wanted to especially emphasize my focus on grades. I guess I was hoping to save the knobs from the same kind of damage I put myself through during my first semester.

Having that first squad of freshmen was an eye opener. I had two slack ones, Powell and Flynn, and one really sharp one, Tompkins. I had to drag my two trouble children along every step of the way, where as Tompkins seemed like he was on autopilot. He was a self-starting perfectionist, and if I hadn't had him in the squad I would have surely considered all freshmen as brain dead. It was rare to even rack him, and since he had good grades to go with his outstanding performance, it was clear he was a knob that would be going places.

My first week as a corporal was so new and exciting that it took a while to realize just how busy I had become. Along with my intense study and workout schedule, I now had a million things to do with the freshmen. Being the new man on the block, they assigned me the job of supervising the knobs in getting the banner made for

Homecoming that would take place the following weekend. There was just so much to do, including making social arrangements for the second biggest weekend of the year. I learned quickly what Cornelious meant by taking it easy with the "private life."

Homecoming weekend was again its usual invasion as crowds of visitors and alumni returned to campus for the scheduled activities. The football game on that Saturday was a tough one since the Bulldogs were playing Marshall, but they played their hearts out, and pulled off the biggest win of the season. After the game there was again an announcement made by the President granting overnights for all classes, and I thought everyone would go nuts. For the Corps of Cadets, life was good.

As I walked back towards the battalion through the jubilant crowd, I could hear my name being called. I looked around, and for the second year in a row, I saw Mr. and Mrs. Johnson from Kingstree.

"Looks like we're going to make running into each other an annual event," said Mrs. Johnson.

"That's right. I saw you last year after the Homecoming game."

"I only wish we could make every game," said Mr. Johnson, "but we spend so many weekends now going up to see Cindy that it makes it hard sometimes."

"How's Cindy doing?" I replied with curiosity,

"She couldn't be doing any better," answered Mrs. Johnson. "She really loves Columbia College, and it just seems to be an atmosphere that brings out the best in her."

"It's good to hear she's happy there," I said.

"Hey, look at those stripes," said Mr. Johnson. "So you made Corporal, huh?"

"I hate to say it, but I've only been a Corporal a week."

"A week?" said Mr. Johnson.

"Some guy went AWOL and got busted."

"I can remember back in the old days when that was a pretty common occurrence around school."

"Yeah," I laughed, "it still happens, but you sure hate to see it when it does."

"Well...we'd better be going," said Mr. Johnson. "I know you're probably in a hurry to get back so you can hit the town."

"It was good to see you again," I said. But as I started to walk off, I turned back and shouted, "By the way, when you see Cindy, tell her I said `Hello' and that I still appreciate how she helped me out during high school. Tell her if she's ever in Charleston to drop me a line and I'll try to pay off that debt I still owe her."

"Ok," replied the smiling Johnsons as they walked off.

As I headed towards to the barracks I thought back to the struggle I had gone through, and how Cindy helped me get through it. It somehow seemed so very long ago. I laughed knowing that Cindy would be shocked if she knew I had a 3.4 GPR in Electrical Engineering.

I was in a really good mood that evening, and was ready to take advantage of the Senior Party. I had been pushing myself like hell to maintain my normal schedule and take on the additional duties. I also knew that this would be the last party of the semester, since Thanksgiving was less than two weeks away and exams would immediately follow. It was indeed time to let it rip.

When I picked up Julie, I could see that she too was fired up for the party. There just seemed to be an over-abundance of excitement, strongly due to the evening's line up of music. Not only were there two very good rock-n-roll bands to kick off the evening, but the third and final act would be Mother's Finest which was a kick-ass band that was very popular among Cadets. Their sound was a driving mix of funk and rock-and-roll, with a beat that carried the force of a Mack truck. Their music would just grab you and force you to dance.

There was electricity in the air as the first two bands did an excellent job of getting the crowd warmed up. But around eleven o'clock, the crowd was placed on high alert when a distinctive sound of a synthesizer started playing a loud, familiar chord that was the beginning of the popular Mother's Finest tune "Piece of the Rock."

With a flash of stage lights, the band cut into the full song, and at that instant, there wasn't a person in the place that wasn't in full-tilt motion. People were everywhere…on the dance floor, on top of chairs, and even on the tables. There was even a handful of fools up in the balcony that surrounded the huge auditorium. It was an experience to watch even after already witnessing eight other wild-ass senior parties that were no less than a formalized drunken riot. But this was like mass hypnosis, with a command for everybody to go crazy.

One by one, song after song, Mother's Finest seemed to attack the crowd with their music and its driving beat. As we all watched the crazies in action, we couldn't help but notice a cadet in the balcony who was standing on the outside edge of its guardrail. He must have been nuts since it was well over fifteen feet above the floor. People down below him were motioning for him to get down, but this lunatic was actually standing there making motions as if he were getting ready to make a swan dive. Everyone was yelling for him to get down before he really did fall and break his stupid neck. But this guy obviously was some sort of certified military fruitcake. He had on army fatigue pants, a green fatigue T-shirt, and what appeared to be jump boots. He was dancing around on the ledge as if he were a part of the Soul Train gang. Then the real fools arrived on the scene. They were the devil's men, sent to coax the guy to go ahead and jump. Hell, this was a party! As those below yelled at him to both get down, and to jump, the idiot grabbed his nose as if on a diving board and jumped! He landed feet first on one of the long tables that were covered with coolers, cans, bottles, and cups. As he hit the table, the crowd below him dispersed by practically running over each other. Even with the music blaring, there was an atomic BOOM and crash as the table collapsed and its contents exploded into shrapnel, with ice and liquids of all kinds flying everywhere. Without missing a lick, the guy stood up and began to run away, knowing that right behind him was a crowd of pissed off cadets who just had their booze smashed to hell. I thought I would die laughing. I looked at

Julie who was shocked at the sight, and I rebel yelled above the music and cheers of the crowd.

It was a classic sight to see several thousand people trying to dance and laugh at the same time. The whole incident left everyone in stitches. Everyone wondered how it didn't somehow kill that idiot, but assumed him to be one of those Airborne Ranger psychos who you could only hurt with a bazooka. But one thing was for sure. The pain he would feel if those cadets caught him would far exceed that which the jump had yielded.

The insanity seemed to linger on as cadets did other crazy things, all fueled by alcohol and music. By the end of the night, Julie and I were both worn out. We had danced more than ever, and with all the excitement of watching the three-ring circus that the crazy cadets had provided, it turned out to be one of the best Senior Parties I would ever attend.

As I drove Julie home, we were both in the best of spirits. We were tired, but from having such a great time. We talked about the many fun dates that we had, and Julie said she seemed to have the best time when she was out with me. But I told her it wasn't me, but merely the insanity of the school that just seemed to intensify everything. Citadel life was full of extremes.

CHAPTER 23

Thanksgiving furlough finally arrived, and on my return home my mother indicated that Charles and my father were down at the barn, preparing to barbecue the traditional hog for the big feast. When I asked how Charles and Dad were getting along, she simply answered, "Well...OK I guess." Without pursuing it any further, I took it to mean that things were probably the same, and that Charles' venture remained a tender subject.

But I was not home for controversy, nor was I looking to get in the middle of anything other than some good barbecue and decent hunting. I jumped back in my car and headed towards the barn where I found Dad, Charles, and several workers preparing the pig for the barbecue. I couldn't help but notice the great mood Charles was in, either because it was Thanksgiving, or maybe because he had won the battle with my father and had some real feelings of control. Whatever his reason, it was nice to have Charles in a mood other than the sour one that made my life in Kingstree hell.

As the weekend progressed, I really enjoyed the usual hunting and visits with family. There were many observations as to how much better I looked than the previous Thanksgiving as a freshman. My hair was longer and I wasn't sporting those dark circles under my eyes. The weight lifting and running had also put many pounds of muscle back on, and my physique was pretty near to that which I had in high school.

I couldn't believe how quickly furlough passed. It seemed that just when I had adjusted to being back home, it was time to return. I appreciated the little break, knowing I was going back to nothing but tests and final exams. I was motivated because I would soon be back for a nice three-week break for Christmas.

At muster formation I happily found that all of my freshmen had returned safe, and I asked them if they realized that they had returned to the most critical time in the academic semester. Tompkins seemed both aware and confident, but I could sense an attitude of fear as the other two predicted a desperate struggle to the end. I decided that I had arrived too late in their semester to be of any real influence. Except for some advice and words of encouragement, grades were all up to them now.

I also had my own academics to worry about. I immediately started getting into my final chapter quizzes that would finish me out in the regular semester grading period. But those tests were mere play compared to what was coming. The hard work I had put in over the previous months had me in a great position to take on what were always killer inquiries of the mind.

Finally, exam time rolled around, and I was happy to see the Fourth Class System lifted since it provided relief for both the knobs and for the upperclassmen.

When I finished my last exam, I was exhausted as usual. I felt like I had done really well, and the early results certainly indicated such. But it would not be until my grades arrived in the mail a week after getting home that I would truly know the official outcome.

When I returned home, I found Charles already in the construction phase of starting his new business. He was building a fish tank facility to hold the little catfish in their infancy. Although I was on break, I certainly didn't mind diving right in to help out, which Charles really appreciated.

Charles had also brought in a backhoe to dig a large pond that would eventually hold the catfish once they reached maturity. They would have to be transferred to the larger pond once they outgrew the smaller tanks. Between the construction of the new building, the tanks, the sophisticated equipment, and the huge pond, $50,000 could easily be spent in just getting started. On top of that Charles would have to buy several thousand baby catfish from a hatchery, as well as tons of fish food to feed them until while they matured to their maximum sellable weight.

I helped Charles right up until Christmas Eve, when everyone stopped to take a break to visit with the family and to open presents. I once again became the object of attention as Mom and Dad told everyone about the new "genius" in the family. My grades had come in the mail and I had indeed made the Dean's List with a 3.4 GPR. The fact that I also was promoted to Corporal left most everyone nearly in shock, and they wondered just what the hell was going on down in Charleston to turn such a reckless young man into a disciplined scholar. I loved how the success made me feel, and how it seemed to erase what was once my very negative image.

But even with the positive attention, Christmas at the O'Bryan house seemed to lack in its usual zest and happiness. There was obviously still a hint of uneasiness over what was going on with the farm. Things were going well in the building construction and in the pond digging, yet that wasn't enough to take away the anxious feelings of the two senior O'Bryans. Charles assured them at every opportunity that he had everything under control and was moving forward according to plan. Their faces, however, did not reciprocate that look of comfort.

The day after Christmas, construction resumed. The concrete slab and pools were then completed and big creosote posts were set in the ground around them, ready for trusses to be mounted so that a roof could be put on. The pond was about fifty percent complete, showing a pretty deep hole with water gathering in the bottom as it seeped in from the ground. I worked as hard on the project as Charles did, with the days quickly clicking off. By New Year's things were really taking shape.

The New Year's Eve celebration I attended had a very nice crowd, and it was held at the same old house that hosted the party from my first Thanksgiving furlough the year before. Some faces in the crowd seemed new to me, but there were still many familiar ones from high school, which was a treat since it was Fourth of July when I last saw them. Everyone seemed happy to see me, and appeared not so shocked by my appearance. I guess I now better understood why people looked at me so strangely the previous year. It was clear that my life had changed drastically by going to The Citadel, but in those early days, it seemed so much for the worse. But I was now looking much better, and apparently to most of them, the only difference between my present state and the old John, was the difference in hair length. I guess the joke was on them. I actually was changed more than ever.

The party was fun, and after many beers and conversations, I decided it was time to head on home. On my way out, I noticed a couple just arriving. Just my luck, it was Donna and her boyfriend Thatch. From where I stood I could tell they were both pretty wasted, and I prayed they wouldn't see me. Since they were standing right at the door, I had no choice but to hold-up where I was until they moved. Eventually they made their way further into the room, and that's when Donna spotted me. Her eyes opened wide, and she immediately made a beeline towards me. I cursed myself for not leaving earlier.

"John," said Donna making her way over towards me, "My little soldier boy! How are you?"

Donna walked up and threw her arms around me and gave me a big hug. Though I remembered her as quite a socialite, I could never recall her being so blatantly friendly. As she released me, I could see her glassy eyes, and that she was as high as a kite.

"My gosh, John," she said, "You're not skinny anymore."

I could see Thatch walking up behind her, not exactly thrilled to see me, but extending his hand anyway.

"Hey John, how ya doin'?" said Thatch.

"Fine," I answered firmly.

"So, how's The Citadel treating you these days?" asked Donna with authoritative concern.

"A lot better," I replied. "I guess you could say I'm on 'easy street' now."

"Good! I always think about you down there in that damn school," she said quite slowly, but with put-on feeling. "You guys looked so cute marching around with your little rifles and all."

"We think it's cute too, and it gives us something to do."

As I looked at her, I not only noted her condition, but also could see that she, in a strange way, had somehow lost some of her luster. Her clothes, hair, and make-up were all pretty lax, but there was also something different about her face. It was as if she wasn't as healthy as she had been. She may have just been tired, or not eating well at school.

"How are you and Clemson doing?" I asked.

"Oh, I don't know. I guess it's there. You know our football team is doing well, and I just really love to go to the games. We always have such great parties during football weekends."

"So I've heard."

Thatch reached down and grabbed Donna by the hand. It seemed to remind her that he was standing there.

"Come on," said Thatch, "I see Jim. I need to talk business with him a minute. It's good to see you again, John."

Thatch pulled Donna away by the hand. But as she got halfway across the room, she glanced back at me as Thatch pulled her on through the crowd. The look she gave me as she moved away would puzzle me forever. I never understood the message that seemed to be written in her sad smile.

As I drove back home, I thought about Donna, and her condition. For so long, I had really hurt over her, and was torn up by the way she had dumped me. Now, I felt nothing but pity, knowing that my worse suspicions from Fourth of July were true. She had dumped me for a different lifestyle, which at this point, appeared to be one laced with approaching tragedy. It was hard to imagine that she was the same girl I once thought so much about.

I worked with Charles my last few days at home, hoping to see the end of the construction that had started almost three weeks earlier. The building was almost complete, and the digging of the pond was practically finished. Once Charles got the equipment installed, and the coating on the inside of the concrete tank, he would be in business.

On the day that I left to go back to school, my father and I found ourselves riding over to Kingstree together, which gave us a chance to talk about things. I was pleased that Dad saw no use in discussing Charles' new operation since he knew I was obviously caught in the middle. He did, however, express his continuing delight for me having made the Dean's List and how amazed he was that I was doing so well under such rough conditions. He told me he received constant inquiries from others in town as to how I was doing, and that he often saw Mr. Johnson who had told him of our chance meetings after Homecoming football games, and how he was so thrilled to see me doing so well. I could see that Dad took great pride in hearing such praise from his peers.

But I just couldn't help but think as my father and I talked, that there was now always some hint of apology in his voice, possibly from realizing that he may have been wrong in his approach to Charles and me as we were growing up. He never came right out and said anything, but I could see something in my father that was not there before. He made me feel like an O'Bryan. It made me feel like his son. I guess I just couldn't understand why it also still brought back for me so many deep memories of painful alienation.

***

When I got back to school we had our normal muster formation, and the next day it was class registration and rifle pick-up procedures that marked the beginning of a new semester. Change was always the common rule at The Citadel, and it didn't take long before we all discovered that some adjustments were going to be made.

The first order of business was rank rotation, where from the senior class down through the sophomores, some would lose their rank so as to give others an opportunity to show what they could do. In the senior and junior classes, the changes were few. But in the sophomore class, the changes were massive. It was questionable why some guys lost their rank, while for others it was a no-brainer.

With all the new corporals, the next order of business was a rotation of platoon and squad assignments. Instead of three freshmen, I now would have four to deal with. But this time, I would get them at the beginning of the semester where I would have a real chance to influence them relative to grades. I now had Watson, Owens, Hay, and Allen, and since I had so little contact with the freshmen during first semester, I really wasn't sure whom I was getting. I was truly starting from scratch with them, but saw it as a real opportunity to do some good.

To go along with all the other changes, there was also a change in room assignments. I was certainly open to that since I had occupied the worst room in the battalion during first semester, and now it seemed, in all due fairness, I deserved an opportunity to get a room that was larger and without pipes in it. It didn't take long for me to confirm that having rank had its benefits when Larry and I landed a nice room up on 4th division. The only drawback now was climbing the three flights of stairs to get to it. It was a small price to pay to literally move up in the world.

With all the changes, I felt like there would be a lot of eyes on all of us since we were in the final stretch to see who would receive rank junior year. There were only three possible positions in R Company that would allow me to qualify to go out for Sword Drill. First Sergeant, Assistant First Sergeant, or Cadre Platoon Sergeant. Understanding that there were well over 40 sophomores in the company, the chances of getting one of those positions would be statistically difficult. Even though I had made the Dean's List the previous semester, and had almost a 3.0 during the second semester of my freshman year, my overall GPR, though quite good, was nowhere near that of some of my classmates. Both Danny Burn and Hank Rosellini had excellent grades, and they had constantly been in the limelight, with Burn being the Guidon Corporal first semester, and Rosellini now having it second. Assuming that Burn and Rosellini would get two out of the three high ranked positions, it would only leave one position open that I had to beat over 40 others to get.

I also soon found myself in a familiar situation of having a Senior Party coming up which was the first of the semester. But this had become a piece of cake, and all I needed to do was make a call to Julie, which around ten o'clock I decided to do.

I called up Julie and quickly popped the question to her about the upcoming senior party. But to my shock, and amazement, her answer for the first time was not what I expected to hear.

"I'm sorry, but no John, I can't."

"You're joking, right?"

"No, I'm afraid I'm not. You see...well...I met this guy over here at the college, and over the last two months, and even some during Christmas break, we've been dating, and dating pretty steady. And now...uh...I guess that's it. I'm going with someone."

"Oh no," I replied, "You're my senior party buddy. You can't do this to me."

"John, come on. All kidding aside. You're a good-looking guy, and I had more fun with you than with any other guy I've ever been out with. You could date any girl at the College you want to."

"Thanks for the vote of confidence."

"I mean it John. Look, you and I had some really good times together, and I'm going to miss that, but like I said, I'm just dating somebody steady now. I guess we couldn't just keep freewheeling forever."

"I know, I know. Well, if you and this guy ever bust up, you will tell me?"

Julie laughed, "Sure. Maybe I'll see you around, although I guess I won't be seeing you at too many senior parties now since my boyfriend goes to school here. I'm really going to miss those good times, and I must say, I'll also miss seeing you."

"Thanks," I said not really knowing what else to say. "It's been fun."

Damn. I couldn't believe it. I knew it was just a matter of time before a good thing would have to end. Julie was a super sweet girl who was obviously going to make someone very happy. But based on chemistry, or something, we just didn't have what it took for some serious relationship. We were more like good drinking buddies. At least that was the way I saw it. Maybe Julie, as a mature girl of twenty, desired love over just good times and friendship.

As I made my way back to my room, I wondered if I too was missing out on something by not being in love with someone. But I quickly thought back to Donna, and how I got burned so terribly bad with her, and how love just seemed to be a deceptive, complicated game where people get hurt more often than they stay happy. I also thought of all the many cadets who like me had received "Dear John" letters. That and the memories of Donna were enough to squelch any desire to meet some girl and fall head over heels. Certainly sometime during the rest of my life it might happen to me again, and if it did, I would then address the problem.

But for the moment, I would have to take the hint that I was just better off skipping senior parties and the huge amount of time they consumed. I could better use that time to study so that I would make the kind of grades that I knew I had to have. I smiled about it as I walked along, knowing that this would appear to be a move that only the insane would make.

On the Saturday morning of the Senior Party I rose as if it were a weekday. I worked all day long, jumping from one subject to the next as I completed assignments and then advanced even further in the course syllabus. As the late afternoon approached, I worked through the last of my most difficult subjects, and found that I completed all my major assignments except for English. I had put it off until last since the biggest task I had was to read a long poem that had some pretty difficult verse to interpret. The professor encouraged us to work through it with as few interruptions as possible since it was going to be a story that we would probably enjoy, but would also find time consuming. Therefore, I saved it until last. The odd thing about the poem was that the author didn't bother to leave his name. He was simply referred to as the 'Unknown Poet' who had

277

penned several very good poems. *Sir Gawain and the Green Knight* was by far his very best work.

I started to read the poem that was like none I had ever read before. It was well over 50 pages of difficult metrical writing that was in small print. I began around 1630 that afternoon, and read continually until 1800, when it was time for evening mess. But I was already so enthused by the story, I decided to skip the mystery meat at the mess hall and continue. I would have to make a burger run later since I knew that I could not go all night without something to eat. But at that moment, I just couldn't put the book down. The old poem was that good.

The story was set in the time of King Arthur and his Round Table of royal knights. Sir Gawain was one of his best, and he held a reputation of being a perfect knight, having led a life based on purity, chivalry, and honesty. These were all strong traits found among King Arthur's most loyal knights, but Sir Gawain stood far and above every other.

During one of the meetings of the round table, an ugly Green Knight stormed into the court, and issued a challenge of a fight to anyone who would accept it. But the Green Knight was mighty, and none of the knights wanted to take him on. But Sir Gawain knew that the honor of the King was at stake, so he accepted the Green Knight's challenge, and agreed to fight him at a location that was far away from King Arthur's kingdom. It was almost a situation of sure death for Sir Gawain, as all could easily discern that the Green Knight was the mightiest warrior that any had ever seen. Yet Sir Gawain, honoring the acceptance, met the challenge and embarked on the journey to another land.

On the way, after traveling long and hard, he stopped at a castle as he neared the site where the battle was to take place. At the castle, he was greeted by a most generous host, who asked that he stay at his house, eat his food, and use his servants as Sir Gawain waited for the time of battle to arrive. He graciously accepted the invitation, and remained there while his host left to go on a planned hunting trip for wild boar. While away, the host's wife made three passes at him, all of which were quite tempting and serious. But with cunning conversation, Sir Gawain managed to talk his way out of each of the situations, knowing that even though she was both beautiful and desirable, that his honor and duty as a gentlemen was to pass up the opportunity with grace such as to not offend the lady.

On her third and final attempt to seduce him, he again managed to talk her out of any actions that would be dishonorable, while doing his best not to insult her. But based on her insistence, he accepted from her a green colored scarf that was laced in gold, which she said was to be kept as a token of love when he went forth to battle the Green Knight. Although he sensed it wrong, he felt almost obligated to receive it. Therefore, he did.

After the host returned from his hunting trip, Gawain found that it was time to journey on to fight the Green Knight. Upon his arrival at the Green Chapel, an immediate battle began with Gawain fighting against an obviously more superior warrior. The Green Knight soon got the best of Gawain, and in what seemed to be the end, raised his ax to chop off his head. But he let the ax fall short, leaving only a small cut on Gawain's throat. Gawain quickly jumped up and recovered; grabbing his sword, ready again to fight. Yet, the Green Knight reminded Gawain of his superiority as a fighter, and then indicated that Gawain's entire journey was merely nothing more than a test of his honor as a knight. The castle in which Gawain had stayed while waiting for the battle was the Green Knight's, who was disguised as the generous host. The beautiful temptress was his wife, and he declared that Gawain had done well to act as a gentlemen, and conduct himself with the true honor expected of one of King Arthur's knights, yet he did fail a bit by accepting the green scarf, and therefore was given just punishment by a simple nick with the ax for the violation he had committed. Gawain understood then what the battle and challenge had been all about. After asking the Green Knight to forgive him for his misdeed, he parted in great friendship with the Green Knight, and journeyed back to the courts of King

Arthur, and on to other gallant adventures that lay before him.

I was blown away by the story. It seemed so relevant to the way I felt about Sword Drill: the chivalry, the commitment, the quest, the battle, and even the penalty. I could see that for me to make Drill, the same degree of discipline would be required.

Whatever variation I was to take from purity, I would eventually pay for one way or the other. Sword Drill was going to be a long and hard journey for me, with odds similar to that which Sir Gawain faced with the Green Knight. Drill was an honorable challenge I had accepted. It was something so few others would ever dare to embrace. There would be monumental trials along the way, ones that would tear at my heart and coax me to stray from what I knew was true and honorable. There were so many seemingly impossible things that had to happen just to get me in the running, much less to a successful end. And if I were so lucky to even see it, the eventual day of reckoning would be the final night of cuts, where the measured penalty based on my performance would be dispensed. Would it be a lethal blow of not making the Drill, or the honored victory of joining the ranks of the elite? But before I could even enter the battle, I was going to have to first become a member of King Arthur's court by getting the rank necessary to even sit at the round table. Then, and only then, would I be in the position to accept the challenge.

It took nearly seven hours for me to read the poem since the writing was so hard to interpret. It was nearly midnight when I finished, and I could hear freshmen and other cadets out on the galleries as they returned from the party. I loved Senior Parties as much as anyone, and I somehow thought I would have been depressed over missing it. Instead, I was only moved and inspired. Exchanging the event for the story had been a worthy sacrifice.

CHAPTER 24

As I was coming back from my last class one afternoon, I could hear my name called, and then noticed it was George Porter.

"Hi, John," he said. "Got a minute?"

"Sure, what do ya' need?"

George was hesitant to talk on the gallery, so I followed him to his room where he then told me to have a seat. He seemed to have something serious on his mind.

"John, are you considering going out for Sword Drill?"

I stared back at Porter, feeling as if I couldn't speak.

"Look, I know it's risky to confirm one's desire to go out for Drill, but you assisted me through the 14 Nights, and I can't help but notice how you seem to be obsessed with your grades and that you go the extra mile on the military stuff. So if this is your desire, it's now time for certain things to start happening. So I ask you again, are you wanting to go out for Drill?"

"Yes," I said as if surrendering a guilty plea.

"You know what you're getting into?"

"That's a hard question to answer," I responded, trying to be honest.

"You don't!" answered George with conviction. "And before you start asking me a bunch of questions, I can already tell you that I can't answer them. Even though I didn't make the Drill, I'm still sworn to secrecy. What I can tell you though, is that there's significantly more to it than meets the eye."

I just sat there, not knowing what to say. I could ask no questions and really had no idea where the conversation was going.

"But, if you're absolutely sure you have the desire to make the unwavering sacrifice, then I'm willing to help. There are certain things that I can show you, such as sword manual. We'll be starting Spring Roach soon, and getting a jump on it will help."

"What does Spring Roach involve?" I asked.

"It provides aspirants with a taste of Drill to help them decide if they want to pursue it. It's also to introduce sword manual to practice over the summer."

"Sounds like a smart way to approach it."

"All of this is harder than you can imagine John. These guys are going to expect you to put your heart and soul into this, and that absolutely nothing comes between you and your desire to make Sword Drill."

"For over a year now, Drill has constantly been on my mind. It's been the driving force that has helped me turn my cadet life around."

"I had suspected that."

"Then you must know that I am committed, and any help you can provide will be greatly appreciated."

"I'll admit, I can see your commitment."

George turned and walked to the door and pushed it closed, then pulled out his sword from the rifle rack. "This was my Night's sword, and although it was a loser for me, it's a good one. You're welcome to use it as much as you'd like."

"Thanks. That does solve a major problem. Surely if I checked out a sword from the Cadet store, word would spread like wildfire."

"That's true, but as soon as Spring Roach starts, there'll be no way to keep it a secret. Everyone will know then that you're bucking for Sword Drill."

"I guess I never thought it would get out so soon."

"There are other risks. Quite often, someone will go through that whole ordeal only to find he didn't get the rank. And contrary to popular belief, roaching in the spring does not help one get rank. Unfortunately, you've got a hell of a lot of sharp classmates that you're in competition with for the three slots here in the company."

"I know," I said with some concern.

"Again I ask you. Are you absolutely sure this is something you want to take on? It could yield a lot of embarrassment to reveal your desire only to find out you don't even qualify."

"I understand the risk. I want it that bad."

"OK then, stand up."

I stood up from the chair.

"This is how you hold a sword," instructed George.

George then proceeded to show me some of the most basic aspects of doing sword manual. Right off the bat, I found it cumbersome, and felt stupid having so much difficulty. Seeing two Drill performances made it look easy and disguised the true complexity of the movements.

The weekdays seemed to fly, as I remained consumed with all of my commitments. I would always find a moment or two during the week to go by George's room to both learn new sword manual and show him how well I had improved on earlier lessons. George was impressed with the speed at which I was learning, though that was due to my devotion to practice.

I lived under a rigorous schedule, using my time to its fullest, sticking with it week after week. By the time the mid-term grading period arrived, I had several achievements to be proud of. To start with, I had straight A's, and a perfect 4.0 GPR. I had busted my tail to get it. Yet, I realistically knew it would be damned hard to keep it that high. My ultimate goal was to have at least a 3.7 or higher at the end of the semester. That would win me Gold Stars, which were worn on the collar of formal cadet uniforms and were the ultimate statement of academic excellence in the Corps.

My physical condition was also a source of gratification. All through the year it had been constantly improving. I not only reached the size and physique that I once had during my peak years in high school, but had far surpassed it. Not only had I gained in bulk, but I also made significant gains in strength and endurance. I actually had to push just to tire myself when running and working out.

Soon grade results became official, and word of an Electrical Engineering major having a 4.0 GPR spread like wildfire. It was an unusual feat all right, but for those classmates I was closest to, it was easy to see how I did it. I was in the books constantly, every day, every weekend, and every free moment.

After the stoking derived from midterms, I pushed myself hard all the way up until Spring Break, where I was truly ready for a whole week off from my own self-imposed intensity of school. Before leaving, I asked George if I could take his sword home with me to Kingstree. It was a good time to do so since I really had no plans of doing much of anything except relax.

After my last class I gathered my things and made the drive to Kingstree. As usual I was greeted with excitement, and my parents couldn't believe how I looked, since the weight lifting and running had done so much for me. They were also shocked and thrilled that I had made straight A's on my midterms, having already received the grades by mail. Dad then asked what my plans were for the week, knowing that a break was well deserved. He was surprised to hear that my plans were to hang around home all week.

"What could you possibly find to do here in Kingstree, son?"

"In my car I have a sword that I borrowed from a guy at school. There's a group on campus known as the Junior Sword Drill, and I want to try out for it."

"When are try-outs?" asked Dad.

"They're not until next fall, but we start learning the sword manual this spring, and with my busy schedule, I just really haven't been able to practice with the sword the way I've wanted to. So if it's all right with you, I'd just rather hang out, take a little break, and work on my sword manual."

"Of course that's all right with us, John," answered Dad. "But son, it sounds almost like you're pushing yourself too much."

"It's just something I really want to do. You have to trust that it means that much to me."

"Ok," said Dad, "but if you want to go take off somewhere, you know you're free to go."

"Thanks Dad. I'll just play it by ear this week."

"Ok, but I don't want to see you blow your vacation time like you did during Christmas by doing work around here."

"I promise. No work. By the way, how's Charles's fish operation coming along?"

"Quite well," answered Mom jumping in. "He's gotten his fish, and the tanks are full of water. Everything seems to be going smoothly. Right, dear?"

I could see that Mom was trying to push a positive response out of Dad.

"It's really too early to say yet," Dad said. "But yes John, at least now, after spending thousands of dollars we don't have, it's going."

I was sorry I asked, as I could see that tensions were still high.

"Why don't you go take a look," said Mom. "You might even find Charles out there now."

"Let's hope not," said Dad. "He still has plenty of equipment to get in shape before planting season. That's his responsibility, as per his demands I might add!"

I remembered that Charles not only wanted to start the fish operation, but he had continuously pushed to get more of a stronghold on the farm operations. We normally would work all during the winter months to have everything ready to go by this point. But Charles' fish operation was apparently taking up a lot of his time, and therefore should have turned his other responsibilities back over to my father. But he had argued hard to get them, and probably wasn't willing to give them up.

I knew just to mind my own business, and get down to the more pressing job of perfecting sword movements. I had to make my clumsy executions into precise ones that would be second nature. I also couldn't let up on my running and lifting. So I filled my days with different activities that I had a notion to pursue, and enjoyed the lack of urgency as much as anything.

Spring break passed quickly, and although I had no wild stories of exotic trips or wild parties to take back, I really enjoyed the opportunity to relax and to give my mind a much needed rest. I had done well in getting my sword manual form up to a respectable level, and I couldn't wait to show Porter.

CHAPTER 25

When I arrived back at school the Corps went through its normal struggles to get back into the formalities of cadet life. For some, the return from Spring break was the hardest to deal with, as it could lead many a cadet to believe that the year was in the final stretch. That could mean trouble as a result of slacking up on things that were still important such as grades and military requirements.

But for those of us considering Sword Drill, everything was about to shift in the opposite direction. It began when the announcer at noon mess asked the Corps to give their attention to the Commander of the 1979 Junior Sword Drill. I stopped eating and nearly froze as Richard Kraft, Delta Company First Sergeant and head honcho of the '79 Drill started to speak.

"All sophomores wishing to aspire to become a member of the 1980 Junior Sword Drill are invited to attend a mandatory meeting in Jenkins Hall Auditorium at 1600 hours. Don't be late!"

Though it came with surprising impact, this was the word I had been waiting for, and was happy to finally hear something. I glanced around the mess table at the faces to detect if my special attention to the announcement had been noticed. All seemed normal, other than a few laughs from some as they considered the opportunity just offered and the hell that came with it.

At 1550 I walked through the side door of Jenkins Hall, shined up and in perfect uniform as if going to an inspection. I was not alone as other sophomores nervously moved in, and I just followed the flow that led into the briefing room. Milling around up front were what seemed to be all of the '79 Drill, and scattered in the rows of auditorium chairs were other sophomores who had already arrived. Once I signed in I anxiously moved to take a seat in the middle.

There were no stragglers, and the meeting kicked off at exactly 1600. Richard Kraft opened with a welcome, and I was surprised by his mild voice and the absence of threat in his manner.

"Gentlemen. The Junior Sword Drill is the most elite organization on The Citadel campus, and also, I might add, the hardest to get into. I'm pleased with the turnout today, since the stiff competition will help insure the quality of the 1980 Drill. It is our job to uphold the standards of this pristine organization such that only the best of your class will take the floor on Parents Day next year."

Kraft turned to a '79 Drill member and summoned him to rise.

"Please give your attention to Ronnie Bourbon, Second Battalion Sergeant Major. Mr. Bourbon is the Voice of the '79 Drill. For those who don't know, he is the guy who makes the siren sounding commands during the performance. Mr. Bourbon also holds the distinguished title of "Low Cuts Man," gaining such a title by virtue of having received the fewest cuts during the final two evenings of the 14 Nights. I've asked Mr. Bourbon to now illustrate the high standard of performance which will be expected from those who aspire to be Sword Drill material."

Bourbon, wearing a sword and gloves, proceeded to amaze the crowd with a series of moves that seemed quite complex. He was good all right, damn good, and he left us all dazed by his ability.

"One of you will be in Mr. Bourbon's position next year, and I challenge each of you to work hard to be that person."

With the large number present, it already seemed hard enough to think we might be one of the 14, much less Low Cuts Man.

"We will take the names of those present and divide them into small groups of two or three. We will then schedule you to visit the rooms of the Sword Drill members. After those visits, we will throw you a little stadium party. These activities will be your introduction to the Drill, and a mere taste of what is to come in the fall. I want to conclude with both words of encouragement and caution. I hope all of you are willing to make the sacrifice necessary to secure a place on the Junior Sword Drill. But I warn you; it will be the challenge of your lives. Seriously consider the commitment you are making. It's best not to even start unless you are certain this is really what you want. Dismissed!"

I was happy that Spring Roach was finally starting. Time had arrived such that at least some of my burning questions would finally be answered, not necessarily by someone's response, but by actually going through the motions of being a roach.

I heard later that 43 sophomores had attended the meeting. This was an impressively high number considering the Drill's infamous reputation of abuse and the small number of available sergeant positions that qualified a guy to go out. There were only three positions in each of the 17 companies, and a few elite staff positions, given only to the superstars of each class, consisting of four Battalion Sergeant Majors, four Regimental Master Sergeants, and one Regimental Sergeant Major, all of which seemed impossible to get. Among the 43 that attended the meeting were others like me who were long shots for getting the rank they needed, yet were willing to take the risk of going through Spring Roach with the hopes that a decision would somehow go their way.

The initial large number meant that each member of the old Drill would have to deal with two or three potential roaches each night. Actually, I really hated to see that so many people were interested in going out, since statistically that made the odds of making it much less favorable.

But George Porter told me that it was normal for a lot of guys to sign up in the beginning, but that many would become disillusioned once they discovered the real sacrifice it would take. I understood the theory behind what he was trying to convey, but knowing that there were only 14 positions, even a dwindling 43 was cause for concern.

I soon received a schedule of room visits that the old Drill had created. From it, I saw that my first visit would be with a guy named Cliff Malone, India Company's Assistant First Sergeant. I didn't know him at all, but just having a name gave my anticipation an added boost of reality. The schedule also said that my Spring Roach partner would be my R Company classmate, Chris Davis. To a certain degree, I felt some security knowing there was at least one other person from R who had signed up for Drill. Chris had teeter tottered back and forth as to whether he was going to give it a try, but surprised everyone by attending the initial meeting to get his name on the list.

I had suspected that if anyone else were to participate from R Company it would have been Danny Burn or Hank Rosellini. Both seemed to be shoe-in's for the rank since they were squared away guys with outstanding grades and military performance. But in my discussions with them, I discovered that Danny simply feared that his personality, which was at times that of a real hard-ass, had caused some genuine friction with some in the upper classes. He was a strong-willed person, and didn't mind tearing someone's head off at a second's notice. He also took great pride in showing his quick wit by cutting others down with a razor's edge tongue, using accuracy in malice like no other I'd ever seen. He often found class standing as a weak barrier, and had burned a few juniors with his mouth. Nothing he could be written up for, but enough such that his escapades would compel some of the old Drill members to get extremely rough with him as an attempt in attitude adjustment.

Rosellini, only slightly milder in his approach, had several of the same traits that Burn possessed. Hank, however, possessed a very strong desire to go out and have a good time. To commit to Drill would cut tremendously into his babe chasing and drinking. His weekends were too important, and there was no question in his mind that Drill was not for him. The social sacrifices would be far too great.

Even with strong reasons, it was hard for me to imagine that someone would voluntarily pass up on the chance to go out for Sword Drill. I guess I could respect both Danny and Hank's good sense in that they understood the commitment and knew themselves well enough to know that it just wasn't for them.

But Chris Davis, on the other hand, had been an effective and popular squad corporal, having served on cadre as well as retaining his rank through second semester. Chris was in excellent physical shape, a star in company intramurals, and had maintained a decent GPR since first semester. He was probably one of the nicest guys in the Company, and I looked forward to us both going through the challenge together.

But as much as I liked and respected Chris, there was a significant problem with him going out. I remembered that George Porter had said going out for Drill would have no impact on rank boards, but it was hard for me to believe that it would be totally ignored. With Danny Burn and Hank Rosellini definites for the First Sergeant and Assistant First Sergeant positions, this left Chris and me in competition for the one remaining slot of Cadre Platoon Sergeant. There was a remote chance that either Danny or Hank would be considered for the Battalion Sergeant Major slot, thus leaving another position open, but not likely. The Battalion Sergeant Major position was extremely political and exceptionally hard to get. Not only did the cadet have to be more than qualified, but also he had to have someone going to bat for him. For Danny and Hank, with their cutting personalities, I couldn't imagine anyone willing to help them out. It appeared that it was going to be a dual between Chris and me for the remaining sergeant slot.

There was at least one positive aspect of my challenge. At least Kevin Schmidt was now graduating, and although he would have some influence over how the senior officer positions would be filled by the juniors, he would have nothing to do with the NCO slots. This was extremely comforting to me, especially knowing that Schmidt was still my worst enemy, and that all the trouble he had once caused me would be no more. My consideration for rank would be outside of his negative bias. If I didn't get it, at least it wouldn't be a result of his continued spite.

Around 2200 on the evening of my first Spring Roach visit I changed out of my gray nasty uniform and into my PT's that were considered the official roaching uniform. But this PT uniform was like no other I had. I had gone over it with a fine tooth comb, making sure that there were no blemishes or stains on any part of it, and that all the loose threads had been removed, and that my socks, shoes, and every other item was in perfect order.

George had indicated that roaches would be required to bring fresh popcorn to the old Drill member they were visiting that evening, supposedly to compensate them for their time to teach us the art of sword manual. I had a popper in my room, just as I was sure all of my roaching classmates with any foresight had. Chris had one too, and we agreed to split the popping responsibilities. The real trick was to find out whether your host even wanted popcorn or not, or if he wanted it with butter, and what kind of soda to go with it. All of this, we would have to figure out without much help from the old Drill. Word of mouth between roaches would become the number one way of communication in finding out what was expected of us. It seemed that the old Drill had a little game to play with us in that it was rare for them to come right out and say what they expected. We had to work through our experience and constantly communicate to determine who expected what. It seemed so trivial, but Porter said that in the end it had real purpose. Though frustrating at times, it quickly brought all the aspirants closer and forced us to work together. You just couldn't do Sword Drill alone.

Chris and I had neither fact nor hint as to what Cliff Malone wanted since this was the first night and we had no way of knowing. We felt we needed to bring something, but knew that to make a wild guess would also be wrong. Of all the options it seemed best just to bring nothing. It made sense that as an orientation Malone would probably tell us his preferences so as to inform the others.

At 2220, I met Chris in his room. At 2225 we left for 3rd Battalion, allowing five minutes to get there without being either late or early. I knocked, and then stood there with Chris as we heard someone moving towards the door. I thought my heart would come through my chest.

"You must be Davis and O'Bryan," said Malone.

"Sir, yes, Sir," I answered.

"That's 'yes Sir.'"

"Yes Sir!" I said.

"That will be your first lesson. You are no longer knobs. You are

Roaches, and you don't have to sandwich your answers. And when we ask you a question, there is no answer such as, `Sir, no excuse, Sir'. We have a lot to do here and so very little time. Everything we ask you to do has a purpose. And the final purpose is for the Class of 1980 to provide to the Class of 1979 the best possible Junior Sword Drill performance it can. That was our goal as the '79 Drill, and this, without question, will also be your goal."

"Yes, Sir," answered Chris without me.

"You two were early to arrive for this meeting," said Malone.

Here it comes, I said to myself.

"In a Drill performance being too early is just as bad as being too late. Obviously, there's a coordination problem between us, and we are out of sync. And that's bad. Were you not told to be here at 2230?"

"Yes, Sir," we answered.

"You were a minute early," said Malone. "At this time please position yourselves in the lean and rest."

Chris and I immediately went down into the push-up position.

"Another problem of coordination...I wanted popcorn. Where's my popcorn? I don't see any popcorn. Who told you I did not like popcorn? Popcorn is filling. I am hungry for popcorn."

Damn, I thought. I had everything I needed sitting right in my room. There's no way to win.

"Roach Davis," continued Malone, "where is my popcorn?"

"Sir, no excuse, Sir," answered Chris.

"I've already told you Davis. Are you fellas not listening already? We have a very short time and much to do. I've already stated that the answer is incorrect. We're really getting off on a bad foot here. First, you were not coordinated in a timely arrival. Second, I don't have my popcorn. And third, you fellas are not listening to what I'm saying. We're really doing poorly here. I'm not used to this. I have problems with this. This is not good. Sword Drill is good. Where's my popcorn? I really want my popcorn. With hot butter on it. And a Dr. Pepper."

I thought to myself that this guy was some sort of rambling

lunatic. His brain seemed to have been locked on one track like a stuck record."

"This really is not good," Malone continued to babble as his voice raised in volume. "But Sword Drill is good. Sword Drill is exact. Sword Drill is on time. Sword Drill is popcorn. I have no popcorn. Come, Roach Davis, arise from your push-up position."

Chris quickly stood up while I stayed down.

"Come and rest my son," said Malone in a compassionate voice.

Chris followed, but had no idea where Malone was going with this.

"Please, rest your jaded torso upon this bed."

Chris climbed onto the bottom bunk in a complete state of confusion as to what was expected of him.

"Please Roach Davis," said Malone in a quiet and mellow voice, "rest your weary head, for the tasks of this Drill seem to have already tired you."

"Roach O'Bryan," screamed Malone as he quickly turned towards me, "I ask of you, where is my popcorn?"

"I did not know you wanted it, Sir."

"Extremely good answer, O'Bryan! Now we are making progress," said Malone in a once again calm voice. "You see a fault within your actions. Recognizing one's faults is an important part of the procedure to have a perfect Sword Drill performance."

Malone slowly looked towards the ceiling, putting his hand to his chin, "But as I stand here thinking, my heart is saddened. We know that there's a problem, but it is too late. Our chance to correct it shall never be. For you only have one visit here to my room. A visit marred by a mistake that will be marked in Sword Drill minds for all eternity. One that shall always be remembered. You shall always be scarred, knowing that I had no popcorn and that I was hungry. You had one opportunity my roaches, to perform well as you entered into my room, but that opportunity has now passed, and you will never again in this lifetime have that opportunity again.

Roach O'Bryan, why are you here?"

"I am here because I want to go out for Sword Drill, Sir."

"Are you not going out for it now Mr. O'Bryan?"

"Yes, Sir," I answered, confused by the question.

Malone squatted down so as to look into my face as I remained in push-up position. "Well, then your statement was incorrect. You said you came here this evening because you want to go out for Sword Drill. Does that mean you haven't started yet? Does it mean that this visit doesn't count? Is that why you did not bring me popcorn?"

Malone stopped talking and started into my face. He did not move for at least a full minute, nor did he even budge. I stayed in the lean and rest while Davis was now lying on the bed, obviously feeling very uneasy about where he was. After our full strange minute of silence, Malone rose and walked toward the telephone and began dialing. There was no question in my mind now; this guy was a certified fruitcake.

"Hello, Chip? This is Cliff. Spring Roach was to start tonight was it not?" A pause. "But I have no popcorn." Another pause. "But how can it be Spring Roach if I have no popcorn?"

Enough of this bullshit already, I thought. Damn, he ought to just let me get up and go get him some fucking popcorn if it was that important. Another pause went by, and then Malone finally hung up.

After waiting about a minute in silence, Malone again began to speak. "I just spoke to another Junior Sword Drill member. He has indicated that he too did not receive any popcorn. I thought it was the first night of roaching. I truly did."

Malone stood, then walked over to the door and opened it, shoving me out of the way in the process while saying, "Excuse me, excuse me." I had to crab walk forward so that he could get the door open. He then walked out and closed the door behind him, leaving me in the lean and rest and Davis still on the bed. I had been staring straight ahead while the whole escapade was unfolding, but as soon as he was gone, I looked over at Chris in the bed and just shook my head. Chris was smiling a bit, but with a puzzled look on his face. We knew not to open our mouths, though there really were no words that needed to be said. It was unanimous that this was a very strange introduction.

I remained in the lean and rest for the five minutes Malone was away. Then the door suddenly opened, and he walked back in. Stepping over me, he walked over to his desk where he pulled out his chair and sat down. He then took a book off the shelf and began looking at it as if the two of us weren't even in the room.

I had been in the lean and rest for over ten minutes, and my back was beginning to feel the effects, and it wanted to bow. I was still holding on, but it was really beginning to hurt.

So far this display of insanity was nothing close to what I had expected. I thought I was going to come to this guy's room to learn sword manual to practice over the summer, but this was obviously some sort of demented mind game. There was pain in my back, but I didn't want to be where Chris was either.

Finally, after I had been in the lean and rest for almost 15 minutes, I moved a bit by shifting my weight so as to help ease the stiffness and pain of having been in the same position for so long. As soon as I did, Malone popped his head up and around.

"What's this? A roach! On my floor!"

He stared towards me for a moment then said, "Mr. O'Bryan!"

"Yes sir," I answered.

"Why are you here?"

"I am here as a cadet who is now aspiring for the 1980 Junior Sword Drill. It was made known to me to report to your room, Sir."

"Oh, good. Do you have my popcorn?"

"No sir," I answered.

"Obviously shortsightedness on your part, Mr. O'Bryan. Please stand up."

I stood up not knowing why I was now the center of attention.

"I have come to a conclusion," said Malone as he stood and walked towards me. "This is not a Spring Roach night. You know why?"

"Yes sir," I answered.

"Tell me why," said Malone.

"Because there's no popcorn, Sir."

"Outstanding O'Bryan. You now understand. Please step forward Sir, while I manifest what it is you seek."

Malone reached back into the corner where the rifle rack was and pulled out his sword. He then took it from its scabbard and handed it to me.

"Mr. O'Bryan, there's something I want to show you. It's what's known as 'arch swords.' Get up Davis!"

Chris sprang from the bottom rack, and stood at attention where he landed.

"At ease," commanded Malone. "Get over here, I want you to watch this."

Chris moved close to watch, and as if his mind and attitude had completely shifted gears, Malone suddenly became a teacher. With surprising care and detail, he walked me slowly through the movement of bringing the sword up to full arc. He spent the remaining fifteen minutes of our time together going over the fine points of the maneuver that actually only takes a fraction of a second. Position of the fingers, angle of the blade, cocking the wrist, straightness of the arm, it seemed there was no end to what demanded attention. Malone stressed that it would take hours to master the movement so that it would become second nature, perfect and capable of passing the testing eyes of the old Drill during "cuts."

From fruitcake to professor, Assistant First Sergeant Clifford Malone was one hell of an introduction to Drill. He was as sharp as any cadet I had seen, but was somehow compelled to convince us that we had left the real world for a unique experience of some sort. Little did we know just how mild that first encounter would comparatively be.

The following Monday evening, Chris and I found ourselves in the room of Kevin Grant, Echo Company Staff Sergeant, who we heard wanted lightly buttered popcorn and a coke. He seemed determined to use every minute of time we had together to teach us how to go to "present arms" with the sword. He seemed the academic type, mild in his manner, and somewhat soft-spoken. He was far from the stereotypical Sword Drill guy who wanted to intimidate and run you into the ground. We learned a lot from him, and left there with a feeling that Spring Roach would be nothing but a casual learning experience. But the surfacing stories concerning what the other old Drill members were doing soon made that feeling short lived.

On Tuesday evening, Chris and I went to see Bert Randolph, Alpha Company 1st Sergeant, who lay to rest any thoughts that we would skate through the visits. Randolph never pulled a sword out, and he used the entire thirty minutes to rack the living shit out of us. It was by far the worst rack session I had ever experienced, bar none from freshman year. I thought that at some point he would stop with the physical games and show us some stuff, but he didn't. We did push-ups, sit-ups, ran in place, and hung from the pipes. Randolph stayed completely calm and focused on the torment as he wore us down to exhaustion. We weren't knobs, so he used every rack technique that was barred and considered as against the rules when dealing with freshmen. Chris and I even did push-ups under the bed, having to lift not only our bodies, but also the set of metal bunk beds and mattresses. He killed us with a surgeon's precision, and I had never before felt such physical taxation, especially when compressed into a thirty minute time period. At 2300, we struggled to get our sweaty bodies off of the gallery after he literally threw us out the door. I was sore for days after that visit, and knew then that we would be facing the challenge of a lifetime in our Sword Drill pursuit.

On Wednesday, rumors of guys already quitting started to circulate, and I was actually not surprised to hear it. That night we spent time with Lamar Jordan, Regimental Band Platoon Sergeant, who told us we were wasting our time going out for Sword Drill since the numbers trying out from our class were high and that there was a less than 50% chance we would make it. He was an asshole all right, and did nothing but test us on different sword manual moves, most of which I knew well from George Porter, while Chris had little idea of what to do. Chris spent most of the evening doing push-ups on his already terribly sore arms, while I got yelled and cursed at for not doing everything exactly right. I did my fair share of push-ups too, but nothing as compared to Chris. I was grateful that I had helped Porter, and he in turn had helped me.

On Thursday, we had a great teaching session with a really squared away cadet named Ronnie Bourbon. I remembered him well from the initial meeting. How could any of us forget? He was both the Voice and Low Cuts Man of the '79 Drill. He was straight forward and calculated, and a guy who seemed to have it all together. He worked on our sword manual from the moment we got there until he had to let us go. He was one of the few who wanted no popcorn, and as busy as we were, he would have never had time to touch it anyway. I learned more from him than any other old Drill member, and through him I discovered the class and integrity of Drill.

With the first of three weeks of Spring Roach behind us, we had the weekend off, and along with my studies, I worked to perfect and burn into my brain all I had learned so far. With 5 down, and nine more to go, I decided to write down what each had told me, and to work hard to master all I was privileged to learn. No one had to tell me about the advantages of staying ahead of the game.

In the two weeks that followed, we had good and bad nights as we found each of the old Drill giving us their version of 30 minutes in their room. Though there were some similarities, no two visits were ever the same, and some would remain more memorable than others.

On Sunday, our first evening back at it, we met another top-notch cadet. He was Dan Trout, Regimental Sergeant Major and the junior class's highest-ranking NCO. He was sharp all right, but far from being kind. He seemed short fused, and every time we made a mistake he would make us do push-ups. He was showing us the "draw swords" movement, and like the others, it too was loaded with details and potential pitfalls. It was a tense and nerve racking half hour with Mr. Trout, and though he taught us many things, I was so rattled by the time we got out of there that I wasn't sure if I even understood all that he was trying to show us.

Then there was Bob Fox, Mike Company Platoon Sergeant, who in my opinion won the award for being the most bizarre of all the '79 Drill. When we entered his room the lights were off except for a black light, and there were candles lit throughout the room. He immediately started his stereo blasting into Iron Man by Black Sabbath, and then made us hit it and pump 'em out to the rhythm of the heavy metal standard. I really don't know what his intentions were, whether it was to try to scare us or to just be entertaining. I can say it was motivating to help us get through all of the pushups, and I loved it when he put on "In-a-godda-di-vida" by Iron Butterfly, and cut on a strobe light. He was a pretty wild dude.

Over in Delta Company we met Assistant First Sergeant Richard Kraft, who was also the Commander of the '79 Sword Drill. He was probably the most distinguished and formal of them all. He did no racking or instruction, and mainly gave us a big brother sort of talk relative to the high standards of the Drill and the conduct that was expected of us as we roached. He made it clear that the organization was far more than what it appeared to be on the surface, and that those fortunate enough to survive the challenge of making it would set a precedent for success in their lives. Kraft made it believable, and you could tell that his love for the Drill came from the heart.

The biggest waste of a visit was when we went to see Ken Lindsey, who put both of us in his full press for the entire duration, and would beat on it from time-to-time as he laughed and shot the breeze with his roommate.

The maddest we made someone was Kilo Company's First Sergeant Andrew Green when we put way too much butter on his popcorn. We heard from the others visiting before us that he liked it on there heavy, and that he often racked those who couldn't get it right. We put it on heavy all right, and by the time we got to Third

Battalion, the brown paper bag was saturated and turning to mush. When I handed it to him and the bottom broke out and half of the soggy kernels hit the floor. Needless to say, he was not a happy camper. It was the first and last time I would ever eat buttered popcorn off the floor while in the lean and rest.

Through our own miscues, and the often strange behavior of the old Drill, it was an interesting three weeks. Night after night, we went to a new room and discovered either new ways to do sword manual or new ways to catch hell. By the end of Spring Roach, 38 out of the original 43 remained. Some became disenchanted once they understood what was expected in order to make it. They saw enough to decide that the Junior Sword Drill was just not worth the sacrifice. In retrospect, they were smart to leave when they did.

I was certain that what we had seen during those half hour sessions was mild foreplay to what was to come, but more than enough to scare off those who may have been straddling the fence. It was great to get an introduction to the sword manual so those who were truly motivated could practice over the summer. There were a few times when it was physically tough, or when my nerves got a little flustered with the mind games, but I knew it was nothing compared to what we would experience in the fall. It was hard to forget what Porter and the other '79 roaches looked like after returning from a night in McAlister.

Both Chris Davis and I remained in the running as potential aspirants after Spring Roach, but we still had to survive something called the "Stadium Party." That event would take place during the final days of the semester, which really wasn't that far away since we were only three weeks from graduation. The old Drill had talked about it often during our times together, and spoke of it as an event that would again "thin the ranks" of the weak and unmotivated.

But not all would be there. The real mystery now was over who would get rank, and the Stadium Party would take place after positions were announced. That issue still lingered as my greatest concern, and if I were unsuccessful in that quest, it really wouldn't matter at all how hard the Stadium Party would be.

The final weeks of school would be tense ones. The beginning of the end would start with the ever-critical rank boards. Right after would be final exams, recognition of the knobs, graduation, and the closing up the barracks for the summer. The seniors could already see a light at the end of the tunnel, and their lax attitudes, even among some of the officers, were starting to surface. Rank and class standing would mean little once they had sheep skin in hand, as few from the outside world would care much at all. A Cid grad was a Cid grad.

The ranking juniors slowly started to take over responsibilities as the seniors became preoccupied with parties and other pre-graduation activities that held a greater priority. As power was being passed, you could see individuals within the lower classes feeling the tension of the approaching change, knowing that they would soon be considered for new positions, and worried just where they might end up. Though they covered it up well, even Burn and Rosellini were nervous and preoccupied by the deviation from what was once a stable and established power base.

When rank boards finally started, it was easy to see that most with the potential for rank were edgy. After all I had been through, it was impossible to ward off the anxiety the process created in me. Getting rank meant everything. It would take effort to keep my wits about me and stay calm about what was going on.

But all of us in the junior class would remain in limbo until the critical officer slots were filled. Those selections would involve strong input from the TAC Officers, faculty, and the high-ranking members of the departing senior class. It was a time consuming process to conduct the interviews and sort through the possibilities, and the strain was evident on the faces of those whose futures were on the line.

One evening as the upperclassmen were standing around waiting for formation, several guys decided to ease the tension and pass the time by joking around with some of the knobs. It was an old Citadel tease concerning the Civil War and who actually won it, and my classmate Hector Reddick starting it off by asking the freshmen in his squad "Who won the war?" Hector, a Yankee, was obviously going to play out the role in favor of the North. In doing so, he soon gathered a crowd around as he got things going. My squad was right beside his, and I could see he was giving the Southern freshmen in his squad a whole lot of grief. I felt a responsibility to act as a counter-balance to help the joke along, and defend the Motherland. I would just have to dish out some crap to the Yankee freshmen in my squad. It was an old joke, but actually harmless, and often funny to the freshmen that were so close to being recognized.

Hector and I drew in a crowd that included both privates and those with rank, including the Company Commander Kevin Schmidt. Kevin had always been the most serious individual in the senior class, but he too was beginning to loosen up a bit as graduation quickly approached. Even he was standing around with a smile on his face as he watched the escapade begin to build. Knowing the history between us though, I couldn't help but notice his presence, which subconsciously affected my approach to the game.

After Hector had asked his four freshmen one-by-one the infamous question, he had an even split with two from the South and two from the North. The two Yankees expectedly answered that the North had won, and the two from the South, living out the inbred pride of generations, answered, "The South did, Sir!"

Hector of course, immediately made them hit it. As the laughing crowd cheered them on, he would ask them again, "I'll give you smacks another chance, who won the war?"

"Sir, the South did, Sir," the two answered.

"Down," said Hector, indicating that they were to pump out a push up.

"Okay, I ask you again! Who won the war?"

"Sir, the South, Sir."

"Down," said Hector laughing.

I could see it was time for me to step in. As I started to speak, I couldn't help but notice Schmidt laughing and enjoying Hector's work. Old anger suddenly felt resurrected, and negative emotions were renewed.

I approached my squad of three freshmen, two of whom I knew were from South Carolina, the other from Boston. I walked in front of them and asked, "How many of you knobs are from hometowns that are south of the Mason-Dixon Line?" I asked loudly. "Raise your hands with pride!"

The spectators suddenly turned their attention to my act, and the two knobs from South Carolina raised their hands. I moved close to the motionless one from the North. "Hey knob, where are you from?"

"Sir, I'm from Boston, Massachusetts, Sir."

I heard a low snicker from the gallery.

"Fine!" I stepped sideways and in front of the first freshman from the South and said, "Knob, where are you from?"

"Sir, I'm from Chester, South Carolina, Sir."

"Hit it," I said.

This brought an immediate groan of misunderstanding from the crowd.

I moved to the next and asked, "Knob, where are you from?"

"Sir, I'm from Atlanta, Georgia, Sir."

"Good. Hit it," I said.

I could see that the crowd couldn't understand my motives. I squatted down close to the two knobs in an appearance to get close to talk to them. I could see Hector had even stopped racking his knobs since he too was curious as to what the hell I was going to do next.

As I began to speak, the look of fun disappeared from my face. "Listen here you knobs, there's something I want to explain to you. You see, there are a lot of upperclassmen that think that since you're from the South and they are from the North, that you have it much easier than they do." I slowly lifted my head with a serious look then stared straight at Kevin Schmidt. "You see knobs, I don't want any of these homesick, cry baby, Yankee ass wimps, for one single minute, to think that you have any advantage whatsoever over them. So while these mama's boys from the North watch, I'm going to rack the piss out of you, just to help them deal with their tender feelings."

I could see the smile on Schmidt's face quickly disappear. The crowd was laughing, and pleased with my innovative approach, but before I commanded them to do the first push-up, I just had to drive the point home. "You don't mind if we show these ladies how to act during their visit to our school?"

One freshman quickly answered with an enthusiastic "Sir, no, Sir," and the other freshman, obviously really into making this point said, "Sir, let's do it, Sir!" with a lot of gritty feeling, opting to risk bypassing his standard answer.

"Atta boy," I said.

I stood up and started commanding, "Down! Up! Down! Up!"

I racked the knobs, and racked them hard, but I could see in their faces that they were enjoying every minute of it. They were shaming the Yankees, both classmates and upperclassmen, as enthusiasm and pride radiated from their voices and movements. I looked back over towards Schmidt, and could see that he understood exactly where I was coming from. He was apparently not very entertained, and looking down and away, he walked off. He moved into the Company Commander position and put an end to the whole ordeal by calling the company together for formation. I told my two rebels to stand up saying, "Good job boys. You won't believe the point that you just made."

"Sir, yes, Sir," they said, quite happy to assist.

"Now roll out!" I commanded.

My three freshmen ran out on the quad, and as I also moved to get to my own spot, I could not help but notice Schmidt glancing over towards me, and then turning his head away. He didn't appear to be mad, but he was obviously thinking. What had started as an old knob harassment joke turned out to be a serious statement, one that I had always wanted to make to Schmidt.

But as formation passed, and we marched over to the mess hall, I began to question the intelligence of doing such a thing so close to rank boards. Even though I knew Schmidt was graduating, I knew better than to take stupid chances. He would have some influence over the selection of the rising officers, but nothing to do with the selection and placement of the rising juniors. I felt sure the little episode would pass without any negative results.

Rank boards for the rising senior class were soon underway, and word began to trickle down as to who had received Staff positions. As usual, R Company found itself slighted on Regimental Staff selections. Knowing that politics played a major roll in getting these high visibility slots, being in the right place and knowing the right people really made a difference. We actually experienced better treatment relative to 4th Battalion Staff as R Company snagged two of the eight officer openings.

Once all the senior staff positions were filled, it only took a day before the officer positions for the companies were announced. R Company would see Lonnie Mauldin promoted as its new Company Commander, with Don Henderson getting the Company Executive Officer's slot. This was a surprise since I thought George Porter would have received one of the top two slots, but instead he received First Platoon Leader. He was sharp in the military stuff, and I assumed they must have wanted him in a position to teach freshmen during Cadre. He wasn't exactly thrilled about it, yet was glad to at least be an officer. Al Rosamino took the Academic Officer's slot, and Bill Kay, George Porter's roommate, was the new Athletic Officer.

After all of the positions were announced, it was easy to see that some were quite pleased, while others were equally disappointed. There were always more qualified and deserving senior cadets than officer slots to place them in. Feelings were usually hurt and accusations of under-the-table dealings ran rampant. Some of the time the politics and deal making did influence the results, but most cadets accepted it, and viewed it as a taste of the real world that they would face after graduation. Whether in the military or in some large corporate structure, promotions work pretty much the same way. But for those who came up short, it was still a huge letdown.

The rank selection process moved on, and junior rank boards soon cranked up. I was anxious, and considered the situation as life or death. I had invested everything, devoting almost a year and a half to the prospect of making Drill. Now was the critical moment of truth to qualify.

I was scheduled for a rank board interview in front of a panel of TAC officers and cadets who had already secured a high-ranking senior staff position. I was nervous, but concentrated on looking calm and composed. There were a lot of people in the room, and the interview moved quickly, lasting only about ten minutes. I assumed that most of the information that really counted was already there in front of them, including records on academics, discipline, and peer ratings. Most of the questions posed were about leadership and goals. They even asked me what rank I hoped to obtain. I shot high, though I knew there was little chance. I gave R Company First Sergeant as my first choice, and Company Assistant First Sergeant as my second. I said that if I had to, I would settle for Cadre Platoon Sergeant.

An immediate response came back from a cadet member of the panel, saying "Sounds to me like you're going out for Sword Drill."

I laughed a bit, and then indicated that I hoped I could. The same individual returned with the statement, "You know that doesn't matter here," and I replied that I indeed understood, and further stated that I felt my performance record was in itself enough to justify any one of the positions. It may have been a bold, even somewhat arrogant statement, but I knew that I had to present myself that way. I had to believe I was qualified, and pass that belief on to the selection board.

At the conclusion of the interview, I left the room feeling as if I had adequately presented myself, and that there was nothing else I could have done. I went back to the barracks, and I started the excruciating wait.

The next day, various announcements of rank began to trickle in. The first were those going to the Regimental and Battalion Staff NCO slots. As with the seniors, I was very disappointed to find that none of my classmates in R had made Regimental Staff, and that Jim Pearl from T Company, who was also a roach, had received the position of 4th Battalion Sergeant Major. I had hoped that either Burn or Rosellini might have gotten it, opening up one of the company slots. Instead the opportunity was created for someone in T since Pearl would have surely filled a top company slot over there.

To my bad luck and misfortune, there would be no juniors leaving R Company, making the competition stiff for the highest slots that remained. All of them would now be filled on mainly the decisions of the company senior staff of Lonnie Mauldin, Don Henderson, and the company TAC Officer, Captain Donnel. I felt pretty good about my chances since Mauldin and I had always gotten along. He also was very much aware that I was going out for Sword Drill. He saw me roaching, and had to remember me helping George Porter out during the Fourteen Nights. I felt confident, yet I knew that someone, whether it was Burn, Rosellini, Davis, or myself, was going to be greatly disappointed. For all I knew, there might even be a dark horse to take more than one of us out.

Word passed through the company that there would be an afternoon meeting in Jenkins Hall between the rising officers in R and the Company TAC Officer. They would take the results of rank boards and sort through them to decide on the remaining junior positions. George Porter, being the Cadre Platoon Leader, was required to attend.

On his way to the meeting, Porter stopped by my room.

"Don't worry. I think you'll get what you want," said Porter.

"I wish I could be as confident," I replied nervously. "Somehow or another, everybody seems to get screwed in these things."

"I know, but your grades and performance are excellent. I just can't see how you can lose out. Besides, even though this is really a decision between Lonnie, Don, and Captain Donnel, I'll still at least be sitting in there and can put in a good word. Don't sweat it. Go take a run. Hopefully there'll be good news waiting when you get back."

"You've gotta be kidding. I know you're giving me good advice, but it's just too important. I think I'll just wait right here."

"OK then, I'll see ya later."

"Watch out for me!"

"OK," laughed George as he exited the door.

The meeting was to start at 1600. Although I believed that the board would consider the facts carefully, I hoped that their decisions would not be based on old conclusions. I knew Lonnie Mauldin would take the process seriously, and so would Captain Donnel.. I just hoped that the meeting would not drag on all afternoon, leaving me to wait and wonder in agony. My roommate Larry also had the meeting on his mind. Like everyone else he had a stake in the matter, and wondered if he would come out on the winning or losing end.

"I guess our lives are in the hands of a bunch of assholes now, huh?" he asked to help ease the tension.

"I'm afraid so," I replied.

"We'll know in a little while what's going to happen, and maybe this is a bad time to bring this up, but you know as soon as rank is announced, there'll be a lot of quick decisions made. Maybe it's premature, but do you wanna be roommates again next year?"

"Sure," I said.

"But we don't know what rank you're gonna get or if I will even get it at all. If you should luck out and get First Sergeant or Assistant First Sergeant, you will probably want to room with whoever gets the one you don't."

"Let's just see what rank we get, and if it's possible, then we'll room together."

"OK," said Larry with hesitance, "but you know that most everyone has already decided who their roommate is going to be, so if you end up having to room with someone else, it's going to leave me stranded. You know what I mean?"

"I guess I do."

"All of the good guys will have roommates and I'll be stuck with some slob who snores all night."

"Look, don't worry about it."

"Easy for you to say. Not only am I probably going to get screwed getting rank, but I'm also not gonna have a roommate for next year."

"Damn son, I'm the one that's supposed to be nervous here. Hell, we may both end up as privates."

I couldn't believe how Larry was so obsessed with the roommate issue. I took it as a compliment that he could put up with me for another year, but also knew that I usually blitzed the room for every SMI and always kept everything perfectly neat. It also helped that I usually left the room during every ESP to go study in another building, leaving him with the room to himself. Larry obviously had it pretty good, and wanted to take no risks in losing a good setup in exchange for a troublemaker or pig.

But to me the roommate issue seemed trivial at the moment, especially when compared to the anticipation and hopes I had concerning rank and Sword Drill. The wait made minutes seem like hours as Larry and I grew impatient to hear the results. By 1700 I was racking my brain with scenarios, and I prayed that good news would soon arrive.

Finally, around twenty minutes after five, after what seemed like an eternity, I watched as my door opened and in walked Porter. He was neither smiling nor frowning as he moved into the room. He had a serious look on his face, and I wanted to grab him and choke whatever information he had out of him. I was jittery, and wanted to hear the right answer, but seriously feared the somber look on his face. My confidence said he was playing with me, but I was in no mood for jokes.

"What about it?" I said as I stood up in my chair.

George just said, "I'm sorry John, but it didn't work out."

"Don't kid around," I said smiling. "This is serious."

309

"I'm being serious," answered George. "You didn't get the rank."

I couldn't believe what I heard. I had not gotten the rank?

Larry immediately yelled, "What do you mean he didn't get the rank? He was a top runner for First Sergeant."

"You're right," said George answering Larry. "He was in the top running alright. As a matter of fact, it looked really good for him. And just as we had suspected, it had boiled down to Burn, Rosellini, Davis, and him.

"I can't believe what I'm hearing," I said.

"The board got into a discussion as to how the three positions would be filled by the four of you."

"Did they not consider Sword Drill?" asked Larry.

"You know that's not supposed to be a part of it, but it was mentioned. It obviously didn't make any difference."

"What happened?" I asked as I trembled.

"I really hate to tell ya' this John. You're just not going to believe it."

"What?" I yelled, now obviously quite upset.

"Your name was first to be eliminated from the running."

"Why? What did I do to deserve that?"

"Again, you're not going to believe this, but sitting in on the meeting was...well...Kevin Schmidt."

"Kevin Schmidt?" I yelled. "What was that asshole doing there?"

"I'm not really sure, it's just when the whole matter of the four of you being considered for the three positions came up, Schmidt said that he wanted to speak with Captain Donnel and Lonnie Mauldin for a second in private. They walked over to a corner to talk and then returned to announce that you were eliminated from being considered."

"That asshole!" I screamed as I was quickly slipping into a rage. "That mother fucking asshole!" I reared back and hit the full press with my fist. "How could he do this?" I yelled. "That son of bitch is a graduating senior. He had no damn business in that meeting. Who in the hell let him in? Damn, why did Captain Donnel and Lonnie

Mauldin listen to that jerk? He had no right."

I moved into a full-fledged rage, something that neither George nor Larry had ever seen out from me. Obviously, my heart was broken. Everything I had worked and hoped for was now gone.

"Then who got the positions?" yelled Larry.

"Burn got First, Rosellini is Assistant, and Davis got Cadre Platoon."

"I can't believe it," I said while wailing away on the full press, hitting it each time squarely with my fist, mad as a hornet. "That stupid asshole Yankee son-of-a-bitch Schmidt! Why can't he mind my own damn business?"

As soon as the words left my mouth, I turned to see Kevin Schmidt walking into my room. My eyes nearly fell out of my head. In behind him entered Carl Andrews who was the current First Sergeant of T. They came in without knocking and stood right behind George Porter staring at me, obviously arriving in time to hear every word I had just said. Schmidt even had a smile on his face, and the blatant nerve of the asshole immediately consumed me. This prick had screwed me over like no one ever had, and now he was in my room to rub it in? My fists immediately balled up, and I felt myself moving towards him to knock every tooth out of his head.

"Boy, you've got some kinda fucking nerve showing up here," I said.

"Why do you say that?" replied Kevin, still smiling with a sick grin.

"You asshole. It's not enough that you can just screw me over, but now you want to come here and rub my face in it."

I could see that not only was Kevin Schmidt smiling, but so was his audience Carl Andrews. They both somehow seemed to think that the whole matter was humorous. I could remember that Andrews was a real good Yankee friend of Schmidt's, and that they always shared rides to and from home during furloughs even though Schmidt was a year ahead of him. Schmidt had brought along his butt fuck buddy to help rub it in, or to obviously jump in between knowing that I would surely beat the snot out of him. Maybe Andrews hadn't thought clearly. I now had nothing to lose, and I was more than willing to also kick his ass in the process.

Larry and George knew that I was riding an uncontrollable rage. They too couldn't believe that Schmidt was actually crazy enough to come to my room right after doing such a dirty deed. But George spoke up knowing that at any second something bad was going to happen, and in his most serious tone asked, "What are you doing here Kevin, and with Carl with you? I think O'Bryan is mad enough as it is."

"Mad? Look," said Kevin laughing and looking at me, "I know you really wanted one of those three positions, but my buddy Carl here found himself in a real pickle. Seems that dumb shit Pearl in T Company would rather have the First Sergeant position in his own company instead of leaving for the Battalion Sergeant Major job. I told him I thought you were the best man for the job anyway. I just wanted to bring him over to properly introduce you to him."

George, Larry, and I stood there with our mouths wide open and our eyes looking like plates. Carl was laughing hard, and calmly turned to Kevin and asked, "Does he always cuss so much?"

Kevin smiled and answered, "I don't know. Maybe he's just a home boy too and wants to stay in the company."

I just stood there realizing I needed to breathe, having gone from rage to complete confusion. Carl could not stop laughing, but straightened himself out enough to say, "Just answer the question, O'Bryan. Will you be my Battalion Sergeant Major?"

Still shocked beyond belief, I mumbled the word "Yes," which immediately made Schmidt smile. I began to shake my head in disbelief, then Carl grabbed Kevin and said, "Come on, I gotta go tell the other guys about this one."

The two turned and walked out of the room and started heading down the gallery. Not saying anything, I ran to the door and watched as they started walking back towards T Company. Carl was still laughing loudly, and turned to Kevin and said, "Stupid Yankee asshole son-of-a-bitch?" He then laughed harder, almost cackling. "I always knew you were a Yankee, and an asshole, and stupid, but not a son-of-a-bitch? That means that your mother was a dog."

"My daddy didn't think so," said Kevin as they moved away, "and besides, I had Gold Stars last semester, asshole."

Their voices faded to mumbles, and they continued to laugh as they turned at the end of the gallery. I just stared in shock. I didn't know what to say. Battalion Sergeant Major was the highest-ranking junior in all of Fourth Battalion, and here I had been worried about making Platoon Sergeant?

Larry immediately spoke up yelling and I was really confused to see him mad. "You piece of shit! I knew it. I knew you would screw me over. This means I don't have a roommate now."

I turned away, obviously too baffled at the moment to worry about roommate problems. But for Larry, it was the only thing on his mind.

"You douche bag, now look what you've done," continued Larry.

Still dazed, I slowly began to smile. Larry started moving towards me saying, "Hey man, don't worry about me. You're a big shot now!" But as the words exited his mouth, Larry grabbed me by the throat and pushed me through the closed screen door, causing it to swing wide open. He was actually mad about the whole incident.

"Damn it, now look where I'm stuck," screamed Larry.

"Calm down you maniac," I grunted while trying to get loose.

Larry then went from a choke to a headlock, and then twisted me down on the gallery.

"Man, are you fucked up?" I yelled. "Let go of me."

"I'll let go of you alright, right after I kill ya. I always knew you'd screw me over."

We began to wrestle pretty hard as I struggled to get that nitwit off of me so I could celebrate. George Porter was just standing there in the doorway, having just witnessed the craziest set of circumstances he had ever seen. As he watched the two of us wrestle he started to walk away down the gallery. He passed one of his classmates who had arrived after having heard all the cussing and yelling, and was staring at Larry and me trying to kill each other on the gallery floor. Smiling at the sight of it all he asked Porter, "What's going on here?"

Half dazed and not even breaking stride, George simply answered, "This place is a friggin' loony bin!"

CHAPTER 26

Word traveled fast about the results of the junior rank boards, and as usual, there were several guys pretty ticked off with coming up short. Larry, however, was pleased to find that he had made Squad Sergeant. He and I agreed, after he managed to calm his ass down, that we could still room together. I would still have to leave the company and physically relocate to the Staff area that was on the other side of the battalion from R. But I would be the only junior on staff, so I would have to bring a roommate.. Larry was willing to move rather than take a chance finding a new roommate, which was a good deal for us both.

It was also nice that everything had worked out so well for Danny, Hank, Chris, and me. We all deserved rank, and all managed to basically get what we wanted. We were lucky though that Jim Pearl was so adamant about staying in his company, which from time to time was the case with some cadets. For me it seemed as if the weight of the world had been lifted from my shoulders as my greatest hurdle had been crossed. I still faced exams, the Stadium Party, summer, the 14 Nights, and cuts before I could even get close to my ultimate dream, but at least now I knew I was qualified.

When exams arrived, I had to put my victory aside and forget about Drill for a while. Academics were a big enough challenge to deal with at the moment, so I had to quickly regained my focus, and as usual, use every free minute to study. I had to. It was a monumental task just making it through the huge tests in my highly technical courses. With rank in hand, I did feel less pressure. But my goal of getting Gold Stars was still intact, and I had managed to hold on to my mid-term 4.0 GPR to that point. I still wanted Stars badly, even if it only happened once during my entire cadet career. With a perfect GPR in place, this would be my best opportunity to get them.

As each exam came and went, I felt satisfied with my performance, and my confidence continued to build. After turning in my last quiz, I was as usual relieved and completely worn out. I had already received some of my test scores back, and was confident my goal could be reached. But just after my last test I walked to check the posted results, and my confidence was shattered when I found my first B. I had obviously choked on an exam where my average was already borderline, just barely hovering above the A cut off point. The exam, however, killed that thin margin, and my perfect 4.0. This left me with a 3.83, which still at least had me in the range for Gold Stars. But it wasn't over, and one more B in anything would end it. I had two more exams that I had not received the results of, and the only thing I could do was wait and hope.

The day after my last test was a busy one. First, there was knob recognition. I really enjoyed the event, remembering back to the previous year when I had gone through the same ordeal. It seemed proper to make their last few minutes as freshmen a real challenge. But after the knobs were racked to the extreme, then finally recognized by receiving handshakes from all of the upperclassmen, there was a moment of anticipation as we waited for some freshmen to come up and slug someone. But like the year before, it just never happened. It seemed the combination of exhaustion and knowing that their life of hell was now in the past helped to put aside ill feelings. I could think back to how much I truly hated Schmidt. Even though he had treated me wrong, I was awfully glad that I never gave into anger and punched him out. Though often times strange, The Citadel's 4th Class System was a unique and cherished experience that one had to pay dearly to receive. It was that personal investment out of one's own hide that seemed to make it such a treasure, and it was something no one could ever take from you.

But the event marked the end of their suffering and provided them with the ability to wear their newly acquired Corporal Wings or threes. It also meant that the rising upper classes would also pin on their new rank. The graduating seniors were basically out of the way now, and although there was still time left in the year, it was time for them to step aside and cruise. All they really wanted to do anyway was enjoy their big moment.

There was also the Stadium Party, which would take place right after recognition. I was nervous, and got the jitters each time I thought about it. According to Porter, this would be a real taste of what the 14 Nights would be like. Rank was out, and only those actually qualified would be there, and indeed there were those who didn't make the grade. After Spring Roach we were down to 38, but 7 more bit the dust after falling short on rank, and we were now down to 31. The old Drill would know that the fat had been trimmed, and that those remaining had to be serious. It was time to reveal what really lay ahead in the fall.

At 0930, we met near the bleachers on the parade ground where the old Drill formed us into a platoon. They immediately started giving us hell and yelled at us to brace and keep our eyes straight ahead. We got a speech from the Commander, Richard Kraft, who observed how the ranks had indeed thinned, and that those of us who remained would need to get serious as the real tests of desire were about to begin. He told us to get smart and use the summer to train and practice what we had learned during Spring Roach, that in the fall, there would be little time to do much of either. We had to be ready the day we returned. He told us what uniform items and equipment we would need, and emphasized that it would be too late come August to start getting them together. Finally, he warned us that the fun and games of the process were over. Sword Drill would turn into the serious challenge it was always meant to be.

Kraft gave the command for our platoon to move out saying, "1980 Roaches! Forward march! Double time, march!"

And that began a two hour PT session I would never forget. It was mid morning in May, and already in the low 80's. We ran around campus in a deceiving jog that lasted about twenty minutes, and just when I started to think it wasn't going to be such a bad day after all, the pace picked up dramatically. We turned to go out Hagood Gate, then jumped into a near sprint as we ran down the avenue towards Johnson-Hagood Stadium. It was only about a

317

quarter mile run, but the blistering pace, after already having run for a while, hit us all pretty hard. Only half of the old Drill had run with us to get there, and the other half was waiting; they immediately took over and tore into us, yelling for us to form back up as we stopped and collided into a loose platoon of gasping bodies. The yelling still hadn't stopped when we started into the stadium through a roll-up service door, and moved through a portal out to the seating area.

This would be my first time to ever run wind sprints on bleachers. We ran up the aluminum bench seats of the stadium to the top, where our legs quickly began to throb with each step up, and then had to concentrate hard as we ran back down. I was sure someone was going to miss with his footing and bust his ass, but instead we all just slowed down to a pace that our legs could manage. The old Drill yelled like mad as we strained, but even the yelling couldn't make us go any faster.

Just when I thought guys would start to fall out, they took us back down under the stadium and made us all hang from the girder beams underneath. It was hard to do, but at least we weren't running. It didn't take long before grips weakened and those who let go fell to an angry, yelling group who made them start doing push-ups. We did them until our arms felt like rubber, and then changed to doing sit-ups until my stomach muscles were in a knot.

We then broke up into small groups, and the individual members ran us through every nook and cranny of the stadium facility. We were an hour into our experience when I thought I would die from thirst, and our hosts then decided to take us back to the bleachers for more up and down trips. I knew then that my existing need for liquids was far from reaching its peak.

Some roaches were faring better than others, and I felt I was doing well comparatively. I soon saw one guy surrounded by screaming old Drill members, as he seemed to struggle just to keep a walking pace. They soon had us running while carrying things such as trashcans, sections of spare bleacher seating, you name it.

Then they moved us onto the field where they made us do

piggyback and wheel barrow races on the grass. They then moved us back to the bleachers so we could do push-ups while angled down the slope. From the difficulty I was having, and the amount of yelling and grunts from the strain, it was easy to see they were killing us all.

We were then formed in our platoon, and in an act of mercy we each got a piece of ice placed in our mouth as we stood there bracing and panting for air. It was heaven to just stop, but a short-lived pleasure as we took off again in a platoon run around the football field. We were told we were going to run 80 laps to represent our class, but I knew they had to bullshitting. Not one among us could survive such a thing, no matter how badly we wanted Sword Drill. I just kept telling myself that it would soon be over, and I would have the whole summer off to recover. But the ice had done little to address my thirst, and as I noticed guys falling out and way behind the platoon, I wondered just how much more of this I could take. If the old Drill was trying to make us think that August would bring a killer challenge, their point was well made.

During our fifth lap around the field, it was evident by the scattered stragglers that only a few of us were able to stay with the front pack. We stopped and waited for the strays to form back up, and it seemed clear that they had gotten out of us all they were going to get. I knew it had to be after 1100, and that they couldn't keep us out much longer.

We started back towards campus in a slow jog, which was actually hell to maintain in our whipped condition. When we stopped at the bleachers where we had originally started, the old Drill took their last opportunity to yell at us as we stood there dripping in sweat, fighting for precious air. Kraft warned us that our little jog was pale in comparison to one of the 14 Nights, and that the old Drill had merely done us a favor to warn us of what was to come in the fall. We were then told to immediately head back to our battalions to shower and dress for noon formation, and that we were not to be late. With our dismissal, our contact with the old Drill ended until the

319

next school year.

Though I had considered myself to be in great shape, I felt like hell as I struggled up the stairs towards my room. As I moved I passed some of the freshmen who were already tooling around on the galleries, probably just because they could. Few knew where I had been, and I talked with no one as I rushed to get showered and back into my nasties. Larry showed me a set of Sergeant Major collar insignia on my bed as I rushed, and said that the past year's owner, Chip Walsh, who was being promoted to Regimental Adjutant, had left them for me to wear as a continuing tradition of passing on the same set worn by others throughout the years. It was an appreciated gesture for him to honor the tradition, especially since Walsh was also a member of the '79 Drill.

I could see Squad Sergeant insignia already on Larry's collar as he explained that I was expected to be wearing my new rank at noon. With no pomp or circumstance, I removed my corporal wings and pinned the significantly larger Sergeant Major emblem in place. I could hear the first bugle of formation, and was moving down the gallery as I changed the insignia on my cunt cap, and struggled to make my aching legs get me down the stairs.

The moment I stepped out onto the quad I saw strange reactions from classmates and guys from the other classes. They would start smiling when they saw me with my new decorations, although I could not see them myself as I walked around.

But things were still awkward, and I wasn't sure if I was to stay in the company or go over to the area reserved for 4th Battalion Staff. It really hit home that I was confused when time came to line up, but once I saw the new battalion staff forming up in the sally port, I knew then that I had better get my butt over there. But as I walked, I got a feeling of separation as I left the group I had grown to respect and appreciate as friends. I felt I was somehow walking away from them forever, or at least for a year. I glanced back, wondering if my friends would forget about me.

I arrived at the sally port to find myself surrounded by the new

Battalion Staff. They were all there, the officers, and the newly recognized upperclassman, the Administrative Corporal. If I thought I was nervous, this poor ex-knob of two hours had to feel like a chicken in Ethiopia.

The first to greet me was Kevin Schmidt's buddy Carl Andrews, the new Battalion Commander. It was easy to see why he got the position. Most knew he was smart academically, but he was also well spoken and had a knack for getting along with people. He seemed to possess all the leadership abilities expected from someone going into such a high-ranking position. He introduced me to the others on staff, and welcomed me as the only junior they would be working with. I appreciated the reception, and started to feel a bit more comfortable about my new place within the Corps of Cadets.

We moved awkwardly through our first formation and then marched over to the mess hall as the new 4th Battalion Staff. The old seniors from 4th marched over separately as one large group, having stepped out of the way of those who were now in charge. It had to be an emotional moment for them, as the reality of an approaching end to their four-year journey was upon them.

Following mess, I was still whipped from the Stadium Party, and felt the need to just go back and hit the rack for a while. But I also had a burning desire to know the final results of the semester. Gold Stars were hanging in the balance, and curiosity alone would power my painful legs over to the engineering building to face my moment of truth.

I was a bit anxious, yet I didn't want to put off knowing. I decided to first check the exam I felt had been the least problem, and was pleased to see that there was indeed an A right beside my cadet ID number. This only made me more nervous. Everything now rested on the last course, and I knew that I had only a borderline A going into exams. I had felt pretty good about my effort, but knew that academics were just like baseball in Yogi Berra's eye in that "it ain't over til' it's over."

I walked quickly over to the other classroom. In an instant I saw my ID number, and couldn't help but see the A gleaming right beside it. I broke down in a squat as if I had just scored a game-winning touchdown, and began jumping and dancing around knowing that I had indeed succeeded. I had a final GPR of 3.83. Gold Stars were mine. I threw my arms up in the air, and yelled. I would wear those golden jewels as proudly as I would my Sergeant Major stripes.

"Damn," I said loudly.

I couldn't help but think that I was the luckiest guy in the world to have so many good things happen.

Suddenly a door opened, and a professor stuck his head out to see what was the commotion.

"You alright son?"

I quickly gained my composure and answered, "Sorry Sir, everything is just A-OK! Well, I must be going now. Please, do have a good day."

I turned and walked away, only to hear the professor say, "crazy cadets" and then close his door.

As I walked back to the battalion, a saying came to me that one of my professors had brought out in class in that "luck was when preparation meets opportunity." I thought back to all the weeknights and weekends that I spent studying while most everyone else was out drinking and having a good time. I had truly sacrificed and made the preparations such that the opportunity presented was fully taken advantage of. I now had one more major task ahead of me. I had to make Sword Drill. I just had to. It would be a challenge as big as anything I had ever taken on. But now I possessed the confidence that I could do anything. I had the experience of victories that would push me through whatever the old Drill had to dish out. I knew I could make it.

I spent that evening with the three guys who seemed to be the most appropriate, Danny Burn, Hank Rosellini, and Chris Davis. Like me, Chris was dragging his ass from the punishment the old Drill had dished out earlier in the day, but it wasn't enough to steal our desire to cut loose. Big John's was calling, and with no classes and no responsibilities, we savored the rare opportunity to just sit around and drink a few beers as ranking juniors. We were each happy for the other, and felt fortunate that no one was left disappointed.

Immediately following graduation the next day, I hung around for an hour or so to fulfill my obliged duties as Battalion Sergeant Major, and watched as cadets literally ran out through the sally port as if on fire, ready to go home for the long summer's break. I had thought little about the upcoming summer, except for the running, weight lifting, and practicing of my sword manual to be ready in the fall. I assumed otherwise that it would be a really boring three months in Kingstree with nothing but farm work to help occupy my time. It was summer furlough, and the hell of being at a maximum-security college was now curtailed. What was weird was that I almost didn't want to leave.

I said goodbye to many of my friends for the summer, and to most of the seniors as they left for good. I even saw Kevin Schmidt standing with his family who came down from Yankeeville to see him walk across the stage. I walked over and shook his hand and wished him well in his new career as a Naval officer, and he smiled and wished me luck with Sword Drill. He had been both my nightmare and dream maker, and I never even got to ask him why.

I walked out of the battalion at noon when there were only the Supply Sergeants and a few stragglers left, then got into my car and started driving off campus. As I drove through the main gate, I knew that I had accomplished more than I had ever imagined I could during my sophomore year, and I looked forward to my return in the fall to hopefully claim the true prize. Everything else was just the result of wanting to make Sword Drill.

CHAPTER 27

When I got home, my parents and I sat at the table and talked for an hour. They were floored with my report on academic performance. They questioned me in disbelief, and wondered what had come over me. They struggled with emotions of overwhelming pride mixed with wonder. They worried that maybe I was getting just too serious about things. They were concerned about my lack of a social life, and the drastic transformation from hell raiser to model student. It was a radical swing that was almost too good to be true. It actually scared them. There had to be a catch to all of this.

Even through questions of my uncanny evolution, my folks were really proud of me. It was great news, something sorely needed at a time when things seemed to be going so wrong in the O'Bryan family. Apparently Dad had to make a decision just after I had returned to school following spring break. He had reached his fill with preparations dragging for the upcoming planting season. He approached Charles and made it clear he could no longer wait for him, and would be taking back full control of the farm. Too many critical responsibilities had been put on the back burner so that Charles could tend to his fish business.

Charles, as I guessed, was outraged. He insisted that he had everything under control, and set out to prove he could keep up. He concentrated on getting the equipment repaired and ready. He really worked hard, knowing he couldn't lose control of what he had gained. But to make up for lost time, he had to put every waking minute into the farm, and had to ignore the catfish. Unfortunately, an aerator pump failed that provided water circulation and critical oxygen to the two fish tanks. The pump casing had cracked, and went unchecked while Charles labored to catch up. The tanks drained completely overnight, resulting in a lot of dead catfish. It was nothing less than a disaster.

Charles was livid. He blamed everyone but himself. He claimed that he would have had things under control had he not been pushed to get the equipment ready for planting season. He said he would have noticed the pump in time to save the majority of the fish.. But he didn't, and the few remaining fish wouldn't bring in enough money to justify the operating expenses to raise them. He would have to pay out thousands more to get a new stock.

His catfish became some very expensive fertilizer for the fields. Dad and Grandfather were furious. It was the kind of problem they expected would happen. Charles was angry with them for not lending the kind of support he needed to make the operation work. It seemed everyone was upset or mad. But the real concern was over whether the investment in the buildings, equipment, and fish would ever pay off.

I myself couldn't believe the stroke of misfortune. Even with our miserable past, I had so badly hoped that Charles' venture would work, for everyone's sake. But it appeared the first problem would be a costly one. Thousands of dollars were lost in those little dead catfish, and profits seemed so far away since Charles was basically starting all over again.

Even though I truly cared about the difficulties of the family, there was nothing I could do other than lend a hand to make a positive contribution towards straightening the problems out. I could actually see where the hard labor and heat of farm-work would lend itself well as the perfect training ground for Sword Drill. Yet, it wouldn't be enough. I was still going to work out and run everyday like I never had before. I knew that no matter how good a shape I was in, the old Drill would push me way beyond my limits. I could only hope to extend those limits, hopefully far enough out so that the old Drill would have to work hard to get to me.

I started work first thing Monday morning. Dad put me on a tractor pulling a disk making the first cut on the land since the previous year's crop. Most of time I was alone, working in some field in a distant corner of the farm, thus running into Charles only occasionally. There were few words said between us, but I could see that he was still sore over the whole situation with Dad, and probably even suspected that I was supporting our father's side. But I was comfortable with the arrangement, as staying away from each other made it easier for us both.

The endless days of plowing soon got pretty boring, and the nights weren't much better either. I concentrated on running, lifting, and practicing my sword manual, and though I stayed busy, I really felt lonely. I tried to look at it as a great opportunity to train, and remind myself that my sacrifices usually worked out for the best. But I indeed had no social life, and hardly anyone, other than my parents, to talk to. I hadn't heard of any parties, and I had lost touch completely with nearly all of my high school friends. It seemed no one even knew I was back in town. It was as if every social tie I had once possessed had been severed. I avoided thinking about it as I was beginning to hate even being home.

My first five weeks of summer passed with few events. It was in the sixth week that it would all change, and my arm's length relationship with Charles would come to a screeching halt. It all started when a truckload of fish food arrived. It rolled up in the yard about mid-afternoon when most of the workers were scattered throughout the fields. Realizing how much work it would be to unload the hundreds of bags, Charles decided that it was time for the "college boy" to do some real work for a change. The flat bed trailer had to be unloaded quickly so the driver could move on, and in his scheme of things, Charles decided he could only spare one other man to help me.

I started unloading by myself, and after a while Charles rode up with Isaiah, who was probably the weakest worker on the farm. Small in frame, the guy had a heart of gold, and what he lacked in strength, he made up for with determination. He would always do what was asked of him, constantly pushing himself to the limit so as to always do a fair share. But in his efforts to keep up with others, he once pushed himself a bit too hard and injured his back. Lifting was hard for him, and Charles knew it. I would have very little help unloading hundreds of bags of Charles' fish feed.

"Here's your help," laughed Charles as Isaiah got out of his truck. "You fellows hurry it up now. This man's got to get on down the road."

Charles chuckled as he drove away. The driver of the truck found a cool spot under an oak tree, and sat down for a quick nap while we worked. He was not in that big of a hurry, at least not enough to want to help unload on a really hot day.

Charles was an asshole and I knew it. But all he had done was thrown the rabbit into the briar patch. I guess he thought I would be ticked off, but he couldn't have picked a better task for me, even with the heat. This was simply an opportunity for me to lift weights and build some stamina.

Isaiah and I began to work, and I was like a human forklift. I loved the opportunity, and was almost running as I picked up two bags at a time, one on each arm, and carried them to the edge of the truck, then would hand them down to Isaiah who would stack them in a row. It was an inefficient method of doing it, but it seemed the only way with just two guys.

After about thirty minutes, we only had about a third of the trailer unloaded. I then came up with another idea. The shed we were unloading the sacks into was large, and since the truck driver was asleep, I took the liberty of repositioning his rig. I backed it in at a different angle so that I could unload off of the side. I could already see that Isaiah's back was hurting him. He probably had a pinched disk, and pain was obviously shooting through him each time he would try to lift a bag. If my idea worked out, I would provide him some welcomed relief.

The feed was packaged well in strong sewn, triple skinned paper bags. I figured I could pick them up one at a time and throw them off the trailer right into position. Isaiah would have nothing to do but make sure they were positioned flat after they landed.. Seemed like a stroke of genius to me. Besides, I would get one hell of a workout.

I took off my shirt, and then started turning bags of fish food into projectiles. Working the smarter way, I was able to unload the truck at twice the speed and save Isaiah's back at the same time. It was working so well it was funny. Isaiah could see that I had both the strength and stamina to keep the bags flying. I was feeling good and cocky, yelling and talkin' trash as I moved. Isaiah decided to contribute some James Brown tunes as he positioned my less than precise shots, and the work soon became a show. Even the truck driver woke up and took pleasure in watching me perform. Soon Isaiah began to dance as he sang. Feeling good from the workout, I did the same. The work pace continued at a blistering rate, and the driver swore it was the fastest he had ever seen any one man unload a truck. I was enjoying myself as I impressed the hell out of my audience.

I could hear a vehicle driving up, and looked up to see that it was Charles' truck, but didn't break stride. I had less than fifty bags to go, which at the rate I was moving, I would be finished in no time. Charles had driven up fully expecting to find me completely worn out, along with Isaiah sitting down since he knew his back would have never been able to take the strain. But what he found was a truck that was almost unloaded, and I in an excellent mood, actually having a good time as I threw the heavy sacks across the open space right into position. Charles was furious. His plan had backfired. I was having a ball, and Isaiah was tickled by the whole situation. He did, however, stop singing and dancing when Charles had arrived on the scene.

"Hey, would you mind telling me what the hell's going on here?" shouted Charles.

"Just unloading your fish food, man," I answered, still be-bopping around and throwing sacks.

"What the hell do you think you're doing throwing my sacks of feed? You'll break 'em open."

"You see any busted sacks?" I asked.

"That's beside the point."

"No it's not. Why don't you get back in your truck and go on back

328

to what you were doing. Me and my man Isaiah here will be through in about ten minutes. As a matter of fact, you can go get us a couple of Pepsi's for having worked so efficiently."

Charles was really mad now, not only had his plan backfired, but also I was being a smartass towards him in front of Isaiah and the truck driver.

"Listen here, college boy," fired Charles. "I'm just about tired of your shit."

"Who cares?" I said, and I picked up another sack and threw it over in place.

"I don't know what you think you're pulling here, but you need to remember one thing. I'm running this farm now, and I won't have you talking to me that way."

I picked up another sack and threw it over towards Isaiah. "Well tell me then Charles, how do you want me to talk to ya?"

"You know what I mean," said Charles. "Isaiah, walk over to the edge of the truck and let him hand you those sacks. Quit throwing them John!"

Charles had picked a bad time to mess with me. I was not only feeling cocky and fired up from the work out, but was also getting increasingly pissed. Not only did he lack appreciation for my effort, but also he was interfering with the most efficient unloading operation in the history of catfish food.

"Tell ya what boss," I said as I reached down and picked up another sack of fish food and held it up over my head, "If you think it's so damn easy, you catch 'em."

I then threw the sack down at him and hit Charles directly in the chest, knocking him squarely to the ground and almost knocking his breath out. I picked up another sack and nailed him again as he scrambled to get out of the way.

"Here's the next one," I said. "You're working too damn slow."

I threw another sack at him with Charles desperately jumping out of the way. The truck driver was in stitches, but Isaiah fought it, knowing his job was on the line.

"You're fired," yelled Charles. "I don't care if you are my brother. You're fired!"

"I'm not fired," I said picking up more ammunition, "I quit! Take your fuckin' fish food and shove it up your ass."

I began grabbing sacks of fish food and started side-slinging them off the trailer just as fast and as hard as I could in every direction, yelling as I did. Isaiah, the driver, and Charles all ran out of the way, seeing that I was basically going crazy. But the moment soon wore me down, and when I finally reached my capacity to throw, I jumped off of the back of the truck onto the pile of bags I had thrown at Charles.

"But before I walk off the job, I gotta unload one last sack."

I reached down and picked up a bag of fish food, grabbed the end of it, and ripped it open. I got a running start and threw the gaping bag right through the open door of Charles' truck where thousands of little pellets disbursed throughout it. Charles couldn't believe what I had done, yet he could see I was flaming, and knew better than to take me on.

I picked up my shirt and started walking towards the house. With some volume, I started singing the old Johnny Paycheck song "Take This Job and Shove It," leaving Charles standing there with his truck still running with the interior now decorated with fish food. The truck driver was literally rolling on the ground, about to split his sides from laughing so hard. It was a humiliating situation for Charles, but one he had asked for.

I soon found myself inside the house in front of my father, with Charles screaming away.

"Dad, it's just not fair I tell ya," said Charles. "He wants to make me look stupid in front of the men. I must keep their respect."

"What respect?" I said. "They all think you're an asshole."

"John!" scolded Dad.

"You see Dad? You see what I'm talking about?" charged Charles. "It's obvious that he wants to do nothing but cause trouble. Things are already bad enough around here for me as it is. You and

Grandpa don't support me with the catfish, and then want to raise hell about everything else I do on the farm, and now I've got John causing me trouble. You folks are just after me, and I don't have to stand for it."

Charles turned and started walking towards the door, but then stopped to turn around. "I'm telling you Dad, if I'm running this farm, then I say I don't need John around here causing trouble. Why don't you just go back to college and leave those of us who have to work for a living alone?"

Charles turned and stormed on out the door, almost knocking it off the hinges as he left.

"Listen John," said Dad calmly, "You shouldn't antagonize Charles like that."

"But Dad, Isaiah and I were working our butts off. Even the guy driving the truck said that we were doing it faster than anybody he'd ever seen."

"I understand that. It's just that Charles is under a lot of pressure, which I know is by his own doings...and...well, you don't have to tell me how difficult he's being with everybody."

"You know I want to cooperate Dad, but the more I try to contribute, the madder it makes Charles."

"I can see how that would be true with him."

"I think it's best if I just not hang around. Maybe I can get a job in Kingstree for the rest of the summer. That way I'll be out of Charles' hair."

"No son, you don't have to go to that extreme. Anyway, that may cause Charles even more embarrassment once the word gets out that you had to go get a job in town just to get away from him."

"I do have one other idea," I suggested.

"What is it?"

"Next fall I'll be trying out for the Junior Sword Drill, and it's going to take a tremendous amount of my time. If you think we can swing it financially, I could take Charles' suggestion and go back to Charleston to catch the second semester of summer school. I could take two courses and get ahead for next semester, and according to what I've heard, it's a laid back way to lighten your load. I also heard summer school is actually quite fun, and almost like a vacation."

"Oh really? Summer school like vacation?"

"You have to understand, the courses are still difficult, and the most you can take are three in one session. It'd be fine with me just to go and take two, and work at them kind of leisurely. What makes it so nice is that you're usually through with class by midday, and you have the rest of the afternoon and evening to knock around Charleston as a civilian, something we cadets rarely have an opportunity to do."

"That seems like a great idea. Not because I want you to leave here, but your mother and I have noticed you never have fun anymore. We're thrilled with your commitment and all, but son you need to take a break before you burn out. If you think that going to summer school would be like a vacation, then by all means, your mother and I are all for it."

"I'll call the school and see what the schedule is. Hopefully I'm not too late to sign up."

I immediately made a call to The Citadel and found that registration for summer school was a simple matter of showing up a few days before classes begin to pay for room and board and the cost of the courses. They said that summer school quarters were set up in one of the battalions, and that life was similar to that of a normal college dorm. Students were even allowed to wear civilian clothes. There was no military whatsoever, and the whole session was built around a very relaxed atmosphere. It seemed like an excellent opportunity to get ahead in my courses and to have some fun at the same time. I would also have access to the weight room in Deas Hall and all the other facilities that would be real assets in getting prepared for Drill.

I really had to rush to get my things together so I could leave the next day to get moved in, registered, and buy my books. Mom and Dad were sad to see me going away again, but pleased to know I would have an opportunity to spend some time in a more leisurely atmosphere. They knew I would study hard, and therefore insisted I not take any more than two classes. Leaving time for pleasure was a condition for me going. I laughed at the idea that they were pushing me to have more fun. It was amazing how times had changed.

CHAPTER 28

After making the familiar drive back to The Citadel, I found that third battalion had been set up as the barracks for summer school. Registration was a breeze, and it was far more pleasant than the hassle experienced during the regular year. With the limited course schedule and the small number in attendance during the summer, there were no lines or crowds and everything was hassle free. It actually felt weird to be tooling around The Citadel campus, walking wherever I wanted, including across the parade ground that was normally a senior privilege.

Ready to move in, I looked at the roster of those in the barracks to see whom I knew, and whom I might find as a potential roommate for the session. In my search I indeed found a few of my R Company classmates there, but they were already rooming with someone. I did luck out and found Albert Sessions whom I met in my ROTC class. He was rooming by himself, and was more than pleased to share, and I felt fortunate to room with such a compatible guy.

After hauling my stuff up from my car and unpacking, I immediately donned my workout clothes and took off towards the gym. For the first time ever, I had all the time I needed to lift like a madman. I enjoyed myself, pumping iron until my arms were about to fall off.

I arrived back at the barracks just in time to find Albert getting ready to go over to evening mess. I grabbed a quick shower then walked with him to the mess hall, which was now set up in a buffet style for summer. They provided pretty decent food for summer school, and it was all you could eat. This would be an asset as I worked out really hard. Sitting at the table, I could see lots of familiar faces from the Corps, and I knew the summer setting would provide an opportunity to meet other cadets whom I had little time to get to know during the regular year.

Several of the cadets at our table had been there first semester. I assumed they used summer school to make up courses they either failed or dropped during regular session, while some, like me, used it as an opportunity to get ahead.

After eating, Albert and I walked back to the battalion. On the way he asked, "You headin' out to Harry's tonight?"

"Harry's? What's Harry's?"

"Captain Harry's, down on Cumberland Street."

"Oh yeah, I've been there. I hadn't planned on it. You going?"

"Sure am. Cheapest beer in town, and I'm not sure if they've got a band tonight, but it's always the place to go in the summer."

"I'd be glad to tag along."

"That'll be great. Several of us'll probably go. It's gettin' to be a habit, you know?"

"Sounds good to me. I want to pull down some good grades while I'm here, but I also want to have a decent time."

"I want to have a great time while I'm here, and if I pass, that's fine too!" said Albert with a laugh.

It was easy to see why Albert was going to both sessions of summer school. He had his priorities set, but academics didn't rank highly among them.

Albert, myself, and several other guys made an early start towards Captain Harry's Blue Marlin bar. I knew I wouldn't stay out too late since the next day was the start of classes, but I had promised myself to take a more relaxed approach. I would do that, as long as I was sure to get an A in each course.

I really enjoyed myself while out, seeing a few of my friends from school, and lots of girls, those attending the various summer school courses and those home on summer break. I loved it. I had hair and was wearing civilian clothes. I felt near normal, and was surrounded by women. The summer nights of Charleston were alive, and for once, I was able to enjoy my furlough. Harry's didn't have a live band that evening, but they did have music playing through a stereo. The good tunes created a perfect atmosphere to shoot the breeze and mingle with friends in the warm summer night. It was such a pleasant feeling, I was actually sorry I hadn't come to previous summer school sessions. I really looked forward to the five weeks of two classes in the morning, working out in the afternoon, and then hitting the town to reclaim a part of my life I had abandoned.

The first weekend arrived with an air of excitement. There was so much happening. Albert was a live-in social director, who along with the others in the barracks, continually extended invitations to me to go to the beach, attend parties, hit the bars, or seek out whatever the most appealing event in Charleston was at the time. Never before did I have so many opportunities to meet girls, and under such favorable conditions. In Charleston, everyone understood what cadets were going through, and although we were different, we still seemed to fit right in to the summer crowd. In Kingstree, I always seemed to stand out like a sore thumb. Having restored my physique to premium condition, I actually felt that I was once again attractive, even with my still shorter than normal hair. Life was really good.

But I had to push myself to move aggressively with women, as I was still lacking total confidence, even though it seemed like all the pieces were in place. Opportunities for dates were there, but my period of inactivity had been too long. I was actually shy, and also in no hurry to rush into anything knowing that I had many more weeks still ahead of me. For the time being I found it satisfying enough just knowing I was able to play in the game. I was free, and able, and there was no need to hurry things.

When that first weekend was over, I knew for sure that I had died and gone to heaven. I was so very grateful to Charles. Had he not been such an asshole, I probably would have still been in Kingstree eating a daily ration of dust on a tractor and bored to insanity at night.

The next Monday brought back the routine of classes in the morning and studying and workouts during the afternoon. I started saving the workouts for last so I could give it all I had and not worry about being too tired to study. I worked every muscle in my body to the max. I even brought my curling bar from home, which allowed me to put a whole lot of time into working my arms. I was proud of them, and knew that the huge rocks under my skin were just what would be needed to get me through the 14 Nights.

After class on Tuesday I went to Deas Hall and put in a really kick-ass workout. I gave it everything, doing five sets of maximum weight with each exercise, leaving my curls to be handled back in my room.

Once back, I started a routine of memorizing formulas at my desk, then reciting them to myself as I pumped out yet another set of reps on my curl bar. It was an entertaining rhythm that worked both my brain and body at the same time. I felt good. I felt smart. I was moving forward.

I worked my arms until I thought their swollen veins would explode. I was about ready to quit when I heard my name being called out on the quad. I was sure it had to be Albert yelling, probably wanting me to throw him something, too lazy to climb the stairs to get it himself.

I strolled out onto the gallery, and looked over the rail down to the quad only to see that it was not Albert, but one of the guys employed to work the guardroom.

"John O'Bryan," yelled the voice from the quad.

"Yeah, over here!"

"You gotta visitor down here at the front sally port."

"OK, I'll be right down," I answered, not knowing who in the heck it could possibly be. I grabbed a towel to wipe off some of the sweat as I was heading down. When I walked out the front sally port, I saw several people standing there. There were two guys who appeared to be summer school students, and a female that was an extremely good looking blonde, yet I didn't recognize her at all, and knew that if I had ever met her before, I would have never forgotten it.

"John, is that you?" I stopped cold. This girl knows me? I quickly turned and looked back at her answering, "Yes, it's me. Who are you?"

"You don't know who I am?" she asked.

This was fun. I walked over closer to her and looked at her square in her face.

"I don't know," I answered. "I'm sorry, did we meet this weekend?"

I knew I had not met this girl. She was gorgeous. I could never have forgotten her, even if I had tried.

"John, I'm Cindy. Cindy Johnson."

For a second I had to think of who Cindy Johnson was, and then it all of a sudden hit me. This was Cindy Johnson? This was the fat girl in high school who had helped me study? My mouth dropped open in shock.

"No," I said. "It can't be."

Cindy started smiling and simply said, "Well look at you. You don't look the same either."

I hardly heard a word she was saying. This girl was an angel, and by far the prettiest female I had ever seen. Yet, as I looked at her face, I could indeed see a faint resemblance.

"Cindy, I don't know what to say. What happened?"

"What do you mean what happened?" laughed Cindy. "Oh you mean the weight? Oh, well, when I went to Columbia College, I kind of went on a diet."

"Holy shit!" I said, then immediately put my hands over my big vulgar mouth, not meaning to cuss. "I mean, darn, Cindy, I just can't believe it's you."

"Well darn John. I can't believe you didn't recognize me."

"Uh, I do, sorta. But...it's just that the Cindy...I remember... well, you know."

"Yeah John, that's the Cindy that I kind of forgot about."

"Oh well, I understand, I mean...I'm sorry."

"There's nothing to be sorry about. It's just that I've changed a little bit. But I'm still the same person I was."

"I guess so," I said.

"But really John, look at you. Your hair is so short now. Last time

I saw you it was down past your shoulders. And look at your body! Are you on some sort of weight lifting team?"

"Oh no...I mean, I do lift weights, but I'm not on a team, and I guess you're right about the hair too."

"I guess we've both changed."

"I'll say we have. It's just hard for me to believe that you're Cindy Johnson."

"You have to quit saying that. You're gonna make me paranoid."

"OK! But how did you know I was here?"

"My dad said he saw your dad in Kingstree, and you know my dad, being a Citadel graduate and all, he asked how you are doing, and that's how he found out about you being at summer school. I only came by because you told my parents if I was ever in Charleston to look you up. They said you were dying to pay me back for getting you out of your studying jam back in high school."

I thought back and remembered having said that to Mr. Johnson following the last Homecoming game.

"I did say that didn't I?"

"Did you mean it?" asked Cindy.

"Of course I meant it. I just didn't think you'd take me up on it, knowing that you were going to school in Columbia."

"I'm not going to school in Columbia anymore. I put my two years in at Columbia College, and now I'm transferring to the Medical University to get my last two years in nursing."

"That's right, your mom's a nurse, and you always said you wanted to be one too. Are you in school now?"

"Yes. I decided to catch a semester of summer school just to help me get orientated before the fall. I'm sharing an apartment with two other girls over on Bee Street. I made the arrangements through a friend of a friend type deal. There's only two of us here during summer school, but during the regular year it'll be three."

"That's great Cindy. You know I think this is the first time I've laid eyes on you since high school."

"And me with you. I guess there's a lot of distance between

Columbia and Charleston, and our paths never seemed to cross in Kingstree."

"I can see why," I said. "I hardly ever went into town."

"Tell me about it. Whenever I went home, I usually ended up sitting around the house. I was lucky I could stay on my diet."

"I know the feeling well," I said. There was a moment of awkward silence. "Uh...listen, where do you want to go? Is there something you would like to do?"

"I don't know. You're the one who extended the invitation."

"Yeah...I guess I did, didn't I?"

"So I'll just leave it up to you."

"I really hate to say this, but the place that I go most often is really nothing but a hole in the wall."

"Where's that?"

"Captain Harry's Blue Marlin bar."

"I think I've heard of that place. Let's go there."

"Are you sure? I should do something decent for you."

"That's decent enough."

"Okay...uh...do you want me to come by and pick you up?"

"That would be nice," said Cindy in a smart tone.

"Yeah, I guess it would. How's about around 7:30?"

"Sounds good enough to me." Cindy started to walk away, but then said, "I'll look for you at 26 Bee Street tonight at 7:30. I'm in the upstairs apartment."

"OK, I'll see ya then."

I turned to walk back into the battalion, but just as I was entering into the sally port, I turned back around to watch as Cindy walked away, checking out her new body as she moved down the sidewalk.

"Damn," I said out loud, "That can't be Cindy Johnson."

I turned and continued on into the sally port, and as I walked across the quad towards my room, I felt almost dizzy from the confusion. I couldn't accept what I had just seen. An ex-200 pound study mate was now the most beautiful girl I had ever talked to. It was about all I could do to absorb the encounter.

Throughout the rest of the afternoon, I couldn't help but think of how Cindy had changed. I thought of myself standing in front of the battalion, looking intensely into her face to find some trace of the old Cindy I once knew. She had lost so much weight in her body and in her face, and her blonde hair was now long and curled. She was even wearing some makeup. She looked so healthy, and not like someone who had just starved herself in order to drop a hundred pounds. It was the weirdest thing I had ever seen. It was even awkward to think that it was really Cindy Johnson. I couldn't put the two together. I almost didn't want to.

At 6:00 PM I walked over to evening mess, where when asked about my plans for the evening I indicated that I had a date. I calmed the ooh's and ahh's down by indicating that it was an old friend from high school who had looked me up. I just didn't mention that this old friend also happened to now be a breathtaking beauty.

After mess, I took a shower and got dressed for the town. Under the circumstances of going to Captain Harry's, I actually overdressed by wearing my best pair of shorts, a pullover Izod, and my Topsiders. It was really an upper crust look for the joint, but I had a date. I just hoped that Cindy knew enough about Harry's not to overdress for the occasion. She did say she had heard of it.

I walked to my car and drove towards the Medical University and I found the street and the house as if I knew where I was going. I became nervous as I pulled into the crushed rock parking area located right beside the huge structure. I could see that it was an old Charleston home converted into a duplex apartment that was likely used solely by MUSC students. I sat in the car, looking up at the top apartment, and used the moment to try to let my feelings of awkwardness subside.

I made my way up the stairs and knocked. Cindy opened the door, and I immediately could see that she understood what Captain Harry's was all about. She was appropriately dressed in shorts, casual shirt, and tennis shoes. Although dressed down, she looked gorgeous, and I was once again stunned.

"Come on in and take a look at my apartment before we go."

"Sure," I responded. "Looks like this is a converted house."

"I think it is. It's old, but they've fixed it up nicely."

I walked in and saw that it had indeed been an old Charleston home with hardwood floors, plaster walls, high ceilings, and a huge fireplace in the living room area.

"You see," said Cindy, "We have a kitchen, two baths, three bedrooms. Pretty neat set-up I'd say."

"And it looks like you're close to the Med U campus."

"I'm pretty lucky. A friend of mine at Columbia College helped me arrange this. I'm indebted to her. My roommate is a real gem."

"Oh yeah, what's her name?"

"Susan Burns. I'd introduce you, but she's gone out to run some errands. I haven't met my other roommate yet."

"Sounds like you've got a good situation."

"I'm ready, if you are?"

We walked out of the apartment, and Cindy immediately recognized my car. Once inside, she said, "Gosh John, this car hasn't changed a bit."

"Not really. How long's it been? Two and a half...nearly three years ago since you were in this car last?"

"It seems so long ago."

"Sorry it took me so long to pay you back for the help."

"Next time you're failing off the football team, see if I care. By the way, you happen to have your Eagles tape?"

"Eagles tape? What makes you ask?"

"I don't know. It's just what I remember about this car."

"I think I have it, but it's so old. Maybe it works. You want me to try it?"

"If you don't mind."

I thought it curious she particularly wanted to hear that tape, but I reached behind the seat and pulled it out of my 8-track storage box. I was surprised it still played well, being so worn and old. Cindy was pleased, and looked at me and said, "Just like old times," but it was hard for me to agree. I thought to myself that other than her name, this wasn't like any of the old times I remembered. There was a totally different person sitting beside me, nothing like the girl I once knew.

It was a short drive downtown to get to Harry's which was tucked away on a back street, and I had unusual luck finding a parking spot. But it was early on a Tuesday evening and the crowds were much smaller than on the weekends. We walked into Harry's and found the place sparsely occupied by the early birds as the sun was just beginning to set. With so few people, it was an excellent opportunity to walk around and look at the unusual way that the place was decorated. It was an old commercial garage that was adorned with nothing less than junk. There were bits and pieces of old boats and water gear on the walls and hanging from the ceiling. Harry had even suspended a canoe up in the rafters, occupied by a mannequin holding a beer. Everything was tacky with a purpose, and I personally loved a serious smartass. Cindy asked what the main attraction was to the bar, and I found it hard to explain, and made an attempt by saying it was the place to be to just not give a damn.

We sat at one of the few tables and I got a couple of beers from the bar. Cindy took a liking to the place, saying it had real personality. "This is the most unique bar I've ever been in."

"Not exactly what you would expect to be the most popular joint in Charleston huh?"

"It must tick off all the others who spent thousands creating atmosphere. This guy takes a dumpy old garage and turns it into a killer night spot."

"He's either the luckiest or the smartest guy in Charleston. But you know, it's the weekends that really make it thrive."

"Oh really?" said Cindy.

"It's the bands. They're really good. Whether you're just listening, or want to dance, it's the place to be."

"I love to dance," said Cindy. "It's actually good exercise. As a matter of fact, that's kind of how I lost a lot of my weight."

"Dancing?"

"Not really dancing per se. Have you ever heard of aerobics?"

"Not really."

"Didn't think so, but it's really becoming popular. They had an excellent aerobics program at Columbia College. It was hard at first, but along with a diet, it's a good way to lose weight."

"You know, I just can't believe the way you look. I mean, not only do you look thin, but you look like a different person."

"Thanks! I'm glad you think it's an improvement. Lots of people say the same thing you do. I've almost gotten used to it since everybody I see has about the same reaction. No one recognizes me anymore."

"Aren't you happy you did it?"

"Of course I am," said Cindy thinking. "Let there be no question. It's just, well...kind of a weird thing to go through."

"I bet."

"Let's talk about you," said Cindy. "You've changed too. You really are pumped up these days. You look like one of those guys on the cover of a muscle magazine."

"Thanks," I laughed. "But I haven't looked this way for long."

"You just got this way?"

"I worked out a good bit during high school, but when I came to The Citadel, I got tangled up with this guy who didn't want to let me eat."

"That's crazy," said Cindy. "There's no good reason to not let someone eat?"

"The Citadel's 4th Class System is crazy alright. But through its good points and bad, I survived my freshman year. During my sophomore year, I recovered, and even put on a good bit more."

"You've certainly changed. Your haircut, and all the added muscles. It would cause anyone to have to look hard to see that it's you. I guess we've both changed our appearance."

We sat at the table and talked for hours as people slowly trickled into the bar. The noise began to crank up all around us as the stereo competed with the chatter. I was enjoying our conversation, catching up on the news, and revisiting old times with someone I had grown up with. It was really weird though, talking with Cindy about the past. Even though we had studied hard together during that critical moment in my life, our lives during high school had actually been distant. We were in the same classes, and knew the same people, but we just never had much to talk about back then. I knew why, and so did Cindy, but we just didn't discuss it. We acted as if we had always been friends through school. She couldn't see it, but at times I felt awkward making the conversation work. I had to be careful. It actually hurt a little to think of how everyone used to make fun of fat Cindy Johnson, especially since I too was one of the guilty.

But the entrance of my summer school friends eventually broke up our conversation. Albert led the group over to our table, and finding that I was talking with an exquisitely beautiful girl who was "just an old friend," they didn't hesitate to pull up a chair to join us for the rest of the evening. Our privacy was gone, but it was still a fun time. We talked about The Citadel and Charleston, telling endless cadet war stories which really entertained Cindy.

The fun of the evening seemed to make the time move faster, and it wasn't long before 10:30 rolled around, which was pushing my limits for staying out. Fun or not, I had classes starting at 7:30 in the morning, and by the time I could get Cindy home and get back to campus, it would be well after 11:00. Cindy understood, and leaving my buddies behind we made our way out of the bar and towards the car. As we walked, Cindy thanked me for the opportunity to go to Harry's. I think she genuinely had fun, and was now able to say she had been to the place that everyone was talking about. I enjoyed it too, having an opportunity to reminisce about high school, and in a strange way, enjoy the company of a beautiful girl.

Cindy was so very different. It was so obvious that her incredible beauty blew away my friends from school, not knowing that years ago they would have shunned her at first glance. It sure had me confused. Though all of that was behind her now, I still had a true understanding of her past, and could see straight to her heart and soul like no other guy sitting at the table enjoying her company that night.

Arriving at my car, I opened the door for Cindy. As I walked around the car, I felt a real sense of being on a date. It wasn't supposed to be a date, just a gesture of being grateful for her help. My mind raced as I asked myself the question, Did I want to be on a date with Cindy Johnson?

We started back towards Cindy's apartment while chatting about our evening at Harry's. I tried to stay focused on the conversation, but I couldn't help but feel some awful sense of confusion about where I was with this person who was sitting beside me. She was the loveliest girl I had ever laid eyes on. I watched her in the dim glow of the passing streetlights as she smiled and talked. It was an awesome sight.

As I pulled into the parking lot of her apartment, I felt the seed of confusion grow into a flora of uneasiness, not really knowing what my next action would to be. I continually told myself that this was nothing more than returning a favor, and not really a date. The outing was just a re-acquaintance of old friends.

But the anxious moment passed as I stopped the car and Cindy opened her door saying, "I can't tell you how much I enjoyed going to Captain Harry's. I also enjoyed the company."

"Great," I answered. "I'm really glad you did."

"I would ask you in, but I realize I've kept you out much later than you wanted, and I have classes tomorrow too. It's a good thing you're the responsible one."

"Amazing how people can change, isn't it?"

"You're a prime example of that," said Cindy who was now most of the way out of the car, obviously not expecting me to walk her to the door. It seemed appropriate under the circumstances.

"Drive safe, and stay in touch," said Cindy.

"I'm sure I'll see you around this summer."

"OK," laughed Cindy and she closed the door.

I watched as she walked up the stairs, and she waved as she

opened the door and walked in. As I backed around in the parking lot, I wondered about Cindy's statement to stay in touch, and my totally brilliant response that I would probably see her around during the summer. We both sure left enough vagueness in our plans to see each other again.

Although I was comfortable in her company and found her easy to talk to, there was really something weird about our time together. Here we were, two decent people, each with a past filled with skeletons. I was no Rhodes Scholar in high school, and Cindy was no Miss America. Nearly three years later, we meet again with our negative pasts behind us. It was a renewal of an odd friendship that carried an added burden of painful memories, ones that seemed to taint my assessment of the present. I could see that our friendship that developed so many years earlier was still there, but I wondered if I would really see her again, and if so, where this new chapter in our lives would take us.

CHAPTER 29

It had been a later than usual evening, and the next day I found myself slightly tired from the outing. I still couldn't come to grips with seeing the new Cindy Johnson, who up until the day before I considered a soul who required sympathy. It had once taken effort to overlook her physical drawbacks, which I felt obligated to do since she had so generously helped me out in my time of need. But the situation had now changed drastically. I now saw her in splendor. She was the girl of any guy's dreams, but was placed before me in the light of our past, one that left me confused and fighting myself internally.

I thought back to our night in the pizzeria, and how I was embarrassed entering the crowd in her company. After getting to know her, I could see through her appearance problems, and past my own prejudice. I could see Cindy Johnson for the sweet, helpful person that she was.

I also remembered how careful I had been not to lead her on, worrying that she would mistake our time together as the beginning of some romantic tie between us. I was thankful that she was intelligent enough to know there was no chance for us.

Our past was a strong blemish in my mind, yet when I looked into Cindy's face during the previous evening, I had to fight to find a resemblance to the wreck of a girl that I once pitied back in high school. My real cross to bear was that had I not known that this girl was once "fat Cindy Johnson," I would have gone to any length just to talk to her. I would have made every attempt to get a date, and maneuver to take full advantage of her beauty, pushing my advances with zeal. Yet the ghosts of our past impaired that instinctive drive, causing a disorientation of my senses, and the resurrection of a once buried guilt. To make matters worse, there was doubt. Our parting statements to each other at the end of the evening left a big question mark as to where this reunion was headed, if indeed it was even going anywhere. For all I knew, she may have come to see me just to rub my nose in my iniquity.

I had this desire to call Cindy right after class and ask her to go with me anywhere during the evening. No matter how clouded my emotions, there was no question in my mind that I wanted to see her again. But my own conscience gave me continuous doses of reality, reminding me that she was now a goddess in every sense of the word. For a girl of her looks, attending summer school classes at the Medical University would automatically mean all the dates and invitations she could stand. Guys would flock to her in droves. For me to call her would probably be setting myself up for a dose of deserved rejection. I'd be surprised if she didn't already have plans. Her classes would surely contain guys, who if sitting in the classroom would notice her the moment she stepped into the room. They would discover a beauty of a lifetime, and would work to find an opportunity to get close to her.

My confusion and turmoil only increased as I tried to decide what to do. Though I had a clear desire to see Cindy again, I struggled to convince myself to just take it slow. But as the day went on, my desire grew stronger, and I began to put together a plan. I elected to just let the entire day pass, and on the next day, which was Thursday, I would call and ask her out for Saturday night and hope that evening would still be open.

That night I went out on the town with the boys, but thoughts of Cindy often filled my mind, and I caught myself looking around Captain Harry's, thinking she might somehow wander in. I had thoughts of her being out with some other guy, who probably wouldn't bring her to a hole in the wall like Captain Harry's. She certainly deserved something more elegant.

I pushed myself to forget her, and just enjoy myself with my friends. But it was hard, as thoughts of her crept into my slipping imagination. My buddies were no help either. They were still impressed after seeing her the night before, and they began questioning my sanity for being out with them and not her. I

349

considered their point valid, and couldn't even provide a reasonable argument. I wanted to see her all right, but the guys didn't know about our history, and I wasn't about to tell them either. With some reluctance, I was stymied by the past.

Class the next day seemed long knowing that I was going to try to call Cindy right after. I thought through so many times what I would say, and where we would go, which would again be Captain Harry's. Granted, it wasn't the best place to take a date, but I could see that she really loved it. I was certain that the live music during the weekend would be even more impressive to her, and worth the second trip.

Immediately following class I walked back to the barracks and then to that battalion's phone room. She had registered her phone number in the student directory at the Medical University, and after obtaining it I took a deep breath as I dialed her number. I waited nervously as telephone rang, and it actually surprised me when the phone was picked up on the other end.

"Hello," said a voice picking up on the other end.

"Hi Cindy, this is John."

"Hi! What's going on?"

"Just got out of class and had a wonderful lunch over at the mess hall."

"I wish I had someone to fix my lunch."

"What? You're not eating in the cafeteria?"

"No, there really wasn't any use to buy a meal ticket. You know...I'm still kind of dieting."

"Still dieting?" I asked with concern. "I thought you were right where you wanted to be."

"Yes, but you know, it's hard to get pounds off, but easy to put them back on."

"Well… the reason I'm calling is to see if you wanted to go out Saturday night to see Captain Harry's in a different mode...you know...with a band and all."

"That sounds great. It seemed like such a fun place the other night as it was. I can't imagine it packed with people."

"It gets crowded, alright, but it's still a lot of fun."

"I'm looking forward to it."

When I arrived at Cindy's apartment Saturday night, I found her dressed down, but still with a look that was dazzling. She seemed happy to see me, and excited to once again be heading to Harry's.

The band at Harry's that night was the "Killer Whales," which was Charleston's most popular bar band. Their music was great, and really intense. They were a three-piece band that hammered out new wave rock-n-roll with a very unique sound. I knew without question that Cindy would love them. The only problem was that any bar featuring the "Killer Whales" was doomed to be packed to capacity. During the hot summer months, this sometimes made it almost unbearable. Even though Harry's was big, the crowd was usually enough to have everyone shoulder to shoulder.

Cindy and I entered the bar at 8:30 and the band was already into their first set. It made for a wonderful entrance with the bar already rocking. You could just feel the energy in the air, and as I had hoped, Cindy immediately lit up to the environment.

It was already hard to move around even though it was still early in the evening, and I knew it would get worse. We made our way over to the bar for a couple of beers to start the night off. The Whales were in prime form, and as they played I could see Cindy getting into them. She was having a wonderful time, dancing in the small space that she stood in, smiling.

Arriving in the middle of their first set, it wasn't long before the band was ready to take their first break. This allowed us an opportunity to take a breather as the crowd disbursed.

"Wow," declared Cindy "those guys are great."

"I'm glad you like them," I replied. "They've got an unique sound. It takes some people a while to get used to their style, but once they do, it's easy to see they're the best band around."

"I can see why," said Cindy. "It's the beat. Their music makes you want to move."

"Except I'm sure you don't want to move much in this heat."

"It's no different than when I run."

"You run?" I asked with some surprise.

"I sure do. Every other day."

"I didn't know that."

"Aerobics classes aren't always available, and I needed regular physical activity to go with my diet. So I run."

"How far do you go?"

"It varies, anywhere from two to three miles."

"That's great. I try to run every other day too."

"Where do you go?"

"Right around The Citadel, but I sometimes break outside of the gate to other parts of Charleston."

"Gosh, we've got to get together! But I guess I shouldn't say that since I know you must run much faster than me."

"I doubt there's that much difference. I don't push too hard."

"I'm pretty slow," said Cindy modestly. "I just move along at a jog, although I'm certainly open to picking up the pace a bit. Maybe we can get together and give it a try."

"Sounds good to me!"

Cindy and I talked about how we worked out, each of us having our own routines. I was surprised to hear that she put in so much time and effort, especially knowing that she had no end result in mind other than just to lose weight.

"Dad said you weren't playing football for The Citadel. Are you on another sports team that pushes you to work out so hard?"

"Not at all. Have you ever heard of the Junior Sword Drill?"

"No, not that I can remember."

"It's a precision drill unit that puts on a performance in honor of the seniors receiving their class rings during Parents Day weekend."

"Yes, my father has talked about Parents Day. That's when freshmen get to see their folks for the first time."

"That's it. The senior class selects fourteen juniors to train and perform on Friday night that weekend."

"What kind of drill performance is it?"

"It's hard to explain, but it's a precise formation where they march and do sword manual."

"Yeah, I saw those guys at a football game halftime once."

"No, no," I quickly replied, "Those are the Summerall Guards. They're a precision drill team too, but they perform with rifles. The Junior Sword Drill performs indoors, and only with swords."

"Oh. I guess I haven't seen them. Are you on that drill team?"

"No, I'm not. I'm getting ready to try out for it."

"When do you start?"

"In early fall. As a matter of fact, I've only got about six more weeks until it starts."

"Six weeks? I thought it was at least two months until school starts back."

"For some," I said, "but I have to come back early to help train the incoming freshmen. It's called Cadre."

"Did you volunteer for that?"

"Not really," I laughed. "It comes with the rank I received."

"What rank are you?"

"I'm a sergeant," I answered modestly.

"Oh, and so because you're a sergeant, you have to come back early and help the new guys learn the ropes."

"That's right. And all sergeants who are eligible to go out for Sword Drill have positions requiring them to report for Cadre."

Cindy and I continued to talk about the Drill, and she took a great interest in what it was about, yet remained a bit confused over its purpose, and why one would be willing to work so hard to make it. She tried to relate it to the band back in high school, and how they marched in long parades carrying instruments, but could never recall anyone running or lifting weights in order to make it. It was hard for her to grasp the intensity of the commitment, or that of the performance.

The Killer Whales started into their second set, and immediately our conversation took a back burner. The band played another full hour set, rocking out Captain Harry's which was swelled to capacity with patrons. Cindy and I were having a blast, caught up in the good music and enthusiasm of the crowd. Everyone was moving as best they could, occupying and guarding their own little space. The heat really built up inside, and by the time the second set ended, everyone was ready for some fresh air. Most moved for the exit, including us, and the sweltering crowd stood on the sidewalk and in the street, chattering through their quest for relief.

This time, Cindy and I got into a conversation about our majors and future plans. I found it interesting to hear about her ambitions, and where she wanted to be after graduation. I wished I were as clear about my post-graduation goals. She hoped to stay in the area, and get a job in one of the hospitals as a nurse. She then asked me about the military, and I answered that I had not ruled it out as an option, but had no existing desire. I told her that before entering The Citadel, it had never even crossed my mind. She said her father chose not to go into the military, but from time-to-time, claimed regrets having not done so.

The band soon started into their third and final set, and everyone left the fresh air for the stuffy heat of the bar. People were once again dancing shoulder to shoulder, getting sweaty as if in some sort of athletic event. I kind of enjoyed it being that way. Like Cindy, I too was looking at it as a workout. I was getting a taste of her aerobics as she claimed Captain Harry's was almost like the real thing.

The band played their best and most powerful set. Everyone in the place was at full tilt with excitement. But because it was Saturday night in the conservative state of South Carolina, the bar had to close by 12:00. We soon heard "last call for alcohol," and the Whales started into their final song. Even with the warm evening and late hour, Cindy and the rest of the crowd were disappointed to hear that it was time to shut down the fun. South Carolina law was strict, and everything came to a screeching halt at midnight, just as it seemed to be really taking off. It didn't take long for everyone to make it out of the bar and into the cool and fresh air.

We strolled back towards my car, and gained a new appreciation for the night air, and the gentle breeze that blew in from the Charleston harbor. It was a strong contrast to the oven-like environment of the bar. Once we were driving, the rushing wind coming in through the open windows fueled a burst of appreciation for good times, and we both smirked at the wildness of the night.

The drive was short, and I soon pulled into the parking lot of Cindy's apartment. But with a shot of reality, I soon realized where I was, and what I was doing. I was not on an outing to pay back a favor to a friend. I was at the conclusion of a true to life date. I suddenly realized exactly what I was supposed to do, and possibly what might be expected. As a gentleman, I was supposed to walk her to the door.

But there was something really wrong. Something I just couldn't explain. I felt so uncomfortable with the task. My heart rushed, and I felt a sense of anxiety. I looked at Cindy sitting in the faint light, stoned by her striking beauty while also fighting my nerves.

This was all too crazy. I was a full-grown adult male. I wasn't some virgin from a life of caution and scruples. I was the same guy who was used to getting slapped in the back seat. Yet, the thought of kissing Cindy seemed to terrify me.

I tried not to look shaken, and as I opened my door, I noticed Cindy doing the same. She didn't wait for me to do it, and she looked a bit tired and worn out from the evening. She had an opportunity to wind down during the ride home, yet she was attentive and waited for me to catch up to her before we headed up the stairs. I almost felt obligated to do something like take her hand, but shuddered at the thought. I just walked right beside her as we ascended the stairs to the landing in front of her door. As we moved, it was deathly quiet between us, with neither of us uttering a word. It was as if we were both expecting the other to say something, though the words never came. Most likely she was feeling as nervous as I was. Without looking at me, she reached into her pocket and pulled out her key, and slipped it into the bolt lock above the knob. She turned it, and then turned around back to face me. I almost collapsed.

"I enjoyed it, John."

"Did you enjoy yourself tonight?" I said, then closed my eyes and cursed myself for the brain fart.

"I sure did."

"I was worried that it got too hot in there."

"No, I'm a bit tired, but it's a good kind of tired, the way you always hope you'll feel after going out."

"I'm glad you enjoyed it. Well...when do you want to run?"

"I don't know," said Cindy answering with a surprised look. "When's the next time you're scheduled?"

"I guess tomorrow. You interested then?"

"Sure," said Cindy. "But I always wait until late in the afternoon when it's cool."

"That's fine with me. How about around...oh, say 6:30 or so?"

"Yeah, that would be fine."

"I'll drive over and we'll leave from here. That way you can show me your route, since my Citadel route is kind of boring."

"That'll be fun. I guess I'll look for you around 6:30."

"OK," I said, stepping off towards the stairs. "Maybe I'll be recovered from the cigarette smoke and the sweat from tonight."

"Me too," said Cindy smiling, still standing at the door.

"I'll see ya tomorrow then," I said as I trotted down the stairs.

"Bye," said Cindy as she moved inside and closed the door.

I almost ran to my car. Inside, I let out a breath, relieved I had made it through the situation. I actually wished I had kissed Cindy, but for some crazy reason, I just couldn't. But the way she continued to stand at the door, led me to believe she may have been expecting me to. Damn it. What was wrong with me?

I cranked the car, then stared up at her door. I hoped that I had not offended her. Maybe she wasn't expecting it. Maybe she just considered us still as friends, and romance was the furthest thing from her mind. Whatever the case, what was done was done. I at least had the comfort of knowing that I was going to see her again the next day. Maybe by then I would figure out what was wrong, and what I should do about it.

***

The next day was Sunday. There were no classes, no commitments to be anywhere. I was able to sleep late, and felt I needed it after the semi-late evening. The slow start was a preamble to an unstructured day, one that would be spent just knocking around, doing a bit of studying, resting, and thinking. I thought about Cindy a lot. I couldn't help it. Though confused about what stood between us, I knew there was something there I just had to understand. I felt that I needed to pursue our friendship, and whatever else that may result from it. The only thing that was clear, but hard to admit, was that I really wanted to be with her.

The relationship Cindy and I had experienced through our lifetime of knowing each other had seen many changes. In our early school years we were oblivious to many of the pains and prejudices of life, and our differences were hardly noteworthy. But as we became practiced in the harsh realities of the world, barriers began to rise, separating us. The distance grew as we sought those who were like we were, and by the time we entered middle school, fat Cindy Johnson was a punch line to our strings of lardo jokes, and a distant target whom we thought deserved little of our consideration. Through our years in high school, our bigotry gained structure, and we concealed our thoughts and comments by keeping them within our little groups, taking great care not to allow admission to those who were so vulnerable to our discreet put-downs. Open criticism was merely used to keep an outsider in place, educating them as to their status, and displaying a warning not to consider approach much less inclusion. I knew the rules of that playing field, having been on both sides of it in my transformation from skinny nobody to an in-the-clique football star dating little Miss Popularity. I worked hard to become one of them, and I became just as cruel and snotty the moment I was in, forgetting the underlings and misfits I left behind, including fat Cindy Johnson.

But those barriers were gone between us now. Cindy now qualified. With her new found looks, I was sure that she would pass the litmus test of even the most snobbish of cliques, ones that would probably turn their nose up at some low-life cadet like me.

So, what was this existing barrier in the way? What held me back from pursuing Cindy? Was it my own guilt and shame? I certainly felt like a hypocrite. I was a master of the double standard. I had acquired her friendship because I used her. I let my personal preferences for a girl's appearance and peer pressure override the situation, and I basically ignored her after she had worked so hard to help me. Now that she had lost her weight, and adopted the acceptable appearance practices of the crowd, I should just sweep under the carpet all of the jokes and the constant ridicule we put her through. All should be forgiven since she was now on the opposite end of beauty scale, now measuring at the redline level. Wasn't I nice to qualify her as one of "us" now?

With my history of being a true-to-life horse's ass, it was hard to see why she would ever even talk to me, and why she didn't just spit in my face. Maybe she would now use me for some personal gain, and then just walk away. After three years of not giving Cindy the time of day, I now wanted to spend time with her? I guess I first had to get past a little thing called guilt, and step around a conscience that rightfully deserved a swift kick in the ass. Even worse was that I wasn't even sure if I had in reality overcome my own weakness for intolerance. As much as I hated it, I still possessed a deep-seated negative prejudice. Even though she was now gorgeous, I couldn't forget who she once was. I knew I was wrong for feeling that way, but my mind could not let go of her previous image, nor could I pardon myself for condemning her for lacking an acceptable physical appearance. Society had ingrained it in me. I was programmed to consider her as a substandard human. It was an appalling way to feel, and a truly disgusting truth about the populous of that day, and about me.

I could see that the problem I faced was more than an analysis of standards of conduct. It was an emotional issue. It was an attitude that came as naturally as blinking my eyes. Maybe it was a flaw in my character. I resented my own intolerance of those who were less than perfect or not fitting in the molds of society. I was ashamed of my narrow-mindedness. Cindy never deserved it. She was the sweetest girl I had ever known. Now, like some perverted weakness, I found her a pleasure to be with.

As if these confusing mind battles weren't enough, I still had other wounds to deal with. It had been almost two years since my breakup with Donna. She had shattered my heart in a way that I thought would be impossible to put back together. Love was a cruel and dirty word to me. I truly hated the concept. It was a waste of productive time, and there were more important things in life than sitting around and looking starry eyed at one's sweetheart. There were more consequential and useful things to pursue. Sword Drill was a prime example. I could see countless positive results the pursuit had yielded. Women were nothing but trouble looking for a man to make it happen with. I remembered how much I cared about Donna, and how I so badly wanted to be with her. I couldn't fathom ever letting myself get so dependent and vulnerable again. Even after all that time, the whole episode was still painful. Heartbreak was something I wanted no part of ever again. With Donna, it seemed that was all I could remember about our relationship.

I felt frustrated as I sat in my room, thinking about how precious Cindy would be to anyone lucky enough to have her, yet here I was fighting with myself to accept her. I could only laugh at my arrogance to assume that Cindy would even want me. How could she after the way I had treated her? If her intent was to lead me down the primrose path of heartbreak as revenge, I knew that she had every right to do so. But I also knew that she was too nice and decent to do such a devious thing. I had to remember that just because I had the tendency to be an asshole, it didn't necessarily mean everyone else did too.

I burnt and exhausted my brain, trying to sort through my feelings to understand the situation, but soon grew weary of fighting the scenarios. I wanted to spend more time with Cindy, and whatever resulted would just have to happen. It was just going to take some time for me to sort things out.

That evening I dressed in what I considered my most presentable running gear, then drove over to Bee Street. As I pulled into the parking lot, I could see Cindy already outside, doing stretches in preparation to run. Before I could get out of the car, it was obvious, even at a distance, that she looked awesome in her running shorts. I looked down at the rags I had on, and thought of how she probably would be embarrassed to be seen with me. Faded shorts, a T-shirt, and ragged looking socks inside worn and dirty running shoes. Cindy had on a nice looking tank top with matching runner's shorts, with anklet socks and fairly new running shoes. Her exposed legs and arms were tan and brown. She was a picture of health and beauty, and I was cautious not to let her catch me staring as I approached. I had a hard enough time comprehending her new found looks while she was fully clothed, but the short running outfit revealed even more to admire. Just the sight of her sent my passions swimming.

"Hey John. You're right on time."

"Yeah," I said, still shaken up from the sight of her.

"What's wrong? You seem tired."

I quickly snapped out of it and answered, "Oh no, I'm fine."

"You sure? We don't have to run if you're not feeling well."

"No, no, that's not it. There's not a problem."

"Oh, OK. You must have a lot on your mind."

"Yeah, I guess so. I've been studying a good bit today."

"That's good. Don't want to see us having to go through any last minute cram sessions again!"

We both laughed.

"I see you're all stretched out," I said.

"Just waiting on you."

"I'm ready, so if you're waiting on me, you're backing up."

"Oh really?" she said with a touch of arrogance. "Let's do get started then."

"You know the way, so I'll let you lead."

"OK, but I told you, I don't go that fast."

"That's alright, we'll get used to each other."

"I hope so," said Cindy, looking at me with a smile.

Her words were enough to stop me from breathing, and her look made my heart skip a dozen beats. Having successfully thrown me a curve, she just turned with a grin and took off before I had a chance to react. I watched her run a few feet, and then abruptly decided it was time to follow.

Cindy started running towards the downtown area. I was expecting a slow jog, yet she surprised me with a pretty quick pace. It was slower than my normal gait, but was good enough for me not to feel like I was being slighted on a workout. We moved down the side streets around the Medical University, then worked our way out to Calhoun Street. We took to the sidewalk as we passed Roper Hospital, and then moved steadily towards the College of Charleston campus in the old downtown area.

I watched and waited for Cindy to get tired, and slow her speed, but that never seemed to happen. Even two miles from our starting point, she still appeared strong, though she felt we had probably gone far enough and started back. I had never run through downtown before, even though I loved to run outside the gates. From time to time, I would break out of The Citadel and hit the residential areas just outside of it. The historic district was quite a stretch from campus, and I had never deemed it necessary to go such a distance. It was a wonderful place to run with the tree lined streets and old historic homes to look at. There was a late Sunday afternoon crowd, running, walking, and bicycling, and it was a perfect time of day to be outdoors. It was still warm, but past the blistering heat that most of the Charleston days of July brought.

I was enjoying the run, and turned to look at Cindy every couple of blocks. I could see that she also liked it, and was still doing well on stamina, not looking too tired to continue. She was obviously not a rookie at this, and had been running a lot more than I had suspected. Her stride was sure, and her pace steady, and she was much quicker than I had expected. During the last half mile or so, as we neared her apartment, she began to show a little wear, and the pace slowed just a bit. I guessed that we had gone about four miles.

By the time we reached the parking lot, Cindy was breathing pretty hard. She walked around the gravel lot as she tried to catch her breath, smiling every so often at me.

"That was a pretty good run," she said, huffing and puffing. "I enjoyed it."

Darn, you're not even winded."

"Sure I am," I said, making obviously fake breathing noises.

"Your nose is growing as you speak!"

"I just recover a little bit faster than most."

"If you want to go run some more, I'll be glad to wait for you here."

"Are you crazy? You must have me mixed up with some marathon runner. This is good enough for me."

"Bull!"

"OK, I admit I run a little bit faster than that, but it's no big deal. I enjoyed the change. Just leave it at that." "OK, OK," said Cindy smiling. "I just don't want to hold you back in your training." "You don't have to worry about that. Of course, I'm quite impressed with your pace."

"I am too! I usually don't run that hard or that far."

"Oh really?"

"Yeah! I just didn't want to hold you back."

"I swear, if I hear you say that one more time..."

"OK!" said Cindy throwing up her hands, still breathing deeply.

As Cindy walked around, I could see her occasionally slap her legs, until I too noticed that the sand gnats were beginning to serve us up for supper. Even though the evening air was quite pleasant to be in, the aggravating little bloodsuckers were doing their best to ruin it all. As long as we kept moving, they weren't much of a problem. But as soon as Cindy caught her breath, and sat down on the steps, she realized we were under attack.

"These darn gnats," she said swinging her hands.

"Don't they make outdoor life a joy here in Charleston?"

"Let's go inside. These things are nothing but pests."

When we entered into the apartment the air conditioning was noticeable, especially since my room in the barracks had nothing other than the usual box fan in the window.

"Want some water?" asked Cindy.

"Sure!"

Cindy walked over and flipped on the stereo as she moved towards the kitchen. I stood listening to the music and the sounds of her putting ice into glasses, and felt compelled to sit down. My sweat covered skin canceled out using a chair, so I decided the next best thing was the floor.

When Cindy walked out, I was happy to accept the glass of water and took a few big gulps to kill my modest thirst. Cindy was also ready to get off of her feet, so she too sat on the floor, leaning up against the opposite wall.

"I can't believe how good of shape you're in," I said.

"Same here. You barely broke a breath."

"I've been working out pretty hard for over a year now."

"It's been almost two for me."

"Two years?"

Cindy forced a laugh saying, "One doesn't lose a hundred pounds overnight you know."

I was stunned. Speechless. One hundred pounds! I guess I should have known it was probably that much, but it was still a shock to hear it.

"I guess it did take quite awhile."

"I've only been at my current weight of a hundred and ten for about four months now."

"You look really good."

"You mean that? You don't think I need to lose any more?"

"No Cindy, I honestly don't think so. Especially since you're in such good shape. You have good stamina and run at a nice pace."

"To be quite honest, I would hate to think I would have to lose more."

"After what you've lost so far, I can understand why."

"It's not as bad as it was. I had trouble with my knees when I first started, especially with all the extra pounds on. I had to jog at a snail's pace. It was tough on my joints, and I was so out of shape. I also had to endure all of the stares from everyone watching a fat girl run."

I couldn't believe her statement. She had a smile on her face, but I could feel my own pain with that sobering statement. It had to be humiliating and hurtful to bear the obvious stares. I could imagine there was even some laughter attached to the looks, and that she would have surely heard it. It was hard to believe she was so cheerful and light hearted about the whole thing, smiling as she discussed it.

"I guess I'd better head back to the barracks. I know you need to get a shower and probably hit the books. I need to get back and do the same before it gets too late."

"I hate to see you rush off."

"I have a couple of books I need to look over before classes tomorrow," I said, again feeling a bit uncomfortable from the pressure of parting again.

"I understand," said Cindy.

I stood up and moved towards the door. I opened it, then turned around to say, "If you can get past your guilt trip of thinking you're holding me back, you want to run again on Tuesday?"

"Sure, if you're absolutely sure."

"I'm sure."

"OK then, I'd love to."

"Alright," I said, while turning to go down the stairway. "I guess I'll see ya then."

I walked down the stairs as Cindy stood in the door, watching as I made my way to the car. Then she suddenly yelled out, "Hey John. Why don't you take a break from Citadel food and have dinner over here tomorrow night? I promise not to poison you."

I stopped and smiled, appreciating her taking the initiative to ask.

"I'd love to," I answered. "What time?"

"What time do you normally eat?"

"Six."

"Why don't you come over then? I might not have it ready by then, but six is a good time to come over."

"Perfect! I'll be here then."

With a smile on my face, I climbed into the car, and breathed a long sigh. I had a pleasant, satisfied feeling overtake me. I was once again leaving with plans made. But this time, they were initiated by Cindy.

The next day, I daydreamed a bit in my classes, thinking of how comfortable I was feeling about what was happening with Cindy. Time spent with her was wonderful, but I knew I could never let it affect my grades, or my preparations for Drill. The real damage wasn't the time away from the books, but my fading concentration as I seemed to often analyze the situation between us. I sometimes had to fight to stay focused, and that was a habit I had to break quickly.

At 6:00 p.m. I knocked on Cindy's door thinking that this was one great way to start what would normally be a slow Monday night. Cindy answered the door, and seeing her standing there, I wondered how long she would continue to have such an effect over me. This time she was wearing a white sundress with exposed shoulders, and it highlighted the brown color of her perfect skin.

"Come on in," she said.

"Great," I replied weakly, trying to get over her looks.

"John, I want you to meet Susan Burns."

I quickly looked over and spotted the semi-attractive girl who was sitting on the couch, fumbling in her purse. "Hi John," said Susan. "It's so nice to finally meet you."

"You too Susan."

"Sorry to be rushing so, but I'm running late," she said with frustration in her voice. "Here's my directions," she said pulling out a piece of paper. "I'll leave you two alone." Susan jumped up saying, "Nice meeting you John."

"I'll see you later," yelled Cindy who was already moving back into the kitchen. "How about a beer John?"

"Sure, why not?" I could see that Cindy already had the table set, and it looked really nice even with the cheap dishes that must have been furnished with the apartment. The stereo was playing at a pleasant volume as I walked into the kitchen, and Cindy had already pulled out a beer and had popped the top on it as I walked in.

"Here you go," she said handing it to me.

"Hmm, Miller Light. You just happen to have my brand huh?"

"I noticed at Harry's."

"Thanks for getting it. You know, wasn't I supposed to bring a bottle of wine or something?"

"Don't worry about it, I have a bottle."

"You're gonna make me feel guilty! I took you to a dump like Captain Harry's and you reciprocate with a wonderful dinner."

"You can pay your compliments after you've eaten. You don't even know if I can cook or not. You may hate it."

"It sure smells good."

"It needs to simmer for another 45 minutes, then we'll eat."

"What is it?"

"It's chicken cacciatore."

"What's that, if you don't mind me showing my ignorance?"

"It's a lot like spaghetti sauce, except you use chicken instead of hamburger."

"Hm, sounds pretty good."

"Let's sit down in the den while it cooks."

We moved into the next room where I sat on the couch on one end, and Cindy sat on the other. She seemed relaxed and pulled her legs up under her as we talked about our summers. I even told her about how I ended up in summer school, and how I had Charles to thank for it. It took little to convince her just how happy I was to be in Charleston versus the isolation of the farm.

As soon as I finished off my beer, Cindy returned to the kitchen to start the spaghetti noodles and put the garlic bread in the oven. I stood and talked with her as she worked, and secretly admired her as she moved about. She then asked me to sit down at the table where she served the salad as the main course finished cooking.

We ate our salads with her getting up and down. I made a token offer to help, but luckily she declined the assistance, probably knowing I would just get in the way. She soon walked in with our plates prepared and placed one before me with steam rising and the wonderful aroma of the sauce and the garlic bread mingling. She then emerged with a chilled bottle of wine, popped the cork on it, and then poured some into the long stemmed glasses on the table. It was then that I realized the magnitude of the dinner, and that Cindy Johnson had her act together in many ways.

"Would you like to taste it first?" said Cindy giggling.

"Sure," I replied, picking up my wine glass, trying to move with an air of sophistication. I took a small sip, acted as if I knew the ropes of wine tasting, and then said, "Emm, Mad Dog 20-20, 1978. Very good! Proceed madam."

"It is not!" laughed Cindy. "I'll have you know this is a fine bottle of wine."

"I wouldn't know Ripple from Gallo."

Cindy laughed, "You mean you're not a connoisseur of wine?"

"If it's not Miller Light, then I'm afraid I'm lost."

"OK, Mr. Kingstree."

She filled our glasses, and then sat down. She looked towards me and asked, "Shall I say grace?"

"Sure," I answered, then bowed my head and closed my eyes.

Cindy said a beautiful blessing, much softer and sweeter than the usual formal prayer I heard in the mess hall.

"Please, go ahead and start," she said.

As mannerly as I could, I picked up my fork and knife and began to eat. We sat on opposite ends of the table, and I appreciated the distance between us just in case I made any mistakes. The food was delicious, and I could see that she had put almost twice as much on my plate as she did on her own.

"What's this? I eat hefty and you feed like a bird?"

"It's not that much, especially for a growing boy like you. And besides, I still have to diet a little."

"No you don't, you look fine."

"Mind your own business and eat," said Cindy laughing.

As I ate, I struggled a bit with the spaghetti noodles to get them in my mouth. It was all excellent, and because I was hungry, I had to force myself to eat slowly, and not act like I was back in the mess hall.

"Do you like it?" asked Cindy.

"This is great. Can I take some home in my pocket?"

When we finished the cacciatore, Cindy took the plates away and I moved to the couch. When she returned from the kitchen, she again took her place on the other end.

"I want you to tell me more about the Sword Drill," said Cindy. "You seem to be preparing so hard for this thing, yet you never really said much about it."

"I hate to say it, but I really don't know that much. You see…there's quite a lot of secrecy that goes with it."

"Secrecy? Why do they have secrecy?"

"I don't know, I guess that's a secret too," I said with a laugh. "When guys go out for Drill, they don't talk much about what happens. During the 14 Nights, they start their activities while everyone else is at evening mess, and then you don't see them again for three or four hours. When they do come back, they really look bad."

"What do they do to them?" said Cindy with concern.

"I'm really not sure. The old Drill inspects the aspirant's personal appearance, and then they form up in a squad and leave the battalion.

They end up in McAlister Field House, which is where they will eventually perform, but no one really knows what goes on inside each evening."

"Do you have any idea?"

"I know it's very physical, and these guys obviously have to push themselves to the limit to make it through each night."

"Do they try to hurt you?"

"I really don't know. Sometimes guys get injured, and it's always said to be an accident, or at least that's what they claim."

"John, are you sure you want to do this?"

"Cindy, there's something you've got to understand. I've wanted this in a very serious way for over a year and a half. That's why I study so hard, and that's why I work out constantly."

"Yes, but why? Do you get some extra privileges at school if you make the Drill?"

"No, just the prestige, and the thrill of doing the performance on Parents Day."

"You only do that one performance?"

"Yeah, and that's only for fourteen minutes."

"All this for one fourteen minute performance?"

"That's right."

Cindy just sat there with a confused look on her face. I continued to try to explain to her everything I knew about the Junior Sword Drill, and made my best attempt to convince her that it was all worthwhile, and that there was much more to this thing than just strutting in front of a crowd.

As I talked, I could only think back to the two performances I had witnessed, and how the crowd reacted, and how I was blown away with the precision and beauty of it all. Cindy could see that I was very serious about this, even more than I was about football back in our high school days. But there were so many things she just couldn't grasp. Why were good grades required? Why the need for so much physical strength and endurance? Why only one performance? She really wanted to understand, and for the rest of the evening she listened as I tried to make sense of it all.

I later felt bad that I let Sword Drill dominate the evening, but I enjoyed talking to her about it, and she really wanted to know the facts. I could see she had real concerns about the physical aspect, and I assumed it was because she really cared.

Around 10:00, after having talked for hours, I realized it was a week night and getting late. I really had to get back to campus since I had a 7:00 class the next morning.

"I'm sorry Cindy, I really didn't mean to take up your whole evening talking about Sword Drill and school."

"I really wanted to hear about it. But I must be honest with you, it actually sounds almost dangerous. I can't help but fear for you in your upcoming quest to make it."

"I appreciate your concern. I must admit that I too sometimes wonder about the sanity of it all. It takes a lot to make Drill, but I have my reasons, and I'm totally committed to making it."

"I can see that. I think anyone can. I really hope you will make it."

Cindy's understanding touched me. The combination of her concern and support for my pursuit brought forth a certain new affection for her that I had not realized existed. Even though I knew she didn't fully understand the process, it appeared that she at least had a respect for what I was doing.

"I guess I'd better get going," I said. "I know you've got classes tomorrow too, and mine will be early."

As I stood up I at once got nervous, then watched as Cindy also rose. At this point there was no question in my mind that even if I could find a good reason for not kissing her good-night, I somehow at least owed it to her. We were relaxed, and had enjoyed each other's company, and I could see by the way that she walked in kind of a stroll, that she was anticipating something happening. My nerves jumped like knobs during mess, and I feared what I might or might not do next.

"I really enjoyed the meal," I said quite anxious. "It was awfully nice for you to go to all that trouble."

"My pleasure," responded Cindy in a sexy voice. "I've really enjoyed the time we've spent together."

"Me too. I feel that we..." All of a sudden I could hear footsteps coming up the stairs. I stopped, turned towards the door, and then watched as Susan walked in. What timing. It could not have been any better or worse.

"Hi guys! I hope I'm not getting back too early, am I?"

"Oh no," I said politely. "I was just leaving."

Susan walked on in and plopped down some books and her purse on the couch, with herself sitting down beside them.

"Well my evening was a pain," said Susan. "I took these directions down over the phone and made one mistake which caused me to be even later than I already was, but they got over it."

"I see," I answered distantly as I started walking out the door that was still open. "I guess I'd better go," I said to Cindy.

I looked back over at Susan who obviously didn't realize she had walked in at a bad time. I could see the frustration in Cindy's eyes, but also knew that I did not want to embarrass her, or myself, by trying to salvage a moment that was already awkward. I just walked on out to the landing of the steps, then turned around and looked back, and could see Cindy's disappointment.

"Good luck in your classes tomorrow."

"You too," I said walking down the steps.

"Are we going to run tomorrow?" asked Cindy.

I stopped and looked back up at her.

"Yes, let's do that."

"Is seven all right?"

"Sure, that's fine with me."

"OK, I'll see ya then," said Cindy.

I could still see a tinge of dissatisfaction on her face as she closed the door and I walked away.

"Damn," I said, knowing that Cindy was probably disappointed that nothing happened. I could feel there was definitely something there, yet our feelings were never consummated through a kiss, or a touch of any kind. I wondered what must have been going through Cindy's mind. I knew that I cared very much for her, and felt like she cared for me. Yet, I hated to think that something as simple as a kiss was providing so much frustration.

CHAPTER 30

In the late afternoon the next day I made my way back over to Cindy's apartment. Susan answered the door, as Cindy was in her room just getting changed and ready to run.

Soon she walked out saying "Hi John," in a very bright way.

"How are you?" I answered, quite pleased to see no visible negative feelings from the night before.

"Good, I'm ready to run."

"I am too, but I'm a bit worried about the weather. It sure has clouded up."

"I know. But it's not raining, and it'll sure provide a break from the heat. It ought to be a nice run."

"We'd better get started before we get caught in a storm."

We made it down the stairs, and after a minute's worth of stretching we took off, heading in the same direction as our first run. We were moving back towards downtown, cutting through the Roper Hospital area, and as Cindy had guessed, it was really pleasant.. The lack of heat provided an extra boost of energy and a higher tolerance for an outdoor workout. I wasn't stressed at all, and I could tell Cindy was feeling good in the milder atmosphere.

But like all good things, it was not to last. As we ran through the College of Charleston, I heard loud thunder in the distance. Because isolated thunderstorms during the summer were so common, a rain cloud could easily pass near our location and we would never feel a drop. We ran, thinking our luck would hold out as we moved through the business area and on towards the Battery, into the most beautiful part of the historic district. But I could feel small drops hitting my exposed arms and shoulders, and the cool, tingling feeling soon became a concern. A glance at Cindy said it had her attention too.

"Uh oh," she said, puffing as she ran. "I think we're in trouble."

"I do too," I replied. "We'd better keep an eye out for some place we can duck into before it starts pouring down."

"Here, cut down this street. I know just the place."

I stepped up my pace as the frequency of droplets increased. We needed to get to wherever it was she was taking us. The real rain was starting to come down, and Cindy yelled that we were almost there. I couldn't imagine where we were headed, but we soon ducked inside an unusual tunnel-like doorway that apparently led into a little gift shop that had obviously closed earlier in the afternoon. It was an architecturally pleasing portal made of concrete, with its vertical walls leading up to a rounded ceiling. The outside was decorated with wandering vines of ivy that draped the entrance with touches of green. It was a perfect place to escape the rain. Moving all the way in, right up against the door, not one single drop could touch us.

"Whew!" uttered Cindy, still panting for breath. "We made it."

"Yeah," I said, shaking off the drops that had hit me.

As the large drops multiplied into a downpour, we stared out into the street while we caught our breath. The rain was beating intensely on the sidewalk and overhang, and I grew thankful that Cindy had thought of the place so quickly before we would have surely been soaked to the bone.

"Wow, look at that rain coming down," I said.

Cindy was walking around in the small dry area of the entrance, trying to shake off her lack of breath and the strenuous exertion from sprinting to beat the approaching storm.

"I hope this isn't going to last too long," I said.

"We could be stuck here for awhile. I guess I should have listened to you and stayed close to my apartment instead of running all the way down here."

"Don't worry about it. These showers come and go. It probably won't take that long."

I stood right beside the doorway, barely keeping myself out of the mist from the rain as I watched the street, noticing that no one was on the sidewalks. It would be insane to be out in such a cloudburst. The only thing we could do was wait in our shelter until it at least slacked off.

For quite some time, the rain continued to pour, and after about ten minutes we saw signs that it was going to ease off from a downpour to a light rain. We decided to wait for a drizzle.

Cindy was all the way in the doorway, leaning up against the wall with her back up against the cool concrete. Having checked the rain status, I walked back in and leaned up against the opposite wall from where she stood. I could feel the chill against my back.

"Man, this concretes feels nice?" I said.

"Yeah, it is. I'm just starting to feel comfortable. It's almost as if we haven't even run."

We stood there, not saying much more. The clouds made our sanctuary a bit dim as we stared out at the rain falling on the street. It was dark inside the gift shop, and the sun's normal illumination of the late afternoon had been robbed by the storm. As I looked at Cindy standing across from me, I couldn't help but admire her beauty. Even after the run, she looked as pretty as ever. As she stood there looking out at the rain, the faint glow seemed to highlight her face in the most wonderful way. It was hard to believe that I had access to such a stunning girl, and had not shown any affection at all towards her. The emotional conflicts that I had harbored in my mind now seemed so very distant. There was no question that I wanted to get closer to her.

Cindy turned from looking out at the street only to catch me staring at her. She must have been embarrassed, as she shyly looked down towards the concrete floor. But her glance would not stay there, and she looked back up only to find me still locked on her in a way that was foreign to her. I gave her a slight smile, and she returned it in equal magnitude, then again in her shyness, looked away. I knew I was embarrassing her, and felt it best that I too should look out at the rain, only to quickly realize the soggy streets were not the calling of my interest. My eyes wanted to behold her lovely face. As I turned my gaze back towards her, I could see that her head was once again raised, and that she was now looking at me, yet this time, without being so bashful.. Both of us could tell as we stood there in the meager glow that there was definitely something between us beyond friendship. I pushed myself away from the wall and slowly walked forward. I stopped at arms length in front of her, and we continued to stare into each other's eyes. I reached out with my hands and grabbed hers, then pulled her gently from her wall towards me. Without breaking eye contact, we looked at each other through the dimness, and then with the speed of a last raindrop, I slowly kissed her. I judged it to be the most pleasurable thing I had ever done. We stood there hand in hand, consumed by the moment, until our grips weakened, and our hands parted only to find their way around each other, pulling our bodies close. I could feel her arms clinging to me with both the intensity and gentleness of someone who truly cared. The kiss that had been so painstakingly hard to initiate, was something I didn't want to end. For the longest time, I just stood there holding her, kissing her, and releasing those passions by way of touch that had been denied for so long. We ended our kiss, and just stood there, holding each other in the silence.

It felt so good to be touching Cindy. For some reason, it was better than I had imagined. I gave her a firm squeeze and said "Thank God for the rain."

Cindy hugged me back and replied, "I was beginning to think we would never do this."

Feeling like the weight of the world had been lifted off my shoulders, I answered by saying, "I did too, I'm sorry."

"It's not your fault," she said, holding me close with the side of her face up against my chest.

"Maybe. All I know is that you're the one person I don't want to find myself too far away from in the near future."

"I feel the same way," said Cindy, again holding on with her squeezing arms wrapped tightly around me.

We stood in our shelter, locked to each other, talking softly and kissing, hardly noticing that the storm had finally passed. We decided it was clear enough to start back, but running no longer seemed important, so instead we walked down the sidewalk, sometimes holding each other's hand, sometimes moving close enough for me to put my arm around her. All the anxiety was gone. I felt a cheerful freedom. The mind games that had left me so unsure had vanished.

We walked casually, and smiled at each other with the confirmation and knowledge of the way things were. When we made it back to Cindy's apartment, we couldn't wait to get up the stairs and inside, where we could once again resume holding each other and kissing. It was official now. We had confirmed what we both had suspected. It had taken too long to break the ice, and get by the shyness and emotional obstructions of the past. Without saying so, I was hooked, and had a very strong feeling that Cindy was too.

I soon modified my daily routine to include time with Cindy. I still attended class and lifted weights, but every evening I was with Cindy doing something. I wanted to be with her all the time, and it seemed we were both obsessed with each other. Unless we absolutely had to be elsewhere, we were together. We even started studying together, either at The Citadel's library or at Cindy's apartment. When we weren't studying or running, we were out on the town or at the beach, or anywhere we could enjoy each other. It really mattered little what we were doing. Our time just being together was pure pleasure, somehow even precious. We both felt ripped off having missed time together during the first week and a half of my summer school, since neither of us knew the other was in town, and that we were so slow in finding out that we cared for each other.

One Friday evening we went out to a beach bar called The Windjammer where we saw a really great band called The Sockets. They were a really hot band out of Atlanta, and they packed in a crowd much like the Killer Whales. But the mob and the heat soon got to us, so we walked on the beach for what turned into a late night experience that lasted for hours. It was a crystal clear night, and once we reached the far end of the Isle of Palms, the stars stood out like fireflies at arms length. I sat in the dunes with Cindy in my lap, with one's lips constantly finding the others.

We watched the moon rise over the water, and it lit our walk back as we returned from our adventure. It was a night to remember.

Our greatest escapade of the summer came with my idea to check out a Sunfish sailboat from the Citadel's marina. We packed a great picnic lunch and even a bottle of wine to sail out to Castle Pinckney Island located in the middle of the harbor. Cindy Johnson learned a real lesson that day about the caliber of yachtsman that comes from Williamsburg County, which has only ponds and rivers. Turning over twice on the way out, we soaked the sandwiches, but at least rescued the wine from sinking. I'd never seen Cindy laugh so hard, and I'd never felt so stupid. I swore I would paddle the damn thing the next time, sailboat or not.

We even played tourist a few times, and I finally got to see some of the museums, plantations, and old historic houses in Charleston. They were marvelous. It took Cindy's persuasion to get me to go, since I would always make a bee line to a bar or party on my rare and privileged times out of the gate during my freshman and sophomore years. She le d me to some of the most pleasurable discoveries of what the old town had to offer as we saw its well-preserved history and learned about the past that made us who we were.

Cindy and I went everywhere. There was always something to see or do, and even with our light classes, there was never enough time to catch it all. There was music and food, and an unbelievable cultural atmosphere. Summertime in Charleston with Cindy was like a dream. I loved where I was, and whom I was with, and for the first time ever, I knew just how good life could be. I didn't want it to end.

But time was not about to stop, and my precious days of summer were fleeting. Final exams would soon be upon me, after which would leave only a few days before the start of Cadre. I would then have to report back to school to prepare for the incoming freshmen. Shortly after their arrival, Sword Drill and the dreaded 14 Nights would start. It didn't take a genius to figure out that my life would then be totally consumed by it.

Cindy could not help but see my genuine concern for what I was getting into. She felt frustrated not understanding more about Drill, and wished that somehow she could help, but knew there was nothing she could do. I hated leaving her each night, knowing that I was one day closer to a major change, and the end of my ability to see her on a daily basis. I wanted Drill as much as ever, but I now feared its isolating commitment, only because of Cindy.

Once Drill started, the very first thing that would happen would be to once again have my head shaved. Following that would be the visible wear and tear of the Nights, such as weight loss and the tired, worn-down look in my face. George Porter endured a harsh pounding through the Nights, and I remembered how his physical well-being deteriorated as the weeks went by. I could only think back to freshman year, and the reaction Donna had when she saw me for the first time. It was the beginning of our end, and I couldn't help but think I could be headed for the same conclusion with Cindy.

Most females I had known had held two things as high priorities in their relationships. Spending time together and having someone they could be proud of. Once Drill started, both would be a problem for Cindy. I told myself that our relationship was strong, but the ghosts of Donna haunted me terribly. The last thing I wanted was for Cindy to see me in that ragged condition, then lose her as the reality of dating a cadet finally sank in.

My summer exams came before Cindy's. Even though they were hard, I managed to conjure up enough conviction to study well enough to make an A in both of my courses. Cindy was proud of me, and laughed as she thought back to how badly I had struggled during high school just to get a D. I thought it was funny too, mainly because she really had no idea just how well I had progressed in academics, having not told her about my regular session work.

Cindy's exams would take place during the following week, so we decided to spend our last full weekend together, then I would go back home during the two days she had exams so I wouldn't distract her. It would also allow me the time to get together the things needed for Drill before getting swamped in the activities of Cadre.

That last weekend together was great. We tried to do the things we loved most. Friday night we saw the Killer Whales again at Captain Harry's, and again danced in the heat until we were drenched. Saturday afternoon was spent at the beach, and I nearly passed out when Cindy removed her T-shirt and shorts to reveal a small bikini that showcased her now perfect body. I tried not to stare, but she was way beyond gorgeous. She had the attention of every male that came within 100 yards. Her looks made my stomach hurt, and my nerves completely unstable. I often wondered if she actually realized just how stunning she was. She was so painfully attractive that I feared she would discover that she had me wrapped around her finger. But I knew she would never take advantage of that. She also just happened to be the nicest person I had ever known.

That evening we went to a restaurant located on Shem Creek in Mt. Pleasant called RB's. It had a deck, and we got a table right beside the water that gave us a view of the shrimp boats as they moved up the creek, and the sun as it slowly dipped behind the tree line. Cindy wore a pastel dress that was cut so as to once again give me stomach cramps. Planned or not, the day was an all out assault on my male instincts, and I mildly suspected she knew just what she was doing. We drank several beers before we ordered, and talked and laughed until the creek became dark and the candlelight gave me an enchanting view of Cindy's face. Maybe it was the beer, or my overwhelming lust, but it was very clear that I wanted to attack her. She was making me crazy with desire.

After dinner, we chose the solitude of her apartment, and I addressed some of my desires of the day as we kissed and held each other on the couch. I felt a need to move forward with her, but saw it as tacky to play the game of getting around the bases. Testosterone pushed me towards being more aggressive, but I couldn't bring myself to start. I wanted her. I wanted to know she was mine. But I was actually unsure, and scared to risk offending her. I knew what I was feeling, but just didn't know how to express it.

Whether good or bad, my dilemma was short lived. With her usual timely entrance, Cindy's roommate Susan came home, and that ended any further debate within my mind as to what to do. It was indeed a frustrating drive back to school that night.

Sunday evening I felt like a sore thumb, as Cindy had to hit the books for one last test before exams. I watched TV as she studied, but suspected I had taken up too much of her time. She didn't want me to leave, but I knew I was a distraction, so I kissed her and left for school. I felt alone as I drove through the gates and walked up to the nearly deserted barracks, wishing I were with her.

Monday was my last evening in Charleston before three lonely days at home. Since I had to report in for Cadre that Saturday, it was clear that time was running out. That night before leaving, I found Cindy getting emotional about the separation, since over the previous three weeks we had spent every spare minute together, separated only by me having to return to the barracks to sleep and attend classes. Considering we had been dating seriously for such a small time period, one would question how we had become so close, so quickly. We probably spent more time together in those days of summer than an average couple would spend together over several months. We were consumed with each other, and when we were apart, it was a heart wrenching time for us both. Maybe this was to be a trial separation; one that would help prepare us for the real void Drill would create. Cindy had to fight to hold back her tears, and though I tried not to show it, it was agonizing for me as well.

CHAPTER 31

The next day I found myself back home in Kingstree. For the first time since entering into The Citadel, it was actually disappointing to come home since my heart and mind was in Charleston with Cindy. My parents knew nothing about my new relationship, and I saw no need to tell them about it. They welcomed me back home, yet it didn't take long for me to see that something was really bothering them. It took effort for my parents to maintain their enthusiasm and pleasantness while talking, and after a while, I couldn't help but ask what was wrong.

"It appears our worst nightmare has come true over Charles' catfish farm," explained Dad. "Apparently the batch of replacement catfish Charles obtained had a few infected ones mixed in that had a fungus-type disease that was a real killer. Even though Charles tried to stop it by applying a chemical treatment to the water, it was too late. His entire catfish population died again."

"All of them?" I asked in shock.

"The ones that are still living will probably pass away soon," answered Dad. "It's just a matter of time."

This was terrible news. I felt sorry for my parents as they were obviously taking the news hard. Charles' get rich quick scheme was now a serious financial problem for the family that wasn't going to just go away. Even with our differences, I also felt sorry for Charles. I knew this was all his idea, and that he alone would have to shoulder the blame since he insisted on taking such a risk.

"How is Charles taking all of this?" I asked.

"Very hard," Mom answered with both despair and concern, "it's tearing him apart."

"It's tearing us all apart," said Dad with anger. "We've invested in buildings, ponds, fish food, and God knows what else, and we have nothing that's even salvageable. Along with that we have the additional problem of Charles' attitude. He blames everyone but himself, claiming we never supported him."

"John, you know that's not true," said Mom. "We all knew that if Charles failed it would be bad for the entire family."

"Now we have a fifty thousand dollar mortgage against what was once debt free land," said Dad, "with nothing but the crop income to pay it off. And if Charles keeps up his attitude, we won't even have that."

"Is there a problem with the farm too?" I asked.

"Everyone is upset, son. Your mother, myself, even most of the workers. No matter how hard we've tried, Charles resents everyone, and that has spilled over into the operation of the farm."

"I'm sorry for everyone concerned," I said.

"I'm sorry too," said Mom, now showing tears. "I've never seen this family so torn apart. It's affecting every part of our lives."

I truly felt bad for what was going on, yet without even asking, I knew that there was nothing I could do. Over time, the failure that Charles had experienced would probably go away, or at least would not be so harsh in everyone's mind. The farm had survived for generations, from year to year, even in other times when things were tough. Although this was a real setback, it too could be put behind us, that is if Charles' attitude didn't destroy the farm and us before the wound could heal.

I was happy knowing that I would only be home for a few days. Forty-eight hours was all I had to stay clear of Charles, and I spent most of my time getting my things together for the coming year. I had heard from the old Drill members that the week preceding the 14 Nights would be filled with hard work in getting our equipment ready. It would require great effort to get things right, especially the metal parts like my sword, scabbard, and brass.

I went out to my father's shop, and with his permission, gathered up the many tools that I would need to do some of the work. I even grabbed a blowtorch and lots of solder and brass welding rods, knowing that they would be needed in the upcoming weeks. My time passed quickly while searching for, finding, and packing together all the items I would need.

I was successful in avoiding Charles right up until the last day. I was within an hour of leaving, and was putting the last few things into my car when his pickup truck came rolling up into the yard. I was prepared. I had decided previously that if by chance I ran into him, I would do everything within my power to make it a pleasant meeting, even if I had to swallow my pride. But as soon as Charles jumped out of his truck, he immediately took a bite.

"Well, if it ain't the old college boy home again."

"Hello Charles," I said.

"Ya here for a while, or just long enough to cause trouble?"

"Listen Charles, you need to understand something right now. I'm not here for trouble. I'm home just to get my stuff and then get the hell outta here, so don't start."

"Don't start? That's a real good one. Last time I saw you, you were the one that started it, and then hauled ass. It was awfully nice of you to plant the seed of destruction between me and the farm hands, then just get in your car and go off to Charleston to have a good time while I'm stuck dealing with the mess you left behind."

"I didn't start the trouble, I was only doing as I was told."

"Yeah, so was Isaiah, who's now fired because of you."

"Not because of me Charles, but because of your ignorance to realize that everyone's not out to get you. You're your own worst enemy. You create more problems for yourself than everyone else combined."

"Let me tell you something little brother. I'm YOUR biggest problem. So it's best that you just pack up your little fuckin' car with your shit and get the hell out of here. 'Cause as long as you're here on my farm, there's gonna be trouble for you."

"Fine, I'll be gone in an hour."

"Good," said Charles, "but don't consider that just by leaving that we're anywhere close to being even. I owe you a lot of problems for the bullshit you've created for me. I don't forget, and I'll get ya, somehow or another."

Charles walked over to his truck, slid through the door and slammed it. I just chose to let it go, not saying another word as I watched him spin the tires in the dirt, tearing out of the yard back towards the highway. I wasn't even fazed by the visit, and just considered it impossible for Charles and I to make it through life without being at each other's throat. Charles had complete control of the farm, and I had voluntarily moved out of his way. It seemed he still wasn't happy with that. The only way to keep peace with him was to avoid him altogether.

I wasn't going to move any faster for Charles' sake, but I wanted to finish packing up my car and get on the road. As I worked I wondered if somehow this mess with him and his desire to get revenge would indeed mean real problems. He was stupid enough to do anything, but I hoped he would at least stay the hell out of Charleston, and away from The Citadel. What I was facing was going to be hard enough. I needed no negative outside influences from anyone, especially my trouble-making older brother.

With my car packed, I sat and once again talked with my parents. I explained to them that I was now going to be getting quite serious about Sword Drill, and put a vague spin on the challenges I would face. They felt regret that I had to come home to experience problems before going back to such a formidable venture, but encouraged me to do well, and gave their full blessings for anything that could be so positive. They had no idea what I would soon be going through, or what I expected to gain. Dreams are often hard to explain to one's parents, including mine. They promised that they would keep open the Friday night before Parents Day, and that nothing could keep them away from the performance. I found humor in their confidence that I would make Drill just like that. They wished me luck in my quest; I too wished them strength to survive the situation with Charles. I walked to my car happy to be leaving such an atmosphere of problems and resentment.

When I made it back to Charleston, I found 4th Battalion already open and was able to make my way up to my new room in the Staff area. There was a long standing room established for the Battalion Sergeant Major, so I began unloading my car and lugged all the clothes, tools, and other gear up the stairs. I knew I would have quite a chore getting all of my things unpacked and put away, but at that point, all I wanted to do was get them inside of my room. Cindy was my most immediate priority, and since her exam was during the morning, it was only a matter of securing my possessions before I could make my way over to her apartment.

When I arrived, I was barely out of my car when I noticed Cindy coming down the steps to meet me. We met each other with an enthusiastic embrace and kiss, and you would have thought we had been separated for months, and not just three days. Our reunion was intense, yet reflected our feelings that the separation was almost too much to handle. Until Cadre started on Sunday, we had the weekend with no classes or outside interferences to deal with. It would be two days of pure Heaven.

I was tempted to suggest that I stay with Cindy in her apartment, but somehow felt that she may take it as some covert suggestion of sex. I wasn't sure where that issue stood in our relationship, but based on Cindy's descriptions of the few dates she had in her life, I felt certain fooling around had never before been even a remote consideration. In my past relationships, sex had been a strong part of my agenda. But I didn't want to push my need for pleasure above what had to be a really sensitive issue for Cindy. I knew the way we felt about each other would more than justify the union, but for now, it seemed to be pushing things a bit. If sex were to enter into our relationship, it would happen at the proper time. As far as I was concerned, that was whenever she was ready, and I was sure she would make that known when she was.

Cindy talked a lot that weekend about an event that would take place on the Saturday night that was a week away. It was some big shindig for her cousin, who by Cindy's description was also quite a looker. I thought of how attractive Cindy's mom was, and how it must run in her family. Cindy explained that her aunt had married well into a prominent Charleston family. Dr. William Maybank and Cindy's Aunt Jean had several children, one of whom, Michelle, was very close to Cindy's age.

It seemed that Michelle and Cindy, in their early years, were quite close as the two young families grew up. Unfortunately, as the two girls matured, they drifted apart. Cindy was never positive, but had always suspected it was because of her appearance. Michelle was a very pretty girl, and very popular with the Charleston boys. She always found herself well seated in the "South of Broad" crowd as she made her way through high school. And though she was now attending the College of Charleston, she never missed a beat in maintaining her top rated status in the local pecking order.

Saturday night would be Michelle's debutante party, and based on her reputation, and the wealth of the Maybank family, it was sure to be one heck of an affair. Not only were many members of the family invited, but also it was sure to be a parade of the local social roster. It was to be a formal dance to rival all others in a long history of girls coming out in the South. It would be one that the Battery of Old Charleston would not soon forget. Like any other female I had ever known, Cindy viewed the forthcoming occasion with the kind of seriousness I reserved only for things like Sword Drill. These formal events were the highlight of any girl's social life, and strategy and planning would rival that of many fierce battles throughout the world's warring history. Cindy approached this female ritual with a vengeance. She had lost her weight and she now had a boyfriend. You could see it in her pretty eyes. She was ever so ready to be seen by her family under her new set of circumstances, and especially by Michelle.

I didn't fully understand what debutante parties were all about, having never been invited to one. They were certainly rare in Williamsburg County. My etiquette would be tested, but I was more than happy to go anywhere with Cindy, even if it meant having to pull out my formal full dress uniform. Any time spent with Cindy was quality time, even if it meant going to some stuffed shirt wingding.

My only real displeasure with the event was knowing it would take up so much time on our last real weekend together. Considering the amount of involvement that Cindy and her family would have with the event, it would overshadow the importance of us being alone. It would be our last night together for a very long time.

In many ways, the summer seemed almost at an end when I was less than an hour from our first meeting in the Battalion Commander's room. Cindy was actually excited that she would now get to see me in my uniform. After two years, the thrill was gone for me, and I could only think of my loss of freedom. It was an anxious moment, hearing Cindy's words of enthusiasm for the change, knowing she had no idea that she was saying auf Wiedersehen to the John O'Bryan that she had come to know best.

As I held her close and gave her a last kiss, I felt like I was saying goodbye to her and to the best summer of my life.

I le ft Cindy's apartment and drove to 4th Battalion. I arrived early for the meeting, finding those already there still in their civilian clothes like me. I had barely gotten to know the members of staff before we left for summer, particularly those from the other companies. I had a feeling I would see these guys a lot in the school year that lay ahead.

Carl Andrews, 4th Battalion Commander, called our meeting to order, and the start of my junior year was officially underway. Within minutes, I heard the expected. There was a tremendous amount of work to be done seeing to it that the staff was set up. Since I was the one and only junior on Staff, my 'to do' list seemed to grow with Andrews' every other sentence. With what the senior staff members called the "privileges of rank," it was guaranteed that I would be busting ass right up until the new freshmen arrived.

Following the staff meeting, I wandered over to R Company to see whom I could harass. I was thrilled to see many of my classmates, especially my pals Danny Burn, Hank Rosellini, and Chris Davis. The cuts were flying at the same time we were shaking hands. These guys just never let up. We quickly breezed over our three-month furlough, and gave a *Readers Digest* version of the better war stories. It seemed we all had cherished the long and relaxing summer break, but were ready to get down to the business of being Cadet Sergeants. We all had power now like we had never known, and Danny and Hank seemed the most anxious to use it. Chris seemed so low-key that I wondered if he was nervous about Drill.

"I sure hope you worked hard over the summer to get ready for what we're about to go through," I said to Chris. "You are ready aren't you?"

Chris stared back and there seemed to be an anxious silence as we waited for his reply. He then answered by saying "No I'm not ready John. As a matter of fact, I think I'm going to let you handle Sword Drill."

I stood staring at Chris in silence. No one else said a word.

"Are you serious?" I finally asked.

"I had time to think about it over the summer, and I...I just don't think it's worth the sacrifice for me. That's an awful lot of shit to put up with until Parents Day."

I was floored. Chris had an opportunity most people would kill for. He had the rank, and had gone all the way through Spring Roach. Now, for some reason, he wasn't going to see it through.

Rosellini broke the silence and said laughing, "The son of a bitch just did the roaching thing to get the rank. You fuckers oughta know that!"

"That's bullshit," yelled Chris. "I had every intention of going out."

"Yeah, yeah, yeah," said Burn. "Sure you did."

"I don't see you two assholes practicing sword manual," scorned Chris.

"We were smart enough not to ever get involved in the first place," laughed Rosellini. "You think we're crazy?"

"I got racked enough when I was a knob," said Burn. "Tell ya what John, why don't you come on into Hank's and my room and let us get you warmed up for Drill. We'll rack the piss out of ya."

We all started laughing, and I could see the summer hadn't taken the edge off of either Danny or Hank's asshole abilities.

"I wouldn't give you cunts the pleasure," I said. "But I think I oughta rack Davis here for backing out. The wimp!"

"Get off of it John," said Chris, "we'll be rooting for ya."

"Thanks a lot!" I said.

I was disappointed that Chris wasn't going out. I wanted to see the losing streak of R Company roaches broken. Now, that burden was on my shoulders. I would be going at it alone.

The next day started off busy for me. I hoped to get a jump on the crowd at the warehouse and get the entire staff's storage boxes back to the battalion. They contained our uniforms, and it was awkward to conduct business while in civilian clothes. The pressure was on me to perform, and fast. There was also the added stress to get things done so I would not run into the evening hours. I had somewhere to go, and I didn't want to lose a minute's time I might have with Cindy. I knew everyone on cadre would be going out that night, probably to grab a few beers to toast the new year. I was going out all right, but not to go drink beer with the guys.

I managed to perform well getting my own uniforms and room squared away. I also had an urgent need to lose some extra hair, as I looked really stupid with my summer growth while in uniform. I stayed focused, and by the time I got everything to the point where I could stop for the day, it was after 1800. The leave uniform was gray nasties, so luckily I didn't have to change before heading out.

When I arrived at Cindy's, she couldn't believe how I looked, and started making a big deal over the conversion. She really thought the uniform made me look sharp, but was honest in saying she preferred my hair longer. She laughed, and stared, and made me feel like I was some kind of friggin' model, and after she had some fun, she tried convincing me that she didn't mind the transformation. She said that it brought even more excitement to our already wonderful relationship. I learned instantly she was one hell of a politician. She simply stated in a faked sexy voice, "I've always been a sucker for guys in uniform," then wrapped her arms around me and began to kiss me as faithfully as ever. I didn't buy the whole story, but it was a joy to have someone so understanding and supportive. The change was not a big problem with her, and I was relieved, at least for now. This was only a small sample of what was yet to come. Once Drill started, she would see a shaved head, drastic loss in weight, and a long separation..

I spent the rest of that first week working hard attending to a surprisingly full schedule of training and strategy sessions and getting everything squared away for Cadre. I had somehow underestimated the workload, thinking there would be an abundance of slack time to work on other things. But I stayed busy and strapped for time the whole week, and had to work hard to maintain my running and lifting schedule and then have my evenings free to spend with Cindy. The week was frantic, and it just flew by.

Friday was both a busy and informative day. I found out some sobering news as a rumor surfaced that the 14 Nights would possibly start during the very next week. It was expected, but still brought on a fair measure of anxiety. The old Drill made it known that we were to use the weekend to get ready, since it would be our last one with freedom and spare time. I already knew that it was going to be a bust ass week starting Sunday when the new freshmen would begin to arrive since ranking sergeants carried the greatest burden for issuing uniforms, equipment, and supplies. Leave during the evenings would be ridiculous to consider, and daytime Charleston passes out of the question. It became clear that Saturday night's party would be a privileged break from my schedule, and without a doubt my last chance to see Cindy for a long time.

Even though it was Saturday, I found myself back in the grind the next morning. I still had a mountain of tasks that required my attention. Being the only junior on staff left me overwhelmed at times with the constant flow of problems passed down to me by the seniors. I didn't dare complain, since I somehow knew that this was by design. My CO was a member of the '79 Drill.

Despite the busy schedule, I had taken great care during the week to get my act together for the big debutante bash. I had unpacked my full dress blouse and had my new Master Sergeant stripes sewn on. I had it and my dress pants pressed and cleaned. I even blitzed down my shoes. For Cindy's sake, I had everything in perfect shape.

In the late afternoon I hit the showers and then began the process of getting dressed. I had given myself plenty of time, so when I reached the moment of putting my new Gold Stars on my uniform, I performed the task with a feeling of ceremony. It was the one part of my uniform I was most proud to wear. Few cadets wore those symbols of academic excellence, and I knew I had earned them at the price of extraordinary sacrifice and effort. After shining them up, I took great care to place them perfectly on my collar.

Once fully in my uniform, I stood in front of the mirror to look for flaws as if I were going to the quad for an SMI. I was pleased with what I saw. I was proud of the new Master Sergeant stripes on my sleeves, and the gleaming Gold Stars that one could not help but see when looking at my face. It was my greatest moment of pride in wearing a Citadel uniform. It not only looked impressive, but it symbolized the accomplishments of my labor.

When I arrived early at Cindy's apartment, she was still in the final stages of getting herself dressed.

"Just have a seat John. I'll be out in a sec," she yelled from her bedroom.

I awkwardly sat on the couch in my snug uniform while Cindy rushed around. Through her slightly cracked door, it appeared she was pretty darned close.

"OK, I'm ready," said Cindy as she exited from her bedroom.

As she walked out, I could hardly comprehend what I was seeing. Her beauty was extraordinary. It was the first time I had seen her in a formal evening gown. No matter what she wore, she was always incredibly pretty, but on this night, she reached new heights. She wore an elegant, yet seductive evening gown. It was a sleek, royal blue number that matched the color of her eyes. Its strapless design elegantly presented her beautiful skin and shoulders, and it was cut low to expose the upper portions of her breasts. It was a classy look, only so very sensual. She spun around and asked, "What do you think?"

I was speechless. She was breathtaking. I wanted to just stare and admire the image. I yearned to reach out and possess her. My attraction was nearly more than I could handle.

"What are you trying to do to me?" I asked with a weak voice.

"What?" smiled Cindy slightly. "Do you like it?"

I walked over to her, and took her by both hands, then slowly pulled her close, giving her a slow easy kiss.

"I just don't know how to handle you sometimes. You look gorgeous, you look ravishing, you look superb."

Cindy just smiled at the conquest, then lightly kissed me as she said, "Glad you like it. You don't look bad yourself."

Cindy then stood back, and turned her full attention towards me, and for the second time she made a big deal over the way I looked in uniform. She honed in on the ribbons and medals, and then asked what each represented. The Gold Stars quickly grabbed her attention, and when she asked what they stood for, I was succumbed to an overwhelming feeling of modesty and felt almost embarrassed to tell. In our conversations during the summer we had rarely talked of academics, and I never once mentioned the miraculous change I had made in my approach to grades. So when I revealed that the stars represented having a GPR exceeding a 3.7 during the previous semester, she was floored.

"You've got to be kidding!"

I hesitated, and then shook my head in the negative.

"Wait a minute, for weeks now, I thought I was dating John O'Bryan. Are you the same John O'Bryan I knew during high school?"

"Of course I am," I answered, playing along with her.

"The same John O'Bryan who I struggled with so hard to help pass his exams?"

"Leave me alone," I said smiling.

"The same John O'Bryan that used to throw spit balls and break wind during class?"

"That's enough," I said.

"The same John O'Bryan that never took a book home?"

"Enough already," I laughed. "Can't somebody change around here without a big to-do?"

"I just can't believe this. A 3.7 in Electrical Engineering? That's one of the hardest majors around. What's happened to you John?" she said with a very pleased, yet serious look on her face.

"Nothin'," I said. "I'm just good ol' John."

"No you're not. I liked the old John, but I really like the new one.... This is such a drastic change. I mean it, what has happened to you?"

I could see that Cindy was quite serious about her question. Without having to think, I knew the answer, yet felt curiously uncomfortable in revealing my explanation.

"It's because of Sword Drill."

Cindy just stood there and looked at me with a small but growing smile on her face.

"In order to get the rank that I needed to go out for Drill, I had to be outstanding academically. That's the bottom line. If I wanted to make Drill, I had to make the grades."

Cindy stood there looking strangely into my eyes, probably finding it hard to believe that someone could be so focused on such a goal.

"You know John, through these last few weeks, I've tried hard to understand what attracts you so to this Sword Drill thing. But the one thing that seems to continually stand out is your utter commitment to making it...no, let's call it an obsession. I've never seen anything like this before. But I just want to say that I'm so very proud of you for doing this. Maybe I'm beginning to now see why my father loves

The Citadel so much." Cindy pulled me close saying, "But I'm really glad that you're letting me hang around to see it," then kissed me sweetly.

"For your protection, I think we should get to the party!"

We left Cindy's apartment and headed downtown to one of the most beautiful antebellum houses I had ever seen. It was a huge three-story home down on East Battery Avenue with very large porches on all three levels. As we walked towards the building I could see females in evening gowns and males in tuxes standing out on one of the upper level porches. The courtyard was manicured, and quite a showpiece to introduce what appeared to be the perfect place for a formal party in Charleston.

Cindy and I entered into the vestibule of the house, and started our climb up the long spiral staircase that was already busy with others going towards the gathering above. At the top of the stairs, we could hear music and see a large crowd in the room that was accessed through a set of huge double doors. About twenty people stood in what appeared to be a receiving line as they patiently waited to enter.

We joined the line, and moved slowly forward as it progressed through the doors. We could soon see a portion of the crowd inside, and Cindy scanned the gathering constantly as we moved ever closer.

"Do you know if your parents are here yet?" I asked nervously, feeling intimidated by the formality and the crowd of strangers.

"They should be," answered Cindy. "They came earlier today to help out. Do you see them?"

I scanned the sea of humans, saying, "No, but there's too many people to tell."

As we stood in line, I couldn't help but notice the abundance of beautiful girls in formal dresses. Accompanying them were sharply dressed guys, most wearing black tuxedos. But there were exceptions. There was apparently a wilder crowd present, possibly trying to make a statement in protest of conservative formal evening wear. These guys were obviously going for a look that would make them stand out by wearing colorful tuxes apparently meant for groomsmen at Ronald McDonald's wedding. If they were trying to be different, they certainly hit their mark.

There were a lot of older adults present too. More than I had expected. There were almost as many of them as there were those our age. I assumed that the adults in the receiving line were Cindy's relatives, probably the immediate family of Michelle. I didn't know another soul there, but I felt good that I at least wouldn't be struggling during the evening to remember anyone's name. This would be Cindy's unfortunate burden since this was her family.

One couple in line was Cindy's grandparents. They were thrilled to see Cindy, and genuinely happy to meet me, saying they had heard so many nice things. Her grandparents were very flattering and complimentary towards me, and openly impressed with my uniform, and especially my short hair. Little did they know I felt completely out of place with my cadet look. But they carried on about Cindy dating such a polished gentleman, and I just wished the line would move along.

We finally made it down to Michelle's parents. Talk about a big deal. They went nuts when they saw Cindy, acting as if she had been raised from the dead. They stopped the whole line, and I prayed it would all be over with quickly. But it only got worse as they turned their compliment guns on me, and started calling me handsome and sharp and clean cut. I felt like a goody two shoes, and had an urge to use some foul language just to calm them down. But the tone shifted back to Cindy as she connected with Michelle. It went from peachy to hysterical. They screamed and laughed and made a big spectacle as they hugged, and I could see that Michelle possessed her share of the beauty that ran in the family bloodline. Cindy then introduced me, and Michelle grabbed her composure and greeted me as if I were the Prince of Wales. She seemed impressed, and complemented me on how wonderful my uniform looked, a compliment that was now making me paranoid. I then shook hands with Michelle's boyfriend, then moved on as the flow of the line finally resumed, and I was spared any further nauseating formality.

Cindy could see her parents standing in a crowd across the room. They had obviously seen her and were just allowing us time to make it through the line.

"I see my parents!"

Cindy reached back and grabbed my hand, and we started walking across the room to where Mr. and Mrs. Johnson were standing.

"Hey sweetheart," said Mr. Johnson, "and would you look at this fella here. John, how are you doing?"

"Fine Sir. I guess I haven't seen you since the last Homecoming football game."

"That's right, it's been that long hasn't it?"

"It sure has. Hello Mrs. Johnson, it's nice to see you again."

"Why thank you John. You look so handsome in your uniform."

I laughed and then said looking around, "I'm glad you like it. It's just... well...I don't see too many other guys wearing uniforms in here."

"Don't you worry one bit about that, John," said Mrs. Johnson, "we'll try not to feel sorry for the other boys who aren't."

I smiled, grateful for her hokey, yet well meaning comment.

"Tell me John," said Mr. Johnson. "What kind of stripes are those? Are you a company First Sergeant?"

"No sir. 4th Battalion Sergeant Major."

"What?" yelped Mr. Johnson. "My gosh, and look at this Elizabeth, he's even got Gold Stars."

I looked at Cindy, knowing well that my face had to be flushed by the attention. She just smiled at her dad as she grabbed my arm, and there seemed to be some unspoken confirmation as to the significance between the two of them.

"What on earth are Gold Stars dear?" asked Mrs. Johnson.

"It means he had over a 3.7 GPR last semester," answered Cindy.

Mrs. Johnson looked at me very puzzled, then said, "My, I guess you've kind of changed your...I mean...oh I'm sorry John."

"I know Mrs. Johnson," I said, "I was kind of slack during high school, wasn't I?"

"I didn't mean that in such a harsh way, John."

"Don't worry about it. Please!"

"Yeah, don't worry about it, dear," said Mr. Johnson with authority, slapping me on the back. "I told you the school just seems to bring out the best in these boys. And see, he's solid there too. You working out with weights or something, John?"

This was getting out of hand. "Uh, yes Sir, a little bit. I try to stay in shape."

"He's going out for the Junior Sword Drill Daddy," said Cindy.

Mr. Johnson stopped breathing, and then brought a serious look to his face. "Sword Drill? You've got to be kidding me John. Aren't you an Electrical Engineering major?"

"Yes, sir, I am."

"I can't believe you're a double E with Gold Stars, Battalion Sergeant Major, and you're going out for Sword Drill?"

I could see that Mr. Johnson was genuinely taken back by all of this. "Yes, sir. I somewhat decided a long time ago to do it, and I've just set my mind to it."

"What is Sword Drill, honey?" asked Mrs. Johnson.

"You know dear. It's the performance given during Parents Day weekend. Don't you remember back when you and I walked through that big ring, and those guys were standing there arching swords."

"Oh yes, I remember. And they did all that neat marching."

"Mom, you've seen it?" asked Cindy with enthusiasm.

"Yes dear, you knew that your father and I dated through his senior year when he was at The Citadel."

"Yes, but I didn't know you had seen the Sword Drill performance. They had them way back then?"

"Watch it young lady," said Mr. Johnson laughing. "We're not that old you know."

"But still, it's hard to imagine that the Sword Drill has been going on for that long."

"It was going on back then, and I'm really glad to hear that it's still around. I don't know how it is now John, but that was an awfully tough thing to make back then."

"It still is," I answered.

"Are you ready to start on it soon?"

"As a matter of fact, I think this is going to be my last weekend out for awhile. We should start roaching next week."

"Gonna get a hair cut huh?" said Mr. Johnson smiling.

As I stood there shaking my head in an affirmative manner, Mrs. Johnson asked, "What's roaching?"

"A lot of hell dear," answered Mr. Johnson.

"What?" asked a puzzled Mrs. Johnson.

"I'll explain it later."

Cindy's father looked back at me and very sincerely said "John, I just can't tell you how proud all of us are of you for having done so well. I was so pleased to know that you were even considering the school, much less finally finding out that you had decided to go there. But now that I see that you have not only survived, but are just tearing it up, it just brings me a lot of great pleasure. I'm also pleased to know that you and Cindy are such good friends now."

I was really touched by Mr. Johnson's compliments, and his approval of me seeing Cindy. "I appreciate it Mr. Johnson, not only the praise, but also you taking the time out when you did to even mention The Citadel. I guess had you not done so, I probably wouldn't be standing here right now. So I guess I owe you one."

"Not at all," said Mr. Johnson. "Just keep making us proud."

"I'm sure he will," said Mrs. Johnson.

As Cindy and I mingled through the crowd with her parents, I was introduced time and again to friends and relatives who all continued the endless chain of compliments and references concerning my uniform and choice of school. Cindy soon recognized the painful redundancy, and out of compassion asked if I wanted to go sample the food. I praised her as a savior, and we escaped to dine and take an intermission from the introductions and attention of the crowd. I made Emily Post proud as I elegantly gorged myself on the tasty hors d'oeuvres. I also hit the bar a time or two, and felt a new appreciation for debutantes and the finer side of life.

While consuming our edible delights, the bandleader asked for everyone's attention. It was time for the first dance of the evening, which by social order was the privilege of Michelle and her father, Dr. Maybank. I guess it was a special moment for them, but I would think being the only ones on the dance floor would embarrass them both. But Michelle and Dr. Maybank seemed well versed in the social graces, and turned an awkward experience into one of showmanship. The crowd watched with delight as the two danced slowly across the floor, and the females in the crowd seemed taken away by the whole deal. I concluded that this was their Sword Drill.

At the conclusion of the dance, the two received everyone's approval of such a touching moment between father and daughter. I clapped with tongue in cheek, but was pleased that the performance seemed to kick the party into high gear. Everyone moved to the dance floor, and Cindy and I were both obliged to do the same. We had danced together many times, yet under very different circumstances. This wasn't Captain Harry's Blue Marlin Bar, and we weren't in shorts and topsiders. I had to produce my more reserved and refined dance abilities, the ones I never knew I had. I just thought a lot about Lawrence Welk shows.

Cindy and I danced well together, yet I was quite aware of the attention we were drawing. I would later learn that most of the stares I had presumed to be gawks, were actually looks of envy. Many girls of Cindy's age were covetous of the moment. There was just something very nostalgic and impressive to females about a Southern gentleman in uniform at a formal dance. Mrs. Johnson would later say it was almost something out of a storybook. But to paranoid me, I just wondered why all of the women kept staring.

But not all there were impressed. To many of the young men at the party, I provided a reason for them to make a lot of monkey suit jokes. I was intimately familiar with being the object of resentment while out on the town, and it was the first thing I thought of when I saw someone looking at me. For whatever reason, I found many civilian guys my age quite aggressive towards me and my fellow cadets. I never knew if it was resentment or jealousy. I just knew it was there. I could see their reactions as they were cutting me down and laughing. They were unaware that I couldn't give a shit. They all seemed dateless as they stood there laughing in their own clown suits, and I was waltzing across the floor with the ever so beautiful Cindy Johnson. I made sure to pass close by, and I winked at them with a pretty smile. I think it was at that point that a few of them wanted to beat my ass.

Cindy and I had many dances together, and I soon grew comfortable that I was becoming less of a wonder. But then we took a break and moved around among Cindy's relatives and the other guests, and it all seemed to start again. No matter where we went, we were both inundated with compliments. Though the attention was a little much for me, Cindy acted like it was a dream come true.

But eventually we both grew tired of talking with other people and not having any time alone, especially when it was our last night together for quite some time. At our first free opportunity Cindy grabbed me by the hand and led me out towards the two large French doors that opened up onto the large side porch. The Charleston night air was warm and fresh, and there were several others out also catching a breath. Everyone was scattered in groups around the banister, and Cindy and I soon found our own spot to hold. The beautiful Charleston harbor lay before us like a picture, and the lights from boats and Fort Sumter could be seen off in the distance. It was a breathtaking sight. The night was clear, and the half moon dimmed only the stars around it. It was a perfect night to be with a perfect girl.

"Privacy at last," said Cindy who leaned up against the rail, then pulled me close.

"I know. I thought we would never get a break."

"You'll have to excuse my parents, especially my Dad. He's so proud of you for what you've done at school. And I am too, John."

"Hey, don't put it all on me. They're proud of you too. You've accomplished as much as I have."

"I have accomplished a lot. I've got you now."

"That's not what I meant."

"Yeah, but that's what I mean. I really thought this would never happen."

"Us coming to Michelle's party?"

"No. I mean us. You and me."

"Why not?"

Cindy stopped talking for a second and looked around at the couples standing near us. She was suddenly concerned with privacy.

"Here, follow me," she said.

Now I was really confused, but didn't question her as she grabbed my hand and started pulling me to follow. She made her way back through the large room and out to the winding staircase and down to the next level. We then walked out to the matching side porch on the second deck immediately under the one we had just left. This time, it was just the two of us. She once again led me over to the rail closest to the harbor, and though one level lower we still had our magnificent view.

"What's going on?" I asked.

"What I wanted to say was that I'm just glad that you and I have had the opportunity these last few weeks to go out."

"I am too Cindy, you know that."

"But John, I'm just so sad now. I know this is our last night together for a long time. I just can't help but feel worried."

"Worried about what?"

"There's just something I want to tell you, yet at the same time I don't."

"What's wrong?"

"Oh, nothing's wrong now. It's just that, well, you remember back when you got yourself in trouble with your grades at the end of our junior year?"

"Sure, how could I forget? You saved my life."

"I may have saved your life, but you changed mine forever. I'm afraid that something happened then that was both good and bad."

"And that was?"

Cindy looked down at the floor for a couple of seconds, and then looked back up with her eyes filling with tears.

"It was that I fell in love with you."

The statement caught me off guard, and my mind raced as I thought back, and remembered well how I had worried our time together would have led to a possible "misunderstanding."

"You see," continued Cindy, "by my own doings, I had made myself a social zero. It was something I hated, yet it was something that I felt like I deserved."

"What do you mean deserved?"

"This is so hard to say John, but somehow I just got off track, and around the age of ten, a vicious cycle started. I just developed some bad eating habits, and even though my mom tried to correct them, I was always stubborn about her guidance. I was always overweight, and well, the more I put on, the more I became an outcast. You remember. I was overweight all through both junior high and high school."

"I remember."

"Then you must also remember that I very rarely participated in school functions, or anything social, sometimes by choice, and sometimes not. These were very painful years for me, John. I was so depressed. I neglected myself by not wanting to dress up, or wear makeup, or even mess with my hair like all the slim and beautiful girls in our class. It was sort of a rebellion against them and what they held as important. I had convinced myself that the appearance game was overrated and silly, yet, that attitude made me even more of an outcast. I was never invited to parties, or out on dates. Even though I asked for it, it made me even more depressed. I addressed my misery by eating more, thus, the vicious cycle."

I could see the anguish in Cindy's face as the tears rolled down her cheeks, yet I really couldn't find any words to say.

"But then something happened, John. You asked me to help you, which I was more than happy to do. But if you remember, that was the first time you had ever really talked to me, other than an occasional 'hello.' As a matter of fact, it was one of those rare times in high school when any boy talked to me other than to either make a smart comment about how fat I was or to ask me if they could copy my homework. You see, during that time we spent together, I couldn't help myself. You were so good-looking and popular, and you were so nice to me. Over the week that you and I spent together studying, I grew quite fond of you. I looked forward every day to our next meeting so we could be together."

"So that's why you worked so hard to help me."

"Yes. I would have done anything to help you. The more time we studied together, the more time I could spend with you."

"But why didn't you say something?"

"John… I knew. I knew as well as anyone I had no chance with you. Yet I couldn't help it. My heart was torn apart every time I thought about test day, and us not being able to study together anymore. But worst of all, my mind went crazy after we went to eat pizza together. I started to think that you and I had a chance."

I closed my eyes in pain, and drifted back as if I were sitting in my car, feeling those exact feelings of wonder as to where our relationship was heading, worried that she would get the wrong impression.

"I remember that night," I said with regret.

"Oh, it was a wonderful evening. One that I will never forget. But then came the test, and you passed, and after thanking me out in front of the school on our last day, it was all I could handle to think that you and I would not be together again."

I stood there with my eyes closed, ashamed that I had simply used Cindy to help me pass, all the while knowing that there was a high probability that I was going to mislead her.

"I'm so sorry I did that Cindy. I really am."

"Oh no, John! There's more to the story. And first of all, I don't want you to be sorry, because even though I suffered greatly through that summer, I never gave up hope that during our senior year I would have a chance again. During that summer I tried to lose weight, yet it never seemed to work out. I just didn't know how to diet, and just wasn't willing to do any physical exercise."

"I remember when you lost some weight, and you came back from the summer slimmer. You were also dressing a bit nicer."

"You're right, both Dad and Mom were encouraging me since they could see that it was causing me a lot of problems, both mentally and socially."

"Why didn't you stay with the diet?"

"I stayed with it John, all the way up until our Homecoming."

"Homecoming? Why Homecoming?"

"Remember the party after the Homecoming football game, where you intercepted that pass and ran it in for a touchdown. I went to that party. It was one of the first ones I had ever gone to."

"I didn't see you there."

"I'm sure you didn't. You were the man of the hour, John. There wasn't a girl in that gymnasium that wasn't after you that night, and I, in my foolish thinking, had planned to go to the dance for weeks, hoping it would be an opportunity to get close to you again, and maybe even get a dance."

"Oh my God."

Cindy's eyes again filled with tears.

"My Mom had taken me out to buy a special dress for that party, and I looked forward to it like no other event that had taken place during high school. I really let my mind paint a lot of wild scenarios of you and me and what might happen that night. But I was standing in the corner of the gym, and watched as you and Donna danced on the floor, and eventually started kissing. It tore me apart. I was so hurt that I quickly left the gym, barely making it to my car before I broke out into tears. It was then that I started hating myself for ever thinking that you and I ever had a chance. How stupid I was for thinking that the most popular guy in the school was going to have anything to do with a fat girl."

I could see that Cindy was truly crying now, and almost had anger in her voice as she spoke. I thought that I should speak to calm her down, "Cindy, I..."

"No wait a minute," she said with authority, "let me finish."

She was now quite visibly angry, and still crying. "I was hurt, and I drove home, and I cried for what seemed like hours in my bedroom until I finally fell asleep. I was devastated for weeks, months really. I wasn't mad at you for what you had done, but mad at myself for all kinds of reasons. It really didn't take long until all the weight that I had lost was regained. I was consumed by depression again, and I hated every thin girl I saw. I rebelled by once again stuffing myself, and the progress I had made in keeping myself up also went to hell."

Cindy wiped the tears from her eyes, and tried to gain some composure.

"After I started Columbia College, I found some wonderful programs for girls like me who were overweight."

"So did you enter one?"

"No, I didn't. It wasn't until I came home for Thanksgiving, that I made the solid commitment to change."

"What happened during Thanksgiving?"

"I came home that weekend for the holidays, and that Sunday at church I saw Jane Fulton. We were just talking about everyone, and it was then that she mentioned, and I'll use her words, that 'Donna had dumped you because she couldn't put up with all the restrictions of you going to The Citadel.' As I drove back to Columbia that night, I thought deeply about what I had heard. I couldn't help but think about how, even after almost a year and a half since you and I had studied together, that I still cared for you more than anyone else I had ever known. It was then and there that I made the decision of my life. Even if I had to wire my jaw shut, I was going to lose the weight. I had suffered through humiliation and disgrace for too many years. The embarrassment and shame had to end. But most of all, I saw an opportunity. As ridiculous as it may sound, hearing that you and Donna were no longer dating, somehow revealed to me that the door might open again. I had a vision that I might have a another chance to have you.."

"I can't believe this."

"Well you must. I thought about you all the time, and it was you who got me through the days and nights of being desperately hungry. It was you who got me through the insults and ridicule as I walked and ran down public streets, and heard people's comments.. It was you who got me through the pain in my knees from exercise and fatigue. In other words John, it's been you ever since our study time together junior year."

I was flabbergasted at the story I had just heard. I had suspected that our study time together may have created the potential for a misunderstanding, but never had I suspected something of such magnitude would have developed.

"You see John," said Cindy as tears continued to stream down her face, "it's always been you. After so many years of wanting and being without you, these few short weeks have been like heaven. And now, I'm going to lose you again, and I don't know for how long. I'm just scared John. I'm just scared."

I stood there looking at Cindy, feeling more emotions than I could handle. Here standing before me was the girl whom I cared for, and because of me, she had suffered terribly, and was now crying because I was going to hurt her again. It really tore me apart to see her that way, and I felt so bad that I had been the cause of so many years of heartache. Even though I had no idea what she was going through, I had a clue during the time that we were studying together that something was going on.

"Cindy, you must believe me. You may not understand why I say this, but I was wrong when I used you to help me pass my test."

"But I wanted to help you, John."

"That's not the point Cindy. You just have to understand that I suspected that our time spent together would result in something misleading, and believe me, I have dealt with a lot of guilt about the way I felt about you then, and the way I treated you."

"John, I'm not saying these things to make you feel guilty."

"I know Cindy, but just as you said you could not help but feel love, I could not help feeling the guilt. But there is one thing you've got to understand, and that is that I'm truly sorry for what happened in our past, but more than anything else in the world, I love you."

Cindy looked up at me, hearing those words. I knew she had probably dreamed of them for years, but I deeply felt the meaning of them, and was sorry I hadn't said them sooner. In a happy way, she once again started to cry, but this time, pretty hard. I pulled her close, and she squeezed me tightly. She cried with her face in the middle of my chest, holding me as if I would somehow get away.

"Listen," I said, "I'm not going to go out for Drill."

Cindy quickly pulled her face away from my shoulder, shocked by what I had said.

"What did you say?"

"I'm not going to go out for Sword Drill Cindy. I cannot bear to part from you again. It's been tearing at me to have to leave you, and I've hurt you once before, and I never want to hurt you like that again."

"John, no!"

"Yes, I've made my mind up."

Cindy became angry again, and with all the power her small body could muster, grabbed me by both of my shoulders, "Now wait a minute, John! You'll do no such thing. You can't do that to me, you can't do that to yourself, and you can't do that to us."

"What do you mean, do that to us? I am doing it for us."

"No, I've got you now, and believe me, I would be thrilled to death to have the old John from high school, who couldn't pass a test and was as wild and undisciplined as the wind. But John, look at you now. Look at what you've accomplished. There's not a soul in that room upstairs that can't help but think about your success."

"But what about us?"

"Whether you like it or not, we have now become a part of one another. Over the last month or so, I've tried hard to understand the Junior Sword Drill, and even though I know I could never conjure up the strength or determination to get through something like that, I want so much for you to make it. It has meant so much to you. It has changed your life. I won't let you throw away the best influence you've ever had. I simply won't stand for it."

"But again Cindy, what about us?"

"You've already answered that question John. If you truly love me, which you say you do, then that's enough to carry us through Sword Drill, and whatever else that may come up, no matter how long it takes."

"Are you sure about this?"

"There's no question in my mind. But if there ever is, there's always something you can say to drive it away."

I looked at Cindy, and saw that her tears were now drying up and she now had a hint of a smile on her face.

I looked at her and smiled, knowing exactly what I needed to say. "I love you, Cindy."

I pulled her as close as we could get, and we kissed each other with more intensity and affection than ever.

"You know," I said in a matter of fact way, "that's about the most amazing story I think I've ever heard."

"Not when you've had to live it," said Cindy squeezing me tightly.

I kissed Cindy again, then held her in my arms as our emotions settled down and we absorbed where we were in our lives together. "I've got to go by the restroom and fix my makeup, my mascara must be running."

"You wear makeup?" I asked as a compliment.

"Right," said Cindy, calling my bluff.

We walked off the porch, and headed straight for the restroom on that floor. I waited outside as Cindy went in. When she came out, she looked wonderful, with only a slight tint of redness in her eyes from her cry, which in the dim lights would be undetectable. We walked back upstairs, holding each other close with each step. As soon as we walked into the room, the band began playing a very slow and beautiful song, trying to match the romantic atmosphere of the muted lighting in the room. It was great timing on their part.

"Shall we dance, Miss Johnson?"

"Why certainly, Mr. O'Bryan."

I held my arm out, and Cindy smiled, almost laughing as we moved towards the middle of the dance floor. Others soon joined us, but they seemed miles away. We danced to the tender music, and I loved the dizzy feeling of my vaulting senses. I had a connection with Cindy that was previously untouched. I could still feel the passion from our conversation, and could see that Cindy was being taken away by the moment. We were together dancing in a strange and wonderful world of our own, unaware that the crowd and dimness of the room did little to conceal the infatuation we had for each other. Cindy's parents, who had wondered what had happened to us while we were gone, stood and watched intensely as we danced, alert to our obsession, but unaware of our burning love..

With a small, yet inviting smile, Cindy looked at me, and I kissed her with no regard to our location. We were miles away as we swayed back and forth to the music.

"Honey, do you see what your daughter is doing out there on the dance floor?" said Mrs. Johnson to her husband, trying to sound concerned.

Mr. Johnson just stood there watching us dancing and kissing in the presence of a few hundred people. He then said, "Lay one finger on those two Elizabeth, and we'll have words."

Mrs. Johnson, slightly surprised by her husband's comment, only looked up at him and smiled, then turned back to once again observe us on the dance floor.

When the song ended, the band immediately changed tempo and started into a faster song. Cindy and I shook our heads, and wanted no part of the mood change. She looked up at me and said, "I think it's late, and since this is our last night together, I think we'd better go."

I looked at her and smiled. "Let's say goodbye to your parents."

We found Mr. and Mrs. Johnson standing on the side of the dance floor, completely oblivious that they had been watching us since we had walked in.

"Mom, Dad," said Cindy, "it's really been fun, and I guess we need to be getting on."

"OK, dear," said Mrs. Johnson, "we'll soon have to be leaving ourselves."

"Well young man," said Mr. Johnson reaching his hand out, "it certainly was a pleasure to see you again, and I know you've got a lot coming up here with Sword Drill and all. Just remember, we're all behind you one hundred percent."

"Yes, John," said Mrs. Johnson, "don't you let those boys make a mess out of our favorite cadet."

Mrs. Johnson reached up and put her arms around my neck and gave me a kiss on the cheek.

We made our rounds to each of the hosts, extending gracious thanks for the wonderful party, then made our way out to my car.

Other than a few words about how nice the party was, there was very little said between us as we drove. As we moved up the stairs to her apartment, we held each other as we walked side by side. Cindy unlocked and opened the door, and as she turned the light on I asked, "Where's Susan this weekend?"

"Oh, she went home," said Cindy, slowly turning around and facing me with a serious look. For the longest moment, I stood there staring back at her. I wondered how someone could have gone through such a long party, cried as much as she did, and at such a late hour still look so good. It was unthinkable that I had once caused her so much pain. But now it seemed for the first time, I knew clearly the way I felt about her, and that she knew it.

Without a word, I walked over to the table that held both the telephone and the lamp she had switched on. I picked up the receiver, dialed seven numbers, and stood waiting for it to ring. Cindy just stood there, looking at me in wonder.

"Hello Fred? John O'Bryan. I'm sorry to call at the last moment like this, but you did say to let you know if we weren't going to come in, and well, this is my phone call."

I could see a smile come on Cindy's face, and after what was obviously a confirmation from the other end of the phone, I quickly said a few words then hung up. I looked back at Cindy, and she returned my loving gaze. I reached up and turned the lamp off, then walked over to her, leaving a small distance between us when I stopped. In the darkness broken only by the streetlights coming in through the windows, I put my hands on her shoulders, and pulled her towards me. I kissed her lightly on her lips, then after doing so, I reached down and removed my sash, and threw it over the couch. I unbuttoned my dress blouse, and then released the collar. Removing my blouse was a wonderful feeling as I dismissed the restraint that came with it. With a new feeling of freedom, I once again pulled Cindy close to me, and we kissed with an increasing vengeance. She grabbed the back of my tee shirt, and we stopped kissing just long enough for it to come over my head. She seemed to love the access to my now bare chest, touching and exploring the lines and valleys the muscles made in my upper body. She ran her hands over my arms, shoulders, and back, holding and squeezing them as she moved. I reached behind her and disconnected the back of her dress, and then pulled the zipper down, making it loose enough to fall to the floor. I felt skin against skin, and held my breath with the sensation. Our hearts raced, as we fought to control our overwhelming desire for each other. We kissed wildly, slowing down only when my hand touched her breast. I felt light-headed, yet determined to take in the overpowering feeling of the moment.

I picked Cindy up in my arms and moved into her room where I gently lowered her onto the bed. I rid myself of my remaining clothes, and then helped her to do the same. I slowly moved beside her, where we quickly found each other's body to hold. We touched and held each other, nearly passing out with the pleasure of the moment. The newness of unexplored regions consumed our every thought, and we tried to know all that we held. We were frantic with the vulnerability, and as our passions gained a state of composure, we slowed ourselves down to comprehend the presence of one another. I looked at her beautiful face in the faint light, and then moving tenderly, positioned myself to have her completely. We made love slowly, and with ease. I found patience and care I never knew I possessed. Cindy trembled, and held me tightly, loving every minute of the pain and pleasure that she was going through. It was all two hearts could handle. It was as close as we could get.

We eluded sleep until the early morning hours, not wanting to miss any part of our first night of truly being together. It was the greatest love that I had ever known. For Cindy, it was the only love she had ever wanted.

The sun rose the next morning only to find us asleep in each other's arms. Several times, as the sun rose and peeked in through the blinds of Cindy's room, we would awake and discover it wasn't all just a dream. I looked at her clock each time I awoke, and then got concerned as I watched the hours pass. Twelve o'clock was my curfew, as I was required to be back in the barracks to assist with the incoming freshmen as they arrived. Through my off and on sleeping, I managed to get enough rest to get through what was going to be a busy afternoon and evening.

It had been an amazing night for us in all kinds of ways, and one that we both hoped would never end. But with the arrival of the eleven o'clock hour, I had to tear away from Cindy's bed and her arms to get myself dressed to go back to school. Even though I had just spent an entire evening with her, I was not ready at all to leave, and I could see she felt the same way. We both understood that it would be nearly an eternity before we would see each other again. For two people who wanted nothing more than to have and hold each other, it was an anxious moment of separation to face.

413

I sat on the edge of Cindy's bed, now fully clothed in my full dress uniform. I could only hold her in my arms and tell her how much I hated to leave, and how much I was going to miss her. It was almost unbearable.

"John, I want you to remember one thing. No matter how short a time, or where it will be, I want to see you the first chance you have. I want you to let me know, even if I have to sneak inside the barracks."

"I'll let you know Cindy, you can count on it."

"I'll be waiting."

"I've got to go. I'm on my final minutes of being able to make it back in time."

"Please be careful, and I'll be expecting a call from you at least every day, right?"

"You've got it."

I stopped in the doorway of Cindy's bedroom, and looked back as she lay in the bed, eyes filled with tears, and once again I told her I loved her, and she answered with the same. I forced a smile, then turned and walked out. I instantly felt sick.

CHAPTER 32

The incoming freshmen were told by letter that noon was the earliest they would be allowed to initially check in. With all of the cars out front with civilians, it was obvious some wanted to get an early start.

Wearing my full dress uniform, I got a lot of stares as I walked back into the barracks. I made it in only minutes before the high noon hour, and with everyone appearing to already be busy, I headed straight to my room and quickly changed into my gray nasty uniform. When I hit the gallery I could see people coming in, and I immediately found myself busy assisting parents and their sons in finding their rooms. The parents were worried about what was going to happen the next day, and I spent an endless amount of time trying patiently to answer their many questions. I was quietly amused at how nervous the knobs-to-be were, and it brought back memories of when I was in the same situation two years earlier.

The next day at 0800, we lit the fire on the 4th class's introduction, and the cadre began to process in the recruits as soon as they joined the check-in line. We introduced them to the basics of marching and a haircut they would never forget. They got new uniforms and an earful of instructions they were too nervous to even understand. It was hard not to laugh, as they didn't know whether to stop or go. I constantly thought back to my first day, remembering it as the longest and most grueling of my life. They weren't even getting racked or chewed out in a serious way, yet that first day would scare anyone shitless. It was even long and hectic as a junior sergeant. There was a lot that had to be done, and it was up to us, the cadre, to make sure it all happened before the sun went down. It took a balls-to-the-wall effort, and we nearly killed a few recruits, but we made it.

I didn't expect to hear anything about Sword Drill during those first few days since it was so chaotic. There was no way any activity outside of cadre could be addressed, as everyone was overwhelmed with handling the freshmen. Things were a bit better on Tuesday as our attention was much more focused, though it was still quite frenzied for the knobs. But the supply end of things was slowing down, and I finally started to see the urgency for my actions cull off. But Wednesday evening was "Hell Night," and that would mean intense changes and a wild ride for the knobs.

As I moved around in 4th Battalion attending to my duties, I would occasionally run into a member of the old Drill. They never said a word, just smiled, never providing any information. I found myself waiting for some communication that never seemed to take place. I only got those shitty little grins. The waiting and lack of information actually got pretty nerve racking, and I hated having to look around every corner. When I passed the other aspirants, I could see the pressure was equally taxing on them.

During Wednesday evening's mess, the air was filled with anticipation and fear as the freshmen racked their brains over the rumors we had planted about Hell Night. Later, as they stood out on the quad, their concern peaked as they heard taps play and the front gates close. We then gave them their first experience of what it truly meant to be a freshman at The Citadel. We killed 'em. I gave those knobs as much hell as I could muster, racking the piss out of them as they struggled, scared out of their wits. I could only think that I too would soon be facing nearly the same thing.

Hell Night went well. There were no serious injuries, and the meat wagon had only a few customers campus wide. We had a handful of freshmen passing out from the heat and exhaustion after being racked badly in the showers and the alcoves, but that was to be expected. It was really quite an interesting evening, especially since I had once lived through their plight, and was now observing from the other side of the fence.

The next morning there were again some adjustments necessary as the freshmen were educated in some of the finer points of getting racked and popping off to upperclassmen on the stairs. Freshmen would threaten to quit, and then we would talk them into staying, and then throw them right back to the wolves. It was a pretty tough game, but I knew there was no other in the world like it that could yield such life altering results. It wasn't for everyone. We all knew that. But we wanted to give the gift to as many as we could. They just had to pay the price, and it wasn't cheap.

Thursday's noon mess arrived, and more than any other meal, this was the most intense. The 4th Class System was now fully in effect, and the cadre members were expecting perfection out of each freshman's performance. There was yelling everywhere. I found myself staying on one particular freshman's case who just couldn't seem to do anything right. He was an idiot, with all thumbs and no brains. I was getting increasingly frustrated with him since he had been on my mess for several days and I was not seeing any progress out of him at all. During the announcements, I was barely listening, thinking more about how I was going to ask the little fart to drive by my room after mess so that I could rack his brains out. But that train of thought was quickly derailed as an announcement caught my attention and I stopped everything.

"Please give your attention to the Commander of the 1979 Junior Sword Drill."

"All juniors, having the rank of Cadre Platoon Sergeant or above, wishing to become an aspirant for the 1980 Junior Sword Drill, are requested to meet immediately following second rest at the rear steps of the mess hall. This meeting is absolutely mandatory for anyone who wants to participate in the upcoming selection process. Don't be late!"

A sound of "ooh" came over the mess hall as smiles covered the faces of those who knew the significance of the announcement. For me, I wasn't expecting the first meeting to be right after noon mess, and I was caught off-guard. But before I could think too heavily about what I had heard, the announcer said, "Rest!" which was equivalent to a gun starting a foot race. Without taking another bite I pushed my chair back, grabbed my cover, then scrambled towards the door. I almost leveled a waitee with her tray as I desperately moved through the packed mess hall. I could see everyone laughing at me and the other aspirants as we scurried towards the exit. Having a seat far away from the doors, I found myself the last one getting out. In a full-fledged run I hotfooted it around the building, and yet found myself as one of the last to arrive.

"You're late mister," said one of the old Drill.

"Form up! Form up according to height," said the Commander of the '79 Drill. "Come on! I don't have to tell you how to do this. Two by two, form up from the tallest to the shortest."

We started scrambling around, looking at each other and comparing height, then quickly formed up into the best descending height formation we could get.

"We don't have all day," said the Commander with disgust.

After about thirty seconds of switching around, we finally had ourselves into almost perfect position.

"As you guys continue to arrange yourselves in proper order with the assistance of the old Drill," said the Commander, "we will utilize this time to get some business done. In case you don't remember, my name is Richard Kraft. I'm Delta Company Commander, and also the Commander of the 1979 Junior Sword Drill. It is our mission here today to start your journey down the road to becoming the 1980 Junior Sword Drill. My first question -- is there anyone here who did not participate in Spring Roach? If so, raise your hand."

No one raised his hand.

"Very good, we have no stragglers. How many do we have, Dan?"

"Twenty-seven."

"OK gentlemen, I want you to stand at firm attention, look straight ahead, peering into the back of the head in front of you. Again, we will utilize our time as best we can, so while I speak to you, we will have an inspection. This will be the first inspection of many you will go through. As an aspirant for the 1980 Junior Sword Drill, we expect perfection, not some of the time, but all of the time.

Your personal appearance must be outstanding in every way. We certainly hope that each of you came to this first meeting sporting the absolute epitome in personal appearance."

I began to think just how awfully nice it was of the old Drill not to let us know there was going to be a meeting. I thought about the condition of my brass and shoes, and knew that they probably looked better than average, but certainly not perfect.

"As the old Drill inspects you," continued Kraft, "I must brief you on the most important aspect of today's meeting. The history of the Junior Sword Drill, as I expect you know by now, is one that has always been conducted under a blanket of complete secrecy. There are many reasons for this, reasons that you will come to understand as you enter into and complete the 14 Nights. What is important now is that you must clearly recognize that the business of the Junior Sword Drill is only the business of the Junior Sword Drill. We are allowing you roaches the privilege of trying out for what we have already aspired to be and have become. You must not view this as anything but an extreme privilege. Each of you is here under your own free will and has volunteered for the journey which you are about to take. If there is anyone here who is not here based on their own choice and free will, please at this time raise your hand."

No hands were raised.

"Good. If there is anyone here who does not understand that this is a privilege granted to you by the 1979 Junior Sword Drill and those that came before us, then raise your hand."

No one raised his hand.

"And finally, is there anyone in this group who does not truly understand that the business of the Junior Sword Drill is only the business of the Junior Sword Drill, and that what takes place with you in the coming days and weeks is to be held within the strictest of confidence such that it is not only never discussed with anyone else, but is not discussed between each other in the presence of others? If there is anyone in this group who does not agree with this, please at this time raise your hand."

No one raised his hand.

"Therefore, I will ask you a question, at the end of which, I ask you to repeat the answer of 'I will.' Stationed around you are all of the members of the 1979 Junior Sword Drill so that each of you will actually be seen as you respond to this question. If you do not respond with an answer of 'I will' in a clear, concise voice, you will be asked to leave this privilege which the Sword Drill has extended to you."

I could see out of the corner of my eye that the old Drill had indeed surrounded the group of aspirants, so that when we did speak, everyone would be observed as they answered.

"Listen carefully gentlemen, this is your question. Do you, the aspirants of the 1980 Junior Sword Drill, swear upon your personal honor, The Citadel Honor Code, and to the God that has made both man and this world, that you will uphold the secrecy of the Junior Sword Drill in every way, both during your time as an aspirant, as well as after the selection process, successful or not successful, and will continue to uphold and preserve that secrecy for the rest of your living days? If you agree with this statement, please answer by saying, 'I will.'"

With an unquestionable volume, the entire platoon answered, "I will."

Kraft continued, "Members of the 1979 Junior Sword Drill, were there any aspirants who did not answer the question with a resounding 'I will'?"

There was nothing but negative headshakes from the old Drill.

Kraft continued, "Was there any member of the 1980 Junior Sword Drill aspirants who did not answer with a clear a resounding 'I will'? If so, please at this time raise your hand."

There were no hands raised.

"Fine gentlemen, let there be no violations of the secrecy you have now sworn to uphold. This, understand you, will be the most important aspect of the Junior Sword Drill. Welcome to your journey. 1979 Junior Sword Drill, please complete your personal inspections of the aspirants."

I stood at rock-solid attention as I could see a Drill member step up to the guy standing right beside me. I suspected it was Ted Rontelli, who was Foxtrot's First Sergeant, but I could clearly see it was Dennis Goldburg, Third Battalion Executive Officer, who was inspecting us.

"Mr. Rontelli," said Goldberg, "I can already tell that your personal appearance is appalling. Your shoes are only shined on the tips, they should be shined all the way around."

Goldberg continued to inspect Rontelli saying, "I can't believe this shit. You've got tarnish on the back of your brass. This is disgusting!"

With a lot of theatrics thrown in, Goldberg quit his inspection of Rontelli and moved in front of me, grumbling as he moved. He then began to look me over. "Not bad on the shoes there, Mr. O'Bryan," said Goldberg looking down at my name tag. He then looked at my brass, finding that for the most part it looked pretty good. "I see that you at least don't have any tarnish or green grunge growing in your brass like Mr. Rontelli here, but you'll have to get these pits and scratches out from the inside portions of your brass, not just the surface."

Goldberg backed up a bit so he could address both Rontelli and me at the same time. "Let me make one thing clear to you. Your personal appearance is far below the standards that I expect to see from a roach. Your brass must be blitzed inside and out at all times, whether at formation or simply going to and from class, and under no circumstances, Mr. Rontelli, is there ever to be tarnish or grunge found on any part of your brass. Your shoes are to look like mirrors. There are to be no personal appearance violations from this point on. You can count on the fact that we will inspect you."

"OK gentlemen, time's up," yelled Kraft.

As Goldberg started to walk away, he turned towards Rontelli and simply stated, "I'll see you during the Nights, Mr. Rontelli."

I couldn't believe I made it through the inspection as well as I did.

Even with my noontime inspection brass and shoes on, they certainly weren't perfect. Rontelli probably got caught with his class brass and shoes on. It was understandable, but it was going to cause him some trouble as soon as the Nights started.

"OK, listen up gentlemen," said Kraft. "The 14 Nights start next week, and you must be ready. Uniform for the Nights will be shako with feather plume, PT-tee shirt, sword, scabbard, scabbard webbing with both breast plate and waist plate, duty pants, belt, brass buckle, white high top tennis shoes, white socks, and white gloves. Needless to say gentlemen, you are to have your personal appearance at its absolute best. Failure to be prepared will result in fitting punishment. And finally, you are to have the proper haircut, and I don't think I have to indicate to you what that is. Who is currently in the 14th position out of our 27 roaches?" One of the roaches shouted to Kraft, "Sir, Chin is my name."

"OK, Roach Chin is now the timer for you aspirants. He, and only he will provide adequate time measurement for all of you. You are to remain here, standing in complete silence and at attention for fourteen minutes. We, the old Drill, will part. These fourteen minutes are for you to think about what we have discussed today, which is your solemn vow to secrecy. At the conclusion of that time period, you are all to proceed directly to the barber shop, and from that point on, we expect you to act like a Sword Drill aspirant, displaying the proper personal appearance and conduct. You are excused from any other obligation you may have for this time period. Gentlemen, we will see you next week. Mr. Chin, start your fourteen minutes. 1979 Junior Sword Drill, dismissed!"

I could see that the old Drill members walked away from our platoon, walking in the opposite direction of where we were looking so we could not watch how quickly they moved away, or if indeed they were still standing behind us. By no means did any of the 27 roaches move a muscle. It was at that point that we all assumed that Chin was estimating when fourteen minutes had passed.

We all just stood there in silence at full attention, thinking just as

Kraft had indicated about what was said. I thought about the oath we had taken, and knew then why George Porter had always been so adamant about remaining silent about what took place even though he had not made the squad. He had obviously taken the same oath we had. I too would no longer have the privilege of discussing the secret matters of the Drill. Without a doubt, I took this to be a very serious matter.

It seemed like a long time as we waited for Chin to announce that fourteen minutes had passed. When he did, the 27 of us moved around cautiously, and for the first few seconds, spoke to each other quietly. Chin then spoke up saying, "Gentlemen, unless there are any questions among us, I would suggest that we make our way over towards the barber shop immediately."

"I have something," said Thomas Karl, who was Regimental Sergeant Major. "We must quickly organize ourselves. I know this because I've gotten some hints from some of the old Drill on Regimental Staff that our own communications will be the only method of knowing when things will happen. We must immediately set up a network to share information, and from what I understand, it will be critical for all of us. I hope the rest of you don't mind, but I would like to ask permission from each of you to allow me to set up this network. We have very little time, and I feel that I'm in a position to do it. Does anyone have any objections to that?"

Everyone quickly shook their heads no.

"Then let's set something up here quickly. If there are any objections, please let me know and we will try to find a better way. From what I understand, we have every Battalion Sergeant Major roaching except for 3rd Battalion, is that correct?"

"That's true," answered Harry Andrews, who was 2nd Battalion Sergeant Major.

"Is there a First Sergeant from 3rd Battalion?"

Only one hand was raised -- it was Cedrick Middleton.

"OK Cedrick, you're 3rd Battalion rep. Battalion reps need to quickly put together a list of names, companies, room numbers, and phone numbers of the individuals in your battalions that are roaching, then call me, and we'll establish an overall list. From what I understand from the old Drill, this is going to be crucial. They're not going to tell us anything. The only way we're going to know things is by rumor and by word of mouth. That's all I needed to say."

"OK fellas," said Lu Chin, "let's quickly head over to the barber shop. I suggest we march over in a platoon. Fall in!"

We formed up quickly, and with Chin calling cadence, we marched from behind the mess hall towards Mark Clark Hall. It seemed almost weird as we marched, with some of the guys talking quietly, but being cautious and quite serious. I cringed a bit as I thought of where we were going and what we would face once there.

When we entered into the barbershop, we were shocked to see the old Drill waiting for us. Along with the four barbers present, they all had shit eating grins on their faces, and as some of the favorite sons of our class were spotted by a special acquaintance from the old Drill, they were grabbed and pulled into the closest barber chair for a massacre. Some of the old Drill started cutting hair all right, but decided to make shapes like hearts, squares, swastikas, arrows, and even a few mohawks as others snapped away with a camera. It was one big humiliating joke as the old Drill laughed and made a mess of our heads before letting a barber finish taking off the rest. It was at times funny to us too, but other than a few reserved smiles, we knew better than to laugh.

One by one, each roach took a turn in the next open chair. When my turn in the hot seat arrived, my own Battalion Commander, Carl Andrews, tried to cut a star in my hair, but botched it up pretty good. I was just happy not to get my ear cut off. After his fun, I looked across in the mirror as the barber took his first cut right down through the center of what was left. I forced a tiny smile, but felt a lump in my throat and a strong feeling of indignity as the razor glided across the top of my head. I had been through this before two years earlier, but experience didn't lessen the impact. I only thought of what Cindy would think. I looked at the event as locking me into not seeing her for a long time. But I had to look at the bright side. This was the first step towards something I wanted badly. Suddenly, I felt better knowing that my journey was now underway. I was a roach now. No doubt about it.

CHAPTER 33

Life quickly got serious for us as roaches. There were many things to do now that we found ourselves at the edge of the storm. We worked constantly on our equipment, burning up the phone lines as we sought out scarce information and planned our strategies to meet the prerequisites of the 14 Nights. One immediate task was to get coordinated with my newly discovered partner, Ted Rontelli. By virtue of height, he ended up beside me in the formation, making him my Drill partner. We would go through cuts together, and it was expected that we would be perfectly coordinated in everything by the end of the Nights. Not only was our personal appearance required to be in tiptop shape, but also we had to be the same. The old Drill wanted to see a mirror image between partners in the way that our equipment and uniforms were set up.

Partner coordination would remain a huge challenge for us in that if a roach were to drop out, it would cause some to have to shift up, thus creating the necessity to re-coordinate with a new partner. But by way of our newly established network, all 27 of us worked quickly to standardize all that we could so there would be few differences between the pairs, hopefully making partner changes less of an excruciating problem. No one wanted to think that they might be the one to quit, or get knocked out by some unfortunate circumstance. But in case it happened, the coordination efforts would surely lessen the impact.

I was impressed by how swiftly and without a lot of debate we agreed on the standards. We defined the details concerning how each piece of brass, including the breastplate and the waist plate would be shaped, finished, and blitzed. Decisions and standards were established for our swords, which after some negotiation, we decided would all be welded together as one solid piece versus the four pieces that could be taken apart. They too would be blitzed down to a smooth finish. Every other item including shoes, pants, belt buckles, belts, shirts, gloves, and shako were all discussed and standardized as tightly as possible. No one wanted to stand out in any way, since that person would be viewed as a non-conformist, and would certainly suffer for it.

Every free moment during that Thursday, Friday, Saturday and Sunday, the 27 of us worked hard to beat, grind, weld, and polish the metal equipment into shape. Some things however, were just a bit out of our league, so we cut a deal with a local jeweler to work on our more delicate and detailed brass to insure that all pieces would be just alike. On those that we thought we could do ourselves, we used drills with grinding wheels and small polishing instruments to modify and shape them to spec. Using torches like skilled metallurgists, we welded and shaped our equipment to the strictest of standards. We adopted the skills of a seamstress as items were sewn, tags were removed, and loose strings were cut. With all the work, it was a race against time from the very start. By 1800 Sunday, I was exhausted, but amazed at what we accomplished.

Sunday night also provided the significant event of a muster formation as the rest of the Corps not on cadre made its return. I definitely had to be there as my duties as Battalion Sergeant Major weren't excused because of Drill. The impossible workload was considered a part of the overall Sword Drill test of planning ability and getting one's act together. Considering all the work required on my equipment, plus my requirements with the knobs and the returning upperclassmen, it was a hectic weekend.

At the conclusion of the muster formation, an hour was lost as friends visited and we greeted one another for the first time in months. Everyone made a big deal over my skinhead, and I reminded them all that it wasn't the first time they had seen me this way. But I soon had to bypass the fun and return to my equipment. No one knew for sure, but there was a strong feeling that the following evening would be the first of the 14 Nights. It gave me chills to think about it, but based on the Drill's desire to keep us guessing, it could even be Tuesday or Wednesday before something finally happened. No matter what, I was determined to be ready to go by the next afternoon.

The next day I found myself engulfed in my duties. The return of Corps brought a repeat of a yet larger situation of getting boxes from the warehouse and rifles issued for the year. This added an enormous amount of pressure to an already super hectic schedule. By the time noon arrived, I was tired, but desperate to hear if further rumors had surfaced. But the communication network had not revealed any substantial information. There was always more that I could do to my equipment, but as I promised myself, I would be ready to go by mid-afternoon no matter what.

At lunch I ate as quickly as I could, rushing back to my room to use every spare minute to put just one last shine on some piece of equipment. New chores seemed to fly at me with each tick of the clock, and I found myself going in and out, rushing and working almost like a madman. Then around 1500 the telephone rang as it had so many times during the day, but this time, it was the call I had been expecting. Delta Company First Sergeant Scott Morris had picked up on a signal from 79's Sword Drill Commander that that evening would indeed be the first. At exactly 1814, all aspirants were to be in front of their company letters in full roach uniform, ready to be inspected, ready to begin the Nights.

With the news my heart started pounding and my breath seemed short. It was here! All that I had thought about, all that I had worked for was now upon me. But I had no time to waste. As 4th Battalion representative in the network, I had to quickly get the word out to the other five guys in the battalion that it was show time.

As soon as I made the phone calls, I scrambled, knowing that I only had less than three hours left to be ready. I knew this would be the most intensive personal appearance inspection of the Nights, and that the old Drill was probably chomping at the bit to catch us with a flaw. I was determined not to satisfy their desire.

The six of us in 4th Battalion agreed to meet in my room before going down, and at 1800, one by one, the other roaches nervously entered my room, each jumping quickly into a request for a quick inspection. We all searched feverishly for little flaws that might yield huge penalties during the evening. Even if we had found any major ones, it was actually too late to do much about it. We made small adjustments, nervous corrections more than anything, right up until 1813. I then gave the word that it was time, and with a huge sigh, we carefully filed out of my door and ran around 3rd division to our respective company areas. Then with a wave at the stairwell, we all started down the stairs at the exact same time. We moved onto the quad, and then stood at full attention in front of our company letters.

As I stood in front of the R, I could see Casey Peppercorn directly across the quad. He was bracing, not moving a finger as he stood in front of the big blue N that was painted on the corner wall of the stairwell. Cutting my eyes to the right, I could see both Jim Pearl and Fred Erving standing in front of the T, and to my left, Buck Edwards and Immanuel Consecos, standing in front of the O. The battalion was deathly silent as the six of us stood at attention, bracing our asses off, not making a move, not knowing who was watching. We stood there for what seemed like forever.

Finally, all at one time, three individuals appeared on the quad. It was Dave Morris, Chip Walsh, and Carl Andrews, the three 4th Battalion members of the 1979 Junior Sword Drill. With only three, it was obvious that someone was not going to be inspected immediately. By luck, good or bad, that someone was me.

I stood and tactfully watched as the three split and made their way over to the opposite corners from me. I could hear them talking softly, not able to understand what they were saying. I could see, however, that the guys were being inspected quite thoroughly. The old Drill was even taking off several pieces such as the waist belt and sword sling so as to get a closer look, then casually draped them over my classmate's shoulders when done. I had expected this to be similar to a knob's inspection, in that no matter how much work you put into it, there was no way to pass everything. If the old Drill looked hard enough, they could always find something, even if it was just a piece of lint falling out of the wind onto your shako.

I could also see that both Jim Pearl and Fred Erving over in T Company were now arching their swords as Carl Andrews dispensed the first bit of punishment. To increase the stress of holding the sword at full arch, their shakos were removed from their heads and placed on the tip of the sword, thus adding a nuisance weight at the end, requiring much more force to keep the sword arched in its proper position. I could see the same actions taking place with Casey Peppercorn over in N Company as Chip Walsh inspected him. When Walsh finished up with Casey, he turned around and headed my way.

As Walsh approached, I made sure to "space out" with my eyes, looking straight ahead, not focusing on him.

"Good evening, Roach O'Bryan," said Walsh as he walked up. "How are you feeling on this fine evening?"

"Fine sir," I answered.

"That's good. I want you to concentrate tonight, Mr. O'Bryan. Do not fail to call out to one of us if there is an injury or you believe that you are physically in trouble. Is that clear?"

"Yes, Sir."

"We both share in the responsibility that you not get injured. No one wants to see you out, but if you are hurt, you must tell a member of the '79 Drill. Is this clear?"

"Yes, Sir."

Walsh then began to look me over quite seriously, taking a microscopic view of every part of my personal appearance. Like the others, he took off my belt and sling to get a closer look, throwing them over my shoulder as he progressed. After several minutes of intense inspection without a word, he finally spoke. "Apparently Mr. O'Bryan, you are using too coarse of a towel for the finish work on your brass. I can actually see a slightly detectable indication of how you shined it. That should not be there. I do not see this in your other brass at all, only on your breastplate. This must be corrected. On command I want you to draw your sword, Mr. O'Bryan. Ready, draw..." I reached down and pulled my sword up half way and held it. Walsh then finished the two part command by saying, "...Swords!" whereby I finished drawing the sword out, put it up into an arch, then brought it down to "carry swords" position.

"Arch swords," commanded Walsh, and I then arched my sword. He then removed my shako and looked it over in detail. After inspecting it for about thirty seconds, he positioned it at the end of my sword, putting me in the same position as the other aspirants.. Walsh continued to look me over, checking out my scabbard, shoes, belt, and belt buckle, finding nothing wrong, yet making suggestions to provide for future maximum performance. He then walked away as I held my weighted sword in place with difficulty.

Walsh joined Morris and Andrews in the center of the quad where they appeared to compare notes on their observations. They laughed as they talked with ease, and their leisure seemed a real contradiction to the strain in my arm, but I held fast just the same.

The three old Drill members soon decided it was time to get down to business and yelled for us to put back on our equipment so we could form up. I worked fast, but with care, in that I didn't want to have it on wrong and catch hell for it later. We were soon formed in a small group in our rows of twos, and the old Drill began to run us around the quad. For our very first time, we were told to start our chant of "We love, Sword Drill." It was a thrill, but somehow I knew that my love for the phrase would not last. It also occurred to me as we circled the quad that I had an immediate awkwardness of running with a sword and scabbard strapped to my side. I always knew that it would be with me, but for some reason, I had not anticipated it would be so much in the way. It took a few moments for me to realize that the only way I could run with the thing was to keep my left hand on the butt of the sword to prevent it from jumping up and down in the scabbard and also to stop it from swinging into and between my legs. I instantly knew that this was something significant that I was going to have to reckon with for the entire run of the Nights.

I felt fortunate that the blistering heat of the midday had passed into the milder late afternoon. The heat stored in the ground waved at the sky as it paid tribute to the end of a scorching day, and I was thankful that the physical challenge that lay before me would not have to be faced during that peak. I liked where I was simply because Drill had finally started. I had prepared for this until I was sick of doing so. I felt a sense of pride that I was finally there. But I knew that this was only the calm before the storm, and that my present course was set for an ocean of physical sacrifice.

After our small group had circled the quad a full seven times, I was beginning to feel my storage of energy being tapped. I was starting to breathe harder as I chanted, and the light spring in my stride began to flatten out. The old Drill had taken the edge off of the thrill, and I could see they were ready to get down to some serious PT.

The old Drill yelled that we were to begin Indian races, and I remembered from the Stadium Party just what that meant. As a freshman, and as a sophomore corporal, I thought I had experienced every possible physical exercise ever conceived. But in the 4th Class System, there were never any runs solely designed to destroy stamina. When doing Indian races, the last two men had to run forward and pass the rest of the squad to assume the leading positions. This went on as a constant rotation, with me cycling through five or six times. It added a new dimension to running which significantly increased the difficulty and effort required.

The old Drill eventually stopped the Indian races and joined us at the front of the squad. They led us out of 4th Battalion and we ran towards 3rd. We entered through the front sally port finding another squad of roaches circling the quad as we had been doing. We joined them, yielding one group of twelve. Shortly after, I heard an old Drill member yell to again start with the Indian races, but this time, with a much further distance from the back to the front. I wasn't sure how many laps we ran in 3rd, but I was pleased when we left heading towards 2nd.

When we came through the front sally port, it wasn't long before we were formed up into one squad and were again made to do even more difficult Indian races. We soon had the full picture of what was happening, and after more than enough running, we finally found ourselves in 1st Battalion with the full group of twenty-seven roaches. As we circled the quad we chanted in a thunderous echo that sounded really impressive.

As we circled I felt the weight of my body becoming a reality. The newness had worn off, and I was completely into an effort mode. The Indian races, with a full-length squad, brought out the need to dig deep. I had no idea how much time had passed, but I was really feeling the strain, and was ready to do something other than running. I felt the anticipation of relief when the old Drill formed up at the front, and with no more battalions to go through, I felt we were probably going on to McAlister.

As we exited through the sally port, we made a turn towards the Field House, and within seconds we were there, since it was right across the street from 1st Battalion. But my anticipation of stopping was short lived as I found that we ran right past the entrance and moved around towards the back of the building. We circled the building once, and then I heard the commands from the old Drill to once again start with the Indian races. It was disappointing news, and the realization of where I was, and what I was doing began to hit me again. In a fast way these guys were tapping heavily into the physical stamina I had built up. I still had a long night ahead of me, yet I was already getting tired. I even asked myself if I was going to make it. I looked at the other roaches, and most appeared as worn as I felt. I found some comfort in that, thinking that the old Drill surely would measure our appearance from time to time, and adjust how hard they needed to push us. Or would they?

I soon realized it was again my turn to assume a position at the front of the squad. As I ran, I felt the eyes of the old Drill on me, and it made me feel like I was back in my football days, where I often sensed the need to make the coach think I was really putting out. I had a feeling that if they could see you were trying hard they would likely leave you alone. But I also knew I had to conserve. We had a long way to go.

After we ran four laps around the Field House, I was beginning to feel really weary. I could see that others were also starting to weaken badly, and the pace set by the constantly alternating old Drill was only maintained by real effort. Finally, as we approached the front of the Field House, we stopped on the concrete pad out front. The old Drill was right there yelling at us to form back up as roaches bumped into each other, weak and wobbly from fatigue. They screamed for us to get into our positions, and we moved quickly to oblige. We stood at attention, breathing hard from the run. Within seconds, they told the front half of the squad to follow two of the old Drill who took off running, with the back half following a different two. I was thankful for the 30-second stop, yet disappointed that it was so little rest.

Again, to my disappointment, those damned Indian races resumed, and I could see real struggle on the faces of the other roaches as they ran past me going to the front. We were running at a blistering pace, and coupled with fatigue, it was a bear just to make it to the front.

I wasn't really sure how many times we circled the building in our divided groups, but when we finally stopped again on the concrete pad in front of the Field House, I could only wonder if we stopped because Donny Gant was puking, or if the old Drill had finally decided they had run us to death. They once again yelled at us to form up in one squad, and we scrambled to get into position, bumping into other scalding hot bodies as we moved. My early thoughts of lower afternoon temperatures were completely gone as sweat dripped from my face and body. Little did I know that it would be the coolest spot I would be in for the next few hours.

After forming up, we marched into the Field House, moving through the lobby and out onto the basketball court in the middle of the huge arena. The silence of the massive room was broken by the echoing sounds of our footsteps and the commands given by the old Drill. The darkness gave the building an eerie look, as the only light was that which came in through the windows at the top of the walls at the north and south ends. There was heaviness to the air inside, and I had a feeling that there was no air conditioning running, and no windows or doors open to provide ventilation.

The '79 Commander, Richard Kraft, walked to the side of the squad, which stood in the middle of the floor, and commanded, "Roaches, left face."

We all turned with some degree of precision to the left. I could see Kraft standing there surrounded by several of the old Drill while others were walking around us.

"Welcome to the armory, roaches," said Kraft. "Over the next 14 evenings, we will challenge both your physical and mental capabilities. We will test your ability to perform under pressure, and your desire to become a part of this most honorable organization. The long running standard of the Drill is high, and we fully intend to present that same standard for you to meet or exceed. Failure to meet this challenge is a failure to become a part of Sword Drill. There are currently 27 of you here today. Only 14 will survive this process. We fully expect that those 14 will truly be the very best that the Class of 1980 has to offer. It is our duty and responsibility to this Drill, school, and to the Class of 1979, to insure that only the finest will be performing on this floor come Parents Day weekend. The challenge is before you roaches. It is up to you to meet it.

"There are several important rules that you must understand clearly. These are firm, and without exception. Know them, and live by them.

"First, we will have 14 nights of training that require your mandatory attendance. Failure to start all of these nights is your failure to make this Drill.

"Second, if we see that you are not putting forth your best effort, we will pull you out of the training and send you back to the barracks. This will be a warning to you, and will occur only once.

The second time will be your last.

"Third, you are responsible for taking care of yourselves throughout this training, both while in the armory, and back in the barracks. If you should become careless, and have an accident, and cannot complete a night, you are allowed to be sent back once. Failure to finish a second night is an automatic failure to meet the standard, and you will not be allowed to continue.

"Fourth, you will not be allowed to commit any sort of violation of school rules during the 14 Nights. If for some reason you are busted, and loose your rank, you are automatically disqualified from continuing. Are there any questions about these important rules?"

There was no response from any of us.

"I want to again emphasize that you are to maintain the highest standard of personal appearance during the Nights. Everyone on campus knows who you are, and what you are doing. You are a walking advertisement as to the kind of standards we set forth. Expect to be checked by the old Drill at any time, including between classes.

"Also, any time you see a member of the 1979 Junior Sword Drill, you will salute him. This includes all outside areas of the campus. When indoors you will use the greeting, 'Good morning, Sir' or 'Good afternoon, Sir'.

"Finally, it's in your best interest to maintain the right attitude throughout these nights. I'm sure that I don't need to go into detail, just as I'm sure you know what will draw negative attention to you. Are there any questions?"

There was no response from any of us.

"Let me then get on with our first presentation. We have quite an honor to bestow upon one of you roaches," said Kraft, who grabbed a completely white plume from one of the old Drill. "This gentlemen, is the white plume. It is an honorary symbol that we award to that roach which has most prominently stepped on his meat with the old Drill. Now we know that with this being the first night, that there are quite a few of you who very much deserve to wear this based on all of the fuck-ups made to date. But through our deliberations, we easily concluded who would be the first.

Roach Stall, please step forward."

Stall moved out to where Kraft and the other old Drill members were standing.

"Ah, Roach Stall," said Kraft as Lamar Jordan reached up and pulled the shako off of Stall's head, "Isn't it nice to be so popular with the '79 Drill?"

Baxter Stall just stood there in silence as Jordan pulled the black plume from his shako and replaced it with the white one. There seemed to be an air of confidence on the face of Stall as he watched, and I couldn't help but both admire and fear what he was doing. I had heard that he had shot his mouth off several times about his confidence in surviving the Nights. Rumor had it that he actually made the statement that there was nothing the old Drill could do to get to him. Even if he believed it true, surely he would regret ever saying something so stupid.

The time it took for Kraft to give his talk was a blessing. I thought I was at my rope's end with the running. The five minutes or so of rest was enough to at least take away the severity. I wasn't fresh again, but I was past the point of gut wrenching effort to breathe.

"Please follow me, Roach Stall," said a smiling Emerson Vaughn.

Vaughn was 1st Battalion Commander, and probably heard a lot of the rumors about Baxter's comments since he too was in 1st as B Company's First Sergeant. He grabbed Baxter's breastplate webbing and pulled him away from the rest of us.

"OK roaches, the first thing I want you to do is to get down in the lean and rest position," said Kraft with a smile, "that's it,' he said as we reacted quickly and went down to do push-ups. "No you idiots! Take off your shakos first!"

I could see those who had not done so already removed their shakos and placed them out in front of them.

"Now," he yelled, "down!"

We all went down, with most saying, "Sir, one, Sir!"

"Wrong…you must now do push-ups the Sword Drill way. When I say down, you say, 'We love,' and when I say up, you say 'Sword Drill.' We will do the counting for you."

"Isn't that nice of us!" said an unseen Drill member.

We did push-ups for what seemed like forever. I was happy that we at least had stopped running, but now the attack came from a different front. My shoulders and arms soon started to burn as we moved through countless sets, and just like freshman year, I started to see backs give way and bow towards the floor. I knew it was a matter of time before mine too would also start to droop.

I could hear Baxter Stall off in a distant part of the armory as he chanted in his single voice "We love, Sword Drill." I wondered if the pain he was feeling was of any comparison to that which was in my back. His voice sounded clear and strong, while the strain I was feeling was killing any sort of clarity I might have been able to muster.

The old Drill must have reached a sadistic point of satisfaction in that they had adequately killed us push-up wise and felt the need to move us on. There seemed to be a gleam in their eyes as they led us off the gym floor and into one of the back corridors that surrounded the huge auditorium. There we found exposed steel trusses that supported the rows of elevated seating.

"All right roaches, let's see all of you grab some of that beam up there," yelled Kraft.

There was a lot of yelling by the old Drill as we went through the motions of giving each other boosts until we were all finally hanging. Their yelling never ceased as they started to threaten us with penalties for being the first to drop. I was surprised at how hard it was to just hang there, and the weight of my body soon started to put a strain on my hands and arms. It seemed that just keeping my grip was the greatest challenge; even though my sweat soaked white gloves did help some as I tried to hold on. I fought hard not to be the first to fall, and the swarming threats were enough to forecast significant penalties for doing so.

A roach down the line finally lost his grip and hit the floor. The old Drill, every one of them it seemed, went towards him with their mouths a blazin'. As I struggled to hold on, I felt relieved not to have started the failures, but knew that my defeat was not long coming. As several of the old Drill verbally whipped the roach that fell and was positioning him to do push-ups, another commotion started as another's feet hit the floor. Those not occupied with the first bust went quickly for the fresh meat, and our chamber became a bath of threatening noise. Then, the roach beside me fell, and I could feel the immediacy of the commotion as the old Drill brushed against my dangling legs as they went for him.

The fall of the roaches now started in steady progression, and as more hit the floor, the less old Drill there were to harass as they started to spread thin. It was all the coaxing my hands needed to accept their impending failure, and my feet soon hit the floor where I was immediately yelled at by two assholes.

"You wimp dog roach! What the hell do you think you're doing on my floor...?" they yelled at maximum volume. "You couldn't last more than..."

But their attention towards me turned as the roach that was hanging just to the right of me fell, and their wrath turned on him. They soon had more roaches to yell at than they had voice to deal with. An old Drill member then pushed me down towards the floor and yelled for me to start doing push-ups. There was already a cadence going from my predecessors, and I picked up on the down stoke of "We love…."

One by one, the roaches hit the floor, and the yells at them became less severe as the final few hung in there. The threats were soon sounding more like encouragement as the game of who could last the longest became serious. But to my utter amazement, I could hear the old Drill coaxing the names of Kellowski and Stall! I had not realized that Baxter had rejoined the group. I also couldn't believe that he was still hanging on. I thought they had taken him off to really wear him out, but must not have had adequate time to do him in. Thoughts of trying to conserve myself as best I could had long since entered my mind, but needless to say, Baxter Stall wasn't thinking about conserving anything.

It really seemed to light a fire under the old Drill when Kellowski finally hit the floor, leaving only Stall hanging there. I couldn't believe this guy's balls. Even if he did possess the strength to hang in there so long, he had to know that drawing that kind of attention was not the thing to do while already wearing the white plume. He must have been crazy, stupid, or Superman.

Finally, Baxter went down, and every old Drill member present seemed to go for him as soon as his feet hit the floor. What should have made him a hero, seemed to sign his death warrant. Someone whisked him away, and the old Drill informed us to stop with our push-ups and to die. It didn't take me long to realize what this meant, as we finally got our very first break of the night. They wanted us to take off our shakos and lie face down on the floor with our throbbing arms extended out in front of us. The cold tile over concrete floor was heaven, as it seemed to draw out some of the enormous heat that burned inside my body. It became almost quiet as only a few of the voices of the old Drill could be heard as they mixed with the distant sound of Baxter Stall chanting out the Sword Drill cadence. I knew that he was missing out on a very necessary break.

After what seemed to be less than a minute, the tranquility of the rest ceased as Kraft commanded that we assume the sit-up position, and we quickly found ourselves doing them. Without any instruction, we all did them to the cadence of "We love, Sword Drill." We were catching on quick to the format of our abuse. It even had a pattern.

It became a real challenge to do sit-ups with a shako and plume on my head and a sword and sling at my side. The shako was tight fitting to start with, and the heat inside had only the small brass vents, smaller than a dime, to escape through. The feathered plume also seemed to provide additional resistance as I cycled through my sit-ups. The sword was just in the way, and the breastplate webbing that wrapped around my chest only further restricted my breathing and increased the resistance in my movements. It was one hell of a uniform to be in while doing such extensive PT.

It seemed we were going to do every callisthenic ever invented before the night was over, and would probably do some that we had never seen. I was always surprised at the ingenuity of cadets to find new and effective ways to dish out physical abuse. With no holds barred on us roaches, I felt confident that I was going to experience every conceived form of corporeal anguish ever imagined.

The old Drill soon reached their satisfaction point with sit-ups. They demanded that we quickly rise to our feet and form back up into our squad, and we were marched back into the gym, where we stopped at one end of the basketball court.

"I want you roaches to now show us just how willing you are to help carry your classmates through the Nights," said Kraft with a laugh. "I want the two lines of you to race each other in some good old fashion piggy-back races. Mount up!"

I could see in front of me two pairs of guys trying to get mounted on the backs of the other, but having trouble as the sword and scabbard got in the way.

"Ready," said Kraft, giving them little time to prepare, "Set! Go!"

The pairs took off running down towards the other end of the court, and as they moved, some of the old Drill yelled, as they demanded maximum effort, while others warned the next two pairs to ready themselves to be tagged. It was awkward to get on securely with our swords in the way. The rider had to have it moved so that the carrier could grab his leg without also grabbing the scabbard. The rider also had to wrap his leg around the carrier's sword since there was just no other way to do it. It was hard enough to carry someone the distance in a full run while already worn out and sweaty, but it was a multiplied nuisance while wearing a sword and shako.

Our next event would really throw us for a loop. Individuals within the old Drill pulled us from the platoon in groups of twos and threes and told us to follow them for a little personal attention. Along with another roach, I was grabbed by my sword sling and was pulled along behind an old Drill member named Ken Lindsey.

Looking quickly at who was with me I could see that it was Dennis Miles, who was a Master Sergeant on Regimental Staff. Lindsey pulled the two of us along in an awkward and uncomfortable fashion that made us both stumble and collide in our efforts to follow.. We both eventually got into a rhythm as he dragged us, but it remained a challenge to anticipate just where he was going. He dragged us around the gym floor once, then headed towards the stairs that led to the upper balconies. The stairs were tricky to ascend while holding my sword with one hand, the handrail with the other, and still keep my balance as Lindsey pulled away. He ran us all the way to the top, and then releasing us and sitting down himself, he ordered us to run back down. We did, then ran right back up again. This began a continuous up and down trek that would last for ten minutes.

The armory was loud with the echoing chant as it sang from every part of the building. Dennis and I contributed our share as we traversed the stairs, which soon became a real bitch. My muscles burned as I ascended the 50-foot elevation time after time. My wind was short as I breathed and chanted. But I could not let my condition get the best of me. To slip and fall would yield a major busted ass.

Lindsey ran us until we were struggling to maintain even a sluggish pace on our ascent. Then finally, he followed us down, and once we all hit the floor, he again grabbed our webbing and pulled us across the gym and out to one of the surrounding corridors. He let go of us, but then took us on a complete running tour of the Field House facility. As my legs throbbed with fatigue and I struggled to breathe, I could only feel lucky that at least we weren't on the stairs anymore.

We came upon Kevin Grant, who had his two roaches doing push-ups with their feet propped up on a long bench. Lindsey told us to join them, which was a welcomed, yet tough alternative to punishing our legs any further. Doing push-ups with our legs elevated put more weight on our arms, and there was no way to get any relief by slumping our backs. After only ten or so of these,

Dennis went down and could not get himself back up, with me straining like hell to make the lift. Lindsey ordered us to our feet where he again grabbed our webbing to pull us off to some other adventure.

We found our next castigation to be "bandstands." It was an interesting exercise that took advantage of our chant. We would stand facing the folding bleachers and would step up each foot on the bottom row with the one-two rhythm of "We love,." We would then step down in a one-two motion as we yelled "Sword Drill." It was a simple activity that kept you on your feet and in one place, but it played havoc on what were already beaten legs. I could at least alternate which leg I used to step up with, but it was really a killer. We stayed there for almost fifteen minutes until we were straining through the chants of "We love, Sword Drill." The vocalization required extra energy that just wasn't there, in addition to oxygen that my system already found so hard to extract from the stuffy, blistering atmosphere of McAlister.

Kraft finally shouted for the old Drill to return their roaches to the floor. As Lindsey ran us back towards the center of the floor, my legs knotted as I tried to use them to now move on a horizontal plane, and I thought that at any moment they would fall out from under me.

I scrambled back into my established position, and stood there in a full brace as I waited for the others to make it back from whatever dark corner of the building they had been in. I stood there breathing hard, competing madly against the others for what seemed not to even be there. I could smell the sweat through the steamy luster of the air as I stood at the best attention one could muster while gasping. Each chest in front of me inflated time and again, and the dripping PT shirts that housed them expanded as they clung to burning skin. The only sounds were that of cycling lungs, and the distant discussions of the old Drill who were positioned behind us, out of sight. I was thirsty beyond comprehension, and wondered if I would ever again feel liquid on my lips other than my own sweat.

We stood there for about thirty seconds as my heart pounded and the sweat started to burn my eyes. I couldn't imagine what time it was, or just how much more pounding this first night of hell would bring. It all seemed worse than I had ever imagined. The old Drill had a no shit attitude about putting us through the hoops, and I began to wonder if I, or any one of us, was going to survive the torment.

"Right face!" commanded the now familiar voice of Kraft.

We all did a proper turn to face him and the old Drill.

"Ready to play a few more games guys?" asked Kraft. "I know that this is going to be a real favorite for each of you. Now I want the roaches here in the front row to hit it. Now!"

Everyone, including me, that was on the front row side of the squad went down into the lean and rest.

"Good," said Kraft, "now I want you roaches standing behind them to grab their legs just like you were getting ready to push a wheelbarrow."

Everyone started to move.

"That's right," said Kraft, "you all know how this game is played."

Ted Rontelli reached down and grabbed my legs and pulled them up as I labored to keep them stiff. The first thing I noticed while in the wheelbarrow position was the sharp pain that the snaps on my gloves produced as the hardwood floors acted as a strong base to drive the little metal knolls into my palms. I moved my hands forward to slide the painful snaps out of the pressure point, but knew that my success would be short lived when I started moving. My sword and scabbard dangled at my side such as to provide a significant distraction, and I could feel Rontelli trying to get a good balanced grip on my legs by grabbing further up on my thighs. In doing so, it helped to reduce some of the weight on my hands and strain in my back. He was a good partner.

"On your marks!" shouted Kraft. "Get set! Go!"

I took off across the floor by walking with my hands as fast as I could. The snaps wasted little time in again becoming a sharp little pain in the palm of my hand. But I concentrated hard on not tripping up with my hands and arms, knowing full well that a whole lot of pain would come with kissing the moving floor if I lost the support of my arms.

I could hear and see one of the old Drill walking beside me, yelling to hurry up and move it. I just kept my mind on what I was doing, not caring that he was there. I soon could see that we were at the end, and the guy started yelling for Rontelli and me to switch.

We changed positions quickly and I tried to grab Rontelli the best I could to make it easy on him.

"Go, Go, Go!" yelled the old Drill member.

We took off, and I tried to watch Rontelli's back and neck for any signs of trouble as we moved along. I still had a member of the old Drill yelling in my ear to keep it moving, but I again just ignored him as I kept an eye on my partner. What could he do to me anyway, rack me?

Rontelli and I got to the end of the court, and again the Drill guy started yelling for us to switch. We changed places, and quickly took off again. But that stupid snap started hurting again as soon as I got going, and about halfway across the floor, I lost my concentration due to the pain and lost my hand coordination. I was at least quick enough to turn my face away from a direct hit with the floor and used my now collapsed arms to help shield the blow. The worst thing about the mishap, other than banging my head on the floor, was that it knocked my shako off. With Rontelli still holding my legs, I got myself back up with one arm, grabbed my shako with my other hand and pushed it back on my head as best I could. We took off again and I tried not to think about the painful snaps, concentrating just on keeping my hands moving and getting to the end.

We finally did make it, and Rontelli and I again switched, then took off back towards the other end. I watched close for any trouble Rontelli might have, but he was able to keep it together the whole distance. When we reached the end of the court, several of the old Drill started yelling at us to get down in the lean and rest and to start pumping out push-ups as we waited for the other roaches to finish their two round trips. I could see as I got down that there were still quite a few of them out on the floor, and was a bit proud that Rontelli and I had done so well in pulling off the exercise. It was too bad that we weren't rewarded with a rest while we waited for the others, but I knew free rests were not a part of the old Drill's curriculum.

Our push-up cadence grew louder as the others finished with their wheelbarrow ordeal, and we continued with them for quite a while. I could feel the muscles in my arms burn and ache as my back began to break down to a point of total collapse. I just couldn't keep it straight anymore, and could see I wasn't the only one.

"Ok, roaches," yelled Kraft, "Die!"

I dropped right there, removed my shako, and then put my hands out on the floor. I lay there thinking of an old saying that compared an unpleasant activity with hitting yourself with a hammer, and how it felt so good when you stopped. It felt so good not to be abusing my now battered body. The heat was still stifling, and the air was just as thin, but compared to being in the lean and rest, it was heaven. My clothes were soaked, and my sweat was now puddling on the floor. I could hear the old Drill moving around us, but I just kept my eyes closed and breathed hard. I was startled when I felt someone's cold fingers on my face, and opened my eyes and saw an old Drill member leaning over me with a piece of ice in his hand. I opened my parched mouth without moving anything else, and he put it in. I could feel it melt on my heated tongue, and savored every drop that made its way towards my throat. I felt both ecstasy and desperation as I moved it around to treat the dryness of my mouth, and feared for the moment it would be gone.

But the pause was to be precious. Just when I wondered if there would be more ice, I could hear the old Drill shouting for us to get up. I couldn't believe the puddle I was in as I lifted myself from the floor, and reached out to retrieve my Shako. As I was placing it on my head, I could hear the Drill shouting for us to form back up, which we did with speed.

"Roaches, right face," commanded Kraft.

We all turned towards him and the other members of the Drill. I was sure every roach was asking himself, 'What's next?'

"During cuts, you will be asked to perform to the best of your ability a series of marching maneuvers that will demonstrate your capacity to perform as a part of this Drill. We will teach you what you need to know to prepare, and it is up to you to learn and perfect what we show you. You must practice at every opportunity to insure that when the time comes you can do your very best. Now, please give your attention to Mr. Bourbon and Mr. Walsh as they demonstrate the cuts series."

Standing at a distance from us was Ronnie Bourbon and Chip Walsh. They stood side-by-side at the end of the basketball court, bracing. They both wore swords, and were apparently waiting for a command.

"Forward, march!" commanded Kraft.

The two started marching forward, then split with head snaps as they turned and marched away from each other. They stayed in step, and moved around the center court circle that was painted on the gym floor. When they met each other on the other side, they turned together with more head snaps to again be side-by-side. They continued to march forward several more steps, and then stopped. After a brief moment, they both turned and started again marching away from each other, and then they both stopped and turned at the same time, which completed the series.

It was nothing simple, but it also didn't look like anything that couldn't be perfected with a bit of practice.

"This is the most important series of moves you will have to know to do well in cuts. It's not even in the same league as the actual performance, which will take you many difficult weeks to learn, but it's enough to show us whether you have the ability to take on the greater task.

"Mr. Bourbon and Mr. Walsh will show you once again the series. This time, pay close attention to detail. It will be up to you to take it from this point to practice and perfect it."

Bourbon and Walsh went through the routine again, in almost a mirror image of the first. They obviously knew it perfectly, especially since Bourbon was the '79 Drill's Low Cuts Man.

The exhibition was to be the longest break we would have that evening. It was an essential opportunity to partially recover from the endless abuse that our bodies had taken. But the need to watch what was going on momentarily took my mind off the pain and heat that consumed my body.

But like the ice, the desperately needed respite was soon gone. The Drill ended the demonstration by again grabbing individuals and pulling them away in small groups to go for runs through the armory. This time, I was grabbed by Dennis Goldberg and pulled into a group along with Lu Chin and Casey Peppercorn. Goldberg took off running, yelling back that we were to follow him as he ran away.

We randomly fell into a line as we each started to run. I found myself running behind Chin, with Peppercorn bringing up the rear. We took off in a sprint in order to catch up with Goldberg. He was fast, and was sparing nothing as he moved across the gym floor and then through every cavity of the building. It was the fastest I had run since starting, and it took everything I had just to keep up. Goldberg was trying to lose us as he poured on the speed in the open corridors, and changed directions without ever looking back. It was a killer run that quickly took back everything I had regained while watching the demonstration.

We finally caught up to Goldberg when we found him waiting for us near a small platform. He chewed us out for being so slow, then demanded that we get under the two foot high structure and crawl on our stomachs the 30 foot distance to the other end. We did so quickly, and I found the scabbard to again be a real bitch to deal with as I tried to move my legs through the tight space and over the wooden braces. Goldberg ran to the other end, and was waiting there, yelling for us to hurry up. When Lu popped out in front of me, I could hear Goldberg commanding him to now get up on the top of the structure, and crawl its length back on his stomach. We followed Lu as Goldberg ran down to the other end. He was waiting for us to start the crawl underneath all over again.

We must have slithered under and over that temporary stage ten times. The tight space caused my scabbard to beat the hell out of my knees along with banging they took against the hard concrete floor. It was almost a relief to see Goldberg change our poison as he again took off running. But he didn't bother to wait for Peppercorn and me to get out from under the stage, so we really had to bust ass just to even keep Chin in sight. We ran as hard as we could to catch up, but Goldberg was pouring it on as he ran up into the balconies, and down the upper level corridors, and then back downstairs. The whole building rang with the different chants of "We love, Sword Drill" that came from every group.

We ran, and crawled, and jumped over every square inch of the huge facility. We carried trashcans, and chairs, or anything heavy that would make our runs more difficult. It was an endless attack on our desire to do this thing called Sword Drill, and I was sure that each roach in that building was measuring the worth of it all.

When we were all brought back together, we found out that someone's measurement of value came up on the short side for Sword Drill. Apparently, Gary Edmonds, C Company's Assistant First Sergeant had gone through enough. I never saw him leave, but like salt in a wound, they let us know with pleasure that one more was gone.

"You are now down to 26," said Kraft. "Apparently Roach Edmonds could not cut the mustard here with those of you who remain. But that's one less we have to cut. It was smart for him to quit now, before it really gets hard."

I was not surprised at all that someone had quit. This was brutal stuff, and if I was surprised by anything, it was that only one had dropped out. You had to really want this to endure even this one night of abuse, much less consider that there were thirteen more to come. It was a real testament to the desire my fellow roaches had, and a clear indication as to what my competition would be to get one of the fourteen slots. I truly began to believe that the Junior Sword Drill would indeed work out to be the very best that the Class of 1980 could offer.

"OK, I want you roaches to give me two long lines up on this end of the basketball court," yelled Kraft. "We're going to run some sprints."

Oh great, I thought. As if the other running through the building had not done us in. Thoughts of football practice crossed my mind again as we quickly moved into the lines, and I wondered if I still had the sprinting speed I possessed back then, or if I wanted to even use it if I did. I was dead tired, and really had no desire to prove anything at that point other than I could survive this night of holy terror and live to tell about it.

I was in the first line, and could see several of the old Drill lining up with us to run. Whatever their reasons, I knew that their presence would only cause the pace to be quicker.

"First line. Go!"

We took off running, and I could see from the start that no one was holding back much at all. Those who were running close to the Drill were really letting it eat. I guess they knew they were being watched and measured, and that anything other than their best effort would be recognized. As I ran hard I could hear the second line receive their start command, and it was a matter of seconds before they crossed the line behind us. There was a group of old Drill waiting there to line us up to run back, and moments later we heard someone shout to once again go.

Each time we ran there was old Drill right there with us. They would run several sprints, then step aside to let fresh guys in to continue. They ran us into the ground. I thought I would never get enough air as I gasped to take what I could from the stale source. I was terribly thirsty as all the chanting and the heavy breathing had parched my mouth and throat. I was weary beyond my worst memories of football camp, and I really didn't know how much longer I could last, and I could see that I was not alone. Some looked worse than others, but there was no one who looked as if he were doing well. Even Baxter Stall, who was easily in the best condition of us all, looked as if they had finally tapped into his last few ounces of strength. I almost wished that someone else would quit right then and there, just to send a signal to the old Drill that they were taking this shit too far, that no one would be stupid enough to stay for thirteen more nights of this, no matter how badly they wanted it. But no one stopped. We just kept pushing what was left of our battered bodies with energy we never knew we had.

I finally crossed the line after what had to be the 25th wind sprint, and I buckled over with my hands on my knees as I tried desperately to get something out of the air that would at least stop the panic my lungs were experiencing. I could see others doing the same, and there was almost a complete lack of concern that we were supposed to be at attention and bracing at all times. The Drill went berserk, and started yelling at us to form back up into a squad. We moved into position, fighting hard to stand straight, and show some semblance of trying to brace. The noise of heavy breathing was unbelievable, and I could feel the air being released behind me on my neck.

The Drill had to know without a doubt that they had effectively destroyed us all. But they walked around us yelling their heads off for us to get our eyes straight ahead, and to tuck our chins in, and to stop moving around. I could see that they had no ideas of backing off, probably hoping that someone else would indeed call out to quit.

But during the next minute or so, we just stood there with them giving us hell, and pulling on our arms to make sure that we were bracing. This was, without us knowing it, our final minute of rest.

I could see most of the Drill moving around on the floor, apparently dividing into groups, for what kind of game now, I did not know.

"First battalion roaches, over here," yelled one of them.

"Second battalion roaches, fall in," yelled another voice.

"Third battalion, let's line up," yelled a third.

And then I heard my call, "4th Battalion, fall in over here."

We all shuffled as quickly as we could to where our calls came from. I had an uplifting feeling that this may have been the beginning of the end of the night. It just had to be. I was ruined. My commitment to make Drill would carry me through anything they could dish out, but physically there was no way I could do much more. I could hardly stand, much less run. The muscles in my arms, shoulders, and back were gone, and I hated to think what would result from any further taxing. It was, for all practical purposes, over for me. If they put me through anything else, I was sure there was no way I could make it.

The six of us roaches from 4th quickly got ourselves into two rows, and followed Carl Andrews and the other two old Drill members as they started running around the perimeter of the gym floor. All roaches were running behind the old Drill from their respective battalions, and as we circled, we closed the gaps until we were one unit. We ran out towards the front vestibule, and then exited through the front doors held open by a Drill member.

The night air hit me like a splash of water. It was cool, fresh, and plentiful. I felt a small bit of rejuvenation as I took my first few breaths between my shouts of "We love, Sword Drill." I only guessed that this gift of air would not have been given if there was more suffering to endure. I felt certain that this dreadful night was finally going to end.

As we ran down the street, I could actually hear our chant start to pick up in volume, whether from getting into the fresh air or because we all felt that we were going home. For a brief moment I had some small suspicion that these sadist bastards might force us to go on some long campus run to further punish us and play with our heads. But as we ran by 1st Battalion, I could hear the rear-most group peal off from the squad, and enter into the sally port with that distinctive echo that would ring if someone shouted while going through it. As I heard the cheers inside the battalion raise, I knew then for sure, the first night of hell would soon be over.

One at time, each group veered off as we ran by their battalion, and the cheers as they entered made me want even more to get to 4th. As we made our turn into the sally port, I felt a bit of strength return, as a glory part of my dream was about to become reality. Because it was the only part of the Nights that I saw as a sophomore, it was the one thing I had thought most about.

As the roar of cheers and applause rang out, my spirits lifted a bit. Under normal circumstances, I would have been beside myself that hundreds of my schoolmates were cheering me on. But I was hurting, and the support was enough to help me run around the quadrangle, and apply at least some amount of feeling towards the saying, 'We love Sword Drill'. It was a real privilege and an honor to be where I was, and I appreciated what everyone was doing. But at that moment, I just wanted the nightmare to end.

After we circled the quad once, the old Drill left the squad and walked towards the middle. We made another lap on our own, until the old Drill motioned us to come over. We ran to the middle where they stood, then quickly got down into the lean and rest as they instructed us to do so.

The ache in my back and legs seemed to bite harder, and I scarcely heard the instructions from the old Drill. The clapping and cheering was ceasing as everyone watched and tuned in on what was happening. I wanted so badly to keep my back straight, but I just couldn't. I heard the Drill tell us to pump out fourteen push-ups, but missed what little else they had said as I strained through the aches. When we reached fourteen, we all got up and ran towards our companies. As I ran I remembered when Porter used to kiss the company letter painted in the corner of the battalion, and I did the same. I then started up the flights of stairs to my room. I could hear my name being shouted, and everyone was cheering and clapping loudly for me. I guess it was the only thing that got me up the stairs and down the gallery to my room. When I ran in, Larry closed the door, and I fell on the floor in pure exhaustion. I had made it back. The first Night was over.

I just lay there on the floor, and savored the feeling of being at rest. My body ached and I was thirsty enough to drink a lake. Larry caught my attention when he asked me if I was all right, and if I needed something to drink.

"Please!" I answered as I panted.

"You look awful," he said as he got me some ice water.

"I feel awful," I said as I gulped down the liquid, intentionally spilling some down my throat and chest.

"Is that water or sweat all over you," asked Larry.

"It's not water douche bag. You think I just got back from the Riviera," I said, not in the mood.

"Looks like you had one hell of a time," he answered.

The door flew open with a bang up against the metal full press, and in walked both Rosellini and Burn as if they owned the place.

"Hey, man," said Hank laughing. "Looks to me like they kicked your ass."

"Yeah, did anyone else get hurt in the wreck you were in," joked Burn.

"Fuck both of you," I answered while drinking and out of breath.

"Don't talk nasty like that," said Burn. "We didn't tell you to volunteer to get your ass kicked."

"You pussies couldn't make it through a debutante, much less Drill," I said. "By the way, Danny, is that your mama I hear callin'?"

"Listen goof ball, you've apparently had your ass kicked hard once tonight," said Burn, "don't make me have to do it again."

"Could you fart heads tell me what the hell you're doing in here," I said as I stood up with real difficulty.

"Hey," answered Rosellini, "we're just here to tell you that you're our hero, and that we too wish that we could get beat up by the senior class."

"It's going to be one broken up junior that beats you up if you keep fuckin' with me," I said as I moved over towards my chair.

"Ok then drilldo, tell us what kind of fun stuff they did to you," said Burn. "Did they use whips and chains?"

"Did they grease you up first before they gave it to you in the ass," asked Rosellini.

I just shook my head and put my face down into my hands, too exhausted to take these guys on any further. "You know, I'm really not in the mood to fuck with you bozos," I complained.

"Aw, come on, you let the senior sickos have their fun, now you don't want to play with us?" said Rosellini.

"Come on, Hank," said Burn, "We know when we're playing second fiddle. Let's go back to R Company where they love us."

"Forget how you got here," I said as they walked out the door laughing.

"Those guys are your friends?" asked Larry.

I just sat there in my chair for what seemed to be the longest time. I could feel my muscles tightening up, but I was too tired to strip down out of my wet and dirty clothes and head towards the showers. I settled for taking off my shoes and releasing my poor dogs from the heat of their encapsulation. I checked my feet to assess the damage, and I could see that I had the beginnings of a few blisters. I was happy that I had listened to George about wearing two pairs of socks and a thick coat of Vaseline. That probably saved my feet from some really nasty wear and tear. I only wondered if the other roaches had been warned or if they heeded the advice. I never could have imagined, even with my years of running, that one could abuse a set of feet so badly.

Over the next twenty minutes, I moved around slowly, taking off my clothes a little at a time, still drinking water like the spigot would run out. When taps blew, I knew I had wasted enough time and that I needed to take a shower and get to bed. My body had a lot of healing to do during the night, and it was beyond me how I was going to be ready to do it all again in less than twenty-four hours. I only knew I had to.

CHAPTER 34

The next day started with a very annoying alarm that went off at 0630. I just let it ring, even though I knew it was my clock. Larry finally got up and turned it off, then proceeded to get himself going. I knew I couldn't just lie there since I had so little time before formation. But as I moved my arms and legs, I realized what a task I had just to get up. I felt like hell, and the soreness in my muscles was enough to make me want to take the demerits and just stay in bed. But I knew that was not an option.. So I pushed myself up with my aching arms, and then pulled my battered legs from under the covers. The jump down from the top bunk was excruciating, and moving around to find my uniform was a real task as the aching stiffness made itself known. The room was a mess, and I knew I would have to clean it up before going to class. But for the moment, I had to shave, get dressed, and make it down to the sally port. I couldn't start my first day after by being late, especially since Carl Andrews was right there to take note.

I moved as fast as my body would respond, and made it down with only a minute to spare. Everyone on staff was looking at me, wondering how I had survived the night before. But I was in no mood for a lot of chitchat about what had happened, especially since one of those dishing it out could hear everything. I just answered with a lot of vagueness. I was not about to make matters worse, having not forgotten about the white plume.

My day was a real drag, and I had to really bust ass to clean up the mess in the room. Larry understood, but I knew that his patience would quickly wear thin if I didn't get my act together. I would hate it if we were to ever get burned during morning inspection because of my Drill mess.

My duties were immense that day. I had to deal with the freshmen as they continued to learn the ropes of being a knob, and the upperclassmen as they processed back into cadet life. Classes would start the next day, and it was a mad rush for everyone to get registered and get their rooms in shape. There seemed to be an endless amount of work that fell on the shoulders of the sergeants, and it was a bad day to have so much responsibility, even though I knew it was something I would have to get used to.

After a busy morning I was trudging along down the gallery towards noon formation when I heard my name being called. I turned around to see Tompkins, the sharp knob I had in my very first squad as a corporal. He was now R Company's Guidon Corporal.

"Hi John, I just wanted to let you know that if you need any help with any of your Sword Drill equipment, I'd be happy to give you a hand," he said.

"Gosh, thanks, uh..., Tompkins," I said, not remembering what his first name was.

"Sure," he said, "just give me a yell if you need me."

He turned to walk away as if he had some place to be, and I smiled knowing exactly what his motivations were. He was probably as nervous about saying something as I had been with George Porter. But I very much appreciated his offer.

Noon mess was a pain, as the knobs seemed to get on my nerves more than ever. I felt less patient with everyone, but I had at least enough sense to know it was because I was so tired and sore, and that it was making me cranky. I was hungry, yet felt too bad to eat much. I knew that the fuel to move me through the Nights would come from food, and want it or not, I had to eat. I forced myself to down two pieces of the mess hall's pizza, along with all liquids I could stand.

My afternoon was scheduled for me as I had a multitude of tasks to accomplish for my CO, Carl Andrews. I think in his mind he was giving me a reasonable workload, but it was no real break as far as I was concerned. I guess he just didn't want to show any sort of obvious favoritism. I had several things to do around campus, and moving about was no great pleasure. It was hot outside, and my legs, and whole body for that matter were sore. I thought often of conserving my energy for the approaching Night since I had a strong idea of what it would hold for me, but I just couldn't ignore my duties. With each step I felt I was tapping into the precious well of strength I would draw from that evening.

My real displeasure of the afternoon came when I happened to run into some of the boys from the old Drill as I was coming out of Mark Clark Hall after checking my mail. It was F Company's CO, Clarence Thompson, and Regimental Band's CO, Lamar Jordan. They quickly spotted me as I was walking out and they were walking in. They seemed to be in no hurry as I saluted them.

"Hey roach! Halt."

I stopped, and then cursed silently, not in a mood to be fucked with. Their smart-ass grins told me they were going to be a pain.

"Glad to see you knew who we were there, Roach O'Bryan!" said Thompson.

"Yes, Sir," I said with a dry seriousness.

"Nice to see you up and about," said Jordan. "Goin' to the canteen to take a break?"

"No, Sir, just checking my mail."

"That's good," replied Thompson. "Thought you may have had some spare time on your hands. I think most of the other roaches are working on their equipment by now. Guess you've got your stuff ready."

"I'm part of the way there, Sir."

"OK then, let's take a quick look at your brass," said Jordan. "I'm sure you have it blitzed."

Jordan reached down and turned the face of my belt buckle up, and then flipped it over to the back.

Jordan frowned saying, "Looks pretty borderline to me, O'Bryan. When did you last shine this brass?"

"This morning, Sir?"

"And not after lunch too? Mr. O'Bryan, as hot as it is out here, you will need to shine your brass at least twice a day if you want to maintain a Sword Drill level look."

"Yes, Sir," I said.

"All I can say is that borderline is not Sword Drill, Mr. O'Bryan," said Jordan, who started to walk away as I stood there in silence.

"No, Sir," I said in a normal tone of voice, knowing well that he had no way of hearing me as he walked into the building

That was a real joy, I thought to myself. I already felt like hell from the abuse these guys had dealt out the night before, and now they wanted to give me a hard time while off. It's not like I wasn't warned about it, and I really did expect to be inspected, but not right after my first night.

As much as I hated to admit it, I was having a bad day. I felt really tired and beat up. Desire to perform my duties was low. I felt drained, and I just wanted to get through with my work and then get into the rack. It sounded good anyway. In reality, I had more than enough to do before 1800 to nullify any real hopes of a nap, even though logic would dictate that being rested was far more important than being shined up. I guess I just couldn't convince myself that I could get away with going down to start my second night looking like hell, even if I did need the rest more.

I had a feeling that this rest versus work dilemma would remain a problem through the Nights. There was no way to do everything and still get the rest I required. There just wasn't enough time, even if I wasn't half dead with fatigue. I needed help. I needed Tompkins! Hell, I could remember back when I was almost begging Porter to let me help him. I considered it an honor. But all Porter ever asked me to do was to bring him back dinner. He never asked me to help him with his equipment. Would I be doing something wrong by using Tompkins?

As I walked back towards the battalion, I forced my tired mind to think through the options, and I considered what was really most important. Survival! It was much better to let personal appearance slip and concentrate more on taking care of my body. Only one night was down, and there were 13 to go, and I was already feeling like death warmed over. I needed to get Tompkins in on the act.

As soon as I walked in through the sally port, I headed towards R Company. I had no idea where Tompkins' room was, but thought that I should use discretion in my search for him. I smiled at the potential for the ragging he would face if his classmates were to discover his willingness to brown nose a junior, or possibly reveal his "secret dream."

After a few questions that seemed harmless, I found his room. I knocked on his door as I walked in, and found him in a bull session with two of his classmates. I had to fight a smile when one of them popped to attention like a freshman when he saw who I was. Having an audience, I honored my intentions to be discreet, and opted for a less direct approach.

"Hey, guys, how are you doing?" I asked.

"Fine, how are you?" replied one of Tompkins' friends nervously.

I still had to fight my smile, and started losing my strength as I spoke, "Tompkins, if you are not too busy in the next half hour or so, there's something I would like to talk to you about."

"Sure," he answered without elaborating. "We're just shooting the shit here. I'll come see you in about five minutes."

"Thanks. I'll be in my room," I said.

I turned and walked out, now wanting to laugh. I guess those new upperclassman privileges hadn't set in fully, or maybe freshman habits were just hard to shake. I'm sure my rank didn't help either.

Tompkins was in my room in no time. He was a bit nervous, but tried to hide it. I was pleased to see his enthusiasm and willingness to assist. It made it easier for me to ask for some real help, and count on him not to let me down. I was wise enough not to trust him with anything critical, but there were more than enough chores to be done, critical or not. I would start him off slow and then let him watch as I prepared my equipment. He could ease into assisting me as he came to understand the criteria. For now, I just needed him to help me do something with my uniform from the night before. It was almost cruel to ask him to do such a nasty job right off the bat, but if I didn't soon wash out my shirt and pants and hang them out, the smell would soon ravage the room. That would soon cause real problems with Larry, and he was not someone I wanted to piss off. He too was more than willing to help, and had already assumed the role of bringing me food back from the mess hall. I also had to live with him.

When Tompkins finished washing out my clothes, I asked him to pull up a chair and watch me as I worked on my brass. He looked on with great interest, and was amazed that my once perfect breastplate and belt buckle were in such bad shape after only one Night. From the nicks, scratches, and even gouges that were in the surface, it was hard for him to believe that not 24 hours earlier they were perfectly blitzed. Now, they were little more than junk, yet acceptable for the Nights since it was too expensive to expect roaches to buy a new set of brass for each outing. But tarnish or dirt found on them would surely spell painful recognition for the offender.

Because I had to spend extra time explaining to Tompkins what I was doing as I worked, I became a bit pushed to finish all I had to do before the 1800 hour arrived, but it was indeed an investment worth making, even though I had not gotten my much needed nap. I at least had the knowledge that I now had some additional relief available for an overbearing load.

At five minutes after the hour, the other roaches started to file in. They all looked as beat as I felt, and I just couldn't imagine how my battered body could again go through what I had experienced the evening before. Though I knew that the anticipation and adrenaline would soon be kicking in to prepare our minds and bodies to meet the challenge, my only real comfort was the knowledge that many others had survived the Nights throughout the years. If they could do it, so could I.

There was little said between us, and so little newness to our one-day-old experience. We had nothing significant to wonder about. We knew we were facing many hours of pure hell, and the moment was upon us to go down and once again face the music.

My legs ached as I ran down the stairs to first division, and thoughts of not having the stamina to make it through the night filled my mind. I knew even then, determination would be the only way to survive, and that my desire to make Sword Drill would surely be measured that evening.

We all took our positions in front of our company letters, and I soon saw the first pair of Drill members walk out from the O Company area. One walked straight towards the roaches from O, and the other made a bee-line for me.

"Good afternoon, Mr. O'Bryan," said Dave Morris as he reached up and took the shako from my head to inspect. "How are you feeling?" he asked with seriousness.

"Fine, Sir," I replied.

"No, I want to really know how you're doing. Are you sore, having cramps, nauseated?"

"Sore, Sir. Very sore," I said.

"I'm sure you are. We kicked your ass last night and we plan to do it again this evening. Did you stretch before coming down?"

"No, Sir. I did not," I answered with reluctance.

"Then do it. And do it well. I don't want any of you guys dropping out because of pulled muscles. Go at ease and stretch out everything. Then start pumping out push-ups for poor planning. But stretch out first."

I hated having screwed up, but I was thankful Morris had been concerned. My muscles were in knots, and the last thing I wanted was to fall out of Drill because of a pulled hamstring or other muscle. I quickly started doing stretches knowing that I had been given a privilege that meant my survival. Morris then left me stretching to go inspect Jim Pearl and Fred Irving over in T. I saw the other roaches also stretching, and wondered if it was because they too had forgotten or if this was just a measure of caution by the old Drill of 4th Battalion to protect their own. But soon the moment of concern and grace was over, and I could see that we were all doing push-ups. It hurt to do them right off the bat, and I could see across the quad that a few backs were already breaking down. The old Drill soon grabbed us up out of the lean and rest to start us on a running tour of the battalion. We were broken up into two separate groups, and we started to run up the stairs, down the galleries, and back down the stairs again. It didn't seem bad at first, but after about fifteen minutes of this, the stairs became a real burden. There was soon a trade-off as the soreness in my legs was replaced with a burning feeling. I became winded in no time, and sweat started to pour in the late afternoon heat. The Drill then increased our haul by making us carry trashcans made of thick, heavy metal. They were awkward to hold while trying to run the galleries and stairs. I could hear a tremendous noise of a trashcan bouncing down stairs, and a subsequent flurry of yelling as someone had obviously taken a spill. I could only hope that there was no injury. If you weren't constantly mindful of what you were doing, an aspiration for the Junior Sword Drill could quickly end.

The old Drill eventually ceased with the games and formed us up. I was sure they had used up every minute available and that we would have to rush if we were going to make it into the field house before the Corps started to return from evening mess. We circled the quad only once in 4th, and circled in the other battalions only long enough to pick up the other roaches. As we left 1st battalion, I indeed saw cadets on their way back from the mess hall, and we went directly into McAlister.

As before, it was stuffy and hot inside, and I hated the feeling in my lungs as we circled the huge floor as the chant thundered and echoed. The old Drill stood in the middle and watched as we circled countless times, and the fatigue and lack of breath became painful. I prayed that the laps would soon stop, and grimaced at the thought that the night had only just started.

"Form up over here," yelled Kraft finally.

The front of the platoon turned in towards the middle of the floor, and we stumbled down to a stop. The old Drill members were yelling as usual for us to get into our established positions, and we sloppily ran into each other's sweat slinging bodies as we got into

463

position. No one could breathe. Only gasp. The air seemed void of oxygen, and the heat was that of an oven.

"Good afternoon roaches!" said Kraft. "I welcome you to this, the second of the 14 Nights. You may have noticed that there is a hole in your ranks today. Another has decided not to proceed with the Sword Drill journey."

I was not surprised.

"Roach Donnatelli has determined that the challenge far exceeds his desire. He is not the first to leave your ranks, and I'm sure he will not be the last. There are now 25 of you left!"

Such encouragement at this point was like switches on Christmas. They were going to kill us. I could see that. There seemed to be a real need for them to do it with a passion, as if that were indeed their true mission.

But my thoughts were soon broken as someone stepped right in front of me. I was breathing hard, so he angled his face towards the side of mine, only inches away. It was that cock sucker Lamar Jordan. "Remember me, O'Bryan?" he said in a low but clear voice of meanness. "Think I was going to forget about your shitty lookin' brass? Well I didn't."

All of a sudden I felt someone pull at my arm that was braced as best possible, but nowhere enough to withstand the tug. The yelling then started from both Jordan and whoever was behind me.

"What in the hell do you think you're doing? Brace asshole!" screamed Jordan.

A harder yank came at my arm, causing me to lose my balance as I tried to brace harder and stand at attention. The yelling seemed to increase from behind, and Jordan stayed in my face, looking like I had just pissed in his Corn Flakes.

"I can tell you right now, O'Bryan, you're history. I don't want a slob like you in my Sword Drill. You just don't fit the mold. Why don't you just head on back to your room. Save yourself some trouble, and a whole lot of pain, cause if you stay boy, I'm gonna kill you. You hear me. I'm gonna run your ass in the ground. I'm gonna make you do my bandstands. You're gonna drown in your own sweat doing push-ups. You hear me maggot?"

Someone again jerked hard on my arm, testing to see if I was bracing, again making me lose my balance. I was exhausted, and I didn't like dealing with the shit that was happening to me.

"I tell you what I'll do for you, O'Bryan," continued the deathly voice of Jordan, "I'll even walk you out quietly so no one will see you leave. There's no need to make a big deal out of this. You can bow out real graceful like. Want to do that O'Bryan? Huh?"

I gasped to get enough breath to answer with a yell, "No, Sir!"

"What!" yelled Jordan with gritting teeth. "I've offered you a nice way to get out of here, O'Bryan, and you don't accept? Maybe you didn't understand what I just said to you. You don't fit the mold. We don't want you here. You're a friggin' slob. You wear shit for brass around my campus and now you want to call yourself Sword Drill? Well forget it! Just get the hell out of here. Now. Now I said! Get out of here asshole!"

Jordan slipped into a partial rage. His nose was almost touching mine since he was so close to me.

"Are you not listening, you idiot, get the hell out of my armory. You're not gonna make it. I've told you that. Are you deaf?"

"No, Sir!" I yelled.

"OK, OK, now I see that you're gonna be a real dumb ass about this shit. Fine. I'll just run your dirty, sloppy ass into the ground. Then you can decide if you want to stay."

Jordan grabbed me by my breastplate webbing, and jerked me so hard that I thought I had whiplash. I started running behind him as he literally pulled me through the air and cussed.

"Let's go douche bag! Run!"

I took off, and worked to get my run in sync with Jordan's pull. We ran around the floor with him pulling and jerking at me in a really annoying way. We ran through the corridors, and up the stairs, and into the balconies for what had to be an hour. He then made me carry trashcans and crawl under the portable stands. I was dying as he sat and watched me do bandstands for the longest time, and then kept his seat as he jeered and yelled at me to run up and down from the floor to the top of the auditorium seating. His attention towards me went on and on, without the slightest hint of giving me a rest. I found little comfort in passing several others who were also getting some special treatment. I was almost amused to see someone come by me wearing the white plume, wondering how it was possible for him to be catching hell worst than I was. I was convinced that Jordan was trying to take me out. At first I had a slight notion that this was all a joke, but I soon could see he was indeed trying his best to run me into the dirt. I was past tired. I was dizzy with exhaustion. I was thirsty beyond any previous thoughts of liquid desire. I had little doubt that I was not going to make it through this Night.

I was running in place, with a metal folding chair over my head, sweat burning my eyes, and thoughts of collapse on my mind, when Porter appeared in front of me, yelling to follow him, and Jordan commanding me to stop as Porter pulled me away by my webbing.. I was on the verge of collapse, but Porter never looked back as he pulled me off the main floor, running fast into one of the corridors. He ran me down the darkening halls, but then stopped suddenly when we reached a corner.

"Stand-up straight, Roach!" he yelled, and I did so as best I could through my now spastic breathing. He started yelling at me about something to do with bracing harder, but it was all I could do to remain standing and focus on any of his words. I was burning up. My mouth was so dry it felt like leather, and my thirst was beyond comprehension. My whole body felt like one huge throbbing bruise. Porter looked around, and then quickly shoved a piece of ice into my mouth. It stung the parched skin of my mouth and tongue, and it almost choked me as the drops moved down my throat. I had to be careful not to suck the large cube down as I continued to fight for air, while at the same time consume the precious drops of liquid.

I was beyond grateful. Porter had surely just saved me from falling out. I was also worried. What would they do to me if they knew he had done this? But what in the hell was that fuck stick Jordan trying to do to me anyway? Did he think that I was going to be able to go on all night at such a pace?

"How are you?" asked Porter.

"Better," I said as best I could talk with the ice and the breathing, "but Jordan…almost…killed me."

"I know," replied Porter. "What's his beef with you?"

"Bad brass... today...in front of...Mark Clark."

"What? It's got to be more to it than that."

I just shook my head no in disgust.

Porter reached up and put another large piece of ice in my mouth and then said, "OK, get down and give me some sit-ups!"

I moved as quickly as possible into the sit-up position, basically lying on my back, sucking on the ice, and waiting for Porter to say up. But I heard nothing. I just lay there, worried about being seen, but so thankful I was off my feet, and that I was getting both a break and some liquid intake.

"Up!" Porter finally said as I heard the sound of footsteps coming. I went into the up position of a sit-up, and grimaced at the sharp pain in my stomach muscles. "Down," yelled Porter with feeling as I saw an old Drill member run by with two roaches.

I waited for Porter to tell me to go up again, but heard nothing. I didn't argue. I breathed long and hard, and started to feel the panic of my condition start to subside. The ice was melting fast, and my thirst was now tolerable, yet not quenched. I looked at Porter with a better sense of comprehension, and I could see a look of concern and protection.

"Up!" he said, and I sat up, again with a great deal of effort. It hurt, but was far from the pounding punishment that Jordan was dishing out, and I felt thankful for the chance to rest, even if it was attained while doing sit-ups.

George Porter had saved me from what I knew was going to be the total collapse of my body. I was in the best shape of my life, but not to the point where I could survive such strenuous exercise at a blistering pace in the heat. My body was hurt, and I knew it. It would be a real struggle to finish out the night, and the only way I would make it was to radically pace myself. It would be a risk, and all it would take was for a '79 Drill member to say I was sloughing off and that would be it for the evening.. George had saved me from the death race Jordan was putting me through, but I knew that his redeeming protection would soon have to disappear. If he owed me anything for the little help I had provided while he was a roach, he just repaid the debt in full.

I must have been out of sight for about five minutes while I did slow, well spaced sit-ups. I knew the risk of receiving such favoritism, and understood fully when George finally said, "We've got to go!"

We started running at a very reasonable pace. I followed George as we ran through the outer corridors of the Field House, passing other '79 Drill members and their trailing roaches. It was a far cry from the unwavering tempo I had weathered in my previous hours, but just as difficult after already being butchered. My brief period of sheltering and rejuvenation could only last so long, and it was completely over as soon as Kraft called us all in.

From that point, we went into the more group-based activities, starting with push-ups, and then on to hanging from the pipes, piggyback races, and endless running. I ached and felt wounded as I struggled through each movement. I again thought for sure I wasn't going to make it, fighting desperately right up until we were allowed to die. It was a long, hard, devastating three hours. It was much worse than the night before, and I thought I would collapse before Kraft finally called us together to return to the barracks. I could see others who were hurting badly, and I knew then that despite the desire, we all would not make it through this agony. It made hell seem like a furlough. It made falling out seem like welcomed relief.

We ran, some stumbled, back to the battalion. I could see Baxter Stall holding a fellow roach's arm, helping him run to finally make it in. Seeing this, I gained a respect for him that would last a lifetime, and I knew that he just couldn't be human. Though I had been singled out early on, the group as a whole looked injured, and there was extreme struggle on the faces I could see. The thunder in our voices the night before was now reduced to a mild noise. My own energy level did not rise as before as the applauding support of my fellow cadets did little to ease my gut wrenching exhaustion. I was running and chanting by sheer determination, thinking I would fall at any moment. We circled the quad, and stopped in the middle to do our push-ups. To my disgust, I knew there was no way I could do them with my back straight, and I hoped that I would not suffer the shame of not being able to do them at all. There was so little there to perform with, and I just faked them as best I could. I got up and ran towards my letter, kissed it, then fought a tremendous battle to ascend the stairs. I stumbled twice, and towards the top I thought my legs would not get me there. They were throbbing with a biting pain, and ignored most commands to move.

Larry had the door open for me when I arrived, and I fell on the floor in a hard collapse. It hurt when I hit, and I rolled as I experienced a deluge of agony. I could say little, but the single word of "water" was more than sufficient. Larry apparently understood my condition, and responded. He filled a cup with water from the tap, and after handing it to me, grabbed the running fan from the window and placed it right in front of me. My hands trembled as I tried to drink, and I spilled half of it as I desperately tried to extinguish both the pain and desire of a fiery thirst. It was relief to desperation, and I felt a panic to both drink and breathe at the same time. When the cup was empty, I dropped it and fell back to the floor and rolled in my torment. I wanted more water, but couldn't move to get more. Larry seemed scared and in a panic as he wet a towel in the sink.

"My God, John! You guys are going too far with this thing. You look terrible, but I mean real bad this time."

I couldn't answer. I just tried to get my breath, and wait out the pain. Larry put the cold towel around my scorching neck, then filled my cup with iced down Gatorade from the cooler, and I pulled myself up to sit against the half press. Again I tried to drink, spilling as I swallowed. I felt some relief, and sat there as the heat escaped from my body, and the sweat ran a river on the floor.

I sipped at the Gatorade, trying to drink it slowly. After a few minutes of silence, I felt I could talk, and that I needed to give Larry an explanation.

"They tried to kill me," I said.

"Wrong! They did kill you. You look like a walking corpse."

"I feel terrible. Real dehydrated. Sore."

"It's too damn hot out there for this kind of shit. Don't those idiots know that?"

"Apparently not. Or maybe they do. Maybe it's what they had to go through."

"Well, this is stupid. Nothing's worth this. Nothing!"

I could see that Larry wasn't kidding around. He could see this was no joking matter, and that it was much more of a serious game than he had ever imagined.

Recovery was slow, and just as my thirst subsided, and my body temperature worked its way towards normal, I felt my muscles start to knot up. I stood up with great effort, and I took my sword and scabbard out of my dirty, sweat soaked sling. I removed nothing else, and walked out of the room and down to the showers. I walked in and turned one on, then sat on the floor underneath it, propped against the wall. I was already soaked, so the water changed little, other than to provide its fresh form of relief. I lay down, too weak to even sit up, and marveled as the water cooled and quenched. I lay there until I heard taps blowing outside, and I knew I had to get to bed. I took off my shoes, webbing, and clothes, then carried them dripping as I walked naked down the gallery back to my room, too tired to care. I threw them across the gallery rail, and dropped my shoes by the door. I took a few seconds to dry off, then crawled into the rack with enormous effort. I was asleep in less than five minutes.

I awoke at 0247. My right thigh was locked in a cramp, and I woke up Larry as I tried to move my battered arms to massage it out.

I remembered a trick from P.E., and grabbed my toe and pulled, and the knot in my leg slowly went away. It was an unwelcome disturbance to desperately needed sleep.

CHAPTER 35

The alarm the next morning had been buzzing for some time when I finally awoke. It was actually Larry yelling at me that brought me out of my deep sleep. I then had to work through real agony just to get through my morning routine so I could get down to formation wearing a look of death on my face. I didn't know what sort of information those outside of Drill had about my personal trauma during the previous evening, but those who saw me come in had to recognize that I was haggard and whipped. There were a few small comments, but most knew that the 14 Nights for the 1980 roaches had taken on a very serious focus. I was sure I had to be the worst of the wounded out of 4th Battalion, but knew that the others had to also be in pretty bad shape. The armory was like a broiler, and just to sit in it would have been uncomfortable. The lack of water was the most damaging, and I couldn't help but think this was somehow wrong. Nearly four hours of a punishing workout without liquid was not smart. It may be necessary to weed us out, but it was too stressful in the long term. I had little doubt that it would quickly take its toll. I wondered how I would ever motivate myself to make it through another night. There had to be others seriously questioning their own desire.

Breakfast was a chore. I had to eat, but felt sick and really weak. I forced down some toast, grits, and eggs, and drank as much milk, orange juice, and coffee as I could stand. I made it back to my room to shine my brass and shoes before my first class of the year started, fully aware of the challenge ahead of me just to make it through the day.

It was hard to stay focused in class. I often had to fight sleep, and knew that the professors would have little sympathy for outside interferences if they saw me having problems. My shaved head had already alerted them that I was doing something extracurricular, and I didn't need to draw any more negative attention by nodding off. It was a struggle all morning.

Noon brought an inspection before lunch, and because I had changed into my inspection brass and shoes, I passed without a hitch. I certainly had nothing to worry about with my hair. Of course, with Carl Andrews doing the looking, it was a high-pressure examination nonetheless. He checked my uniform, brass, and shoes, and then looked into my eyes for a few brief seconds towards the end. I could see his concern. There was little doubt he knew my condition. He had been there.

Lunch was again a real task. I felt better than I did at breakfast, but my desire to eat was insignificant, so I again had to force myself. I drank water constantly, and gave the knobs at my mess a challenge in keeping my glass filled. I let the corporal raise hell at them when they didn't, since I was too tired and frazzled to get involved.

Afternoon class was not as bad as the morning since it was a lab, and that kept me up and moving. My legs hurt as I stood, but I didn't have to fight sleep like I would if I were in a lecture. Walking back to the battalion afterwards, I saw and saluted a member of the old Drill without incident, and then hurried back to my room before trouble somehow found me.

I was pleased Tompkins came through for me as I noticed my clothes gone from the rail when I returned to my room. I had more than enough to do, and the help was very much appreciated. I worked on my equipment first, then on my uniform. I worked with a new sense of efficiency, and with a more realistic idea of the degree of effort my personal appearance required. I was only going for the minimum. I needed rest, and Wednesday was a very good day for me to get it. There was no drill with the staff and no significant cadre or supply work to do since classes had started. By 1600 I had everything ready, and the only thing that delayed me from climbing into the rack was a visit by Tompkins. I was short with him and he understood. I told him I would work with him to further his knowledge when time and getting rest were not so critical, and I thanked him for taking care of my clothes. As rare as it was for me, I was asleep in no time in the middle of the afternoon.

The alarm went off at 1730, which gave me 45 minutes to be ready to go down. I was groggy, and my muscles had again tightened up while I slept. Stretches would not be something I would forget again. My uniform was on within minutes, and I put on my two pairs of socks with Vaseline packed in them, then finished by adorning myself with the hardware. Putting my shako on my head, I suddenly felt a real dislike for what I was dressed in. Motivation was scarce. I had no idea how I was going to make it through the approaching four hours of misery. I just couldn't see how it could be done with legs that already felt like huge rubbery wounds.

I already felt tired as I stood in front of my company letter. In no time I was inspected and again down in push-up position. I was terribly sore, and somewhat groggy from my nap, so my enthusiasm was lacking. We ran around the battalion for a while, and then made our way over to the others to group up. We ran and did push-ups for a long time outside of the armory, and I cursed the clear weather that allowed three days of direct access to the sun. Inside, McAlister was roasting hot as usual, and the familiar sounds of roaches breathing desperately arrived quickly. Edward Peagler was the lucky recipient of the white plume, and at the same time I felt sorry for him, I was thrilled it wasn't me. Baxter Stall was also again pulled off for some special treatment, and the rest of us started into the normal games of torture. I felt drained as usual, but because I knew I had to, I held back just a bit to conserve my energy. To give 100% at all times would almost certainly be my end. I had to be smart. The goal was to survive the night, and each that would come after. There were no awards for the roach that tried the hardest, only punishment for those who really sloughed off, and the ultimate penalty for those whose bodies couldn't last the duration.

It seemed that no one had any special beef with me that night. I caught my fair share of hell with the pack, and didn't stand out with anyone. When we hung from the pipes I fell early, but wasn't the first. During the piggyback and wheelbarrow races, my partner and I finished somewhere in the middle.

Though I was personally surviving, things went sour for everyone shortly after we broke up into groups to run through the corridors. Along with two others, I was selected by Dan Trout to follow him. He ran us over every square inch of the building. We passed several of the other groups as we ran, and after going hard for what seemed like half an hour, we passed through the main floor where we immediately saw a group of old Drill members standing over a roach who was lying on the floor. At that moment I was exhausted, thirsty, and burning up, and I was sure someone must have passed out as the third day of torture finally reaped a victim. I would later find out otherwise.

It seemed that Bob Fox was not pleased with the speed at which his group was following him. Jim Pearl, who was right behind Fox and actually putting out the hardest, was grabbed by his sword sling and was pulled around the armory floor in an attempt to speed up the others. But luck was not on Pearl's side that day, in that as Fox pulled him, his sword swung between his legs and he tripped. It was a violent fall, and the rigid scabbard did some real damage as Jim tumbled. The result was torn ligaments in Jim's right knee. It was over for him. He faced the end of a dream, a trip to the hospital, and major knee surgery, all at the same time.

I felt terrible for Jim, and prayed it was somehow not serious as the old Drill only told us initially that his knee was injured, not knowing that it was far worse than we ever suspected. During my later moments of torment that night, I couldn't help but think of my own shattered dream of playing college football, and how it too had ended as Jim's dream had. I became concerned for my knee that had the potential to go out again with the slightest mishap, and I recognized that it could have easily been me riding in the meat wagon to have my second round with surgery. From that point on, this concern would be ever present.

The old Drill was not happy with what had happened. Even though they tried not to show it, they knew that the circumstance of

Fox pulling Pearl when the accident happened was not good.

Certainly someone in the administration was not going to like this, even though it was an accident.

The rest of the night was hard, yet a bit different. There were less threats and yelling. The old Drill seemed to be worried, more careful. Their sense of meanness and dedication to dishing out torment had been dulled by the incident. Little did I know just how serious the matter would be to Jenkins Hall.

By the end of the night, I was, as usual, dead on my feet. I was not in a desperate state as was the case the night before, but I was definitely hurting. The return to my room left me at least sitting in my chair this time, still out of breath and in pain, but at least not reeling in desperation on the floor. I was able to function like the first night, but with a great deal of effort. I showered, hung my dirty uniform on the rail, and then threw on a pair of shorts. I limped over to T Company as my shin splints ached with a vengeance. I knocked on the door of Jim Pearl's room, and I heard his roommate answer for me to come in.

"Hi, John, I know why you're here. His leg is pretty bad. Torn ligaments. They plan to operate tomorrow. He's in a lot of pain, but they will soon have him so doped up, he won't feel a thing."

"How's his spirits?" I asked.

"He's more upset about being out of Drill than anything. He knows he's through."

"I'm sure he does. I'm sorry this happened."

"He feared many things about going out. This was one of them. He said he would have stuck it out to the end, although it's been really tough on him so far."

"It's been hell."

"I wish you guys luck. It's more than I was willing to do."

"Thanks. And if you talk to him, tell him to put another bed in his room. I have a feeling he's just the first."

I hobbled back to my room and crawled into the rack. I lay there thinking about Jim's accident, and how my leg had the potential to be re-injured with very little help. I thought about all that could be lost in a matter of seconds as you turned a corner and found an injury gremlin waiting to take you out. That scoundrel got Pearl, and he was out of the running in an instant. We were now down to 24 roaches. I hoped not to be the next out, and I fell asleep with that prospect on my mind, and dreamed of awful things as my physical pain and subconscious mind took away some of the value of my sleep.

The next morning was the usual struggle. Repetition had no value. Experience didn't make the process any easier. It seemed to be one big measure of my commitment through every waking hour, and sometimes even in my sleep. I had to admit that my dedication to the endeavor had eroded, and that the wonder and envy was now replaced by anxiety and fear. I really wanted this. And the more I invested, the more I had to have it. But with only three of fourteen Nights complete, the light seemed but a flicker at the end of the tunnel.

After my classes, I had my first afternoon drill of the year. I was fortunate to now be carrying a sword, and had to only work on the limited requirements that Battalion Staff had during parades. It was so simple compared to Sword Drill that it quickly became boring. I could only think of the things I had to do before the night started, and how this waste of time assured that I would not be taking a nap that afternoon.

Preparations for the evening went well. I had finally reached a point where I felt that I could trust Tompkins to work on some of my brass. I showed him many times just what was expected, and then watched him as if he were disarming a bomb when I let him work on my shako. He knew the seriousness of the matter, and in truth, I really had nothing to worry about. He was the best knob I ever had, and his personal appearance was always perfect. The fact that his grades were also good told me he was someone I could count on. It was just hard to let go and trust anyone with something that could potentially cause me so much pain. It was impossible to relax.

I found great comfort in the fact that this would be the last night of the week. I would have almost three days to recuperate. Sunday evening would then be our next time out, the first of a five-night week. It would be hell. But for now I just had to make it through this next night. You had to take the Nights one at a time.

Everything went as usual except for the blessing of a late afternoon thunderstorm. It had been threatening during the hour before we came down, and as we stood in front of our letters, you could see the lightning popping, and hear the thunder as it blasted and echoed off the walls of the battalion. The old Drill went about their business as usual, and even when the rain started, their only concern seemed to be that of the lightning.

Because it was really coming down, we skipped the usual trips from battalion to battalion to assemble the full platoon, and each group just formed up and ran straight over to McAlister separately. We were soaked when we entered, and the building was strangely different as it was darker and noticeably cooler inside. I had a feeling that it just wasn't going to be that bad of a night with such a tremendous break in the heat.

The Drill started putting us through the usual hoops all right, and indeed it was challenging, yet nowhere as harsh as it had been in the sweltering heat. I felt a bit of guilt that we weren't receiving our full dose of misery, and was concerned that the Drill might figure out that we were getting away with something. The way they were yelling at us made it seem that they had some hint that we weren't catching our normal brunt of hell, and they yelled constantly that we had to move faster and try harder to make ourselves miserable. It was a tough night all right, but it was becoming clear that the old Drill wasn't impressed.

It was actually pretty amazing how the old Drill was giving all 24 of us so much of a hard time at once. It was as if they were mad at us because of the break in the weather, like we had something to do with it changing.

"That's it! That's enough!" yelled Kraft after a couple of hours had passed. "Line-up roaches! Get up off your lazy butts now and fall in."

I wasn't certain what was going to happen, but I knew that something was coming that would be different. We fell into formation, and the old Drill hovered around us like vultures, giving us constant grief for being so slack, yelling and pulling on our arms to see if we were bracing.

"You roaches think that just because it rained today, and it's nice and cool, that we're just going to take the day off and lollygag around. Well you're wrong! You guys are not putting out. You're not giving your best, and I won't stand for it, not during the Nights, or during cuts, and I sure as hell won't stand for it during your performance, that is if you are allowed to give it. You ladies may not realize it, but you've got to make it through us. You will have to perform to our satisfaction before we will ever allow you to represent this organization in front of thousands of people. We will not accept second best. We will not accept the minimum. I hope and pray that what we are witnessing tonight is indeed not the best that this class has to offer. You must, through your own pride and discipline, ALWAYS give 100%. We will only accept your very best."

Kraft walked over to a group of Drill members who were standing near, and spoke to them in a loud and irritated voice. "Get these slack dogs out of here. I'm sending them all back."

"All of them?" asked one in the crowd.

"That's right, all of them. They have got to learn to push, and right now. They're completely unmotivated. They're not Sword Drill. They're not even close. Get 'em the hell out of my sight."

Kraft stormed out of the huge room to the front lobby and slammed the door loudly as he left the building.

"You heard the commander, roaches," said Ronnie Bourbon, now assuming command, "Right face. Forward march. Double time march."

So off we went back towards the battalions. We had apparently not pleased the '79 Drill in our efforts. I didn't like that they were sending us back, but I somehow found it hard to believe that we weren't putting out as much as we had been in our previous nights. Because it was so cool, we probably weren't suffering and breaking down as fast, but that didn't mean we weren't doing all that was asked of us. Maybe the old Drill just became frustrated in that they weren't as efficient in their delivery of abuse.. I took it seriously only because of the rule saying that each of us could be sent back only one night for not meeting the standards. I had viewed it as a small bit of insurance in case anything ever went wrong, and wondered if this was that one mark against our small balance. On the other hand, I couldn't help but recognize a bit of planned execution in the incident. There was no argument, no debate from anyone from the old Drill on such a radical move. I couldn't help but wonder if this was just another one of their mind games.

Being so early, there were no crowds or cheers as each group broke off from their silent platoon and entered into their respective sally ports. When we entered 4th, we never even circled the quad. We were told just to stop, and instructed to silently proceed to our rooms. Their final words to us were laced with a bit of compassionate satire in saying that it was too bad that this night would not count as one of the 14.

Count or not, I was happy to be back in my room so early. Larry was shocked to see me walk in at 9:05, and was immediately concerned with my presence.

"Oh shit! You didn't quit did you?"

"Hell no! Never. They sent us all back," I answered with a slight shortness of breath.

"What?"

"Yeah, they said the night wouldn't count. I guess the rain made it cool enough to where we weren't all dying, so they sent us back."

"No shit. What does that mean?"

"If the night doesn't count, I guess we'll be doing fourteen and a half nights for this Drill."

"Those sadistic assholes," said Larry with feeling. "If they can't kill ya, they don't want to play."

There was a moment of silence as I started to undress, and continued to think through the ramifications of the half night.

"Aren't you getting your fill of this shit yet," asked Larry with disgust. "I mean... these Drill jerks are off their rocker. I used to think they were fucked up, but now I know they're really psychos. Know what I mean?"

"Yeah, from a distance I'm sure it's a bit strange."

"From a distance? Are you crazy? I'm not sure if you've been awake for the last week, but these nuts have been steadily kicking your Master Sergeant ass. Ain't you got the picture yet?"

"Yeah, I got it. I know it sucks. But I want this. I want it bad. I won't quit no matter what they do. They're just testing our desire, and my desire has no holes in it."

"Yeah, but your fuckin' head does. You're just as sick as they are. Put me on record to say I wouldn't do this crap if there were a hundred naked whores at the finish line. You're all nuts."

The next day was a breeze. I was totally conscious all day of my renewed sense of comprehension and ability to deal with things. I was still sore all right, but the half night of abuse and the full night of sleep were enough to make a world of difference. There were plenty of wounds left to heal, but I didn't have to fight to stay awake in class.

I rejoiced in the fact that I had enough time. Time to rest and time to study. Time to shine-up, do my duties, and take care of all the things I was forced to put off because of Drill. I always felt rushed to get prepared for the approaching Night. But there wasn't one. There was only parade with the Corps, our first of the year. I shined up my normal cadet brass for the event, knowing well the need to present myself well at all times. I could feel the eyes of the old Drill around every corner, across the parade ground, wherever I was. I had my freedom until Sunday evening to put out fires, and I didn't want to strike any other matches before then.

481

I quickly learned that carrying a sword was not going to take away all the pains of parade. It was hot and humid and the sand gnats swarmed in clouds. The whole thing seemed like a waste, mainly because I had more important things to do. It was my duty, like it was for every cadet, but even that reasoning did little to ease my stiff muscles and my aching legs as I tooled around on the Parade Ground in the heat.

Our great Friday afternoon chore was over at 1645, and from that point I was supposedly free. However, our first SMI of the year was scheduled to make sure the Corps had rooms and uniforms back up to standard. That, along with having to practice the cuts routine we were shown with my partner Rontelli and having to put in some time working on my personal sword manual meant it was to be a busy weekend.

But I had to make time to call Cindy. My contact with her had been scant, and I really wanted to talk to her, just as I wanted so much to be with her. As I thought about making the call, I walked over to look in the mirror. The reflection had once again become my enemy. My hair was again gone, and due to the hellacious physical exertion, lack of sleep, and poor eating, I could see a deathly unpleasant look in my face. I had already lost weight, and there was a familiar darkness about my eyes. I looked rough, and I had only gone through three and a half nights, with possibly eleven more to go if indeed the previous Night did not count. I was surely going to look bad if I managed to make it to the end.

As I surveyed my condition, the demons of my terrible experience with Donna came strongly to mind. I was on my way to looking every bit as abused as I did when I was a freshman. I was convinced that my grim appearance was the starting point of Donna's loss of love for me. I knew Cindy really loved me, but I thought the same was true with Donna before she saw me as a cadet.

These were not pleasant thoughts. I cared for Cindy deeply, and I just couldn't help but think that wasn't good. I swore I would never let myself become so emotionally attached again, and now, here I was very much in love. All I needed was for her to see me and then have her dump me right in the middle of the Nights. I would surely not make Drill after that.

I just had to make sure Cindy would not see me until the 14 Nights were over. By then, some of my hair would be back, and I wouldn't look so much like a P.O.W. As bad as I wanted to see her, I could not do so if I had any hopes of keeping her. Presented right, I knew I could somehow make her understand.

I picked up the receiver and dialed her number. I wasn't sure if she would be there, especially on a Friday night. Even without me, there was plenty to do on the MUSC campus.

"Hello?" she said in her unmistakable voice.

"Hi, it's me," I said.

"John! I'm so glad to hear your voice. I've missed you terribly."

"I've missed you too."

"How's Sword Drill going?"

"Really hard. I don't have time to do anything."

"I'm sorry. Is there something I can do to help?"

"No," I responded with a laugh, "not unless you want to come over and shine my brass."

"Be right over!"

"Right. Which uniform are you coming in?"

"Which ever one they will let me in with. Oh John, I hate this separation. I know you can't leave, but I just miss you."

"Stop! I can't take it anymore. You will soon have me sneaking out of here."

"What else can I say to make that happen?"

"I'm sorry, Cindy. I want to see you too, but I just can't leave. We both know that."

"Suppose I just come see you?"

There you go stupid. You just led her to ask exactly what you wanted to avoid.

"I wish you could. But you can't. I know it sounds crazy, but I have about a thousand things I have to do before Sunday night, like open my books for the first time. But more so than that, I just can't be seen doing anything except Drill related stuff. They would make things very hard for me if they saw me."

"OK, John. I don't want to make it rougher on you. But as soon as you're allowed, please let me come over just to hold you for at least one minute."

"I hate being apart as much as you do, but believe me, we will have all the time in the world after these 14 Nights are over. You'll see."

"OK."

"Well, I hate to go, but I'm nowhere ready for tomorrow's inspection."

"Darn John! I can't see you and now I can't even talk to you on the phone. OK, I know...I know. I won't complain anymore. I realize you are really catching it with Drill and I don't want to make it any worse. Just promise you'll call again when you can."

"I will. I promise. And don't worry, this will all be over with before you know it."

That was tough. I wanted to see her as much as she wanted to see me. Probably more. She sounded so sweet and strong about us. Maybe I was wrong. Maybe. I didn't want to lose her, and didn't want to take the risk. The Nights would be over in a few more weeks. I hated not to see her, but I had more than I could handle at the moment and our relationship would just have to wait.

I had my best night's sleep in a week. The SMI was a breeze, and I easily filled my day after its completion. Rontelli and I met at McAlister and put in our first two hours of practicing our cuts routine. It was an odd feeling to casually be in a place that had provided such pain and anguish in the previous days, and knowing that more would be endured in the weeks to come. The remainder of my afternoon and evening was consumed with getting my equipment in order and playing catch-up with my studying. With five nights on tap for the approaching week, I knew there would be no time to do anything, other than survive. I worked hard to get ahead, and tried to cover all the bases of planning for the crunch.

In my previous two years of attending The Citadel, I had rarely attended church. It seemed like my Sunday mornings had been reserved for suffering through hangovers or getting in some extra studying in my more responsible days. But on that Sunday morning, I felt a calling, and a real need to be there. I felt a touch of guilt in going only when I was in need, having previously ignored the doors of Summerall Chapel until then. It was something I hoped God would understand. Maybe my eighteen years of near perfect attendance at the Kingstree Methodist Church would provide a bit of redemption for my most recent life of heathenism.

Walking into the Chapel I found that its cool air grabbed my senses, giving me a feeling that there was something different inside. I took a seat on a pew near the front as I listened to the glorious sound of the organ, which was both powerful and beautiful. The Citadel Chaplain, Colonel James, was an eloquent and talented man of God, having served both his maker and his country through the same career. He had a remarkable talent of connecting with cadets, and understood both the value and struggle of the Citadel life they had chosen. He was respected by everyone, and held a special place in the hearts of those who for years had passed through the Corps. His sermon that day, was on the subject of John the Baptist, and was as entertaining as much as moving. At times he was even funny, especially in his descriptions of the wild man in the wilderness, who on the surface was uncivilized and crazy, but had the faith and heart that would exceed that of even the most devout historical Christians. It was a wonderful story that was brought to life by a wise and talented Chaplain, and it was easy to see that every Cadet in the Chapel understood his message in their own personal way. I left the church that day with a stronger will and better understanding of life. I only regretted not having come to hear the Chaplain sooner.

CHAPTER 36

Sunday afternoon was warm, yet peaceful. The rest received over the weekend was rejuvenating for both the body and mind. I now knew well the taste of the abuse poison one had to consume in order to make Sword Drill, and that the secret of surviving was to withstand the near lethal dose given each night. Having a clear understanding of just what I would face in the coming week converted fear and concern to a solid plan that gave me assurance. My equipment was in excellent shape. I had all the supplies I needed such as tape, Gatorade, Ben-Gay, and Vaseline. I had help available from Larry and from Tompkins who was now adequately trained. It was up to me to utilize those well-placed assets to withstand the old Drill's pounding. I was ready and poised to do battle with the demons of survival.

Study consumed most of my afternoon, and I thought it both good and bad to be inside on such a clear summer day that was indeed marred by the extreme heat. It was down right hot in my room, even with the sun blocked out and my window fan on high. The early September day showed no signs of breaking the chain of summer scorchers by yielding to the cooler approaching fall. Though the clear weather was a superlative ingredient for Labor Day vacations, I knew it would make the armory dangerously potent.

At 1814 we all stood in position in front of our company letters. Everyone was back, and that was no surprise. The half night on Thursday and the weekend off did nothing to chase anyone away. As the old Drill was inspecting and running us through the battalion, they were quick to make note of our "vacation." As their reference to our lengthy rest became frequent, I somehow gathered that a payment had come due for the luxury.

It may have been the rest, but for some reason, the initial workout of getting to the Field House seemed not as draining as usual. I thought with the old Drill's comments that they were surely going to kill us for our few days of rest. It was certainly hot, physical, and demanding, but there was a noticeable absence of desperation, a sort of normalcy that went with a challenging workout versus our usual death run.

In the armory, the surprise reason awaited us. To our utter shock and confusion, there was a large cake with yellow icing there for us, and it was decorated to say "Well Wishes to the 1980 Junior Sword Drill." Suspicions raced like our heartbeats, and the gesture was immediately surmised as deceitful. You could just feel the distrust among us, though no one ever said a word. The old Drill went through the ceremony of cutting the cake, and making sure there was a nice big piece for each of us. After running so much in our journey through the battalions to get to McAlister, dry cake with sugary icing was not a desire at all. Water would have been nice, but gracefully declining the treat never seemed an option. Having been handed my portion on a floppy paper plate, I took a generous bite as commanded. I recognized the cake as a product of the mess hall, and even on my hungriest day, I never experienced the urge to ever indulge. My desire to eat was created only by direction.

After two big bites, the overpowering sweet taste of the frosting and the dryness of the cake became choking to my arid throat, yet the old Drill was still more than obliged to step in to assist. It started with them helping us to eat, and like the devilish play of a bride and groom at a reception, the confection was terribly misguided towards our mouths. Both cake and frosting got all over our faces, and then it spread quickly to our necks and shirts. It was a terrible feeling, and I thought I would croak when one guy grabbed a hand full and pulled my shirt collar wide enough to smear it on my chest and back, then worked his way up into the fine bristles of the hair on my head. The sticky frosting on my sweaty skin touched a sensitive nerve in me, normally reserved for things like fingernails scraped across chalkboards and eating greasy food while nauseated. I hated, even despised that sticky feeling on my back and neck as it formed an adhesive between my shirt and skin. It was a direct hit on my grit,

487

disguised as an offering of kindness.

Wearing our cake, and eating it too, the old Drill set us up for a visit to hell. They stopped with the culinary games and went quickly into a monumental torture session. The dessert both choked and annoyed us as we crawled under the bandstands on our backs and bellies, and did the usual piggyback races, push-ups, sit-ups, and hanging from the pipes. Rested or not, I hated every second of that sticky feeling as they worked our asses off. I began to understand the effectiveness of Chinese water torture as the nuisance became obsessive. Like insult to injury, there was dual strain on my body and mind. The control, and the plan to conserve my energy fell by the wayside. The added feature broke my concentration like a stone on glass. I started to really hurt again as we ran through the back corridors, and a form of panic soon grabbed me. I cursed the Drill as I ran, and reached in my shirt to remove the flat, pancake-like pieces of cake. I breathed with desperation, and a monster thirst soon overpowered my concern for the cake. This really sucked. For the first time since the Nights had started, I was actually mad. I felt like they threw a curve ball, and it made me hate the old Drill's twisted forms of mistreatment. I fought hard through that night with each push-up, sit-up, and stride, each requiring more than the normal effort. The call to return to the battalions was the beginning of the end of "Cake Night," which would mark the most disgusting night I would experience.

After climbing the stairs, I bypassed my room and headed straight for the showers. I drank most of the initial flow, and then quickly stripped off the nasty, adhering shirt from my skin. Still breathing deeply for air, I washed the remnants of cake and frosting from my neck and back, then sat down in utter exhaustion and disgust under the cool sprinkle of water. I breathed, drank, cussed, and cringed as I coaxed my body and mind to forget the previous hours of frustration and anguish.

The next day I once again found myself in a terribly sore condition. Sleep was not solid during the night, probably from my frazzled nerves. I had to fight to stay awake in class, and a sickly absence of appetite ruined my meals. The bodily aftermath of a torturous Sword Drill night was again upon me. Like some wicked hangover, it consumed my normal mental and physical well-being to produce a far less than functional person. I just wanted to get through my day, since there was no doubt I was going to get some rack time in during the afternoon. I trusted Tompkins enough at that point to leave all but the hardest stuff to him. It had been a long day of classes that included several agonizing walks from one side of the campus to the other to get to my various classrooms. It was a real bitch going here and there while my legs hurt so bad, and I felt so unmotivated to even try.

But the 1400-hour finally arrived, and I walked through what seemed like the hottest day of the year back to my room. I hadn't seen a thermometer, but knew that the temperature had to be at least 100. I knew that a very difficult night was coming. Rack time would be more than just a nice thing to do.

Things actually went well for me. I did the critical work on my equipment and found Tompkins anxious and honored to get the increased responsibility. I was out by 1500, and slept well until 1730 when the alarm brought me out of a deep sleep. I worked through my lingering grogginess to get ready to descend the stairs to yet another night of pure misery. Little did I know what lay before me. Coming off of the previous evening with the trauma of having cake, I actually expected a better night.

Everything started as usual, but the wickedness of the heat became instantly apparent as we started running and chasing after the old Drill through the barracks. Those sadist bastards must have seen it as an opportunity to further thin our ranks, and they kept us running through the battalions and around the Field House for a maximum amount of time. The air was hot and we breathed with a vengeance as we labored to get oxygen. Sweat poured like we were in a shower, and you could see the toll the heat had taken in the faces of its victims. With a few quick, careful glances, I could see that even the old Drill members had to really struggle to keep up with the lethal pace they themselves were setting, even though they had the luxury to switch out and catch a breather. Though I thought it was hot outside, the move into McAlister brought an even worse environment as it felt like an oven the very moment we entered. I was concerned, and viewed it with seriousness. I felt a sense of real danger, and hoped these assholes weren't in the mood to exterminate a roach.

We formed up in our platoon, and turned to hear the words of Kraft. We were all puffing away, and trying to stand straight and brace as he talked. The words were almost insignificant as he spoke, that is until I heard my name come from his lips. To my horror, I realized he was awarding the white plume, and at that very moment I was certain this would be my final night as an aspirant for Sword Drill. My shock was so great that I had to force myself to momentarily forget the ramifications of the circumstance, and tune in to what Kraft was saying. I missed part of his explanation, but understood enough to know that in my exhaustion and drudgery to make it through my day, I had apparently missed saluting two members of the old Drill. Kraft didn't say when it happened, and I judged quickly that it really didn't matter. In this heat, I was a dead man under white feathers. Within an instant I heard only a monogamous block of yelling voices. It was a mixture of questions, comments, and foul names coming from six old Drill members as they stood in my face to address the miscue on my part. Their yelling may have actually affected me if I weren't facing the grave reality of my immediate future. Someone grabbed me by my webbing, and the noise engulfment quickly became distant as I was pulled away at a rapid pace. My worst nightmare had begun.

Like a tag-team wrestling match the old Drill traded off as they took turns running me into the ground. There were times when I was sure I was not even audible as I tried to say, "We love, Sword Drill." My throat was so dry that no moisture whatsoever existed, and the heat from inside my torso was like that of a boiler on a steam locomotive. I ran up the stairs, down the corridors, around the main floor, and through the lobby on what seemed to be an endless sprint. While running down one of the back passageways, I wasn't sure if I had passed through a dark spot, or if I was about to pass out. I stumbled several times as I felt light headed, and my current escort must have detected my condition. He stopped me long enough to demand I start crawling under the now familiar temporary stage, and I was actually grateful to him for the deviation. The dark spots had been a warning that I was on the verge of losing it, and just the mere opportunity to get down on my knees to crawl was enough to terminate the approaching blackness. I moved under the plywood platform and crawled slowly over the two-by-four bracings. I thought about being smart, and slowing down to a minimum speed where I could get through the moves but without being chastised. I was pulling in dusty air as I crawled, but thought little of the choking debris. I needed oxygen of any kind. I wasn't picky. I could hear my pacesetter becoming irritated as he noticed my fallen tempo, but I knew that to quickly increase would be confirmation that I had been sloughing off. Maybe his ego would work to my advantage if I remained steady, and he gained a confidence that he was doing a splendid job of killing me. He knew I was hurting. No need to make him think otherwise. And with that thought, came a plan. A plan that I knew would be my only chance to survive the torment that was ahead. I had to give no more than 90% at any given time. The white plume would be with me until the night was over, and there was no way to go another three hours at full pace in such heat. I had barely escaped unconsciousness already, only because my tormentor was observant enough to recognize my plight and react. Maybe the next wouldn't be so astute. I had to remember, the old Drill had no pain meter to measure by. There was no award for the most effort. I kept telling myself, to reach the goal, you just had to survive.

I crawled for a good while. It was a real task as my sword and scabbard banged everything, especially my left knee. It was a real pain under that platform, but I kept a reasonable pace, and reclaimed myself to a level of controlled weariness. But my next event would make it a critical break.

Andrew Green got a hold of me and took me back down to the main floor where he put me through his signature assault of making me "do his bandstands." I could hear the rest of the aspirants behind me, going through what sounded like push-ups. I could hear someone's voice off in the distance as he ran and chanted. I could tell it was Baxter Stall, and I thought of how he must be tired of receiving all of the special treatment. He was a rock, no doubt. Although this was my first award of the white plume, this was the second night for me to receive special attention. It was far more than I had wanted. Unlike Baxter, I had nothing to prove.

I went from doing bandstands to push-ups. Then I joined the other roaches to hang from the pipes, only to be pulled away once again as they received a chance to die and rest. I again went on a run, and as Emerson Vaughn started to run away from me, I held my pace. He turned to give me a hard time about it, but that was it. He could do no more, except maybe consider sending me back for not putting out. But that just didn't seem possible. The whole idea was to really run someone in the ground when they were singled out. For them to think that they could never reach that goal would be ignorant on their part, and mine. Vaughn just slowed his pace and continued to yell as if it were his duty. I kept my pace.

I never got to rest at all during that night. The closest thing I got to a break was doing sit-ups and crawling under the wooden stage. I did push-ups, carried trashcans, chairs, and even a bench for a while with Baxter holding one end and me on the other. It was one hell of a night with terrible heat, endless PT, no rest, and no water. Constant thirst kept my mind focused on the torture, and it seemed to make the night lag. I often guessed at the time, and wished that Kraft would command us to form up. But time dragged on, and I cycled through every conceivable exercise five or six times. Each Drill member took a turn at killing me, and not a one knew what I had been through with the others.

The worst part of the evening came towards the end, when I started to feel as if I wasn't going to make it. I had tried to hold back to conserve what I knew was going to be desperately needed energy, but after hours of being battered, it soon took everything I had just to do the minimum. It was amazing that I had made it to that point. I didn't think that the human body could withstand such endless agony. In the last hour of that terrible evening, I brushed often against my ultimate limit. My legs just wouldn't carry me at times, and I started to fall. The old Drill would just yell at me until I returned to my feet, and I started to run again. I wondered where the sweat was coming from after pouring for hours. I saw patches of black as I ran, and often felt that it was from the lack of oxygen, even though I had constantly breathed with a vengeance since I entered the armory. Finally, I was running through the corridors with all I had left, then noticed I was on the main floor as we turned through the lobby doors. I could see everyone was formed up, and I was told to fall in.

I knew that it was over, and that I had made it. But my joy was precluded by the lingering agony from many hours of a non-stop, waterless workout. Though motionless, I had to fight just to stand as my legs wanted to just fail. I trembled from degenerated muscles that were now spastic. The thought of drinking something, anything at all, controlled my thoughts. I completely missed the command to go to right face, and turned only when I noticed everyone else had.

On the run back I gathered everything I had left just to keep up, and I became frustrated as my legs refused to cooperate. I was afraid I was going to fall on the asphalt as we ran in front of the battalions, and I could hear my fellow roach Immanuel Consecos coaxing me on, saying we were almost back to 4th. I hated that I had been reduced to this condition, and embarrassed that I needed the encouragement. I learned that night about the white plume, and was sure that I would never again experience such exhaustion and pain again in my life. It was an act of discipline not suited for the most hideous of crimes.

My push-ups were poorly faked when I reached the quad, and I grabbed the last ounce of strength I had to ascend the stairs, but it just wasn't enough. I was reduced to a crawl as I climbed the last set of stairs. My legs were gone, and so was I. I felt a hand under my arm, and I could see it was Porter. He pulled me up from my crawl and on up the stairs.

I soon fell on my floor, and I could hear Porter yelling at Larry to get me some water. I was in the worst condition of my life. I felt faint, and I could hardly function to obtain relief. Porter and Larry lifted me from the floor enough to prop me up against the half press, and they handed me a cup of water, which I spilled terribly as I drank. Porter removed my shako, and pulled my sword and scabbard from under my legs. They gave me several cups of water, and each was spilled and barely consumed as my shaking hands tried to hold it. I couldn't manage to both drink and fight for air at the same time. Larry took the fan from the window, and put it on the floor in front of me. I felt weak, and lay over on my side. Even in the worst of times while working in tobacco, playing football, and enduring knob year, I had never experienced such painful heated exhaustion. I felt dizzy, and I rolled over on my back in the middle of the floor. I felt sick, and for a minute thought I may have been damaged seriously. I was scared I would be sent to the infirmary, and started telling Porter and Larry I would be all right, even though I felt terrible, and they weren't even asking.

"Just lay back down for a minute," said Porter. "It will pass, just give it a few more minutes."

I put my head back to the floor, and I closed my eyes. I could feel my heart beating blood through my veins, and for the first time in hours, there seemed to be oxygen in the air as I continued to gasp. At that moment, I felt there was a chance I was going to make it.

I lay on the floor for five minutes as Porter and Larry gave me wet towels and water. Concerned classmates, and even my CO Carl Andrews came in to ask of my condition. There was little hiding the terrible shape I was in when I entered the battalion, and there was genuine concern for me. I even heard Rosellini tearing into Andrews over my treatment, but I heard no response come from him. I was in too bad a shape to even care. I didn't really need to see anyone, despite good intentions. I couldn't even take a call from my fellow roach, Thomas Karl, who had phoned to see how I was, and to say that Scott Morris was fed up with the abuse and had quit, leaving us now with twenty three.

I was still in my room, barely sitting in a chair on my own when taps blew. I knew I had to shower, and get into the rack as precious recovery sleep was being lost, but my arms and legs pounded with pain, and I couldn't control the throbbing long enough to start them moving. Larry gave me some aspirin, and reminded me that it was getting late, so I hobbled through my aches to the showers, where I again sat on the floor in my clothes under the stream of water and didn't move for ten minutes. After a major struggle to get out of my clothes, I wanted to wash, but my arms hurt too much to use them, and I just settled for a soapless rinse of the surface dirt and sweat. I dried little, and struggled to get back to my room, not even bothering to pick up my stuff off the shower floor to hang out. I crawled wet and naked into my rack, too tired and sore to bother with any clothes. I was asleep within minutes.

I saw myself riding on a white horse, a great stallion of beauty and strength. I was in a slow canter, making my way over a grassy knoll, looking from its peak at a castle in the distance. I rode with an obvious pride as I could see myself fully clad in a suit of armor, and my sword Excalibur hung at my side. I arrived at the door of the castle where I knocked boldly, not knowing however, why I was there, or who was inside. The door opened, but no one was there. I walked in and observed a richly decorated vestibule of gray stone walls and floors, and a darkness broken only by the few small flames that burned in silver candelabras. I saw several passages, and through instinct knew which one to follow. Candles passed at distant intervals as I strained to see my path, and I soon found myself standing at a door that I feared to open.

"Come in John," a female voice said from inside. "I've been waiting for you."

My left hand reached for the butt of my sword, and I felt its familiar shape in place. I felt comfort that I was armed, and walked in to meet the voice.

I entered an elegant chamber, draped in colorful silks hanging from the walls of stone. The furniture was towering, all of which was ingrained with gold leaf and leather. I saw a great bed, luxurious and gaudy. It was garnished with lace and embroidery, and contained the faint image of a woman, scarcely seen by the candles found throughout the large room.

"Come closer John. I can't see you," said the coaxing voice.

I moved forward towards the bed and the figure in it, and then I noticed the familiar face. It was Donna. She was lying against a mountain of satin-sleeved pillows, smiling with the enchantment of a sorceress. Her beauty was stunning, and her lazy nightgown of silk provided little cover to her alluring breasts. I was mesmerized by the scene, and my attraction of old rose from its grave.

"I've been waiting for you John. Do not linger in the cold darkness of this room of stone. Come to me. Let me warm you."

I stood there in awe, and I felt an inner circulation building a desire to do as she wished.

"I cannot," I said.

"Why John? Why can't you attend to me? I too am cold, and in need of your warmth."

"I find my comfort with another now, one to whom I am faithful."

"There is no other John. You know that. I was wrong. I left you, and it wasn't your fault. Forgive me, John. Love me again."

Donna looked at me with unbearable enticement. I battled myself in conscience, and labored with agonizing temptation. I felt myself moving towards her. But only her smile stopped me, and I gained control of my desire.

"I cannot come to you. I am not cold. I have been sweltering in the heat for so long. I am thirsty only for drink, and rest."

"You are cold, John. Look at yourself."

I looked down to see no armor, no sword, no clothes of any kind.

"You see. You are cold. I have wine, and a soft place for you to rest. Come, you are weary."

I felt myself moving towards the bed, yet had no command in my mind to do so. My lust overruled my strength of contention, and I watched as she drew back the sheets to expose her bare body. I entered her bed of silken richness, and she pulled me slowly to her, and all was gone to oppose. I touched my lips to hers, then to the softness of her breast. The sensation was overwhelming, and my craving became unbearable. She rotated from her side, and I followed to the crest of her body. With no conscious effort, I was inside of her. The feeling was painfully exquisite, and I became lightheaded with the sensation.

A scream rang out in the room, one that possessed the horror of torture. I leaped up from Donna and her bed, and turned to see only a faint shrieking figure. Guilt instantly consumed me, and I roared out in my shame, and turned around to the temptress of my fall. But what I saw was not the beauty of Donna, but the grotesque face of a demon hag. She was laughing in hysterics.

The walls seemed to come alive. There were men, many of them, all with swords. They walked towards me, smiling at the notion of their mission. I reached for my sword, and again realized I was naked, and without my weapon. The old witch laughed harder, and the approach of the men hastened. I turned and began to run. I ran through the doorway, and into the dark corridor that had led me to the bedroom. I ran as hard as I could, knowing a lack of effort would mean my death. I ran until I reached the entrance, and found that it was secure. I could hear the swordsmen coming, and I chose one of the many halls before me, and ran for my life. I looked for a weapon, or some way to get away from this trouble. But I saw nothing. I could only run as I could hear footsteps close behind. I ran for what seemed like forever, and as my body began to fail me, I tripped and fell to the cold stone floor. As the steps approached, I became terrified. They stepped from the shadows, and I could now see their faces. It was Richard Kraft, and Carl Andrews, and Ronnie Bourbon, and Bob Fox, and Emerson Vaughn, and every other member of the '79 Drill. They walked towards me with evil smiles on their faces, swords drawn, and a lust for death in their eyes. They started slashing away at me, and the blows from the dull blades only bruised, and never cut. I tried to crawl away but there was no place to go. They just whaled at my body, breaking bones, and drawing enormous whelps.

"Enough!" rang out a voice, and the swordsmen all came to attention. "Prepare him for justice," said the strong, approaching voice.

The swordsmen grabbed me, dragged my broken body across the stone floor to a chopping block, and laid me face up with my neck in its saddle. The huge towering figure behind the voice approached, and through the dim light of the candles, I could see that the enormous man was dressed in green armor. He carried a huge ax as he walked, and when he was standing over me, he raised it high, ready to strike a lethal blow. With his other hand he raised the cover of his helmet, but I saw only the angry face of Cindy inside who said, "Your just reward, my love!" and with both hands she grabbed the handle and brought the ax down, and it removed my head at the neck.

I sat up in my bed screaming. Larry awoke and reacted, yelling, "What's wrong? Are you alright?"

I was trembling, and there was enormous pain throughout my body. I felt that I was naked, and remembered not dressing before climbing into bed.

"Hey John, man, you all right?" shouted Larry as he got up from his bunk in the dark.

"Yeah," I said through grogginess and pain. "I'm sorry, I must have had a bad dream."

"I'll say! You scared the shit out of me."

"I'm really very sorry. I know this must be getting old for you. I

498

guess I'm just in so much pain. My muscles are really sore."

"You want some more aspirin?"

"Yeah, but I'll get it. I need to put some clothes on anyway."

I crawled from my bunk with immense stiffness and pain and put on a T-shirt and a pair of shorts. I took three aspirins and crawled back in my rack. Sleep was delayed only by the remnants of trauma from the dream. It was too real, and I didn't like the message of the vision.

CHAPTER 37

The next day started with me feeling as if I hadn't slept at all during the night. I was the sorest ever, and my stomach burned from taking so many aspirin on an empty stomach, and not having touched the dinner brought back by Larry. Movements getting dressed and shaved were painful and restricted, and when I stepped into the sally port to join the rest of the Staff, I was looked upon with pity. Some even questioned my sanity. The previous night was enough for any rational person to have left halfway through. But quitting never crossed my mind. Passing out was my greatest concern. But I survived. The old Drill had to know that I really wanted Sword Drill.

My movement that day was nothing more than a hobble. As bad as I felt, I watched for old Drill like a hawk, and saluted them even if they didn't see me or were halfway across campus. Another night under the white plume would be impossible. A night of any kind was even questionable. I was at the edge of failure, and I needed no more self-imposed assistance in getting on over. I feared the night that approached. My body was bruised and battered. My mind was weak, and the heat had gotten even worse. It was a record high temperature for September, with the noontime thermometer reading in the high nineties. Triple digits were expected before the day's end, and I dreaded the thought of another four hours of pure hell. I had to do it, but how could I? It was hard to ignore the reality of even a conservative assessment of my condition. I was hurt. I desperately needed rest, but the prospect of an afternoon snooze was doubtful. There was Tuesday afternoon drill with the staff and the rest of the Corps. As a battalion, we looked pretty bad at the last Friday's parade, and I had special work to do to help correct the problem. Sword Drill or not, I was still 4th Battalion Sergeant Major, with regular duties and responsibilities, and XMD or Excused from Military Duty status was the only relief from them. However, that was also automatic disqualification from Sword Drill. Though I easily qualified for XMD, you couldn't have dragged me off the parade ground at 1500.

After drill, I had about two hours before show time, and I still had to get my stuff ready. A nap seemed impossible. My equipment was a mess, and I was moving too slowly to get it back in shape fast. Tompkins showed up within minutes after the companies returned from the parade ground, and insisted that I allow him to do it all, knowing I was in bad shape. He really wanted to help, and I felt I could trust him, though instinct said I just couldn't release such a responsibility, and place my certain death in the hands of a sophomore. But he had not failed me yet, and he asked if I had thought about what was most important. I looked at him for the longest time, then released my most important work to him, things I had never even walked him through. Things he had never done. He told me to trust him. I slept solid for an hour and a half.

I stood in front of the R at 1815 and waited as a member of the old Drill inspected me in detail. I was nervous as if it were the first day, not having had time to even check Tompkins' work. I could see that all the others across the quad were through with inspections and were doing sit-ups in a group. After a thorough look, my inspector told me to join them. It was great news. Tompkins had done it. He got me through the inspection. I hated to think that I was so deeply indebted to a sophomore. Even though I was miserably sore, his assistance allowed me to get the rest that improved my condition from critical to stable. I owed him big time.

My only mental agenda was survival. The run through the battalions getting to the Field House was treacherous, and it took little time for the heat to make its afflicting presence known. Sweat poured and lungs pumped, and I was amazed at my survival with each passing minute, straining to move with each step. I had convinced myself to push until my body refused to move, and reason indicated that it wouldn't take long to reach that threshold.

I ran in agony, but with a sense of having nothing to lose by continuing to try. I watched as others around me struggled with their own turmoil, and my heart went out for Richard Kelly as he was endowed with the white plume. It was an awful time in the Nights to mess up and win the dreaded adornment. It was serious enough just being a roach in that heat.

The old Drill acted as though oblivious to the severe conditions. They dispensed their woe upon us as if it were just another night. Maybe they didn't realize that this was a critical time for some of us, but then maybe they did. There were 23 of us left, and 9 left to cut. Not an excess to take to cuts by any means, but enough not to have to worry about attrition. Pouring it on at this point could only test character, stamina, and desire such that only the cream would continue through such a trial. But a year can make one forget and lose touch, and the old Drill seemed unfazed by our degree of suffering. They had a high standard to sustain, and their concern was stifled by pride for the Drill. Their mission was to weed out those showing the slightest hint of being unmotivated or weak. Their goal was perfection. Little else mattered.

We went through the maneuvers. Hanging from the pipes, where I was the first to fall. Piggyback races, where I fell and procured a nasty scrap. Wheel barrow races, where I ate the floor. And bandstands, where my legs started to fail me and I was threatened with being sent back for not putting out. I continued with all I had, and sweated bullets from the strain as much as from the heat. It seemed I was always just moments away from failure, but somehow managed to survive by the skin of my teeth. I often heard Kelly off in the distance, vocalizing the now torturous slogan of our quest. His agony was real as he passed by us, and my lingering afflictions from the night before were a veritable measure of his present state. He was where I was, and I wished that horror on no one.

That night introduced a new class of desperation as I struggled through each step and movement with supreme effort. There was no getting used to the pain. You fought it each second with the knowledge that at some point, it will end. That is, if one's body can withstand it such that your legs and arms are able to respond. But even the parts of the finest racing motors sometime break. Bodies, like machines, have their limits too. There is an ultimate strength even to steel.

The old Drill stopped everything when Kelly fell. We were in the middle of a marathon push-up session when all attention turned towards the lobby. We were told to go to attention, and we just happened to be on the opposite side of the floor from the main entrance and could see the action taking place. First, there was a sudden rush of the old Drill to the area, then an appearance by the Officer of the Day. The stretcher used to haul off knobs during Hell Night came in and out in a flash, sagging from its fill as it moved through the door. I wasn't surprised at all, only ashamed that deep inside I was so grateful for the break. Granted, I didn't know the seriousness of the matter, although I knew that a roach down was always serious. If there was any way at all to continue, any one of us would.

The only thing that told us that the problem was critical was the look on the faces of the old Drill as they returned to us. There was real trouble, and they couldn't hide it. They scrabbled to regain their composure and move on, but Kraft was visibly shaken, and was spared the chore of proceeding as he was forced to speak with the Officer in Charge, a commissioned Air Force officer, who was not pleased at all. There was genuine trouble, and for whom I did not know. Something told me it was Kelly. I knew his plight. I remembered the dark spots in my eyes as I ran. I prayed for my downed brethren, and that God would forgive me for relishing the delivering benefit from his pain. His crisis provided critical recovery time for those who remained, but I somehow knew this was not going to be some minor injury.

We soon returned to our routine, but there was an obvious absence of enthusiasm on the part of the old Drill. Their hearts were torn. Their minds drifted. Then Major Jim Tyler arrived, who was the TAC Officer for Sword Drill, and this only deepened the old Drill's expressions of concern. They immediately shifted to a quasi-form of mistreatment. There was little yelling, and a complete absence of threats. Physical training was reduced to a slow run at first, and then a member of the old Drill jumped into a lesson in performing the cuts routine. This actually lasted a while, and then there was another relatively slow run around the floor. The time went by fast, and had it not been for my sad state, it would have been a breeze. In the absence of Kraft, we finally formed up in our return formation, and then exited towards the battalions. It was a shorter Night by at least an hour. We still returned to the usual cheering, but concern among us overshadowed our pride. In the lean and rest in the middle of the quad, we were told that Kelly had collapsed and they couldn't revive him. They knew no more than what they saw. I immediately thought he must have died. It wasn't hard to imagine.

We pumped out 14 push-ups, kissed our letter, and then ran to our rooms in an early arrival. I was still in a state of agony, but not as desperately winded. The night that I feared would have surely resulted in my end, had taken another.

I was in constant pain as I stripped out of my nights uniform and went to other roach's rooms to get more information about Kelly. But there was no information available beyond what we already knew. Thinking the old Drill would be on top of it, I even went to Carl Andrews' room, only to find that no further details had been passed to him either. I went to bed in bad shape both physically and mentally, miserable from the torment and concerned from the absence of news. I slept terribly, and at morning formation there was still no word to ease my anxiety.

It wasn't until my return from breakfast that the full story was heard. Kelly had experienced a serious case of heat stroke. He was rushed to the infirmary and packed in ice, but problems persisted, and he soon required serious attention. He was then rushed by ambulance to the Medical University Hospital where he was placed in intensive care.

At noon, more news was received, but this time it was a somber announcement to the Corps that revealed that an unfortunate injury had occurred. Nearly 2000 cadets fell silent as a request was made to pray for Cadet Kelly. His condition was still very critical, and he was hanging on to life by a thread. I felt ill, and the reality of our goal, my goal, hit home.

It wasn't until I returned from my final afternoon class that I learned that the 14 Nights had been suspended. The '79 Drill had a lot of explaining to do. To the administration, the Junior Sword Drill was an organization out of control.

I didn't know what to think or say. I didn't know where to even start. I called the other roaches, and found only the facts I already knew, along with a lot of speculation and rumors. Some said there was to be a Commandant's Board, and others said that Colonel Dick had already decided to ban Junior Sword Drill activities forever. We all feared that our steep investment to date would end with nothing to show for it.

***

At 1600 sharp, Richard Kraft walked into the office of the Assistant Commandant of Cadets. The secretary announced his presence over the intercom, then sternly instructed the nervous senior officer to go on in. His heart rate soared when he saw Colonel Dick rocked back in his chair, locked and loaded.

Lieutenant Colonel Harvey M. Dick, United States Army, was a large man who had the face of a pit bulldog. He looked as if bred for battle, and he was both respected and feared by the Corps of Cadets. He was as consistent as time. He was fair. If you broke the rules, you were punished. No exceptions. The Commander-in-Chief himself would find no special exemption in the conviction or sentencing of a Blue Book offense. Colonel Dick's favorite expression was, "If you can't do the time, don't do the crime." He handed out confinements and tours in groups of ten, sometimes going into triple digits when the offense was serious. A can of beer in the barracks brought 120 tours. That's twelve weeks of restriction to campus, walking back and forth across the quad with a rifle during free times. He had the Honor Code on his side, which made confessions and straight facts easy to gather. He would award stiff punishment without a blink once he was sure in his mind that the offense was committed. He was just as quick to send a cadet to the Honor Court if a lie was discovered, and see him on out the gate once convicted. Colonel Dick was a no-shitter. To a high-ranking cadet, he was normally a best friend and ally, but come before him in trouble, he was instantly your worst nightmare, previous supporter or not.

"Mr. Kraft. Trying to kill this young man Kelly?"

"Sir, I can..."

"You just go to at ease Mr. Kraft," said Dick with quickening firmness. "I have already sent word to you that all Sword Drill activities are to cease. You've already been in this office before with excuses, back when Cadet Pearl had his leg destroyed, and it was then that you assured me that this was an isolated accident."

"It was, Sir..."

"I said at ease!" yelled the Colonel as he stood up from his chair and leaned across his desk. "I have a young man barely hanging on to life and you want to talk. Your time for extenuation is over, Mr. Kraft. Over! And as far as I'm concerned, so is the Junior Sword Drill."

Kraft was at attention, dying to respond, but knowing better than to make a peep.

"Right now I have his parents to call, to explain to them just what in the hell their son is doing in an intensive care unit when he should be in class. I'm sure that's what they thought they were paying for."

"Sir, I..."

"I'll tell you what I want to know here son. Save the other crap for the Commandant's Board. You'll need more than a bunch of excuses to defend the existence of this nonsense on campus. I want to know what happened without all the bullshit. You understand me, son. You have jeopardized the very existence of this school. I want the full story."

"Sir, Mr. Kelly was receiving special training due to his failure to follow the rules of the Drill."

"Special training? What the hell kind of training results in heat stroke? Don't you mean punishment, son?"

"Yes sir, punishment is probably the more appropriate term."

"Mr. Kraft, I've asked you to cut out all the double talk. What the hell happened?"

"Sir, he was being punished for not being shined up."

"Not shined up? When?"

"Between classes, Sir."

"Between classes? I don't understand."

"Sir, the Junior Sword Drill considers its members the best that a class can offer. During the 14 Nights, aspirants are easy to spot. We prefer that they maintain the very best in personal appearance at all times."

"Sounds like a set-up. But go on. I'm all ears."

"Sir, Mr. Kelly was observed by a member of the 1979 Junior Sword Drill to have very poor personal appearance as he was inspected between classes yesterday morning."

"To what degree was his appearance bad?"

"It was my understanding that his brass was scratched and tarnished and that his shoes were not shined."

"So what's the story on the heat stroke?"

"When a roach...excuse me...aspirant is found to be in violation of the rules, he is awarded for one evening a white plume. This is symbolic of having failed, very similar to a dunce cap in a classroom. Wearing it, he draws and receives extra attention from the '79 Drill during the physical training portions of the night."

"In other words Mr. Kraft, you half kill the poor bastard who gets caught violating one of your impossible to meet rules."

"Sir, not in so many..."

"Hog wash, Mr. Kelly. I know that game. It's the same way you boys do the freshmen, and sometimes some of you crazies get out of line with them too."

"Yes, Sir."

"We want The Citadel to be a challenge son, but not hell on earth. You're one of the highest-ranking Cadets in the Corps Mr. Kraft. You were placed there because you were deemed a leader and a man of above average intelligence. Those same attributes probably inspired your election as Commander of the Sword Drill. But look at the results son. You have another cadet in very deep trouble, needless to say yourself, the Junior Sword Drill, and this school."

"Yes, Sir."

"I'm constantly amazed at the ability you boys have to get off track. But son if this trouble should somehow find an end, and God help us it's not tragic, then you can damn sure bet that the Junior Sword Drill will have an uphill battle to even exist. You had a perfect chance to control this organization without interference, but now we will have to step in."

"Yes, Sir."

"And one other thing, Mr. Kraft. You had better hope that young man comes out of this thing."

"Yes, Sir, we all do."

"I will be in touch with you concerning the Commandant's Board. That is all."

***

When 1800 hours arrived, I felt out of place and lost. My whole perception of being where I was supposed to be was warped as I marched with the staff over to evening mess, and sat down to a normal supper. There were questions from everyone, but I felt it best not to talk about the incident. This was Drill business, and not a topic suitable for public debate. There was trouble already, and adding fuel to the fire would not be smart.

Later during ESP I sat at my desk and forced myself to study. It took effort. Even though I was still bruised and battered, I had a feeling of both heartache and relief. There was a lot of anxiety about the future of Sword Drill, and with it a fear that the administration would end the very thing that had been my reason to study in the first place. It was clear just how much of an influence this one campus function had become. It had changed my life, and I found new dreams in just its pursuit. Now, as my greatest desire hung in the balance, I felt a real lack of motivation to study even casually. Drill had become almost everything to me. Good or bad, that was the simple truth.

There was only one other thing that even mattered. Cindy. I loved her. And that too was the simple truth. She was a light that shined inside of me, and kept emotions like happiness and love alive. She was a source of sanity, a feeling of natural order. It was as if she had become a part of me. Someone who understood me for who I was, and not for what the world thought I should be. I never found that sort of feeling with Donna. I thought I loved her too. I really just loved who she was: beautiful, popular, adventurous, every schoolboy's dream. But in the year we dated, slept together, pretended to love, we never really connected. I was her best showpiece for the time being. I had my allotted time in her schedule of steady boyfriends. But like those before, and those who would follow, I fell out of fashion. There was a new look for the season, and I was an outmoded style.

Everything was there for a love to exist between Cindy and me: her story of adoration through the years, her work to become what she thought I wanted, her sincere expressions to me. I had every reason to believe that she cherished me. But I just couldn't forget what I also knew was true. I was in a school that made it very hard to carry on a relationship. There were real and constant obstacles. I was going out for Sword Drill, and one look in the mirror was a painful vision of what that pursuit cost. After having my head shaved, and getting the shit kicked out of me, it was plain to see I was far from being attractive. It didn't help that Cindy was the prettiest girl I had ever seen. It was phenomenal. She could seriously consider modeling, and expect a Ford contract as a start. She was breathtaking, and I would have been blind not to see the way other guys looked at her when we were out during the summer. She could have anyone she wanted. Guys would kill to have her. There had to be a bunch of swinging dicks at the Medical University hitting on her every day, including guys in med school who had tremendous futures as wealthy doctors. Guys in her classes would have every opportunity to convince her that she was letting life pass her by while dating someone who was locked away. What kind of beau would leave a girl like her sitting at home just so he could pursue a single 14-minute performance that required an unthinkable sacrifice?

My experience with Donna and sense of reality gained from reading the regular "Dear John" column left me gun shy when it came to any cadet's relationship. I'd seen hearts torn out of guys just when they needed support the most. It was a helpless, violated feeling as gates and curfews thwarted opportunities to work through troubled times. I had already experienced that dreadful scene and swore to never go through it again. I loved Cindy with all my heart. I loved her more than Sword Drill. I loved her so much it terrified me. I could face the Nights, endless PT, the white plume, and even, God forbid, even not making Drill. But I couldn't face losing her. I couldn't. I cringed at the thought of her seeing me, and that look of pity and embarrassment she would surely bear. Time was what I needed. Time to get through the Nights, and back to a semi-normal life. That's why the delay was so devastating. It would mean that much longer until I could see her. It seemed silly, almost childish that I just didn't go ahead and face her. The total separation was killing me. I needed her, but feared losing her more.

Half way through ESP I called her. I thought contact would help relieve my mind from continually wandering to her. I closed my eyes as I heard her voice. I could feel her through the phone, and could almost see her face as she waited to hear me say when we could be together. It was something I, in truth, could not answer.

"If they have suspended all activities associated with Drill, then why are you still restricted to campus?" she asked.

"I don't have an answer other than we haven't been told that the restriction has been lifted. Under the circumstances, that's enough. For all I know, we could be back at it tomorrow night, or we could be finished for good. We haven't been informed either way."

"If they do release you, will you call me?"

"Of course I will."

***

Further word on Kelly filtered in from the hospital in painstakingly infrequent intervals. The next day at noon mess the Corps was updated with the good news that his condition was upgraded to stable. There was a sigh of relief. Like Sword Drill or not, the entire Corps had been pulling hard for one of its own.

Later that afternoon at company drill more information was received when Kraft returned from a Charleston pass to visit with Kelly and his family at the hospital. Kraft said his visit had been a positive one, but that Kelly was devastated in knowing he was out of the Drill, even though he knew he was lucky to be alive. His family showed no ill feelings, and they accepted Richard's condition as an unfortunate accident in the quest of a dream. The Kellys were a Citadel family with Mr. Kelly having graduated back in the early 50's. They knew the advantages of Sword Drill, and they knew the risks. Like any parent who watches a son participate in sports such as football or boxing, the chance to experience a problem always existed, and was accepted. The Kellys were pleased that their son appeared to be doing better. They held no one from the school or the 1979 Drill accountable. Colonel Dick, however, was not so understanding.

There was a meeting called in Kraft's room at 2200 for all aspirants. Kraft wanted to inform us of Kelly's status, the investigation, and the scheduled Commandant's Board. He also told us what would be expected of us until a decision was made on the future of Sword Drill. He was optimistic, and held the opinion that the Nights would continue after a Board met, and that we should continue to practice our sword manual and cuts routine, work on our equipment, and catch up on studies that he was sure had been ignored. Based on our appearance of being a knob as a junior, he felt it was not a good time to be out in the eye of the public. But he and the other Drill members had no idea how long the delay would last, and knew there was only so much that could be accomplished with the resulting free time. He encouraged us to rest, and make the best of the time available. But if the need to get out for a reasonable period existed, then there would be no penalty for exercising General Leave privileges, but added that the use of good judgment should be a priority while taking advantage of the intermission.

Everyone left the meeting with concern for our Drill, but pleased to know they could venture out beyond the walls of the campus to eat, drink, or see a girlfriend. My mind raced as I walked back towards 4th Battalion, wondering just what I was going to do with this bittersweet news. The next day was Friday, and I had a gorgeous girl waiting patiently to see me. I tried to sort out my options, and delayed calling Cindy with the news until I had things figured out. Though I fought with the choices, I went to bed that evening without even making a call.

The next day at noon mess brought an announcement that Richard Kelly was completely out of danger and the Corps cheered in sincere relief. They said his condition was now considered good, that he would hopefully be released during the weekend, and was expected to fully recover. That afternoon before parade, Kraft was told to use the weekend to prepare for an appearance before a Commandant's Board on Monday. The future of the Junior Sword Drill would be discussed and recommendations made. It would be a meeting of utmost importance.

As usual, parade was a pain. The heat wave that had caused injury and heartache earlier in the week was still with us. I even heard a cadet behind me pass out and make that unmistakable thud as he kissed the ground. The crowd in attendance was large, probably because there was a home football game that weekend. The added eyes provided little motivation to enjoy the weekly event that seemed such a burden. The chance to see the pretty girls waiting in front of the barracks at the end was the only consolation. Being on staff allowed some of the first looks as we led the four companies off the parade ground, down the street, and back into the battalion. One had to be shifty eyed with good peripheral vision to inconspicuously catch the sights since a lot of looking around was not a good idea while trying to present a formal image. But once we turned to march down Jones Avenue, we were officially finished. I was still trying to be less than obvious about my looking around, but then I almost snapped my neck as I saw the most beautiful girl in world in the crowd. Cindy just waved and laughed as I marched with difficulty and shock completely filled my face. I didn't know what to do as I got myself back in step with the rest of the staff as we turned into the sally port. I only caught a glimpse of her still smiling face in the crowd as I entered through the gates. As usual we stopped on the side of the quad and were dismissed. I stood and stared at the companies as they entered through the sally port, and wondered just what the hell I was going to do. I saw her. She saw me. She saw that I saw her. Shit! I couldn't run. I had no choice. The decision had already been made for me. I had to go out and see her, and she would have to see me.

When the last company of cadets entered the battalion, I knew that the moment of truth had arrived. Would she laugh, cry, or run? Would I see that it was all over for us in her face, or would it be just a subtle change in her expression? I walked towards the gate that was now crowding with visitors. I didn't see her among those in front, but knew she was probably in the back waiting. I walked out and turned towards where I last saw her, and there she stood. She was stunning. Her eyes indicated nothing but delight, and I walked towards her with a smile I had not consciously created. She only said "Hi!" as she wrapped her arms around me.

I thought about how hot and sweaty I was, but marveled at having

Cindy in my arms again.

"I'm so sorry John. Really. I just had to come over. I heard parade was open to the public and I..."

"I'm glad you're here. I should have asked you to come."

"I know you are at risk being seen with me, but I thought I could at least say hello really fast and then go. I promise I won't stay long."

"Don't worry about it. They told us it was OK. They've lifted the restriction."

"They have? John, that's great!" said Cindy as she hugged me again in excitement.

"Yes, it is."

"So what does this mean? Can you leave? Can we go somewhere to be alone?"

I suddenly felt a need to talk to her. There was a mismatch of emotions, and I felt like she would soon see that something was bothering me. But I could see that people surrounded us.

"Cindy, let's walk."

The expression on her face showed a mix of happiness and confusion. She was thrilled at the information, but baffled by my lack of joy and immediate need to talk. We turned and walked towards the parade ground, and found the shadows of an oak tree to shade the blistering sun. I turned to look at Cindy who placed her back to the huge trunk of the tree, and I wanted so much to kiss her right then. But I couldn't. I felt ugly. Sweaty. Unworthy. She had to see the monumental negative difference. She had to hate it. She looked at me with her eyes of loveliness, only to see a rogue. I was nervous, and I was afraid.

"Cindy, I've missed you, and..." I lost my introduction, as it was wrong.

"I missed you too, John. But what's wrong?"

"Cindy, look at me."

"I am looking at you."

"But look how I've changed."

"You have on a white uniform now," she said controlling her

smile.

"No Cindy, I'm serious, look at me!"

"OK, what? Your hair is shorter. You've lost some weight. Is that it?"

"Yes, that's it. I look like hell."

"You told me before Sword Drill started this would happen."

I did tell her that.

"But look how bad I look, Cindy."

"You look bad," she said in a poor attempt to be serious while again controlling her smile.

"Cindy!" I yelled between gritting teeth, pacing back and forth. I looked at her as she stood leaning against the oak with an innocent face and raised eyebrows. I smiled, and realized she could care less about where this conversation was going.

"Listen," I said as I removed my hat, knowing well I wasn't supposed to while outside, "Would you feel comfortable walking around Charleston, around the Medical University, in front of your friends with someone who looks like me?"

"Yes!" she answered.

There was silence. I scratched my burr head and then rubbed my eyes. I was getting nowhere.

"John," she said walking towards me, "have you by chance forgotten who I am? This is Cindy Johnson. You know, the one who loves you. The one who could care less what your hair looks like or how much weight you have or don't have."

"I know, but I just look so bad."

Cindy suddenly grabbed a semi-serious look, then walked up close to me. "Listen here, you're gonna look even worse if you just stand there going on about your appearance. I've not seen you for three weeks, so I risked coming over here, thinking I would be the cause of you getting shot at sundown, and all you want to do is talk about your hair?" She balled up her fist and put it up to my nose, "Suppose we add a couple of black eyes to your plight, cause if you stand here and waste anymore time on this, I'm gonna belt you."

"OK," I answered meekly.

"Now John. Your mother would be so ashamed of your manners. Aren't you supposed to kiss your girlfriend when you see her?"

I reached and pulled her close. We kissed each other with appreciation.

"Oooo, you're sweaty. And your after-shave smells like bug spray. I'll tell you this, I won't go around Charleston, or the Medical University, or my friends with you like that."

"I knew I'd get to you sooner or later."

"It's later! Put on something decent and let's get out of here. And take a shower!"

"Yes, Ma'am!"

***

I rushed to my room to shower and change. Cindy had returned to her car and pulled it in front of the battalion by the time I returned. I jumped in and she kissed me. "Much better!" she said, and we drove away.

We drove out towards John's Island to a small but nice restaurant on a tidal creek called Cappy's, and we sat on the deck outside and drank beer, ate oysters on the half shell, and talked about Sword Drill. Cindy wanted to hear everything. I tried to ask about her activities, but she was genuinely more interested in mine. It seems she had done little, except go to class, study, and run. It was such a hard thing to imagine, that a girl so pretty would spend so much time alone. I felt awful about her sacrifice. She felt awful about mine. We seemed so close because of that, and she seemed to want it that way. The oysters were enough for her, and with her encouragement, she watched me eat a huge dinner. We saw the sun set into the trees to the west, and the warm air of the late afternoon turned into a pleasant breeze. I felt more comfortable about myself in the dim light, and I often caught myself staring at my girl.

We drove back to her apartment, and found it empty as her

roommates had left for the festivities of back-to-school parties. Although it had only been three weeks, it felt like forever since I had been there. I removed my blazer, and sat down on the couch.

"Oh no," said Cindy, "We don't have much time."

She took my hand and pulled me towards her room, turning out the lights as she walked.

Later, we just lay there in her bed, cool from the air conditioner, warm from our activity. She ran her hand across my sparse hair, and laughed after doing so.

"How would you like for me to throw you on the floor?" I asked.

"Oh, sensitive about our mane, are we?"

"Wouldn't you be if you were me?"

"No."

"And why not?"

"Because I would know, without a doubt, that I had someone who loves me, no matter how I looked."

I stared down at the faint outline of her face, then asked, "How can you say that?"

"I've been at both ends John. Remember? It makes you understand things."

"I see."

There was a long silence between us.

"John?"

"What?"

"Will you do something for me?"

"Yes. Anything."

"Never again, ever, doubt that I love you!"

I thought for a moment, and confirmed that I believed it was true. But I loved her to the point that I feared losing her worse than I feared my own death. I had to ask. "OK. But will you do something for me?"

"Yes. Name it."

"Promise you will never leave me."

There was only a slight pause, and a smile in the dark. "I

promise."

A kiss was never stronger.

***

The next day I awoke with a strange feeling of peace. It was a comfort based on knowledge. It was the realization that I carried with me something extraordinary, yet in previous weeks, hadn't realized the possession. I had someone. I really had someone. It felt comforting. It felt secure. It was amazing, Cindy and I.

I rushed over to McAlister first thing that morning to buy a ticket for the football game. Prior to the previous day's parade, taking Cindy had not been a consideration, so I was fortunate to get a decent seat for her in the junior date section. I would have a chance or two during the game to talk with her as I carried out my duties of being an usher for the event. Usher was only a name used to describe my real job of being a guard. I had to be a bad ass and make sure that the Corps did not get out of hand during the game. I heard it wasn't really all that necessary, but just a deterrent for those who had the potential to get too rowdy.

After getting the ticket I met Rontelli at his room at 1000, and we watched each other do sword manual to detect flaws we could not see on our own. By 1100 we were at McAlister where we worked on the cuts routine and labored with it until noon. I was just able to catch lunch, and after returning to the battalion I changed into my leave uniform and used some discretion getting to my car. In less than ten minutes I was knocking on Cindy's door. Her two roommates were there, looking rough after a wild night of parties. Susan was shocked at my change in appearance, and Cindy's other roommate, Darla, seemed lukewarm towards me in our first ever meeting. I knew my looks were reason enough for her to stand off. We didn't chat long though, and left to drive back to campus.

I arrived back at the battalion, and changed into my uniform for the game, which was dress whites, sash, and sword. I walked over to the stadium with several other guys who also had usher duty, and I sat with Cindy in the stands as the Bulldog fans arrived and the Corps marched in. It would be my longest visit with her during the game.

I didn't even return to the barracks to change after the game. I had my hat, and I just removed my sword and put it into the trunk. We drove out to Folly Beach, and we walked out to the waves, I in my white pants and leather shoes, she in her skirt. We walked in the warm September ocean breeze, and we must have held each other for every minute when we were there, never tiring of the privilege. It was an excellent place to be after the crowds of the game. We could have sat together in the sand all night, but I had to be in by 0100. I walked through the sally port with only ten minutes to spare, and I considered the crazy risk I had taken.

We couldn't see enough of each other. I met Cindy again the next morning at Summerall Chapel. I wanted her to hear Chaplain James. She loved his style, and said she could see why he was so well-suited for cadets. We followed his positive words with lunch downtown, and then I had to leave her again to practice.

Rontelli and I spent several hours working on the cuts routine, getting down to the most precise details. It was a very productive session, probably because my mind was so at ease and my body had recovered from the pounding of the Nights. I truly felt that we were starting to get it down.

I returned to Cindy's apartment, knowing that I couldn't stay long. Cindy's roommates were coming and going, so we sat in her room for privacy. We talked about our week ahead and my possible re-entry into the Nights. She was sad that it would be the weekend or possibly longer before I would see her again. I held her close and could feel her genuine need, squeezing me ever so tight as if to stop me from leaving. I didn't want to go, but knew I just had to study. But the more I tried to leave, the tighter we held each other. There was something in the touch, something magic and medicinal. We struggled to get closer, and we were soon making love without effort. She said nothing as I held her. I didn't have to ask why. I felt it too. We just absorbed each other until there wasn't a minute left to stay.

During formation and at mess, I just wasn't myself. I missed her that quickly. I fought to keep my mind on my work as I studied, but it was hard. For the first time in my life, I really understood what real love was.

***

At 1530 hours on the following Monday Cadet Captain Richard Kraft walked into the Honor Courtroom in Mark Clark Hall, and after being sworn in, was asked to sit in the witness chair. Several select Who's Who members of The Citadel's administration occupied the other seats, and Kraft knew instantly that this was going to be a serious discussion, but felt confident he had come prepared.

"Mr. Kraft," said Colonel Dick, "Would you please describe to this Board the events leading up to the injury of Cadet First Sergeant Kelly?"

Kraft, a high-ranking Cadet, had no doubt been under pressure before through his three years as a cadet. He was one of the few Air Force scholarship recipients in the school. Along with Sword Drill he could claim Gold Stars, Deans List, Summerall Guards, and high rank each semester as an upperclassman. But the pressure was on his shoulders to put out a fire that burned to the core of who he was. The Junior Sword Drill was in trouble. He alone would have to answer for that, and possibly be the determining factor in its very existence in the future. He had prepared and memorized a statement, and knew not to veer too far from the well-rehearsed story line and strict train of thought. Only he knew how nervous he was as he told the truth of the events that evening.. The Board then asked very specific questions concerning the activities of the 14 Nights, and about the precautions they had assumed were in place. Kraft felt under the gun as the board fired inquiries about the previous problem with Jim

Pearl and his knee, and why that was not enough to warrant some serious evaluation and change in the '79 Drill's approach. Strong interrogation ran continuously as the Board's ammunition of difficult questions seemed endless. When the shooting finally stopped, Kraft was asked to leave, and he knew a decision would be made in the discussions that followed.

He left exhausted, but thinking he had done well.

The next day Kraft received the results of the Board's findings. It was documented in a brief but complete memorandum from the Office of the Commandant of Cadets. The document gave instant gratification to Kraft as he read that the training for the 1980 Junior Sword Drill would resume, but further spelled out conditions by which it would be allowed to continue:

1. All training activities will be observed and supervised at all times by the Tactical Officer for the Junior Sword Drill, Major James A. Tyler.

2. There will be proper ventilation provided within the confines of McAlister Field House at all times, starting one hour prior to entry.

3. Rest breaks will be provided every fifteen minutes.

4. Fluids will be provided at rest breaks.

Kraft was pleased that the Drill would be able to continue, but disappointed with the recommendations. He knew the others in the '79 Drill would not like the interference. He would have quite a job ahead of him to find consent.

Tuesday evening Kraft broke the news to the old Drill, and as expected, they were not pleased with the recommendations. They understood that there had been problems, but to install such changes was to completely remove the harshness of the challenge. This was not a high school marching band, or some kind of intramural sport. This was the most prestigious and sought after honor on campus. To water down the Nights was to lower the high standards of the Drill. Like the performance itself, the method of training was developed through years of tradition, a system built by past generations of those who were so honored to be selected. The administration had no right to step in and make such major changes. They obviously didn't understand the process, the standards, the reasoning. These recommendations were not acceptable, and the 1979 Drill decided unanimously to fight them.

The Roaches of 1980 were not fully aware of the controversy, but a few were privileged to information as bits and pieces were passed on from the old Drill. The network was alive and well, and although pieced together, we at least had some idea of what was going on. It was sort of strangely ironic, that we all supported the position of the old Drill. We wanted to go through the full program, as hard and dangerous as it was. We didn't want to go through the rest of history known as the half-trained Drill. We were proud. We wanted the full honors of being one of the elite, even at the price of some not making it. Certainly injury and accident should be avoided, but just like playing football, there were acceptable risks.

Accompanied by two other members, Kraft returned to Colonel Dick's office the next day. This was a meeting scheduled by Kraft, and he brought along the additional comrades for moral support. There was a lot of big talk back at the barracks, about what the '79 Drill would and would not accept, knowing well the person to confront was Colonel Dick. They pulled together what they considered as a more than reasonable compromise, and sent in their delegation led by Kraft to present their solution to the problem.

Colonel Dick leaned back in his chair and listened with unusual silence as Kraft presented a proposal which completely threw out the recommendations of the Commandant's Board and proposed adopting what the '79 Drill considered minor, but more than adequate changes to the curriculum of the Nights. Colonel Dick allowed Kraft to finish, and even asked if he was sure he had made his full case. Kraft answered yes, though he could see he had sold nothing, and that a tongue-lashing was forthcoming.

"I really don't think you boys fully understand the severity of this situation. You see, you are lucky, damned fortunate to be able to proceed at all. Does it even matter to you that you almost killed a fellow cadet? Do you not understand the seriousness of this matter?"

"Sir, we do understand. That is why we feel that these changes as recommended by the Commandant's Board are unreasonable. Sir, the Junior Sword Drill has been around for decades, and it has been more than successful in setting standards which are high, and policing its own in the practice of carrying out the training of those who wish to achieve the honor of participating. Sir, to be perfectly frank, this outside interference is not necessary. We had an unfortunate mishap, but that is no reason for Jenkins Hall to step in and take over the Drill. This is an organization that is run and controlled by the Corps, not the faculty."

It was easy to see the fire in the eyes of Colonel Dick. "I can't believe my ears. The Junior Sword Drill, Mr. Kraft, is an official function of this college, and not some renegade group with free rein to abuse cadets in the name of tradition while the faculty and staff sit back and assume it's none of their business!"

"Sir, this is not as bad as you make it out to be!"

"A cadet's life was in danger and you question its seriousness?" yelled Colonel Dick.

There was silence from the three seniors who had just gained additional knowledge as to the stature of their opponent.

"Sir," said Kraft in a toned down, now meeker voice, "we only want to do what is right. We have had two very unfortunate accidents, and we know we were responsible for the safety of the aspirants at the time the mishaps occurred. But we have a responsibility to the tradition of the Junior Sword Drill. It is our duty to keep the standards high, to weed out those who are not Sword Drill material."

"By killing them, Mr. Kraft?"

There was a silence of frustration with the three seniors.

"No, Sir."

"Then I say to you men of Sword Drill, your standards may be high, but your methods are far from sensible. The Junior Sword Drill is a precision marching group, not a test of endurance with the penalty of a hospital trip as a result of not meeting some so-called standard. Standards are only as good as your ability to measure them. Your measurement is apparently based on bodies dumped at the door to McAlister Field House. That's a poor measure, son."

Colonel Dick sat back down in his chair and looked at his desk for a moment, then looked at the three sets of eyes across the room. "The decision of the Commandant's Board stands. Accept and adopt them fully, or don't proceed at all."

"Yes, Sir."

***

Kraft was silent as the members of the old Drill filed into his room. He was in a serious mood, and the occasional laughter of those not so in tune with the dilemma could not ignite the humor tucked away in him. He was nervous. He had bad news for his comrades. There would be changes. He stood up after the majority was there and the meeting time had arrived. He told them in a few short sentences the results of the meeting with Colonel Dick. They bitched and moaned, and he allowed a moment for them to vent. He then took control of the meeting. He was the Commander. He informed those present that the guidelines would be adopted, and to the letter. He was convinced that to proceed was indeed a privilege, one that included little room for variance. He was a smart young man. He had not risen to the top of his class because he lacked the ability to measure a situation, especially when it was one so serious. He loved Sword Drill. He loved who he was and what he had accomplished because of it. He also knew that graduation was in sight, and that a promising career in the Air Force awaited him. He believed in The Citadel, the 4th Class System, and the Honor Code. He trusted the judgment of those before him, and those who were in command. He had every reason and intention to follow the orders of the Commandants Board and that of Colonel Dick. He understood his position. He understood his commitment.

Kraft's meeting with his classmates was hard. He used his position, and every bit of tact and talent he could muster to make his stance clear. He recognized the insurrection, and held fast in his determination to guide the others to accept what had to be accepted. He was indeed a leader. He was truly one of the best that the Class of 1979 had to offer.

CHAPTER 38

The next day I got word through the usual channels that the old Drill's problem was solved. We knew nothing of the results, other than some sketchy rumors that there would be changes. The most important information was that Sunday would bring a continuance of the Nights. It was good news. I actually wanted to get back into it.

Sunday afternoon was soon upon us, and like seasoned veterans, the 22 that remained were prepared to perfection. At 1814 we were once again in front of our letters. I was calm and unruffled. I was a professional at this now, and ready to take on the old Drill's next round of desecration.

They arrived in their usual manner, and inspected us with detail. There were push-ups, sit-ups, and a small amount of running in the barracks. We moved quickly towards the other battalions, and didn't tarry as we linked up with our fellow roaches. Everything seemed to be progressing smoothly, and I was curious as to what the catch would be. I was only further surprised to find McAlister not like an oven, but pleasant. We were worn from the running, but there was a real lack of struggle in our need for oxygen. I braced with a passion as I savored the difference. There was an air of restraint in the old Drill's demeanor, and we didn't have to guess why. We started into our normal nights routine, but were shocked when we took a break only fifteen minutes after arriving. I was grateful for the rest, but couldn't help but wonder about the new format. We moved on to other activities, and there was a large amount of attention to detail in our execution of the acts. We removed our swords and scabbards for the wheelbarrow races, and we died at what seemed like every fifteen minutes. No one had received the white plume, and there was a change in the voices of the old Drill. What were once blistering verbal attacks were now firm commands. There was also an officer sitting in the bleachers, whom I soon discovered was Major Tyler, the JSD TAC, and I wondered how long he would be there. He was watching like a perched eagle, and I assumed that was why we soon had another chance to die. I felt as though the process was under a microscope, and that the old Drill was pulling punches in a big way. I knew what it meant to desperately need rest and water, and I was nowhere near that threshold. My eyes met with the other roaches from time to time, and I could see the look of question on their faces that also was surely on mine. I knew not to look a gift horse in the mouth, but I somehow felt guilty. I knew what a Sword Drill night was, and this was a far cry from it. I was thrilled to know there was now some restraint in the process, but I couldn't help but feel a bit babied. I had the guts. The passion. The will. The desire. I was Sword Drill. I could make it. I wanted to prove myself. I wanted the prize legitimately. Never, ever, did I want to hear that my Drill didn't have to go through the full test, and that we were somehow half of a real Drill. If there were those who couldn't take the heat, then they needed to drop out. This was never supposed to be a tea party. This was the Junior Sword Drill.

The time moved quicker than usual. There were regular breaks at short intervals. There was water and Gatorade. Baxter Stall looked as if he were out for a Sunday jog. For the sake of the old Drill, I wanted to look as if I were getting tired. Towards the end of the Night I was, but it lacked the gut wrenching anguish and effort that was the signature of the previous nights. I couldn't complain about the new attention to instruction. I actually had a feeling of having been productive. We were getting intense yet constructive critiques of our sword manual and the awkward style of marching found only with the JSD. It was tiring to work with such concentration, but it was a far cry from those first nights of living hell.

The TAC Officer never left, and the attitude of the old Drill remained professional and subdued throughout the entire evening. Even our run back to the barracks was a new experience. I felt good, yet confused. I didn't know whether to celebrate our new prosperity or mourn the passing of what I thought was a tradition. I wondered what the gossip would be. I wondered what the old Drill would say about the Class of 1980, and how we had missed the full experience of Drill the way it was back in the "Old Corps."

Things seemed normal as we entered through the sally port and were once again greeted by the applause of the upperclassmen lining the galleries on every division. There was an unusual reserve of energy available to do the meager fourteen pushups, and after a peck on the R, I floated up the stairs to my room.

I sat there consuming liquid as if I had just finished eighteen holes of golf, and almost felt it a requirement to finish off my second quart of Gatorade. Night number eight ended as easily as it had progressed.

The next day was a whole new experience. Thoughts entered my mind as to whether a bit of acting was in store as I moved among the staff and the rest of the Corps. We were, after all, supposed to be receiving the workouts of our lives. I was sore, but the whipped, almost crippled look of the early Nights was gone. I knew there was little reason to put on a front. Everyone knew as I did where the true power of the administration of The Citadel came from, and with the near death announcements of Richard Kelly, everyone was sure to expect intervention by the Commandant's office, and that there would indeed be changes, possibly drastic.

That Monday was my most productive of the "next day" classes. No nodding off. Lots of comprehension. I even got some homework done between classes. There was no need to panic or even be concerned with my equipment. Tompkins was now a professional at getting my stuff ready, and besides, I felt no need or desire to take a nap. Things had changed drastically all right.

It seemed so casual as I readied for the ninth Night. I actually had to tell myself that it wasn't wrong to have this break. Whether I crawled across the finish line with my last breath, or just strolled across with power to spare made little difference in the long run. "Old Corps" or not, my approach to the Nights had not changed. I still had to survive.

As we stood in the silence of the battalion I had to remind myself that this was only the ninth of fourteen, and that the cockiness I felt had to be suppressed. The entry of the old Drill brought me back to some amount of reality, but it was funny, I knew their hands were tied. There would be no more open season on our ass.

I ran with vigor as we entered and circled the quads of each of the four barracks. Glances at the other roaches revealed a consensus. I wondered if they had the same sick thoughts I had, which was that there would be no more casualties. This thing was now going to go down to cuts, and who was truly the best with his sword and marching. I felt it almost unfair. Not everyone wore the white plume the way I had, or suffered an additional night of pure shit from a couple of jerks preaching the personal appearance ethic. Along with Baxter Stall, who asked for it, I was sure I had suffered more than my fair share of pain and agony, and proved I had what it took to make it through the hard way. I had the stamina because I worked hard to prepare. I had the desire and the heart to take all they could dish out. I wondered if the others could have withstood the same. I knew some couldn't; yet they might still have a sword in their hand on Parents Day as I sat in the bandstands and watched. It was a wicked thought, but I didn't care how they were taken out. It was clear to me that even though we were classmates, and we often worked to help each other through the torment, we were indeed enemies in the pursuit of a hallowed place in history. Whether through not being able to survive the Nights or cuts, there were still many aspirants left in the way of my dream.

I experienced no surprise when I saw the green and khaki Marine uniform waiting when we entered the Field House. I was sure the Major would be with us for the remaining duration. It was a sign that once again there would be no funny business, or singling out of individuals for "special training." It was obvious that another comparatively easy Night was ahead.

But as we got into our activities I could see that there was a bit more aggression present than during the previous Night. The old Drill had gained a bit of confidence. Major Tyler was there for some reason, and they must have tuned into his expectations. We did a lot of the regular stuff, and there were times when it wasn't so easy anymore. Granted, there weren't any moments of desperation since we were still getting the mandatory breaks and liquids, but in those minutes in between, the old Drill poured it on as the physical challenge started to creep back in.

At what seemed like the three quarter mark of the night, we went into a series of sit-ups. It was right after our break, and I smiled at the sound of liquid sloshing around in my gut as I cycled through the up and down position. Sweat poured from my body, as I'm sure it did from each of the other roaches. Even with the perks, it was still intense physical activity.

We rose from our sit-ups and broke off into a hearty and somewhat high-spirited round of relay races. We were divided into six teams of four, with a few of the old Drill members filling in on the teams that were short. The idea was to run around the full circumference of the court, then tag the next man in line who would then take off for his sprint. It was a race for pride, one if held during the first Nights, would not have seen such effort from the roaches. Compared with the past, we all had strength to spare..

When the first group left the starting line it appeared there was little holding back. I was second in my group, and in a split second decided that I was going to give it my all. I took off as another roach from my team touched my hand, and I accelerated with the sprinting ability I knew I had. My shoes held on to the wooden floor like a stock car's tires at Darlington as I banked into the first turn. I was flying, and I poured it on in the straightaway heading for the second turn. I entered it with my legs straining to hold both the power of my stroke, and the centrifugal force of moving hard to the left. As if I had hit a banana peel, I felt the traction of my shoes go to non-existent, and in an instant, too fast to comprehend, I then felt a terrible pain on the side of my head as it struck the floor, and I was on my side, sliding. I then heard the noise and ache of crashing into a row of metal folding chairs. I was consumed with pain, and several seconds passed before I realized in my agony that I was holding my injured leg from high school football. My body turned into a knot, and the old Drill soon crowded around me, and I heard someone say, "My God, he's blown out his knee."

I reeled in agony, and then felt the pain of disbelief work its way in to take its fair share of my attention. I was horrified, anxious, and very scared. Drill was over. My dream was dead. I couldn't believe my luck. My dreaded bad luck. I was defensive as the old Drill offered assistance. My leg was killing me, and so was my broken heart. It was more than I could bear. I wanted to survive this, get up and walk away, but reality said no.

Major Tyler walked up, and my irreverence was not at a level to exceed his seniority. I withstood the pain, and in my assumption I told him I had reinjured my knee, a statement I would later regret. I learned a lesson in the power of suggestion, and I wished I had never heard the old Drill member say my knee was destroyed. My past injury, and that one statement, was enough to override the chance it was the type of injury I could recover from.

I could see a look of death on the faces of the old Drill. They were all filled with fear. There was even a bit of resignation in the look of Major Tyler. There was frustration in his voice as he asked me to lie back and try to relax. As the pain subsided, I was able to do so. At his insistence, he asked me to try and move it, and I did. There was no indication of a break. There was an instant look of hope from the observing faces.

"Actually Sir my leg struck the chairs, it may only be bruised," I said through the remnants of pain.

"Can you walk on it?" asked Major Tyler.

"I can try."

With a little help, I came to my feet. It hurt as I put my weight on it, and I grimaced as I took a step. The cadet Officer of the Day arrived on the scene, and in my relief to know that it wasn't broken and that there was hope to recover, I realized this wasn't going to be a freebie.

"Take him to the infirmary," said Major Tyler.

"But Sir," I said in protest, "can't we just wait and see?"

"No, I'm not willing to take any chances. OD, you and the others get this man to the doctor and have him checked. Right now."

"Yes, Sir!" replied the OD. There was no further discussion.

My sword and shako were removed. Maybe for my comfort, or maybe so as to not attract attention. I was helped to the OD's car and taken to the campus infirmary. It was an in and out deal in a matter of minutes. By the time I got there, the pain was gone, except when I walked or stood on it. The doctor checked it for a break or sprain, but it was easy to see it was just a nasty bruise. It was also an early end of night number nine. I thought about the one freebie we were supposed to have, and prayed it wasn't spent the night we all got sent back.

My return to the barracks involved a hobble through the sally port and a slow accent up the stairs. It was hard to walk, just as it was hard to sit and wait for the rest of the roaches to return. Only then would someone be there to let me know if I was still in the running. I waited and cursed myself for being so passive. I should have insisted I was all right. I should have faked it through the pain. Even if it was killing me, I made a drastic mistake of thinking it was all over. This was much too important to just give up without a fight. I made a critical mistake all because of sweat on the floor, and a bruise on my leg.

Around 2200 I heard the sound of the Drill in the distance. It was a haunting deja vu created many years earlier by the same echoing sounds. I walked out onto the gallery outside of my room, and heard the thunder of the 1980 aspirants from a different perspective as the group came in through the sally port. They looked good. Everyone appeared strong, not too worn. I felt cheated not to get the easy credit. I felt embarrassed to be on the gallery, and I got a lump in my throat as the thought that I might find this as a permanent situation, watching from the sidelines. There was so much at stake.

I watched my fellow roaches go through the normal routine, and as they ascended the stairs, I started walking towards Carl Andrews' room. I had to climb one flight myself to get there, and I felt the whelp of the bruise on my leg with each step. I walked towards the CO's headquarters, and then saw Andrews step off of the stairs at the other end of the gallery. Our eyes met, and I could see he was not smiling, or showing any kind of reaction. I took it as a bad sign, even though I knew he was by nature a serious guy who rarely showed emotion.

"How's the leg?" he asked, waiting at his door for me.

"It's bruised, Sir. But I'll make it," I answered.

"Cut the Sir crap. Come in and get off your leg."

I hobbled in as he held the door open, and he rushed over to his desk and pulled out a chair for me. I sat down, and he sat at the other desk. We looked at each other in a moment of silence, each waiting to hear the news.

"Tell me the bottom line," said Andrews.

"I had hoped to hear that from you," I answered.

Andrews looked at me confused, then said, "Are you going to be able to continue?"

"If I'm allowed to?"

"Are you able?"

"Absolutely."

"Then you can continue. Why would you think you couldn't? This is the only Night you have fallen out."

"What about when we were all sent back?"

"That was bullshit. That's tradition. Every Drill is sent back at least one Night. It doesn't count against you. But tonight did. Will your leg work tomorrow Night?"

"It will."

Andrews looked at me sternly. He knew I meant it.

"Good. Anything else."

"No. Thank you."

"Go rest your leg. You'll need it."

I hobbled to the door, and just as I opened it, Andrews spoke again saying, "You know, it was almost over for us all tonight."

I looked at him in silence. I knew exactly what he meant.

"Hang tough," he said.

My leg ached most of the following day, mainly when I walked, or touched it against something. It was tender, and would talk to me regularly. I knew we would be in a full conversation once the night started, but I would eat the pain like it was candy. I had to.

If I had asked, I could have gotten XMD status. But I begged to avoid it. I would pay the price for that request when afternoon Drill arrived. Even though I needed to be off my feet, I had to march through another practice for parade, and I had to keep up and not limp. Doing so would draw attention from any number of those in charge and they would surely insist on me being placed on XMD, and that would be the end of Drill for me.

I knew by 1814 that my efforts to rest my leg had been in vain. It was sore, but at least it functioned. The pain would just be a nuisance, and with some luck, and the new format of not killing us, I could get through it. If we went through a night like one of the first, I would surely not survive.

The evening started like any other. The pain was a nuisance, but it didn't consume me. The old Drill was fully aware of my injury, and no one seemed anxious to make things worse. The minimum would be hard enough for me to endure, and they had nothing to gain by advancing my injury.

We entered into the armory and received an immediate address from Kraft. It was apparently "Thousand Push-up Night." By tradition, the aspirants would do at least one thousand push-ups before the night was considered over. I was thrilled that it wasn't some tradition requiring a lot of running.

I wasn't sure how to read the Major and his look of concentration, but I had a feeling he was not comfortable with the proposed format for the evening. Just the thought of such an extreme goal had to bring concerns for excess physical work, and the possibility for another injury. We started right off the bat doing push-ups, and they continued to come through the evening in groups of 50. I would usually see the Major standing close, watching with the intensity of a driver testing a racecar at top speed, looking for signs of impending breakdown and disaster.

We moved through the night swiftly. All of our normal events of working out were short and quick, always followed by another 50 push-ups. There was a lot of instruction on sword manual and marching. More detail than ever was put into the finer points, and we actually learned something as we waited for our arms and shoulders to recover from the most recent round of push-ups, and prepared for the next wave that would soon start. It would have been a good night, had it not been for the aggravating pain in my leg, and the building fatigue in my arms and shoulders. Our backs were starting to break down, and after we crossed the 500 mark, the challenge then took on a more realistic character. I began to wonder if I could indeed make the mark.

The old Drill never let up. We stayed on course with our pursuit. Thirst was never a problem, and I was grateful for that. But I soon was able to hear others groan as they strained to push themselves up. More and more you could hear the sound of brass touching the floor as contact was made. Both the watchful eyes of the old Drill and Major Tyler were upon us. We strained to complete each movement, and prayed for the final number to arrive. The stress and strain of the effort began to spread through our backs, and then on down to the legs. My bruise started to throb. Effort increased. The night started to feel like the old torture routine. What should have been a break by going on a run through the corridors quickly turned into a struggle as I couldn't help but now limp as I ran. The old Drill asked me constantly if I was OK, and I always answered with an affirmative. But they worried nonetheless. I wasn't sure if their fear was totally due to Major Tyler, but I too shared that fear. If the Major saw me and decided I was in too bad a shape to continue, it was all over for me. There was no more grace period. My one freebie was gone. Spent. I had to keep up. I had to look healthy.

As we hit 800 pushups, I wondered just how we would make it. I could see the Major talking to Kraft, and I was sure that the night was approaching his threshold of reason. Tradition or not, the previous circumstances had made everything critical. We roaches were looking ragged, and this quest would soon have to end.

The frequency of doing groups of push-ups lessened, and there was a reduction in the number down to 30. We had covered what seemed like every possible detail of sword manual and marching, and at a time when we really needed nothing but rest, there was little left to fill the time except for exercises that required running. This was bad. My leg was killing me, and I couldn't cover the pain very well as I was limping badly. I became very concerned, almost panicky about my condition. The old Drill could see I was in trouble, and there was a genuine look of anxiety on their faces.

I was limp-running through the corridor when Ronnie Bourbon stopped me. I had had little contact with him since the Nights had begun. He stopped me and the others continued. He made me go down into sit-up position. He commanded, "Up!" and then "Down!" in a slow but steady progression. I did them constantly, seeing a group come by me only occasionally as they continued to run through the Field House. The sit-ups were hard, especially after so many push-ups, but they kept most of the pressure off my leg. When time came for more push-ups, I joined the rest of the roaches. It was my saving grace, but it was also killing my upper body.

We finally arrived at 950, and it was easy to see that we had reached our maximum. The Major and Kraft agreed to something, and they formed us up shortly after our last set. I strained to run with some degree of health, and soon was aided by Baxter Stall as we moved towards the battalions. It was bad that 4th was the farthest from McAlister, and the pain was now overwhelming as I tried to maintain my speed with the platoon. We soon were at the sally port, and with everything I had, I tried to look good for the battalion. There just always seemed to be the potential for someone to say I needed to be taken out, and I just couldn't take that risk. I know I had to appear to have a limp, but I felt I hadn't raised anyone's concern to a critical level. To my surprise, we did our last 50 push-ups right there on the quad. I could have cared less that my back was in a full slump. There was just no other way to do them. It was all I could do just to make it to a thousand. But a thousand did come, and I limp-ran to kiss the R, and then hobbled up the stairs to my room. I had survived my bruised leg and the traditional Thousand Push-up Night all in the same evening. I felt no extra consolation. Night ten was history.

CHAPTER 39

The next day my knee felt a good bit better, and with no practice parades I had time to rest it further. I would need it. There were rumors flying through the network that we were facing the first "Feats Night." I wasn't sure I could pursue the events because of my leg, but I knew I had the desire to try.

The inspection that night was a piece of cake. I wasn't sure if there was a more important agenda or if the old Drill had just gotten tired of messing with it. Naturally the old Drill from 4th Battalion wanted the home team to do well, and the need to push the personal appearance issue at that point was moot. This was night number eleven, and for all practical purposes, it was the next to the last night of physical hell. Nights thirteen and fourteen would be consumed with cuts. If we could just make it through the next two evenings, we would be left with the final deciding test. But the gremlins were alive and well, anything could still happen.

Our arrival at McAlister brought a seemingly more relaxed, carnival like atmosphere, and the old Drill was primed and ready to get started. So as to be as fair as possible, the old Drill said they would make the very first activity the "50 Lap King" event. It was a survival test where the old Drill lined up in a squad, and we roaches would fall in behind them in ours. We would all then run around the floor of McAlister for fourteen laps with both the old Drill and roaches in the one group, where the old Drill would then leave the court, except for those who had been successful in the event the previous year. Ronnie Bourbon and Cliff Malone would set the pace for the final 36 laps, and it was up to them to make up the almost full lap of distance and catch the roaches. If they touched you, you were out. If you could stay ahead of the old Drill through the full 50 laps, you would hold the honor of being a "50 Lap King." As silly as it sounded, it was taken seriously. Successful roaches would have the honor of standing out, both in front of the old Drill and the Corps.

The names of those successful would be announced at noon mess, and it was an ego boost to have your peers think that you were some kind of a rock. It was also rumored to affect cuts. It made sense, but there was no way to prove it.

This was the only feats event I was interested in, but I could think of nothing but my bruised leg. If it could withstand the pain, I knew I had the speed and endurance to make it. Make it or not, I felt I had to at least try.

Kraft gave the command for the combined squads to start. We took off in what could only be considered as a very easy pace. Easy as compared to some of the other running we had done through the Nights. I couldn't help but think that the easy pace was for those members of the '79 Drill who had not maintained their shape since making the Drill. It was an easy start, but definitely a deception. As soon as the initial fourteen laps were complete, there was a quick increase in the pace. It wasn't a sprint, but it was fast enough to leave no doubt that some of the slower roaches would soon feel a tap on their shoulder.

When we reached the halfway point, all of the roaches were literally still in the running. There were, however, several who were starting to lag behind the main group that was still on the heels of the two '79 Drill members. To lag at this point was a clear indication that they weren't going to make it to the end. It seemed pretty clear that the only real way to insure success was to stay right with Bourbon and Malone. That would be a challenge.

After 30 laps, three of the roaches were already out, with many more scattered at various intervals and only a handful, including me, still glued to the heels of Bourbon and Malone. I was really winded, and my leg was starting to hurt. Fifteen more laps at the blistering pace would be tough, but I at least thought I had a chance to make it.

At that point it seemed that with each lap another roach was tagged. I felt really winded, and my leg was starting to take a toll, and I cursed my bad luck from two days before. With eight laps to go, there were only three of us left in-tow, and another handful scattered. But the old Drill guys kicked in their afterburners for the *coup de gras*, and one of the three in-tow faded back behind me. I watched as others were tagged out, and soon I felt my ability to hang with the front disappear. There were five laps left, and the lead group began to pull away. I wasn't surprised in the least to see that Baxter Stall was the only remaining roach to stay right with them. I struggled to keep their pace, but could see I was losing ground as the three crept away. Then I watched as Ronnie Bourbon got a second wind, and he then left the other two. For a moment, Baxter stayed behind Malone, but in an unprecedented move, passed and left him to stay with Bourbon. With Baxter on his heels, Bourbon soon reached Gregg Alston, and he too was out. Apparently Bourbon had his mind made up to get all he could. We all knew he could never get Baxter, but as I looked at him across the court, he was pouring it on to catch me in the two and a half laps that remained. From the looks of his and Baxter's pace, they were indeed on the way to catching me before I could finish.

I reached deep, and grabbed all I had. I was too close to lose now. I ran with everything my legs had to offer, but I could still see I was losing ground. The Field House soon came alive with the sounds of my classmates and the old Drill as they cheered us on. With about a lap and a half to go, I could hear Bourbon coming like a freight train. He was grunting like a Marine, and I could tell his adrenaline was really pumping. He wanted me. He was a man with a mission to seek and destroy. He was a jarhead down to the bone. He was coming for me with a passion to kill. As I crossed the line to start the final lap, I could hear him getting even closer, and I reached even deeper. I felt as if I ceased all other body functions to put all my effort into my aching legs. I poured it on and felt as if I increased my speed by only a modest degree. With half a lap to go, I could hear his footsteps and Marine grunt seemingly inches from my ear, and it was enough to scare an extra ounce of energy out of me. I crossed the finish line and he ran into me the second I slowed in exhaustion. He had been inches away from his goal, and I was inches from failure. But I succeeded, with nothing to spare. We were covered with slaps on the back, and cheers filled the building from the small crowd that was there. I gasped for precious air. I was happy but too exhausted to enjoy it, and I forced myself to receive the congratulatory remarks.

Just as I got my wind, Bourbon walked up and said, "I had you in my cross hairs."

"I was just playing with you, Sir," I said with an exhausted smile.

Bourbon smiled back, "You made it, that's all that counts."

We formed up and resumed the normal activities of the night. There was a lot of instruction on sword manual and marching, and it felt like this was being done despite any recommendations from Jenkins Hall. The time for mind games and physical abuse was over. Cuts were only days away. We did go through more than enough exercise, and my bruised leg remained a real nuisance since the 50 laps hadn't helped. It wasn't brutal, but it was a hard night.

The next day at noon mess Baxter Stall and I had our names announced over the loudspeaker as having been successful in the 50-lap run. Both the battalion staff and everyone from R Company applauded and cheered. I acted like it was nothing, but deep inside, it was everything. This was a hard group to impress. To win their approval was extraordinary. I would savor that moment forever.

At 1814 I stood on the quad for what was to be my last regular night of hell, and I felt a bit of accomplishment. There was a feeling that I had passed through the worst of it, even though two nights of cuts would take place the following week. The inspection by the old Drill was hardly more than a quick look. There were no activities in the battalion, and little time was wasted gathering the fold through the four battalions while getting on to the armory. Once inside, we heard a lot of verbal instructions from Kraft and others from the '79 Drill. They apparently worked from a checklist, wanting to cover the minimum requirements for cuts, both in personal appearance and in sword manual and marching. There were many details left out on purpose, but those were the elements of surprise that would truly test us. They warned us to expect anything, mental and physical. These guys had already established credibility with me in their ability to be innovatively proficient in the art of trauma. They didn't have to warn me twice.

After the guidance, Kraft described several feats events that would fill the remainder of the evening. These would determine the best in push-ups, hanging, sit-ups, and arching swords. Participation to a minimum cut-off point was mandatory for everyone in all events, after which, those who chose to could try to establish himself as a king in that event. It was a chance to prove one's talents and stamina. It was a chance to show the Corps that you were a rock among rocks. We were all encouraged to go for what we could, and warned not to think one man could take it all. But cuts were only days away, and in my mind, it was a bad time to destroy one's arms for glory at the cost of losing the real prize.

The first event was the search for "Push-up King." The minimum was that each of us had to do 80 push-ups that represented our class year. After that, we would continue on until there was only one roach left. He alone would own the honor and title of "Push-up King." If he was a real rock, he could continue on to beat the existing all time record of 1078, set two years earlier by a guy named Frank Darton, a member of the 1978 Junior Sword Drill. Each had to be a perfect military push-up with no bending of the back, resting on the floor, or stopping out of cadence. It only took a moment for me to decide it would be the minimum for me. I was satisfied just being a "50 Lap King."

We were lined up across the floor in one long row. Observers were posted to watch for violations such as slumping backs. I assumed it wouldn't be cool to show problems before at least the minimum was reached. After that, I knew I wouldn't go much longer. Perfect military push-ups, 80 of them, would be hard enough. I couldn't imagine someone doing 1080.

The cadence was started by Kraft. He used his best command voice to say, "Down!" and we all lowered ourselves. "One!" he yelled, and we all rose. "Down!" he yelled again. "Two!" and we rose again. This continued, and I felt fine until about 50, and I knew then that 80 couldn't come fast enough. I didn't know how the other roaches were doing, but I had to struggle to make the minimum. I didn't stop at 80, but before we reached 90, I was asked to fall out of line because my back was slumping. No yelling, no penalty. I was just excused to the side and found comfort in the fact that I had company. "Push-up King" was apparently a title that only few could ever hope to obtain.

The cadence continued, and when 200 were done, there were far less than half still going. By 300, there were four roaches left, and by 500, only two. I stood in awe as I watched Baxter Stall and Buck Edwards from 4th Battalion hang tight. They were rocks all right. I also thought they were crazy.

To everyone's surprise, Baxter dropped out at 700. No slumping back, no chest on the floor. He just stood up, and said, "That's it!" I thought for sure that Edwards would have gone ahead and stood up in triumph as we cheered, but he never broke his concentration or the cadence. Our cheers quickly fell back to silence, and we heard Kraft call out the next order of "Down!" I smiled at the adventure. I respected the drive. We all loved his ambition, his commitment. This was what Sword Drill was all about.

Edwards moved in perfect form through the never-ending calls from Kraft. There was a pool of sweat under him, and as he moved past 900, strain found its way into his face. His expression changed, but his form didn't. At 950, we could hear him starting to grunt ever so slightly. He could see the goal, and Kraft moved closer for volume, as we couldn't help ourselves but to loudly cheer him on. We all wanted it, maybe as bad as he did. We wanted the record with our class, and no one had to guess that his goal was to make 1080. It would be impossible for me, and probably most everyone. But for Buck, the determination was there. He passed 1000, and we had to be told to quiet down by the old Drill. He had to hear, and they had to watch. If he were to do it, it would be legal. One momentary bow in his back would end it all. Down to the last push-up they had to be perfect. I looked for a change in his expression as he reached 1070, but he stayed on track and pace. He was a machine, programmed for success. He changed nothing until he pumped 1078. He smiled with gritting teeth as he performed 1079, and then after 1080 he stood up and was smothered by his classmates and even the old Drill. It was a triumphant moment. No one knew how he could have possibly done it. I was honored to have witness such power and determination.

We were formed back up, and formality returned as order was restored. Water was given to us as we stood in formation. Only Edwards sat on a bandstand and drank. He had earned it.

The next event was the search for the "Hanging King." There was little explanation needed for this contest. We all grabbed a piece of the steel I beam, and hung on as best we could. We had already had dress rehearsal for this many times during the previous nights. I guess we all had our ideas as to who would hold out the longest. I was sure it wasn't going to be me. So as to be fair on time, several of the old Drill assisted some of the shorter roaches in getting up to the girder, and we hung there as someone took a lot of pictures. I held on as I heard others begin to fall. No one was giving them a hard time, but I just didn't want to give in too soon. But my arms set my limit, and my ability to keep a grip weakened until I soon slipped. With little fanfare I walked over to the wall and stood as those remaining continued to struggle. Some had a real look of strain as they held on, while others seemed to just hang there effortlessly. Dennis Miles had his eyes closed, and Fred Irving was zoomed out. They seemed to be in another world, and I was not surprised to find them as the last two hanging on as the final few fell. It was a point where there was no cheering. We all wanted them both to succeed, but knew only one could take the title. They both seemed to be in a peaceful state, able to hang with no effort, hanging on long after others had conceded to the power of gravity. But their faces soon told the story of success and failure. Irving remained composed as he hung there with his eyes closed. Miles' face began to grimace, and his body started to shake. Irving never opened his eyes, even when Miles fell. He was locked into another world, and he opened his eyes only after we yelled at him over his victory. He was happy, and seemed fresh enough to hang much longer. His method of zooming out worked well.

The final event in the last night of feats was that of finding the "80 Minute King." This event tested a roach's ability to continuously arch a sword for the number of minutes that represents one's class year. It would start with each of us arcing our swords perfectly for fourteen minutes, and then we just had to hold it above our heads for 52 more, then again in a perfect arc for the final fourteen. It would be nice to take the honor to go along with "50 Lap King," but I could only think of the real goal of making Drill. To push to hold a sword above my head for that length of time might possibly damage my arm at a critical time so close to cuts. It just didn't seem to be worth it.

With the command of "Arc swords!" we all raised our swords up into position. But after the minimum requirement of fourteen minutes, I lowered my sword with plenty of strength left and moved to the side. It was a tough decision, but I yielded to my ultimate plan for getting through the Nights. Survive! It wouldn't matter at all that I was successful in two feats events if in conclusion I failed to survive cuts and make the Drill.

I stood on the sideline and watched guys drop out until it was down to Stall, Middleton, and Chin, all of whom held on to the end. Their efforts were admirable, but I couldn't help but think that I too could have made it if I had tried. I soon felt regret for not staying with it and gaining the additional title.

Kraft then had us all line up facing the bleachers, where the old Drill members were seated. He then explained that there would be one final competition, one of great honor and significance. The Voice of the '80 Drill had to be selected, and the old Drill traditionally chose him. One by one, each of us were asked to take a shot at giving a specific command in our best siren voice, and we went through the platoon several times as we let out the various commands found in the performance that some of us would eventually learn. Each member of the '79 Drill had a grading sheet that they marked on a scale of 1 to 10 for each attempt. The sheets would be tallied and the Voice for the 1980 Junior Sword Drill would be revealed to us following cuts.

After completing our final test, we were formed up into our normal squad. The old Drill seemed relaxed. There was no yelling. No threats. No racking, or even PT. Everything considered, we were into the final moments of the physical 14 Nights. The last two, 13 and 14, would be totally devoted to cuts. Other than surviving, it was the most important test in making Drill. It was the final point of judgment. All we had worked and practiced for would be graded. There was little to be gained at that point by proceeding with further physical taunting. Kraft stood before us and again reviewed in detail the requirements of cuts, continually reminding us to pay attention to details as we prepared. Details were the heart of Drill, the magic of the performance, and sure death during cuts.

After Kraft covered what seemed to be every aspect of the two days of trials, the old Drill positioned themselves at the front of the platoon, and after a high spirited pair of laps around the floor of McAlister, we headed back towards the battalions one last time. We were rested. We felt a sense of victory. Our spirits were high and our voices proclaimed it. We had survived. The rest would be a test of our abilities and strength of mind. The physical terror was behind us. For all practical purposes, we were somehow almost there. Twenty-two of us were on our way to cuts.

As we entered into 4th Battalion, our voices thundered and echoed like no other previous night. The normal crowd of supporters probably didn't know why, but they had to notice there was a real difference. We were light on our feet, and there was strength in our presence. As usual we circled the quad with the old Drill out in front, then circled a final time by ourselves. The fourteen push-ups were a piece of cake, and the run to my room was a declaration of victory. I meant every word of "We love, Sword Drill."

CHAPTER 40

Though Fridays normally represented the end of a workweek, for me and the other roaches it was the beginning of a packed schedule. Ready or not, the first night of cuts would start at 1814 on Monday afternoon. Many things were already done, but so much was still left to do. Rontelli and I had talked constantly over the Nights about each part of our uniform, and how we wanted to have it prepared. We had to be twins. It didn't matter what the other roaches were doing, we had to be exactly alike in everything. There were so many details. A cut would be awarded for any problem or deviation, big or small. And equipment was only a part of the requirements. We had to practice as much as we could. Every spare minute had to be used to prepare. Each was precious. We had been told that often in the past that only one or two cuts had separated the 14th and 15th ranked roach when all was over. I could think of hundreds of little things that could lead to receiving the dreaded negative mark, some of which took only a minute to correct. I didn't want to fail making Drill because I was a few minutes short on time.

The uniform for cuts was a slightly altered version of that used during the 14 Nights, with the only difference being a long sleeve gray nasty shirt instead of our PT shirt. All the personal appearance work and inspections over the first twelve nights left little doubt as to the condition it should be in, but understanding and delivering was still a challenge.

With so much to do, I adopted a plan of working my way up, dressing myself, and perfecting each item as I went. Since there were two days of cuts, I had to have two of each item, all of which had to be blitzed and made to conform in every way to the standard that Rontelli and I had agreed on. Starting with my shoes, I spent an hour just putting white polish on the fabric and rubber portions of my high tops. The brand tags had already been removed, and my old shoestrings were replaced with new ones that measured the same length as Rontelli's and were laced in the same order we had agreed upon.

When my shoes were finished, so was my time. I spent a quick fifteen minutes in front of the mirror practicing my sword manual, then it was off to McAlister to meet Rontelli. We talked for a bit, as questions about our uniform coordination couldn't seem to wait.. I could tell he was tense, and I was sure he could see it in me.

When we got into our practice, our jittery nerves were really apparent as we often missed our timing just so slightly. We didn't get upset, but conceded that we just needed to calm down.

On Saturday morning I decided to get my clothing out of the way first since my brass could tarnish before cuts, which was still two days away. I first worked on my socks, underwear, and T-shirt. They were all brand new from the Cadet Store and the same size as Ted's. I went over them in detail to trim loose strings and to look for other flaws, then put them away carefully until they were ready to be worn. I then moved on to my pants and shirt. The pants were my best pair from the lot issued when I was a knob.. My shirt, however, was one from the old Corps, back when they had long sleeves for the winter months. Porter had passed several of them on to me, and he told me to guard them with my life, and make it or not, to pass them on to a member of the next Drill.. I had little work to do on them since they were pressed and already in perfect shape from years of detailed inspection and care. I checked both my pants and shirt in detail knowing they were potential mine fields for cuts. I checked for strings, buttons, fuzz, you name it. I looked in every pocket and at every seam, and I indeed found plenty wrong. I worked carefully not to wrinkle the starched and pressed garments as I explored every square inch of fabric with small finger nail scissors in hand.

Once an hour I would stop working and spend ten minutes on statics and sword manual. I worked to make sure that obvious things were covered like my chin being in and the cheerios of my fingers were always perfectly round. They had to be perfect, and second nature. I would think through what every part of my body was doing as I manipulated my sword. Checking the details gave me confidence that everything was in place, and I felt confident that after all the many months, the basics were mindless reactions.

During the afternoon Carl Andrews visited me. He checked on my progress, then spent some time giving me pointers on making it through cuts. I appreciated his consideration, and was surprised as he made it clear that he was one of my strongest supporters. He said he knew Porter was from R, and he had done well in seeing me through to this point, but realize it or not, I was now under his wing too. He said he felt just as strong about me making it as he did the guys from his own home company. I felt my confidence and support move up a notch as he walked out the door.

I filled my afternoon working on my gloves, pants belt, scabbard belt, and webbing, going over every minute part, then putting them away when I knew there was nothing more to be done.

My sword manual started to get nerve-rackingly redundant as I continued to practice once each hour. I had a feeling that I already had it down pat, and that I was looking for flaws that just weren't there. I was worried more about my cuts routine with Rontelli than anything.

I called Rontelli and we agreed to practice after the game that evening. We both had initially assumed it would be too late after to get any real practice done, but we were getting anxious about our slight miscues. They were small, but they were there. We needed to be perfect before cuts. It would be bad to go in knowing we weren't flawless under the best conditions, much less the worst.

I was lucky enough not to have usher duty that evening, but was required to march over to the stadium with the rest of staff. Of course I again had tickets for Cindy in the junior date section, and was thrilled beyond measure to see her. It would have been a wonderful reunion had I not been so high-strung and nervous about what I had left to do. Cindy could see I was wound up like a clock, and I think it was all she needed to see to fully understand what I was going through.

After the game I returned to the barracks just long enough to change into my practice uniform. The campus crowd was still thick from the game as I hurried over to the Field House. I was only minutes ahead of Rontelli, and we wasted no time getting down to business. We started with a quick critique session as a warm up. Even though we had both spent many hours in front of a mirror, there was nothing like a second set of eyes to help one pick up on flaws that were hidden from sight. It was just another check to help shave off cuts.

We then proceeded with the objective of going through our routine. We knew exactly what we needed to do, having practiced it what seemed like a hundred times. We were now looking for that feeling that would make the process instinctive and second nature to us. We had to feel what the other was doing. We had to be together or it would mean cuts for us both, no matter who was out of sync.

We had moved successfully through our series twice, and had completed our third run when we heard someone clapping, and wondered what smartass was there to ridicule us. Looking towards the source of the noise, ready to do battle, we saw only an older man, clapping as he stood there wearing a Citadel windbreaker and baseball cap. He appeared to be in his forties, and he smiled and said "Bravo" as he moved towards us.

"Excellent, gentlemen! Excellent!"

"Thank you, Sir," I said with curiosity.

"I couldn't help but notice that the lights were on, and I came in here just to have a look at the old Field House." The man walked right up to us and extended his hand to Rontelli, and then to me. "Dan Ethridge, Class of 1957."

"Nice to meet you, Sir," I said.

"You guys practicing for cuts?" he asked.

"Yes Sir, we are!" answered Ted.

"How did you know, Sir?" I asked.

"I was a member of the '57 Drill. That was the reason I wanted to see the place." Both Rontelli and I silently shifted gears into a state of shock. "I've got a son here this year. A freshman. This is our first trip up to see him. Wanted to see the game too.."

"What company is he in?" asked Rontelli.

"He's down in 3rd, "L" Company. Know him?"

"No, sir," I answered. "I'm from 4th. Romeo."

"I'm from Foxtrot, Sir," replied Ted.

"Good. I don't have to worry about you killing him. Say, would you guys do that little series again? It looks familiar."

"Sure, that's why we're here. To practice. You being here will put a little more pressure on us, like cuts," said Ted.

"And we could use the extra set of eyes to see if we're together," I said.

"Great. Glad to help. Let's see it again."

Rontelli and I moved back over to our starting positions. With all the concentration we could muster, we started. I could feel the eyes of Mr. Ethridge on us as we moved, but then I quickly reminded myself to forget him and concentrate. I got in tune with Ted, and tried to anticipate and move as one. We seemed to be doing well, then miscued slightly on our finish. It was a small goof, but we could tell.

"Great! Great!" said Mr. Ethridge. "You've got it down pat."

"Thank you Sir," I said.

"Guys, may I be so brazen as to ask a favor?"

"What sir?" I said.

"Anything for a member of the old Drill," said Rontelli.

"Could I borrow one of your gloves, and a sword? No one else is here. Could I try it? I have this crazy notion in my head that I can still do it. I really think I remember it."

With amazement, I was pleased to make the loan. This old guy couldn't be serious. What in the world could he remember after almost twenty years? He had to be dreaming.

"Here you go, Sir," I said. "My glove should fit your hand."

I handed the gentleman my glove, and after he put it on I gave him my sword. His face lit up as if I had given him a free vacation, and he immediately re-gripped the handle as a firm gesture of love, then snapped it down to carry swords with precision as if still in the Corps. He then went to present arms, then to order arms, all without a single hitch. My mouth had to be gaping as he walked across the floor to position himself at our normal starting point. I looked at Ted and he looked at me. We said nothing, and just smiled.

Mr. Ethridge stood at the launch, and we laughed as he put the sword down into the leather belt of his pants. I later called it his "civilian scabbard." He killed us as we saw him zoom out, and then with his own command, go right into the routine. We were in awe as we watched this old guy do it, and do it well. He wasn't as polished as us, but he never missed a step. He had good sword manual, and made outstanding head snaps as he turned the corner. We were astonished. Absolutely speechless.

"How was that?" asked Mr. Ethridge as we stood bewildered.

I started clapping, not knowing what to say, and then Ted followed.

"How did you do that? How could you possibly remember?" asked Ted.

"You know, I think if you got the fourteen of us back in here tonight, we could still do our performance. I'm not saying perfect, but there is very little of it I've forgotten."

"You're not serious," I said, still amazed.

"How could I forget it? How could I? We went over it a million times. It's ingrained in our minds forever. Like me, you will probably never forget yours."

We were impressed. It was a real statement about the history of the Drill, and that it was always taken seriously. We needed to practice, but Ted and I had a million questions for Mr. Ethridge. He had to meet his family though, and could only chat with us for a moment more. He told us that the 14 Nights weren't quite the same back then as they were today. A lot more emphasis was put on marching and sword manual skills than on endurance and desire. But he was pleased to see that the standards were still high..

It was a treat to experience a voice from the past, but as soon as Mr. Ethridge left, we knew we had to get back to work. It was getting late and we only had time to go through the series a few more times. It was weird though. After our visit with the past, we performed our routine the best we ever had.

Sunday morning I woke up with brass on my mind. I had perfected every other part of my uniform, and was now ready to start on the massive task. I had my belt buckles, breastplates, waist plates, shako brass, sword, and scabbard to blitz to perfection. They were all practically finished as far as being set up, but this was to be the ever-important final run on them. They had to be handled delicately. They had to be shined with a care that exceeds handling the finest crystal. One ping of an item against the desk could mean a complete loss, and it was far too late to get a new one and have a jeweler in town match it to Rontelli's. If push came to shove, I would have to borrow an old one from Carl Andrews, but there would be cuts for the mismatch, even if it were perfect otherwise.

There was just so much to do, but I had to do nearly all of it myself. Both Larry and Tompkins offered to help, and I did let them join in, but only in a few things. Larry was given a pretty important task of making our cuts number cards. Though they would be different numbers, they would have to be the same otherwise. One of our other classmates was in Civil Engineering, and had his drafting tools in his room. Larry got with him and together they drew some really nice numerals. I was impressed with his efforts. He worked both that day and some again on Monday to make them perfect. Both Rontelli and I were grateful, and we both realized that preparing for cuts was not a task that could be conquered alone. Even if we hadn't wanted the help, we had to have it.

My entire Sunday was filled with a killer schedule as I alternated between practicing on my own, practicing with Rontelli, and working on my equipment. I tried to stay calm, but I couldn't help but feel the pressure. Even though our routine was now flawless, my partner and I were both on edge. We had talked, planned, and practiced together for over a month, and our greatest dream was held in trust with the other. We needed to get through this before a natural saturation of each other's company set in.

Exhausted as I was, I tossed and turned during my first hour in the rack that night. In less than 24 hours I would be taking the test of my life. All I had worked for would be nullified if I failed to perform. It was hard to ignore the significance.

I was on edge the next day, although I tried not to show it. I deserved an Oscar for my acting and false air of calmness. I wanted to remain tranquil and not burn precious energy worrying. I went through my classes and duties, trying hard to concentrate on them instead of the approaching trial. But it just wasn't possible.

At 1500 I stood at the door to my room, seeing it in perfect order. I knew that in the hours that would follow it would come to life with activity. It seemed so quiet, and I absorbed the moment of peace before walking over to my lock box drawer and opening it to see my most prized possessions. I slowly pulled out the pieces of glowing brass, and laid them out one by one on my bunk, holding them as if they were my own beating heart, respecting them as if they held the fate of the world. From my full press I retrieved my shako and shoes, and added them to the collection of treasures. Finally, I put a pair of gloves on and carefully lifted my sword from the gun rack behind the door. It was cloaked in a red velvet sword bag, and with care I pulled it from its refuge. Drawing it from the scabbard, I moved to the mirror, and placed it up to present arms, with it spaced perfectly from my chest and brow as if I wore both my breastplate and shako. I felt good. I felt like success was just a matter of going through the motions. It was too late to practice or prepare. There was no need. I had it down. I merely had to execute.

I called Cindy, and told her I only had a second to talk. She understood. There was nothing really that I wanted to say to her. She knew my schedule, but I still told her it was time for me to get ready and I wanted just to hear her voice. She told me she would be with me every minute, and if I felt nervous, that I could take refuge in knowing there was someone out there more worried than I was. I laughed, told her I loved her, and then we hung up. Even with casual words over the telephone, she made me feel invincible.

Having laid out my equipment, I started into my process. I pulled out a brand new razor blade, and then with care shaved as close as anyone could without taking the skin. I then struck out towards the showers, and by agreement with Rontelli, washed my entire body with Ivory soap. Nothing else. I used Sure unscented deodorant, then pulled my brand new size 32 Hanes from the plastic bag I had sealed it in, then put on the new medium 38/40 size Hanes "V" neck undershirt. Rontelli and I had made sure to keep them folded around the shipping cardboard, even after we worked them over looking for loose strings and other defects. Their creases were exact matches.

Soon Larry, and then Tompkins arrived. They were in the right frame of mind as they stood back and moved on my queue as we continued the process. Next, they laid a towel on the floor and pulled a chair in front of it. I then put on a new pair of Haynes white socks, and then stood on the towel to insure no dirt was picked up from the floor as I worked. I looked back at the chair knowing I would not sit down again for many hours, but said nothing and moved on. Next were my gray nasty pants, and I struggled to stay balanced as Larry and Tompkins helped me get in them, working diligently not to damage the crease, or cause a wrinkle. The gray nasty long sleeve shirt followed, and I did nothing as the other two gave me a shirt tuck like I never knew existed. I then got nervous as I told Tompkins to get my belt.

"Stop!" I yelled. "I forgot. Put some gloves on. Good ones. Please. And for God's sake be careful."

"We will, douche bag," said Larry. "Calm your ass down!"

"Sure man, I got nothin' to lose," I said firmly.

"Remind me to whip your ass after all this is over, OK dick weed?" said Larry.

I said nothing more, grateful for the help, but not in the mood to fool around. Tompkins never opened his mouth as he got a pair of gloves from my drawer. He was focused and without emotion. He was definitely future Sword Drill material.

Larry gave me a pair of gloves, and I held the buckle of my belt as Tompkins pulled the webbing through the loops of my pants. I gave it one last close look before I buckled it. I inspected it intensely, searching for some flaw that may have mysteriously crept into what was supposed to be perfect. I saw nothing. I buckled it with care, and then asked for my sword sling. Tompkins handled it cautiously and put it over my head and adjusted it into position. I checked it over as Larry brought the breastplate. I was especially nervous about it since it was easily seen, and I looked it over for something that wasn't supposed to be there. I had this feeling there was tarnish on it, having been shined the day before, and not that day. But there was nothing. Next was my scabbard, and I had Tompkins look at it closely. I feared some remnant of Brasso being hidden in one of the many grooves and curves. It took only the slightest bit of it to soil the pure white webbing, and every square millimeter of metal was cleaned with it. I had used the precision of a brain surgeon when I worked on it, and then checked it a hundred times after I had finished. But there was always a chance that I missed something. A second set of eyes might find it, but they didn't. Both Tompkins and Larry scrutinized my sword, and like everything else, it too was fine.

Next on was the waist plate, and with it the fear that there was now the potential to get careless and bump metal to metal as it was carefully placed near my sword and scabbard and then over and into my belt buckle. I thought I would die as the two guys worked to pull it all off.

It was now time for the toilet tissue. I had Tompkins start wrapping it around all exposed pieces of brass, begging him to be careful not to let the fibers fly to create lint as he worked. I could see he took his time, and was providing all the care one could muster to do it right. He wrapped my breastplate, waist plate, belt buckle, scabbard, and sword until they were nothing but toilet paper mummies. Without bending at all, Larry and Tompkins helped me into the shoes I would wear over to McAlister, one keeping me balanced and the other putting them on and tying my laces. I would carry my cuts shoes and put them on once inside. I wasn't about to risk getting them scuffed or dirty walking over.

I was down to my last item, and well within my time schedule. I had wanted to finish at 1730, giving me more than ample time for problems found and the walk over. The only down side was that once in the Field House, I would have to stand, and wait. To be too early would not be wise. To be late would be a disaster.

Tompkins placed a ring of toilet paper around my head, and then brought my shako to rest on top of it. I knew it would be soaked with sweat before long, but considered the paper a better choice to absorb the moisture than my shako. Tompkins checked for flaws, and then wrapped the brass of my shako in tissue. With the brand new gloves in my hands while still wearing some old ones, I was ready. I was nervous and edgy and was set to leave. Larry agreed to walk with me over to pin the cuts numbers on us that he had made and to help carry the other things. Tompkins handed him a bag I had packed with emergency items such as toilet paper, Brasso, shoe polish, a shine cloth, and tape. I just knew something was going to happen on the way over, and I didn't want to be scrambling for what I needed, even though I knew that the others would probably be bringing the same stuff. But it was a long haul back to 4th if something was needed that couldn't be found.

As I moved towards the door, I asked Tompkins if he wanted to come. He declined, saying he would if I needed him, but for right now he preferred a bit lower profile. I understood fully. I shook his hand and thanked him, and he wished me luck.

It hadn't rained in days, so there were no puddles to fear. But there was dust and lint everywhere. Bugs were flying, and if they couldn't bite me, they would at least try to get me some cuts. I even imagined some stupid bird laughing as he pulled up from a bombing run. The real problem was the heat. It made you sweat fast, and sweat made clothes stain, and brass tarnish. I walked at a careful pace, trying not to kick up any kind of debris or get heated. Already nervous, the latter was hard to avoid.

I entered McAlister to find several of the other roaches already there. A few of them were balls of tissue like I was. Others had nothing at all over their brass. I had wondered if it was a mistake to wrap everything. The extra handling brought the added risk of creating a flaw, or causing lint or fibers to fly from the tissue onto the black felt of my shako. It was a gamble by both those who did and those who didn't. I guess I was never comfortable with the 'just do nothing' approach.

We all stood and passed the time in nervous reviews of procedure and last minute checks of items that were exposed. Rontelli soon arrived and we worked together to make sure all of the bases were covered. He was nervous and so was I, and we wished it would just start. We were ready and wanted to get it over with. Larry made us stand side by side, and using "T" pins, he attached the cuts numbers to our shirts in the exact same locations. The cards looked great. The 7 and 8 were perfect. Admit it or not, Larry was into this, and really cared if I made it or not.

At 1800, I could see some of the others unwrapping their brass, and I felt compelled to do the same. Cuts would start in fifteen minutes, and I wanted to be ready. Larry put on a fresh set of gloves from the bag and began the slow process of removing the paper. He was careful, and more serious about the work than ever. He knew it was down to the no-shit final hour. There was an obvious lack of humor in his voice, and he had an uncharacteristic deep attitude of concern.

After unwrapping all the brass, Larry carefully used several large pieces of masking tape to brush for lint. He lightly brushed my shoes with the toilet paper as a check for dust, then spent the remaining moments inspecting me as if he was sure he could find something wrong. But he couldn't, and that made me even more confident. I knew he wanted to find something, anything, and the fact that he could produce nothing told me I was as ready as one could get. He smiled and wished me luck as the old Drill called for us to form up. I thanked him sincerely, and then carefully moved to my place beside Rontelli. The preparations were over. Night number thirteen was upon us, and with it our first round of cuts.

The old Drill made us stand at attention, but told us to save our energy and not to brace. They explained the process would be short for some, long for others. Inside the auditorium, the old Drill had set up various stations, each of which would be used to inspect and test for certain skills. We would spend ten minutes at each station, and would progress through two at a time. On this night they would start at the front with roaches number one and two, and then work their way back. The following evening they would start at the back and work forward. In total, everyone would have to wait the same amount of time. You were allowed to check yourself, make any final adjustments, and even have another roach help you while you waited. But there would be no getting out of line, and while not checking or adjusting, we were to stand at attention. With twenty-two roaches left, the last two would go through after standing in line for almost two hours, and we were told that would be easy compared to the night of the performance when we would arch swords for over four hours. Despite those words of assurance, the immobile wait would be a real challenge on top of what we would find inside.

For the first two in line, it was show time. The doors opened and closed as they walked through. We stood still, and waited in silence as the first few minutes passed. Number three and four roaches were the first to move as they did one last check of each other, probably realizing their time to make corrections would soon be gone. I thought it wasted motion, since there was little now that could be done except make something worse. If Rontelli wanted to check as our time approached, I would make it clear not to touch my brass. It was too late. I was confident everything was in place.

Time passed, and I seemed to be on a constant plain of anxiety. Roaches three and four moved through the doors, and I watched as five and six directly in front of us gave each other a last minute check. Time was eaten up as I watched them go through the motions. Before they were through, it appeared that they were no better off, and that their shirt tucks weren't quite as tight. As their time on the starting line expired and they moved through the doors, I wasted little time in getting straight with Rontelli.

"Listen Ted, we are as ready as we ever will be. No need for any further checking. We have our shit together better than anyone. Let's just go in there and kill 'em."

Rontelli smiled, then said, "We're gonna tear this thing up. I was thinking the same thing, no need to adjust. We're in sync. Don't change a thing."

I smiled at our paralleled minds, and let the satisfaction of the coincidence settle in as confidence. I stood and stared at the door, then prayed for strength of mind, and that this was a day where I would at least be able to perform my best, which I knew was better than most.

The doors opened, and we were commanded to follow. I felt as if I should be marching, but a member of the old Drill led us somberly to the far side of the court, where we saw roaches five and six helping each other adjust their gear as we walked forward. We were told to stand and wait at a line that was part of the basketball court, and we stood and braced as five and six finished getting themselves together.

"Are you guys finished," asked one of the old Drill.

"Yes, sir." responded six.

"Good! Move on quickly to the next station," he then said.

"Roaches seven and eight, please come forward to this line," said Ken Lindsey.

We moved forward and stood with our toes on the line. Bert Randolph walked forward, and stood in front of me and Lamar Jordan seemed to follow him with a clip board. I kept my eyes straight ahead, and braced my ass off. I could tell two others had moved over towards Rontelli, but I quickly focused in on Randolph as he started to look me over.

"Good afternoon, roach number eight," said Randolph.

"Good afternoon Sir," I said.

"Two cuts Mr. Jordan," said Randolph, "Did I ask you to talk, number eight? Huh? No I didn't. Keep your mouth shut unless I tell you to talk. Hear me. Hear me!"

I said nothing, and Randolph just smiled. He then looked with detail at my breastplate, and after staring at it for a good ten seconds he flipped it over to look at the back. He had gloves on, and pulled it off the sling webbing to inspect the back of it. He looked it over good, and then placed it on the floor without a word. He then went to my waist plate, looked at the front of it, and then slowly removed it. He stood there and looked over every square inch of the two brass pieces, and then moved along the webbing. He draped it across my shoulder, and then went for my sword. He removed it from the scabbard, and I heard Rontelli's inspector say, "Cut" very loudly. Randolph looked my sword over, holding it inches from his eyes as he moved up and down the blade, and spun it in his hand as he looked over the handle. He laid it down on the floor, then pulled my scabbard from its sling, and looked it over with the same precision. He then picked up a clean white rag and wiped both the sword and scabbard firmly, then looked long and hard at the rag for whatever he could find. He found nothing.

"Ready with the sword," asked Chip Walsh, who was inspecting Rontelli.

"Yeah, guess so," said Randolph as he looked closely at my scabbard.

He reached down and picked up my sword and scabbard, then held the two items up beside Rontelli's that Walsh held.

"They don't match," said Walsh.

"Three cuts to each," said Randolph.

"Bullshit," I thought to myself. They said we didn't have to have matching swords.

""Three cuts is a lot," said Walsh to Rontelli. "You guys not have time to get matched swords?"

Rontelli didn't answer. I just stood there pissed, but didn't show it. Randolph then removed and inspected my sling, then after throwing it too over my shoulder, he moved on to my belt. He loosened the buckle from the back, and then pulled it out through the loops of my pants. He held it close, and looked at the buckle first, then the belt tips and webbing. He then removed the buckle and looked on the inside, and explored every nook and cranny. I noted the speed and precision with which he looked. He was moving fast, but was thorough. I supposed that after years of looking at knobs, he could spot a problem in an eye blink. But he said nothing, then put the buckle back on the belt, and draped it across my other shoulder.

I could hear a lot of unnerving yelling across the court, but remained focused and kept me eyes glued straight ahead. I had worked my ass off not to get cuts on my equipment or performance, I certainly didn't want any for looking around.

Randolph next went for my shako, and spent nearly 45 seconds on it as he twisted and turned it to see the noteworthy items. Near Rontelli I heard Walsh say, "Cut" again. Randolph then finished with the shako, then plopped it back on my head, both backwards and crooked. He grabbed the items from my shoulders, and then handed them to Jordan to hold, while he proceeded to remove my shirt. He looked at it inside and out, especially inside. He eyed the seams, looked in the pockets, and looked at the button threads. He looked at my pants, and then as best I could tell, was on his hands and knees, looking closely at my shoes. He checked the front and back, and on the sides. I couldn't tell for sure, but I felt him doing something with the laces, probably making sure I put polish on the tongue. He then got up and unsnapped my pants, and pulled them to my knees. It surprised me, but I didn't flinch. Randolph looked on the inside at the seams as they were piled down around my knees. He then flipped the tag on my underwear, and said, "Hanes, size 32."

"Yep," replied Walsh, whom I could not see.

"Time?" said Randolph.

"One minute," said Lindsey, "better get em' movin'."

"I've seen enough," said Randolph.

"Me too," said Walsh.

"OK, roaches," said Lindsey, "get your stuff back on, and move it, or you'll be late to your next station."

I reached down and picked up my shirt and put it on. With lightning speed I pulled my pants up, gave myself a shirt tuck, and then put my belt back on that was held and presented by Jordan. I then moved swiftly as I put on my sling, waist plate, and breastplate.

"Take enough time to get them on right," said Lindsey, "You don't want them in the wrong place when you go through the rest of the stations."

I agreed without saying anything, and made sure things were right as I continued to work fast. I could hear roaches nine and ten being led up behind us as I was turning my shako around and getting it back on correctly.

"You two look each other over. Carefully!" said Carl Andrews, who I had not seen until now, but made nothing of spotting him.

"Make sure the other has his stuff on right," said Randolph. "But hurry!"

We turned towards each other, and I knew exactly what was important. Our breastplates and slings had to be just right, or we would be in big trouble doing our sword manual. Everything was routed correctly and in their proper positions with Ted, and he confirmed that I was fine just as Kevin Grant started yelling at us from across the floor that we were late.

"You slow pokes are gonna get a cut for every five seconds you are late if you don't hurry!" he screamed.

Rontelli and I took off in a full run as we moved to get over to the next station. There was a huge crowd of old Drill at this stop, but Kevin Grant grabbed us and pulled us into position on the side of the court. As a formality, he told us that we were to perform our marching series, and he emphasized that he would be the one and only commander at this station, and in complete control of the series. I knew exactly what that meant. Dave Morris immediately got right in my face, and I looked right through him as I braced my ass off. He just stood there, with me breathing his breath.

"You're gonna fuck up here number eight," said Morris, "I can see it in your face. They give you a hard time over at the personal appearance station? You look flustered."

"The series is," yelled Grant from afar, "the 1980 Junior Sword Drill Series."

"What the hell is this shit?" said Morris. "Your sword's in backwards!"

"Hey Morris, get the hell out of the way," said a voice from behind my head.

"I say again, the series is, the 1980 Junior Sword Drill Series," commanded Grant.

"I'm giving you a cut for your sword being in backwards number 8, now stop what you're doing and fix it."

"Move out of the way Morris," a voice yelled loudly from behind my head.

"Commence series on my command," said Grant.

"Fix the fuckin' sword number eight, or I'm gonna give you another cut. Now move!" yelled Morris.

"Your gonna screw him up, man. Get out of the way," screamed the voice from behind.

"Forward..." said Grant.

"Stop number eight don't you move!" yelled Morris an inch from the side of my face.

"March!" commanded Grant.

I immediately started marching, in perfect form, in sync with Rontelli.

"Stop number eight," screamed Morris as he jumped up and down beside me as I moved, "I order you to stop. Now! OK, have it your way asshole! A cut for every step! Cut, cut, cut, cut..."

"Five, six, seven, seven, seven,..." said someone as he passed just in front of us, barely missing a collision with me.

"Stop you idiots," screamed a now berserk Morris.

564

We turned with head snaps right on time to start around the circle. Someone was whacking loudly on a clipboard with something, and someone else, other than the still screaming Morris was counting an out of sync cadence loudly. But I had them all tuned out. I was fixed only to my own count, and stride, and the instinctive feeling of my next turn and shako pop when Rontelli and I met at the completion of the circle. I had him in sight, and could see our steps were at least still in sync. I could feel the correctness of where I was, how the steps would work out as we neared each other. We made a perfect turn, and I didn't let the noise from the old Drill's mouths, nor the guy again passing just inches in front of us counting throw me off.

"That's it! That's all you dorks. You're through with Drill," yelled a pissed Bob Fox. "Stop! Stop!"

It was truly all I could do to keep my wits, and keep the old Drill tuned out as I finished the ten steps into the turn where I went left, and Rontelli would split to the right. Someone was right in my ear, making them ring with false counting, but I moved with precision, until I hit my fourteenth step, stopped tilted with my right heel elevated, then stayed motionless for three counts, then went to attention. As usual, I couldn't see Ted as I did my final right face to complete the series. I just stood there, as what seemed like a wall of yelling surrounded me.

But the yelling quickly subsided, and the old Drill disappeared behind me, and I stood there not knowing or hearing a thing. Thirty seconds, one minute, two minutes, I stood there silent, bracing, not moving a muscle. I didn't know if Ted was doing the same, or was somewhere else. Finally, Grant appeared in front of us, just barely in sight, then commanded us to move quickly to the next station. I could see the crowd of old Drill standing where we had started, and waiting like vultures for nine and ten to come. It was the most nerve-racking experience of my life, and I knew without a doubt, not everyone would survive that ordeal.

The old Drill at cuts station 3 were less in numbers than found at station 2, but they shared the common threat of cuts if we didn't get over to them faster. As we ran I felt good about my performance to that point, though I had no idea at all what sort of cuts I had received at the last station. I only knew I hadn't made any obvious mistakes, at least ones I could notice. I reminded myself to stay focused, and to keep my wits about me. I was lucky to have the strength of mind to survive the surprise attack I had just experienced, but I took it as a warning to expect anything at the next station.

Cliff Malone seemed in charge as we arrived, and he quickly showed us just where he wanted us to position ourselves. Andrew Green stepped in front of me, about three feet away, and Emerson Vaughn stood beside him. They stood there so that I could see them, just as another pair of old Drill stood in front of Ted. I gazed a hole through them, resisting all temptation to look around. Cliff Malone then explained in a fashion similar to Grant that he, and he alone was in charge of this 3rd and final cuts station.. I again understood the significance. Green's attention seemed to draw in on me as Malone commanded, "Draw..." and I reached and drew my sword to a half up position. Vaughn was right there with his clipboard, and he placed it on my arm as Green watched closely to see if I moved, which I didn't. Vaughn then laid a pencil on the clipboard, and turned it several ways to see if it would roll. It didn't, and even though I heard the word "Cut" come from near Rontelli, I didn't move a muscle, and the pencil remained stationary. Vaughn removed the pencil and clipboard, and then Green stepped in for a closer look. He seemed to look at everything, including the position of my fingers on the sword. But I kept my mind off of him, and zoomed out, and listened for the next command from Malone.

Green hurried and positioned himself in front of me. Then I heard Malone command, "Swords!" I finished pulling my sword from the scabbard, then held it perfectly arced above my head, then brought it smoothly down to the carry swords position. It felt perfect. Green didn't say a word as he moved in for a closer look.

Malone soon barked another command, "Present...swords!"

In one smooth motion, I raised and twisted my sword, then with a single click, snapped it against both my breastplate and the rim of my shako. My mind made note that the breastplate was now history, but that was expected. I quickly chastised myself for drifting, then zoomed back in. Green and Vaughn moved about me, searching for flaws. They said nothing.

"Carry...swords!" commanded someone standing near Rontelli.

I didn't budge. Didn't even blink. Malone hadn't given the command. Someone near Ted said, "Cut!"

"Carry...swords!" said Malone.

Green and Vaughn moved about, but said nothing.

"Arc...swords," Malone fired.

I snapped my sword back up to a full arch, and I could see Green moving in close to inspect. I could feel that my fingers were correctly positioned on the handle, and that I had a good "cheerio" on my left hand. Vaughn placed his clipboard beneath my hand, matching it to the butt of the sword and the hilt, making sure that the angle was parallel to the floor. I concentrated, and tried not to move a finger, or flinch. It shook me a bit when Green said "Cut" and Vaughn pulled the clipboard away to write it down. But I didn't budge. Just wondered what the cut was for. They continued to look me over, and then Green stood directly in front of me, probably to check that the blade bisected my body.

"Carry...swords," commanded Malone, and I immediately snapped it back down to carry position, and was again inspected.

"Cut," came a voice from near Rontelli.

"Cunt," I thought I heard Green say.

"Return..." ordered Malone, and I raised my sword to half up position, then dropped the blade over perfectly to meet my thumb and index finger that collared the top of the scabbard. It was a perfect hit on the tiny opening, and I let the tip slide in several inches."

"Cut," I heard someone say near Rontelli.

I stood like a statue, peering in a laser stare across into the stands in front of me, keenly tuned to where I was, and ignoring the uncontrollable thought that it was almost over.

Green and Vaughn moved quickly in search of a mistake, but again, could find none.

"Swords!" commanded Malone, and I pushed the rest of the sword on into the scabbard, then glided my hands down by my side.

I watched as Green, Malone and the others walked behind us, and I could hear them softly discussing what they had seen, but couldn't make anything of value out of it. We stood silently as the noise from station number 2 subsided, and I knew we were nearly through. I could only fight to hold back my smile.

"Dismissed!" commanded Green.

I didn't move.

"Dismissed!" commanded Malone.

I turned to get instructions, and a member of the old Drill escorted us quickly to the door, saying "Good job, we'll see you again tomorrow!" as he shuffled us away.

Rontelli and I moved through the doors into the corridor that surrounded the auditorium, then stopped and looked at each other. I was ready to celebrate, feeling pretty good about my performance. But I could see that Ted was not in the same frame of mind. He seemed disgusted, and happy to be free from the pressure of the testing.

"I'm glad to have that behind me," I said.

"I wish I had a few parts to do over again," said Ted.

"Why? Did something go wrong?"

"Yes! Brain lock on my part. I blew it a couple of times in there."

"So did I."

"I heard them giving out cuts, and I know I got at least two or more for every one you got," said Ted.

"What happened?"

"I don't know. I was trying to stay focused on what I was doing, and I must have missed something. It was hard to know what to do sometimes."

"Yeah, they did everything they could to throw us off."

"I feel like I blew it, man."

"Oh no. Don't say that. They were laying it on pretty tough in there. I'm sure there will be a lot of cuts handed out before the day is over. Don't worry about it."

"You did great, John. I hope you did exceptionally great. Because if the number of cuts you received are the norm, I'm up shit creek."

"You're alright! I'm surprised we both didn't get more."

Rontelli and I moved through the corridor towards the exit. We knew better than to go back to where the others were still waiting to enter the cuts process. Unlike the other Nights, we were to just walk back to the barracks and wait for the others to finish. Rontelli was upset, convinced he had blown it big time. I wasn't sure what to think. Even though I got less than him, I still had received several cuts that I knew of for certain. But we had nothing to gage it all on. How could we know if we were above or below average? There was no way to tell.

Rontelli left me as we passed his battalion, and I walked on feeling bad about both his and my cuts. But deep inside, I was satisfied that I had done as well as anyone considering the conditions. The old Drill tried everything imaginable to throw us off. It was tough, but I had every confidence that all of us had been treated the same. It seemed impossible to have been perfect.

I walked into my room and just sat at my desk. Several guys came by, but I was in no mood to talk. I was tired, both mentally and physically. I had been on my feet for hours, and I was stressed out to the point of being emotionally drained. The thought that it would all start again the next day was a source of discomfort, but I was ready to see an end to the ordeal of the 14 Nights. I only prayed that the end would be a happy one.

I called Cindy and spoke with her in a tone of wear and tear. I wanted to lie down in my rack and find her there to hold. But she wasn't with me, and her voice was the only serenity I would find. There was work to be done to prepare for the second and final round. All that would be accomplished in the remainder of the evening was the careful removal, cleaning, and storage of the items that would be used again the next evening. The need to study was nothing compared to what I had to do to be ready. In 24 hours I would have the answer to the question I had pondered for nearly two years. I would work hard until the effort would no longer count.

CHAPTER 41

The next day brought no feedback on our performance, as the old Drill was completely silent about the first night of cuts. They had nothing to gain by commenting, and could very well establish either a false sense of security or doubt. They had dropped their arms-length attitude towards us, and were treating us like normal human beings as they encouraged us to stay focused and give it all we had in those final moments. The time to weed us out with threats and hard times were gone. The mark of a pencil was our greatest threat, and there was nothing else we feared more.

I used every minute of free time to get my equipment back in order. It was a busy day as classes were a real struggle and Tuesday afternoon drill with the Corps was a complete waste of time. If there was one thing I didn't need, it was time to practice Corps level marching and sword manual.

I moved swiftly towards the showers after coming off the parade ground, and once again started the delicate procedure of putting on more brand new undergarments, freshly pressed shirt and pants, and perfectly formed and polished pieces of brass. I had worked my sword and shako back to perfection during the day, and had Tompkins look them over while I was in the shower. There was little to be explained as my squire and Larry worked to prepare me for battle. They knew the process as well as I did, and their assistance and understanding helped to ease the tension. They worked like surgeons as they carefully moved, inspected, and placed each item on me. I felt calmer than the day before, yet stayed attune to every detail of the process.

I felt an air of experience as I walked over again with Larry to McAlister, yet felt just as stupid as I looked like one big roll of toilet tissue. Time in the dressing room seemed to move well, and there was slightly less tension, as we all knew what we faced.. The few conversations that took place were vague assessments of the previous night's performances. There were some who were confident, and some who were worried. No one was sure of anything.

At 1800 there was real movement to get one last look from our partners, and the missing tension among us returned. We were getting close to the end, and everything would be over with in less than three hours. It was an intense moment as all we had worked for was coming down to the wire.

At 1814 the old Drill formed us up, and spent little time explaining what was to happen. Their only significant information to pass on was that we were allowed to return to the barracks after our trip through the cuts circuit if we chose to, but within minutes of the last two roaches going through, the results would be tallied and the names of the 14 successful aspirants would be revealed. We were to be back at the Field house at exactly 2100.

The first two through the doors were from the short end of the platoon, and I felt lucky to be a mid-sized guy near the middle. I would have a longer wait than the night before, but it would not be the forever duration that one and two were facing.

The pairs moved steadily through the doors at ten-minute intervals. I went through sword manual and marching moves in my mind as I waited, and tried not to think of what I might have forgotten with my personal appearance. Like the night before, there was little that could be done at that point.

After numbers nine and ten walked through the doors, I looked at Rontelli and confirmed that we were ready. He was nervous, and I encouraged him by saying we had it made. He smiled, but lacked the confidence he had the night before. I wanted to tell him many things to get him psyched again. But there was not enough time to even begin. The doors to the auditorium opened, and it was time to sink or swim.

A member of the old Drill led us over to the personal appearance cuts station, and there waiting was the same group from the night before, except this time Chip Walsh inspected me, and Bert Randolf inspected Rontelli. They tore into us with speed, knowing they had a limited amount of time to seek and find the evidence they needed to prove us not worthy of Sword Drill. I found comfort in the consistency from the day before as Walsh inspected my equipment in the exact same order that Randolph had. Near Rontelli I heard Randolph say, "Cut" twice, but Walsh said nothing as he worked through my gear. I had a weird feeling of confidence. I knew my equipment was as good as it could get, but my suspicions of the selection process being political told me that I would not get away with getting zero cuts. I had checked and rechecked everything, and then had Larry and Tompkins confirm and corroborate my micro inspection. I knew Tompkins was a whiz, and that he would rather French kiss a rattlesnake than let a flaw go undetected. I had the confidence. I was borderline cocky. I was so sure my equipment was perfect, that a cut would have to be political. Piece by piece, I was stripped down to my essentials. Walsh seemed intent on finding something, anything. If I learned one thing that day, it was that politics had nothing to do with the selection process in the Junior Sword Drill. Other than a few complementing observations, Chip Walsh never opened his mouth.

We again had to bust ass to carefully put ourselves back together. They tried to rattle us with continuous threats of cuts, but I refused to take a step until I was sure my equipment was where it was supposed to be. They could cut me all they wanted for time, but I was not going to rush and cause a disaster at the next two stations. They could threaten until they were blue in the face.

I took my free ride through personal appearance as a shot to further boost my confidence. Like station 1, the same crew was back for station 2, except I now had Rontelli's inspector from the previous night, and he had mine. They were again locked and loaded with exceptional distractions, but I was fixed on the instructions of the station commander. The series was nothing more than a simple matter of procedure. I knew the sequence like a razor knows how to cut. I wasn't going to do it right; I was determined to do it perfectly.

Rontelli would have to deviate if we were to err.

Threats and noises filled the air at the command to start, and the bodies of old Drill members went by in constant near misses. They presented wildly different cadence as they marched in view and counted loudly. But they were wasting their time with me. They had nothing to do with my agenda, and I knew it. I ignored the word "Cut" which was said many times. I didn't know who said it or why, but as far as I was concerned, it was all bullshit. I was prepared, and in full execution without flaw. At least it felt that way. The only indication that there was something wrong was seeing Ted slightly out of step as we rounded the circle, and slow on where he was supposed to be. I knew that I had not faltered, and made no effort to correct. He must have lost it somewhere. He adjusted somehow, and amid a shower of the words "Cut," we managed to make a fair turn together. From there it went perfect from what I could tell, right up until we turned away from each other, and I had no way to tell from that point. I moved with the rhythm of a Timex, and stopped and made the final turn with a feeling of a job well done. The noise died instantly, and I waited in a trance for some further command. I felt like a machine, and it was a good feeling.

A member of the old Drill was soon in our ear to move us over to the final station. I could see Andrew Green now positioned and waiting for Ted, and Dan Trout was there for me. I guess I should have been nervous being the center of attention with the Regimental Commander. Fuck him and his Cadet Colonel rank. I just zoomed out the instant I got on line, and from that point hung on every word that the station commander, Cliff Malone, said. Trout had his trusty clipboard, and moved around me as he checked the angles and position of alignment. He made a real and significant effort to make me lose my shit. I was surprised as I just stayed calm, and unnerved. The old Drill yelled at deafening levels, and someone even dropped a metal folding chair on the floor right behind us. I thought of them as newly crowned flame-on corporals. Just noise. The real bite was in Malone's commands. He was the only sound that mattered. Like the eye of a hurricane, I stood there, calm, surrounded by turmoil, moving my sword with the strike of a cottonmouth, flawless in execution, focused on the kill. My confidence was real. I never once had to reassure myself. I was on the mark, alert, and no one could thwart my resolve, or overwhelm my determination. Malone bellowed out the requirements, and one after the other, I moved to execute. It seemed so quick, so short, such a rapid test for something that held so much significance. But with a word from Malone it was all over. The fourteenth and final night was complete, and my once in a lifetime chance to make the Junior Sword Drill was now history. Try harder meant nothing. No further effort could be made.

We were dismissed and led to the door as the next two roaches were shuffled to the line. I felt a lump in my throat as I walked. It was really over.

Once in the corridor, we were abandoned quickly with few words, and Rontelli and I stood and stared at each other. I had always thought that this would be a moment of great celebration, but for my partner, it was one filled with despair.

"I blew it," said Ted.

"Of course you didn't," I replied.

"I did. I must have gotten a hundred cuts."

"They were yelling Cut right and left! What makes you so sure they were giving them to you."

"Because I was fucking up."

I stopped talking, and took in Rontelli's seriousness.

"How bad?"

"Hard to say. I just lost it a couple of times. They were distracting the hell out of me."

"They were loud alright. Nerve-racking. But don't sweat it. We all had to go through that same shit. It took everything I had to ignore them and stay focused."

"But you did, and I didn't. I'm happy for you, but I'm worried, man."

"You'll be alright. I bet ya. Five bucks says you make it."

"You think so, huh."

"Five bucks, douche bag. Shake on it. Everybody else has to go through the same thing, and they will get their share of cuts too."

Ted seemed to feel better, and he shook my hand. Though I couldn't see him throughout the testing, and I heard the word "Cut" come from his direction many times, but I was sure he was going to be fine. If his personal appearance was like mine, which it was supposed to be, then he was probably ahead of the game. He would make it. I would make it. We both were in there. I was certain.

We walked down the corridor and returned to the dressing room where we found a waiting crowd of roaches who had completed the circuit. Spirits were both high and low, and there were a thousand questions as to how we did. Self-analysis flowed like water, and feelings of frustration were very apparent. Everyone talked of cuts being handed out in massive doses, and the conversation worked well to ease the worries of Rontelli. It took him from scared to concerned. I thought of my own experience, and I didn't recall such a large portion of the black marks. I was zoomed out. I wasn't paying the old Drill any attention. I subconsciously heard the word "Cut" said many times, but couldn't say if they were directed at me. I had an underlying feeling of confidence since I just couldn't remember making any mistakes. But I just didn't know, and the information void made my mind race, and I too soon felt the anxiety. The talk was unnerving, and tension in the room was high. Some felt worse than others, and like me, some had no idea. Wild guesses and gut feelings were all we had.

Two more roaches soon entered the room, and the game of a thousand questions started another round. It was a frenzy to find someone who had done worse, and there were plenty of negative critiques to be found. I listened passively, then moved over to a metal folding chair against the wall. I sat and felt the relief of being off of my feet, and I could feel the tension in my body take a turn for the better. I again noted that it was all over, but the reality just wouldn't sink in. My mind reserved the right not to let go until I knew if I had made it or not. There were others yet to finish, and I was too tired to sit there and pass the time discussing and beating the possibilities to death.

Roaches three and four soon came through the door, and I could see the strain among us getting worst. The latest to arrive were just happy to have it over with, while the early birds had moved on to ponder the outcome, and had twisted the results through a myriad of scenarios. They couldn't wait for one and two to make it through, and when they finally did, they were mobbed with more than their fair share of the unrest.

It took a while for the group to gain its composure. We were never loud, just quietly in a state of turmoil. Some paced, some whispered, some gestured as they relived their experience to others. All were worried. It was an emotional free-for-all. Some had left for a while, most never had the chance. For Rontelli it was an hour of pure hell.

At exactly 2100, two members of the old Drill entered the dressing room, and asked us to put back on our shakos, and to move out to the main floor. I thought I would die. Fear grabbed us all, and in what seemed like a walk reserved for those on death row, we moved to the center of the huge, nearly dark, and deathly quiet McAlister Field House. The old Drill seemed serious and somber. They probably saw little of the good in what they now had to do. While they knew they were about to make fourteen dreams come true, they were also about to place a dagger in the hearts of six others. It was a profound moment. They had been there.

"Members of the 1980 Junior Sword Drill Platoon," said Richard Kraft. "You have much to be proud of. You have completed your journey. You have all been successful in completing the Fourteen Nights. This is something you can be proud of for the rest of your days. I congratulate each of you on this accomplishment. But the purpose of the Nights is steadfast. It is to determine who is best capable of shouldering the task of honoring my senior class as we celebrate receiving the most prized possession that this school will provide to us. The ring. We have taken this selection process seriously, just as I hope you, the Class of 1980, will take the performance. A year ago, the highest of standards were presented for us to meet, and we ask nothing less of those who follow.. Only fourteen of you have met that standard."

There was a moment of chilling silence.

"The cut sheets have been tallied and triple checked. I will now read to you the cuts numbers of those who have made it. You are the new members of the 1980 Junior Sword Drill. Please remain silent. I emphasize this. Remain silent. If your number is not called, you will be dismissed, and are to immediately leave this place, never to return. Are there any questions?"

There was complete silence, and the tension was unbearable. I felt my heart throb, and found it difficult to breathe. I concentrated as hard as I could, and locked my mind in to listen for the number eight. "The 1980 Junior Sword Drill is as follows: Numbers 1, 3, 4, 5, 6, 8, 9, 13, 14, 16, 18, 19, 20, and 22."

I heard it! I sighed with my eyes closed, and teeth gritting. I made it. I struggled to contain myself, and then quickly sobered at the sound of a slight groan through the silence.

"If your cuts number was not called, then listen carefully. About...face!"

I heard the sound of squeaking shoes turning on the floor, and the feeling of someone moving beside me. Rontelli!

"Dismissed."

The silence was broken by the sound of footsteps walking away, then out of the door until there was again silence. I trembled as the quiet moments passed.

"I congratulate each of you," said Kraft. "You may now celebrate!"

The McAlister Field House roared as we all jumped and screamed and hugged each other. It was over. We had done it. I had done it. My dream had come true. I was a member of the Junior Sword Drill.

"OK guys, settle down! Settle down! You can raise hell back in the barracks, as I'm sure they will be waiting for you. I want you to form up now. This will be the first time you will ever be in your performance position. I'm sure I don't have to show you where to get. Now move it."

We moved quickly. I was now number 6.

"I will now tell you at this point who your Voice is," said Kraft as we settled into our positions. "After the sheets were tallied, we were very pleased with the result. I'm proud to say that the Voice of the 1980 Junior Sword Drill is Roach Stall."

As the cheers rang out for Baxter, I couldn't think of a more deserving guy to receive the honor. He caught more hell than any of us, yet remained solid in his quest. He was truly a rock, and a premium image of what Sword Drill is all about. We were all happy for him, and smothered him with a loud recognition of his title.

"When we pass your respective barracks," continued Kraft over the noise, "just fall out and go through your sally port and kiss your letter. It's your night from there on. Forward march."

We marched out of the Field House, and then with a command of "Double time" we were running, heading back towards the battalions. We were running with our feet barely on the ground. I don't know who started it, but we went into our chant of, "We love, Sword Drill!" It was the strongest I had ever yelled it. It was the best it had ever felt. I howled it with passion, right up until I saw a roach walking alone and silent over on the sidewalk. I almost choked, and the sound of the whole platoon took a turn for the worse. I thought about Ted, and looked to see if it was he, but I couldn't tell. It hurt. I suddenly felt a paradox of emotions, and I struggled to keep chanting. I knew he was hurting with an almost unbearable pain, and it was hard to remember I was supposed to be exuberant over my own success. I fought to forget it as a group peeled off to run into the massive and exploding cheers in their battalion. I would celebrate the victory, but it was hard to forget Rontelli's defeat.

The quadrangle was loaded with cadets as I came through the

sally port. I could see "O," "R," and "T" companies alive and kicking, and "N" was silent. The roar was deafening as I ran across the quad and down the line of knobs that were standing in their bathrobes and uniforms, all arcing brooms or transom sticks. The whole company was there, and I was barely able to kiss the R when I was mobbed and then hoisted up in the air by the upperclassmen. The cheering and laughing was blaring, then a gush of water hit us all from above, and its shock did nothing to douse the noise or excitement. The R Company jinx had been broken. There was much to celebrate. It was a huge victory for my class, my company, my battalion, and me. I could barely comprehend as hundreds of guys congratulated me, and it just went on for what seemed like forever. They carried me around the quad a few times, then up the stairs into Rosellini and Burn's room, where they beat the hell out of me as they showed a genuine pride in the conquest. It was a win for us all, and I marveled at their sincere involvement. Someone produced a beer, and they held me down as Rosellini tried to pour it down my throat, claiming they were going to bust me, and that the effort was all for naught. I laughed madly as the brew spewed everywhere, and I loved every second of what was happening to me.

Over in 3rd Battalion, F Company was silent. Cadet First Sergeant Theodore Rontelli sat in his dark room alone, and tried not to hear the noise of the celebration outside as his tears stained the breastplate he labored for hours to perfect. Sword Drill was now a painful part of his past.

CHAPTER 42

At 2300 taps blew, and things finally calmed down enough so that I could call Cindy. She was ecstatic with the news, and claimed she never had a doubt I would make it. She then made a point that she hoped my priorities would soon be reordered so that time with her would be on the increase. I told her that other than the hundreds of hours needed to learn the performance and catch up on grades, I was available. She didn't think it was funny.

The next day, the old Drill once again got serious with us. There were no threatening tones or intimidation, only stern warnings that time was of the essence. The delay during the Nights had robbed us of precious time to learn and perfect our performance, and there wasn't a minute to lose in getting started.

The first order of business was to elect a commander, and the old Drill immediately pulled us together for the vote in an attempt to ward off any opportunities for politics to play a part. They emphasized that this was not a time to pick a good ol' boy, but that we needed to concentrate on someone who could organize and control a group of guys who were all used to being in charge. It was a position loaded with work and responsibility, and one that was sure to catch hell from Jenkins Hall. The new Drill was full of great guys, any one of whom could be considered for the spot. But the one guy who seemed made for the role was Jack Capragetti, M Company First Sergeant. He was intelligent, calculated, and normally soft spoken. Even in his past positions of power as Company Clerk, Battalion Clerk, and First Sergeant, he had performed with excellence, and was liked by nearly everyone who knew him, which was unusual for someone who held such authority. He was perfect for the job, and after he was elected, it was immediately clear the right choice had been made.

Capragetti didn't need much convincing to realize we were starting with an urgent situation. He knew we would have to fast track our education in order to make a decent performance on Parents Day, but that he also had a bunch of guys that had been on campus for weeks and were hammered from the stress of the Nights. He called us all together that afternoon and posed a question to us. It was simple, yet one that carried a huge hidden liability. "Is our goal to have a perfect performance?" he asked. There were a few who spoke right up with an affirmative answer, but Capragetti quickly dismissed their rapid responses.

"You have elected me as your commander, and I know a perfect performance is my goal, but I have to know that it's really yours too. But you must realize just what you are committing to, and understand the price of such a desire. A perfect performance means practicing often with lots of focus. Kraft says I can expect to see many of you lose a large part of your resolve, having obtained the goal of making the Drill. We can do this anyway you guys want, but if you so choose to go for perfection, you must understand that we will be practicing day and night. So consider your answers carefully. Are there any comments?"

"Yes," said Thomas Karl. "I, for one, have no question in my mind. Even if we do have to work at it around the clock, I want people to remember that the Class of 1980 was the best there ever was. You guys all know that there hasn't been a perfect performance that anyone can remember."

"I don't want to approach this thing half-assed," said Baxter Stall. "Either we do it right, or not do it at all."

"Yes, but is there anyone willing to talk about the reality of this decision," said a sobering Lu Chin. "I want what you guys want also. But I think we all need to know what we're committing to. Some of us have other commitments, and my grades have already suffered some significant damage. Tell us Jack. What do you see is required to achieve a perfect performance?"

"First, we must work with the old Drill to learn their performance. We then have to create a unique change or addition to the performance that will make it our own unique series. After that it's just a matter of doing it over and over, perfecting and fine-tuning. There's a lot to do."

"What sort of schedule will this require?" asked Gregg Alston.

"I would guess about every spare minute we have between now and Parents Day," replied Capragetti.

"Not all of ESP!" said Cedrick Middleton with concern.

"No, they won't run that long. Kraft has already explained that it's best to run through the performance only one or two times each practice. I think that would require at least three to four short practices a day."

There was a silence of reality in the room.

"That is a lot," said Ed Peagler. "Do you think that much is really necessary, even to get it perfect?"

"If you want to make sure we can do this thing even in our sleep, then it's not a schedule filled with excess. This is why I asked the question. It requires 100% out of each of you. If one of the fourteen is not in agreement, then there's no need to even start with such a commitment."

"I guess this is what the nights were all about," I said, finally throwing in my two cents. "I guess I always thought the old Drill was full of shit when they would preach to us about the commitment. Maybe now I see that they weren't."

"This is not an organization for those with other priorities," said Capragetti. "I know that all of you have other things pulling at you, and this is just going to make them pull that much harder. It wasn't our fault that the Nights were stopped, but the burden is still on us to perform. I can't make the commitment for you. We all have to want it."

The discussions continued as Capragetti tried to make the situation realistic. As much as my grades were suffering, and as badly as I wanted to be with Cindy, there was still no question about the route I wanted to take. Even so, I was surprised to see the vote go unanimous for the pursuit of perfection.

We all agreed to practice four times a day. This included early in the morning before class, in the afternoon, right after evening mess, and again at 2230. It was an aggressive schedule, and one that would require unimaginable commitment. But this was far different from the 14 Nights. We were now on our own. The old Drill was there only to educate and instruct. It was now our job to make it all work.

Capragetti had taken the liberty of arranging for our first practice that afternoon, and the old Drill immediately started to teach us the performance. They explained that they would start from the beginning, and then day-by-day would add on the pieces until they had introduced the entire performance. This would allow us to practice what we learned in between their instructions.

The old Drill began by explaining that most of the moves in the introduction were there primarily to allow us to get on the floor, calm down, and give our eyes time to get used to the bright spotlights. It would all start as soon as the bagpipes were leaving, with us in our platoon formation in descending order of twos. We would be shoulder to shoulder, half an arm's length behind someone. We were packed together like sardines, and if one guy tipped an inch, so would his neighbor. Our Voice, Baxter Stall, would then command through the darkness, "Sword Drill...Fall In." I could remember well how that piercing voice cut through the silence, and caught the crowd off guard. Stall would then command, "Forward...March," and we would then march forward, and with a stomp, stop with our chins in our chests to protect our eyes as we readied for the introduction of the spotlights. When the lights were on, our heads would lift together with a snap, all based on a barely audible sniff.

The old Drill thought this a good time to explain the "silent count." It was silent only to the audience, but for us, it was a collection of small, nearly undetectable sounds used to start a movement. A sniff or a breathing sequence would become our most important cues, and we had to recognize and distinguish them from noises in the crowd. Missing , or mistaking them would mean a major error.

The next movements started with slow marching that led right into what we would call "statics" that included dress right dress and parade rest. To get us into position to start, we would begin with the distinctive Junior Sword Drill slow march, where our feet would appear to be going through a backwards motion of peddling a bicycle. It was much harder than it looked since keeping one's balance was difficult with the lengthy stand on one foot while moving the other. The steps also involved precise hand movements the old Drill called "clicking," where the hands shifted in from side to side while maintaining brilliant "cheerios." All of this was accomplished with spotlights in our faces, while we braced our asses off, nervous as hell. The difficulty of our task was swiftly becoming apparent.

The old Drill further explained that most of our movements would be symbolic. Each would represent a part of the ring, since the whole purpose of the performance was to honor the seniors as they received their most prized band of gold. Our first movement was to split the platoon and fast march around the giant ring that the seniors would walk through when we arced swords for them after the performance. Once moving straight again, the platoon would again split, this time with each pair turning away from each other by two's, then marching out to just far enough to form a single line with everyone marching in place. After stopping, we would do a series of ripples with our swords utilizing different movements such as arch swords and present swords.

The old Drill then decided they had given us enough to work on, and we wondered how the hell we would ever recall all we had seen. Kraft said we had just clipped the tip of the iceberg, and we knew then it would be a long, hard road to get to performance.

The old Drill stuck around as we struggled with what they had shown us. It was frustrating and tedious, and we all felt like a bunch of dorks. But time soon ran out, and we had to rush to make evening formation. Capragetti informed us that we would practice what we learned immediately following mess. As I ran to make it back to formation, I realized that the days leading up to the performance would be just as busy as they were during the 14 Nights. It wasn't a pleasant thought.

After mess we returned to the McAlister, and worked hard to put the pieces together in the absence of the old Drill. We worked until 2000, and then broke for a two-hour study break. But 2200 came quick, and I had to sprint back to the Field House to avoid being late. The next hour was filled with improved but still-lacking attempts at what we had learned. We had enough time to go through it twice, and then it was another sprint back to 4th to get in before taps.

I called Cindy and we talked about my new schedule. It didn't seem very different to her, but I managed to calm her frustrations with a promise of time together during the weekend. Capragetti said we would only practice Saturday morning and Sunday evening if things went well. If they didn't, he would have a riot on his hands and a blonde haired beauty in his face.

The next morning the alarm went off at 0520, and I cursed as I crawled out of the rack to get into my PT's. I ran while half asleep through the dark towards McAlister, and wondered with my sluggish mind if I was going to survive this schedule until Parents Day. One Drill member slept through his alarm, and we went through the routine three times with a hole in the squad. We made lots of mistakes, as we were all still groggy from the mere six hours of sleep. By the third time through, it seemed to have gained additional structure, even though still riddled with blunders.

I ran back to the battalion with only minutes available to shave, get dressed, and get down to formation. Though not beaten up, I still lacked sleep. I had many classes and a day dominated by a killer schedule. An unclear and tired mind was the last thing I needed.

The fact that it was Thursday meant that we would have drill that afternoon with the rest of the Corps. As usual it seemed a waste. Rack time, study time, you name it. I could think of a dozen more important things to do.

Fifteen minutes after drill was over, I was once again standing in McAlister. We went through our learned series as we waited for the old Drill members to show. It was a definite improvement since we first saw it 24 hours earlier.

Once the old Drill arrived, we started where we had left off. We learned all of the other moves that would encompass "statics." There was dress right dress, drawing our swords, arc swords, and several snaps of our swords to our breastplates on a sniff. The old Drill explained that the snap of the sword up to the breastplate was symbolic, and that it usually indicated that a major movement representing a part of the ring was about to be performed. Our first snap made was to indicate we were about to do a maneuver representing the shank of the ring, which involved a series of very difficult moves.

It took over an hour for the old Drill to show us "the shank," after which they said it was all they would show us for the day. It was indeed enough to add to what we still had to work on, but the old Drill indicated that their biggest reason was that the next moves would be so complex that they wanted to dedicate an entire afternoon to them. They were called the "cartwheel" and the "pinwheel," and they warned us that we would come to both hate and love them both. It was what would make or break a Drill, and drive everyone nuts trying to make them work.

After the old Drill left us, we practiced the new stuff until our time was out, then was again back at McAlister at 1900 and at 2200. Each time we saw a bit more improvement, and tried to forget we still had a long way to go.

At 0520 the alarm was once again ringing, and another day of pushing my tired body through practice and class was upon me. I had the added bonus of having a parade to march in that afternoon, and as the rest of the Corps was changing into leave clothes, I was getting back into some PT's to run over to McAlister. For the first time, I was already getting tired of being a part of Sword Drill.

Only Richard Kraft, Ronnie Bourbon, and Carl Andrews were there from the old Drill. They were dedicated enough to delay their leave plans to show us "the cartwheel" and "the pinwheel," and we couldn't have picked a better three to help us through such a complicated series of moves. It was enough to test both their patience and ours.

The "cartwheel" was demanding, but not impossible. It looked like one big propeller from an airplane that rotated a full turn. But the "pinwheel" was a close quarters move that required balance, timing, and extreme concentration. The movement started with the Sword Drill slow march, and through a series of fancy steps and turns, we would end up in a six-by-six "X" that crossed out the center court circle. The two extra guys where stationed on the perimeter, and they would arc swords at various stages of the movement for show as the "X" rotated inside the circle. The difficulty factor matched the depiction the old Drill had always presented. These were complex moves, and there were more yet to come.

We stopped long enough to go eat dinner, but were back at it at 1900. But before we resumed, Capragetti accurately observed that we had been really busting ass, and concluded we needed a break more than the 2200 practice. Besides, we were going to have a long Saturday morning practice to try to perfect the "pinwheel." After finding not one ounce of resistance, the decision was final. It seemed we were all more than ready to get out of there, and it was probably the most intense I had seen everyone work.

At 1945 Capragetti called it quits, and we almost tore the doors off of McAlister getting out of there. I wasn't sure where everyone else was going, but my destination was clear. I took the fastest shower of my upperclassman career, and my car slid in the gravel of Cindy's apartment's parking lot as I turned in.

At the door Cindy and I grabbed each other with an obsession, and I hoped no one was looking as we tripped and fell to the floor.

"You don't look any different," said Cindy laughing.

"What do you mean?" I asked.

"Other than an extra eighth of an inch of hair, you don't look any more Sword Drill like."

"Ah, but you can't see the lash marks on my back. Our new

commander works us like slaves. We don't sleep and barely get to eat."

"And I thought making Sword Drill was to be a good thing."

"Oh, we're having fun all the time. As a matter of fact, what am I doing here? I could be practicing right now!"

"I'll tackle you if you move towards that door."

"How about I move towards your fridge? Please, tell me you have a beer in it!"

"What are you willing to do for it?"

"Crawl across a mile of broken glass!"

"That's wanting it bad enough. But I'll think of something better that involves me."

Cindy brought out two Miller Lites, and I beamed at the sound of the top being popped, and I drank half the can on the first swig.

"John!"

"I attack. That's all I know. I've been treated like a dog, so I act like one. I'm like an animal."

"I can't wait."

"You know, you're not helping matters here. I'm really a gentleman, and a scholar. I'm doing all I can to be nice, and gentle, and easy. I'm disciplined and in control, even though I'm dying to attack you."

Cindy smiled, stood up, and walked into her room, and I grinned as I followed her. I knew that even with the rotten practice schedule, things weren't all that bad.

But as the evening progressed, that killer schedule made itself known. I was exhausted, and even with my precious freedom in hand, I was falling asleep, and knew that as much as I wanted to be with Cindy, I had to get some rest. With a promise of being back the next day, I left Cindy's that evening at 2300.

At 0730 the buzz from the clock awoke me, but I felt like a million bucks after eight full hours of sleep. In no time I was at the Field House finding all were rested and ready. We started the morning with a run through our series as a warm up, and our fully rested minds made an obvious difference. It was our best ever, and it gave us a proper mindset to tackle the "pinwheel" and fight through the details. It would take many more days of practice to get it right, but we knew that in time it would eventually become perfect.

It was a long morning, but we stayed busy repeatedly working on what we had been taught, trying hard to bring in some of the details. Like cuts, we knew there would be distractions, and that we would have to know the performance backwards and forwards so every movement was natural and automatic.

We called it quits just before noon. We had accomplished much, and there was a new snap to our runs through the sequence. Capragetti gave us 24 hours to do what we pleased, and it was initially hard to comprehend so much time off. What I really needed to do was study, but I was dying to get away from campus and spend some quality time with Cindy.

The blistering heat of summer was gone, and the temperature in the low 80's made it a gorgeous fall day. That afternoon Cindy and I took a boat out to Fort Sumter. We both had been there as kids, but thought it would be cool to go there again as adults. It was where the Civil War had begun, and was a real part of The Citadel's history since cadets actually had fired the first shots. The boat ride was informative, and at times even a bit romantic.

I used an overnight that evening to stay at Cindy's apartment, but the 24 hours I had thought would be lengthy were gone in what seemed like a flash. I never knew just how fast time could fly until I became fixated on spending it with Cindy.

On Sunday the fourteen of us were back in McAlister at 1500, and the "pinwheel" was again number one on our agenda. It was important that we work on it while the old Drill's instructions were still reasonably fresh in our minds. It was so very difficult to do, and it turned out to be the only thing we would work on that afternoon, and Capragetti was soon questioning the time we had taken off.

We practiced the pinwheel again following evening mess, then at 2200 gave it a temporary rest as we made a futile attempt at doing all we had learned as one continuous series. We left the armory that night in frustration as we raced back to our battalions before the gates were locked at 2300. We indeed had a long way to go.

At 0530 we had our Monday morning practice, and at 1500 the old Drill once again joined us in McAlister where we resumed our education at the conclusion of the "pinwheel." We then learned next what would be known as cross rifles. It was a huge rectangular "X," which represented the crossed rifles on the ring. We were then introduced to "the mesh," where the platoon would hard march across the floor in two lines facing each other. Each of the lines swung like two huge gates, first passing through each other and then continuing around like two opposing hands of a clock.

The old Drill then indicated we had reached the closing stages, and proceeded to show us how the introduction portion of the performance would work. We would first position ourselves shoulder-to-shoulder in a line facing The Citadel President's box where he and other distinguished guests would be seated. We would then do a series of our best ripples, and then the MC from the podium would introduce each Drill member's name, rank, company, and hometown to the crowd. The old Drill said that it was a proud moment, curtailed only by the fact that at this point, we would be totally exhausted. As each man was introduced, he would lift his sword in a slow and difficult twist, and then snap it to his breastplate. To an observer, it appeared as one simple, continuous move. But simple it wasn't, and we would later break it down and spend many hours working on it.

The old Drill called it a day at that point, saying that the following afternoon they would show us the final part of the performance. They left us to again struggle with what we had learned, which we indeed fought with over the next 3 practices.

A day later, we were ready to be introduced to the final movements of the performance that started with a series of moves that split the platoon into two halves on opposite ends of the floor. In a tough about face move, we would all go up on one leg and balance ourselves in what was know as the "tabletop." The move got its name since it looks like you are standing there with one leg resting on a table. Once everyone was in place, the lead men on each side would start to mark time, and one at a time we would all join in with a stomp each time a new pair would start. Once we were all marching, we would then silence our footsteps to barely audible, and then Baxter would command "Forward March." This was the last command of the performance. We would move forward, turn at the corner of the basketball court, then turn again when we were near the center, then move out in our two single file lines towards the center with shako pops at each turn. Partners would have to be perfect on that last turn, and we would each take a total of 43 steps. We would then stop, turn, and then go to full arc. That was it. That was the performance.

There in the middle of the Field House we all stood, both old and new Drill, staring in silence at each other. We knew that our work was cut out for us in a big way. The silence was broken by Kraft when he said, "You can make it, if you have the heart!" Our minds locked in on both the encouragement and the doubt of the statement. Of course we would make it. We were no worse, and probably even better than most previous Drills.

"Piece of cake!" said Donny Gant.

"I hear you," said Carl Andrews with a more than obvious lack of enthusiasm. "The true test of whether you are Drill material is just starting. You'll soon think the Nights were easy."

There was a silence as the old Drill stared at us with cold, stern faces. You could tell there was some serious experience behind their position. It had our attention, though I knew there wasn't a member of the 1980 Drill who didn't feel that we could pull this thing off with style.

"You know where we are if you need us," said Richard Kraft.

In silence, broken only by the sound of echoing footsteps, the old Drill walked away. It meant something. They knew there were gremlins out there just waiting for us.

CHAPTER 43

On Wednesday we practiced that morning, afternoon, and evening without a single member of the old Drill present. It was not our first practice alone, but it was the first time we felt as if we were on our own as we struggled to remember what to do. How many steps? Who does the sniff? How do we hold the sword? Questions that were once answered in seconds were now a debate. Though we knew help was just a call away, pride curtailed any communication with the old Drill. The 1980 Junior Sword Drill did not need baby sitters.

We worked hard, always including in each practice an attempt at doing the performance. There were screw-ups by the dozens. Frustration grew, yet was rarely expressed openly. Control was in place, and there was a professional air about our work. We were high ranking juniors. Leaders. We were veterans to the pressures of both the 4th Class System and the 14 Nights. We were going to get it. It was frustrating, but we knew it would come to us.

We stayed true to our practice schedule through Thursday and Friday. Capragetti called it quits on Friday evening until Sunday night. That amounted to 48 hours, and he noted soundly that it was a long time off. He said it was time for us to think about the series, and to work out the slew of problems that plagued it. "We've got to get through this without a single screw-up." That was our goal. I was sure we would be there by the end of the next week, and actually wondered what we would do with the remaining time.

Capragetti also said that he was going to use some of the free time during the weekend to ponder over what addition we, as the 1980 Drill, wanted to make to the performance in order to give it our own personal touch. He said he was open to suggestions, and that anyone with an idea needed to see him during the weekend. It was the last thing he said before we scattered like a flushed covey of quail.

I was back in the barracks by 2200. The battalion, usually dead on a Friday night, was livelier than usual. There was a home football game the following day, and there were few cadets taking overnights. I already had a ticket for Cindy, and I was thrilled I would be sitting with her again. Only to myself would I admit that I really liked being seen with her, right in the plain and open view of the Corps. I was sure it was both pleasure and torture for cadets to see such an angel, and I loved it. She was all mine.

The weekend was outstanding, spoiled only by the burning need to study and the time away from Cindy when I did. Sunday evening's practice was centered on the change that Capragetti and several others had come up with over the weekend. After numerous ideas and much discussion, a short series of moves was added between the "introductions" and the "tabletop." The transition from one to the other was just too simple. It was decided to put in a backwards-double gate swing, and then have each pair of partners head out to their table top positions in a crisscrossing diagonal direction. It was well received by the guys, and put into place. With a real awkwardness, we tried it out, and discovered that a bit more planning, and a lot more practice would be required before it was workable.

On Monday, the 9th of October, we found ourselves eighteen days away from Parents Day. It seemed like more than ample time. We knew we had a lot to do, but our confidence was high, being fully rested from the weekend. All the same, the alarm at 0520 seemed just as nagging, and the effort to get out of bed just as hard. There were strong thoughts of the morning practices not being worth the trouble, but I wasn't going to be the one to complain. I just put on my PT's and ran through the darkness towards McAlister. Spero Kerretsis missed the practice, and later said he had had too much weekend. The rest of us gave it our best shot, which with sleepy minds was pretty pathetic. We left McAlister thinking it had been a waste of time, and with Capragetti not pleased. I heard one guy say Jack just needed to lighten up.

The afternoon practice was much better than the morning's, but far from being the perfect performance we were seeking. Mistakes were constant, including a multitude of small ones and still a lot of big ones. Guys would just turn and march the wrong way. Some would drop their swords. Losing one's count was the most common booboo, and that always yielded a blatantly obvious mistake. But Capragetti did a pretty good job keeping his cool. He would act more as a cheerleader than critic, though I was sure his patience was being tested. Surely as we got better towards the end of the week, the pressure on him would start to lift.

The mistakes started to go away with each practice. But by Wednesday the eleventh, there were still too many to even begin to count. Progress was evident, but slow. Some guys would just get hung up on one thing or another. Someone would always lose count on "21 Steps" and run into the guy in front of him. The flip in the "pinwheel" was a joke since we were yet to do it right just once without a major tilt or fall. We even had three guys who couldn't even do the awkward sword twist during the introductions. You could see the frustration, and the hard blows to egos, as time after time someone would make the same mistake over and over again. Those who could execute couldn't understand what the problem was. No one had freaked out yet, but on Thursday, I could see it wasn't far from happening.

I had never been a superstitious person, but everything I had ever heard about Friday the thirteenth came to fruition on that day. It was the last of a long, hard week. Four frustrating practices a day stacked on top of classes and being a ranking NCO made life one big cruise in the sewer. Complaints had surfaced all week about the early morning practice and its worth at the price of being tired all day, yet Capragetti always answered with a reference to the obvious need. While I thought we would have reached the "perfect performance" run by the end of the week, we were still struggling just to make it once through the "pinwheel." Dennis Miles soon took a shot at Capragetti when he asked how it was possible to do anything right without sleep. Capragetti insisted that the morning practices were required, at least until we were able to do the performance right at least once. But the mutinous multitude balked. Even me. I hated that morning practice, and especially how it ruined my day. I was tired not only at practice, but also in class and when I had the rare privilege to study. I wanted to support the 1980 Drill and Capragetti in every way, but not at the price of having continuous bad days. We all had too much to do, and so little time. We had to be super-efficient and productive every waking minute. This was a tall order for those who were always tired.

Capragetti could see he was outnumbered. I found new respect for him, as he had to dig deep and give in. But he did so through compromise. He reduced his demand. "Do the pinwheel right, all the way through, and the morning practice will be dropped." It was accepted, but the end seemed far away as we wrecked the "pinwheel" in the run through the performance that followed. The calm of the compromise was short lived as some Drill members cursed openly as they left to get back to morning formation. I knew then our commitment had suffered a setback.

Classes, as well as Parade, were their usual bitches to get through. I was tired of being behind and only seconds away from where I had to be next. Nerves were on edge as we assembled for our late afternoon practice, and one had to be blind not to see the approaching confrontation. Failure during the "pinwheel" broke the bands of silence, and after a massive assault on one another, Capragetti called it quits for the weekend as some guys walked out. We were all tired. Our nerves were shot.

Cindy could see that I was distressed. I knew that time could heal the wounds of the 1980 Drill, but time was something we sorely lacked. We were a long way from being ready, and now we couldn't stand another minute working together.

I spent that entire Saturday with Cindy, but my spirits were further dampened when The Bulldogs played Western Carolina in an away game that day and lost. Nothing seemed to be working right. My disposition was that of someone who had lost a loved one, and I was not very good company for Cindy. Thank God she understood. I was worried, almost scared. If '80 Drill didn't get its act together soon, the '79 Drill might be performing on Parents Day, and we would go down in history as the Drill that never was.

CHAPTER 44

At 1900 Sunday evening all fourteen of us sat in McAlister Field House and there wasn't a member of the 1980 Drill who wasn't concerned about what their conscience was telling them. The warnings of the '79 Drill seemed to echo in our heads. Our dreams were in a murky haze, and we all ached with the reality of the dilemma. Penitence filled the air, and we were silent when Capragetti stood before us with what we hoped was a bulletproof game plan for success. Instead, he had a poem. I looked to see if the others considered this a sentimental shot in the dark when something more concrete was surely required. Indeed, there were uneasy looks on the faces of most.

"I'm sorry if this is my fault that my lack of leadership has taken us to this point of frustration. I'm as disheartened as anyone that things are so tough. I spent the weekend agonizing over what we should do, and I actually found answers in a poem that was passed to me by a member of the '79 Drill. It was written years earlier by a cadet named William Hendry, Class of 1973, who was Regimental Band's Assistant First Sergeant. It reads like this:

We Die Proud

Where is the honor of yester-year
Of Thermopglae and the Spartan's lack of fear?

Where is the ambition to give one's life
In the fight for Freedom, Truth, and Right?

Is to be honorable such a sin
That it brings scorn from friend and kin?

Oh God, to be a man is such a struggle
That I wonder the meaning of the life of trouble

598

Yet, from the back regions of my mind
I hear a lonely echo rise

An echo that pierces my very soul
And helps me remember my goal

"We Die Proud"..."We Die Proud."

"The poem is pretty deep," continued Capragetti, "but it really made me think, about Sword Drill, and about life in general. I wanted Sword Drill the first time I saw it, and I felt the experience would be my only chance to ever really do something so unique, so extraordinary. It's a chance to be a part of history, something that would be extinct if not for Drill. It's an opportunity to taste the honor reserved only for knights of days long since past. We not only have an obligation to see through our responsibility, but we have the extreme privilege to experience it. The poem reminds me, sadly, that the "honor of yester-year" is dead, except for Sword Drill. My interpretation of "We Die Proud" is that in the instant we die, we part with a momentary sense of what our time on earth stood for. Sword Drill is our chance to make a statement loud and clear. It says firmly that we believe in honor and commitment, even to the point of sacrifice."

What I thought was going to be a sentimental pep talk, turned out to be a moment of reflection for all fourteen of us. We sat there in silence, and thought about who we were and the opportunity that lay before us. Deep inside, we all knew something that we would never dare speak out loud. We were indeed the best of the best. No matter what we had done in the past, we had now risen to the top, yet faced the responsibility that came with that ascension. Like us or not, we were the cream of the crop. There were others, both in and out of The Citadel, who would surely debate our status, but no one could question what it took for us to get there. We had accepted a challenge few would be willing to embrace just by even entering The Citadel. But we took it further. We had the discipline to get the grades, and the rank, just so we could even attempt the endeavor. Then there were the Nights, where even the best of the best were thrust into the trial of their lives. Somehow, we all had made it. For some reason, we were the chosen, and we had to act like it.

What happened to us as a result of Capragetti's talk that day was not something that took us like a sudden flash. It was like a new attitude was planted in us, and that poem was the seed. Capragetti would later give us each a copy of "We Die Proud," and it would become the theme that would bind us together as a Drill, and change all of us for the rest of our lives. It was from that point on that we knew we had to work hard together to make this the best Drill it could be. From that day forward, I don't think we ever argued again.

We formed up after Capragetti's revelation and gave our performance a shot. We were focused more than ever. We made half the mistakes we made in the best of our previous attempts. We didn't make it through the pinwheel, but we did it well by comparison. We knew then it was to plague us forever if we didn't attack it with a passion, so we worked only on the "pinwheel" for the remaining hours. The mistakes started to fade, and in our concentrated attempts, it began to fall into place. When it started getting late, Capragetti called for one last attempt at doing the entire series, hoping to do it well, hoping to do the pinwheel perfectly. Before we left McAlister Field House fifteen minutes later, Jack Capragetti made the announcement that there would be no more morning practices. I felt alive as I ran towards 4th Battalion to make all-in. I felt like I was Sword Drill again.

I had the best Monday of the semester the following day. It was different, almost strange, not to be tired in class. I felt good and my spirits were high. Though I looked forward to our practice at 1500, I stayed focused in class. I had to be good at all I did.

We learned something from our experience with the pinwheel.

We knew that just knowing the series wasn't going to cut it. We had to perfect it by concentrating on the details. We had to feel it.

We had to break it down and work on the moves individually. There were only twelve days left to make a miracle happen.

We soon started doing the series in small sections. We would do a portion then analyze it. We ate our pride and asked the old Drill to help us by providing spotters, and encouraged them to tear us apart. If it was wrong, we needed to know it. We left our egos at the door. No one cared who made a mistake, just how it could be corrected. There wasn't a man on the '80 Drill that wasn't sharp as hell. That was fact. We just had to execute. Passing blame became an obvious waste of time. Solutions. Performance. Precision. Teamwork. That's all that counted. It was all that mattered.

Capragetti soon became pleased with the elimination of the morning practice. There was a lot of discussion about quality time versus quantity. If you showed a monkey a trick a thousand times he would learn it. But we weren't monkeys, and there was no time for endless repetition. We had to think, and concentrate. Care had to be taken with every step, with every flip of the sword. We had to harness those skills that got us there, and use them to their maximum potential. It was an exercise in the fine art of self-discipline and control, only now in a group sense. We were living on the edge. We were fine-tuned human machines with a mission.

We would end each practice with a complete and continuous final run through the performance. We concentrated and performed as if it were the real thing. Our hearts were in it. We chased the elusive perfect run as if it could shoot back and take advantage of our mistakes. We were at war with our own weaknesses. The frequency of mistakes and miscues declined at a remarkable speed. Major mistakes became rare, and little blunders were easily counted. The gremlins were growing weary. Our concentration and state of mind had elevated to a higher plane.

Each of the fourteen of us started to change. There was something different steadily growing among us. We all seemed to talk less and think more. I personally became withdrawn as an eerie sixth sense that I never knew I had revealed itself to me. It was an emotion, a sensation. It was a bond to reason, and an understanding of the true and sobering facts of life. It was joyous and strange, almost supernatural. Most uncanny was that we all felt it.

On Friday the 20th, we found ourselves exactly one week away from the performance, and five days from our pass or fail test with the old Drill. The progress we made over the previous week was nothing less than phenomenal. We were working on details now that meant nothing to us two weeks before. Positions of fingers, exact placement of steps, perfection in timing on ripples, and mirror image movements by all fourteen every time we would execute. It was a tall order, and reality gave strong evidence that a perfect performance was just impossible to achieve. Every Drill had some memorable flaw in their performance, labeling them as precisely as their class year. With such difficulty, perfection was an ambitious undertaking, missed year after year by each Drill dedicated to chasing that dream. It was nearly absurd to conceive that we, starting with a two-week deficit, would even try. The '79 Drill was realistic, and hoped only for something that would pass. Their doubts and fears were real.

During the weekend, Cindy could see that I was acting different. She said I was being too quiet.

"There's not a whole lot to say," I told her.

"Are you guys prepared?"

"I don't know. We still make mistakes. You know, the kinds that just happen. It's not because we don't know what to do, or how to do it. It's just that it takes so much hard and continuous concentration. If you let your mind drift for a mere second, you could crash and burn the performance for everyone."

"I guess it's a lot of luck."

"I once heard that luck was when preparation met opportunity. We're working as hard as we can to prepare, but there's something more to this than practice and repetition."

"Like what?"

"I don't know if I can describe it. It's a sense of concentration that comes from confidence. A confidence that comes from being at peace with yourself, and having a state of mind that is geared to a single purpose."

"Are you getting worried?"

"No. I mean yes. I mean...I don't know."

"What else can be done, other than to practice?"

"It's in our minds now. How do you rid yourself of the potential for brain lock?"

"Find the answer to that question and you'll rule the world. Making mistakes is a part of life."

"Yet some make less than others. Some can do impossible things while under the worst conditions. We have to do something perfectly in front of thousands of people that we can't even do while alone."

"Then you'll just have to do the best you can. That's all anyone can ask of you."

"We know we can do it perfectly, just as every Drill before us could have. But for some reason, it never happens."

That weekend was filled with thoughts of the performance which was only days away, and I conducted a constant mental search for the key to perfection. We had a practice on Saturday, which was well done, but again not perfect. Saturday afternoon brought more sour news as the Dogs once again lost while on the road playing Appalachian State. Saturday night Cindy and I ate dinner at Bushy's on Folly Beach, then sat on the remnants of the burnt Folly Beach Pier as we watched a windy, overcast sky churn up the ocean. I rambled on about my life and where it was going, and Cindy listened patiently as I thought out loud. I think she knew what was happening. She could see my life was changing, and she had a front row seat to watch it happen. Everything of meaning in my life was being examined. I was forming values and opinions that would never leave me. My life after Sword Drill would never be the same.

In church the next morning, I struggled with prayer, feeling it too selfish to ask God to intervene in my Sword Drill struggles. I even doubted if I was worthy of such a gift, and thought back to the countless sins in my life, with anger and hate topping the list. It took a long time for me to realize, but it was my disgust and the pure hatred for my family situation that had so driven me to lash out at the world. I hated family traditions, and I hated the very name of Charles O'Bryan, and the imperial arrogance that its relative birthright brought with it. It had deprived me of a happy childhood, and made me the whipping post for the next crowned prince of Kingstree. It was that hatred that led me to rebel against all that was formal, and filled my mind with an obsessive need to escape, and prove I was not just a burden to some far greater plan. But through The Citadel, and Sword Drill, I had risen above that. It was now all a part of my past.

On Sunday afternoon we gathered again in McAlister. The weekend had been many things to the fourteen of us, and there were signs of anxiety as we discussed the approaching performance for the old Drill, now only three days away. We formed up to start practice, and there was a fresh formality to our movements, and an obvious lack of chitchat. There was an absence of emotion as reactions to problems were treated with cold professionalism. We moved through the series, doing what we had already done a hundred times just a few times more. We were looking for something to improve. It was hard to imagine that it was simply down to a matter of execution. The education was complete. With every run through the performance, we got a little better. Our hope was to peak on October 27th at 2000.

On Monday we came very close to a perfect performance. Two mistakes were all that kept us from our goal. On Tuesday we started getting nervous, and the number of mistakes took a turn back up. Our last run of that day was a good one, and we prayed that our time before the old Drill would be as good or better.

On Wednesday the 25th, we stood in performance formation as the entire 1979 Drill positioned themselves on the floor to get a detailed view of what we had learned, and hopefully had perfected. It was late afternoon and there was enough light to see our every step, twitch, and eye blink. I was nervous, yet relatively composed considering the circumstances. Some of the other fourteen were not as calm, but they just had to work through it.

They did. We ran through the series with a total of five mistakes, with three pretty minor, two pretty bad. The verdict was passing, and the old Drill was both complimentary and encouraging. It had been a real ordeal to learn the series, but learn it we did. But knowledge was no longer the problem. Execution was everything.

On Thursday, Capragetti spent his day making sure that the spotlights and seating in the Field House were arranged just as they would be for performance. That evening was going to be our dress rehearsal, or what was better known as "Picture Night." During the actual performance on Friday, no flash photography would be permitted. There would be a request for complete silence, and no one would be allowed on the floor, therefore the reason to have Picture Night. It was also a good chance to have a go at our performance while under the lights, which according to the old Drill was a really different environment from that of a well-lit floor. It was open to the public, and there would be many present to put the pressure on us to do well. Our hopes were high to make a good showing.

That afternoon I shined my performance brass to perfection. I picked up my full dress blouse from the cleaners, and then went over it with a fine tooth comb. My shoes were blitzed, and my sword was perfect. My nerves were the only item in need of attention.

At 2000 we stood in the dark silence of the Field House, and we heard the noise of the gathered crowd die as our narrator went through his run on the introduction to the performance. This rehearsal was to be the spitting image of what was to happen the following evening, and we even had the bagpiper there to set the initial mood. Everything clicked right along up until the darkness was broken by the brilliance of the spotlight which, even with our heads down, tore into the tender backsides of my eyes. One guy actually made a grunt as the beam appeared, and it became obvious why a previous Drill added in having our eyes to the deck at the launch. The nuisance was short-lived as our minds locked onto the performance. I concentrated on nothing but what was immediately next, and tried to blank out the annoyance of the endless flashes from the cameras that seemed to surround us. It wasn't as easy to do as I thought. Guys came right up to us as we went through statics. As we marched around the ring, I could see people everywhere, and I almost lost my count when my mind questioned whether someone might get in the way. Concentrate! Concentrate, I thought. Zoom out.

But my ability to zoom lost its intensity as I witnessed a major mistake when we turned during "21 steps." My heart sank knowing a perfect performance was not to be on that night, and the bad feeling deepened as I heard a foot stop late when we came to a halt for the "cartwheel." Everything seemed to settle down fine until we got to the "pinwheel," and there, disaster of major proportions bit us as an outside man tipped in, causing two others to loose their balance. It didn't crash and burn the move totally, but there were three guys obviously out of sync with the program. One guy nearly dropped his sword during the introductions, and to cap off a pretty rotten performance, I lost my balance during "tabletop," and made my own personal contribution to what we would later consider as our "disaster with pictures." The applause was generous considering the many mistakes, but obviously less than what those present could have provided. When Capragetti, called for "order swords" and then "dismissed," there wasn't a one of us who didn't know we had just blown it. I felt sick, and I wanted to yell obscenities. If this was a sample of what was to come the following evening, we would be the Drill that everyone would try to forget.

CHAPTER 45

"I don't know what it's going to take to make you understand that I have no interest whatsoever in going! Once in a lifetime or not, I really don't care," said a heated Charles.

"I think that's a selfish way to be, Charles," said my mother. "This is important to John, and no matter what your differences, the two of you will always be brothers. You should respect that."

"Right Mom. Just the way John and the rest of this family respect me. It's bad enough to have everyone on my case around here, but then I get little brother running kamikaze missions on me every few months. Now you want me to take time out of my busy schedule to go watch him march in some show! Give me a break. Not a day goes by that I'm not reminded of the debt that I supposedly alone created, even though I got no support from anyone."

"We've been through that a thousand times, Charles!"

"And a thousand times I end up with all fingers pointed at me."

"I just think you owe it to your brother. He's a junior, and you've never once visited him at school. Not once. If you won't do it for him, then do it for me."

"This is crazy. I don't care about John or his stupid marching squad."

"Will you go, Charles? Tell me no now so you can finally alienate the last person in this family who supports you."

Charles stood silent and stared at Mom, knowing there was fact in her statement, and contemplating the loss of his last source of understanding.

"Alright, Mom. You win. Even if I'll hate every minute of it, I'll go for you. I don't need things any worse around here."

"Good, and I want you to enjoy it, and by no means cause problems by having an attitude. It will only spoil it for the others, especially for your father and grandfather. They're proud of John. Trying to run him down will only hurt you, Charles."

"OK, OK! I'll be quiet. I don't need to give them more ammunition."

***

At 4:10 p.m., Bob Johnson pulled into his driveway. He knew he and his wife had no time to waste getting to Charleston. The several urgent projects on his drawing board made the hour off early all the time he could get. Mrs. Johnson waited as her husband changed into a suit and tie, and encouraged him to hurry knowing that it would be a close schedule to get through the traffic to both pick up Cindy from her apartment and then meet my parents in front of McAlister Field House at 6:30. Though never before close friends with my mom and dad, they were delighted to be included in their plans to attend the performance. Mr. Johnson wouldn't have missed it for the world, and Cindy had long since invited her parents down for the event. It would be the first time her parents and mine would see each other since Cindy and I started dating, and also the first time my parents would see Cindy since high school. Both sets of parents looked forward to the meeting.

***

At 4:30 p.m. my grandparent's big Buick pulled off the long driveway from the house onto Highway 52. It would take just over an hour to drive to Charleston, leaving plenty of time to meet the Johnsons. Charles stared silently out the window, feeling surrounded by the enemy as he sat in the back with Mom and Dad.

Charles cringed as he endured the conversation that centered on my life at The Citadel. It was hard for the elder O'Bryans not to be proud over what I had done, but probably didn't realize how much their words of praise for me would sting as they fell on Charles' ears. Though they tried to restrain themselves, they were compelled by the circumstances of the event and the long drive. Charles remained silent until he could stand it no more, and then started into a slow offensive.

"You know, I have friends who went to The Citadel, and they said that most of the guys who are on this Sword Drill thing are a bunch of weirdos."

"That's a bunch of bologna," said Dad.

"No, I'm telling you," said Charles in an unusually calm, almost intellectual tone, "they say these guys go through some really bizarre rituals to get initiated into this thing. Rick Canty said it was really a cult."

"That's nonsense, Charles," said Granddad, "The Citadel is one of the finest schools in the country. They wouldn't have a cult in it. Do you think they would let some whacko group have such a big public performance every year?"

"I'm telling you what I heard, and several guys who would know said the Junior Sword Drill is nothing but a bunch of sickos."

"I heard that the performance is breathtaking," said Mom.

"From who, John?" asked Charles.

"No, from Mrs. Johnson," said Mom.

"Who?"

"Elizabeth Johnson. Cindy's mother. We're meeting them tonight to see the performance."

"Why?"

"Because John and Cindy want us to."

"John and Cindy? No! They aren't dating, are they?"

"Yes, you didn't know that?"

"John is dating fat Cindy Johnson?" said Charles starting to laugh. "Please tell me you're joking!"

"Charles, you be nice! I understand that Cindy has lost some weight."

"How much?" laughed Charles. "She must have weighed 300 pounds. Old Lee Bradford ain't got a hog as big as that girl!"

"That's enough, Charles!" interjected my grandmother. "John can date whoever he wants to and it's not your business or anyone else's to pass judgment. Besides, it's what's in a person's heart that counts."

"Yeah, but you still have to look at what surrounds that heart, and that girl is a sow!"

"No more, Charles," said Granddad with disgust.

"OK, I'll shut up. But just remember, I was the one who told you first. Having a shaved head must have sent brother dear off the deep end. First he joins a cult, now he's datin' fat girls. Sounds like college has been real good to him, alright!"

The older O'Bryans just let the conversation die. It was an obvious counter attack to what good they had said about John. The car remained silent until it reached Charleston.

CHAPTER 46

Parents Day weekend was always an exciting time. The fact that the performance of my dreams was just hours away made the other highlights seem unnecessary, and Friday's parade was its usual pain. The place was crowded with visitors, and shortly after the big marching spectacle cadets showered and left the battalion to join family and girlfriends.

My uniform and equipment lay ready on my bed. Larry was gone with his parents, and I sat alone in my room, staring at the back of the door. In a few hours the dream of my life would be upon me, and I felt like I wasn't ready. The other guys on Drill had to be feeling it too, frustrated still by the performance from the night before, still searching for answers as to what went wrong. It seemed that every mistake was always a new one, found while doing something we had previously done right a hundred times. We had beaten the performance to death, looking for something we could do to make it all better. Practice was good, but not the answer now. In every pursuit of a solution, it all came down to the same answer. We had to concentrate. We had to stay calm. Think. But even that seemed all too obvious. We were all frustrated from looking for an answer that never came after exploring every possibility.

I put my face into my hands, and wondered why it wasn't easier. I knew I would be nervous, but never imagined I would be looking for answers on the day of the performance. I thought about how my lack of confidence was in itself the reason for my fear. My mind was not solid. Even though I knew what I had to do, I just wasn't sure that it could even be done. It seemed that a perfect performance wasn't possible. I always tried to look for the positive, but we had failed too many times. At that moment, even a good performance seemed at arm's length.

We had agreed to meet in the locker room in the Field House at 1830. That was early enough to beat seeing the crowd and late enough not to spend endless moments racking our nerves. But just sitting in my room was not the answer either, so I started putting my uniform on, knowing an early arrival at McAlister was better than just sitting around by myself playing mind games.

I dressed with care, though there was no need for the type of detail that came with cuts. I did want everything secure and looking its very best, so I used caution with all my equipment. At 1745 I was ready. I picked up my shako, stood at the mirror, and looked in almost a trance as I gently placed it on my head. I stared at the figure in the glass, and thought about the same night two years earlier when I first saw Sword Drill, and the night later on when I stared in mirror after my world had crashed after Donna had dumped me. Things were so different than they were then. I tried to look into the dark centers of my eyes. Somewhere in there, was the mind that would make or break me in the hours to come.

I left my room and received sincere wishes of luck as I walked down the gallery and out of the battalion. The crowds from parade were gone, and other than a few visitors at the front gates of the battalions, the campus seemed unusually quiet.

I walked towards McAlister, passing in front of the other battalions in the process. I found stares at each meeting, because of the formal uniform when I passed civilians, and because I was obviously Sword Drill when seen by other cadets. When I crossed the street from 1st Battalion over to the front of McAlister, I stopped to look back over the parade ground, and the view of the campus on such a sunny and cool fall afternoon seemed almost a gift. I thanked God for such a beautiful day, and then saw the cross on top of Summerall Chapel as I did so. I wondered if that was not the place to spend the extra time before the performance.

I walked towards the Chapel, and climbed the granite stairs to its huge wooden doors. Moving into the vestibule, I marveled at the cool air that always seemed so noticeable every time I entered. I walked forward, and then stood motionless in the silence of the empty sanctuary. The afternoon light coming in through the stained glass windows gave the chilly stone interior a dim cloudy look, and as usual I felt consumed by the beauty of the place.

"I've been expecting you," came a voice through the silence.

Shaken by the call, I stood silent, not sure who was speaking, or that it was I being addressed.

"Come in, come in!" said Chaplain James as he stood from a chair at the front of the church, now no longer hidden by the pulpit.

I walked forward, thinking there must be some mistake, that the Chaplain surely was confusing me for some other appointment.

"I'm so glad to see you, son. You're the first to arrive."

"Sir, I'm sorry I have disturbed you, but you must be expecting someone else. My name is Cadet John O'Bryan."

"You're with the Junior Sword Drill, right?"

I stood with mouth open and stared back at the Chaplain in silence.

"Well...yes Sir, I am."

"I've been expecting you, and I'm sure there will be others later. You're just a bit early."

"But Sir, I wasn't aware that I, or any of us had a meeting scheduled with you today. I was just on my way to McAlister and decided to stop in."

"God scheduled the meeting, son. He does this every year. He uses the Sword Drill to drum up a lot of business for me."

I stood silent and was sure I was looking at the Chaplain as if he had lost his mind.

"Come on up, son. Let's talk a bit."

I walked forward and stopped at the communion pew where Colonel James met me.

"You see Mr. O'Bryan, every year you men come in here like clockwork, just before your performance. There's something on your mind, isn't there?"

I was awestruck by what he was saying, and found it hard to speak from the shock.

"Well...yes, Sir. There is something on my mind. A lot to be quite honest."

"Tell me about it son." I looked at him in disbelief, but decided to go with the flow of a very weird situation. "I guess... I mean I think I'm just nervous about tonight's performance."

"That's understandable."

"I'm just not sure why I feel so much like we're not prepared. We certainly practiced enough, and we know the performance backwards and forwards."

"Go on." I stopped talking for a moment, and looked in silence at the Chaplain, as if to wonder if he knew where I was going with this.

"You see, Sir, it's our state of mind. Call it nerves, or brain lock, or whatever. We just can't seem to pull off what we are capable of doing. I know we can...but we just haven't been able to make it happen."

"And you've been searching for the answer."

"Yes Sir."

"Have you found it?"

"No Sir."

"Where have you looked?"

"I've looked at myself, just as I hope the others are doing. It's up to us. The old Drill, the Corps, the administration, they are out of the picture now. It's got to come from us. It's got to come from me."

"What have you questioned about yourself?"

"Many things. But mainly what I have done wrong in my life. Things that were wrong in my past."

"What denomination are you?"

"Methodist."

"Have you gone to church much in your life?"

"Got a string of perfect attendance pins that would impress even you."

"Ah, so you know the rules."

"Sort of. I guess it's the interpretation that often leaves me confused."

"Got ya. So what is it that bothers you so about the past?"

"I guess I haven't always followed the rules."

"I see."

"I used to raise a lot of...uh...heck, Sir."

"I've said hell plenty of times in my life son, have even preached about it."

"Yes, Sir."

"Son, let me tell you something I've discovered in my years as an Army Chaplain. I guess I've seen enough of you boys in trouble in my time, some in pain over losing a girlfriend, some in trouble with the law, and some holding on to life itself by just a thread. I've even seen more than enough off to the better life above, and that, is the hardest thing I have to do. Korea, Vietnam, we lost a whole lot of good ones then. But what is the most important thing Mr. O'Bryan, is that before death becomes so immediate, we must all remember, that we are here to live."

"Yes, Sir."

"It's a common problem son. You see, your faith, and mine, is built around Christ, and the forgiveness His sacrifice brings. That's the real meat of the matter. I know there are others who get wrapped around the axle about "the rules." They're important all right, to live a good life. There's a whole lot of common sense in 'em too, but I'm sure you know that."

"Yes, Sir."

"You need to try to do the right thing son. But you can't. We all know it. It's one of those givens. That's why we turn to Christ."

"I know that, Sir."

"But do you?"

"Sir?"

"You know it, but you don't feel it. Deep in the back of your mind, you keep tucking away all of your little faults and crimes against God and others. Oh, you do the right thing alright, you put all the transgressions and problems of your past in a box labeled "Forgiven Sins" and you try to move on."

"That's true, Sir."

"Son, what I want you to do is to now throw that box away. You've only labeled your past, not cleaned house of them."

"But my past still haunts me, Sir. There are people, family, and situations that fill my heart with hate, and anger. I've been driven by it, and I still do things that I, well...suspect are wrong."

"Does that mean you're out of the club? Does that mean you need to beat yourself up about it? Son, that's not what a Christian life is about. If it was, we'd all be miserable."

"I guess you're right."

"Mr. O'Bryan, you've got a long life ahead of you, and the simple fact that you are on the Junior Sword Drill tells me you are probably destined for greater things. Believe me though, life is hard, and you are going to face many more challenges in the future. God tends to place His strongest in the most demanding spots, and often, it's faith alone, in both God and themselves, that carries them through what your average man could never dream of enduring. Your performance tonight is but one of many tests yet to come."

"I have often felt like this is all leading up to something."

"This institution, son, is the best in the world at preparing a young man for what lies ahead. Citadel graduates always seem to get the toughest assignments, usually because there's no one else to turn to who can get it done. We prepare you boys to be at your best when things are at their worst."

Chaplain James reached into his pocket and pulled out a pair of white gloves, then slipped them on his hands.

"May I?" he said as he reached for my sword.

"Yes, Sir," I replied, and he pulled my sword from the scabbard.

"I'd like to ask you to do something for me son."

"What, Sir?"

"Kneel here at the altar, and pray with me."

"Yes, Sir," I said as I knelt down on the cushion of the communion altar.

"You see Mr. O'Bryan, this sword represents two very powerful things. As I hold it now, it's a weapon of the ages, capable of both

616

protecting and taking life." Chaplain James grabbed the blade, and then held the sword with the handle and hilt on top. "To look at it another way, hold it by the blade, and it's a cross, which represents Christ, and the giving of eternal life. Pray with me son."

I bowed my head.

"Heavenly Father, today, fourteen of your best face a great challenge. One that will cause them to question their very worth, and one that will forever live in their minds. Guide and strengthen them through this trial, and bring with its conclusion a peace of mind that they gave their very best performance. Father, I ask that you take Cadet John O'Bryan, and grant him the peace, and the strength, that comes with Your forgiveness. Amen."

Chaplain James then turned the sword back around, and held it by the handle.

"Son, God needs you as one of His knights. Are you willing to accept His forgiveness, and forget about the past, and all that is in it that burdens you?"

"Yes, Sir, I am."

"Good!"

The Chaplain placed the sword on my right shoulder, then said, "Sir John O'Bryan, I knight thee as a member of God's round table, and with it the strength, and the courage, and the honor that comes with knowing that you are endowed with His full grace, that if you should ever walk through the Valley of the Shadow of Death, that you shall fear no evil. In the name of the Father," he moved the blade of the sword to my left shoulder, "and of the Son," then moved it back to my right shoulder, "and of the Holy Spirit. Amen."

I stood, and Chaplain James placed my sword back in its scabbard.

"Go now, Sir O'Bryan. Let that which you have received, guide and strengthen you, for now, and forever more. God bless you."

Without another word, Chaplain James turned and walked back up to the altar, then sat silently back into his chair. I turned and walked towards the doors, never looking back, thinking only of the inner peace I had just found. I met Jack Capragetti and Dwight Pearson coming in the Chapel as I was leaving, but only smiled as I passed.

CHAPTER 47

I walked on over to the Field House, and joined the only other Drill member who was already there. I removed my sword, then sat down and tried to relax. We struggled to talk as the others filed in one by one, and it became a strange pastime to watch everyone in such a solemn, meditative state.

At 1850, the Johnsons, along with Cindy, walked into Mark Clark Hall, where they found my parents, grandparents, and Charles there waiting. Though there was a bit of shyness between the acquaintances, they were pleased to see each other. They now had a new sort of bond between them in having children that were dating each other. As the parents exchanged greetings, Charles tried to get hold of himself as he blatantly stared at Cindy. He was certain that there was no way it could be her. He didn't even realize that his mouth was open as she spoke to him.

"Hi, Charles, you probably don't remember me."

"Uh, no...I mean yes...I mean, sort of."

"I was two years behind you in school, but I was in a lot of John's classes. I've also lost some weight since then."

"I'll say! I mean, yes, I think you have."

"Aren't you excited about the performance?"

"What performance?"

"Tonight's performance! John and the Junior Sword Drill."

"Oh, yeah, that performance. Yes, it ought to be just great."

"Folks," said Mr. Johnson, "I bet you want to say hi to John before the performance since I know you aren't going to wait around until 1 a.m. to finally get to talk to him."

"Yes," replied Mom, "that would be wonderful."

"Great!" said Mr. Johnson. "Let's get on over to McAlister before he gets too wrapped up in things. Then we can be out of his hair so he can start sweating bullets."

At 1900, a cadet came into the locker room and told me I had

619

visitors outside to see me. I left my shako and sword and walked down to the front lobby. I suspected it was my parents, and was both surprised and pleased to see them standing with my grandparents, Charles, the Johnsons, and Cindy. I was delighted to have such a large cheering section, but was actually shocked with the presence of Charles. I received hugs and handshakes from the group, and then marveled at the sight of Cindy in her evening gown. I gave her a hug, being sure not to do something inappropriate in front of her parents.

We talked about the performance, and I got the expected questions of whether I was nervous and if we were ready or not. They all seemed cheerful and pleased to be there, even though Charles seemed to be feeling a bit awkward. I talked with everyone for about 5 minutes, but knew that I couldn't stay long. I then told everyone how much I appreciated them being there, then started an attempt to leave by saying goodbye to each person and receiving wishes of luck and success.

When I got to Charles, a peculiar feeling struck me as I thought of him just being there. So much went through my head at that moment, as if some mile long videotape of our relationship throughout the years ran fast-forward through my brain. Strictly on impulse, I spoke to him. "You know Charles, I'm probably most grateful that you came. A whole lot of what I have accomplished with Sword Drill is a result of some of the things I got out of you being my brother. I'm glad you're here." I extended my hand to him, and he looked at me in disbelief, and then slowly extended his out to mine. We shook hands firmly, and he said he was happy he came. I think I caught him off-guard, but I was sincere, and I could see he was moved.

I then turned to Cindy, then said the hell with her parents and held her in my arms and kissed her. We expressed our deep love for each other without a single word spoken, and I told her I would see her later. I left them as they all wished me luck.

At 1915, the fourteen of us were all present in the locker room. Except for an occasional visitor, we sat alone. Capragetti asked one of his flunky sophomores to guard the door, and for the next half hour, he asked us to think about what we had to do. We sat in silence, and meditated over the task that we faced. It was Jack who finally broke the silence.

"I'd like to say something," said Capragetti.

Everyone looked his way. And he spoke in a somber voice.

"Tonight, whether we set the standard for all Drills to come, or just end up screwing the pooch, I want you guys to know that this has been a dream come true for me. I wanted Drill ever since I first saw it. I never imagined I would be 1980's Commander. It's been an honor. You guys are the best."

There were silent smiles around the room, and then silence once again became the agenda.

It was Fred Irving who finally broke the stillness once again.

"This school has been a dream come true for me too. It's given me more than I ever imagined. It scares me to even think about it. I look around this room, and I see thirteen other guys who I share a bond with that will never be broken. I haven't told anyone else this, but I was a pretty sad case before coming to Charleston. I should be in jail, but they offered me the Marine Corps as an alternative. After a few tests some idiot figured I was officer material, so they sent me here. Imagine that, a convict or an officer."

We all laughed, but only lightly. Irving was pretty serious.

"You see, I guess it's just a real fine line between making it good, or making it bad," continued Irving. "I look back at where I came from, and I wonder how I could have ever been so stupid. I also think about where I am now, and question how I could have ever been so fortunate. I mean, just the chance...just the opportunity to be here. I appreciate that chance."

The door opened and the conversation halted as Capragetti's sophomore guard entered and walked over to speak with him. He said something too low for the rest of us to hear, and then Jack placed the matter before us all.

"Hey Gant, your brother wants to know if he can talk with us," said Capragetti.

"He said he would probably do that," answered Donny Gant. "You guys know he was Commander of the 1975 Drill, right?"

"Let him in," said Baxter Stall.

Capragetti's guard walked back out the door, and moments later returned with Gant's brother. He seemed so familiar. He smiled as he walked in and shook both his brother and Capragetti's hand.

"Hey, I know you guys are probably getting psyched for your performance, and I appreciate you letting me barge in like this. I just wanted to let you know that this is my first trip back to see the Drill perform since I graduated. It's a privilege to have my brother in the line up. Our whole family is proud, but I'm still walking on air, knowing he has done it too."

There was an obvious look of respect and love exchanged between the two brothers, with Donny a bit embarrassed by the compliment.

"But my main reason for coming in is because I want you to know that not only am I proud of you guys, but so is every alumni out there. You guys represent all that is good about this school, and like I was when I performed on Parents Day, I know you feel as fortunate and honored to carry on the tradition. You're probably nervous, and the likelihood that you guys will pull off this thing with no mistakes is nearly impossible. But what I do hope is that you will be who you are. You're the best. You're Citadel men. You're Sword Drill. Thanks for letting me talk to you."

Bruce Gant turned and walked out with no further words, and the silence was broken only by the sound of the door closing. We were ready.

***

In tight formation, we stood in the pitch black darkness under the stairs as we listened to the bagpipes begin to play. I was nervous, and tried to settle down by thinking about those first few moves that would be so critical. We were silent, but then Mark Kellowski broke the silence. His raspy voice cut through the quiet like some ghostly contact from another world, and chills shot down my spine as he whispered the words to "We Die Proud."

When Mark got to the final line of the poem, without plan, the fourteen of us whispered together, "We Die Proud...We Die Proud."

I heard the bagpipes start to fade, and my emotions kicked in to tell me that the ultimate moment was upon us. I felt an initial rush in my head, and then a sudden feeling of calm overtook me until I actually felt peaceful. I was locked and loaded. I was ready to execute.

I drifted in meditation as I heard the pipes move further away, and then go completely to silence. When Stall's voice tore through the serenity of the Field House with his high-pitched command, it was then that I zoomed.

"Sword Drill...Fall In!" Stall commanded. "Forward...March."

We marched forward, and with a stomp, stopped with our chins in our chests, and I readied for the lights. They were as bright as ever, but I waited for the sniff to snap my head up. There...perfect.

Next, the short marching sequence to take us into "statics." Wait for the sniff...there, leg up...balance...my hands and legs moved, and my clicking was perfect. I felt good. I felt relaxed. Concentrate. Brace. Six steps forward. Stop. Wait for the sniff from the middle of the platoon. There, pop to. Perfect. Wait for the whisper, "Dress right dress." Boom. Perfect. Listen. "Ftttt." Snap back to attention. Listen for the whisper. "Parade rest." Go. "Fttttt." Perfect again. We were rolling.

Five steps to the outside, about face, five steps back, turn, tilt, wait...sniff, upright again.

It was perfect so far. Though consumed in concentration, I knew I would hear the slightest mistake, and there was none. Next, the fast march around the giant ring. Wait for the sniff. There! Stomping now, we marched forward, then two by two separated and marched around the circle where I met my partner on time and the head pop felt great. Count 25 steps, turn away again from each other, mark time in place, stop, and turn forward, "dress right dress." Great! It was a solid pop.

With a sniff, our first ripple to "ready front." Here comes the Voice. "Draw...swords." Great. A sniff from the center, march, and with fifteen steps we turned into two lines to open up the ranks like swinging doors. Stomp, about face, and now we're facing each other. Sniff to "arc swords." Another sniff, down to our breast plates in "present swords." A sniff, and we all go back up to an arc. Sniff and we go back to the breastplate. A final sniff, and we are back down to "carry swords." All perfect. I fought getting pleased. There was a long way to go. So far, so good.

Next, the slow march moving into the "V's" of the diamond shaped "shank." We stopped, leaning forward, then with a sniff, popped back straight. Another sniff, fast march, then snap turns towards the front. With a double stomp as we marched in place, the two rows split at the back and again opened up where we ended up again in one long line across, with the shortest in the middle. With a stomp, we came to a halt.

Now the "cartwheel," the heavy breathing middleman provided the count, and the right half of the line did an about face and with a sniff, we started marching. Our dress was in-line, and the move was flawless. I had a flash of fear knowing we were getting close to the "pinwheel," but got rid of it. Concentrate!

Twenty-one steps would get us there, and on the 21st, all were there in a precise "about face." The single file line marched and curved across the floor, moving and bending around the center ring that we wrapped into our circle. With a turn towards the center, we faced each other. We snapped to our breastplates with a "ripples up," and then a "ripples down." Without any "ripple" we did a simultaneous snap on a sniff, and the single click echoed through McAlister. Next to an arc, then to "order swords." All exact.

A perfect performance so far, but now it was time to face the music. The pinwheel was here. Going back to the slow march, we took our four precise steps in towards the circle, and on the fourth step, our toes were touching the edge of the circle. Everybody tilted forward, then on a sniff, went to vertical. With another sniff we did another arc, and then snapped down to "present swords" with again a single pop. Once we went down to carry, there was the sniff where we all lifted our legs together, once again going into the slow march. One step, two step, three, and we were on line and in position. We took four more steps, and then came the most difficult move of the evening. I didn't even think about it, and with our right legs lifted, we all did our simultaneous spin 180 degrees on a sniff, and landed going in the opposite direction, on the right foot with the left foot in the air. Boom. Absolutely immaculate! Still in a slow march, the outer four men of the groups of three started the stepping out, leaving the other two. They all tilted, then the next four followed, then the final four. When all were tilted, a sniff brought us all back to vertical. Then it was another "ripples up," this time the hard way as we faced away from each other, then followed with a "ripples down." I couldn't believe it. We had survived the "pinwheel!"

With a sniff we all took four steps out, then made a right turn so as to be in a single file line. We hard marched around the circle, making one large turn to bring the line into a diagonal position. After marking time, a sniff halted us with all but three guys doing a 60-degree turn to the left. The three started their slow march to the rear as four others marched forward. Stopping at different intervals, we formed the huge rectangular "X" of "crossed rifles," then did a snap to "present swords" on a sniff.. After "order swords," we took eleven steps in a hard march with the bottom guys in the "X" marking time, and the upper guys moving forward to form the inverted "V." With a double stomp one side turned to the left, the other to the right, then started our long march around the edge of the basketball court. It got tricky as usual as we fought to deal with the echoes and the distance, but nothing went wrong, and we stayed in perfect step. The lead guys stopped us just where we needed to be, then with the double stomp from across the court, we stopped and turned to face the others through the dark distance.

Tired now, and breathing hard, I strained to hear the faint sniff from across the court, and we all started marching together and came across the floor in the two lines facing each other. Once we reached the center and met nearly face-to-face, we did our two moves of the "mesh," which worked without the slightest defect.

We were into the home stretch. I still couldn't believe we were still without incident, still into a perfect performance. We marched out of the "mesh" and positioned ourselves in the line facing the podium where the President of the school and the other distinguished guests were seated, and the very sight of them made me snap out of concentration. But I got hold of myself in time to stop with the others. Bracing, standing shoulder to shoulder, we breathed with a vengeance while covering any movement. The sweat poured down my face, then I put my observations aside and readied for the first ripple from left to the right. This was pure reaction to the movement of the guy beside me. I worked to anticipate, and the sound indicated that the ripple was a great one. Then a man on the right side gave a sniff, and we went back down. On reaction from the man in the center, we rippled up from the center moving out to each side, and then brought our swords down from the center. Finally, there was one breath, two breaths, and on the third, we all did a single snap to the breastplate. Impeccable.

Baxter then commanded in his siren voice, "Carry Swords," and we were now going to get a rest. We were still perfect, and already into the introductions. We breathed hard, and I heard the narrator start to speak, and I came out of my lock on pure concentration. It was time for a mental break.

First to get recognized was Dwight Pearson. His name, rank, company, and hometown were presented to the capacity crowd. Though out of breath and exhausted, it was a proud moment. I soon heard my name, and then lifted my sword in the slow and difficult twist up to my breastplate. I had worked for hours on this one moment in the spotlight, and it showed as I went through the one continuous move. I used my time in glory not in conceit, but silently thanked God and every Citadel man before me for the privilege.

The introductions were soon over. Everyone had their swords up in "present swords" position, and Stall commanded us to go back to "carry swords," and we did a perfect ripple down. We then performed our own "backwards hinge" move that made the performance uniquely ours, then split partners and marched diagonally across the floor and went up on one leg, all of us perfectly balanced in the "tabletop." With a sniff, the lead man on each side started to mark time, and one at a time we would come in with a stomp. I counted the seven stomps, and then silenced my steps with the others such that our footsteps were barely audible. It was at this point that my heart exploded, and I had to fight to keep my concentration, knowing we were almost there, and we were still perfect. Stall called his final command of "Forward March," and I stepped forward and started my count on the forty-three steps. I fought hard to maintain composure, as my chest seemed to burst with pride, and my emotions came alive. I turned the corner of the basketball court, and then turned again near the center. We moved out in our two single file lines towards the middle of the floor. 39, 40, 41, 42, 43, stop. With shako pops, we each turned to face in, and as if in slow motion, I could see us all together lifting our swords. We went to full arc, and the armory exploded with a roar. We had done it. Our only perfect performance.

In the stands, Larry and Tompkins were going berserk, the old Drill beamed with pride, and the rest of the Corps was in a frenzy. They knew. The whole crowd knew it was flawless. My parents were out of control, and Charles was stunned, not knowing how to deal with what he had just seen. Cindy cried and held her mother as Mr. Johnson yelled like a rebel.

The noise was deafening, and the floor seemed to shake in an earthquake of applause. I could hardly bear the knowledge of where I was, and what we had just done. I was where I had hoped so much to be, yet it was too good to be true. My life was forever changed, and my first thing to do was break my most solemn vow.

I didn't move, but just stood at perfect "full arc" as the crowd continued its storm, and I could feel a tear start to roll down my face. I just couldn't help it. From hoodlum to hero, my dream was now a reality. I was Sword Drill.